FLATLANDER
BOOK ONE

iUniverse books may be ordered through booksellers or by contacting:

iUniverse
1663 Liberty Drive
Bloomington, IN 47403
www.iuniverse.com
1-800-Authors (1-800-288-4677)

Because of the dynamic nature of the Internet, any web addresses or links contained in this book may have changed since publication and may no longer be valid. The views expressed in this work are solely those of the author and do not necessarily reflect the views of the publisher, and the publisher hereby disclaims any responsibility for them.

Any people depicted in stock imagery provided by Thinkstock are models, and such images are being used for illustrative purposes only. Certain stock imagery © Thinkstock.

ISBN: 978-1-4917-9992-5 (sc)
ISBN: 978-1-4917-9993-2 (e)

Library of Congress Control Number: 2016910553

Print information available on the last page.

iUniverse rev. date: 09/08/2016

Flatlander

BOOK ONE

OLIVER KRANICHFELD

ILLUSTRATIONS BY: SAM BALLING

C⊙Nͭ€Nͭ₵

ACKNOWLEDGEMENTS

Mom- I miss you so much. I dedicate this book to your memory and your spirit.

Sir Bramius- Thanks for all of the advice and being supportive of me since day one.

Erin K- one of the hardest working, most generous, loving people that I know. Thanks for everything you've done for my family and I!

Chow- My brother and fellow author. I'm so proud of you and all of the adversity you've overcome in life. I can't wait for the next book(s) in your career to come out and for your move to Vermont!

Dad- Thanks for raising me through thick and thin. Thanks for all of the encouragement. Keep fighting the good fight.

Henny- you're the best nephew ever. I can't wait to see you grow up. The sky's the limit, kid!

Aria- When you're old enough, I hope that you enjoy this story. And remember, every family needs a quiet one!

Libby- You've been an awesome addition to the family! It's great to see you guys so often in Vermont.

Sam Balling- We did it! You're a real talent. I had a blast collaborating with you. Hopefully more to come on the horizon!

My colleagues and students at Essex High School, and former colleagues and students at BFA St. Albans, On Top, the Integrated Arts Academy, and the Rye Nature Center- thank you for being such wonderful communities and teaching me how to be a good teacher, and more importantly, a good person.

JD Fox- thank for all of the edits and insights. It was a big help.

Burlington Writers Workshop- Thanks for your input and advice.

Kickstarter friends: Thank you so, so much, guys and thank you for being patient! I'm so grateful to each and every one of you. With your encouragement and financial support, this would have never been made possible. Special thanks to Matthew Payne, Brendan Donoghue, Nathaniel Stratton, Kyle Lemieux, Janet Donoghue, Neil Mendick, Liza Park & family, Chris Healy, Oran Walsh, Mary Alice Keator, Heather Clark, Hank, and to the many other friends and family who pledged!

Joseph Long and Andrea Ardonis of I-Universe: Thank you both for all of the support.

If I'm forgetting anyone, my deepest apologies. I'm grateful for everyone in my life.

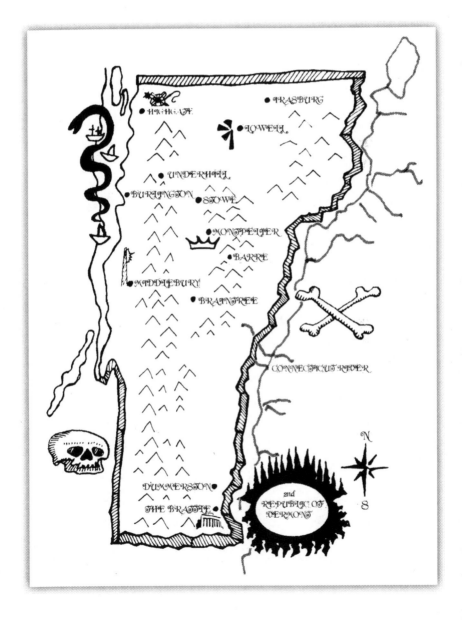

CHAPTER ONE
The Arrival

APRIL 18TH, 2110

A MAN AWOKE NEXT TO a river, groggy and disoriented. He woke with little else but the face he bore, a blue button down shirt, and a pair of brown khakis, which clung tightly to his body in the humid, earthy air. In one palm, a small frog sat calmly, its throat sac steadily inflating in the morning sun. He felt a small bump at the crown of his head, which was tender to the touch. Probing his mind, he

searched for any memory, any hint as to where he might be. He knew the river before him to be just that: a river. He knew the trees around him to be trees, and the frog in his hand to be a frog. But what alternatingly baffled and terrified him was the fact that he could not extract a single memory. He watched as the mud slowly eroded away mere inches from the soles of his moccasins.

He sat up, mindful of his stiff back, and plopped the docile amphibian at water's edge. Scanning his vicinity, he saw that the surrounding wood was deep. The river, its graveled shores extending ten feet on the opposing banks, narrowed around a small bend twenty yards upstream. Downstream, the river disappeared through a dense section of brush and cattail. Much of the forest was free of leaves; spare the occasional sapling, or sprouting weed. Ten paces away, upon a small clump of dirt, a robin tinkered about, probing the thawing soil. He heard a woodpecker knocking away in the distance. An eerie symphony of morning birds gave him the chills. The shrill echoes came from all directions.

Mouth parched, he yearned for drink. This section of the river was fast moving enough, and he cupped both hands and scooped the near-freezing water. Slurping it like a soup, the liquid coated his throat, its excess streamed down the sides of his cheeks like tears. He belched painfully then nodded in newfound contentment.

Then, no more than thirty feet away, he observed a small, dwarfish figure emerging from the woods. Carrying an empty, metal pail, and whistling a joyful tune, the small man frolicked, seemingly, without a care in the world. He stood around four feet tall, and wore a pair of dusty, green overalls, the cuffs of which were covered in mud. A thick, white wool turtleneck sweater covered much of his torso. A pair of oversized, green rubber boots, the tongues reaching halfway up his shins, squeaked incessantly in the morning dew. His thin, brownish hair was parted down the middle in waves, and a thick, stubby mustache graced his upper lip. Gnome-like, and rather disproportionate, the small man resembled a large, stuffed doll more than a human.

Pacing along the riverbank to get a better look at the stranger, he snapped a twig underfoot. The smaller man froze into place. For several awkward seconds, the two locked eyes, and he, even in his fugue-like state, recognized sheer terror in the other's face. With a shriek, the small man tossed the pail aside, as it clanged about the rocks, and frantically ran back into the woods from which he had come.

"Hey, you! Come back! I need help!" he called toward the wood. His calls were answered only by a series of snapped branches and shuffled underbrush.

Who on earth was that? Desperate for answers, he followed what he presumed to be the proper trail. Walking briskly down the forest path, he was determined to follow. The small man's clumsy footsteps resounded throughout the forest, acting as his sole navigational tool.

It was a cool spring morning in Middlesex, a town on the outskirts of Montpelier, Vermont's capital city. The landscape sparkled with morning dew; as patchy, rolling hills and hardwood forests spanned the distance with an angelic quality, fresh from the waking light of dawn. The mist of the Green Mountains spun through the valleys like a fine, silk web. Spring's gentle thaw revealed a land spotted in dull greens and browns, graced with clusters of white and yellow crocuses and daffodils. The Vermont winter often carried with it a great weight, a weight the land was now shedding in this stretch of mid April.

Near a decrepit, gray farmhouse, a rooster crowed from a small pen surrounded with chicken wire. Beside it, the chicken coop lay vacant. A herd of one dozen Holsteins stirred gently from their slumber, mooing for their helping of dry feed. A rectangular retention pond laid fifty paces to their left.

Nearby, three figures assembled on top a wooded hillside ridge. To the untrained ear, the only sounds enveloping this ridge were the waning songs of the morning birds, and the chatter of the various farm animals. To the conditioned hearing of the King Henry, however, the rapid advancement of footsteps could be discerned with crystal clear reception. Henry sensed such things naturally; as he had spent much of his youth exploring the outdoors; hiking in the foothills of the Brattle[1], watching and listening to the animals, the rivers, the wind, and the land, which seemed to carry with them the stories from the Green Mountains[2] and beyond. And just as a man could familiarize himself with a work of art by observing it both analytically and with abstract enjoyment, likewise were Henry's heightened senses developed and nurtured beyond his years, here amidst Vermont's natural beauty.

Today, he wore the dark grey, tanned hide of a wolf, which he had found dead along the roadside near the town of Newfane years ago. Henry's greyish-brown hair was short and well cropped. Stubble covered his cheeks, which he kept shortened with a hunting blade. Though this look suited him well, he had often sported lengthier facial hair throughout his life. He also wore the finest leather boots in all the land; handcrafted by the legendary Jonathan Cerpelli of St. George, who had since grown old and slowed in his production, but whose limited boots had been rendered into fine collectables and treated as near works of art. It was often said that the boots maintained their sheen fifty harvests deep, and judging by the glint of Henry's pair, the rumors appeared to be well substantiated.

Considered the perfect composite leader for the republic, most Vermont residents viewed Henry as tough, smart, and fair. He

---

[1] A cultured city in Southeastern Vermont molded after Ancient Athens, Greece. Formerly referred to as Brattleboro.

[2] A mountain range that spans much of Vermont, north to south.

carried himself in modest fashion. His possessions were more than sufficient, yet unpretentious when compared to many of his contemporaries within the ranks of the upper class. Henry walked the town freely, often times without even the supervision of his lone bodyguard, Franklin. He often interacted with the people of Vermont as if he was a commoner.

He enjoyed the simple pleasures of the world: feeding birds, looking out from mountain summits during foliage season, fishing, hunting, and tapping the first of spring's maples. Yet he also often quoted other wise men in conversation, and was as well read as many of the republic's top intellectuals. Simply put, Henry was a man of the land, one who felt as comfortable in a hunting blind as he did on the throne of the statehouse; qualities which hadn't gone unnoticed during his landslide win in the election twelve years prior and subsequent reelection. Because of these modest and 'common-man traits', Henry was dubbed the "Humble King" by many. Yet those who worked with him professionally knew him not as a 'push-over', but more as a reasonable, good-natured leader.

The 'King' label was terribly misleading, Henry often informed those who would inquire, for the republic was bound and run by the populace as a whole, with each town's elected representatives or "lord" and "lady" holding seats in the senate. Henry was more a 'president' than a 'king', he argued, for he was an elected leader, not some self-appointed tyrant. Yet when Vermont gained its independence from the Old Country four scores prior, the secessionists thought it would be amusing to create the title of 'king' for their leader. To this day, few could fully explain why.

Accompanying Henry were three companions: his bodyguard, Franklin, his advisor, Ellen, and his assistant, Menche, who had recently departed to find the group water by the Winooski River[3]. Franklin of Walden was a brute from the Northeast Kingdom, a rugged land encompassing the republic's northeastern reaches. He stood six foot two and weighed a solid two hundred forty pounds. His fur coat was a thick and black bear pelt, which he had hunted in his hometown of Walden. An axe was attached to the holster on his back, and sharpened by oil and whetstone on a near-weekly basis. Scar tissue lined much of the visible skin on the right side of his chin and lower cheek. His hair was near shoulder-length, a brown tangle with often-visible specks of leaves and twigs embedded within. Franklin's boots, massive olive green creations made of aniline leather, were broken in twenty winters deep, but unlike that of Henry's Cerpellis, showed their true age no matter how much mink oil he applied.

Ellen Parthen, King Henry's trusted advisor and lead counsel, stood in stark contrast to the northerner. Although she too wore a fur coat, it looked snug and elegant on her trim torso, a pattern of brown, tan and cream, made from the pelts of martin and rabbit. Her hazel eyes bespoke a depth: a certain complexity of nature, calculating and knowledgeable. Her dirty blond hair was pulled back in a ponytail. In her hands, she held a small notepad and a quail ink pen. Several sketches with relevant annotations marked an open page, showing the borders of the surveyed farmland. The notes were clean and neat. Not a single line of ink was misplaced on her parchment.

One of Henry's duties was to approve survey lands for public use. On this particular excursion, Henry and his company were looking at a section of farmland in Middlesex that had been auctioned off a day prior. Miles Hakey, a farmer who had dwelt on this land, had become overburdened by maintaining his property. So he sold it to the republic and had taken to the ways of the lake men. *Farmers were a thorny lot, habitually distrustful*

---

[3] An important tributary of Lake Champlain.

of government, mused Henry, so it was a rare treat that the man sold his land to the republic, much less for a reasonable price. A number of ideas looked appealing for the property, for there was an abundance of farms, and always a need for commercial space, lumber yards, and recreation centers in Montpelier's surrounding towns. And the dozen cows were to be picked up by day's end, three to each neighbor.

Dozens of old elms and ashes lay in the overgrown wood, their roots anchored deep. Yet the stipulation in the land-deed declared that not a single tree be cut down in the process. *Farmers can never make things easy,* reflected Henry, drolly. This inexplicable caveat frustrated Henry, but he would adhere to the terms of the deed, as was expected. Then, from his left, the sound of approaching footsteps stirred Henry from deep concentration.

The fog in the near distance gently rolled forward, then suddenly pushed back, as his assistant, Menche, came barreling through at a relative sprint. Breathing rapidly, Menche's belly fluctuated with every step, as his overalls were loosening to the point of falling down completely. His rounded cheeks were blushed a cherry red. He looked terror-stricken.

"Lo...Lo...Lord!" stammered Menche, "there comes a man, a, a stranger, I says."

Henry perked up and peered out towards the fog, as Franklin and Ellen quieted mid-conversation, watching their small friend approach with alarm.

"From where?" called out Ellen sternly, as she followed Henry's gaze.

Menche pointed towards the fog at his back. "Froms the Western Woods!"

"Well, what did this man *say*? Who was he?" asked Henry, as he glanced dismissively at his winded assistant. "Many a stranger comes and goes from the city reaches, Menche. Heavens, one would think that the forest itself was fully aflame by the sound of it."

Menche paused, rested his hands on his knees, while trying to collect his ragged breath.

"Lord, he looked like, looked like one of dem..."

"Looked like one of *whom*, Menche?" asked Henry hurriedly, as he shot his bodyguard and advisor a humorous look.

"Like one of dem...Flatlanders!"

At the mere mention of the word, the air grew thick. The northerner drew his axe, and Ellen, a sharpened dagger. Menche, clearly panicked and winded from his sprint from the woods, hid behind the imposing legs of Franklin. The bodyguard and counsel rushed to flank either side of Henry. Henry looked sharply at Menche's face, now half-obscured by Franklin's monstrous thigh.

"A Flatlander hasn't wandered here in well over twenty five years, Menche. Last month, you supposedly saw an owl talking in the woods. And just last week, you claimed to have downed a catamount barehanded."

"Coulda been a bobcat now I thinks about it," offered his trembling assistant.

Henry shook his head emphatically. "Nonsense. The point is: I'm not sure what to believe from you anymore."

Menche shook his head. "But I tells you, *that* was a Flatlander I saws, milord."

Henry sighed. "I send you on a simple task of collecting drinking water, Menche, and this is what..."

His words trailed off, as a figure staggered out from the dense fog. His gait was off-sync, his clothes unrecognizable, and his frame had a slightly muscular build. The man looked weakened and disoriented, like he had recently escaped from a fight, bruised and battered. Still, the distance was too great to ascertain his class or land of origin.

"Hail, *stranger!*" called Henry, as he picked up a jagged branch lying afoot. He hoped dearly that he didn't have to use it.

"Hey. How's it going?" replied the stranger, casually.

Henry exchanged nervous glances with his companions, who were likewise baffled. The man's dialect was unrecognizable. The Humble King's fur coat rippled in the wind, as he yanked at his collar for protection against the morning chill.

"You speak in an interesting tongue, stranger. Where do you hail from?"

The stranger gazed upon the surrounding farmland, vacantly. "Umm. I can't really say..."

"My eyes still need to adjust to the light of day. Can I see your face up close?" asked Henry. As the figure approached, Franklin tightened his grip on his axe handle.

The man approached and paused within a dozen paces of the party. And indeed, Henry's suspicions were confirmed. His stubble looked juvenile at best. He bore no animal hide, nor the orange vests of the wardens, nor the blue uniform of the lake men, nor the green robes of the monks, nor the overalls of the farmer folk, nor the togas of the Brattle-folk, nor the tattered rags of the mountain traders, but rather, an odd, blue buttoned shirt and strange beige pants. His hair was semi-long, wavy and brown, and his face, slightly awkward, with large nostrils, but otherwise, nondescript. In unison, the group lowered their eyes to his feet. The man's footwear was of an unusual kind, like a boot hacked off in the middle, pure relics of the Old Country. The truth of this man's origins became clear.

"You must be lost, *Flatlander*," remarked Henry, his voice heavy with contempt, "the lands which you seek remain at your back. Please, leave this land at once and don't look back. The Old Country lies in wait."

"But I don't even remember where I came from," replied Flatlander with a shrug.

"From the damned Old Country," interjected Franklin, in a low growl.

"*The Old Country*?" The stranger paused and ruffled his hair. "I'm not sure I follow."

"That's funny," laughed Ellen. "Everything about you screams 'Old Country'."

"Did I do something wrong?" asked the stranger, confused by the sudden note of hostility. "Please, I'm begging you for help. I'm cold. I'm hungry. My head's killing me..."

"Oh gracious, what help could we *ever* offer a Flatlander?" replied Henry, facetiously. "For they must have enough possessions to dispel the very notion of need itself. What on earth could us *wretched* Vermonters provide for such a privileged gentlemen, such as yourself?"

"Vermonters?" he murmured. The name sounded odd, alien to his memory.

"Yes," answered Henry, as he raised an eyebrow to Ellen, who, in turn, exchanged with her king a look of doubt. "*Vermonters*, my friend. That's us. *This* is Vermont, this land on which you stand before us in this moment of need. I've called it home throughout my life, as do my companions. I, King Henry, ruler of this land, have made it my honor and sworn duty to help protect it."

Ellen tucked away her dagger. "What is it you seek?"

The stranger scratched his head. "A meal and a shower. That's it."

"And where would have the river carried thee beyond that, dare I ask?" inquired Henry, his thirst for information from the stranger not yet satisfied. "Clearly you weren't carried to Middlesex, for the river flows west towards Lake Champlain. That part of New York is desolate and abandoned, separated by over a mile of brutally cold water, barely thawed from its winter freeze. Therefore your appearance and alibi strike me as somewhat suspicious."

"I've told you everything I know," replied the stranger.

Ellen nudged Henry in the small of his back, gesturing that they talk amongst themselves.

"If you'd excuse me for one second, Flatlander," said Henry, as he raised a finger, politely.

The two turned their back on the stranger and huddled close, as Ellen stated matter-of-factly. "I don't trust this man."

"I've never been the type to accept a Flatlander with open arms, and you know that," replied Henry.

"Something about him doesn't feel right," she added, as she twiddled her quail pen between her fingers.

Henry glanced subtly at the stranger, who seemed to be shrinking by the second under Franklin's weighty gaze. "It's too early to tell, Ellen, *much* too early to tell. It can't hurt to have him stay one night, though, under our supervision, and then send him on his way to his rightful path tomorrow," said Henry, then after a brief, somber thought, "to wherever that rightful path may be."

"But we can't just play host to any wayward Flatlander wandering these woods, Lord Henry. He could be a thief or worse," argued Ellen. Her eyes cast doubt on the stranger and his odd footwear.

"He could also be a fine gentleman. And I must say, it's unlike you to be so hasty to judge, Ellen," countered Henry. "We don't even know this man."

"Exactly. We don't know him," rebuked Ellen. Her face grew flustered as she spoke.

Henry pounded the oversized branch into the earth. "Ellen, the man is lost. Have some pity, for heaven's sake."

"Pity or blindness, neither attribute is grounds for a king to ignore his advisor," said Ellen with a scoff.

"This is my wish, as I will it, and I expect you to be a gracious host, Ellen," replied Henry. "I'm sorry, but I'm in no mood to debate this."

"Suit yourself," replied Ellen with a scowl.

The sun now peeked through a small slither of clouds near the horizon, but it was evident that the morning rays wouldn't last long, as an endless trail of billowy, cumulus clouds stretched to the west, as far as their eyes could see. The bells from the moving Holsteins now grew in volume and intensity from across the hillside, as they approached the party, restless for dry feed. Henry straightened and stepped forward towards the newcomer.

"Flatlander, you'll be happy to hear that we've decided to treat you as our guest today, despite my better judgment. It is extraordinarily rare that we see Flatlanders in these parts, let alone *house* them, so consider yourself very fortunate." He considered a moment. "Perhaps it's the softening that comes with age, as well as my natural curiosity that comes hand in hand growing up a Vermont country boy. Please, allow me to introduce my party: this is my head advisor, Ellen, my bodyguard, Franklin and my assistant, Menche," as each member nodded towards Flatlander, "and this, at our backs, is the beautiful city of Montpelier, in the Republic of Vermont. This is what we call home."

"Thanks," replied Flatlander, uncertainly. Henry threw down his branch, and they shook hands apprehensively.

"Come, we will feed you and house you, and then you'll go on your way tomorrow. I'll call for one of my men to show you the way back home. Hopefully, the cows will be taken care of by then," said Henry, as he shot a look at the Holsteins then draped an arm around Flatlander's shoulder. "I won't leave a stranger alone and hungry." Henry winked at Ellen. "Not even a wayward Flatlander."

And there they were: four Vermonters and one lost Flatlander, walking shoulder to shoulder, through the sanctity of Middlesex's softening countryside, and straight towards the heart of Montpelier.

Nestled in the foothills east of the Green Mountains, the city of Montpelier lay close to the geographic center of Vermont. Henry spoke to Flatlander of the city that he now called home. Regarded by some as an odd choice for a capital, Montpelier was dwarfed by the Queen City, Burlington, forty miles to its west through the Bolton Gap. The quarried remains of Barre, a now-desolate mining town, flanked its southern and southeastern borders.

They passed through what Flatlander presumed to be the city limits. Rows of shops lined both sides of State Street, Montpelier's main block, as three chimes of a church bell rang out in the distance. They passed a corner store named "Zeek's," painted green with pink trim, and a red-checkered awning. Flatlander deeply inhaled the aroma of freshly baked goods and pastries, as hints of fried dough left him salivating.

The city moved with a morning energy that Flatlander hadn't quite braced himself for. The sounds of men laughing funneled out from a nearby alley, as soon the comforting aromas of eggs, bacon, fish, and baked bread flooded the city streets. Throngs of parents passed the group, escorting their children to school. The children wore school uniforms of heavy, cloth tunics of grey and white, and boots of various styles, colors, and materials. Most of the townsmen and women nodded politely to King Henry and his company, while a few others passed with wary glances at this suspicious, new stranger.

Flatlander's back and neck still ached from the awkward position in which he had awoken by the riverbank. There had been no signs of a struggle. No blood. No dropped objects. No footprints. He'd woken up with a small frog in his palm and a pounding headache, and not much else. Henry's assertion that Lake Champlain resided to the west, downriver, towards New York, certainly left more questions than it answered. It would have been impossible to come by boat, or by means of the river itself, as it would have pinned Flatlander's origins further within the alien realm of Vermont. *Then how could he have awoken so far inland?* It was folly, however, Flatlander reasoned, to try to decipher the past. The more important task was trying to navigate the present before him.

During the walk, it became quite evident that the group's presence in Montpelier began attracting a great deal of attention. An awestruck woman dressed in a silver gown dropped her basket to their left, then a cat-whistle from around the street corner, followed by a collection of gawking schoolchildren, whose faces were pressed firmly against a storefront windowpane. The townspeople's reactions fluctuated between surprise and disgust when seeing Flatlander, to a form of subdued reverence, as they also saw their leader, King Henry, accompanying him. The Humble King's presence alone diffused a simmering tension, keeping the townsfolk at bay.

As Flatlander neared a corner, an elderly fellow wearing a French beret and dark blue pea coat casually spit a huge glob of phlegm directly in his path on the cobblestone walkway. The group stopped dead in their tracks, as Flatlander looked at the mixture of mucus and chew with silent disdain. Before he could respond, however, Henry came face to face with the man.

"You know that you've got a nasty habit, old man," said Henry, inches from the man's face.

"I didn't see ya there, King Henry!" replied the man, in a sudden bout of nervousness. Franklin took position behind the old man, glaring hard at the back of his head.

Henry pointed to the spittle on the ground. "You also know that it's a crime, punishable for up to one month in jail, to spit in the path of a king?"

Franklin removed the axe from his back holster, and began sharpening it slowly against his handy whetstone. Upon seeing the bodyguard ready his weapon, the man's eyes darted from side to side, as he backed slowly from the shimmering axe head.

"Many apologies, ma lord! It was an accident, I swear!"

"An accident, you say?" asked Henry.

"I d-d-didn't mean nothin' by it- it was just I saw that..."

"Let me guess: it was that you saw a Flatlander and didn't think too kindly of him," interrupted Henry "so you took matters into your own hands and summoned up the courage to make your feelings known. Sadly, you also spat into the path of a king and his trusted advisor, bodyguard *and* assistant."

"Jeezum Crow[4], me lord!" The man pointed squarely at Flatlander. "It's that I didn't see ya behind that scuzzy Flatlander! Woulda never done it if I had seen ya too!"

A crowd had begun to congregate at a safe distance from the action. The people whispered and murmured, following every move with morbid curiosity. A mother scrambled out of sight

---

[4] A Vermont expression conveying an array of emotions, most commonly that of surprise.

with her daughter, hands placed firmly over the child's eyes. A few bystanders pleaded for mercy. It was rare for the Humble King to show such an impassioned display of emotions, let alone in a public setting such as downtown Montpelier.

"Watch your tongue, old man," commanded Henry. "While this Flatlander remains in our company, you will treat him with the same respect you would show to us, or anyone in Montpelier. What say you, Franklin? You know, in parts of Vermont, shortly after the dissolution of the Old Country, spitting at a king was an offense punishable by banishment?"

Henry was bluffing, of course, but he delighted in making the old man squirm.

"I say we make him lick it up," said Franklin. The old man's eyes widened, as he reflexively gagged at the mere suggestion.

"Please, sir. I meant ya no harm! *I swear*, I didn't. A Flatlander stole me family's fortune when my pappy was a lad! Was in the family records, mum said. Was unfair! Been meanin' to spits on 'em fer years if they ever crossed me path, lord!"

Henry held his gaze. "What's your name, old man?"

"Barry, ma lord."

"Barry, while I can't change a fool's tune, let this be a warning. The next time you decide to spit in *anyone's* direction again, you'll be answering to the Court of Fools[5]."

"Aye, ma lord. A thousand apologies to ya!"

Henry gestured to his new companion. "And for Flatlander here?"

Barry turned his head, waywardly, desperate to avoid eye contact with Flatlander. A deep scowl spread across his weathered face.

"Sorry fer spittin...." mumbled Barry, his head cast downward.

"Face the man, Barry!" chastised Henry. "Look him in the eye, for it is *he* whom you truly owe an apology!"

---

[5] A court of the absurd in Burlington devoted to making a mockery of criminals as a form of punishment.

"I'm sorry fer spittin' yer way," he said, looking Flatlander in the eye while limply shaking his hand.

"Apology accepted," replied Flatlander, confused. "I don't know why…"

Henry cut off Flatlander with the wave of his hand, and glared at Barry. "Now go foul some other street corner with your wretched devil-chew."

Barry turned, sheepishly lowered his head, and then scuttled away through the gathered mass. The bystanders rapidly dispersed in stunned silence, unsure of what they had just witnessed.

"That was odd," muttered Flatlander, as the party resumed their walk. They passed a small shop selling maple syrup and maple-products. The storefront was painted with a crimson maple leaf, with "Plattner's" written in bold blue on a windowpane. Inside, the store bustled with a large crowd, as a customer haggled prices with a store clerk.

"It takes time to reverse years of teaching, years of stories, years of ingrained hatred. You must understand, Flatlander, that you've wandered into a land that, although *you* perceive as alien; is not alien to *our kind*, nor our parents, nor our grandparents, nor several generations further down the line."

"I feel like I've already worn out my welcome."

"I've said enough for now, Flatlander. Shortly, I'll tell you all. You have my word." Henry then studied the position of the sun in the sky. "As for now, we should eat and talk things over. It's close to eight o'clock by my estimation." Henry paused and looked Flatlander up and down, scanning him as if he were an unfamiliar specimen. "You look weary, Flatlander. It wasn't the warmest of greetings, even I can attest to that; but some of us still take hospitality seriously around these parts. Come, join us."

"Why do you all keep calling me a 'Flatlander'?"

He was just realizing how much the name had begun to bother him. Not only in the derogatory tone that he had first heard the term from their initial meeting in the meadow, nor the way that Barry had recently referred to him; but it was also the general feeling he had sensed that people had waited much too long to use this word and its connotation; as if it were a forbidden curse. *Flatlander. It sounded insulting.* The fresh memory of Barry's darkened phlegm clouded his thoughts.

"Well then, what is your true name? Just say it, and we shall do our best use it from now on," offered Henry diplomatically.

Flatlander tried to dig deep into his memory, searching for any and all clues that would yield his true identity. But it was futile. His memory offered nothing. *Keep it simple and call me 'man' if you have to. See if I care. It's the least of my worries, I suppose.* Flatlander walked on in frustrated silence.

"I guess it doesn't matter," he mumbled. "Does it?"

Henry sighed. "Very well. If it should come back to you at any point, we will oblige. In the meantime, put your mind at ease."

Flatlander thought it over. *Put his mind at ease?* The whole experience seemed crazy to him. He wanted quite desperately to relax, yet discovered each attempt a failure. *Could this be my imagination?* Flatlander tempted the thought. It was like something out of a vivid dream, where every visceral experience was subconsciously meted out in fine detail, though he lacked fundamental control over the characters and plotline. Yet it had become quite evident from the get-go that this was no dream. Even his most vivid dreams could never be this authentic, this genuine. Every step, every emotion, every ounce of pain on his back and head indicated that this was real. Very real.

The outline of a gargantuan building at the edge of town began emerging. White and topped with a golden dome, it loomed mighty against the backdrop of a picturesque, wooded highland. Six massive, white granite columns protruded from its front entrance in a portico. Two stone stairways, encompassing three separate tiers, cascaded down, and then melded into an extended, concrete pathway that led two hundred feet to the edge of State Street. In the middle of these pathways lay six rectangular beds of crocuses and tulips. The golden roof, even in the relative gloom of the morning, gleamed brightly in the distance. Several large black panels, each the size of a small house, were raised above the highlands. Flatlander found himself in a state of natural awe as they neared the massive structure.

"Amazing," was all he could muster.

"Yes, it's quite impressive," agreed Henry, simply.

"We meet there as a government to make decisions, debate, introduce legislation, and hear from the commoners, but *that*", said Ellen, pointing to a three-story, red brick building, "is Henry's house. *That's* where we're staying."

Flatlander turned his head slowly to where Ellen was pointing, shielding his eyes from the golden glow of the roof, to a smaller, cube-like, more residential structure with a greyish-blue roof. Its first two levels contained spacious wrap-around decks, and were covered with a narrow wooden awning. Several gardens lined the yard, and Flatlander could make out in the distance a large white gazebo, which stood alone in the backyard near a shallow, winding stream. And there, next to the front door, sure enough, was Menche, holding the door wide open for his guest, a dopey grin spread on his face.

"Ready for brunch?" asked Henry with a wink. "We're home."

A table built with maple and polished with a dark brown varnish spanned most of the dining room area. On the walls were paintings depicting magnificent wooden temples, which Flatlander learned were actual structures in Henry's hometown of the Brattle. The mount of a black bear's head looked menacingly over the party, bearing three-inch canines. Henry's home was dark, even as late morning approached. Nearest the living room, the house had a pleasant, smoky aroma about it, the source of which Henry identified as the burning of his favorite wood, yellow birch. The hardwood oak floors were kept clean, and the furniture was neatly arranged.

They were served scrambled eggs, bacon, toast, and a side of herb salad with maple vinaigrette, courtesy of Lord Henry's thick, redheaded maid, Gabby. It dawned upon Flatlander just how hungry he had become. For prior to brunch, his stomach churned and moaned. During the first few minutes of their meal, his movements at the dinner table were fast, automatic. Manners would have to wait. Between rapid bites, Flatlander sucked his fingertips clean from any excess grease.

Ellen sipped at a goblet full of milk, nodding to Flatlander. "Most of what we know of the outside world was passed onto us from our parents and grandparents. We know little of the Old Country in its present form, and from what little some of us have heard from the mountain traders, or the whispers from Braintree, it doesn't appear encouraging. Apparently, much of the Old Country has not quite recovered since its fall. As such, Flatlanders are still considered a sworn enemy by many here."

"I want to know about this whole 'Flatlander' thing instead of listening to you guys talk in circles around it," said Flatlander, as he mixed his toast and eggs with his fork.

"Got a tongue on this one, don't he?" chided Franklin, as he shot Flatlander a cautionary look from behind an immense plate of stacked toast and eggs. "I can change that if ya want, boss."

"That won't be necessary, thanks Franklin," replied Henry, as he nodded. "We understand your frustrations. Forgive us. So be it, I'll try my best. There are many different interpretations or definitions on what a Flatlander is."

Flatlander smiled crookedly. "Give me one."

"Very well. A Flatlander is someone who isn't from Vermont."

"Is that all?"

"Yes, umm, and it's also somebody who isn't accustomed to our land, our weather, our culture, our dialect. It's somebody who comes from a flatter land: flatter in terrain, flatter in moral principles, flatter in natural beauty." Henry folded his hands. "Flatlander, you must understand, many people here haven't seen your kind for decades. In fact, most in Vermont have yet to see a single Flatlander throughout their lifetime. That man that you saw in the marketplace, the one who spat in your direction, as old as he was, was likely taught at an early age that Flatlanders are considered the enemy. Family grudges die slowly here. You'll see."

Flatlander wiped his mouth clean with a napkin. "The *enemy*? I'm an *enemy*? What did I ever do to tick you people off?"

"It's not always about *you*," interjected Ellen. "We're talking about years and years of generational hatred. That doesn't just go away like *that*!"

Ellen snapped her fingers, as Menche straightened from a daydream.

Henry nodded. "The Old Country is now an entirely separate nation from us, or should I say, more fittingly, *us* from *them*. For this December marks the 80th year of our independence. There was some fallout from that era, both before, during, and after our quest for sovereignty."

"Eighty years ago?" asked Flatlander, baffled. "Why would Vermont want to start its own country?"

"The road to secession was slow to form, like Lake Champlain icing over mid-winter. Yet when the fall of the Old Country came, it came quick, and with it, the forming of *another* sovereign Vermont republic. The Old Country reeked of war, corruption, environmental devastation, widespread greed, the disparity of the rich and poor, consumerism, laziness. Not a care for nature. Not a care for the needy. Not a care for all that is pure and innocent in this world. Too long had the ideals of the Old Country and

Vermont diverged. Too long had they grown unfamiliar to one another," said Henry, who proceeded to look towards his mantle at a small, framed painting of a blond, teenage girl. "It was like having a family member who had become rotten to the core over the years, despite years and years of trying to save them from a faulty path. So when that last line snapped, the Old Country went into ruin, and so too did our desire to remain a part of this once-great land. The Shelburne Doctrine[6] spread. We adopted a culture that resembled this land during a simpler, happier time."

I get it," sighed Flatlander. "And since then, you have more or less outlawed the entrance of Flatlanders..."

"For the most part, yes," replied Henry.

Flatlander sprinkled a pinch of salt on his remaining eggs, as the clanking of silverware continued.

"So how do you feel about me so far? Am I living up to the Old Country's reputation?" cried Flatlander. The others at the table looked at one another, dumbfounded. Flatlander chuckled nervously as his question was met with awkward silence. "Um, I'm waiting for some form of reassurance here..."

"Gabby the pepper, please!" cried Henry from across the table. Within seconds, Gabby emerged from the kitchen with a large peppershaker and began grinding it furiously over Henry's salad. "You're a curious case, Flatlander, if I may say so."

Flatlander raised an eyebrow. "Because..."

Henry gave Gabby the signal to stop grinding. "In the past, we've at least had an idea where the few Flatlanders came from. Either we'd send them on their way back home, give them permission to stay a night or two, or in extraordinary circumstances, grant them permission to stay for good."

Flatlander cocked an eyebrow. "In *extraordinary circumstances?*"

---

[6] The period of time shortly after seceding in which Vermont modeled much of their culture from the dated artifacts of Shelburne Museum.

"Yes, but I cannot divulge exact numbers or locations to you. Let's just say that an extremely, extremely small number of Flatlanders currently reside here in Vermont."

"There's one," called out Ellen, whom quickly covered her mouth in embarrassment.

Henry shot his advisor an angry look, and then took an aggressive bite from his salad. He turned to Flatlander, his hands folded neatly on the table, a pitiful attempt to exude grace.

"Yes, actually there are two who live together."

"I don't care about any others. I want to know what you're going to do with *me*," stated Flatlander, as his voice rose in agitation. "Is there anyone here who could at least point me in the right direction tomorrow?"

"Quit badgerin' the man," grumbled Franklin, as he downed a bite of egg and bacon. The northerner then eyed down Flatlander's remaining eggs, now reduced to a yolky mess. "The King feedin' ya is more than nice enough fer my likin'!"

"You say that you remember nothing?" asked Henry.

Flatlander glanced down at the table. "Nothing."

"Hmm. Well that certainly makes our decision difficult."

"Decision?" mumbled Flatlander, as he raised an eyebrow.

"Why, of course. Our decision on what to do with you after tonight…"

Flatlander blinked rapidly. He didn't like Henry's answer, or the direction of the conversation.

"If you're going to decide on where I'm going, I'd like to have voice in the matter."

"You wouldn't be the first Flatlander to say something like that," quipped Henry.

Flatlander groaned, rubbing his temples in marked frustration.

"Why does he make that sound, Lord?" asked Menche from his corner of the table.

Henry turned to Menche. "He's just groaning. It's a sound that Flatlanders often deliberately make to convey exasperation during periods of high stress. I've read extensively on this phenomena."

"Exas...por...ation?" Menche fumbled wildly with the word. "What's that, lord?"

"Exasperation, Menche," corrected Henry, calmly. "Is when somebody gets very annoyed or frustrated about a certain situation or event. It's very common amongst Flatlanders."

"Hey, c'mon!" said Flatlander.

"Like that," pointed out Henry without missing a beat. "Or like the time I told you to weed the garden by the statehouse," continued Henry to Menche as a parent would talk to a child, without giving so much as moment's notice to Flatlander's objection. "And then you came back with a wheelbarrow full of roses and tulips that I had freshly planted. One could say that I was... *exasperated,* Menche, by your actions and behavior that day."

"But ya told me to pick the flowers too!" said Menche in protest, his fork held high in the air, as drips of grease streamed to his plate below.

"I said no such thing!"

"Did too!" replied Menche.

"Ya can't argue with the king, ya fool!" said Franklin.

"Can too!"

"Stop it! Both of you!" chided Ellen, as she rang her fork repeatedly against her goblet. Waiting for the grumbling to die down, she then glared at the king and his red-faced assistant. "Excuse me, Flatlander. Sometimes even we Vermonters forget our proper table manners. We'll do our best to accommodate your wishes."

"That's right, Ellen," said the king, as he took a long, deep breath. "Flatlander, I'm curious, do you have a plan in the coming days, hours? Now's the time to speak."

"Honestly? For now, it's just to get through the day without losing my sanity," replied Flatlander in earnest. The terrifying maw of the black bear's mouth made him feel slightly sick to his stomach.

"But as for tomorrow?"

"I want to at least try to get my bearings," interrupted Flatlander. "If you'd just let me stay until then, I'll be out of your hair by lunchtime tomorrow."

Henry glanced at Ellen, who returned a reluctant nod. "Very well, if you'll now excuse us, Flatlander. I'd like to have a discussion with my party."

Flatlander rose slowly from the table, as Gabby walked in to take away his plate and silverware. His dish had been polished clean, save for a slight smudge of egg yolk. He felt the small of his back, which still ached whenever he sat or stood.

Henry took notice. "And please, get some rest today. It's early, but you're going to need it, no matter the decision."

Flatlander shook Henry's hand. "Thanks, King Henry. It was nice meeting you all. Thanks for the hospitality."

"You're very welcome," replied Henry, as Gabby gently took in Flatlander's elbow, and leading him to his room.

Henry and the others watched him intently. Flatlander tried not to show that he took notice of their judgmental gazes, and more so, that it bothered him. Walking casually with Gabby, Flatlander listened half-heartedly to her stories about Henry's house. According to the maid, the home was hundreds of years old, and had the oldest fireplace in the republic, and they had spent years restoring the original decks, and that it was built on an old apple orchard, and that there was a cute barn on the property. This wealth of information, incredibly enough, had been disseminated in a matter of twenty seconds. And as Flatlander slowly crossed over to a hallway near his room, he noticed through a sliver of

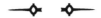

doorway that the four were still staring at him in complete silence, awaiting his late morning rest.

A small cedar desk stood in one corner of the bedroom, with several dust-covered books and an oversized teal lamp. Clumps of browned pages protruded from their worn spines. Flatlander skimmed over the titles. He thumbed through a large hardcover "The History of Montpelier," and then a crumpled, water-damaged paperback copy of "Birdwatchers" half-heartedly, smiling as he glazed over each colorful illustration and caption, particularly that of the Great Blue Heron. Yet, within minutes, his mind began to cloud. He tried to continue reading, partially to distract his mind from his worries; but his eyelids soon felt too heavy for such a task.

The bed was spread with a wildly colored red and green comforter decorated with roses, and raised nearly a foot off the floor. With a full belly and heavy legs, Flatlander hopped pathetically onto the mattress, and stretched himself into a comfortable position. Yet he almost jumped when Franklin came barging through the door just moments later unannounced with a steaming cup of tea.

"From Lord Henry," muttered Franklin, as he handed Flatlander pine needle tea, which looked little more than a toy cup in Franklin's giant paw-like grasp.

"Thank you," replied Flatlander, as he took a cautious sip. Franklin grunted then turned to leave, yet Flatlander had some questions for the burly bodyguard. "Excuse me? Franklin, is it?"

The bodyguard stopped dead in the doorway for a few seconds, then turned to face Flatlander, his massive frame obscuring all light from the living room.

"Yes?"

"Are you from around here? From Montpelier?"

Franklin paused and shook his head. "No."

"But you're from Vermont, I assume?"

"Some might say."

He looked upon the bodyguard peculiarly. "I don't follow."

Franklin sighed. "Ah. From the Northeast Kingdom, Flatlander, in a little town called Walden. It's rugged land, even fer the republic's standards."

Flatlander squinted in confusion. "So it's part of Vermont?"

The Northerner shook his head with a grin. "Only in maps and little else."

"But what brings you here?"

Franklin smiled wickedly. "Another story fer another time. Sleep well, Flatlander. We'll talk more tomorrow if it serves ya."

Flatlander gently sipped the scalding-hot liquid. "Thanks for the tea."

The northerner nodded politely and excused himself. Flatlander laid in bed for some time, thinking of the all that had transpired over the past few hours: the river, the king and his party, Barry the old man, the statehouse, the brunch with his new acquaintances. He drifted to sleep riding a wave of these thoughts and images. And as he neared sleep, he had forgotten that it was not yet midday, and had neglected to notice his tea had accidentally spilled near to where he lay in bed, soaking through his bed sheets entirely, and staining the white satin a sickly brown.

He dreamt that he was caught in a raging river of extreme proportions, like the water itself had been shot out of a giant cannon. He had no way of gripping onto any of the protruding rocks that might hinder him down as he raced downstream. They were simply too slippery, and he was moving at much too fast a pace. Tired and helpless, his body was battered mercilessly against rock after rock after rock. Even his knees were scraped raw by the impacts. This went on and on, like a sick game, as Flatlander's body drained of life.

And, despite all this, in his dreams, Flatlander was more concerned about what lurked beneath the murky waters of the river, rather than the rapids themselves. Each time he was able to catch his breath; he'd look beneath its muddied surface. The rocks would only appear in his field of vision when he was almost right on top of them, and by then, it was often too late to avoid a collision. After a particularly brutal series of strikes, Flatlander's torso was then skirted across a clear, calm section of river, where his last fleeting visions were of a radiant blue just up ahead, and a small school of brook trout darting along the tan, silted bottom of the riverbed. And it was with this dream that he found himself submerged in for quite some time, trying to subconsciously retrace his footsteps back into yesterday, and the days and weeks preceding it.

In the early afternoon, while Flatlander was sound asleep, the party moved to the adjacent living room, where a fire burned hot and bright in the fireplace. It was a fireplace of impressive proportions, large enough to fit three grown men. Burnt birch and the sweet aroma of hot cider filled the air. Henry and Ellen sat together on a suede couch and watched the dancing flames. Franklin made himself comfortable on the floor nearest the fire, warming his knuckles close to its embers. The traditional evening fires had often brought with them great tranquility for Henry and his party. It was often used as a time for reflection and deliberation, for issues grand and small. Yet this night was different, for while Henry and his party gathered by the fire, they were consumed with one thing and one thing only: what to do with the curious stranger, Flatlander.

As Henry finished arranging the birch-logs, he smirked at Franklin. "You know, they had an old joke about taking in Flatlanders when I was growing up. Give them an inch, and they'll take the whole damned foot." Both Ellen and Franklin laughed heartily. Henry smiled in jest, but soon his brow furrowed, and his expression stiffened as he gazed upon the growing flames. "My mind troubles me. I trust both your guidance. I hope that you know this. And I also know that I risk losing face with the people of Vermont for letting the man stay."

"Then spare yourself the harm and let him go," pleaded Ellen. "It's the logical thing to do."

"That's also difficult for me, Ellen. The man has no home, no direction."

"The lad asked me where I was from," interjected Franklin with a chuckle.

"*And*? Did you tell him?" asked Henry, as he took a seat next to Ellen. "I wouldn't ask you to hide anything from this stranger."

"I did," replied Franklin, cautiously. "How do ya explain the kingdom, though? Even a Vermonter would have them a tough time, I'd wager."

"Excellent point."

Henry chuckled in amusement and sipped his hot cider, savoring the sweetness, before placing it on a small, folding table next to the couch.

Clasping his hands together, Henry said, "I'll just get to the heart of it, I suppose. I can't help but feel that this man is special, and will serve an important purpose for us." He looked at both Ellen and Franklin, awaiting their disapproval. "Odd, I know."

Ellen squinted hard. "A special purpose for *what*? He can't even remember his name."

Franklin shook his head, as his tangled mane of hair ruffled loose. "Flatlander's scared. I can see it in his eyes. This land burdens him. I'm one with the lady, Lord Henry. I say we let him pass on the 'morrow."

This wasn't going to be easy. Henry needed to consider an alternative approach.

"The ruling against Lockerby from a few years back. Who was responsible for that decision? Vermonters or Flatlanders?" asked Henry, referring to a recent controversial court case in Montpelier, regarding a cheese maker and the city at odds over regulations pertaining to wooden surfaces used for serving. The artisan saw no problem using wooden boards, but the city thought it unsanitary. The city lost, but only after a prolonged, expensive trial, further alienating artisans and business owners from the government.

"Vermonters," answered Franklin, suspiciously, as he withdrew his toasted knuckles from the fire.

Henry sensed some momentum. "And the judgment of Inepticus versus the republic[7]? Was *that* ruling made by Vermonters or Flatlanders?"

Ellen's face paled. "Those poor cows. They never stood a chance. Quit playing this game, Lord Henry! Why bring up such a gruesome memory?"

"My point is this," replied Henry, as he took in a deep breath, "perhaps we need to use an outsider's perspective during times of conflict; times of decision-making."

Ellen snorted. "You can't really be suggesting that we heed the advice of a *Flatlander*?" Franklin remained silent, though the twitching in his legs spoke volumes.

"I've said no such thing...yet," continued Henry. "Though I believe Amos the Monk once spoke of the meaning of 'truth'. 'There is a reason why mothers can find missing objects so easily',

---

[7] A tragic incident regarding a resident (with a troubled history) plowing a horse-drawn carriage into a herd of cows, killing 3 cows.

he said, 'they see things not as how they *want* to see things, but as they truly *are*'."

"What does that even mean?" asked Ellen. "We're talking about Flatlander, and you're talking about…*mothers finding lost objects*?"

"It means that that we as a people, Ellen, *we as a people*, bury a lot of things deep down and see things the way that we *want* to see them, not as how they truly *are*."

A realization then occurred to Ellen, as she turned to Henry with a sudden glare. "There is another, remember? The last Flatlander, the one in which you relented, and let stay? What of *him* as a reminder? What of *him*?"

She then crossed her arms, as a devilish grin spread across her face.

"He's still… adjusting," stammered Henry.

"A*djusting*? A*djusting*?" gasped his advisor. Ellen couldn't believe what she had just heard, the words spit out like venom. "Even to this day you cannot see the truth as it lays plainly within sight. Twenty-five years is not *adjusting*! It's a foregone failure, Lord Henry! An utter failure!"

Just then, a strong downwind from the chimney chute dampened the flames, and blasted a cloud of black smoke and ash out in a blinding flash. Franklin stumbled back, coughing. Ellen and Henry waved their hands frantically through the thick smoke.

"I've asked Menche a hundred times to clean that flue!" said Henry between coughs.

"Clearly he's been dallying on his chores," cried Ellen.

Tinkering with an iron tong, Henry rearranged the birch firewood with a steady hand. The embers pulsated and hissed, as the occasional spark popped and resounded throughout the living room. The acrid smoke lingered, as he returned to the previous subject at hand.

"You can never live that one down, *can you* Ellen? The man tries, for goodness sake."

"I beg to differ, Lord Henry. The man no more tries to fit into the republic than a lake man in the mountains."

Henry raised an eyebrow. "It's not completely unheard of for the lake men[8] to trade their work as mountain traders[9], and vice versa…"

"You know what I mean," rebuked Ellen, sharply.

"Despite his struggles assimilating, I am actually quite fond of the man."

"And yet you still hide him away in the woods of Colchester like a dirty, little secret…"

"Enough." Henry held up a hand to his advisor. "Ellen, tomorrow you will hear my judgment and you will honor it." Ellen bit her tongue, as Franklin picked off several dangling pieces of ash from his hair. Faint gasps of wind still cried from the chimney flue. Henry continued: "Trust me. I will take your concerns into consideration, Ellen, for they're valid, no doubt. But I must do what I feel makes sense for the people of Vermont. I bid you both goodnight."

"Yes. Good night, Lord Henry," said Ellen through clenched teeth.

Henry got up, and glared in annoyance at the ash-ridden fireplace. "And please remind Menche about the chimney flue. He needs constant reminders, like a child."

The Humble King walked slowly up the stairs with Franklin in tow. The people of Vermont would not be thrilled at the inclusion of a Flatlander into their society, and he knew it. *I'm certainly risking much with his newest proposition.* He turned one last time to see Ellen dousing the fire with the remaining contents of her mead. *This clearly isn't one of my more popular decisions.*

---

[8] A common term for one whose work is tied to Lake Champlain.

[9] Those who trade or smuggle goods using the various mountain trails in Vermont.

After almost twenty straight hours of sleep, Flatlander awoke to a bright ray of sunshine blasting through his bedroom window. Save for a minor ache in his neck, he felt renewed. He cursed as he saw the unsightly tea stain on the sheets. It also reminded him that he had been asleep for a long, long time. He couldn't believe it. *A day gone to complete waste*, and worse yet, he thought, *it couldn't have come at a worse time.* He could use every minute, every waking hour, to try to find his way home.

As he drew the curtains to his room, and soaked in the morning sun, he beheld the capital city of Montpelier in all of its glory. The view from his room was simply spectacular. To his right, rolling hills crested in the distance, ascending gradually above the fertile farmlands, in which farmers with ox-drawn carts were now tilling the recently thawed soil. Looming mountains beyond the pastures dominated the skyline, their peaks still snowcapped. Cows and horses lined the undulating ridges. The other side of his view, in stark contrast, revealed the busy downtown section of Montpelier, which was now brimming with life during this springtime bliss. Residents bustled up and down the cobblestone streets, rushing to their local jobs and schools. Nearby, a small group of nobles and lords approached the statehouse, laughing as they spoke. A teenage boy peddling loafs of bread, baguettes, and croissants pulled his fare in a small, battered rickshaw-style wagon, while calling out for customers in an off-pitch, cracked voice. An elderly, oddly bent woman showered a section of cobblestone with birdseed, attracting a small flock of pigeons, which picked between the red bricks. Flatlander turned from the view, and to his surprise, saw Henry's little assistant, Menche, standing awkwardly in the doorway.

"Mornin', Flatlander. Milord means to meet with ya in ten minutes, out by the gazebo." Menche pointed in the direction indicating the back of the house.

Flatlander nodded. "Be right out."

The back garden of Lord Henry's home was no larger than three acres and well manicured. A thin creek, no wider than an arm's length, winded its way around a large, white gazebo, and subdivided two large, rectangular garden beds, each approximately half an acre. A small forest lay at the back of the property. Henry, Franklin and Ellen sat at the gazebo chatting, while Gabby served them what looked like snacks and freshly squeezed juice.

"Flatlander!" cried Henry, merrily, with a mouthful of pastry. "Please, come join us! Come! Sit!"

He approached his hosts and took the available bench seat between Franklin and Ellen.

Henry finished his pastry, and dabbed the corners of his mouth with a handkerchief. "I trust that you've slept well?"

"Couldn't have asked for better, thanks" replied Flatlander.

"I was unsure if we should hold you a funeral or not," the king quipped.

"Funny," replied Flatlander with a crooked smile.

Where was this going? Would Henry cast him from this strange land? Or partner him up with a guide to see that he leaves for the 'flatlands?' Was there a way to communicate with his family, if he had a family? Something about the King's demeanor, his sheer excitement upon seeing Flatlander, suggested that he had rather pleasant news to share.

"Well," stated Henry, as he placed his handkerchief back into his pocket: "I've done much thinking last night, and this morning as well... and I came to some conclusions." He paused. "First, it's clear that you came from the Old Country. Your attire screams of it. We don't know much anymore about what resides to the west of Lake Champlain and the mountains beyond it, for its cities lay abandoned or ruined from a series of wars and the likes. *But...*we do know that New York encompasses most of that area. *Where* in New York is an entirely different story. So, that would be our first target area for ensuring your safe return."

Henry nodded at the newcomer's footwear. "Plus, there's your moccasins."

They looked at Flatlander's moccasins in unison. Franklin tried, unsuccessfully, to stifle a laugh. Blushing, Flatlander tried to hide both shoes behind the bench stand. Exchanging a nod with Ellen and Franklin, Henry cleared his throat.

"I have come up with a compromise. It's against the advice of my advisor, but I'll stand by it. It's something that I think will benefit all parties…in time."

"In time," said Franklin with a snarl.

"Flatlander, I want to send you on ten quests. And if you complete these quests to my overall satisfaction, then you will be granted full citizenship to the Republic of Vermont. *If* you accept, of course."

"*Quests?*" Flatlander squinted hard at Henry. "What are you talking about?"

Henry's gaze then followed the lazy stream circling the gazebo. "Yes, quests that are designed to help the republic. Helping fix problems that have been festering for much too long. As Vermonters, we sometimes like to think that we're immune to many of the problems that the rest of the world faces, yet that is not so. Concocting the ideas for some of your quests wasn't terribly difficult. There is a lot of room for improvement."

"And if I fail?"

Henry leaned forward. "Fail, and I shall reconsider my offer. Refuse, and you will be removed immediately from our lands."

Why would he be motivated to stay in this strange land with no friends and no support? Ten quests, no less? This was madness. He had the sudden urge to leave at once.

"Okay, this is crazy. No, forget it. I'm out."

"Then Franklin here can see to it that you'll be on your way immediately," replied Henry, with a nod to the northerner. Franklin stood up, ready to pick Flatlander up like a twig.

Flatlander looked meekly at Henry. "And if I agree?"

Henry signaled for Franklin to halt, as the bodyguard took a tentative step back. "At least you'll have enough time to get your wits about you, and from what I've gathered thus far, that may still seem like a ways away," replied Henry with a hint of good humor. "I would, as you might imagine, be delighted if you accept my proposal."

Ellen nodded. "You should be honored."

Flatlander considered his options. The gentle rush of the nearby creek provided momentary distraction. *No. I don't owe these people any favors. Besides, they don't even like me. I was spit at during my first minute walking downtown!*

Still, something tugged at his heart, begging him to reconsider. He supposed that it couldn't hurt a bit longer to stay while he tried to regain his bearings. His severe bout of amnesia made any attempt to return home near impossible at the moment, a mere pipe dream. Home could be hundreds of miles away, perhaps more. A professional escort to the nearest border didn't seem to be the answer he had hoped for. He'd still be just as lost, just as confused. And at least here, he had made new acquaintances of sorts, and had a roof over his head and food.

Flatlander sighed. "Okay, okay, I'll do it."

"Excellent!" Henry replied. "But I must warn you that the quests will not be easy. You will encounter foes of great strength, and prejudice at nearly every street corner."

"Your kind are considered fools here, just remember that, Flatlander," added Ellen.

Flatlander rolled his eyes. "I get it, I get it, *and everyone* hates Flatlanders. I'm not making any promises, Henry. I'm just telling you that I'll try."

Henry nodded in approval. "That's all we can ask. Just remember that we're on your side, and in turn, you have the backing of the king. And as a small measure of protection, I give you this."

Henry then produced a medallion from his pocket, and handed it to Flatlander, who held it in the light for closer inspection. Engraved on the front was a portrait of Lord Henry smiling and a crescent moon above his head. A large bear in an aggressive stance was pictured below his caricature.

"Show it to anyone who poses a threat. And though I can't guarantee it'll always help; it rarely hurts."

Then, from his side, Franklin held out a heavy, green metallic ring. A series of small stars lined its frame, and it had looked quite worn down. The face of the Lynx, a species of large wildcat found in Northeast Kingdom, marked its center.

"Take this as well, Flatlander. Ya never know when yer gonna need it when travelin' in the Kingdom. Just, umm, don't tell them ya got it from me," stammered Franklin, oddly.

Flatlander nodded. "Thanks."

"You will also travel with company during these quests," said Henry, as he rested his back against the side of the gazebo bench. "In fact, I have already chosen your company for the first quest."

Flatlander raised an eyebrow. "*Company?*"

"Yes, of course. You'll need someone to show you around the republic, somebody with a knowledge of this land and our people."

Flatlander looked joyfully upon the massive northerner. "Great."

Henry cleared his throat. "Actually, you will be accompanied on your first quest by Menche," said Henry, as he gestured to his pint-sized assistant sitting on his own by the creek. Menche gave Flatlander a wink and a nod, as Flatlander returned a pained look to the Humble King. Henry noted the exchange wryly.

"Worry not of Menche. Though he can be dimwitted, he knows these lands as well as I, and is loyal almost to a fault."

"It's da truth," concurred Menche, beaming with pride.

"When do I start?" asked Flatlander, sourly.

Henry nodded. "As soon as you can. Your supplies are awaiting you by the front door."

His options were limited, at best. *Perhaps I could muster some memories in the process, string together some semblance of home. Wherever home is, or was.* And as the group remained seated, discussing in fine detail that of Flatlander's first quest, a cold Montpelier wind sang amongst the seedlings and the creek, as it rattled Flatlander to the bones. And it was just an hour and forty minutes later, when the wind had fully subsided, that Flatlander and Menche were gone, departed for the northern reaches of the republic, to the small town of Irasburg.

CHAPTER 2
Pete the Moose

FLATLANDER'S FIRST QUEST WAS TO free a domesticated moose named Pete, whom, according to both Henry and Ellen, was facing certain doom at the hands of republic's game wardens. Pete resided on a farm in Irasburg, a small town just south of the far-northern city of Newport, which straddled the Canadian border, and due west of the fjord-like Lake Willoughby. From Montpelier, they were to travel the Newport Road, a stretch that would take them northeastward some fifty miles. The Humble King advised them to leave at once, for even his healthiest steeds, built primarily for endurance, would be tested on such a lengthy excursion.

The legend of Pete the Moose had roused much controversy in the republic, yet Flatlander had to admit that its backstory was intriguing. Years prior, on a bitterly cold day in February, Pete's mother was killed by a pack of wild dogs when he was just days old, and in the process, had been nearly mauled to death himself. Luckily for the baby moose, a gentle soul named Leyton Myregard had heard the commotion while scraping ice from his gutters, and managed to scare away the dogs before they killed Pete. Miraculously, Pete survived the vicious attack and was slowly nursed back to health by Leyton. Suffering substantial wounds to his legs, chest and hindquarters, Leyton treated the baby moose's wounds by pouring a fifth of Coventry whiskey on them as an antiseptic, then bandaging them with gauze meshed with mint and sage. His goat, Patty, provided milk for the creature. The abundance of pine trees on the farm provided ample pinecones, a moose's preferred winter diet.

Leyton, a widower and retired land surveyor for the republic, had spent a good deal of his career surveying the land of Central Vermont and the borders of the Northeast Kingdom, mostly to see if there were any additional, untapped marble or granite quarries laying in wait. Vermont had built a reputation for its marble and granite deposits. During the days of the Old Country, the state had built an important industry exporting stone to the Flatlands[10], where they had built their buildings, monuments and homes. Most of the quarries had been heavily exploited during these years of supplying the Old Country, and were then summarily stripped to the bedrock during the construction of the wall, an extended stone barrier encircling most of the entire republic. Yet many experts believed there to be remaining deposits in and around the spine of the Green Mountains, and Leyton's job was to prospect many of these supposed hidden pockets.

Years passed. Stone was unearthed in small, well-contained mines. Leyton had proven his worth as a premier prospector and surveyor of the republic. Yet soon, the purpose of these trips changed. Every quarry worth its own hauling road had been excavated, and every mineral worth its spoils, sold. And increasingly, Leyton continued visiting these remote sites for another purpose entirely: to scout out potential farmland for his retirement. And in the autumn of 2100, and at the ripe, old age of 68, Leyton decided that he would uproot from his rather squalid home in Calais (near Montpelier), and relocate to the beautiful, remote hills of Irasburg.

---

[10] Another slang term for the Old Country.

Perceived as an eccentric by the small community, Leyton Myregard was simply hard to miss. He sported a faded, tanned fedora, which complimented his tight, denim overalls and pointy, chest-length beard. His glasses were thick, and he had shoulder-length, glossy, grey hair. Leyton was as old school, backwoods Vermont as they came; a true relic, agreed the few townsfolk of Irasburg, whom he would occasionally bump into at the general store. Likable as he was cantankerous, those who came to know Leyton, knew him to be a stand-up man, his good deed of saving Pete the Moose from harm's way coming as no surprise.

Shortly after rescuing the moose, Leyton wrote a letter to the wardens for advice on the matter on what to do with Pete, for caretaking a moose was unnatural and unheard of in the republic. Responsible for protecting and managing Vermont's wildlife, the wardens were a rugged group of men, and the few in the republic entrusted with rifles; which were now exceedingly rare artifacts from shortly after the dissolution of the Old Country. The wardens told him that he would be doing the animal a disservice by letting him live. According to the letter provided by Chief of Wardens, Filmud Asterbrook, Pete could be harboring a contagious brain disease common in domesticated deer and moose, and could also pose a physical threat to humans after being desensitized to their company. Leyton had a hard time believing it. He had never once seen the animal try to hurt anyone. Despite Asterbrook's advice to "destroy" Pete, Leyton decided, much to the wardens' chagrin that he would keep him. He had grown an attachment to the animal. In an act of sheer desperation, Leyton decided to write to King Henry for assistance on the matter.

The wardens couldn't see what kind of joy the animal had brought to the old man's life, Leyton cited in his letter. If they could only see the first time that Pete walked successfully under his own power, merely days after the vicious attack, reflected Leyton. Or the way he trotted around the fenced yard the two weeks later like a dog at play. Or the time that Pete took some of Leyton's milk from right under his nose, and guzzled down the whole gallon, despite Leyton's best efforts to dislodge it from his jaws.

But one memory that stuck out though, Leyton relayed to Lord Henry in his letter of protest, was an occasion in which Leyton presented Pete with a knot of fur from his mother, discovered near the roots of a juvenile pine. Pete sniffed at the clump of fur, his eyes widened, and he then began to make sob-like wails for minutes, his snout pointed high up in the still air. Leyton "reckoned they were sounds of mournin'. He was sure of it." The former prospector had no doubt that Pete was re-living the very moment in which his mother had died, right in front of his eyes. Pete's life, Leyton wrote, "was worth more than dyin' in a ditch from a pack of 'em dogs. Alone, scared, motherless."

As Leyton took on his new role of foster parent, something inside of him changed. No longer was he purely tied to the land to "get away" from it all. No longer would he spend his days in near-solitude since the passing of his wife a twenty-five years prior. Solitude was only refreshing to a point. His experience surveying and prospecting through some of the more isolated regions of the republic taught him that notion well. Now he had something to care for, some purpose in life, beyond the comforting pastures of retirement. As such, the old man took pity on the creature, and decided to adopt him indefinitely.

The wardens had jobs to do, though. Part of that responsibility was enforcing laws without prejudice or emotional attachment. Hardened souls, sure, but also *good* men, *simple* men: who wanted nothing more than to maintain a healthy and safe environment for any and all creatures under their watch. Yet they did not have the authority to storm the farm and kill the animal, due to Henry's refusal to sign off on that particular request per Filmud Asterbrook. As such, the dilemma had resulted in a legally complicated and tense standoff, right there on Leyton's farm in Irasburg ongoing for six weeks and counting.

The story soon became fodder for the republic, near and far. The standoff in Irasburg became a headache for the wardens. It completely diverted their limited resources from other important areas, as well as highlighted an unsettling lack of support from Montpelier. To Henry and many Vermonters, however, Pete the Moose had become a symbol: a symbol of strength and courage, a symbol of overcoming enormous odds in the face of adversity, a symbol of the republic's fierce independence seared in time's memory.

The history of Vermont indicated that the republic had adopted a chip on its shoulder, a stance influenced by their seceding from the Old Country many years ago. Many Vermonters had grown a sense of fierce independence over the years, as the majority still resided in farmlands, reconciled to a life of self-sufficiency. Thus, few had developed a trustful or positive relationship with the government. The plight of Pete the Moose spoke to their core existence and their very notions of what was fair and just. Many believed that certain legacies should transcend customary laws. The powerful machine of Burlington's newspapers, particularly that of Shay Bromage's weekly[11], championed the peaceful release of the creature back into the wild. Others called for Leyton to keep the animal. Very few, outside the wardens, supported destroying Pete.

The political stakes were higher than one might imagine. Though interested in boosting his trust and popularity with the people of Vermont, Henry was also an avid hunter, and very reluctant to alienate his allies, the wardens. Walking a political tightrope, it had become quite evident that recruiting Flatlander to rescue Pete the Moose was the smart and practical thing to do for all parties involved. With the release of Pete, he could appeal

---

[11] The republic's most popular weekly newspaper.

to the sensitivity of the citizens. If Flatlander was caught, he could tell the wardens that this stranger, this outsider, acted on his own fruition.

Henry knew that there would be risks associated with sending Flatlander on this task, but he saw it as an important goal and a good springboard for Flatlander's introduction to the republic. What more fitting way to present an employed Flatlander than sending him to retrieve the republics' very own newly adopted symbol?

Yet, while Henry watched both Flatlander and Menche depart on horse and carriage, a sense of unease filled the Humble King. He stood there on the porch, long after the pair rode off on his two favorites steeds. As the creaks from their carriage faded, and the dust had settled slowly on the gravel, he remained fixated on the now-vacant road. Henry was still standing, quite eerily, when the bells from the statehouse rang aloud across the rolling valleys and hills of Montpelier, signaling the resumption of his governing duties.

He rode in a britzka carriage with Menche, pulled by two of Henry's prized horses, Bella and Amethyst, a bag of supplies, and no real idea of what to expect upon their arrival in Irasburg. The plan, devised by Henry, was to infiltrate the perimeter disguised as wardens from the Northeast Kingdom, get to Leyton Myregard, and then create a diversion that would ensure the release of the creature. The King had warned him that wardens would be surrounding the farm, and that they weren't the type of people he'd want to upset. They were 'burly folk from remote villages across the republic; types who made it their livelihood to kill not for sport, but for order.' Upset the wardens, cautioned Henry, and they might have to hightail it out of Irasburg, and fast.

Amazed at how quickly the city limits of Montpelier transformed into dense mountain wood, Flatlander came to truly see the grand countryside of Vermont. They passed two imposing mountains that Menche referred to as Mount Mansfield, with its rolling profile of a human face pointed skyward, and further south some twenty miles, Camel's Hump, a mountain aptly named for its hump-like ridge upon its summit.

Mansfield's vast, snowcapped summit shimmered in the late morning sun, yet as the pair traveled north of Mansfield through the towns of Westford and Cambridge, Flatlander caught full view of a strange sight. An odd feature, like a giant plateau, protruded from Mansfield's western front, arising half again or more the full height of the mountain. The feature, unlike the wooded highlands of Mount Mansfield, was mostly comprised of bare, whitish-gray bedrock, and it seemed to span for a few miles. It looked out of place, foreign.

Menche shook his head glumly, and mumbled. "Just a shames, it is."

"What is?"

"Ya thinks the cliffs would be dones taken, is all…"

Flatlander pointed at the bulge of rock. "Menche, what is that next to Mansfield?"

"The ball is all da hope they got, I says. Better get it 'fore it's too lates."

The little man's jargon answered little, and while Flatlander gazed at Mansfield's towering prominence, a strong jerk by his steed, Bella, reminded him of the task ahead. Later, along the border of Belvidere, still thirty miles west of Irasburg, Flatlander noticed Henry's assistant grinning uncontrollably, as he steered the horse and carriage around a bend in the road.

Flatlander glanced at his smirking companion. "What's so funny?"

"Not often that I get to goes on adventures, Flatlander, sir."

Flatlander nodded. "Glad to be of help."

Menche shrugged, and whipped the horse reigns lazily. "Beats carrying water all day from da springs, sir, or diggin' up holes in da garden. Haven't beens on a trip for some time, I'd say."

"Must be nice," marveled Flatlander, as he glanced at Menche again.

It was the first time he had noticed how short Menche's legs were. Even fully extended and dangling carelessly, they couldn't touch the bottom of the carriage floor.

"Yer noticin' me socks, aintcha?"

Flatlander looked away, embarrassed. "Uh, yeah."

Menche lifted a pant leg to reveal a white wool sock, with yellow and green stripes embroidered on the top. Pictures of pigs were etched on the sides with what appeared to be a thick, pink threading.

"Glad ya like 'em. Lord Henry got 'em fer me birthday."

"They're, uh, very nice," replied Flatlander with a smirk.

"Thanks. Much appreciated. Knew you'd like 'em."

Menche then began to hum to pass the time. So loudly, in fact, that the two mares leading the way would turn their heads periodically towards the carriage, and grunt in what appeared to be annoyance. Menche was simply oblivious to his own noisemaking. Flatlander was oblivious as well. He had blocked out the little man's noise, as his mind wandered far and wide. He wondered what would await him back in the Old Country and if it was as beautiful as the wooded mountain terrain, which now graced his sights. He wondered if he had family. He wondered what kind of work he had been in. He fantasized of a large group of people rejoicing upon his return to the Old Country, as he was strongly embraced by friends and family alike. Flatlander shook away the fantasy before it drove him mad.

Luckily for the two, it was a beautiful, sunny day. Birds and butterflies darted around on both sides of the dirt road, between the budding wildflowers and weeds. A red-tailed hawk circled overhead for a few minutes, then disappeared above the eastern tree line. Nearly halfway through the trip, a family of deer lingered no more than ten paces from the roadside.

"Menche, look," said Flatlander, childishly, as he pointed at the herd.

"Aye, ya see them often here, Flatlander."

"Is that right?"

Menche nodded and grinned. "Yer in Vermont now, fer what it's worth. Animals are just part of the scenery. Run-o-the-mill. Ho-hum!"

"Oh," Flatlander sighed, feeling slightly embarrassed from his exuberance.

They rode on some more, but this time it was Menche who broke the silence.

"They taught me growin' up that yer people are bad, sir," said Menche, and then he spoke in a low voice "but just between you and me, ya don't seem that bad to me."

Flatlander smiled; his curiosity piqued, as he recalled Barry spitting in his path and their semi-enlightening talk over brunch.

"What exactly *did* they teach you?"

Menche pulled hard at one of the reins and continued nonchalant. "They taughts us yer kind tried to take over this land once. They tolds us that you only care of moneys and houses and fancies. They told us that you don't cares for dem trees or bunnies or water or none of that. They say dem Flatlanders coulda ruined the world and not just the Old Country, just about did, they said."

Troubled, Flatlander thought hard. His lack of memory presented many difficulties, some just as simple as holding simple conversation, without any notable frames of reference. If what Menche was saying was indeed true, then it was no wonder that Vermonters looked down upon his kind with distaste. If it was untrue, however, then the people of Vermont were grossly misinformed.

"My memory tells me nothing," responded Flatlander, flatly.

Menche chuckled. "So ya says. So ya says."

Flatlander began to wonder about his companion. "How did you get to living with Lord Henry in the first place? You two seem like an odd couple."

Menche itched his arm and then the back of his head, and spoke softly. "Was a failure at everythings I tried, sir. Too small fer farm-work or buildin', too stupid fer schoolin', and too pigheaded to make much friends. Ya see, sir, my parents didn't wants me burdenin' them after school and all. I had trouble findin' work. Turned to mischief. One night gots caught stealin' a chicken from its coop."

Flatlander cocked an eyebrow. "Henry's coop?"

"How'd ya know?" replied Menche, bewildered, as he looked at Flatlander, amazed at the newcomer's quick perception. "Aye. It was hard keepin' quiet with dem wire cutters. Got 'em from me gramps. Coulda woken up every cow from here to Burlington, I swears it. Anyways, as he held me theres, he asked old Menche one good reason why he shouldn't bring me to da court of fools. Then I told 'em me life story."

"And he just took you in?"

"Yeah."

Flatlander felt goose bumps form on his arm. "Even after you *stole* from him?"

Menche nodded enthusiastically. "Oh, he saved me life, Flatlander! Woulda been stealin' chickens still, or worse, in jail, if it weren't for that man. We can argue now till the snow melts from them highest peaks of Mansfield, sure. Ya seen it yerself already! But I never seen him treats others unfair who don't deserves it."

Flatlander considered this as Menche ranted on some more about Henrys moral exploits. Yet Flatlander's mind fixated on the memory of a younger Menche in the chicken coop. *Why would anyone want to take in a thief?* He could almost imagine Menche clumsily working with a pair of wire clippers, fumbling about in a darkened coop, as the chickens squawked in dismay. Feathers, squeals, dropped wire clippers, and a furious Henry standing behind Menche in the dark. Flatlander chuckled softly at the conjured visual.

Then, after their five-hour trek on the fifty-mile course up the Newport Road, the pair heard the faint rapids of the Lords Creek from the woods to their right, swollen from the ongoing melt. According to a map of the area brandished by Flatlander, and courtesy of Lord Henry, Irasburg lay right up ahead. Turning to his left, Flatlander saw a metal street sign for 'Pray Road' half enveloped in a thorn-laden rose bush. He shook his head. *We're getting close.*

Little did the pair know, they were being trailed by a formidable foe. Lurking in the shadows of that Newport Road to Irasburg, he followed in the distance like a wolf. Feared by many powerful men throughout Vermont, he did not overpower through brute strength or weaponry. He carried no magical powers. He didn't possess great wealth or a propensity to commit cruel deeds. The man's only true possession that posed any real danger was his typewriter- but, oh, what power it did yield.

His name was Shay Bromage, and he was considered the most prominent and influential investigative journalist in all of Vermont. His tactics were labeled callous by some, ruthless by others. Like a predator on the prowl, Shay would follow a promising scent until they produced him a story, or dropped dead in the process (according to his critics, in good humor). And it was often joked by inner circles that it was a miracle that Shay had still retained such a large and devout following (or even friends for that matter), after blasting so many people in his articles, from statehouse lords to business owners to maple syrup farmers to mountain traders. For the Republic of Vermont was quite small, they reasoned, and a Vermonter's memory often burned deep.

Dressed in a blue and grey plaid wool jacket, and plain vanilla corduroys, Shay's boots were meticulously shined like new every day, even during the sloppiest of mud seasons. His hair was long and dirty blond and was kept tightly in a ponytail. He wore wire-brimmed glasses. A true muckraker's wardrobe, Shay had once mused. Although Shay was curiously mum on his age, acquaintances put him in his early forties.

Wielding tremendous political influence in the paper that he personally printed, Shay was the brains and brawn behind Burlington's popular weekly, *The Shay Chronicles*. People gravitated towards Shay Bromage's articles for their wit, controversy and brazenness. Just the mere uttering of his name prompted politicians to look over their shoulders and accountants to double-check their audits. And in *that* sense, Shay acted as an important cog in the republic's greased wheels: a holder of moral authority *and* popular sentiment, a dangerous combination of power. He oftentimes relied on information gathered from his informants, and his network spanned from wall to wall, despite the fact that Shay considered himself a hands-on journalist.

Shay's method of transportation was unique. He rode in a small, stand-up-room-only chariot pulled by his beloved mule, Harrison. Harrison was a stout creature with brown and black patterns. His aloof disposition stood in stark contrast to that of his master. For every 'blowhard needs its workhorse' once mused Shay's former colleague, Bailey Johanna Marks, when observing this disparity between the journalist and pet. Shay did a lot of traveling for his stories, often under the added duress of meeting deadlines. It was important that he had a reliable way to travel the republic near and far. Harrison's determination often amazed

Shay. The mule's relentlessness matched only by that of his master, who bore his whip by sheer necessity.

One common misconception regarding Shay Bromage was that he wrote his pieces purely out of spite. Anyone who *truly* knew Shay, knew this to be untrue. Indeed he was a man of strong convictions, but rarely, if ever, wrote pieces in sheer malice. Shay saw the world in a different and more cynical light; and it was in this very nature in which he wanted to reveal the world to his readership.

Subjected to many derogatory names throughout his life, the fact that he had maintained such a fervent group of supporters for close to ten years spoke to the strength of his mind and wit. Shay was not to be tested, and those who often challenged him got burnt in the process. A noble from Shelburne, Ezra Bingham, once found this out the hard way after criticizing one of Shay's articles examining the condition of the Bennington aqueduct. The following week, Shay had concocted a crossword puzzle in his paper listing all of the noble's mistresses by name. Subsequently, Bingham kept a low profile in the following weeks and months, right up until he abandoned his lordship some two years later.

Shay had become a household name over the years: a staple within the political and cultural realms, a dynamo of journalism, a risk-taker, a crafter of fates, and an object of scorn. He held Vermont's court of public opinion in the palm of his hands, and right now, the Flatlander and his partner were unknowingly marching directly into its vice-like grip. Having tailed them shortly after the spitting incident in Montpelier's downtown, Shay had sensed an unusual development from the start. Suspicious of the stranger's garb and demeanor, it hadn't taken long for him to piece together that this was a Flatlander in their midst, a noteworthy story unto itself.

He had been in town a day earlier in order to cover meetings at the statehouse, a thankless task that he had covered dozens of times over. Reporting from the senate floor was a necessary, but often dull aspect of his job. The atmosphere of the statehouse ranged from the absurd to the mundane, but rarely were any substantive issues resolved. Topics ranged from what kinds of trees to harvest for next season, to the maintenance of the republic's wall, to the proper materials used for cheeseboards. The monotony of these meetings often had Shay daydreaming of bigger, better stories to dig up. For it was in this void in Vermont's fabric that Shay had found his niche; searching for the eccentric, the dark, the mythical, the deceptive.

It was nice being his own boss in a sense, admired Shay. He didn't have to answer to a superior, could change stories on a whim, and didn't need to justify certain hunches. And right now, his hunches regarding the Flatlander's activities grew with each passing mile on this dusty, backcountry road to the northern border. For his suspicions were generally well founded, a point in which Shay was known to boast frequently of.

"Whoa, boy!" cried Shay, as his trusted mule came to standstill.

So it was on this stretch of the Newport Road in which Shay decided to hold his ground and maintain a safe distance from his new subjects. He bolted in the woods when he saw the two come to a brief stop. After a half-minute of waiting, his targets resumed their pace. Emerging from behind the shelter of several downed branches of maple, he then mounted his companion and counted off ten seconds in his head before pulling on the reigns.

Two hundred yards separated him from his quarry. He watched them from a distance, as they disappeared behind a gentle descent further up the road. *What are the Flatlander and little one up to? Out of all places, why venture into the Northeast Kingdom? Irasburg, of all places? This is no place for a Flatlander. This could either become headline material, or one long, pointless ride. I hope sincerely for the former.*

"Come, Harry," ordered Shay as he patted Harrison's snout. "I think that we might be visiting the wardens soon."

Flatlander directed Menche to pull off the main road near a soft clearing in the woods. According to the map, the next bend in the road signaled the border of Leyton's farm. He unlatched the corroded lock of the carriage's trunk. Henry had left them a large bag full of supplies, the contents of which were deemed pertinent to the overall success of the quest. Rummaging through the bag, he removed a pair of crusted boots, binoculars, a fur coat, a long grey wig, and finally, a rifle. As Flatlander removed the rifle from the bag, his heart sank.

At the very bottom of the bag, lay a small note. He unfolded it and read: *in case you need it.*

"What's it say?" asked Menche from behind Flatlander, as he tried to steal a glance.

"I'm beginning to think that your master has gone mad," said Flatlander, as he folded the paper and tucked it into his pocket.

"What's he wants us to do?"

"Go through with the plan," replied Flatlander, as he sighed. "I just didn't know that guns would be involved."

"Ya never shots one?" inquired Menche, as he adjusted the rifle's sights.

"How many times must I tell you that I don't remember!" said Flatlander, as he ripped the gun away from his partner's wandering hand.

"Jeezum crow. Only askin'."

Flatlander cradled the rifle gently in his hands. It was heavier than it appeared. As he twirled it awkwardly in the air, Henry's engraved symbol soon came within view. The marking of the moon was large and a bright white. Underneath, the caricature of the Humble King was smiling in exaggerated happiness. These were odd folk, yet it was clear to Flatlander not to underestimate the wisdom of Henry; for the Humble King had meant to send Flatlander on this quest for a purpose. As Flatlander glanced back and forth between the clothes scattered on the carriage floor and the rifle in his palms, he cast a brave glance at the chubby assistant.

"Menche, tether these two a few paces in the woods here," he ordered, as he pointed at Bella and Amethyst. "We don't have a lot of time to spare."

Menche grew frantic. "What is it then, sir? Are we startin'? Don't do nothin' stupid! I'm too young to die here, if it pleases ya!"

"We'll be fine," replied Flatlander. "I think."

After the horses had been tethered to a tree, Flatlander and Menche walked to the edge of the wood where the map had marked the edge of Leyton Myregard's property. They then positioned themselves on a rocky outcrop overlooking the roughly 100 meters between them and the farm. Although the foliage at this time of the year consisted only of the light green potpourri of budding trees, it just barely provided ample cover to the pair.

Flatlander lay down on his stomach, and peered through the binoculars. He could see three separate sets of two wardens each. They all wore orange vests and vanilla trousers, and most of them, yellow-brimmed hats, camouflage and sunglasses. They formed a loose perimeter around the front section of the property along a dirt road, glaring at the home in between spurts of simple conversation. A red two-story farmhouse stood within the middle of this scattered half-ring.

"I count six," whispered Flatlander.

Menche's eyes widened. "Six?"

"No. Eight," corrected Flatlander, as he adjusted the binoculars, catching two more wardens sitting in the shade of a horse-drawn carriage. Seconds later, he saw two more figures crouched down beside what appeared to be the entrance of the driveway, inspecting the trigger of a rifle.

"Nope. Make that ten."

"Ten!" screeched Menche. "I don't knows about this, sir. This ain't lookin' like something Menche would be good at! I can just wait by the horses if ya don't mind, keep them company. Tell 'em stories and the likes."

"Calm down," stated Flatlander plainly.

"What if I goes on and screw somethin' up? Wouldn't be the first time, I'm tellin' ya!"

"And what would Lord Henry say about *that*? I'm looking for a ticket out of here. Just listen and do as I say."

Menche sighed in resignation, wiping a bead of sweat from his brow. From the wooded farmland below they heard faint laughter from the wardens.

Though few within range could tell, Hal Gaudette was smirking beneath the shade of his yellow brimmed hat. His hands, cold and rough to the touch, were placed firmly on a brown wooden fence. From beside him, Jimmy Rhodes shuffled a deck of cards, using a short kiosk as a table. The sun shone heavier than it had in days, as a light dust emitted from a nearby feeding trough.

It was tedious work, this waiting game. He knew it. Not in one million years would Hal ever envision himself one day quarantining an old man and his beloved pet moose. In his childhood dreams, Hal use to dream of riding on a buffalo, an animal that he had studied from the wild west of the Old Country. In this reoccurring dream, he hooted and hollered, as he rode the mystical beast. He shot at deer. He shot at bear and coyotes. Hal smiled at the memory. *Boyhood dreams. Ain't they nice?*

This waiting game, this drawn-out political hand, had become the new reality for him and his group of wardens. And while he served his men and served them proudly, the second in command of the wardens was frustrated at the lack of backing from Montpelier. If only the people of Vermont informed themselves of the danger in keeping Pete the Moose alive. What if he were to escape and injure somebody in the process? Pass on a disease to an otherwise healthy population of moose? Those same people would be calling for Hal's head! *Life ain't fair sometimes.*

He lit up a cigarette with a pack of kitchen matches sitting on the kiosk, tugged down his sunglasses, and glanced over at Jimmy, who shuffled his deck of cards with utter indifference.

"Damn pretty out, I suppose."

"S'ppose," confirmed Jimmy.

"Hey Jimmy, you winnin' that game yet?"

The slack-jawed warden nodded triumphantly. "Yessir."

Hal glanced at Jimmy's wild display of cards. "Though I suppose it's pretty hard to lose when yer only playin' yerself."

"Hmm," considered Jimmy, as flipped over a pair of aces. "S'ppose so."

Years ago, Hal had come to the conclusion early on that Jimmy wasn't much of a talker, more of a shooter. *The man could shoot a sparrow in the eye from a stone's throw or more, but I'll be damned if he could muster enough verbosity to speak in a full sentence!*

"Ya know, you'll be givin' yerself that damn 'thritis if ya keep playin' with them cards."

"Don't bother me much," responded Jimmy matter-of-factly.

"Nope, Jimmy, it don't seem like nothin' bothers you much. My lord, sometimes I gotta poke ya to make sure yer breathin'." Hal laughed shortly to himself, took a long pull from his cigarette, and began walking up the road to the roadway checkpoint. "To hell with him. I've had better conversations with my dog."

As he approached the Newport Road checkpoint, he came upon wardens Dougie and Weekes laughing wickedly. They had barely noticed Hal's arrival until he was practically on top of them. Weekes nodded in greeting, and gestured for Hal to look in the direction of the farmhouse. Hal looked and saw the crazy old loon, Leyton, standing next to the moose. His shirt was soaking wet, as water dripped copiously from his hair and fedora.

"Hal, you missed it," said Dougie, through struggled breaths, as he adjusted his hat. "That damned moose just sipped some of that water from old man Leyton's bucket, and spit it right on the ol' geezer!" Dougie almost keeled over in laughter. "You shoulda seen his face!"

Hal smiled thinly. "That right?"

"The man just looked at the moose all funny, like 'what the…'" said Weekes, as he did his best impression of Leyton's reaction. "He saw us laughin' and stormed in the house angrier than a cornered bear! Woulda been pure gold for ol' Shay Bromage, I'm tellin' ya!"

Hal smiled and glanced towards to where Pete was standing. The moose was still squirting water out of its mouth like a hose, splashing the farmhouse's kitchen window. Leyton opened the window to chastise Pete, but instead, took a stream of water directly to the face, prompting him to curse and slam the window shut. Dougie and Weekes howled with laughter. Hal looked through his binoculars. Several of the other wardens surrounding the premises must have seen the same series of events too, because they were all laughing just as hard. After a half minute, Dougie caught his breath and wiped a tear from his eye.

"I'm telling ya, Hal, I don't know if I can take this any more. Am I just goin' stir crazy or are these two really *this* funny?"

"Certainly somethin' you don't see every day outside Irasburg," replied Hal nonchalantly. "Don't forget why we're here though, boys. If that damned moose gets loose, we may be looking at a world of hurt." The laughing slowly subsided, with a few low grumbles.

Hal nodded. "I'm just sayin', don't let yer guards down."

"You know, I never thought that I'd be sayin' this, but I will truly miss this place when we have to leave town," stated Weekes.

Hal considered that for a moment. "That's because neither of you two rimrods got paired with Jimmy. That man's thicker than a box of bolts."

"Jimmy ain't much of a talker," said Weekes. "I've heard more comin' out of that man's backside than I've ever heard come out of his mouth."

"Oh, c'mon," said Dougie with a scrunched nose.

Hal patted Dougie on the shoulder playfully. "I'm with Dougie," agreed Hal. "We don't need to be hearin' that. Got a question though, what's…"

But before Hal could finish his question, he caught some movement down the road from the corner of his eye. It looked like a man and a boy walking and arguing, as they moved in the direction of the wardens. Hal threw down his cigarette and gripped his rifle in a rush.

"What on earth have we got here?"

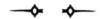

Adorning a pair of Norwich boots, a black fur coat, and a rifle casually tucked underneath his arm, Flatlander tried his best to look the part of a Vermonter. Walking with a determination that betrayed his anxiousness, he approached the wardens gathered near the driveway, kicking up dust with every step. Menche wore a curly, grey wig, and clutched at Flatlander's legs in pronounced desperation.

"Just remember what I said and don't take anything personally. And look convincing!" murmured Flatlander from the side of his mouth.

They eyeballed the odd-looking pair. Standing at least six feet tall and wearing their distinctive orange vests, the wardens looked like a rough crowd from up close. The lead warden gripped his rifle hard, as smoke wafted at their feet from his dying cigarette.

Flatlander and Menche continued their fake struggle. "I'm tired of hearin' all of yer excuses, ya hound!" snapped Flatlander at Menche in his best Vermont accent, as he brushed him aside.

Menche grabbed at Flatlander's leather belt. "Please, sir. He didn't do ya no harm!"

Flatlander shoved Menche. "Not yet, he didn't! Move!"

"My brother loves that animal, sir. Please. Means the world to him."

"Like I give a damn!"

The wardens looked at one another curiously, as the two strangers came to the head of the driveway. They formed a small blockade, sizing up their unexpected guests.

"Hey! What seems to be the problem here, fellas?" asked Hal curtly.

Flatlander rolled his eyes, and pointed to Menche. "Ah, the little twerp won't leave me alone!"

"It ain't fair!" cried Menche.

"*Life* ain't fair, little man!" replied Flatlander, without missing a beat.

"Whoa, whoa, whoa," said Hal, as he held up his hand, incredulously. "Just what the hell's goin' on here?"

"Little weasel here tells me I shouldn't be shootin' his brother's moose! I says to hell with him! Nobody's givin' me orders, tellin' me what I can or can't do!"

Hal gripped his gun and cocked an eyebrow at Dougie and Weekes. The others followed suit as they lifted their rifles chest-high in unison. Flatlander tried hard to keep his cool.

"The only peoples who are goin' to do any shootin' around these parts is *us*," responded Hal, matter-of-factly.

"Says who?" demanded Flatlander.

"Says *me*," answered Hal, fiercely, as he pointed to his chest.

Flatlander sized up Hal dismissively, then scoffed. "And who might you be?"

"Hal Gaudette. Warden of the Republic. Chief enforcer and second in command to Filmud Asterbrook. And you are..."

"Ripley," replied Flatlander, as he rested the butt of his rifle against the fence. "Got orders directly from the Northeast Kingdom. People in high places. They want this thing out of the picture." Flatlander then produced the heavy ring given to him by Franklin. The wardens huddled around, gawking at the exotic accessory. Dougie began reaching towards it.

"Don't touch it," warned Flatlander, as Dougie recoiled from his outstretched hand. "The true men of the North don't take too kindly to the touch of folks like you. We also don't take kindly to fawning."

Dougie blushed. "Sorry."

"Where ya say yer from again?" asked Weekes, inspecting Flatlander's fur coat carefully. Flatlander had to think fast.

He thought of a name he had read on the map. "Granby."

Ricky nudged Weekes with his elbow and smirked.

"Did you say...Granby?" asked Hal, as he tipped his shades slightly.

Flatlander swallowed and hoped for the best. "Yup."

Hal was real quiet for a second, almost as if he were contemplating something. He inched up close to Flatlander, face to face. So close, that Flatlander could feel the moisture of the warden's breath, and see each individual nose hair and traces of razor burn on the man's wrinkled neck.

"I hear they got big buck up there," he said in a low voice.

Flatlander matched his tone, as his heart raced wild. "They do."

"Like one of them monster bucks," said Dougie from Hal's side. "Seen one once come out of the woods not too far from Granby. The thing was a straight-up bear killer, I'm tellin' ya. Racked like a damned pine tree."

"Everything's bigger in Granby, they say, except the town that is," responded Flatlander in true Vermonter form. The wardens chuckled softly at the jest.

"Got a comedian here," quipped Hal, dryly.

"One of these days, we're gonna have to make a trek up there, fellas," said Weekes.

As Flatlander maintained their full attention, Menche, as planned, eased away from the conversation towards the house. Backing up from the wardens, Menche moved as if in slow motion. Flatlander pretended to be caught off guard by the act.

"And just what do you think *yer* doin?"

"Seein' me brother, and ya can't stop me!" said out Menche, as Henry's assistant sprinted to the front door. Flatlander then burst into motion towards Leyton's home.

"Whoa, bud," said Hal as he caught Flatlander with an extended arm. "Strict orders. We can't go on that property. It's off limits."

"What? Says who?"

"Lord Henry himself."

He remembered one of Henry's requests. *Don't show the wardens my medallion. Only Leyton. This is meant to be a covert mission unless noted otherwise.* Flatlander brushed off Hal's grip.

"Well, I ain't under the same orders."

He then ran past the group of wardens, towards the front door of the farmhouse to which Menche now knocked on frantically. After several seconds, Leyton opened the door, the look of utter surprise spread on his face. Menche jumped onto Leyton's leg, his forward momentum pushing Leyton back into the entranceway. Flatlander followed directly behind and slammed the door closed.

"Wait. Hold up," said Hal, as he watched several wardens from the various checkpoints staring at the farmhouse with looks alternating between befuddlement and outrage. "Damn ballsy, if I say."

"Yup," agreed Jimmy, who had also taken up his arm and watched the spectacle unfold.

"Keep yer eyes peeled for anything funny, fellas," said Hal. "I ain't never heard of no wardens from that far north."

The men stood there in stunned silence, unsure of their next move. The other wardens from around the perimeter gave Hal curious looks; wardens Sam and Fred had their arms up in the air, puzzled. Hal gave them all a thumbs-up gesture.

"Boys, do me a favor and tell them others that it looks like a warden from the kingdom and a family member of Leyton's are meetin' impromptu. But tell 'em to be on high alert. Somethin' about this whole thing don't feel right to me."

Hal removed another cigarette from his now empty-pack, and gently pressed it to his lips. After a minute, he saw the wardens return the thumbs-up gesture after discussing the message with Dougie and Weekes. Listening for any suspicious sounds from the house, Hal was only greeted with silence. *Funny*, he thought, *those two were screamin' like fisher cats a minute ago.*

The impact with Menche and Flatlander spun Leyton around entirely, yet all that the retired surveyor could manage was a muffled yelp. Flatlander was on top of him in a flash, hand firmly pressed against Leyton's mouth. Frantically, the old man tried to wrestle from his grasp, but it was no use. The younger, stronger adversary had him outmatched.

Flatlander whispered hoarsely. "We mean you no harm. We've come to help you and the moose." To his dismay, Menche had already removed his wig, and was itching madly at his scalp.

"What are you doing?" admonished Flatlander in a whisper. "Do you want to get us *killed*? Put it back on!" Menche promptly obliged, embarrassed at his lapse in judgment. Flatlander then turned back to Leyton. "Do we have a deal, sir? I'm going to remove my hands, if you promise to keep quiet." The old man nodded. Flatlander removed his hand, as Leyton's eyes softened.

"Jeezum Crow. Don't see *this* every day," said the old man as he extended his hand, flush red and winded, "Leyton Myregard."

Flatlander shook Leyton's hand. "Nice to meet you. They call me Flatlander," he said, as he then nodded to his small companion, "and this is my friend, Menche. We've come to save Pete from the wardens."

"A *Flatlander*? You don't mean to tell me that they sent a *Flatlander*? Why? And save Pete? Why in the heavens…"

Flatlander waved a dismissive arm. "Where is he?"

Leyton gestured for them to follow him into the den. The walls and ceiling were painted in pastel reds and greens, and an oversized wood stove dominated the small living room. A large painting of a cow hung above a brown Chesterfield sofa. On the far side of the room stood a large, stuffed moose next to the wall. Flatlander neared the moose and touched its antlers.

"Is this…"

"No, that ain't Pete, ya dimwit. Shot that bad boy two years before I even met Pete. Pete's out back."

Transfixed by the woodstove, Menche opened and closed its lid while inspecting its inners.

"Don't play with that," ordered Leyton. The woodstove's lid snapped shut.

Menche looked sheepish. "Sorry."

Leyton held out both arms in exasperation. "What's with this 'save Pete' business? What in the damned hell's *that* suppose to mean? I've raised the guy since he was just a little chum, no bigger than a fox. He don't need no savin! Already been saved by my measure!"

Flatlander nodded and pointed outside the window. "Right now you've got ten wardens waiting outside your home, just one signed paper away from raiding this place and killing Pete."

"*The wardens*? Hmmph," said Leyton with a scoff as kicked at an imaginary opponent. "I've seen better shots from those pellet peckers at the old folks' home[12]. The fools couldn't shoot their ways outta wet paper bags if they wanted!"

"Regardless, your pet's in danger and we need to move him."

"He ain't my damned pet."

"Then what is he?"

---

[12] This is a reference to a small old folks home in Irasburg, which often employs the use of slingshots as a popular activity.

"He's…" Leyton paused, as he contemplated the proper terminology for the creature, "…my bud."

"Well, whatever he is, we need to get him out of Irasburg," replied Flatlander, as he produced the Henry's medallion from underneath his shirt, and displayed it for Leyton to see. "Highest orders."

Leyton toggled with his glasses, and peered closely at the medallion around Flatlander's neck. He sighed deep and leaned against the wall. Gently placing his hat on a nearby wall hanger, Leyton's eyes trained to the floor.

"Had a funny feelin' bout today. Somethin' wasn't right. Pete was actin' too damn odd, if ya ask me! Spittin! Hissin! Makin' a scene about lunch! It's like somethin's been in him all day! Now it all makes too much damned sense!"

Menche leaned up against the wall next to Leyton, and mimicked the old man's look of resignation, eyes cast downward. Leyton looked at the gnomish assistant, unsure if he should laugh or scold him.

"And what's with you, little fella?"

"Pardon my partner. He's strange," answered Flatlander, as he shot his new pint-sized friend a stern look.

"Yer tellin' me," nodded Leyton, with a look of bemusement.

Flatlander carefully tried to steal a glance out of a front window at the wardens. The only warden he was able to catch sight of eyed the house ominously.

"Leyton, we need to act fast."

"This ain't none of yer damn business, Flatlander!"

"It is whether you like it or not."

"I say hogwash! Last thing I needs is a damned Flatlander helpin' me."

"What's hogwash?" asked Menche.

"Shut up!" said Flatlander vehemently, before turning to the elderly farmer. "Leyton, we need your help on this, or there's no point for us being here in the first place. I've got an idea. If you'd just hear me out."

"I'm all ears," he answered. Leyton shuffled his feet, and stared at the floor in defeat. Nodding reluctantly, he wagged a finger at both Flatlander and Menche. "But if any harm comes to that moose, I swear...."

"Nothing," interrupted Flatlander, as he took a gulp, "nothing will come to your moose. That, I swear."

"I'll hold ya to that!"

"Fine," replied Flatlander, as he stole another glance out the window. "Now, listen to me."

As Flatlander divulged the plan in a low voice, the three hadn't noticed the wardens now repositioning themselves along the perimeter. They also hadn't noticed that each warden was now hoisting their rifles directly towards the house. Jimmy Rhodes cards had since dropped to the ground, unattended, and fluttering wildly in the wind. Patty the goat was sitting in the shade of shagbark hickory, snout hoisted high into the air, as she tasted the mountain gales. The farm grounds had grown eerily silent. The laughter of the wardens had ceased long ago.

Leyton directed Flatlander to the backyard of the house where Pete spent most his time. Luckily, the wardens' views of the small enclosure were completely obscured by Leyton's house. The moose's size was impressive, thought Flatlander at first impression. His frame was long and massive and he stood nearly six feet at the shoulder. His antlers were covered in soft brown velvet, which had peeled back in small traces at the tips. Scar tissue stemming from the dog attack of his youth lined both his legs and side, which also converged near Pete's backside.

The moose chewed slowly on a slither of bark. Small clumps of half-chewed poplar lay scattered at his hooves. Reluctantly, Flatlander closed the distance and was now an arm's length from the moose. Pete's eyes then met Flatlander's, yet conveyed no sense of surprise or delight, only complete indifference. Flatlander, on the other hand, was awestruck. The size of the creature was tremendous. He only hoped it to be of a friendly disposition. Pete dropped the bark on the ground and grunted, as a fine mist ejected from his nostrils.

"Whoa, Pete," remarked Leyton, as he stroked the creature's neck, "These fellas mean ya no harm."

The pair approached Pete cautiously, as Menche awkwardly grabbed at Flatlander's pant leg.

Leyton waved for the two to come closer. "C'mon, don't be shy. Give 'em a pet."

Leyton smiled broadly, yet maintained a rather strong grip on Pete's neck. At first, the animal grunted and shifted uncomfortable at the presence of the two strangers. But as Flatlander ran his fingers smoothly over his neck and shoulder, Pete relaxed and, eventually, seemed to actually enjoy the new attention. Flatlander smiled as he massaged the animal, while Menche summoned up the courage to touch Pete's leg.

"Don't poke him, fella. Be gentle. Like *this*," said Leyton, as he modeled the proper way of petting Pete. Menche watched and soon emulated the old man's gentle touch, as he stroked the animal's haunches.

"Hi, Pete," said Flatlander affectionately as he gently pet its snout. He bent down to pick up some of the fallen bark and held it out for Pete to chew. The moose hesitated slightly, then swiftly grabbed the slice of bark and gobbled it down in several chomps.

"I may not know up from down, or good from bad, boy, but I think he likes ya," muttered Leyton, as he sidled next to Flatlander. Placing his hand on Pete's massive snout, Leyton stifled a cry.

As tears welled up in his eyes, he nudged his glasses nervously. "You've been a good boy since I've known ya, Pete. I'll see ya again soon though, boy. Yer goin' to a better place. Goodbye, boy. Take good care of yerself."

The breeze picked up slightly, as a cloud of dandelion puffs filled the air around them. Leyton turned to the two rapidly, his eyes red and fists clenched.

"Don't be thinkin' you can be ridin' the guy for long either, I'll tell ya that much! He don't much like it. He's too proud fer that!"

As he gave Leyton some time to say farewell to his beloved friend, Flatlander heard the moose whimper softly. He felt as if his very presence was somehow in violation of this very tender moment between two friends. Stepping aside, he felt Henry's medallion clinging close to his chest. Time had moved rapidly since his awakening outside of Montpelier, yet now, time seemed to stand still. Legends were evolving before their very eyes in the pastures of Irasburg, as a prolonged silence enveloped Leyton's farm.

Hal signaled to the rest of the wardens with a closed fist, communicating to them to ease up but stay alert. Squinting hard at the house, Hal figured that it must have been a good twenty minutes since those strange men; those 'northern wardens' went inside, and still nothing. He wondered if he should approach the house and demand answers. If things went wrong in a hurry, Hal and his men had these strangers outmanned, outgunned, and plainly within their sights.

But just as Hal was considering these options, a large moose burst from the house with surprising speed toward the outlying forest. Fumbling for his rifle, he began shooting wildly at the animal. The other wardens followed suit. The moose stiffened

---

briefly as it caught a shot on what appeared to be its rear, and Hal could have sworn he heard a very humanlike 'yah.' Yet the animal continued running, very awkwardly, away from the swarm of wardens.

Hal licked off shot after shot at the animal, but in those nerve-rattling moments, he noticed something off with the way the creature was shaped, the way it moved. Its front legs looked way too short and mismatched, and its gait lacked any form of fluidity. Stumbling over a slight ridge, the creature then collapsed out of view near the edge of the woods. Hal motioned for the men to follow him, as they jogged to inspect the fallen moose. A sense of regret immediately began gnawing at Hal, and the warden could feel his mouth go dry as he came upon the forest ridge. The deed had been done, he supposed, but not in the way that Hal would have preferred.

As they inched up to their target, Hal's breath caught in his throat. Lying at the bottom of a depression in the woods lay Old Man Leyton hollering in pain, as he grabbed at the back of his thigh and wounded backside. A hollowed-out stuffed moose lay next to him in a bundled heap. As the wardens gathered around Leyton, a growing suspicion crept upon Hal. But before he could shout his next command, the actual Pete the Moose stormed out of the other side of the house from behind them, with the man who called himself Ripley riding on his back.

"Hold your fire, boys," commanded Hal.

The distance was too great. Their nerves were too unsettled. Hal didn't need card games like Jimmy to tell him when he had lost. The dust from Pete's gallop traced back their route upon arrival, and up Ripley went on that hilly Newport Road from which the two strangers had come not thirty minutes prior. Which got Hal thinking: where had the little one gone? He scratched his head, as several of the other wardens cursed under their breaths.

"Granby, my ass," muttered Hal.

"Yep," agreed Jimmy from his side.

Hal turned to Jimmy, ready to say something, but his mind faltered. While the other wardens muttered in confusion, Hal thought back to his childhood dreams, riding his buffalo, chasing things for the hell of chasing things. In a way, Hal admitted, he was jealous of this Ripley. The stranger was here for a half hour, tops, but in that time had managed more excitement during his brief stay than all of Hal's weeks in Irasburg combined.

Instinctively, Hal pointed his gun skyward and licked off a shot from his rifle. The other wardens jumped back in surprise. Ammunition in the republic was hard to come by, and it was unlike the second-in-command warden to be wasteful with his supplies. It became obvious after Hal's second shot, however, that this was a silent tribute; an odd commemoration to a newly-minted enemy, whose legacy had permanently become intertwined with their very own. One by one, the wardens shot their remaining bullets skyward toward the forest canopy, as the fleeing moose and its rider had become nothing more than a faded silhouette amid Irasburg's wake. And no more than a hundred yards away, from the shadows of Leyton's farm, Shay Bromage recounted the chain of events with exquisite detail.

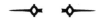

Miraculously unscathed, Menche ran through the adjacent woods terror-stricken. Even during his days stealing chickens, vegetables, and farm tools, he had never experienced a more harrowing escape. He tripped and fell flat on his face on several occasions, as his body went numb from shock. Almost everything had gone according to plan. *Almost.*

Menche had assumed the front half of the stuffed moose during their attempt to flee, and Leyton, the back. They had provided the distraction needed to help Flatlander escape with Pete. However, they had not planned for anyone to get shot in the process. Apparently, they had underestimated the wardens' range. Leyton took a bullet.

Luckily for Menche, the wardens didn't manage to pick up his trail fast enough, and he was gone from sight as they encountered Pete's wounded caretaker. He feared for the old man. Unsure what had happened to Flatlander during his own escape, Menche shook his head in confusion. *The horses. He had to find his way back to the horses before the wardens found them.*

"Ya really dids yourself in this time, dummy," muttered Menche between heavy panting.

Suddenly, sounds of gunshots echoed throughout the forest, giving Menche momentary pause. He gulped and closed his eyes tight, hoping that his new friends hadn't met their fate. It wasn't until close to twenty blasts later that the gunshots came fully to a stop. The ensuing silence was sickening. Several deep breaths later and overcoming a tremendous range of emotions, Menche resumed his escape deep into the woods towards the Newport Road.

On the other side of Irasburg, Pete moved like the wind. Galloping in full stride, the creature had left behind his accustomed life and injured master. And as soon as Flatlander saw the group of wardens, backs turned, converging on the forest ridge; he knew that he stood a fair chance of escape. Yet he was deeply concerned for Menche and Leyton. They had taken quite a spill. He hoped, in the bottom of his heart, that they had escaped uninjured. He had grown fond of the little man during the short time in his company.

As Flatlander rushed down the country road mounted on the freed moose, the wind howled past at a dizzying rate. He placed a hand across the crown of Pete's antlers to calm the animal, like Leyton had shown him.

Then as Pete slowly came to a brisk walk, a distinct memory came back. Looking out of a beautiful framed window at a vast body of water, Flatlander saw himself sitting on a velvet couch, as a hard sea breeze rattled the windows and blew right through his body as if he wasn't even there. He could smell the salt of the ocean, and nearly taste the brine on his lips, as the sounds of gulls echoed across the room. The glare of the rising sun on the water nearly blinded him.

Throughout his entire fifty-mile ride back to Montpelier, he found himself drifting in and out of this pleasant vision. The journey was long and hard, and daytime gave way to a spectacular sunset overlooking west of the Green Mountains, and the peaks of Mt. Mansfield and Camel's Hump. Alone with these thoughts, the only thing anchoring him to his reality were the hard, rapid sounds of Pete's hooves on the winding, dirt road and the creature's ragged breath.

It was well after nightfall when Flatlander arrived back in Montpelier. In the cool evening still, Flatlander led Pete at a slow pace through the pastures and hills on the outskirts of the capital city. He talked to the animal reassuringly. True to Leyton's warning, Pete had let it be known several miles into his journey that he did not like to be ridden, as evidenced by a sudden and violent bucking. As a result, Flatlander had taken a hard fall, but it could have been worse. Aside from a sore back, he had mostly incurred a bruised ego. It had been a very long, trying day for them both, reasoned Flatlander. He was a stranger to this animal.

After daydreaming through much of the journey back, Flatlander then thought heavily of Menche and Leyton: the gunshots, the fall, and the notoriety of the wardens and their shooting skills. None of this bode well for Menche's or the old man's wellbeing. A hard knot formed in the pit of his belly, and he thought hard of how to best describe the situation to Henry. *It happened so fast, I couldn't really see. They could have gotten away, honestly.* He could leave the memory open to interpretation, but Flatlander's senses betrayed his optimism. His gut told him all that he should know. Somebody got hurt back in Irasburg, potentially killed. Flatlander took a deep breath and swallowed hard.

They made their way past the rolling farmland, and into downtown Montpelier. The few younger men and women were out mingling on the streets near the Porter's Tavern. They turned their heads as Pete walked past, and whispered softly amongst one another, continuing to follow the two strangers with bewildered looks. Flatlander looked upon Pete with a mixture of humor and empathy. *A lost, pathetic Flatlander and a fugitive moose. Can you blame them for staring*? Flatlander patted Pete affectionately on the shoulder and continued to think of how to articulate the news to Henry.

As he approached Henry's home, Flatlander could see the kitchen lights on, as the sounds of rinsed dishes and clattering silverware emanated from the kitchen windows. Henry's bedroom was alight in a dim glow, as several candles lined the inner mantle. Before he could knock, the front door swung open with great velocity. There stood the Humble King sporting a long yellow bathrobe.

"Flatlander!" cried Lord Henry, with a wide smile. "You've made it!"

He embraced Flatlander and breathed a genuine sigh of relief.

"Made it," mumbled Flatlander, momentarily taken aback by Henry's hug.

"And what news? How did things work out?" Henry asked frantically. Noticing Pete for the first time, Henry's eyes lit up in joy. Pete tilted his rack to the side, and looked upon the Humble King curiously. "I can see we have our moose! Greetings, large one! Welcome to Montpelier!"

Flatlander nodded. "He's a handful, but he's safe."

"Excellent work, Flatlander," said Henry. "Thank you. The wardens are good men, but are hard to convince otherwise when they get something in their heads. This moose is too special to kill, as you can see. Please, come in. Come in."

"I barely made it out alive," said Flatlander, as he slowly entered Henry's house.

"But made it you *did*!" said Henry in glee.

Henry looked for any visible signs of injury on Flatlander. He checked under sleeves for wounds, inspected the fur coat for any holes or cuts, and circled him curiously before pausing.

"My apologies. You're weary, of course. Your bed is ready, and your room is made up. I'll send for Gabby to bring Pete to the barn. We can talk more about this in the morning."

"Thank you, Lord Henry," he replied. Flatlander slowly began making his way towards his bedroom. Yet Henry hadn't moved from his position near the doorway.

The Humble King hesitated. "But, um, what of Menche then? I notice that he's curiously absent."

Flatlander stopped halfway up the staircase. The truth was, he didn't know, and part of him dreaded finding out the truth in the coming hours. Menche and Leyton could both be dead. *How could he explain what he saw to Henry?*

"He's…I don't know. But he could be badly hurt," stammered Flatlander. "It all happened so fast. One second, I saw them running, the next, I heard a bunch of shots, and they were falling over a small ditch…"

Henry raised an eyebrow. He scratched the back of his ear, a pained expression on his face.

"Is that so?"

"I'm sorry."

"No, no. It's quite alright," Henry said in an empty voice. "Tomorrow we will send a party to look for both Menche, Myregard and the horses. Get some rest, Flatlander. We will speak in the morning."

Henry coughed, but it was readily apparent that the news of Menche had hit the Humble King hard. Flatlander took one last look at Henry before slipping through the living room doorway.

It was merely seconds later that he swore he could hear the king gently sniffling.

Like a worried parent, Henry spent the night with his senses heightened for any hint suggesting Menche's arrival. He had been a wreck since Flatlander arrived with the news. Guilt and anxiety wreaked havoc on his psyche, and despite his tired bones, Henry's bed felt no more comforting than a heavy wooden crate. *Why did I send them on such a dangerous quest, and the first of their tests, nonetheless? Getting the moose was important, but not worth the life of my beloved assistant! How could I have been so foolish to think that nobody would have gotten hurt?*

It was a particularly windy night in Montpelier. A large watering can fell onto the stone patio in the backyard, causing Henry to jump in his bed and listen intently. Minutes later, a small bucket was caught by the wind, and rolled and hurled itself down the nearby cobblestone of State Street. A dog barked in the distance. With each interruption to his thoughts, Henry sat up in a cold sweat, heart thumping.

It was close to two in the morning, according to his antique clock at his bedside table, when Henry heard a knock on the front door. Without any hesitation, nor the wherewithal to put on any pants, Henry sprinted down the stairs and hurriedly opened the door in nothing more than his underwear and a pair of fur slippers. There stood his assistant, Menche, covered in the porch lantern's light. His suspenders and trousers were covered in mud and burs, and he bore several scratches on his arms and face. Menche was shaking. Henry wanted to shout out with glee, but instead gave his assistant a twisted smirk.

"Welcome back, little one," said Henry as he shook his friend's hand. Behind Menche, the carriage sat motionless in the driveway, as Henry's two horses wagged their tales in unison.

"Hi, milord! Quite da busy day in Irasburg, I'd say!"

"So I heard. It was quite the frightful encounter, wasn't it?"

Menche nodded. "Did Mr. Flatlander makes it back, sirs?"

"Aye, he did, Menche. Tired, but in good spirits."

"Been thinkin' of 'em since back before sundown, sirs."

Henry smiled and nodded. "You did well, little one. I'm very proud of both of. If anything," said Henry with a wink, "consider this payback from the chicken coop."

"Ya means it, sir?" said Menche as he brightened up. "Not playin' around with Ol' Menche?"

"I mean it, yes," replied Henry with a wink. The Humble King glanced at the pair of snorting horses, whose legs were now struggling to keep upright. "Now, please let the horses back into the stalls. They must be beyond exhausted."

"Yes, lord," replied Menche.

"Good to have you back, little one," replied Henry softly. Menche nodded and guided the horses slowly back to the small barn in the back. Henry sighed low but deep, making sure that his assistant was out of earshot.

"Good to have you back."

CHAPTER 3
Fish

A HORN BELLOWED FROM AN APPROACHING steam-powered barge across the vast expanse of Lake Champlain, the sound so thunderous that it rattled paintings from the walls, tin cans on tables, and could be heard from upwards of three miles inland. Its freight, several dozen tons of cured meat, had made the short trek from the farms of Grand Isle, the largest of Lake Champlain's Islands, to the Burlington ports. Lord Henry told Flatlander that this was the freighter that they were waiting for. Two wispy clouds of smoke streamed from both sides of its bow, leaving a distinct trail. The lake men had used a metal barrel that had been cut in half vertically, and then reassembled it with a latch, creating a giant grill and cover. The cook was a hefty, bald fellow. He wore a thin white goatskin tee shirt, smeared in blackish grime, and loose-fitting, blue cargo pants (popular with the lake folk). His face looked weathered and red. Despite years of observance, Henry admitted that didn't know the fellow's name.

Three days after their return from Irasburg, Henry and Flatlander rode on horseback, westward, on the Rounding Road[13] to the republic's largest city of Burlington. In Duxbury, they again

---

[13] A well-traveled road that links White River Junction to Burlington, west to east.

passed the notable white-capped summit of Camel's Hump, where the supposed wizard, Vergil, lived, then through the Bolton Gap, which bypassed both Mansfield State Park and Camel's Hump State Park. They passed through Richmond, and the two giant statue whale tails in Williston, and the markets of South Burlington, before reaching their destination of Burlington Proper. Shortly before the pair reached the famed Burlington Waterfront, Henry had promised more details regarding Flatlander's second quest.

"You don't want to miss this," said Lord Henry as he tapped Flatlander lightly on the shoulder.

They hurried downhill to the ports near the giant boat slip, where a small group of Burlingtonians had congregated. The crowd yearned madly for the meat, raising their hands skyward, signaling for the cook's attention. Highborn men and women intermingled with the commoners and the poor, for all had assembled, under a fine morning mist, to receive the finest cuts in the republic. The crowd instantly parted a wide channel for Lord Henry. The barge crept to the dock, as its hull moaned and shuttered. The foreman quickly hopped into action, knotting ropes frantically around several giant cleats and piles. Letting out one last loud, low-pitched rumble, the barge soon came to a complete stop. Seconds later, the hum of the engine fell silent. As the freighter bobbed gently in its slip, commands and curses from the lake men readying its cargo rattled from inside the ship's hull.

"Anyone who knows anything…knows that this is the best meat in all of Vermont," stated Henry confidently to Flatlander, "as fresh as it comes."

Within seconds, an assortment of smoked meat rained down upon them, thrown from beyond the lip of the hull, hidden from sight. The two-dozen men and women assembled at the port smiled and laughed, as some caught the descending chunks with nothing more than their bare hands, while others swooped around their burlap sacks and wooden buckets strategically.

"Bless you! Bless you!" cried a short, stocky man with glee.

An elderly woman dressed in a tattered, sienna robe picked several parts of cooked chicken from the ground. During the brief scrum, Henry had managed to grab a section of what appeared to be pork tenderloin from midair. Tearing it in half, he presented a piece to Flatlander.

"Try this."

Flatlander inspected the meat closely, unsure. Yet hunger won out from reason. After the first test bite, hints of smoke and apple glaze left him salivating for more.

"This pig was slaughtered no more than twenty four hours ago in Grand Isle," said Henry between bites from his tenderloin. "The men and women of the First Slaughter[14] work fast. Though it looks unsavory to throw meat in such fashion, this is a custom, a tradition, which has been in place since shortly after our independence, during the droughts of 30's[15]."

Lord Henry then summoned Flatlander along the Path of the Lake, a trail that hugged the Champlain shorelines from Burlington to the island of South Hero, over a dozen miles northwest. He gestured to the Chamber of Echoes dominating the waterline to their right. It was an architectural oddity. On one outer wall was painted a giant black spire with a glowing ball atop. A large, cube-like concrete and glass structure, the Chamber of Echoes had an assortment of walkways placed at irregular angles, as well as dozens of holes placed at random intervals in its walls. People walked up and around the structure, peaking their heads through these holes, and, curiously, shouted questions into their depths.

According to Henry, the chamber was constructed as an oracle. One would shout a question deep into the building and listen for an echo. Sometimes one would hear nothing. Sometimes

---

[14] A popular farm in the islands specializing in slaughtering cows and pigs.

[15] A series of devastating droughts that affected Vermont and Old Country through 2030's and early 2040's.

one would hear something new in the echo itself, a trickery of tone or pitch. Sometimes one would hear somebody else's echo answer your own call without any trickery at all. Seldom, and only according to the most superstitious folk, the echoes would come to people without any prompting when they needed it most. Henry confided that he had used the chamber only once, yet it was 'partly responsible for molding him into the leader he had become.' Despite Flatlander's request to use the Chamber of Echoes, Henry was adamant that there would be another time, as there were more pressing matters at hand.

The waterfront bustled with activity. Sailboats, fishing vessels, and ferries dotted the horizon close to the base of the sprawling mountains of the west. A dozen Birch bark canoes with rawhide lacing leaned against a fallen tree, as their owners monitored the water draining from their bellies. Nearly a mile directly out in the lake, a small ferry was anchored near to what Henry identified as Juniper Island, to which a home and attached lighthouse were barely discernible. Barges lumbered through the waters from both the north and south, as a few casual spectators cheered on their near-arrivals. On shore, no more than a few hundred yards away, men were loading a freighter with lumber, positioning the heavy trees by pulley and rope one by one into the undercarriage of the vessel.

"Welcome to the Burlington waterfront, Flatlander. My father used to bring me here as a child during our visits to the Queen City[16]. In fact, we would pick up creemies[17] over there," said Henry as he pointed to a small six by six foot shack-like structure. Then he took in the whole lake, motioning its grandiosity with his arms. "For such a small republic, we have an abundance of resources: granite, marble, lumber, highly sought-after materials for builders. Our farms supply massive amounts of meat and

---

[16] A nickname for Burlington.

[17] A type of soft-served ice cream popular in Vermont.

vegetables from town to town. Maple syrup provides one of the most important industries for our economy and culture, and is a valuable commodity when other crops fail.

"Yet Lake Champlain is really the backbone of the republic; for it eases the burden of transporting goods when the mountain roads prove simply too difficult. A single, standard steam-powered or horse-powered barge can haul ten times the amount of our largest ox-driven flatbeds, and even the smaller horse-powered barges can haul close to three times that. Plus, when moving such large quantities, we cannot simply scale the peaks of the Green Mountains with ease like the famed Danario of Stowe[18]."

The rain clouds had completely burned off into the east. The air, fresh and clean, blew in a steady stream through his hair and nostrils. The mountains across from the lake loomed large over the surface, with faded shades of greyish-blue gently cascading softly in the distance. The lake sparkled magnificently in the sun. An odd notion then occurred to him. Flatlander wanted to drink the entire lake up, drink it as if it were a freshly poured grail. It seemed to reinvigorate him. A vast sheet of cumulus clouds spread across the blue sky, their movements imperceptible. The sight Flatlander beheld at that moment was one of pure majesty.

And it was as if Henry read his mind. "Beautiful, isn't it? Those mountains are called the Adirondacks; and form the border of Vermont and the Old Country. You see why this city, this republic, is proudly called home to so many. You also see why we take such extreme measures to protect it, don't you? Flatlander, this is why we keep foreigners, many likely bearing ill will, from of our republic. This fragile treasure is our daily reminder."

Flatlander nodded slowly in agreement. Henry then seemed to quietly contemplate something.

"But I want to show you something else entirely; the reason I brought you here in the first place."

---

[18] The famed messenger of a nearby mountain town.

The two made their way down the Path of the Lake, past docks, past people having picnics, past unloading freights, and the scurrying lake men. They moved past rusted metal train tracks, and a strange, domed building. Past men and women walking dogs, small footbridges, and circle of seagulls monitoring a picnic basket. Past songbirds and stone carvings and stacked rock formations on the beach. Then they walked past a massive wind-battered, granite wall near a long uninterrupted section of the path. Past a curious stone formation resembling a concentric circle, or some type of ancient sundial, until they eventually came upon a big field, which sat adjacent to the Path of the Lake.

A nearby sign indicated that they were in Oakledge Park. From their vantage point upon a short hill, the path meandered around the edge of a field. In the distance, Flatlander saw a concentrated group of people huddled en masse by the waterfront. In the center of this group was a flurry of movement.

"Even the most precious of stones can carry blemishes, and even the finest of diamonds, imperfections. In the same light, even Burlington, the jewel of the waterfront, has darker forces at work."

Was Henry referring to these people?

"I don't understand," remarked Flatlander.

Henry took a deep breath. "You will."

Flatlander glanced at the crowd, and then looked to Henry, whose brow had furrowed considerably. The Humble King concentrated heavily on the gathered people, a look of grave concern heavy in his eyes.

Flatlander stood next to Henry and followed his gaze. "Who are they?"

Henry shook his head in disgust. "You mean who *were* they? They were once people, like you and I. *Real* people, with *real* emotions, and *real* passions in life. No more."

Flatlander squinted hard at the group of people, but the distance was too great to catch any details.

"Are you suggesting…"

"We have much to discuss."

Flatlander tried to peel his eyes away, but couldn't. Then a few members broke away from the mass, and began speaking in a garbled, agitated dialect. One of the people pointed squarely in their direction. The Humble King grabbed his arm hard and pulled him back towards the Path of the Lake.

"Come, Flatlander. We must leave. It's not safe here any longer. Ellen will tell you all in Montpelier."

They rode back to Montpelier, and despite Flatlander's numerous inquiries, Henry was quite mum on what they had seen earlier in the day. Shortly after their return from Oakledge, Menche, Franklin, and Ellen joined them in the living room. Gabby retrieved bags of pine needles from the pantry, which she then used to fix his guests cups of pine needle tea.

Ellen then retold the tale of "Fish," while dusk descended upon them. A master storyteller, she delighted in relaying tales of the past, whether they were tales pertinent to the development of the republic, or simply fun fables with underlying lessons. While not tending to the affairs of the statehouse, Ellen was skilled at the art, sometimes spending entire days studying the lore of her land with the perfect blend of enthusiasm and curiosity. She noted the importance in knowing Vermont's tales, for it sometimes helped inform her counsel. According to her, knowledge of the past better shaped her understanding of the present.

She began: "Not too long ago, in the depths of Lake Champlain there lived Fish. He was a proud fish, though some may have called him *too* proud. He thought very highly of himself, or so they said. He had no siblings, which, as you know, is quite rare for a fish.

"Fish liked to acquire things. Lots of things. Pebbles. Lost jewelry. Zebra Mussels. Food. But instead of sharing the morsels that fell from the animals and boats from the surface like other, more ordinary fish, Fish would take his food and bring it away to his own lair. The other fish in his school would cry, 'Where's the delicious meat that the Gods left us from the heavens, fathers?' To which the fathers replied: 'Once again, Fish has eaten your meals and taken them to his lair, sons and daughters. He cares not for our welfare. Only his own.' One could have felt the dejection and resentment in the water.

"Fish had his own space, with his own toys, and his own gathered food, and his own decor. His mother would always call him the most spoiled fish in town, but Fish paid her no heed. He simply did *as* he liked, *when* he liked, *how* he liked. Word spread of Fish's greed, and it attracted the last person that one wants to attract within the entire republic: Vergil, The Wizard of the Camel's Hump. As old as the land itself, guardian of Vermont and protector of its fate. Vergil visited Fish one day upon the shores of Champlain, and offered him three wishes.

"Fish, incredibly enough, had actually already contemplated these types of offers, long before Vergil had even paid him this visit. He often dreamt of unlimited wealth and possessions. His life at that point had been a constant journey to accumulate more and more things, in both quantity and quality. Rarely ever was there a stone unturned near his home. And as it turned out, Fish requested three things, to which he was sure of.

"Fish's first request was to have the largest home in the lake. Discontent with his modest stone structure amid a small cliff in Colchester, he yearned for something bigger. Hours later, and by no mere coincidence, a freighter carrying stones for masonry sunk to the bottom of the lake. Luckily, there were no casualties, but the ship and its cargo were irretrievable, carved deep within the murk of the lake's bottom, creating a massive castle of jumbled stone and bogged-down wood. It would have been a suitable home for ten sturgeons or twenty gar; yet for a single, smaller rock bass such as he, it was simply gargantuan.

"The second request was the ability to breathe both air and water. Fish had always been curious to see the gods from above the surface, or whom he *thought* were the gods. That's how all fish are raised, you know. All that sinks beneath the surface are 'gifts from the gods.' Never had they been able to see things as they truly are, from above ground. Fish thought of this a pity.

"Fish's third request was to have a beautiful singing voice, to which Vergil did oblige. Having always been captivated by the calls of the seagulls, the horns of the ferries, and the chants of the Wicca[19], Fish wished this perhaps more than any other wish. You can imagine the pain he'd felt in the past when he attempted to sing, only to see trails of bubbles slip clumsily to the surface. He wanted to be capable of more. He wanted to be capable of spreading beautiful songs, even better than those in which he had once relished.

"With his newfound singing voice, Fish routinely breached the surface; sometimes even lying on shore for short intervals singing his original tunes. Often, a crowd would form near to his song, and dance and sing in merry circles at his unique talent, cherishing the absurdity and magic of such an encounter. The papers and journalists loved him. The youth loved him. Even the birds, which had long considered rock bass a delicacy, avoided eating him for the sheer love of his music. People from all over the republic flocked to see the singing Fish, who by now was becoming intoxicated from the endless stream of attention.

"Yet Fish, drowning in his newly acquired wealth and abilities, was still not content. He sought out Vergil, returning to their meeting place in Colchester every night for weeks on end. Finally,

---

[19] A group that adheres to a pagan witchcraft and practice their chants by a stone formation at Oakledge Park.

upon seeing Vergil upon a clear night, Fish asked the wizard for one additional wish. The wizard was completely taken aback at the request. 'What else does a fish need like you need, I wonder?' he asked. 'You have the largest house in the lake, you can breathe on both land and in water, and you can sing more beautiful than any creature of the mountains and beyond.' Yet Fish was still not content. Vergil promised Fish unimaginable wealth, with the freedom to create the wealth of the republic many times over, and all of this in just a matter of hours! But he also warned Fish that the power would be difficult to manage. The thought became too much for Fish to bear, and it wasn't long before he agreed to this mysterious power at any and all costs."

Ellen paused. Henry nodded at the accurate retelling, while Flatlander remained captivated by the odd tale. "The power, as it turned out, was the ability to turn everything to silver upon mere touch. At first, Fish was beside himself. He turned his house to silver. He turned friends' homes to silver. He even turned common driftwood to silver. All who knew Fish were intimidated and shocked by this newfound power. And soon, much of the bottom of Lake Champlain glowed with a layer of silver thicker than any silt."

"Fish learned the sad way, however, that the power of turning *everything* to silver had its downsides. *Catastrophic downsides.* You see, even the food that Fish tried to eat turned to silver before it could even be swallowed. The food! Even a wealthy fish has to eat, right? He tried to use different strategies, sometimes hoping a quick strike of his meals would suffice, but no matter how he approached his food, or whatever he was attempting to eat, it would fall before him to the bottom of the lake in the form of pure silver."

"Musta' been a lot of silver at the bottoms of the lake, Ms. Ellen," remarked Menche, as he rubbed his hands together excitedly.

"Hush, Menche. You're missing the point," chastised Ellen. "And plus, that silver was later salvaged from the bottom of the lake by no other than Vergil himself and used to construct the tower of Middlebury[20]."

Menche crossed his arms. "Mph."

"Now, where was I? Oh yes, as you can imagine, Fish was starving at this point. The only food source he could eat was given to him in the form of liquid. He had burned his bridges with his friends and his community, and he had to eventually lean on the people from the shores to care for him as he aged. Once a follower named Oscar turned to silver while trying to physically console Fish, and his statue still stands as a testament in the woods of the Oakledge Park; a warning, if you will, to those who tempt fate. The people who had come to love his beautiful singing, who had yearned for it during his dry spells, had flocked to Fish's rescue. His body and mind began to deteriorate, and to anyone else outside of his realm of fans, they could see it and notice the change in Fish's voice. The supporters of Fish, however, could not sense his decline. They were blinded by their obsession with the creature. If anything, the return of Fish reinvigorated their interest in the creature's singing, and since it had to spend nearly all of its time on shore to survive, the supporters spent unnatural amounts of time listening to its gasps and wails, their minds warped by a nostalgic glory that had been forever instilled in both time and memory. And this, my friend, this is how a group of loyal fans rapidly became a cult."

"How many are there?" asked Flatlander. He estimated the crowd at Oakledge to number several dozen.

"We have no official numbers, but some say that it totals well over one thousand from Burlington alone, and countless others from neighboring cities and towns," answered Ellen matter-of-factly.

Flatlander shifted uncomfortably in his seat. "I don't get it. I just don't get how a fish could control people like that. It doesn't

---

[20] The famous silver tower in the southern town of Middlebury. Built by monks.

make sense. I mean; it's a fish. It probably doesn't even know what's going on."

"Perhaps you should take another trip to the waterfront and get a closer look with Menche," interjected Henry, calmly. "Only then may the sheer gravity of the situation dawn on you."

Before Flatlander was to venture back to Burlington to observe the cult in action, Lord Henry wanted to go over some details in his office. Folder upon folder lay strewn upon his desk, some neat and trim while others busted at the seams. Each folder had a name and number displayed on a brightly colored insert. Then after rifling through each file, Henry would throw them disgustedly to the floor.

Henry paused as he glanced through a manila folder. "A4202. Classic example. Peter Martinello. Nineteen years old, straight A student, president of his school council, promising oboe player. He received a full-ride scholarship to Hilltop University[21]. Yet now, his mother says that he hasn't been home for days and that he had been 'forgetting to shower because he's too busy seeing Fish down by the lake.' Look, this is a direct quote from his mother, Flatlander. Not surprising."

Henry drew out an even thicker file. "Here's another one. B1016. Liza "Love-Buggy" Putzmann. As you might presume, 'Love Buggy' isn't her birth name. It was a nickname given to her by her fish-loving peers. The child spends most of her days eating cheese on a quilt by the lake, hoping for another set from Fish, yet, sadly…that set will never come. It's been years. Years!" Henry slammed a fist on the table. "The list goes on and on."

Flatlander shook his head. "I don't know. It sounds like these kids just need some guidance."

---

[21] One of the biggest, most popular post-high school academies in the republic.

"They need something, Flatlander! Anything, really!" Henry rubbed his hair frantically, and settled his face in his palms, before looking at Flatlander, troubled. "I'm...sorry, Flatlander. They're good kids, they really are. All of them. These are the sons, daughters, nephews, nieces, and grandchildren of the men and women with whom I work with. These are the future residents of this city, this republic, and this world. They are our future warriors, teachers, merchants, wardens, lake men, and farmers. Without them we Vermonters are doomed. They are our future."

Flatlander nodded. Admittedly, the concept was startling: an entire generation lost to an expanding cult. How could so many respectable young men and women fall victim to this strange phenomena? Henry continued, his frustration growing by the second.

"I hate what Fish has done with my people! It's like he's ripped out their very souls and stomped on their lifeless corpses! They're drones. Puppets. Zombies." The Humble King was on the verge of hyperventilating. He steadied his hands on the top of his chair's armrests. "Pardon me. I have to remind myself sometimes, Flatlander, it's not Fish's fault. He's no longer in control of his own fate, let alone the fate others."

"Relax," said Flatlander, as he thumbed through one of the files casually and cast a smirk at the farfetched anecdotes. "By the sound of it, you would think this creature stole your heart."

Henry nodded. "Not far from the truth. You see, it's taken on quite a personal nature for me."

"Why?" Flatlander placed the file back on Henry's desk. "I mean, seems like you just restrain the crowd, tape off the scene and throw the fish back into the lake. Anybody resists, they get arrested. Simple as that."

"It's not as 'simple as that'," said Henry in a strained voice.

"Why not?"

Henry stood and walked across the room, gazing whimsically out the office window at his garden. Placing his hands on his hips, the Humble King sighed long and deep, and recited from memory.

"A3061. Sixteen years old. She used to like creemees, long walks, and inventing funny songs for various family members on their birthdays. She was a…poster child for future success."

"Sounds like a great kid."

"She *was*, Flatlander. She *was*," replied Henry, forlorn, as a tear streamed down the length of his cheek. "It's my daughter. The cult has my daughter."

During summer trips up to Burlington, Henry would take his wife, Kylie, and daughter, Jess, for long walks along the edge of Lake Champlain. Jess's favorite part of the trip was seeing the way that Fish would straddle the shores, singing its beautiful melodies, while the boats and lake men wandered Lake Champlain's expanse like actors in a play. Her eyes would light up as she listened, and despite Henry's greatest efforts in continuing to engage her in conversation, Jess's attention was focused elsewhere. She would watch Fish in sheer adoration, simply entranced by its songs. The Humble King, on the other hand, was not much of a fan of Fish's music; it seemed too distant, too exotic. It appeared that the younger children really had an ear for it, or were completely enraptured by the image of a singing fish, rather than by its music, but not he. Whatever made Jess happy, however, made Henry happy. And at that particular moment in time, that's all that mattered to him.

When Jess began humming some of those very same melodies in the home, Henry thought little of it. In fact, he thought it was cute. When she asked for a couple of watercolor prints of Fish from the local stores (it was quite a popular draw in town), he was happy to oblige. Yet over time, this pattern continued and became more troubling. He bought Jess a stuffed animal of Fish, Fish t-shirts, and even her first Fish bootleg album on vinyl that he had bartered for her in the market of the Brattle.

A few years later, and after Kylie and he had divorced, his string of gifts proved to be a costly mistake. For Jess became increasingly obsessive with all things pertaining to Fish, blurring the line between simple fandom and cult-like worship. Jess's vinyl collection soon comprised half of her room, with volumes that included rare demos, live sets, and even secret performances in which Fish was unknowingly being recorded).

In time, though, Fish began getting old and weak. He dwelt more in the extremely shallow water, sometimes managing to wiggle halfway up a particular beach. His breathing problems worsened. His skin condition degraded, as lesions and sun blisters took their toll on his chaffed scales. During one of the last walks that Henry went on with his daughter, he swore that he had even heard Fish mumble "help" as they strode by. In vain, Henry tried to rush by the shore-bound atrocity, but Jess had much likely heard its desperate plea. For she refused to continue onward until she saw Fish wobble pathetically back into the waters.

Her behavior became more worrisome in the two years prior to Flatlander's arrival. Jess would leave for days and nights to spend time by the waterfront listening to Fish, rarely coming home. She often tried to be secretive, lying about her exact whereabouts. Unknown to Jess was the fact that Henry had eyes and ears on watch. Most of these spies were lords and commoners whose children struggled with the same dilemma. They often reconfirmed to him what he had already known deep down: Jess was spending inordinate amounts of time at the waterfront with Fish. He had even gone to great lengths to observe this phenomenon for himself, one time even traveling the shore incognito to spy on her. And there she was, listening closely to the dying Fish. He held his tongue and reserved judgment until Jess arrived home later that day.

"The creature is dying, Jess. Why do you still subject yourself to that drivel?" He had once called from the top of the stairs, moments after she stumbled through the front door. "Have you no eyes or ears?"

"Dad, Fish is just hitting his stride again, and his late-nineties run was out of control!" Jess shouted back. "You don't understand!"

"Oh, you're right. I don't understand. I don't understand how a group of formerly kind, highly educated, skilled youth can spend the better part of their day listening to the dying gasps of a decomposing freak!"

But Jess was back out the door before Henry could finish his rant.

He sometimes wondered why Jess had always been so reluctant to share with him the joys of his favorite band from his youth, The Stony Mahoney's. Sometimes, she would make a rude remark in reference to Henry's beloved band, but Henry loved his Stony Mahoney's! He loved the sounds of those beeps and bops and boops! The past year had been a sharp downward spiral for Jess. She barely ever came home, and if and when she did, it was to ask for money or food from the pantry. Her eyes looked vacant. Her speech was often unintelligible. Her hygiene left something to be desired. She made no efforts to wash the strange face paint from her face before bedtime, nor did she wash it sometimes before school, much to the consternation of her teachers. Jess's school attendance was poor and her grades, even worse.

Henry noted that Jess had lost any sense of musical objectivity when it came to listening to Fish's songs. On one occasion, she compared the sounds of the forest to Fish, but 'not quite as cool.' On another occasion, Jess listened to one of Fish's songs on repeat for several hours, despite the fact that it sounded like a series of wet burps. This behavior drove Henry nuts, of course, because to his ears, Fish's songs were but a mere distorted, sloppy mess; a musical travesty of the utmost degree.

He had trouble coming to grasp with this family issue. Although few knew it at the time, he would spend long hours at night mourning the loss of his daughter. One night, upon seeing a wet document at his bedside table, Gabbie had asked him what had happened. Henry had told her that he had accidentally spilt some of his water on it. But no cup was ever seen anywhere near its vicinity.

The next day per Henry's suggestion, Flatlander decided to take a closer look at the cult with Menche. He wanted to see the cultists again and arrive at his own conclusions. Early indications were that these people, these cultists, were dangerous folk; a group with tunnel vision, whose obsession with the creature known as Fish trumped any form of logic or common sense.

They walked up a hill in Oakledge nearest the throngs of Fish supporters. Some were lying on the grass in a half conscious state. Others walked aimlessly from one group of Fish fans to another in a quiet daze. The dense group surrounding Fish, however, appeared to be focused, continuously splashing lake water on the creature in a human chain circulating wooden pails. With each lap of water, Fish wriggled helplessly on the shore, bound by his personal purgatory. It almost appeared as if the creature was trying to flop over but was too weakened to muster the strength. Two men jointly operated a manual pump and short hose, dousing the animal to keep it from drying out and succumbing to the elements. Nobody, however, dared touch Fish.

"What are they doing, sirs?" asked Menche from his spot upon a checkered blanket, which Flatlander had spread neatly upon the hill's crest.

"Keeping the poor thing alive," marveled Flatlander, as he peered closely at the group. He nibbled on a slice of pumpernickel bread with a slice of cheddar. It was Flatlander's halfhearted attempt to remain inconspicuous by staging a picnic.

Then Flatlander's ears caught a troubling sound.

"Do you hear that, Menche?" he asked.

A low and chilling collection of voices drowned out Flatlander's every thought. Like a heartbeat or machine, the sound grew in fervor from cultist to cultist.

"Hear what?" asked Menche, as he cupped his ear.

The sound rose in volume.

"That!"

And beyond a shadow of a doubt, Flatlander soon recognized the sound. It sent goose bumps up and down his arms. They were chanting, all of them. *Fish. Fish. Fish.* Over and over again came the horrid incantation. *Fish. Fish. Fish.* Not so loud that it warranted attention outside of the park. *Fish. Fish. Fish.* But it was loud enough to evoke a visceral reaction from Flatlander and Menche. It was a slow, guttural chant, a cursed mumbling: a primal homage to their flailing deity. Flatlander was horrified. He squinted closer at the group of cultists surrounding Fish.

Something was painted on their foreheads, but the distance made it difficult for him to ascertain. A teenage boy with long, brown hair and overalls passed within fifty feet to his right. He wore a fish-scaled tunic wrapped in decorative algae. *There it was*: a bright blue symbol of Fish painted on his forehead in bold, exotic lettering. It depicted the creature Fish during its youth, when its scales were healthy, and its body was slim and strong. The illustration showed Fish half submerged in the water, crooning to the sky.

"I don't believe what I'm seeing," stammered Flatlander, as his hands shook the binoculars, rendering his sight to a faint blur.

Menche scanned the sky and surrounding park with optimism. "Aye, sir, tis a nice day to be at the park, I'd say, with the sun out and the clouds lookin' like marshmallows and all."

"No, Menche," said Flatlander, as he dropped the binoculars in frustration. "I was talking about the cult."

Then several members of the crowd surrounding Fish looked up at him curiously, as if he were an outsider, witness to a private affair. A small group began to assemble at the foot of their hill, and slowly, deliberately made their way towards the two. Judging by their reddened eyes and zombie-like movements, Flatlander figured that their time observing the cult had abruptly come to an end.

"Menche, quick. Let's get out of here."

Flatlander hurried back towards to Path of the Lake with Menche closely behind. They mounted their carriage close to Pine Street, and rushed off back to Montpelier. The chanting in Oakledge Park faded back into the bustle of the Burlington Ports. Flatlander had seen enough.

"It must die," muttered Henry, as he worked a handsaw jerkily, while Ellen and Franklin held a table leg into place with the help of several clamps.

The grim three-word analysis, barely audible over the grating and splintering of wood, hung heavy in the air. Upon his return to Montpelier, Flatlander found Henry, Ellen, and Franklin in Henry's barn, hand-sawing pieces of wood for the legs of a new kitchen table. Saturday chores, particularly in the early throes of spring, were much needed in the republic. Henry noted that Vermont winters were often long and cold, and citizens of all backgrounds and socioeconomic classes struggled with accomplishing much in the ways of housework or yard duties during the winter months. On this Sunday in early May, Henry only saw opportunity.

Sawdust gathered on the floor near the worktable, intertwined with layers of hay and dirt. On the near side of the barn, pitchforks, shovels, and a single hoe stood upright against the wall. Each tool had looked like they had seen better days. A half-finished canoe hung from the rafters, dangling precariously from three thin pieces of rope. On the far side of the barn, Pete the Moose chewed slowly on a serving of pondweed, watching his new masters with curiosity.

"And how do you suggest we do that?" asked Ellen, as she held a disengaged bolt at the ready.

Henry paused briefly from his task, as he flashed Ellen a wry smile. "Isn't that what I pay you for, dear: to suggest things to *me*?"

"Poison it," Ellen suggested without hesitation. "Find the food source the cult uses to feed it and poison it. No traces. No leads. No suspects. It will perish within the hour. Need I remind you: the alchemist is only a stone's throw away in Waitsfield[22]. You need only to mention his name, and I'll fetch him immediately."

"Hmm. Not my style, Ellen." Henry sawed a leg completely off, as it thudded anti-climactically to the ground. "Dire as the situation may be, Fish doesn't deserve a death lacking dignity."

"Shoot it with an arrow then," pleaded Ellen. "It can't be too hard, even from a distance. You are as true with your bow as any marksman in the republic."

Henry bristled at the thought. "Have you seen the crowd huddled around the creature, Ellen? I'm not going to make the papers for shooting an innocent fan of Fish by mistake. Shay Bromage would have my head, besides."

"They're not fans, they're cultists," countered Ellen.

---

[22] Fedor the Alchemist, of Waitsfield, was famous for his concoctions, poisons and potions.

"They could be Barre-dwellers[23], even. Does it really matter?" Henry fumed. "Does it really matter what title they bear? Titles are just that; titles. They're still people, Ellen, and I'm not going to risk further injury or death for a clean shot at that menace."

Henry folded a sheet of sandpaper in his hands, and began sanding the new edge of the table leg, as Franklin and Ellen took a cue from their lord, and did likewise to the other legs. Sawdust rained on the barn floor. Twenty seconds later, the sound of Henry sanding subsided.

"Do we have to kill it then?" asked Flatlander. "Isn't there a way we could transport it out of the republic safely or keep it in a private aquarium, away from the cult?"

"So it can corrupt *another* set of youth in *another* region of the republic? *Yes*, we have to kill it, Flatlander," Henry answered curtly, as he exchanged a look of exasperation with both Ellen and Franklin. The northerner chuckled under his breath. Henry continued: "Have you heard *nothing* that I have said these past two days?"

"But…"

Henry threw his sandpaper aside and locked eyes with Flatlander. "No room for argument. It must die. Correction- it *will* die." Henry's expression then softened. "See, think of it not as an act of aggression, but rather, an act of mercy. You saw Fish earlier today, did you not? And what did you think? What emotions came to mind?"

"It was a sad sight," admitted Flatlander.

"Absolutely, it's one of the saddest sights one can imagine," answered Henry with a nod. "Think of the potential talent Fish has squandered. For every minute these quacks listen to Fish, a minute is lost for a more productive life. What other emotions come to mind?"

Flatlander conjured up images of some of the cultists at Oakledge Park; how many of them appeared unwashed, unkempt.

---

[23] A slang term for undesirables who dwelt in the abandoned stip-mined city of Barre.

"I was confused. How do they eat? How do they live with themselves?"

Henry hesitated, and rubbed a bead of sweat from his brow with the back of his wrist. "It *is* quite a confusing scene down there with those hordes of teenagers walking around looking shell-shocked. Anything else?"

Flatlander thought hard. He hadn't felt it right away, but shortly into his journey back to Montpelier, Flatlander found himself stewing in the absurdity of the scenario, which morphed into something else entirely.

"Anger, Lord Henry. I was angry."

Henry nodded vigorously, and threw one of the table legs to the ground below. "Aha! And just *who* were you angry with, Flatlander?"

"Angry at the, the…" stuttered Flatlander, as he struggled with an answer. "I'm not sure."

Henry readjusted one of the table clamps, and squinted. "Let me re-phrase that: were you angry with *Fish*?"

"No," replied Flatlander.

A noticeable pause ensued, as Henry approached Flatlander, a tired, somber, look in his eyes.

He spoke very softly. "Were you angry with Fish's fans?"

"Yes."

"Why?"

Flatlander thought back to the hideous sights and sounds at the waterfront. He recalled the cultist who mindlessly directed the hose over his deity, as simply as one would water a garden bed. He recalled the haunting chants. He recalled the creature's fins stirring with each and every splash, as if awakened from near death.

"It should be dead. The poor bastard should be dead. He's just plopped on that beach, baking in the sun like he's being cooked alive. It's sick."

"The cultists have largely forsaken their humanity years ago. They care not for quality of life, for themselves or that *thing*," spat Henry. His answer lingered in the space of the barn, as both Franklin and Ellen took their rest upon a nearby workbench. Henry inspected the new legs of his table, admiring their smooth surfaces. "No. I want it dead, and the sooner, the better. And I don't care if Jess finds out."

"I'll kill the bastard," growled Franklin, as he took a large gulp from a blackened stout beer, as a trail of brown foam streamed down the length of his face.

Henry rolled his eyes, and chuckled darkly, as if he'd heard the suggestion before. "Franklin, I have little doubt that you can kill Fish quite handily, and several of his followers in the process," replied Henry, as he took a deep breath. "But I have elected Flatlander for the deed, as it should serve as his second required mission."

Flatlander stood upright. "*Me?*"

"Yes, of course. You still have many duties to fulfill."

"But how would I kill it?"

"By sword, I figure. It's a more noble and instantaneous death."

Flatlander was sickened by the thought. "But I've never swung a sword in my life."

"How would you know? Your memory betrays you," Henry quipped, as he began collecting the various newly sanded table legs and placing them upon a large, metal worktable. "Besides, Franklin can teach you."

Flatlander shook his head. *Avoiding* death in Irasburg was one thing. *Inflicting* death, quite another.

"They would recognize me from earlier today."

"Wear a disguise," replied Henry.

"Will I get in trouble?"

"The courts should turn a blind eye for they too consider the very existence of Fish outside the laws of nature."

He had run out of excuses and fast, and Henry's request was non-negotiable, particularly if he wanted to stay in the republic for the foreseeable future. During the past several days, he hadn't come any closer to figuring out his real home. Sadly, he didn't see any better alternative.

"I don't want to kill anything, Lord Henry. Fish or no Fish."

"Well, it's not entirely up to you, Flatlander. Is it?"

Henry's question was met with sheer silence, soon broken by Pete the Moose inadvertently clanging the side of his metal stall with his antlers.

"But how will he get close to it without being stopped?" Ellen asked, as she began tracing a diagram of Oakledge Park's layout on a piece of parchment from her journal. "Those fans are clustered around Fish like flies on…"

"Leave that to me," interrupted Henry, his eyes betraying a man lost deep in thought. "Leave that to me."

Shortly after lunch the next day, Franklin grabbed a short sword from a loft in the barn, and led Flatlander down a short path behind a rather scant section of Henry's garden. As it rounded a bend past a small marble fountain, they came to a two-acre section of woods, full of yellow and white birch. An old stump from an oak tree protruded from the ground. No higher than four feet, and bearing multiple scars from sword and axe impacts, the stump was covered in jagged notches, which had browned and withered substantially over the course of time. *This stump has seen better days*, thought Flatlander.

Franklin swung the sword upon the stump with so much force that it imbedded several inches deep. It was a short, one-handed sword, the blade itself barely longer than Flatlander's arm. Its handle was tightly wrapped in blue, coarse tape. On its silver hilt there was the engraving of a single maple tree in dark etches, leafs scattered among its roots. Franklin released his grip, spit to the side, and turned to face Flatlander.

"A beginner's blade from Danville, close to Walden. Found it in an old scrap yard and had it cleaned and sharpened. Figured it was a good starter's sword for ya."

Flatlander stood and admired the sword in its simplicity. The blade widened nearest the curved cross guard, its edges looked expertly sharpened.

"It's yers, if ya can get it out," exclaimed Franklin, as he leaned against a nearby tree, crossing his arms in anticipation. "And I'll warn ya, it ain't as easy as it looks."

Flatlander looked at Franklin, then the stump, then back at Franklin. "I'm sorry but what does this have to do with anything?"

"Consider it a test," said Franklin.

Flatlander placed his left leg on the side of the stump within a small cleft; his right leg crouched behind him. Clamping both hands around the hilt of the sword, he pulled with all of his might. He grunted and blushed a deep red, pushing his every muscle to the limit. Nothing. The sword didn't so much as budge. Not even an inch.

"That all ya got?" mocked Franklin with a grin. "Ya look like my grandma on the toilet fer all I care."

Flatlander stopped, and looked down at the ground, defeated.

"Gross," he gasped between heavy breaths.

"Look," said Franklin. He placed his hands around the hilt of the sword, and swished the blade from the stump with minimal effort. "Piece a' cake."

"Franklin, you're twice my size," countered Flatlander.

"Size means little when it comes to wieldin' swords. It's all about speed and technique. Even pluckin' it from a stump, ya need to really *feel* the sword. Put all of yer energy in it, like this."

Once more, Franklin impaled the sword deep into the stump. The blade reverberated from its stationary position, humming softly.

Flatlander took a deep breath. "I might pull a muscle."

"Well, boo-hoo-hoo. Take the freakin' sword from the stump, Flatlander. Yer givin' me the twitch," responded Franklin, and true to the northerner's warning, his right eye began blinking on cue.

Taking a deep breath, Flatlander then exerted all of his energy pulling the hilt of the sword, using both legs as props for leverage against the stump, back arced; yet to no avail. Collapsing on the forest floor, Flatlander cursed underneath his breath.

"Ah, who am I kiddin'?" asked Franklin, as he shook his head shamefully. Turning from the pitiful display, Franklin lumbered slowly back in the direction of Henry's house "Take a wimpy, little Flatlander from the Old Country. I shoulda expected nuthin' more."

Flatlander stood up. "Hey, c'mon."

"Just a scrawny, hands-as-smooth-as-a-baby's ass Flatlander, probably'll get a cold from bein' out here too long."

"That's not fair!" he called to the northerner's back.

Franklin turned his head slightly to the side as he continued walking away. "Huh, guess I'm just wastin' my time. Better off headin' back to the house and playin' some cards with Menche. I'll just tell Lord Henry the whole thing needs to wait. His daughter ain't too important, maybe."

"Wait! Hold up!"

Franklin ignored his calls and continued onward the path to Henry's house. Mounting the stump once more in a similar position from his previous attempt, this time Flatlander crossed his hands on the hilt, and streamlined the angle of his upper body. He pulled and grunted, wondering, if for a second, the stump was anchored into the ground with bedrock. Franklin halted his departure and watched Flatlander's attempt with a mixture of humor and respect. He yanked with all of his strength until his energy was all but sapped from his body, and a series of veins bulged from his temples.

At last, the sword broke loose from the stump, hurling Flatlander backwards on top of a large, protruding root. The impact knocked the wind out of him, and he lost control of the blade, as it clanged against some nearby stones. Flatlander writhed on the forest floor in agony. Hurrying over to his fallen form, ecstatic, Franklin paused.

"Ya did it! Ya did it, Flatlander! Yer a beast, I'm telling ya!" said Franklin, as he lifted Flatlander to his feet with ease and patted him heartily on the shoulder.

Flatlander winced. "My back," he groaned, rubbing the small of his lower back.

Franklin chuckled. "Ah, yer damned back can wait! Yer a warrior now! Warriors don't have time fer back pains!" The Northerner picked up the fallen sword from nearby and tossed it next to Flatlander. "It's yers now. Ya earned it, kiddo. Ya did good. Ya did real good."

Rubbing the small of his back near the spine, Flatlander smiled thinly and nodded. Franklin's happiness was contagious, even if it had come at the expense of a potential spinal injury. This small victory, however, didn't overshadow the fact that he would soon have to become a killer. Looking up at the jet blue sky through the forest canopy, Flatlander estimated that it was approaching early afternoon. The time was getting closer.

Like two merchants of death, they came upon the field as steady as the wind, which now enveloped their hooded attire. Neither talked or smiled. The assassins walked with a dreaded sense of purpose across the short-cut grass of Oakledge Park. An ominous air befell the waterfront, as the seagulls kept a safe distance from the shore. The rainclouds were thick, and the occasional scattered shower fell gently and sprinkled the placid surface Lake Champlain. The cult's chanting, muffled by the rain, pulsated across the soaked earth. The two men stopped a few hundred yards short from their intended target. Flatlander turned to Franklin, who nodded and removed his hood. Flatlander followed suit. The blue symbol of Fish was displayed on each of the assassin's foreheads, painted on earlier by the steady hand of Ellen.

A concentrated group of cultists still formed a perimeter around the immediate vicinity of Fish. Though it now appeared that an entirely new group of cultists were acting as the human chain, transporting buckets back and forth from lake's edge. *They must have a way of communicating this type of change to one another*, thought Flatlander.

Franklin quietly cleared his throat. "Wait for the signal, Flatlander."

On cue, the mysterious voice of Fish from his younger days rang out from the circular stone formation across the field. Unlike the dying gasps that had become the norm, the wonderful melodies were true songs of beauty, perfect in clarity and harmony. These were songs of Fish's past. The cult members perked up at the sounds of the classic voice, and sprung toward the stone formation in a relative sprint, leaving their spiritual leader and holiest of the holy fully unattended. A lopsided bucket and several discarded pieces of chum were all that remained at Fish's side. Franklin waited until the cultists had put nearly two hundred meters distance between themselves and Fish, right up until they were practically at the foot of the stone formation.

Franklin nodded. "Come, let's have at it. Cut strong and cut quick."

Flatlander hit the field running like a deer in full stride. His adrenaline boosted higher and higher, yet he could feel neither his sword clacking against his hip, nor the compacted mud beneath his feet. Nor could he sense the looming shadow of Franklin trailing him several yards behind, or the fact that even in such a small window of time, several of the cult members had turned their heads towards them in confusion. He was on kill mode: every iota, every nerve of his body, was on high alert and ready to deal death.

As they neared Fish, they slowed and drew their weapons. Franklin assumed a position close to Flatlander's back, facing outwards to the cult members. A female singer named "Katya," hired by Henry for the deed, was provided as a momentary distraction. Katya, dressed in fine, green silk dress, sung her incredible impression of Fish. But it was no use. Several of the cultists who had caught sight of Flatlander and Franklin alerted the group of their presence with a series of grunts. The cultists grunted at one another then began speeding back to Fish in sheer desperation. They stampeded through the meadow of Oakledge back to their vulnerable deity. Mud was kicked up and grass was torn. The rumble of a hundred footsteps resounded from the waterfront.

"Do it, Flatlander. We've no time! The killin' must be done!" said Franklin from Flatlander's back, as he cradled his axe. "They're almost upon us!"

Silently, Flatlander drew his blade and stared gravely at Fish, which was flush on its side. From up close, he could see firsthand the terrible physical deterioration that Fish had endured at the hands of time and fate. Its scales were flaky and bleached a pale gray. Its eyes were glassed over, and fungal-looking secretions gathered within the corner of each eye socket. Fish's ribs popped grotesquely from its underside, and its fins were drooped completely to the side like a wilted flower. What really hit home for Flatlander, however, were its eyes. He had been so quick to dismiss the creature as a truly sentient being all this time, but now, as it lay here before him, there was no more denying it. This *was* a creature of depth and power. Its eyes bespoke a certain regret and sadness, a burdensome intelligence that a creature of the lake should have no business meddling in. It looked directly into Flatlander's eyes and moaned. As the cult saw the drawn sword of Flatlander, they sprinted back to Fish with renewed intensity. Fish's sworn guardians soon reached the assassins, forming a fierce perimeter around the two.

"Do it! Ya haven't any time to spare!" yelled Franklin.

Cult members had begun grabbing at Franklin, and despite his immense strength, he could not overcome their incredible power in numbers. Flatlander raised his sword high up in the air, and despite the foul cries of the horde of cultists at his back, struck down the blade with great force upon the neck of Fish. An explosion of blood, gill pieces, and bone sprayed in the air, and the stomach-turning stench of rotted flesh was released. And as the life itself drained rapidly from Fish's still corpse, the hands of a dozen cultists grabbed, clawed, and shoved Flatlander and Franklin around like a couple of rag dolls. Some cried out in rage, some screamed, while others, still chanted, all of it completely unintelligible.

The crowd of over one hundred cultists now surrounded Franklin and Flatlander, and the closest violently grabbed at them in an animalistic rage. Franklin kept them at bay as best he could, shielding the two by the mere handle of his axe. Flatlander cried out as a cultist scratched his arm above the elbow, shoving him backwards. Franklin too stumbled backwards. Only the lake was at their backs now, and the angry mob stood on the verge of tearing their limbs off, one by one. There was no way out.

"I wish that we had included this part in our plan, Franklin," stated Flatlander matter-of-factly, as he shoved a pimple-faced cultist into the mud.

Franklin reared up like a cornered animal. "They gotta sayin' in the kingdom. 'If yer gonna sheer the lamb, make sure ya take every last bit o' wool!'"

"What does that mean?" asked Flatlander, as a hand flew from the crowd and slapped his face.

"It means there ain't gonna be a single one of these fellas left when I'm done with em," replied Franklin, a crazed look in his eyes.

He swung his axe wildly, forcing the crowd back a step, nearly severing a cultist's hand in the process.

It was just after that moment when something very odd occurred. The frenzied crowd, one by one, began settling down and looking in the distance over the lake, entranced. One cultist after another halted their barrage of fists and grunts, and focused at the water behind both assassins. It took near half a minute for Flatlander's adrenaline to settle, but when he did turn, he couldn't believe his eyes.

Jumping in and out of the water freely like a dolphin on open water was Fish. He bobbed, spun, and flipped in utter joy. Rolling and splashing along the surface, Fish was now freed from the captivity of his own body. The cultist's rage slowly morphed into amazement and joy, as several clapped their hands in unexpected celebration. Oohs and ahhs resounded from deeper within the horde.

"I...don't believe it," murmured Franklin. "You hacked his head clean off."

"I...know," replied Flatlander, as his jaw dropped in sheer awe. The bloody corpse of Fish still laid unmoved at his feet. *If Fish is dead, then what on earth is this?*

Before Fish submerged for the very last time under the shimmering surface of Lake Champlain, it turned towards the crowd gathered at the lakefront. Positioning its upper body half out of the surface, Fish opened its mouth and began to sing. And the song was absolutely beautiful. It had the resonance of an old church bell and the melodic quality of an old, antique harp. For a full three minutes, it sang. It sang with emotion. It sang with heart. It sang with soul. The cultists swayed side to side to the sweet, nectarine voice, humming and whistling to the haunting universal melody, popularized in several of Fish's songs. The upper Champlain Valley and the Adirondacks, half-covered in a fine mist, provided a spectacular backdrop, an amphitheater of epic proportions, for most felt, and in some cases, understood, that this was Fish's last song.

And by the end, all those in the valley within earshot whom had heard the song that fateful day knew it to be true. From that very moment on, they would never forget where they were when they heard Fish's final mind-blowing song. The wind shifted rapidly to the east, rippling Flatlander's clothing and blowing Franklin's hair back from his sweat-covered brow. Then, with one thrusting motion, Fish dove headfirst into the lake, splashing his tailfin dramatically, before plunging deep one last time below Champlain's surface. And from that day forward, Fish ceased to be, and what was presumed to be the ghost of Fish would be remembered as the marking of a freed soul and the rejoicing of the grateful dead.

After waiting several minutes for the excitement to die down, and shortly after both Franklin and Flatlander had fled far away on foot, Henry slowly made his way through the disbanding crowd. Intently, he scanned the small gatherings of cultists, looking for any sign of his daughter. A vast emptiness engulfed the lake. Many cultists openly wept and embraced one another. Under a nearby tree, a distraught, mud-covered couple hummed some of Fish's melodies. He finally found her.

Sitting by herself at a nearby dock sat Jess, arms leaned back, as she flicked the water's surface with her feet. She gazed out over the expanse of the lake, forlorn, jewelry and costume accessories piled up around her, discarded. Her hair was still a beautiful blond, and her skin, tan and muddied. Henry sighed in relief and paused.

"I love you, Jess," stated Henry, his voice cracking with emotion.

Jess turned around, her eyes burning red and bloodshot from crying.

"Will it ever come back?" she asked in a monotone. "Fish, I mean…will it ever come back?"

"The better question is this: will *you* ever come back?" asked Henry with a sniffle.

Jess turned back towards the lake, took a deep breath and sighed long and hard. As she continued flicking the water below with the tip of an outstretched toe, Henry sat down next to his daughter and put an arm around her shoulders. At first, she tried to resist. Henry held on hard, however, and quickly her struggle faded into quiet resignation.

"This is…horrible," she muttered in her father's arms. "*Why* did they do it, dad? *Why*?"

"Now, now," whispered Henry in her ear. Holding her close, he scanned the Path of the Lake. "Do you remember when we use to get creemees and walk this park? I think that this dock is where you spilt your creemee on the ground, and some little dog ran off with it. You chased him as if you were possessed by the devil! Do you recall?" Henry chuckled. "You were so cute then, Jess."

Jess reflected for a moment. "Kind of. What song was Fish singing that day again?"

The pleasant memory was instantly shattered for the Humble King. "It matters *not!*" snapped Henry, as his face turned cherry red. "It matters *not* what Fish was singing!"

"Chill, dad," replied Jess, taken aback by his outburst.

"I will not '*chill*,'" said Henry. "Fish was the background music that day, Jess, that's what you have to understand. *Background music.* The real memories were the times we had together. The creemees, you chasing the dog, gazing through those binoculars and claiming that you saw Champ. Skipping along one of the most beautiful paths that this republic has to offer. Those were the *real* memories, the *real* magic. *Those* are the memories that you should cherish."

Jess scoffed. "You can't tell me which memories to like or not! You're not the boss of me!"

"Actually, I am," replied Henry, assuredly. "Even more so, I am the king."

"In fantasy land, maybe," mocked Jess.

"No, in *reality*, Jess," replied Henry. "But enough with this silly argument! Open your eyes. The ride is over."

Jess looked at her father, distraught. A creeping sensation tugged at her. "You killed him, didn't you? You, Franklin and that weird 'Flatlander' guy…"

Lord Henry met his daughter's gaze with silence. Jess stifled a cry and kicked the water hard. She looked down at her reflection, vacantly. Filth and mud coated her lower calves and ankles. Instinctively, Henry leaned over the dock, and began splashing water on the legs of his unwashed daughter.

"Stop! What are you *doing*?" yelped Jess in surprise, as she recoiled her leg from her father's well-intentioned effort.

"I'm sorry," mumbled Henry, as he halted.

"You're being a weirdo."

Henry fumbled for the words. "Jess, I'm sorry. Your legs…why don't you…I'm sorry. It's just that it's been so long since I've seen you. I miss you. Please, come home tonight. Your room is still the same as you left it."

Jess thought long and hard. "It'll be hard not seeing Fish anymore. He was like family."

"And I love you like family because you *are* family," replied Henry.

Scanning the shoreline, he focused on a young male cultist, no older than thirteen, crouched over the beheaded corpse of Fish. He touched the creature's slimy lips while reciting a song or prayer. Henry had to pry his eyes from the sad sight.

"The Stony Mahoney's will be playing a show tomorrow at the statehouse," offered Henry diplomatically, "perhaps you should come see them if you're feeling able."

Jess scoffed. "Dad, c'mon. The Stony Mahoney's?"

Henry sighed. "Please, give them a chance. For me?"

"But…Fish…." Jess stumbled for the words.

As the surrounding fog grew thicker and darkened, Jess's sobs became muffled by Henry's fur coat. His shoulder was damp with his daughter's tears, yet the Humble King was content. *It was a new day*, he thought. *A new day, and I have my lovely daughter back. All is well in the world.* Henry and Jess remained seated after most of the cultists had left, now lost souls wandering aimlessly in a Fishless republic. The day's battle had been won thanks in due part for Flatlander, but little did Henry know that the war to win back his daughter had just begun.

Shay Bromage woke suddenly in the middle of the night in a cold sweat. He had no idea why. His wife Dawn lay fast asleep at his side. His hands shook madly. The clicks from the grandfather clock from across the bedroom seemed pronounced, as a slight shift in the wind from outside rattled his bedroom window. The journalist couldn't shake a sinister feeling.

"Something terrible has happened," said Shay under his breath.

"Go to sleep," murmured Dawn.

"I can feel it, though. Something terrible has happened."

His revelation didn't even provoke so much as a response from Dawn, whose head was now wholly covered by a large, cotton pillow. Shay stroked his loose hair back from his eyes, cleared his throat, and got out of bed. He felt troubled and the house reeked of certain disquietude. After all, the last time he had felt this overwhelming sense of despair, a large fire had erupted in a home in the Old North End of Burlington, critically injuring a young child and rendering its occupants homeless. He sincerely hoped for something less severe if his instincts proved to be true.

Shay left his bed, and groggily made his way to his desk to turn on the oil-lamp next to some of his current articles, works in progress for the upcoming issue of his paper. Reaching for his glasses in the dimmed light, he nearly knocked over a glass pen jar. Per the norm, he spent many late nights plugging away at his typewriter, making sure that every grammatical error was fixed, every unnecessary detail expunged. His late nights scrambling to finish the paper weren't the most glowing aspect of his job; yet it was a necessary evil. It was mere routine in the field of journalism.

But tonight felt anything but routine. Something felt off. He looked at the various contents on his desk: a sticky-rimmed tea cup, a small, used pastry dish with frosting encrusted at the base, several feathered quill pens perilously low on ink, his blue vintage typewriter, the week's unfinished edition of the paper, and a landscape painting that Dawn had made for him prior to their wedding. He was looking to frame it one of these days.

He needed something to help soothe his worries. Anything. Sometimes, he would rely on Dawn for comfort, for she was one of the few who would actively listen to him, much less help manage his eccentricities. But she was much too deep in her sleep, thought Shay. Dawn needed all of the sleep she could get after a long week of work at the Burlington Daily News, Shay's direct competitor.

Funny, really, he thought. *If I didn't love her so much, I'd want to run her business out of town.*

Then it came to him without warning or sudden premonition. Shay simply did as he had always done when feeling on edge, and felt foolish for not thinking of it earlier. Without so much as a pause, he made his way downstairs, opened a nearby bureau, and removed an old favorite vinyl recording of Fish from ten years prior. Delicately placing the recording, "Fish: Unplugged in Burlington" on the platter, Shay adjusted the stylus, leaned back on the couch, and listened to the aquatic superstar sing his beautiful melodies. *The creature's opus, in my estimation. At least I'll always have Fish to provide me comfort through times thick and thin,* thought Shay. *At least I'll always have Fish.*

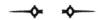

So it is with much animosity that Shay Bromage recounted the misadventures of Flatlander in Irasburg, as well as the assassination of Fish at the waterfront. One article, "Flatlander Steals Diseased Moose From Devoted Wardens," went on to describe the public risk of unleashing a potentially disease-ridden animal, interviewed one particular distraught, yet non-articulate warden, Mister Jimmy Rhodes, and described in fine detail the rash of injuries incurred by the elderly farmer, Leyton Myregard.

The other article, aptly titled "Flatlander beheads Vermont Cultural Icon," went to great lengths in describing the beheading of Fish, in every last, gruesome detail. Shay relayed a story from his past, where, as a little boy, the only thing to cheer him up from a long day of getting picked on in high school was an old recording of Fish that he had found at a garage sale. He also listed Fish's body of music at the end, highlighting some of his own favorites albums amongst them. The article contained no mention of the cultists, nor the miracle of Fish's ghost upon the lake. According to Shay in conversation with Dawn, 'neither merited much consideration, for they pale in the face of this unspeakable tragedy.'

Shay concluded his article with this passage: "The musical genius of Fish transcended both time and space. He took us on a musical journey, without any preconceived notions over what music is or should be. Sadly for Flatlander, he was never provided a ticket for this wonderful ride, so he felt compelled to act on his own behalf, fueled by an unbridled jealousy and an utter lack of culture. Thanks to him, we will no longer be able to enjoy the perfection of a Fish song by the lake. Never again."

The challenge had thereby been set forth: mess with republic and the values to which it holds dear, and you will mess with the likes of Shay Bromage. The issue sold like hotcakes. His printing press on Pine Street churned out papers 24/7 to meet the demand. The emergence of Flatlander in their midst soon became the talk of the republic. And it would be safe to say that, after reading Shay's paper, most weren't becoming terribly fond of the newcomer. In the meantime, Shay had become drunk with his recent success. Surely, there was more folly to come, Shay convinced himself. *But focusing on Flatlander for stories wasn't by mere choice any longer,* he reminded himself, *it was simply an obligation.*

CHAPTER 4
The Miller of Lowell

TWO WEEKS AFTER THE ASSASSINATION of Fish, on a Wednesday on the seventh of May, the statehouse was packed for Henry's bi-annual state-of-the-republic speech. Every noble, lord, and assistant was in attendance, from the white birches of Putney in the southeast, to the marshes of the Missisquoi near the Canadian border. From Flatlander's vantage point atop a small, high balcony,  the statehouse senate chamber appeared as agitated as a hornet's nest. For close to a week, and thanks to Shay Bromage, the republic had been stewing in the tales that emerged from Irasburg and the Burlington waterfront. Many nobles thought that these exploits were outrageous, and fully expected Henry to broach the subject of a Flatlander's connection within his ranks.

Shay Bromage sat at his regular desk near the back of the main chamber, a smug smirk on his face. His paper had set records the previous two weeks for copies sold. Before Flatlander, never before had a person been such a blessing and a burden for the journalist.

Vaulted ceilings reached high into the air, amplifying sounds twofold. Richly carved and painted white, the engraving that covered most of the ceiling depicted a sprawling forest. The floor outside of the main chamber was comprised of the rare black marble from Isle La Motte[24], containing oceanic fossils from its ancient Chazy Reef[25]. A large, multi-tiered gasolier dangled from the top of the room. Red drapes lined the windows, and a sprawling crimson Oriental rug sat below its audience. Rows of richly carved, black walnut desks formed semi-concentric circles around a large silver throne reserved for King Henry.

Three separate twelve by fifteen foot paintings hung at opposing angles of the chamber, equally spaced apart. Near the balcony, a large, dark watercolor depicted the construction of the wall, the manmade barrier surrounding most of the republic. An unidentified builder, bearing a tattered grey shirt and a large, recently unearthed stone on his shoulder, peered out, tired but proud at his admirers. In the second painting, closest the main entrance was a detailed, realistic landscape of a snow-capped Mount Mansfield, with a woman in the foreground, in a heavy white dress, kneeling down in prayer. The final painting, a bright and impressionistic homage to Vermont's road to sovereignty, showed the Burlington waterfront being besieged by boat from Yorkers[26], and the subsequent torrent of arrows raining down upon them from the legendary archers of St. Albans[27].

---

[24] One of several inhabited islands in Lake Champlain

[25] A black limestone formation containing prehistoric fossils.

[26] An older Vermont term for New Yorkers.

[27] A highly trained unit of infantry in the republic that is seldom used.

Stoic, Henry sat on his throne clothed in his heaviest, darkest fur coat. Flatlander remembered what Ellen had told him. The coat was taken from a bear that Henry himself had killed, skinned and tanned. The bear was grazing on Henry's bird feeders, a source of much comfort for the Humble King during his downtime. Finding the story both gruesome and awe-inspiring, the sudden pounding of a gavel soon interrupted Flatlander's thoughts.

"Hush, now! Ladies and gentlemen, please," pleaded a furry looking man wielding a gavel.

Seated at Henry's side, Greg Ulger looked more animal-like than human. His dark brown beard hung low to his chest, and chainmail armor rattled with every motion. A bushy unibrow dominated his forehead, and his brown hair resembled that of an unkempt bush. He continued pounding the gavel until silence descended upon the hall.

Ulger then scanned the lords until he felt it proper, and bellowed. "Now, I will present to you the lord of lords, King Henry Cyrus, The Humble King, the free leader of the Second Republic of Vermont."

Despite the loud applause by most of the audience, a fairly discernable hissing and booing emerged from a number of the lords and nobles. Henry stood up from his throne, letting the mixed reaction stretch out for some time, as he assumed a speaker's stance at a nearby podium.

"Lords. Ladies. Masters. I thank you dearly for your presence today, coming from near and far. I regret the foul weather. It's a shame not only for you, but also my Cerpelli boots, for I have just recently had them shined," he stated, nodding to his feet. The crowd laughed softly. Smiling, Henry positioned himself to the front of the podium.

"Today I bring to you not bad news from Burlington, nor another trivial matter that can be played out indefinitely in the Court of Fools. Instead I bring you news that Vermont is on the verge of change. Much change, perhaps. And I feel compelled to tell you about this change, my friends, because change can sometimes be a good thing."

Henry paused, and nodded subconsciously to the painting of Mt. Mansfield and the woman in prayer. "But I know what you're thinking. Why change something that isn't broken? And I agree to a certain extent. Our republic is in fair shape, despite the growing trouble in Underhill and the Fiskle Cliffs. As of today, our economy is fair, our syrup season, generous, and as we now emerge from winter into the healing touch of spring, our faith in this republic is restored. But even we, in our beautiful hills, mountains, and rivers…even we are not immune to deficiencies. Even we…must remain vigilant in finding ways to better the republic. *Our* republic."

Henry cleared his throat. "We're trying to answer a lot of questions about ourselves, our land, our lives. It's important to keep in mind that we are doing our best, but 'our best,' in my estimation, could always be better. Could it not?"

Some of the lords chattered and grumbled.

"Recently, you all may have read an article from a local newspaper concerning Pete the Moose and his escape from Irasburg. While some may laugh at the absurdity of the events, or the nature in which Pete was freed, the idea of our state symbol freed serves as the perfect emblem for Vermont and Vermonters since as long as time remembers. For Pete the Moose embodies the essence of virtually every Vermonter: pure, independent and free. And while I respect the hard work that the wardens bring to their jobs every day, a part of me finds added comfort in the idea that Pete is a free moose again, undisturbed and unchained. At times, humanity and common sense must trump even laws and dignity, and I stand, unabashed, as a true Vermonter *should*, to the idea of keeping Pete free. As such, I'm now ordering the wardens to leave him be."

The crowd of lords applauded loudly in appreciation. Even Shay Bromage nodded, impressed by the Humble King's spin on the controversial story. The elderly Chief of Wardens, Filmud Asterbrook, dressed in his ceremonious dark camouflage pancho and antique rifle that he used as a walking stick, scowled and kicked the leg of his desk.

Henry continued undisturbed: "Once again, the seeds of change endured these past few days with the passing of Fish. Though tragic by its very nature, I think that we can all agree that removing that animal from corrupting our youth is a big step in improving the city of Burlington, and the republic as a whole. His time was all but done on this earth years ago, and I consider myself very fortunate at being present the day in which his soul was freed, and his life's song filled the whole of the Champlain Valley. My, what a beautiful song that was."

The memory of Jess washed over him. Seeing her, dejected, kicking lifelessly at the water below, filled him with a profound sadness. Henry dabbed away a tear.

"One important thing that I learned was this: it's very easy to attach oneself to the past and grab onto it for dear life, even while the winds of change seem so obvious. It's only when we step outside of this realm, this sanctity of belonging, that we realize there's much potential in Vermont's future."

A great applause ensued, yet as Henry peered around the room, he saw a number of familiar lords and nobles giving one another odd looks. A minute or so after the applause had died down; Henry sat back slowly upon his throne, and mumbled from the corner of his mouth.

"Okay, now let me have it, you twits."

The gavel pounded. "That commences King Henry's speech. The floor is now open for debate," commanded Ulger.

Lord Andreas of White River Junction, adorning his magnificent, white fur-trimmed robe, looked around the hall to see if anyone else shared his suspicions, and indeed, found several nodding him on.

"I think that the question on many of our minds, lord honorable Henry, is whether or not you are you associated with this 'Flatlander' character? And if so, to what degree?"

Henry cocked his head. "Does it matter, Lord Andreas?"

"Well, it just so happens, Lord Henry, it *does*. Many here on the floor don't take very kindly to outside influences."

"Except, of course, for the ones lining your pocket," replied Henry.

An audible gasp from the assemblage of lords resounded throughout the hall. Rarely were references to Lord Andreas's connections to an illegal sugaring operation brought up in such a large, public forum. While thousands of the maples in White River had been improperly, and without good reason, condemned by Andreas's government because of a supposed tree fungus, shipments of syrup had still came and went from his own family farm for months without disturbance. Lord Andreas had pushed for legislation promoting tighter regulation of the sugaring industry, while dozens of other farmers elsewhere in his jurisdiction had lost out on much revenue due to the ordinance. Cornering the market of White River's syrup, buyers were forced to pay high prices for the product. Andreas made off quite well running his very own illegal sugaring operation. The whispers were impossible to ignore. Andreas's attire had rapidly improved these past few months, from gamey to cavalier, as he now dressed himself in the hide of a rare albino wolf. Several heavy necklaces hung from his neck, including one adorned with a large, green gossular garnet.

Andreas blushed. "No need to get testy, Lord Henry."

Lord Henry leaned forward, and admonished the lord of White River with a stare. "Then do not cast stones from glass houses, Andreas." Henry paused. "And as it relates to the Flatlander: a question for you, Lord Andreas...and be honest. If you stumbled upon a great treasure, lost in the deep woods, and were presented with two options, spreading the wealth among your community, or leaving it out in the woods to lay stagnant, which would you choose?"

Andreas exchanged a puzzled look with his comrades. "To spread the wealth with White River, of course, my lord." Lord Andreas stared vacantly. "I don't see where you're going with this."

Andreas only looked upon Henry in cold silence. Other lords murmured in confusion. Knowing that he had to act soon, Henry continued.

"My point being, as a government, we've been at a long, tired stalemate in this republic. We get little done. We bicker back and forth about everything until we're all blue in the face. Do we not, Andreas?"

"But that's our job," replied Andreas, adamantly. "We are elected by our people to argue their positions. We are representatives."

"Indeed. Yet, isn't it also our job to get things done?" inquired Henry, as he gazed dramatically upon the sea of leaders in the statehouse.

"Of course," conceded Andreas, flippantly.

Henry pointed directly at the lord from White River. "Right. It *is* our job, but it is also our tendency to squabble, which is arguably tied to our very nature as Vermonters. We're bristly and we're independent-minded people. Fiercely independent, some might say."

"What are ya getting at, Lord Henry?" asked the droopy-eyed Lord Sarmus of St. Albans from three rows back. "Quit tryin' to dance 'round the issue!"

"My point is this, patient ladies and gentlemen," answered Henry slowly, "I believe that I have found this proverbial treasure in the woods. I decided not too long ago that we needed to use someone from the outside. Someone with an outsider's perspective: someone who, quite literally, wandered into our magnificent republic with no memory, preconceptions, prejudgments, or bias. He is the perfect medium for honest reform. Some may think of him a pest. Some may even think of him an evil relic from the past. But I think of him as my friend. He is Flatlander and he is here to serve republic as I see fit."

The crowd exploded. Several lords shouted, while others threw pens, pencils and papers in sheer disgust. Blushing, Henry tilted his head up towards the balcony with a sheepish look. Flatlander leaned back in his seat very low.

"A *Flatlander*?" said Sarmus in thinly veiled contempt. "You've been seein' to them crucial issues with a *Flatlander*, Lord Henry? Me moms would a been turnin' in her grave faster than a pig roast on Grand Isle!"[28]

Several shouts of agreement followed while a few chuckled loudly.

"A Flatlander couldn't fell a tree if it was held up by a single-thread," added Andreas, as he brushed a piece of lint from his pristine, white coat.

"We don't need a Flatlander any more than a frog needs sideburns," mumbled Lord Hamish of Duxbury, the mustachioed former mountain trader.

Henry bristled. "Gentlemen, ladies, say what you will, but I will reveal this to those of you who haven't yet read Bromage's piece that it was Flatlander who rescued our beloved state symbol, Pete the Moose, from certain doom. It was Flatlander who released our sons and daughters from the merciless clutches of Fish. All in very short time, nonetheless. He's a formidable ally, and now a trusted aide of mine. I'll quote Filmud Asterbrook himself: 'a different hunting blind provides different angles of the same game.' In this light, a new set of eyes, one free from the tutelage of Braintree and Middlebury[29], free from any spheres of influence, may be needed at this juncture."

---

[28] Grand Isle hosts a popular pig-roasting event from the First Slaughter.

[29] The two towns that house the Monks of Middlebury, the leading clergy of Vermont.

There was still a considerable amount of chatter and grumbling in the hall. Several members looked as if they were on the verge of walking out all together, yet sat back down uncomfortably, as if their chairs were torture devices.

Henry continued: "Happy or not, I'm using the man as a fresh pair of ears and eyes, and more importantly, a fresh pair of balls," stated Henry with authority, to a chamber now void of applause. "Keeping him is for the greater good, and for the greater good for the men and women of this republic. We may not all recognize it yet, but it is. There cannot be progress made in Vermont while that pile of laws sits and grows like giant hogweed[30]," said Henry, near-shouting, as he gestured towards a giant mountain of paperwork, pending legislation, in the corner of the room at a clerk's desk. "The decision has been made, and it will continue to move forward according to my rule. And you have my assurance that I will fight for this cause unless the senate agrees to impeach me. Any other topics to consider?"

The grumbling died down from the audience. Tristan Fallon of Lowell sat with his arms crossed in deep concentration. Long, white wisps of hair hung out from his military-style hat like an old mop. His wrinkles and freckles were so abundant that they created a masklike appearance, and he dressed in his old miner clothes, with tan suspenders and thick, wool shirt.

"I'm concerned about certain windmills in our town, lord. I'm getting more and more constituents claiming that they're loud and eyesores to look at," claimed Fallon.

A momentary sense of relief overcame Henry at the changing of the subject. Body sweat had already moistened the lining of his jacket.

"I seem to recall hearing of these windmills," he said, nearly breathless. "Then why keep them, Lord Fallon?"

---

[30] A fast-growing invasive species that can cause severe burns when touched.

Fallon shrugged. "Some tell me that they're good for money and business, help process food and subsidize their costs of living."

"And how do *you* feel, sir?" asked Henry.

"A bit torn, to be honest, Lord Henry. Those are nice, helpful, good folk running those mills. But something about the hills just seems off from when I was a boy. Like something's gone missing- or in a place it shouldn't be. We played on those hills as kids. It just doesn't feel quite right with those mills springing up like that."

Henry drummed his finger on his armrest. "Nostalgia shouldn't trump common sense, nor what's best for the republic's interests, Lord Fallon."

The intellectual Lord Trombley of Middlebury interjected. "I beg pardon, Lord Henry, but what makes Lowell and this republic so attractive in the first place is that we have so much undeveloped land, unlike that, presumably, of the Old Country. Beauty and nature come first before our own capitalistic ventures. One can travel a full day on foot in certain areas before seeing another soul. And some say that a squirrel can traverse the republic without ever having to touch the ground, for we harbor a vast ocean of trees."

"Is that so?" asked Henry, genuinely interested at the suggestion of the normally objective, scientifically-inclined noble. "I'm curious to see your sources on such matters, Lord Trombley."

The noble of Middlebury, adorning his customary green robe, adjusted his glasses and folded his hands politely atop his desk. "Yet one cannot dismiss the possibility as an utter falsehood."

Henry shook his head, annoyed with the straying topic. "There are but few windmills in the republic of which I'm aware of. I doubt they will ever become a common nuisance. Besides, from my limited understanding, Lowell is the perfect location for the windmills. High up. Away from the public eye."

"Like half the blasted republic!" interjected Lord Reigelman of Addison. Middle aged, with a neatly trimmed grey goatee and bleached and brown hair, the noble wore what many suspected to be a toupee. He removed his coat of beaver pelt, and wiped a bead of sweat from his brow. "Soon they'll be sayin' that Addison County is ripe fer windmills, or the hills of St. Albans! And before ya can even blink, they'll be sproutin' up like corn in Danville."

"Not on my watch," grunted Sarmus, as the mere reference to his hometown riled his spirits.

Henry was caught off guard by the shift in the conversation. "Umm. I can't say for sure..."

Riegelman continued his aggressive stance: "Of course ya can't, Lord Henry! That's because every soul in this room knows that this could happen anywhere in our republic, at any given moment! Before ya know it, the whole of Vermont will be runnin' off of windmills, and ya couldn't escape their sound if ya wanted! The wind goes calm, and we'll be sittin' in the dark! The wind goes strong; it'll look like a damned fair! Energy needs in the republic shouldn't be restin' on the afternoon forecast, I says!"

"Now, hold on, Lord Riegelman," replied Henry, "No need for hysterics. Nobody said anything about building more windmills, aside from perhaps Shay Bromage's weekly fodder. I wonder- have any of the fine lords and ladies present at the statehouse ever been to the windmills of Lowell?"

A noticeable silence ensued.

"I have," stated Lord Hamish of Waitsfield in a small voice. Diminutive and elderly, the noble was often dubbed the "lord of time," as no other standing member of the senate surpassed his ripe old age of eighty-nine. He wore a heavy, red-wool cardigan and a pencil-thin mustache. "Passed through several months ago to check up on my daughter in Newport. They produce quality goods, they do."

Henry's curious was piqued. "Like what?"

"Some of the freshest, finest bread that I've eaten since that corner market in Burlington shut down years ago. They also cut some fine lumber too. I bought a half-ton for building a tool shed on my property. Some fine lumber, I'd say too. Harvested from an old patch of hickories if I recall."

Henry leaned forward. He'd always admired the lord from Waitsfield. Hamish was one of the kinder, more amusing senators in the statehouse, though some saw him as somewhat of an exaggerator, or in traditional Vermont dialect, a "spinner of yarn." He had once claimed he 'tunneled through eight feet of snow for six miles to get to school, and despite this, was only 20 minutes late for class.' Henry smiled at the memory of the tall tale.

"Do they now?"

Hamish perked up. "Do indeed! He's quite a nice fellow, that miller. A little peculiar, but he gave me quite a good deal on those items. It would have surely cost me double in Burlington, there's no doubt. So the trek was well worth it."

Henry nodded. "So you say, so you say," muttered Henry in curiosity. "You said that this miller is peculiar? How so?"

Hamish crossed his arms and chuckled to himself. "Some might say he has a funny way of speaking."

Henry nodded. "And you say that this man, this miller, makes bread *and* cuts wood?

Hamish counted off on his fingers. "And corn mash, and mining, and making oil from seeds, and pumping water, and harvesting grain, and...."

"Whoa, whoa, whoa. Hold on just a sec, Lord Hamish," interrupted Riegelman, as the chatter amongst the lords increased. "You mean to tell me that these mills create all of these goods *and* their own energy? How many men and women are workin' for them, and how do they pay for such a large group of workers out in the backwoods of Lowell?"

"Far as I know, it's just the miller and his wife," replied Hamish with a shrug.

Laughter erupted throughout the hall. Riegelman smirked uneasily, and he patted down his bleach blonde hair.

"No, seriously, Lord Hamish, speak to me truly. Your reputation for exaggerating tales precedes you. What size workforce must this man have? Several dozen strong?"

Hamish grew flustered at the insinuation. "The lord didn't bless me to be clever enough to lead you to a bad swimming hole even if I tried. I didn't stutter before and I won't now. I'll repeat- just the Miller and his wife."

There was a muffled chatter in the hall, as Lord Andreas joined in.

"One man and one woman? Tell me, Hamish: do they part the heavens to rain gold upon thee? Heal sick infants from disease? Bring light where there is only darkness? I must know, for the hour is getting late."

Again, laughter erupted from the lords of Vermont. Henry shifted in his seat uncomfortably.

Hamish blushed a deep red. "I'm not the sharpest tool in the shed, sir, but I'd wager you're mocking me..."

"I would never!" rebuked Andreas, as he placed his hand to his chest, his face drenched in mock pain. "On the contrary, I must find these makers of miracles so that I can get my back straightened, my wagon fixed, and my bank account doubled! With that luck, I'd be better off getting into a load of superpac."

The crowd gasped at Andreas's final words. Superpac was a mysterious drug that had been rapidly seeping into Vermont. The drug gave its users an unnatural advantage in more ways than one, and even evoking its name caused strong reactions from many Vermonters who saw these unnatural talents as contradictory to everything that the republic embodied. Although the drug was widely shunned throughout the Vermont community, a growing undercurrent was beginning to affect people from all social classes and backgrounds.

"Enough, Andreas! Leave Lord Hamish alone," interjected Anne Weston of Shelton. Her tight-fitting, magenta corset twisted unnaturally. "He clearly stands by his word, and the only way to find out is by looking into this ourselves."

Andreas looked incredulous. "It's just that I find all of this very difficult to believe, that's all."

"He speaks truth," said Stannard of Milton (pronounced Mil-un). "We have windmills in Milton too. They don't stop movin', they don't. Like sugar on snow year 'round[31]."

Henry turned to the old, eccentric lord, who was donning his owl hat and a pair of usual hefty lamb chop sideburns, and looked at the man peculiarly.

"Come again, Stannard?"

"Got them mills too."

"And just when were you intending on telling the senate of this, Stannard?" asked Henry.

Lord Stannard had a habit of speaking in short bursts without providing much needed clarification. To humor himself, Henry sometimes pondered how Stannard delivered his acceptance speech to the citizens of Milton. Henry once joked to Ellen that it must have been the shortest speech in the history of acceptance speeches.

Stannard shrugged. "Set 'em up two years back. Thought ya knew."

"What he means to say," clarified Sir Trombley of Middlebury, while he twiddled with his black, thick-framed spectacles, "is that roughly two years ago, a public review in the town of Milton approved the construction of several mills along a hilltop."

"I know what I says, Trombley!" snapped Stannard.

"I was just trying to help…" pleaded Trombley.

"To hell with yer help!"

"Enough! Both of you!" chastised Henry. "Lady Anne's right. The only way to help resolve this conflict is by sending a person of

---

[31] A spring Vermont tradition in which maple syrup is combined with snow as a treat.

trust to Lowell, someone who doesn't have a substantial political hand in this. I, for one, recommend my new aide. Flatlander."

Flatlander blushed mightily atop his private balcony, and continued to slink low in his chair. Though the crowd was once again boisterous in their reaction to Flatlander's name being mentioned, few felt the need to argue a moot point. Henry waited for a lord to formally object and voice their dissent, but the dissent never came. Most of the lords knew when to play their hands and to what degree, and this appeared to be a time they swallowed their objections. *They may wait in the wings until things got hairy: for that is the way of the Vermont senate*, mused Henry.

"Pardon me, sir," exclaimed Trombley with his finger raised.

Henry blinked. "Yes, Lord Trombley?"

"It seems to me that we need to strike a negotiation."

"I sense you have a suggestion?" prompted Henry.

"Well, yes," continued Trombley. Whatever blemish he had been trying to rub off from his glasses' lens had been stubborn, and he clanked the spectacles on the front of his desk to rid them of this blight. His green robe, the clothing of choice of the Middlebury monk, shimmered in the sunlight peeking in through the hall's immense windows. "I'm curious as to what these mills produce. A few of our fellow lords speak very highly of them. If we do make a fact-finding trip out of this, I say that we also bring some terms to this miller."

Henry squinted. "Terms? Such as...?" Trombley had Henry's attention. The Lord of Middlebury had his faults, but Trombley was often a wealth of ideas.

Trombley gestured wildly with his hands. "Think of it for just a minute. Bread. Trinkets. Lumber. Grain. If he's selling these below Burlington's market value, and if the products are as good as they say they are, we could always use some here in the Queen City."

"So what you're saying is that we take over his operation?" asked Henry, baffled to where Trombley was going with this whole thing.

"No!" screeched Trombley, before collecting his wits. "I mean, *no*. Flatlander comes to see the place, cozies up with the miller, familiarizes himself with the layout, and then brings back some goods for us to judge its long term viability."

"And then what?"

"If it's a place of agreed value, surely we will be able to tell, and we'll let the miller operate undisturbed, and we benefit from a new formalized trade connection, and maybe a potential model for future production."

"And if not?" asked Henry gravely.

"If not?" Trombley considered the implications for a moment. "If not, we will have to determine whether or not to remove the these mills, and return Lowell to its original, more natural state."

A round of applause ensued and nods of approval spread from lord to lord. Greg Ulger knocked the gavel on his desk several times to restore order to the session. When the raucous had died down substantially, Henry stood aside the podium, and looked upon the crowd of lords.

"Strong terms, but necessary terms," nodded Henry in approval. "So be it. Lord Trombley, you speak wisely on such matters. Tomorrow, Flatlander and a trusted group will depart for these mills and do as we bid them. We will equip them with enough carrying power to bring as many goods back as possible, but with the added stipulation that we pay back the miller its market value when the time is right. Lord Trombley, I'm not a common thief, nor do I intend on sending one to Lowell on my watch. Hamish, I hope that what you say is truthful. I dislike sending out the republic oxen for trivial matters or false leads."

Hamish nodded. "You'll be pleased, my lord."

"I hope so, Hamish. I hope so."

The session was then adjourned. Though it was several minutes later until Flatlander began sitting up straight again. His chair creaked awkwardly in the now-quiet chamber. The lords slowly meandered out of the chamber's main doorway in small clusters, and soon Flatlander felt himself breathing easier once again. He could now see the perception of Flatlanders amongst the republic with more clarity, and it wasn't good, no more of an upgrade, really, than his encounter with Barry in downtown Montpelier. At least during the spittle incident, Henry and Franklin had strong-armed an apology. This was different. There was no opportunity to save face. Not a lord or lady offered him so much as a single word of praise for his two successful quests. In fact, the audience's unease over his presence was palpable. Troubled, Flatlander left the statehouse feeling empty. He proceeding to Lord Henry's abode, his gaze averted mostly to the ground.

Two women and two men constituted the old folk band of Henry's affection, The Stony Mahoney's. Once described as, "traditional folk with a twist," they had grown quite a legion of devout followers during their prime years of the 2080s. The twist? In complimenting the rhythm guitarist/lead vocalist, one of the band members used actual rock as instruments, while one played a highly unusual water barrel for percussion, and a fellow named Sal Solomon played lead guitar. They had never struck up the same following as some of their predecessors, and more mainstream contemporaries of their time. Yet, to Henry, they captured the heart of his carefree youth. They provided the necessary soundtrack to his life through adventure, love, and heartbreak.

Kneeling on the floor of his living room with a dozen vinyl record jackets scattered about him, Henry struggled with the arm of his record player.

"You've got to hear the solo on track six, Jess."

From a nearby couch, Jess rolled her eyes. "Dad, I'm bored."

Henry continued fumbling with the record player's controls, as his fingers became clumsy with anticipation. "Track six. Hold on just a minute. I have to find this song for you. You won't regret it. Sal Solomon's finger-work is exquisite."

As Henry huddled around the record player playing the Stony Mahoney's "Greatest Hits," the Humble King hadn't noticed Flatlander standing motionless in the doorway. *Bad timing* thought Flatlander. He was reluctant to interrupt, but conversely, felt obliged to. *I need to get some things off of my chest. Daddy/daughter time would have to wait.* Flatlander cleared his voice loudly.

Henry looked up from his scattered vinyl, startled. "Oh, Flatlander. I thought the statehouse session went well, wouldn't you say? You've come just in time! You might actually appreciate this. I was just playing Jess some of my favorite music from my youth. Please, join us!"

Flatlander pursed his lips and shook his head slightly. He could see that Jess looked bored and withdrawn, sitting in a non-committal position on the couch next to the record player, legs splayed out. She turned to the wall, strumming her hands on the carpet as if there could be a thousand better places to be- than right there by her father's side. Henry took heed of Flatlander's urgency to talk.

"Jess, if you'll excuse us for a few minutes, Flatlander and I have some important matters to discuss."

Jess breathed a sigh of relief, and hurried out of the room without even acknowledging or making eye contact with Flatlander, nearly shoulder-checking him in the process.

"What's *her* problem?" muttered Flatlander, quietly.

"Oh, I don't know," replied Henry. "It might have something to do with the fact that her father and a flatlander carried out the brutal, unexpected assassination of her beloved deity. Something along those lines."

"Fair enough."

Henry waited until Jess was out of earshot. "I hope that this is important, Flatlander. In case you didn't notice, I was trying to spend some quality time with my daughter."

"Looks like she was having a real bash," quipped Flatlander, as he leaned against the doorframe.

Henry became unnerved and collected his vinyl into a pile. "The effects of Fish have left her devastated. I'm trying my best, Flatlander. When you raise a child, then maybe you can judge. Until then…." Henry replied, wryly, trailing off, as he got up from the rug and peered Flatlander in the eyes. "What's wrong?"

Flatlander felt his frustration surge. "I would have appreciated it if you hadn't mentioned my name in front of that crowd. I was eaten alive out there."

Henry took a deep breath and nodded. "You have to understand, Flatlander, that this is just the nature of politics. Did I not speak highly of you? I used your name to be transparent with the people of the republic. They must know if you truly work for me. I'd rather tell them than that worm-of-a-journalist, Bromage. You must understand- I walk a very fine line between doing the right thing, and appeasing my subjects, at any given moment. Sometimes, they are not mutually exclusive. I often walk on knife's edge, waiting to fall astray at any moment. Vermont politics is a very complicated thing, as you may have noticed this afternoon. I must needle without breaking, strengthen without blinding, and dissect truths and half-truths without alienating. It's tough work. We often spar over matters of the utmost importance."

Flatlander chuckled. "Oh yeah. Like the time you and the legislature spent an entire week debating fencing dimensions for the republic's pig farms?"

"How did you hear about that?" gasped Henry. His face blushed a deep red.

"It's right there in the statehouse logs. I had some free time."

"Tried and true," said Henry, as he took a deep breath. "Look, Flatlander, I know that many of these things may seem trivial to you in the big picture, but to others, these are very important matters. With the pig farm legislation, we were confronted with the fact that large, mutant pigs were being raised throughout several locations in Central Vermont. It was dubbed 'The Central Scare.' Please study up these things before you try to offer insight. The pigs were trampling fencing left and right as if they were no more than common toothpicks. Eating garbage in the streets, mating with wild boars in the forest. It was a nightmare. I didn't have a choice but to devote my full attention to the matter."

Flatlander shrugged. "I just don't really get what my role here is suppose to be."

Henry sighed, picked up the pile of records on the floor, and stacked them delicately on a small, metal stool. "Your role? If I had to use your terminology and assign you a role? I would say that you're a voice of reason, a man of both action and principle. You have very little to lose here. No possessions, not much of a reputation, no family. You don't have any horse in this race, Flatlander. But you can and will collect these things if you complete these quests. Just because you're not established here yet doesn't mean that you're not a critical piece of Vermont's future."

"Funny, the lords and nobles didn't seem to think so."

Henry sighed. "They will, Flatlander. Give them time. Vermonters can be a thorny bunch, especially to outsiders. You must earn their respect. If you keep producing, then people will take notice." Henry paused. "They must."

"It didn't seem like a single lord supported me today," rebuked Flatlander.

Henry patted his new friend on the back. "Ah, true. But consider this: not one noble objected the second time I recommended your presence in Lowell. Sometimes, in politics, much like in life, you have to appreciate the small victories."

Flatlander nodded in silence.

"Now if you'll excuse me, I have a music date with my daughter," said Henry, as he scanned the outlying rooms. *"Jess? Where did you go? Jess?"*

Flatlander walked out of the room, his spirits uplifted, yet still unsure if he was being used as a pawn, and little else. *What's the end game here? Where's all this leading? I may have amnesia, but I'm not stupid.* As he walked through the recently cleaned and dusted living room towards the backyard, some movement on the stairwell caught his eye. There was Jess, sitting halfway up, slightly embarrassed at the fact that she was caught eavesdropping on the two. She gestured to Flatlander to keep quiet with a finger to her lips, as Henry continued calling her name. Giving her a reassuring thumbs-up, Flatlander left Jess atop the stair, and for the very first time since his arrival, saw Henry's daughter smile big and bright.

At the bottom of the Lowell Ridge sat the perpetually lonely minstrel, Benegas (pronounced Benny-giss). Perched on a large granite rock, he sported a long, mustard yellow robe imbedded with odd, multicolored marbles, and an oversized beaver tail hat. The rock was rather large, and folded inward with soft edges, perfectly suiting the minstrel's form. Benegas sat for some time on his rock, tuning his guitar to his fancy. During the previous rendition of "Lowell Hills," he noticed that he had sounded flat, very flat. *Flatter than the flattest flatfooted Flatlander from this side of the flatlands*, he thought in jest. Then in the midst of changing his "E" string, he noticed three companions arriving at the base of the ridge with a long procession of oxen following, sixteen by his count. Three large Conestoga carriages rocked crookedly in tow.

Benegas resumed tuning his guitar as the men passed slowly by. He noticed a large, dangerous-looking bearded man in the front carriage, steering, and then an oddly dressed, medium-built man and very short, gnomish-looking man in the back carriage. The middle carriage carried what appeared to be a dozen or more wooden crates. They all passed with courteous head nods aimed at the minstrel, as the massive caravan shook the nearby earth, kicking up dust in the heavy air. Barely a dozen paces after they had passed the rock, Benegas burst into song.

"Changes comin' to Lowell hill,
Changes comin' but no one will,
The siren sings but her lover's comin',
Drowned out, pity, by the blades a hummin'."

"Say again?" asked Franklin, as he motioned for the caravan to halt, as he faced the minstrel.

"Where ya headed?" inquired Benegas, as he rested a weary arm against his guitar.

The minstrel swung an annoyed hand at some gnats hovering near his nose. Flatlander failed to see this man as a threat, and besides; it must have appeared their destination was obvious. Few used this road for trade or travel, and fewer maintained it, for even in the early throes of spring, the grass had already sprung close to knee-high.

"We're here to see the miller," answered Franklin, roughly. "He up that road?"

"Yep."

"Many thanks."

"That's a lot of oxen ya got there," observed Benegas. "Not every day ya see sixteen oxen makin' their way up the Lowell Ridge. The Miller must have somethin' special planned."

Something in the Minstrel's tone suggested a well-guarded humor.

Franklin squinted at the stranger. "What's it to ya?"

Benegas splayed out his hands defensively. "Oh, many pardons, dear sirs. I meant no offense. Just the excitement that a large caravan of oxen and a trio of strangers can have on a poor, lonely minstrel in the middle of the northern wood."

"He's playing us. Let's go," urged Flatlander to his companions.

Up ahead and to the left, Flatlander eyed the looping mountain road curiously. No clear markers stood at the entrance; only a significant gully at the foot of the mountain with clusters of weeds running rampant.

"Tell them that old Benegas gives his regards."

Flatlander looked queerly at the man. "Who?"

The minstrel nodded. "Benegas. That's me. That's my name."

"Flatlander. Nice to meet you."

The minstrel raised an eyebrow. "Flatlander, eh? Shoulda figured with that strange, buttoned shirt and that stubble of yours. Don't see many Flatlanders 'round these parts. I'd welcome you, but I figure somebody already beat me to the punch."

"Many thanks," replied Flatlander, his tone suggesting a false sense of gratitude.

"Well, in that case, I'll leave you be. I see you're not in the mood for mere pleasantries like us simple folk from the country."

And without so much as a warning or formality, the minstrel broke out again in song. The three travelers looked at one another curiously, shrugged, then rallied up the dawdling oxen onward towards the Lowell Ridge Road. Every now or then, one of the three would turn, awkwardly, and watch the minstrel enraptured fully with his music.

"Trampled dreams and childhood's end,
The Mills a-hum,
Pinwheels on my hill of hills,
They'll break
Before I die.

The horizon doesn't seem the same to me,
The Mills a-hum
Just let them be.
If I should die before I wake,
A Lowell exit I should make.

A siren's song and goods to bear,
A weeping willow in the mist,
The birds, they fall,
A misjudged gust,
And mountains crumble with a kiss."

The minstrel's fading words bore a heavy weight upon the weary travelers. The wind grew and the air began to cool considerably. Darkened storm clouds glided across the sky above. The road began taking a very sharp, steep turn up the narrow mountain ridge. The oxen hesitated upon seeing the new, difficult terrain, but lumbered onward when Franklin smacked several on their backsides with his whip.

Menche finally spoke up from Flatlander's side. "I don't like them clouds, sir."

"Trouble stirs in these hills," agreed Franklin.

Unbeknownst to the party, the quest was taking a particular heavy toll on Franklin. From the moment Henry ordered that he assist Flatlander to Lowell, Franklin's nerves had been on edge. For he harbored a bitter past amid this harsh land, and hoped, for the very life of him, that it would remain a secret for the remainder of the journey. His past was his past, and *his* past *only*. Sure, he had regrets, but his life in Montpelier was a vast improvement from the hardships of the Northeast Kingdom.

He hoped to avoid any suspicions from those at the mills. Luckily Henry agreed, and thought that it would be wise for Franklin to introduce himself with a different alias, "Peter." Periodically, the northerner would dab water from his metal canteen to slick back his wild, mangy hair. He even shed his thick fur coat in favor of a lighter brown tunic, despite the growing chill of early dusk. He actually basked in the darkening skies. *Less chance the miller recognizes me.*

He needed to get a hold of himself. *Get there, set the terms, take the goods, and get out. Like dressin' down a deer 'fore sunset.* Franklin hoped for a smooth trip: step-by-step methodical. *No overthinkin', no storytellin', and no socializin'.*

Gripping the amulet of the north, customized for him for his service to the Kingdom, Franklin uttered an old Walden prayer: *safe keepin' fer the good willed.* He looked briefly upon the old amulet. His name, Franklin of Walden, was engraved on its backside and a quote "o stone be not so," a silly tribute in the form of palindrome, referencing Franklin once mistaking a companion's whetstone for his own. Its edges had smoothed considerably, yet the cold serpentine gemstones from the Belvedere mines had lost none of their olive green luster. The clouds, which had built up in both density and darkness, now spread around the summit of the Lowell Ridge like an ebony blanket. Large drops of rain began to fall, panging sporadically among the nearby leaves. Within a minute, the downpour built up in intensity as they lurched up the ridge. The dirt road had been already muddied from a recent rain, and soon emulsified into a wet, claylike substance.

"Mud season is like no other, I'm tellin' ya," muttered Franklin in frustration, as he attempted to steer the stumbling oxen right and keep his caravan evenly keeled.

"Look, you can see some of the mills!" exclaimed Flatlander, as he pointed to the top the tree line to the right, and what appeared to be windmill blades protruding over the forest canopy. "We're almost there."

Without time for any further distractions, Franklin shoved his amulet deep within his pocket and trudged on with heavy legs and a heavy heart. One more bend appeared in the road up ahead. A sudden torrential downpour ensued, as a series of fierce gales swept over the ridge. The oxen grunted in disapproval. Thin trees bent like guitar strings. Footprints were rendered to muddy oblivion. And deep in the woods at their backs, Shay Bromage huddled as best he could underneath a bent tree branch in the limited warmth of his soaked plaid jacket.

As they approached a clearing in the wood, Flatlander discovered the assemblage of windmills to which they sought. Wood windmills. Stone windmills. Windmills made of copper. Windmills that stood the height of the tallest buildings in Burlington, while others were the height of a man. The field spread close to twenty acres, by Flatlander's estimation, yet there had to be at least ten to twelve windmills within plain sight. In the center of the field, stood the tallest of the mills. A wooden giant made of oak, fifteen stories tall, its blades cut high through the Lowell tree line, emitting a low, engine-like groan with every revolution. Even in the growing gloom, its bright, white exterior and mahogany trim stood out boldly against a dark green, wooded backdrop.

The rain had grown thick, and the wind was particularly strong on this stretch of exposed terrain. The field was overgrown with tall grass, except for a small, rectangular enclosure, which was shaped to accommodate a vegetable farm. The three travelers trudged on, soaking wet, as the oxen grew restless.

"Jeezum crow," muttered Franklin, in awe. "Never seen anythin' like it in me life."

"Amazing," agreed Flatlander.

All of the windmills, because of structural differences in size and style, were moving at different speeds. As a result, when viewed as a whole, the windmills had quite a hypnotizing effect. Each had a distinct sound, from the high-pitched rattles of the smallest mills, to the deep, rumbling groan of the giant.

Menche smiled to himself. "Looks like me pinwheels back home."

"They're windmills, Menche," replied Flatlander. "'The gifts that keep giving' I heard one noble, Hamish, say."

"Aye, so they are," said Franklin, as he wiped away a steady stream of rain from his eyes.

As the three approached the center mill, Flatlander grew nervous. He had no idea what to expect, or what they would encounter. The terms set out weren't exactly of the kindest nature; essentially they called for the miller to fork over some goods, or get shut down. They were strong-arming the man, thought Flatlander, despite the euphemisms laid out in the senate chamber. As far as the miller's response to such conditions was concerned, they were soon to find out.

As they neared the center mill, they could hear not only the soft hum of what sounded like blades turning, but also a loud series of mechanical groans, creeks, and crashes come from inside. Flatlander looked back to Menche, Franklin, and the line of oxen, ensuring that they were all on guard.

They dismounted from their carriages, and approached the front door to the mill. Flatlander gave three pronounced knocks and waited. It wasn't long before the miller answered, opening the door cautiously. He was an ugly man. His hair, knotted and disheveled, fell to his shoulders like matted grey fur. His face was wrinkled and weathered. He wore what appeared to be a wolf pelt over a dark robe, which was oversized and covered in sawdust. His pants were loose and made of wool. Very few of the man's teeth were intact, and the few remaining, had a grim future indeed. The miller gave the party of three an awkward smile.

"Oh, welcome weary travelers near,
What brings thee to mine humble clear?
The weather is not fit for this,
Wandering through this Lowell mist."

"Hello, kind sir!" stammered Flatlander, after a pause, as he reached out a friendly hand.

Flatlander recalled bits from the senate floor. *Some might say he has a funny way of speaking,* mentioned Hamish. Glancing back awkwardly at Franklin and Menche, who flanked Flatlander on either side. Franklin nudged him gently in the back with a closed fist. He brandished Henry's medallion.

"My name is Flatlander, and these are my companions, Peter and Menche. We come from Montpelier at the bidding of our king, Lord Henry of the Brattle, and the Vermont Senate. We've come to strike a deal."

"It surely must concern the mills,
Some villagers, whose voices shrill,

Just like that nasty minstrel sings,
His music- blah, it's spite he brings!"

Flatlander leaned over and whispered in Franklin's ear. "Does he always speak in couplets?"

"A strange duck, this miller," whispered Franklin back, quickly. "Keep yer cool."

"I see," whispered Flatlander back, his attention once again focused on the miller. The rain was relentless, and even the miller involuntarily took a step back further within the doorway to escape the ongoing splash from his gutter. "On a related note, we have met this Benegas, sir, who was quite insistent that we give you his regards."

The Miller shook his head in annoyance.

"Don't confer with bitter neighbors,
Minstrels know not of life's labors,
He sees the mills with vile regard,
The grass is sown, *the minstrel-* barred!

He sits upon that rock and moans
All day, and whilst his parents groan,
Oh petty, petty Benegas!
Leave the mills be; those goods are bliss!"

"Speaking of those goods," replied Flatlander in his most formal tone, making his best effort to remain composed in light of such strange dialect. He thoughtfully recalled the lines that he had rehearsed under the tutelage of Henry. "Let me explain our deal. Think not of it as a bribe but a gesture of goodwill, sir. Your goods have won you select acclaim, and yet only a small group from the capital have seen them with their own eyes, or tasted them with their own tongues. We ask for goods of plenty to fill our carriages, and in return you have our assurance that we pay you later what we deem fair market value, but we also let you be, undisturbed, and will spread word of your goods nearer to the cities of Burlington and Montpelier. The republic also wishes for new trade partners, no matter the distance. We come in good faith and hope to leave as friends." He paused. "Do you accept these terms?"

Franklin nodded his head in approval of Flatlander's delivery. *Here we go*, Flatlander thought, as he braced himself for a fight, *this could get bad*. The miller mulled over the terms, and as his eyes shifted from traveler to traveler, his face alternated between concern and acceptance. And then, most reluctantly, the miller smiled his toothless grin.

"The rain bears upon thee this night,
Will leave you soaked and cold, despite
Your best intentions getting home,
Chilled to the touch, raw to the bone.

Fix your oxen, break bread with me,
So you can dry, you lucky three.

My wife will fix you up some beds,
And I will tend to bake you breads,
If sleeping is your one true will,
Relax yourself; enjoy the mill!"

Flatlander extended a hand once more for an official shake on the matter. "I take that as a 'yes' good man. We thank you from the bottom of our hearts, kind host."

The miller looked at Flatlander carefully, inspecting his buttoned shirt and unfamiliar, plain khakis.

"My, a Flatlander is seldom,
Seen in Lowell; they're unwelcome,
But I must say, you seem quite nice,
Dry off inside, I'll strike a light."

After securing the oxen, the three ventured inside the mill. As he entered, Franklin tried his best to avert his face from the miller's gaze. Aside from a couple of lanterns lit by the entrance and the back of the room, much of the hall was engulfed in darkness. Despite this, Flatlander could tell that the room was quite large, as evidenced by the deep, bellowing sounds of whatever machinations lay full center in the middle of the room. As the miller lit a dozen lanterns around the outlying walls, the full enormity and complexity of the mill emerged from the shadows.

In the middle of the room stood a series of complex wheels, pulleys, mechanical arms, drills, smashers, cutters, and borers. A series of two metal conveyor belts shifted below, each surface moving in the opposite direction of the other. It seemed unfathomable how anyone could put up with the noise, thought Flatlander, but judging by the nightfall's rapid descent and the continuing onslaught of rain, they had but little choice than to stay. The room was massive; nearly one hundred feet diameter was his best estimate, with nearly half of the surface area fully devoted to the functions of the mill.

"How we suppose to sleeps here?" said Menche at his side.

Flatlander whispered sharply. "Shh!"

"Could wakes a bear in winter's slumber!" Menche continued.

"Menche, enough!" said Flatlander.

"Smells nice, though," remarked Franklin after a long, deep breath. And he was right. As the moist, earthy smell of the Lowell ridge dissipated at their backs, in its stead came the wonderful smell of baked bread, mashed apple, and churned hops.

"That's wonderful," agreed Flatlander.

The potpourri of smells was intoxicating, and judging by the drool collecting at the corner of Franklin's lips, Flatlander suspected that the complaining would slow, if not cease altogether. Proudly, the miller gestured to the great operation at the center of the room.

"Our crispy, doughy fresh-baked bread,
Or oak-wood stacked up to your head,
There is much that these mills do make,
Harness the wind for goodness sake!

Need stone cut quick or butter churned?
Energy sought or wood to turn?
Collect clean water for the town?
The mill rules all without a crown.

The miners struck a deal with me[32],
Enjoy my fruits and let me be,
A Miller's mill is no place for,
A miner's brawl, a settler's score[33].

Love my fruits the wind delivers,
Blessed in the sky's own rivers,
Your oxen, you can load right up,
But first, hot cider in your cup!"

The miller then produced a steaming, tin pitcher full of hot cider from atop a woodstove, and poured the three weary travelers a cup each. Menche sipped the scalding cider and smacked his lips in pained delight. Flatlander enjoyed the complexity of its flavor: the sour apple combined with the pleasant aftertaste of spice and a

---

[32] This refers to an actual agreement where the miners of Lowell receive 5% kickbacks of the Miller's goods to allow him in business.

[33] Miner brawls at the local tavern were a fairly common occurrence in Lowell.

hint of maple was phenomenal. Joining them with a hearty cheer, the miller took his own swig.

"We thanks you, sir," remarked Menche in appreciation. "In keepin' us warm and such."

Flatlander added. "You're a very gracious host. Lord Henry will be tremendously honored and grateful."

The miller nodded humbly.

After cider, the crew packed their empty wooden crates full of the miller's goods, then stacked them upon the carriages. Excited by their newfound bounty, Flatlander envisioned the heaps of praise that would be bestowed upon them on arrival. Crate after crate they filled with bottled cider, butter, bread, corn mash, grain, and tea, with each labeled appropriately with a hastily drawn illustration courtesy of Flatlander. The crates kept coming until the wheels of the middle carriage sunk close to an inch in the mud from the added weight. As a gesture of good faith, the miller even included a barrel of specially made blackberry jam that he had just produced earlier in the day. When the party had finished packing, thirty large crates filled their caravan front to back.

Yet much to Franklin's growing unease, the miller began passing him curious looks. As they stocked the goods, the miller kept repositioning himself to get a better look at Franklin's face. But the northerner took quick action, pretending quite cleverly that Flatlander called his name, as he rushed off for assistance. The dusk had now fully succumbed to nightfall, and every crate was accounted for. Shortly after the goods had been stacked, and their clothes thoroughly soaked from the torrential downpour, they re-entered the mill and heard what sounded like a woman's voice from atop an adjacent stairwell.

"Good lord, Earnest. I was resting well enough until I heard all of the commotion. Are you going to introduce me to our new guests, or should I do it myself?" came the voice, as her footsteps made their way gracefully down the steps.

And there, at the bottom of the stairs, in full view for the three guests, approached the most divine woman Flatlander had ever laid eyes upon thus far in the republic. The miller nodded towards the direction of the rare beauty, a stunning blonde of substantial height. She wore a ragged brown tunic. Her pants were made of faded, black leather; used frequently to work outside during the recent spate of rain. Her hair was damp, yet it still maintained a dignified quality. Her body was fit yet curvy. In the palm of her hands stood a candle alight. The miller cleared his throat:

"I'd like to introduce my wife,
Sonia, my one true love in life,
Her hands are strong; her hair so pure,
Always firm, and never demure."

Simultaneously, the three guests all stepped forward and extended their hands. Flatlander's shock rapidly mutated into a raging jealousy; his feelings reconfirmed by the openly gawking Franklin. Menche simply shuffled his feet back and forth sheepishly.

"Pleased to meet you all," replied Sonia, as she shook their hands, one by one. Her hands felt surprisingly rough, like sandpaper.

"The honor is all ours, Lady Sonia," responded Flatlander, as he swallowed. "We've come from Montpelier to deal with your, umm…" Flatlander hesitated, as the word was hard to muster "husband… and yourself. We've collected your goods in good faith and will pay fair market value. The republic is curious of your operation here. And I must say, we're beyond impressed by the quality…"

"Your accent," interrupted Sonia with a raised hand, as she glanced upon Flatlander suspiciously. "And your garb."

He paused. "What about them?"

"What region of Vermont are you from?"

Flatlander looked down at the floor. "That's the thing, mam. I'm not from the republic. I'm a Flatlander, mam."

Sonia's face soured noticeably, and she unwittingly took a step backwards. "So what brings you to *Lowell,* of all places? Why is Montpelier sending a flatlander here, of all people? Earnest, I hope that these people have paid twofold for our goods?"

Flatlander stammered. "Mam…"

"*Sonia,*" she corrected in a more formal tone.

"Sonia then, can you let me explain?"

"Maybe," replied Sonia, quite indifferently. She began to massage the inside of her biceps. "For twelve years, I've toiled in these mills. Twelve years! Wayfaring strangers are rare, wayfaring flatlanders, never! What little I've been told of your kind has *not* been good. Your speech is coarse upon my ears."

"He can't help it, milady," interjected Franklin. "Ya can't control where ya from, only where yer at."

"Pearls of wisdom," retorted Sonia with a smile, as she looked Franklin deep in his eyes. He turned away, abashed. "And you seem familiar as well. I recognize that brutish tongue. It's common here in the kingdom."

The northerner looked directly into the face of the miller's wife. Her eyes held an intense beauty, smart and daunting by nature. They shone a magnificent hazel. And yet, there was a sense of sadness inside of them. Slight bags under her eyes indicated that of a sophisticated nature, but also a life full of toil and hardship. Franklin did his absolute best to keep a poker face, and much to Flatlander's amusement, altered his accent to sound more smooth and traditional in the Vermont dialect.

"From a small town. Ya probably never heard of it."

"Perhaps I have. Tell me," replied Sonia.

Even the miller now directed much of his attention to Franklin, monitoring his every word and movement. Franklin squirmed slightly. He could not reveal his true name and origins. Not now, perhaps not *ever*. Flatlander gave him a subtle and gentle nudge in the side.

"Peter of Ryegate," he lied. The miller's eyes opened wide with delight.

"The gates of Rye, where mills were built,
The River Wells[34]; where riches spilt,
Grain, or wood, or rich, full leather,
Sir, I think of you the better."

Sonia allowed her husband to finish, but her suspicious gaze remained steadily on Franklin. After a few tense seconds, she turned towards her husband.

"Earnest, do you remember the story of the swan that I told you about some time ago?"

The miller rolled his eyes back in his head, as if searching, digging, for any sign of the memory.

Sonia sighed loudly. "It figures. The man can't even remember where he put his shoes the previous night unless I tell him…"

"Sonia do not speak of me ill,
I hate this fighting in our mill…
Our guests are spooked, our…"

"Enough, Ernest!" said Sonia, annoyed. "We'll talk about this later."

The miller removed himself from the group's close proximity, and made his way towards a small table near the back of the room. There, he began whittling a large branch with an oversized hunting knife. Sonia watched him curiously as he whittled away. A long silence ensued. The three guests smiled awkwardly at one

---

[34] A river in Ryegate with several functional, long-operating mills.

another, awaiting the other to restart conversation. The miller continued whittling his branch away defiantly.

"How have I forgotten my house manners? Please come and make yourselves home. Come and sit," she gestured to a two adjacent couches near the front window.

Bales of hay shaped into that of couches, bent and supported by a series of metal wires. A sheet of fine brown leather draped the hay bales, and looked to be quite new; it glistened in the torchlight. The three travelers and their gorgeous host sat amongst the mill's equivalent of a living room.

Sonia sat across from Franklin and jogged her memory. "Where was I? Oh right, the swan! Ryegate! Although I lived just north of there, in St. Johnsbury, I spent three summers as a child on McLam Pond. I'm sure that you've been there, Peter. I couldn't have been older than nine or ten. Yet I remember a family of swans. They were so beautiful. I spent hours watching them sometimes with my sister, Delia. Do you recall much in Ryegate?"

Franklin grimaced then chuckled. "A bit here and there, my lady, though more *there* than *here*."

Sonia laughed softly. "But surely you must recall McLam Pond? Ryegate isn't *that* large."

Franklin swallowed hard. "Aye, I believe so, milady. May have stopped by for a play once with friends."

Sonia eyed Franklin curiously. "I'm surprised you don't recall. Hmm." Shaking her head briefly, Sonia resumed her story. "Well, the swans stood out to me. Not only because they are rare in Vermont, but also because they remind me of a time in my life when I had time to appreciate nature. Truly appreciate it. Delia often told me how the swans were placed there from their old home; like decorations. Maybe she made up the story, I don't know. As silly at it sounds saying it now, it always seemed like they yearned for home. I could feel it. There was a kind of graceful melancholy about them."

"What's a swan, milady?" asked Menche.

"It's a bird, little one," replied Sonia with a laugh. "A large, beautiful, white bird that spends its time on water. Like a giant, prettier version of a duck."

"Hmm."

"Well then. You all look weary. Help yourself to our bathrooms. We have beds ready upstairs. If you need me, just call."

Excusing himself while claiming that he wanted to make absolutely certain that the goods were secured, Franklin stepped outside. Menche left to bathe upstairs. The miller continued to grumble and tinker about in the kitchen. Minutes later, and without warning, came the sudden halt of the mill's blades, as the groans and creaks of the inner workings came to a standstill. The wind outside remained fierce. Cursing under his breath, the miller attributed it to the growing storm. Flatlander saw this as an opportune time to get to know Sonia better, even if it meant drawing the miller's ire. *Life is full of risks.* And it was with this sentiment that Flatlander attempted to rationalize his plans of flirtation with Sonia. He watched as the miller left to tend to his mills, and smiled devilishly, welcoming this godsend.

He had never seen beauty as fine as Sonia's, and Franklin had needed to remove himself from the mill as he could simply bear it no longer. *Finer than the sands of North Beach*[35] *on a summer's day, she is,* he reflected, smitten. He found himself moving against his better judgment, as he scavenged the yard for fallen branches and limbs from the current storm. *A swan. What better gift for the lady than a swan? Just wouldn't be proper to stay at their house without the proper giftin'.*

He hoped dearly that his ploy to stall for time would help, and that the miller's suspicions weren't roused in the process. Placing

---

[35] Vermont's largest sand beach, located in Burlington.

his amulet in the blades was foolish, even Franklin knew that much; but his desire to win Sonia's affections, even if just for a minute, trumped any and all forms of common sense. He wanted to surprise her tonight.

While in the yard, he began to assemble branches and sticks together into what he believed to be a good model of a swan. He knotted the branches together using peeled bark, preventing the wind of making haste to his creation. 'Oh, Franklin!' he could almost hear Sonia weep, 'this is the most magical, most wonderful present that anyone has ever given me! The swan is the key to my heart. A kiss I owe for my thoughtful guest!' He then saw Sonia kissing himself in his dreams, but if anyone had perchance observed the brute from nearby during this strange episode, they would have seen the northerner awkwardly tonguing a large crooked tree limb hanging from a massive oak.

The miller strained his eyes hard against the falling rain, looking for signs of damage to the blades of his windmills. Nothing. The wind was fierce, even more so since the strangers' arrival, and the rain, no lesser. In the distance, he could see that the other windmills were working fine. Whirling and buzzing madly, the wind was relentless. The miller smiled eagerly at the thought of the strong wind: *a week's work, a miller's perk.* And yet there stood the main mill, the mill that housed his home, sitting completely still amidst the torrent of the night.

He began climbing the slippery rungs of the mill to get a closer look about. The explanation had to be purely mechanical, he thought, and although it was a rare event, there had been a few jams in the past. Once, a wayward goose had gotten caught in its gears. On another occasion, a piece from the blade itself had fallen into a small opening, jamming the entire mill for three hours.

They were all somewhat costly mistakes, but corrected rather quickly, with little impact on their operation as a whole. As the miller slowly prodded his way up the rungs, a flash of lightning briefly illuminated the Lowell Highlands and Belvidere Mines in the distance. The resounding thunder shook the mill, yet the Miller continued on his way.

Upon reaching the drive shaft at the center of the blades, his cloak soaked and his hair drenched, the miller cautiously lit the wick of an old mining lantern, coated with the water-resistant oil of Braintree. He then partly sheltered the lantern with his robe. Inching the flame towards the base of the shaft, the miller spotted something rather peculiar. There- wedged perfectly between blade and beam, was a small dark object, half the size of his fist. Curious, the miller gave it a quick yank, careful not to catch his cloak in the blades. In one rapid motion, the miller plucked the object from its dark crevasse, causing him to slip slightly and nearly topple over the edge of the small platform. The small object slipped onto the floor before him. The windmill's blades instantaneously broke into a blinding fury. Lightning struck closer this time, as the thunder rolled for twenty seconds or more, enveloping his thoughts. Regaining his balance, the miller went to inspect the object, lantern aloft.

Lying on the floor, in all of its rugged glory, was the amulet worn by only a select few from the various regions of the Northeast Kingdom. An amulet forged from the Serpentine rocks of Lowell, which was not produced any longer within the kingdom. Engraved with a lynx and fading stars on its face, a crack traced its outer edge. The miller picked it up with a curse, as realization began to dawn on him. He had suspicions of these folk, particularly that 'Peter of Ryegate'. He knew something was amiss. It was the outcast, Franklin of Walden, now an unannounced guest in his home, and traveling under a different name. And worse, the brute was already tampering with his living. And who were these companions? The Flatlander, by mere association alone, could not be trusted. The miller reddened with fury, the rain having minimal effect in distracting his ill-tempered thoughts.

"He thinks of me a doltish clod,
Pity's fool; to me they prod,
But if trinkets strikes their fancy,
All the more to make them antsy."

Franklin of Walden gathered branches in the dark. With each passing flash of lightning, he began to see the structure clearer. The assemblage of branches almost resembled that of a swan. He was close. Whether or not Sonia would be able to ascertain that, Franklin didn't have a clue. From behind, Franklin heard a voice.

"What builds you this, thou northern quack?
I found your amulet whilst back,
In the mills' blades, found deeply-root,
To stall my mill, ungrateful brute!"

Franklin jumped, startled. Dropping a large stick from his clutches, Franklin stroked his slick-backed hair, as if awoken suddenly from a dream. The miller threw an object, which splashed in a puddle at Franklin's feet. The miller stood his ground, ominous looking, his darkened silhouette outlined against the gentle glow of the mill's lantern light. The northerner picked up the amulet, as if for the first time.

"Oh, sir, I'm sorry, sir. I just...I...oh, where did ya find my amulet? I was lookin' everywhere fer it!" Franklin then followed the miller's gaze, which was now fixated on the strange wooden creation, and realized that an explanation was needed. "Oh, don't mind me, sir. Just fixin' both of ya up somethin' nice, to say thanks!"

It was only a half-lie, thought Franklin with an awkward smirk. The miller's voice carried with it a new edge.

"Brute is the name I called you then,
You fled the north, your honor bent,
Franklin of Walden, on your own,
The North, you'll never call your home!"

So much fer nothin', mused Franklin. The gig was up. The miller had found him out. He had warned Henry of the high chances of being found out, but the Humble King was adamant that he assist Flatlander to Lowell. But before Franklin could muster a response, the miller strode past him at a brisk pace, exchanging one more befuddled glance at Franklin's attempt at a wooden swan. Gulping, Franklin watched nervously as the miller approached the front door of the main mill. And it was in that very moment that Franklin spotted something simply terrifying protruding from the miller's back: the outline of a hunting bow. *This could be bad*, dreaded Franklin, *really bad*.

Flatlander and Sonia sat close together at the dinner table over two bowls of cream of corn soup, a helping of fresh bread, and two cups of warm milk. Placed between them stood a lit lemon-scented candle. The candlelight gently flickered from wall to wall, as the unexpected silence continued. As Sonia nibbled on a handful of bread, Flatlander wondered aloud.

"Do you ever get bored around here? What kind of things do you do for fun?"

"What do you mean?" Sonia laughed.

"I mean," Flatlander began, nodding to the machinations in the center of the main room, "don't get me wrong. You guys have a beautiful setup here. It's peaceful. Business is good. I just feel like it might get a little old after a while."

"Doesn't everything 'get old after a while'?" retorted Sonia with a smirk, as she passed a helping of bread to Flatlander.

"Fair enough," nodded Flatlander, as he helped himself, and took a hearty bite into the salted crust. "Sorry, I wasn't trying to be offensive," he managed through a full mouth.

"None taken," replied Sonia, matter-of-factly. "Though I'll admit, there are times in which I become weary of the day's labors. Sometimes, all it takes is one look at my hands," Sonia paused, as she displayed her weathered, rough-skinned palms, "and I start to think about what else my life could have been had I never come here in the first place."

"And?" asked Flatlander, expecting her to continue. "What other life would you have envisioned for yourself?"

Sonia smirked, as a loose bang draped over her forehead. "Don't tell me you've never wondered the same thing yourself?"

Flatlander ripped apart the chunk of bread, and buttered it up with an old, silver knife. "How could I? I can't even remember where I was four weeks ago."

"And yet your garb tells me that you hail from the Old Country, a sworn enemy of our republic," said Sonia, as she pointed to Flatlander's collared shirt and jeans.

Flatlander shrugged. "I am what I am. I can't change that. But while we're at it, do you have any idea how frightening it is to wake up with no memories? I wouldn't wish it upon anyone. I have no idea who I've loved, who I've lost. Whether or not I had kids. What kind of job I worked. My hobbies, even, Sonia. I have no idea what kind of hobbies I use to have. I'm starting from scratch. It's hard to even talk to people without being able to relate to them any of my past, any of my experiences. The only stories I can tell you have to do with releasing a moose from near death and executing a cult-leading Fish. You've probably heard."

"News travels slow in these parts," replied Sonia, with a cocked eyebrow.

"Never mind," said Flatlander with a sigh.

"You poor thing."

"The funny thing is, I keep having these dreams. They come to me at weird times. I've dreamt of being carried down a river, and a house with an ocean view, and some experience on a dock. Weird things, but I feel like they're serving some type of purpose."

Sonia offered with a kind smile. "Memories may come in the form of dreams. Even you should know *that*. The swans that I use to follow as a child in Ryegate they use to, oh, this is going to sound weird to you…" Sonia trailed off, her face turning a bright red.

He leaned closer. "Have you seen the bozos that I travel with? Nothing would sound weird to me." Sonia laughed. Flatlander's heart skipped a beat. *You're doing good, kid.*

"They sometimes spoke to me," replied Sonia.

"*Really?*" asked Flatlander.

Sonia nodded. "Yes, they told me that I could fly with them whenever I was ready."

"Please tell me that you didn't take their advice," replied Flatlander with a smirk. "Because last I checked, humans were unable to fly. Not even in the Old Country."

Sonia laughed loudly, and she took a swig of warm milk to soothe her throat. She looked hard into his eyes, raised an eyebrow, and gave a flirtatious wink.

"You're too funny."

Flatlander beamed. "I try."

"You know, it gets pretty lonely here at the mill," said Sonia with a sigh. "Earnest is a great man, really he is, but not the best husband. Not much of a talker, and even less of a looker, as you can see."

Flatlander then realized that he was treading in very dangerous territory. He could have been mistaken, caught up in his own realm of hubris, yet it appeared that Sonia was leading him on.

Flatlander twitched. "He's been a great host."

Sonia leaned in. "And he's left us all alone for the moment."

Swallowing hard, Flatlander watched helplessly as Sonia looked deep into his eyes, as if searching for an answer. He responded by grabbing a handful of hair, and kissing the miller's wife passionately and slowly. Her lips tasted of sweet apple and cream, and her perfume was as sweet as a field of wildflowers. His heart skipped a beat.

From the corner of his eye, Flatlander spotted movement and heard the creaking of a door. As he frantically pried himself from

Sonia's grasp, he looked up. There, standing motionless in the doorway was the miller. After three emphatic steps inside, he proceeded to slam the door behind him with a kick. Drops of rain from his jacket spattered on the kitchen floor. Flatlander jumped up rapidly from his chair, and shuffled slowly away from Sonia. The miller breathed heavy, and spoke in sheer contempt.

"Thy eyes cannot believe this sight,
You kiss my wife; yet have no right!"

Sonia moved quickly to her soaked husband. "Earnest, you scared me! Aw, look how wet you are! Let me fix you a hot cider, dear!"

The miller pulled down his soaked hood, whereby revealing his true rage. As a flash of lightning lit the room, the miller's breath steamed, and his bulbous eyes glared solely into that of Flatlander's. He wrung a wet sleeve, as water beat off of the hard oak floor.

"I can explain everything," said Flatlander, as his face grew ashen. Suddenly, he became all too aware of the miller's bow and arrow hanging sinisterly from his host's back. Slung on his left shoulder rested a leather quiver full of hunting arrows.

"The lands of flat from whence you came,
Go back to them, and leave thy dame.
Perhaps return; a coffin box,
Take your small man, big man, and ox!"

In one rapid motion, the miller readied his bow and aimed an arrow directly at Flatlander's head.

"No Earnest, you mustn't!" pleaded Sonia.

As the miller drew the bowstring back and held the motion, Flatlander's mind raced. He readied himself to jump on the floor and shield himself under the kitchen table, when all of the sudden, they all heard a rather loud bang come from upstairs. The miller looked curiously to the ceiling planks. He then strode past the two without another word, past the kitchen and the brewing cider, and began ascending the staircase with heavy breaths. Flatlander let out an audible gasp, waved a rushed goodbye to Sonia, then fled outside into the rain, where he found Franklin readying the oxen and securing their goods.

"Franklin, we've got to get outta here. You wouldn't believe what just happened."

Franklin spread a tarp along the backside of one of the wagons. "Heard it all. Every last bit."

Flatlander shot his companion a look of incredulity. "You heard it all and you didn't *do* anything? What if he had shot me?"

Franklin continued fastening the tarp with rope and knots. "The miller's angry, but he ain't stupid. He ain't the killin' type, at least not yet. Just wanted to scare ya."

Flatlander shook his head, stupefied. His heart still pounded heavily and his hands shook uncontrollably. The rain had finally begun to let up, and in the distance, rolling thunder steadily faded from Lowell. Beyond the oxen, he saw a strange wooden formation of branches and tree limbs. He hadn't recalled the assembled sticks upon arrival.

"Building a tree fort?"

Sheepishly, Franklin glanced at his creation. "Somethin' like that."

"Where's Menche?" asked Flatlander.

On cue, a high-pierced scream emanated from the upstairs bedroom window of the mill.

"Menche!" called Franklin and Flatlander in unison.

Menche fixed himself up nicely in the guest bed, fresh from a wonderful bath. Not being use to such fine toiletries in his small bedroom space at Henry's, he had taken full advantage of Sonia's vast array of items. He lathered himself in rose petal chamomile soap, shampooed with honey and mint, and even used a slither of a special anti-wrinkling cream, made from blackberry extract and cucumber (according to the homemade label). After stumbling clumsily on the leg of a rocking chair, he crawled in bed in nothing more than his drawers. Posing suggestively towards the doorway, half of his body in the sheets, half out, with his head resting nimbly on his hands, he imagined Sonia coming through the door to bid him goodnight. She would kiss him lightly, and tell him that there would be a full breakfast with fruit, eggs and bacon waiting for him in the morning. *She'd do that, wouldn't she?*

He wondered what he would say to Sonia, how he would convey his true feelings for the Miller's wife. Sadly, Menche would never get the opportunity. Loud footsteps pounded up the staircase, which made Menche wonder why Sonia sounded so heavy in her walk. Nervously, he peered around the bed. A pair of muddied boots rested at the foot. A large wool shirt rested awkwardly on the top corner of a closet. A book entitled "How to save your marriage" lay half-read on a desk to his right. The realization came much too late for poor Menche, for this was not the guest bedroom as he had presumed. *This was the miller's bed.*

Before he had time to react, the bedroom door swung open with such force that it slammed into the back wall, sending a framed painting crashing to the floor. Menche's breath was caught in his throat. He wanted so badly to explain his predicament. Sonia had directed him to the wrong room to take his rest, he was sure of. It was all so easy to explain. Yet when Menche tried to articulate his predicament, the only sound that left his lips was a soft, high-pitched whimper. The miller walked to the foot of the bed, eyes twitching, gripping his bow with one hand, and he looked upon Menche as if he were vermin.

"I've never seen a sadder sight,
Than this munchkin-man here tonight,
A little gnome within my sheets,
I'm short of breath; can barely speak."

Menche found his voice. "I can explains, mister. Ya see, was a simple mistake. Honest."

"My shock will now slip into rage,
I'm sure you thought you were quite sage,
Now, I will drag you out of bed,
And twist your legs, and break your head."

The miller came around the side of the bed, his bow drawn. Menche shuffled frantically to the opposite side of the bed, ready to call out for Flatlander or Franklin.

"I see why the mill failed to spin,
I'm greeted now; a pool of sin,
To draw me out straight from my mill,
Your treach'ry's sealed; my bow to kill."

As the miller pointed his bow with arrow directly at him, Menche screamed, and faster than a doe downwind, retrieved his soaked clothes from the floor, bolted to the door, and fled down the stairs in nothing but his underwear. Rounding the bottom of the stairs and into the kitchen, an arrow narrowly missed his shoulder, and pierced the wall. Through the corner of his eye, he glimpsed Sonia crying at the kitchen table. While in mid-stride, Menche nodded in her direction.

"Milady," he gushed, then continued to the front door, past the hulking machines, which had only just recently resumed their automated pounds, creaks and hums. He burst out the door. "No! Backs! Backs! The miller's comin' and he ain't happy! Backs! Ready the ox, masters! We needs to leave!"

Scooping Menche up in his massive clutch, Franklin placed him roughly on his shoulder. They sprinted to the caravan of oxen, which had now been quite worked up amid the commotion. Flatlander jumped on the third carriage, as Franklin threw Menche to the floorboards of the middle carriage, before hopping onto the lead.

"All ready!" said Franklin over the dying rain.

And just as he commanded the lead ox, another arrow imbedded itself within his backrest. Franklin barely took notice and rode on with a fierce sense of determination. A whizzing sound then buzzed over Flatlander's ducked head, falling several meters in front of the caravan onto the Lowell ridge road. A third arrow pierced a rested jug to Menche's left, which leaked blackish ooze. Menche dabbed a finger on the leak and tasted the liquid.

"Blackberry jam, sirs. Not too bad."

"Forget about the jam! We're gonna die out here!" barked Franklin, as he snapped the reigns.

The caravan bore down the muddy ridge, the weight of sixteen oxen, thirty barrels of product, and three men complicating its maneuverability in the dead of the night. The road looped the ridge like a figure eight, and on a few occasions, it was difficult for the oxen to negotiate the hook-like turns. Twice, Flatlander was convinced that the oxen would lose their footing and hurdle the carriages over the steep embankments lining the majority of the ridge. He had a fleeting vision of the miller finding their broken carriage, broken bodies and all, as he hovered over them with drawn bow and murderous intent.

Thankfully, Franklin's eyes were well adjusted to the
shadows of the night. He had, after all, spent the bulk of the
night outdoors building his misshapen swan. Franklin guided
the caravan down the ridge, further and further along, until
the mills were no longer visible above the tree line, and the
danger was no longer imminent. Benegas's rock was now empty.
The rain had all but subsided. It was some moments before the
three spoke again, as they all tried to get a bearing on the rapid
sequence of events.

"Wasn't all that bad a visit, I'd say," said Menche in a most
sincere tone.

Before Flatlander or Franklin could scold him, they looked
at one another, dumbfounded, then laughed heartily. The Lowell
Ridge faded fast in the distance. The windmills continued to plod
along at their regular pace. And deep in the shadows of the miller's
realm, Shay Bromage had bore witness to arguably one of the
wildest stories of his long, fabled career.

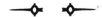

No more than five days after the party's return from Lowell,
Henry paced rigidly up and down the length of his office, with
a long, handwritten letter splayed out before him. Flatlander,
Menche, and Franklin sat in a prearranged line of chairs, shuffling
their legs nervously. Henry cleared his voice and read the letter in
a very loud, frank manner, making sure that his party could hear
clearly his dissatisfaction:

"G'day to you, dear lord, you see,
I have a tale to tell to thee,
I hope you scorn that rotten crew,
They left me cuckold, ragged, blue."

Henry looked at each of the three with a noticeable pause, as Franklin and Flatlander exchanged a wry look. He cleared his throat for dramatic effect.

"Wait, it gets better."

"I caught the brute making a swan,
From fallen branches on my lawn,
I found his charm inside the spoke,
Silence ensued, not but a croak.

Flatlander was not too timid,
His actions left me stunned, livid,
Kissed my wife whilst my wind was out,
Five minutes more, was sure to mount."

Henry looked straight through Flatlander in utter disgust, as the words seemed too repulsive to even utter. He then scanned the bottom of the document.

As I thought it could get no worse,
The third one made me yell a curse,
My interest up the stairs, which led,
The gnome-man disrobed- in my bed."

"He's actually a very good rhymer," remarked Flatlander, impressed.

"Yes, very good," agreed Franklin.

"Unbelievable!" shouted Henry, as his face turned a deep red and contorted in anger. He threw the miller's letter to the floor, and looked with shame upon his three trusted party members. "Five days since you came back, and this is the first I hear of your misadventure? I assume you kept this from me on purpose! Do you have any idea how *bad* this makes us look? What were you three buffoons thinking? *A swan*, Franklin? That's just flat-out bizarre. As for kissing the man's wife, Flatlander- that is simply inexcusable. And *you*," said Henry, glaring directly at Menche, spitting the words like venom. "I have no idea what got into that little mind of yours, but generally speaking, it's not considered appropriate guest-like behavior to lay naked in the host's bed!"

"I thoughts it was the guest bed!" said Menche, desperately. "Plus, she was seducin' me, lord, I'm tellin' ya!"

"Me too!" exclaimed Franklin.

Flatlander nodded. "*She* kissed *me* Lord Henry, not the other way around."

Henry scoffed. "Oh, right. How foolish of me. Because I forgot that it makes perfect sense that a beautiful, successful, young woman would fall in love with a passing-by, strong-arming Flatlander, a pot-bellied garden gnome, and a giant brute of a man who has the social skills of an adolescent bear!"

Flatlander stammered. "Lord Henry...you're not...it's not so..."

"I'm not done, Flatlander!" Henry picked up a newspaper from his desk. "That's just the start of it. Shay Bromage must have had a front-row view of your antics too, boys, because it made front page of his paper today, just like his nasty takes on Irasburg and Oakledge!" hollered Henry, as he threw a copy of the newspaper on the table. Flatlander picked up the issue and focused on the front page.

Henry began reciting the article from memory. "A comedy of errors: the debacle witnessed at Lowell has few such incidents of comparable measure. A sheer abandonment of reason..."

Flatlander continued where Henry left off in a quiet voice, as he read the article with alarm.

"From the same parties who brought you the decapitated Fish, and caused a lovable farmer to be shot in the buttocks..."

Henry then picked up where Flatlander had left off: "comes Henry's fabulous trio; more apt to fit the bill of Vermont's premier comedy troupe, rather than a arbitrary branch of state-level authority," recited Henry with his eyes closed, and hands clasped firmly behind his back. The Humble King gazed outward through his office window at the gazebo in his backyard.

"That's a bit harsh, don't you think?" asked Flatlander.

"It's *embarrassing*, Flatlander! *Embarrassing!*" corrected Henry, as he turned around.

"But more importantly, I just want to know, for my own sake, is it all true?"

The three looked at one another awkwardly, waiting for the other to answer. After a few seconds of awkward silence, Menche giggled, prompting a sharp look of rebuke from Henry.

Henry sighed. "So. It *is* true. These events actually happened. Unreal. I cannot believe for the life of me how grown men such as yourselves can behave so boorishly."

"Sir, if you had seen her with your own eyes, you woulda been love-struck too!" pleaded

Franklin. "It's the devil's tea for a northern bear[36] like me!"

Henry shook his head adamantly. "Incorrect, Franklin! Unlike you barbarians, I know that it's improper to have eyes for another man's wife *while on a diplomatic mission!* And you, Flatlander, this may be acceptable behavior for a man of the Old Country, but around here, you'll learn quickly that this kind of thing doesn't fly with us Vermonters."

Flatlander bowed gravely. "I'm sorry."

"Not sorry enough, I think," muttered Henry, as he paused to think for a few seconds. "Maybe I've been too soft on you. Successfully complete a couple of quests, and the next thing I know, I'm dealing with the next Casanova of Castleton[37]!"

"Lord..." pleaded Flatlander.

---

[36] An expression in the Northeast Kingdom denoting a sense of powerlessness.

[37] A reference to a play about a womanizer from the town of Castleton.

"Don't 'lord' me!" said Henry.

Flatlander shrugged. "We did what you asked us to do. The goods were unloaded at market price. Every lord that I've spoken to has been impressed."

"Until they read Bromage's article out this morning, I'd imagine," quipped Henry.

"We may have found you a new trading partner."

"Are you really *that* dense, Flatlander, to believe that the miller would trade with us again in light of what just occurred?" mocked Henry. "And here I thought that I had brought you on board for your reason…"

"We got them goods, sir," reminded Menche, sheepishly. "Like ya said."

"Oh, that's right. You 'got them goods'. Pardon *me* then! And still, you manage to rustle half of the republic in the process! That's it. I've got quite the remedy for this recent inappropriate display of wife-lust!" said Henry, as he pointed a shaking finger at his bodyguard. "Franklin, you will be on your way to Lowell shortly to mend relations with the miller and his wife. Menche, I don't want you anywhere near that man, his mills or his wife. I fear for your safety. You'll assist me in the coming days in my travels to the Brattle. I have some business to tend. In the meantime, Ellen will handle my work here in Montpelier." Both Franklin and Menche lowered their heads and stared at their laps.

Henry then paused in front of Flatlander and looked him dead in the eye. "And *you*, dear Flatlander. You will embark on a quest soon enough that won't give you a chance to cuckold any wives. Oh yes, I will see to that personally. You have my word. Get your sleep tonight, boys- you'll need it. Now leave me be!"

Henry left the three cursing under his breath. As he shook his head, Henry noticed Jess had watched the whole exchange from the nearby dining area. Before he could call to her, however, his daughter bolted upstairs. It suddenly felt awfully hot in the house, thought Henry. Perhaps it was only fitting. The antics of Lowell had left him in a blind fury. Shaken, Henry wiped the sweat from his brow with a silk kerchief. The unspeakably strong sphere of Shay Bromage's influence was now upon them, and Henry was committed to do anything in his power to keep his house in order. *Anything.*

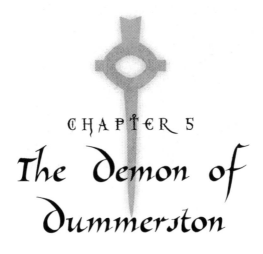

CHAPTER 5

The Demon of Dummerston

RONSON'S TAVERN: THOSE WERE THE only two words
uttered by Henry prior to Flatlander's departure for the
Brattle. He was given no other background information.
No context. No stories. No companions. No location. No words
of advice. No encouragement. Henry's party had curiously stayed
mum on the subject. Eventually, a young, fair headed boot-shiner
near the statehouse told him that Bronson's Tavern was a bar
in Burlington's Old North End section, but he had also warned
Flatlander to be wary, for 'it served mentionin' that the tavern was
of ill repute,' a den for the dregs and misfits of a dark rough and
tumble society.

He still couldn't believe what had transpired in Lowell. Henry,
whom he considered one of his few friends in this land, was now
livid over the incident, and who could blame him? They had acted
like fools, and in this case, Flatlander's amnesia served as no
excuse. Shay Bromage, Vermont's very own wolf in plaid, had
thoroughly dragged Flatlander's already fragile reputation across
needled ground. He was unsure if he could ever recover.

For now Flatlander was at a crossroad. A crossroad in which he dreaded, for while the road he now traveled was chaotic, at best, the other lay almost completely obscured within the shadows of his past. He wondered how much longer he could endure the strange trials and tribulations in Vermont. How long would it be before he would have to abandon his new friends and make for the Old Country, with or without assistance? The republic had so far been unkind to him. His thoughts shifted to his home; his family; now rendered to brief glimpses in a now-alien land.

With Henry's permission, Flatlander rode Pete from Montpelier to Burlington for his travels. The moose had mellowed some since Irasburg and his altered diet of pondweed, trembling aspen and willow trees had bulked the creature up in both muscle and fat. Though he had spent the bulk of his time in the barn, the Humble King allowed for the creature to wander his property after he had built a small enclosure with the assistance of Menche and several workers.

He found the bar just after sunset. Burlington's Old North End was met with far less foot traffic than that of downtown or the waterfront. The singing buskers were nowhere to be seen. Nor were there any street vendors, a near-permanent fixture along the cobblestone stretch of Church Street. The consistent hum and buzz of downtown faded at his back. Now, as he ventured along the corridor of Elmwood Street, a series of nearby yells and foul screams were all that welcomed Flatlander; for the darkened bowels of the Old North End had spoken its greeting.

He knew little of the Old North End, yet judging by its appearance, it seemed an area of stark contrasts. From the faint orange glow of the street lamps, he could see several homes in a state of disrepair. To his left, a large humanoid scurried through a hole in the wall. Several vagrant cats crossed his path at various junctures, while inspecting the newcomer with distrustful glances. Shadows spread deep, and on a few occasions, he saw what he presumed to be people scuttling away from the sidewalks as he approached, disappearing into the darkened cluster of neighborhood homes. As he closed in on Bronson's Tavern, a growing glow in the middle of the dark, he went through great lengths to avoid the shadow-lands entirely.

Located on a darkened corner of Elmwood and North Street stood the bar of mystic renown. During the everyday bustle

and hustle of Burlington life, it blended in seamlessly with the neighborhood. Yet at night, the tavern stood out dramatically, for Bronson's was seemingly one of the only sources of light and vitality in the Old North End. While the derelicts, thugs and thieves of the night roamed the city streets with reckless abandon seeking out their stakes, the patrons of Bronson's Tavern had come to this place, this oasis, to seek momentary reprieve. The patrons, in some ways, were not that much different than the very people whom they were trying to avoid, for they too had brothers, sisters, children, and friends who had succumbed to the call of the night. The key difference being that these men and women had settled on the temptation of drink, lore, and sanctity over the fruits of criminality; kindred spirits united.

Outside, the walls of Bronson's Tavern consisted of white, faded stucco. Vaulted, stained mahogany provided a contrasted trim, glossy from a recent round of varnish. The faint glow of several lanterns lit the immediate vicinity outside the tavern, but little beyond. Shadows danced with unpredictable nature in the flame's shape, which cast light upon the tombstones of Elmwood cemetery across the street, often blurring the line between shadow, man and creature. This phenomena proved even more of a challenge when patrons left Bronson's in the dead of the night, eyes heavy, as the steady stream of beer and liquor plagued their perception and inhibited their judgment.

Upon entering one would notice three circular, wooden tables ahead, the bar to the left, and a game of Colonies to the right. A popular local game in which players used heavy, carved elm branches to shoot polished small, stone balls into four holes in the corners of a table; the concept of colonies derived from its ancestor, billiards, but with a Vermont flavor. Its tabletop was made of polished marble from the Danby quarries[38]. Its frame was built of strong oak. The concept was simple: whoever got

---

[38] A successful quarry near Rutland, Vermont.

the most points at the end was the victor. There lay fifteen stone balls, and each stone ball represented a "colony," with its own unique color, marking, and point total. The green shooting ball represented Vermont. Accidentally sinking the black ball signaled an automatic loss. The "independence ball," painted with vibrant rainbow colors, was counted with the same amount of points as three regular balls.

Bronson's Tavern was anything but ordinary. Its namesake was borne from the tavern's sole proprietor, Bronson Bal Ryeah, a muscular, giant of a man, standing six and a half feet tall. Bewildered by the changing world in which he lived, and the degradation of the Old North End, Bronson sought out the paranormal. The hobby reminded him of when the only things that mattered in life were magic, monsters and ghosts. Bronson exuded the Old North End. He was rough around the edges and spoke in simple language, and yet there was often a depth and wisdom in his words. His patrons knew when to tease him and when to hold off. Few residents, even by the rough standards set forth by the blue collar Old North End, meddled in Bronson's affairs.

The tavern also boasted one of the most eclectic collections of artifacts and treasures in the entire republic. Shelves of amulets, skulls, goblets, weapons, gems, and other oddities and items adorned his walls. Several horns of the Highland Cattle[39] sat firmly in place behind the bar; the preferred drinking devices of only his most trusted patrons. In the corner of the tavern, a skeleton was mounted against the wall on a pole. His bony hand rose high above his head in what appeared to be a waving gesture of salutation, and a smoking pipe protruded awkwardly from his mouth, partially agape.

Bronson had a photographic memory of these items, and as a result, stealing was rarely an issue. Once a stranger had come in

---

[39] A popular drinking device used throughout parts of the republic.

and swiped an ancient photograph from Calais. The photograph was that of an elderly man who was said to have frozen himself annually in a feeding trough to survive the winters, only to be thawed out every spring with warm water and whiskey. The grainy black and white photograph depicted this fellow, Ethan Hungerford, in this vegetative state while lying in the trough. Bronson cherished this artifact, for photographs from the Old Country were extremely rare and a photo such as this one held immeasurable value. Bronson had caught up with the thief before he had made it two blocks. Two broken arms, a black eye, and a concussion later, the burglar learned a hard lesson, and word of this incident only further solidified Bronson's stature as a man whom one wouldn't want to cross.

Peering through the tavern windows, Flatlander hoped for the best. A dozen men and women were scattered around inside, exchanging stories and laughs over copiously poured drinks. He tethered Pete to a nearby tree and took a deep breath. Henry had warned of a darker quest ahead for Flatlander, and it was now easy for him to see what the Humble King had meant. Then a thought occurred to him and it was the only thing that propelled him to enter the tavern in the first place. It was the notion that he was now becoming a valuable asset to Henry and the republic, whether or not he was in Henry's proverbial dog cage, or the whipping boy of Shay Bromage, as a whole. *One step closer to finding home.* He then opened the door to Bronson's Tavern and ventured in.

On the rare occasion that both Shay and Dawn were free from work, they tended to take full advantage. Sometimes they traveled the republic on a day trip with Harrison. Other times, they would visit the local farmer's market of Burlington, purchasing a range of crafts, art, and produce. Because they were both journalists, they loved to keep close tabs on the pulse of the city, from the latest fashion trends of the women in the marketplace, to unearthing city gossip, to the opening of a new shop or boutique. There was almost never a shortage of material. Although many of Burlington's residents warily guarded their interests from the two, Shay and Dawn made efforts to convey to the people that their work and personal lives were two entirely separate entities. Yet that was only partially honest: for the couple used any and all opportunities to keep a watchful eye for potential stories afoot. On this particular Friday late morning, however, under the cool shade of a horse chestnut tree in their backyard, they sat at a wooden table sharing water, cheese and crackers.

"What a godsend to have a day off. No traveling, no assignments and no statehouse. I swear, sometimes I feel like this republic is being run by a bunch of barbarians," remarked Shay as he sipped on his water.

His wife, sporting a white dress with red polka dots, was dressed comfortably for the spring day. She placed a slice of sharp cheddar on an oversized cracker and smiled faintly.

"We've made our own beds, dear."

"Perhaps so," replied Shay with a sigh. "But I can't begin to tell you how crazy it drives me. Just yesterday, Lord Casper of Bristol all but confided to me that he hasn't read a single page from any of this year's passed laws. When I asked him why, he told me that he was a man 'of action, not words.' Is that code for being illiterate? It's scary to think about, really."

Dawn chuckled softly. "Some leaders are more apt than others."

"That they are, that they are," agreed Shay, as he twirled the ice cubes in his drink.

His attention drifted to a group of feeding warblers in the corner of his yard. They must have been trying to feast on surfacing worms, inundated from three days of rain. This was often the mood of Shay and Dawn's off-day afternoon talks: a strange combination of venting and relaxation. Though at times, it became something of a perilous balancing act. It was often Dawn who would call out Shay if his complaints reached a fever pitch. As Shay continued watching the birds, Dawn turned to her husband.

"You were a little harsh in your paper these past couple of weeks," she said, as she strummed her fingers through her crimson hair. "Wouldn't you say?"

"What do you mean?"

"You know what I mean. This whole Flatlander thing. Your article was cruel."

"*Cruel*?" yelped Shay. "I was taking it relatively easy on the bunch if you ask me."

Dawn raised an eyebrow. "You compared the Flatlander's intelligence to a toad's, while preemptively apologizing to all toads in Vermont."

Shay smiled devilishly. "Your point?"

"My point," Dawn said with hesitation, "is that I think you're being totally unfair, Shay. He may be a bit reckless, but he doesn't seem like a bad person. He's become a pawn in the republic's game."

Shay crinkled his nose, the mere notion of Flatlander being labeled a victim was absurd.

"*Unfair*, Dawn? *Unfair*? You want to know about *unfair*? That damned Flatlander coming in and destroying this republic. *That* has been unfair. His systematic meddling in affairs that aren't his own. *That* has been unfair. He can't take two steps down the street without tripping over himself. The problem is that he usually takes out two more people with him every time he falls."

"You're a journalist, Shay, not one of the Gods[40] themselves. You sound so judgmental."

---

[40] The term "Gods" is used more frequently that "God", as most of Vermont has shifted to a more polytheistic religion.

"It's my job, Dawn!"

"It's my job too, and I don't make a career of breaking people down."

"Well, dear" replied Shay, as he munched on a cracker, "that's where both you and I differ!"

Dawn sighed. It was no use arguing over Shay, and judging by his bulging eyes and reddened face, he was growing quite irate by the direction of the conversation. Still, Dawn needed to make one last point.

"Would it be unfair of me to suggest that perhaps, Shay, *perhaps*...this has more to do with what happened to Fish than anything else?"

Shay blinked rapidly. "I'm glad that you think so highly of me. Truly. My own wife. Are you suggesting that I'm shirking my journalistic obligations because of some Fish-borne vendetta?"

"I'm not suggesting it, Shay; I know it."

"Well, that's your opinion, dear. And it's been made clear to me that you've no shortage of those. But please, I beg you, don't bring up Fish's name again in vain. You know how much that animal meant to me."

"It was the right thing to do," continued Dawn, as she leaned over the table defiantly. "What Flatlander did. You and some of the others may never admit it, but it was the right thing to do."

"Dawn," replied Shay, condescendingly. "Perhaps when you reach a point in your career when you're covering real stories like me, you'll realize that you have to take some tough stances on subjects that don't always coincide with popular belief. As fond as I am of the spoon gallery and all..."

Shay had struck a tender nerve, and he knew it. He had meant to. Dawn's paper, The Burlington Daily News, had recently run a news story covering an art exhibit called "Spoons" from The Pine Street Art Gallery. From wall to wall, nothing but spoons had adorned the gallery, as its showcase theme. Big spoons.

Little spoons. Metal spoons. Wooden spoons. Ancient spoons. Paper spoons. It wasn't a very popular exhibit in the community, by anyone's standards, and even Shay had made a demeaning reference to the Burlington Daily's coverage in his most recent issue of the Shay Chronicles. He didn't have to wait long for a reaction.

Dawn sprang up from the table without another word. Stopping at the back door, she turned to Shay, the contempt heavy in her voice.

"You know what? You're a real piece of work, Shay. That ego of yours is out of control, and one of these days, you're going to pay for it. You think that you're better than everyone else, and you know what? I hope that Flatlander *does* prove you wrong, because you've really become something else with all of this success. It's gone straight to that big head of yours…

"Dawn…"

"But you know what? At the end of the day, you're just a pompous brat who takes pleasure in other people's pain more than anything. You're a glorified, narcissistic couch-warrior. You'd sell your own mother if it gave you good writing material."

"Good advice. I'll make a note of that in my next article," retorted Shay, as he dumped his remaining water to the lawn.

"To hell with your next article!" shouted Dawn as she slammed the back door so hard it bounced back and hit the side of the house.

The warblers feasting in the yard scattered. A plate sounded like it was literally thrown into the sink. Shay sat for some time outside, fidgeting with his hair, wondering how he could have approached the conversation differently. Leaning over, Shay grabbed the remaining cheddar and crackers that Dawn had left unattended, and began nibbling on them slowly. *I wonder if she would mind if I ate her cheese?*

"The lure please, Menche," asked Henry, one hand extended, as the other readied his fishing pole.

As the rowboat drifted across the smooth surface of the Pleasant Valley Reservoir[41], Menche fumbled through the tackle box frantically. Jess sat complacently on the bow, rolled her eyes and looked off towards the shoreline.

"The lure please," repeated Henry.

"Just saws it in the back. One sec, milord."

Henry grunted in frustration, as he placed the pole gently against his seat. "It's red, Menche. Red. Like a tomato."

"Red, milord?"

"Yes," replied Henry through clenched teeth.

Menche fumbled around a bit longer in the tackle box, then produced a small, oval red bar.

Henry glanced briefly at the item. "That's a pocket knife."

"Then what's it doing in yer tackle box, sir?"

"By all the cats in Winooski[42]!" cursed Henry. "For cutting lines with, Menche. Let me be more specific then: it's a small, red lure that's meant to resemble a baby Red-Breasted Sunfish, a favorite snack of Brook Trout and other various freshwater species. It should have a frill on it." Henry splayed out the backside of his hand for Menche to see. "It's about the size of my pinkie finger."

Menche scratched his head. "Uh oh."

Henry frowned. "What?"

"I thinks I may have thrown that one overboard. I thoughts it was a live fish by mistakes, sir."

"You thought that it was a *live fish*? It was made of rubber, Menche! Rubber!" said Henry in disbelief. Jess smiled from the bow, enjoying every minute of her dad's agony.

"Looked reals to me, milord."

[41] A small pond located in the Brattle.

[42] An expression conveying frustration. For the record, there is a disproportionate number of housecats in Winooski.

Henry buried his face into his palms then squinted at Menche. "It looked *real* to you? I come here to have a relaxing weekend with my beautiful daughter, here at the Brattle's finest reservoir. I ready my tackle box and rowboat just like I've done two dozen times in the past without incident, and all that I ask is that my lures are looked after and my tackle box organized to my liking. I put you in charge of that box for twenty minutes, and I'm already missing…"

"Dad, you're sounding like a real brat," interrupted Jess under her breath.

"*What*?" asked Henry. Menche's misdeeds had suddenly become an afterthought. "Did you just say what I thought you said?"

"I mean we're here to relax, so why don't you just relax. All you've been doing all day is yelling at people. It's getting really old, like you."

"I'm the elected leader of Vermont, Jess. Part of my job requires me to yell, no matter how harsh or unsightly. I think of it as critiquing."

"Is that what you call it nowadays?" replied Jess, as she turned from the two and looked towards the opposing shoreline of the reservoir by the dock which they had departed from.

Nearby, a small dam broke up the deeply wooded shoreline. She waited for her father's harsh response, but it never came. Henry, ashamed of his outburst, begrudgingly took the tackle box from Menche's hands, and resumed the search, this time for an alternative lure. He cast his reel and took a deep, thoughtful breath.

"My apologies to you both. I'll admit, I have been under much duress as of late, and have let it get the better of me. It's just a lure, Menche. Worry not. Jess, I will try to be more understanding from now on. Let's just enjoy one another's company."

And for a while, the three of them simply drifted on the darkened surface of the reservoir, exchanging infrequent bouts of small talk regarding fishing, home or Jess's past athletic accomplishments, while something bigger loomed just underneath the surface. While there were no more outbursts for the duration of the excursion, an air of tension remained, and hadn't fully subsided until the three were ashore and unpacking the contents of the boat. Desiring a private chat with Jess, Henry sent Menche to ready their cabin and gather firewood. As she sat at a picnic table, Jess fiddled with her hair, which had grown tangled without the luxury of bathroom amenities. Just the way that she had liked it.

"I was out of line, Jess. My apologies…"

"It's just you've just been acting like a jerk to everyone since I've been back."

"Sometimes I get very frustrated with Menche," replied Henry. "I feel like I'm watching a never-ending case in the Court of Fools."

"It's not just Menche, dad," argued Jess. She stopped fidgeting with her hair and scowled at him. "It's me, it's Franklin, and even that Flatlander guy. I heard the way you talked to them the other day. I heard you yelling. They didn't mean any harm, dad. They did their best."

"I thought that you hated Flatlander for what he did."

"You mean what you put him up to do?" rebuked Jess.

Henry rolled his eyes. "Jess, it's more complicated than that…"

"No, dad. No. Actually it *isn't*. All I'm saying is you should start treating people with more respect, and you'll start getting some in return. You know what? You're right. It *is* beautiful down here, but this whole trip isn't worth anything if you don't start chilling out!"

"Chilling out? I don't even know what that term means…"

"Bye dad. I need to take a nap. Wake me up at supper."

She stormed off towards the cabin where Menche had now gathered an armful of kindling. Henry stood there for some time after Jess had left, at a complete loss for words. He threw his fishing pole into the dirt in sheer frustration, kicked an empty metal bucket, and sat at the picnic table, eyes cast downward. *It seems like I can never get things right.* Yet as he lightly kicked at the dirt repeatedly, he began noticing a red object jutting out. Brushing off the remaining grime gently with the tip of his boot, Henry swallowed. There it was, clear as day. The lure, the Red-Breasted Sunfish lure.

"...And the next thing I know, the big guy was layin' belly up on the counter like he was at his own wake!" said Bronson, wet rag in hand, as he gestured to the bar surface.

"Ya gotta be kiddin' me, Bronson," exclaimed a short elderly man with an eye patch.

Roars of laughter filled Bronson's Tavern just as Flatlander strode inside. And while several patrons continued to howl with glee, at least two men took special notice of the newcomer. He pretended not to notice their suspicious glances, and moved to a table by the far end of the bar. From his vantage point, he saw that the bartender, presumably Bronson, was simply a mountain of a man. Bulky and bearded, his hair was long and black, and his beard forked out into two finely manicured points. He wore a black, sleeveless tunic, studded with old copper buttons. On his left arm, a detailed tattoo of an unrecognizable map lined his forearms and bicep, and on the other arm, the picture of a red-curtained shrine was inked into his triceps and elbow. He adorned a broad range jewelry: a bright blue ring on one hand, a silver bracelet on the other, and a rustic-looking nose ring, looking more fit for a bull, pierced his left nostril. A necklace of bones graced his neck.

"What did the old woman say when she found 'em?" asked a heavyset man with a bushy, white beard, enraptured with the Bronson's tale of tomfoolery.

Bronson shrugged. "Dunno. But no kiddin', I saw the man pourin' each and every liquor bottle he had on the curb the next day."

This news was met with a round of chuckles from his patrons.

Bronson continued: "It happened, I'm tellin' ya. But I'd bet half the grain in Fletcher[43] he came back out to lick it off the street the second she left."

The men broke out again in laughter. Flatlander couldn't help but smile. It had been some time since he had been around joyful people. It was refreshing, he thought, to be in the company of happy people. But as the laughter died down, a few of the men talked lowly amongst one another, and turned to Flatlander with noticeable scowls.

Bronson picked up on their cue, as he nodded to Flatlander seated at a table. "Ah, and who's this stranger that wanders from these troubled streets?"

As he approached the seated Flatlander, each footstep rattled some nearby glasses.

Flatlander thought fast. "Name's Remy."

The bartender grunted. "New to town I take it?"

Flatlander shuffled in his seat. The others watched him, and he saw the true grittiness of these men. Two wore black fur coats, and the heavyset fellow, a ragged white tunic. All three looked rough in the eyes. The two in black appeared to be carrying swords under their coats, as a wayward glimmer would shine briefly in the tavern's torchlight. None wore a friendly expression. Regrettably, he had left his sword unattended with Pete.

"You could say that."

Flatlander grimaced. He knew right away that it probably wasn't the best response, but he didn't have the wits about him to fabricate a story while in this particular company.

---

[43] A Vermont town known for its production of grain.

"The boy's as green as a salad. Look what he's wearin'," replied the man in the white tunic, as he pointed in Flatlander's direction. Flatlander looked down. The blue button down shirt stuck out like a sore thumb. He wanted nothing more at that moment than to change shirts immediately.

"Wait a sec, bud," said one of the men in black, as he rubbed his eyes in disbelief, "either yer pourin strong tonight, or that's that damned Flatlander that's been all over them papers!"

"Let the boy speak, fellas," said Bronson. "You can speak, can't ya?"

Flatlander swallowed. "I can."

"Well, that's a start," replied the bartender. He stood right in front of Flatlander, looking over him, large as a bear. Flatlander twitched nervously, but the man extended his hand. "Name's Bronson. Welcome to my tavern."

As Flatlander shook his hand, he was awestruck by the sheer size and strength of the man's fingers. They covered his grip entirely and much of his wrist, as if he were a little child.

"Thanks."

"Whatcha havin'?" asked Bronson, as he waved an arms at an assortment of bottles on the bottom shelf. "Got lots a' whiskey, mead from the Brattle, Northmind Lager, Newport Vanilla Stout, a spicy white ale from the islands called 'Spinnaker', two barrels fresh from Bristol of somethin' hoppy…"

"Get the man what he deserves, Bronson- a Flatlander drink!" hollered the taller patron in black, with long, straight black hair down to his shoulders. The others chuckled.

"What's a "Flatlander drink"?" asked Flatlander softly.

"Right over there," replied Bronson with a sigh, pointing to a small wooden bucket on the floor.

Gnats buzzed in and out from its opening, and a sickly white crust had formed on the bucket's perimeter. The walls of the bucket were covered in a brownish-yellow film, and it was to Flatlander's mild surprise that there was, in fact, skunked, stagnant beer inside of it. Above this foul creation, a crooked sign read "flatland'r drink" in sloppy, bold handwriting.

"No, thanks," mumbled Flatlander. "I'll have a water."

"Suit yourself."

A couple of the men chuckled, and even a couple other patrons from the back of the bar joined the group to watch the spectacle. Bronson smiled and filled him large glass full of water. He slid it across the bar into Flatlander's outstretched hand, as it spilt slightly on his hands.

Heartily, the man in the white tunic pulled in his chair snug with the bar. "Got some flatlander jokes for ya." Those around him perked up. The man cleared his throat. "How is a flatlander and a bad lasagna alike?"

"I don't know Marshall, how?" asked Bronson.

"Neither's got proper layers[44]." The men, including the newcomers, laughed heartily. Flatlander smiled. He needed to show the men that he could play along with this game. He needed to show them that he wouldn't be affected by their barroom banter.

Wide-eyed, the shorter of the two men in black sat up straight in his seat. "A flatlander, a baby, and a horse walk into a bar. Bartender throws each a beer. Don't know why. As can be expected, the patrons look at the bartender with a mixture of shock and amazement. 'No way in hell you're servin' that baby!' yells a man from the other side of the bar. Bartender looks at the man and says, 'You know what, you're right. I ain't in the mood for his cryin' today one bit!' He then promptly takes the beer from the flatlander[45]."

---

[44] Previous records indicate that Flatlanders, as a whole, had a tougher time dealing with and preparing for Vermont winters.

[45] Many Flatlanders also had a reputation for being less tough and hardy than their native counterparts.

Bronson made a real effort to maintain his composure, but even he succumbed to the chuckle train that had now become Bronson's Tavern. The jokes didn't seem to have any ending in sight. A wiry fellow who had joined them late, who had been wearing brown tattered rags, decided to get into the action. His speech came out lisped and strange.

"A child oncthe athed me how to tell when it'th officially winter. I told em it'th during firth froth, firth thnowfall, or when the firth flatlander whineth."

The men laughed heartily. *It's as if I'm not even here*, thought Flatlander. The idea of what it meant to be a Flatlander, the very concept of a Flatlander to these people, was completely ludicrous, and not to be taken seriously. *Great, so I guess my people didn't like the winters here.* He thought back to an earlier conversation with Henry and his party during brunch, and Menche's question regarding his groaning. It was now being made official to him. Flatlanders, when they were still allowed in the republic, had developed reputations as whiners.

Then Bronson threw his washcloth over a shoulder and joined in. "Okay, okay. Here's one, and then we're done. Poor Flatlander. Have some mercy." He thought for a second. "How are a tadpole and a flatlander opposite?" He paused. "A tadpole grows a tail, loses it and eventually learns to walk on its own, as a frog. A flatlander never had a tail to begin with and slimes up any pond he encounters[46]."

This one had the men laughing so hard they were red in the face and in a state of near delirium. It was close to a half minute before the laughter died down; but to Flatlander, the moment felt unpleasantly long. Then, one by one, all of the gathered men looked for an expression on Flatlander's face, gathering their composure for just one reaction from the stranger. He was at a

---

[46] This was a joke originally told by Bronson's friend, Eli Donlon, ten years prior. It relates to the **flatlanders**' corrupting influence.

complete loss for words, and he looked at the men bewildered. As such, the men proceeded to laugh even louder.

When it was all over, the group looked like they had been drugged or beaten. Their faces were flush. Their hair was disheveled. Below their stools and chairs, large quantities of beer had been spilt all over the floor.

The man in the white tunic, Marshall, had laughed so hard, he now dabbed at his eyes with a light blue handkerchief.

"Alright, alright boys. Enough. Give the poor man a break."

Flatlander nodded in courtesy and took his water outside to the back deck without uttering another word. He could hear the men laugh more, but the chatter was immediately cut off as the back door slammed behind him. The deck was approximately the size of a bar itself and contained three large round tables. Bordering the outside was a series of large, black gothic statues towering high above him. Among others, he could discern what appeared to be a gargoyle, a bear, and a foul multi-mouthed blob of a monster. Flatlander took a gulp of his water. The door behind him swung open as Bronson strode outside.

"You'll have to excuse our manners, fella. It just ain't too often we see a folk of yer likes 'round these parts," said Bronson, as he patted Flatlander on the shoulder blade. Though meant to be a friendly, reassuring pat, he thought that he had separated a shoulder.

"I'm use to it. No worries," replied Flatlander, as he swallowed away the pain.

"Hate to pry, but I'm dyin' to know, fella: but what brings you these ways? People don't typically wander into the Old North End unless they're intent on stayin'."

Flatlander breathed in deeply. He would have to tell him. There wouldn't be a more opportune time.

"I was sent here."

Bronson's expression darkened. From Bronson's belt, a dagger was put up near Flatlander's face in the blink of an eye.

"Ya got three seconds to tell me who sent ya!"

"No, no. Please. Nothing like that."

"Who sent ya?!" demanded Bronson. He pointed the dagger threateningly at Flatlander's face.

"Henry, Henry. It was King Henry," replied Flatlander frantically. Reluctantly, Bronson lowered his dagger into an unseen sheath at his hip. Flatlander gasped once more. "It was King Henry."

Then, distantly, as if entrenched in memory, Bronson uttered. *"You'll know when the favor is asked of you."*

His eyes were vacant; he certainly wasn't directing the words at Flatlander.

Confused, Flatlander shuffled nearer the bar. "I can go now if you'd like…"

Bronson scanned Flatlander from head to toe. "What's yer real name?"

"Flatlander."

Bronson chuckled, as recognition dawned in his eyes. "Aha, so *yer* the one they've been rippin' up the news? Without good pictures of ya in the paper, it's hard to tell. Quite the entrance to the republic, if I may say. I think I know why the big man sent ya here." Bronson paused, and glanced back inside of his tavern at the collection of patrons chugging the remaining contents of their drinks. "Stay out here for a bit if ya don't want any more grief. And I can't blame ya if that's yer choice. After I close up and kick these hooligans out, you and I need to talk fer a bit."

Bronson's affable nature was now gone, the humor had left his cheeks swiftly. He spit into a nearby ashtray, and gave Flatlander one last dreadful look before re-entering the bar. He just about had to duck to avoid bumping his head on the doorway. *What a bizarre man,* thought Flatlander. *I'll stay on his good side at all costs.* He gulped down his lukewarm water under the shadow of a stone-carved gargoyle.

It was with certain regret that Franklin agreed to travel back to Lowell to mend relations with the Miller. He simply couldn't refuse Henry in good conscience. He confided to Henry his concerns in private, and in particular, the fact that the Miller had recognized him from his younger days. After all, Henry was one of the few people in Burlington with direct knowledge of Franklin's prior issues in the Northeast Kingdom and his subsequent ouster.

Yet it was also Henry who had once saved his life.

And despite his protests, the Humble King decided that it would be good to "bury the hatchet" with the Miller once and for all. Franklin cringed at the unfortunate usage of the idiom, but ultimately, agreed to leave for Lowell the following morning. Shortly after a brief and awkward greeting with the Miller and Sonia, he offered to down a sickly maple just a stone's throw from the main mill. He brusquely axed away at the rotten, old tree between visions of a dreadful night.

Hours later, he found himself sitting at the dinner table with the Miller and Sonia without appetite and slumped over a plate of crushed cauliflower, green beans, and a sizeable steak. The Miller glared at him for the entirety meal, while barely touching his food. Involuntarily tapping his foot against the floor, the Miller's foot fell into a synchronized rhythm with the mill's creaking gears.

Sonia attempted to break the tension with small talk. "That was so nice of you to split and stack that wood, Franklin. Ernest could always use more firewood before winter. Isn't that right, dear?"

The Miller nodded slowly, keeping his eyes trained solely on Franklin's every move.

"Thanks, milady," he uttered in a low voice, as he averted the miller's eyes.

There was little in life that scared Franklin. Large as a bear and hard as an ox, he bore the scars to prove his mettle. He had beaten several men in a bar simultaneously. He had killed dozens of deer in his time; some with bow, some with spear, and some with nothing more than his bare hands. He had even spent an infamous three days caved up on top of Mt. Mansfield with a black bear during a harsh winter blizzard. And yet, there was something about the way the Miller looked at him that gave the northerner chills up and down his spine.

"You know," said Sonia, as if completely oblivious to the suffocating atmosphere. "I'm not sure how Ernest would feel about the whole thing, but it would be nice having some help around here for the week. We have been unseasonably busy these past few days with all of the press."

The very moment Sonia finished her sentence; the Miller stabbed his large steak knife into the tabletop with enough force to spill his own cup. The sharpened knife pierced the wood a solid inch before he retracted it.

"Oh dear," remarked Sonia, as she scrambled to clean the mess.

But the Miller gestured for her to stay seated, as he kept his glare locked solely onto Franklin. Unable to handle it any longer, Franklin decided that it was time to try to mend things.

"I feel like I owe ya both an apology, 'specially you, sir," said Franklin, as he shifted his plate to the side with his fingers, barely touched. "It ain't the Vermont way, what we did, and I knows it. Can't explain what happened that night. The partners and me were totally outta line. The little one, he's a little slow. As fer the Flatlander…"

At the mere mention of the name, the Millers eyes blurred with a deranged hatred.

Franklin continued hesitantly: "Like I was sayin'….as fer the… Flatlander, he doesn't know the land here or the people, he feels awful fer his behavior. He told me to tell ya both he's sorry before he left."

"I'm sure," answered Sonia. "It was just as much my fault as his. Franklin, we accept your apology." She paused and looked at her husband with renewed hope. "Don't we, dear?" Yet the Miller met Sonia's question in complete silence.

"*Don't we dear?*" she repeated.

The Miller finished chewing on a strip of his steak, he gently dabbed his lips with a napkin, and cleared his throat.

"Though mind and heart still burn with rage,
I soon would like to turn the page.
For Flatlander, I must reserve,
My goodwill; he should yet be served."

Good enough, I suppose. Franklin breathed a small sigh of relief, as he resumed eating the barely-touched morsels of baked cauliflower. At least, for the time being, the Miller's resentment of Flatlander trumped Franklin's own past transgressions. If he agreed to stay per Sonia's request, this would surely be one of the more uncomfortable experiences of his life. At least during that infamous blizzard and the bear, the danger was obvious and out in the open. This was entirely different. And despite the Miller's acceptance of Franklin's apology, there was still something very dark and disturbing about his look. Franklin knew one of the major sources of the Miller's angst, and he would have to address it before he departed. *I just don't know what exactly I'm gonna say. Not yet.* He never got the chance, though. Minutes later, the Miller sent him back home to Montpelier.

It felt like a very long half hour sitting out on the deck, and Flatlander had spent the better part of the time studying the finer details of the statues while bracing himself for the conversation with Bronson. There were six statues total, each with its own personality, each frightening. The one that captivated him the most, however, was the disfigured form of a creature with horse-like haunches, squid like tentacles, and the face of an ape. He wondered to himself what kind of wild imagination would conjure up such a creature. The statues were each carved in black marble with exquisite detail, and to entertain himself, Flatlander could imagine an inebriated patron, on occasion, mistaking them as real creatures. Interrupting his thoughts were shouts and commands from Bronson to his patrons to leave the tavern at once. Despite some of the men's complaints that it was 'too early', and even Marshall proclaiming that he wanted to see the Flatlander again, they obliged. Reluctantly, they drained out of the tavern, wobbly but giddy.

"Ya know, ya could've at least motioned to me fer a drink," joked Bronson, as he stepped outside. "What have ya been up to this whole time?"

Despite the inquiry, Flatlander continued gawking at the creations. "These statues, they're incredible. May I ask who made these?"

"They strike yer fancy I take it? Best stonemason in town. He had some time on his hands at the time, as did I when I planned the whole thing."

Flatlander nodded silently. He glanced at Bronson, who was now admiring the statues himself, chest beaming. His face looked drained. Sweat stains had spread to the entire sides of his tunic, and he seemed to savor the fresh air of the outside, as he breathed in deep gulps. The bartender then nodded to Flatlander.

"Come now. We need to talk and my eyes are growin' heavy as we speak."

Bronson opened the door and motioned for Flatlander to take a seat at one of the few tables in close proximity. Scrubbing the surface clean with a warm, wet rag, Bronson threw it, carelessly, on a nearby stool. He then poured both himself and Flatlander a glass of water for good measure.

"How *is* the big man?"

"The big man?"

Bronson smirked. "I take it ya don't use that title 'round Lord Henry like me."

Flatlander nodded in acknowledgement. "Oh, I gotcha. He's good. A little grouchy recently, I'd say, but otherwise good."

"We all have our days, don't we?" replied Bronson, as he took a sip of his water.

"That we do," affirmed Flatlander, as he did the same. The water was lukewarm, and flavored with a touch of mint.

Bronson unleashed a deep belch, and looked curiously at his guest. "Now that it's just me and you, what brings ya here anyways? The Old Country is far from here and has brought us nothin' but trouble in the past."

Flatlander hesitated. "So I've been told," he said dryly, recalling the old man, Barry, spitting near his shoes in Montpelier. "Truth is, I don't remember. I woke up in Vermont with amnesia. Sometimes, when I lose myself in my mind, or deep thought, or when I sleep, bits and pieces come back to me. Henry was kind enough to let me stay, even though he and his party weren't thrilled about the prospect…"

"Can't blame the man, or his party," interrupted Bronson, nonchalant. "Harborin' a Flatlander would be unwise for even the commonest of commoners, let alone the ruler of the republic. There is much resentment in our land, Flatlander. You must understand."

"After tonight, I'm getting a clearer picture," he quipped. Then, a thought brought him back to a comment made by Ellen at breakfast the day he was found. "What happened with the last Flatlander anyways?"

Bronson raised an eyebrow. "The *last Flatlander*?"

"Henry made reference to this person," continued Flatlander. "He admitted that another remains nearby."

Bronson paused before finally nodding in understanding. "I'll leave that to the big man to tell ya. Not my place, sonny."

"Understandable, I guess," sighed Flatlander in disappointment. "Anyways, the short of it is this: I need to complete ten quests for Henry in order to stay in Vermont. If and when I do, I can either stay here or be escorted home. You probably saw me in the news..."

"Don't read or listen much, and don't care for mindless republic gossip," interrupted Bronson. Momentarily relieved that Bronson had never heard of him, the bartender continued. "But *you*, my friend, are all the talk of the town thanks to that good ol' Shay Bromage."

"Wonderful," replied Flatlander with a grimace. "He *does* have an affinity for me."

"Or the trouble ya cause," added Bronson with a wink.

Flatlander nodded. "Regardless, I was told to come here for my next quest, yet I wasn't told anything, really, other than the name of your tavern. Nothing."

Bronson sat silently, mulling things over. He lit up an old, red and yellow ringed corn pipe, stuffed to the brim with tobacco, and took a long, hard drag. The smoke twirled and danced around his eyes, obscuring the intensity of his gaze. The tobacco smelled minty.

"Excuse me for the smoke, Flatlander. I only tend to use it before bed." The bartender coughed then hocked phlegm into the nauseating bucket of Flatland'r drink. "I got a feeling I know what he wants."

"You do?"

"The big man took a real likin' to one of my ghost stories not too long back."

Flatlander raised an eyebrow. "A ghost?"

Bronson sighed. "Ay. It goes like this. Once, not too long ago, I was as dumb as a doorknob, and as hardheaded as a boar, I was. A few screws loose from a fallen bridge, Flatlander. The thing ya gotta know around these parts is if old man winter doesn't drive ya nuts, surely the vagrants and hedonists will.

"Ya see, when I first started workin' this bar, I did as much drinkin' as I did pourin'. There's a reason that people come to the bar, ya know, for release, to blow off steam. But in *my* case, it's tough tryin' to unwind in the same place that yer tryin' to escape from in yer off-time!" Bronson tapped some ash into an empty beer bottle. "Ya know how they say that there's 'glass half full' people and 'glass half empty people'? Well, I was a 'glass-shattered-on-the-floor-and-covered-in-day-old-ale' type of person. But it was hard to avoid the draw of this tavern. It was hard not to be just like yer patrons after so many months and years of bein' around them.

"Of course, winter brings with it not only the folks who are regulars, but some who look as pale as the first snowfall, I tell ya. But this one fella in particular was a bit different. It had to be three winters ago. This fella slipped in with the crowd long just an hour before closin'." Bronson paused, before looking him straight in the eye. "Flatlander, would you believe me if I told ya I saw a demon?"

Perplexed, Flatlander squirmed in his seat. "A demon?"

"Aye."

Bronson exhaled a thick cloud of smoke, nodding slowly. "He hung around later than the other folk. He was quiet that night, real quiet. Wore a hood so you couldn't make out any features from his face. Last call came and went, and this man just sat in his chair, lookin' straight down at the bar. I closed up his tab, but still, he just sat there. He didn't even flinch when I handed him his tab fer thirty dollars or sufficient barter. But then I saw his bad stare, looked at me like I was see-through.

"Get movin', I told em, 'or I'm gonna have to launch ya out the door.' He took the bill and wrote somethin' on it, but the bill burst into flames. I swear it. *Flames*. Thought he was trickin' me with a candle. But he had no candle and he wasn't laughin' neither. Handwrote him another copy of his bill and this time he turned the paper into dust. Now, I know what yer probably thinkin' 'oh Bronson, he's surely lost his marbles.' But it happened. I swear it by my stars. I know I have a ways of attractin' the weird out of things like ya wouldn't believe, but this was different.

"Now if yer gonna be wastin' my paper, I says, I'll be havin' none of it, mister.' The thing just smiled. So I said 'that's it, ya made me do it.' So I come around the bar to grab em and drag em out, just like I've done a thousand times to men twice his size nonetheless. Now, I'm a large man, Flatlander, case ya haven't noticed. He, on the other hand, musta been five foot eight, maybe 160 pounds. But he didn't budge. Not one inch. I grabbed him. Shoved him. Pulled him. Yanked him. It was like trying to move a buildin', I'm tellin' ya. Now keep in mind this whole time he had his hood pulled low since he burned those receipts. Couldn't really get a good look at the fella's face. 'What in the Gods names' I muttered, 'you need to leave, bud.'"

Bronson pulled hard on his pipe, as its tip glowed a fiery red. "I'll never forget it. The figure slowly looked up at me and pulled down his hood. Its face was animal like, like somethin' I've never seen before. Completely black. Glowing, red eyes. Face was like a blend between dog and pig. I've seen plenty in my line of work in and out the tavern, but I never saw me a face like that before, and I can't imagine anythin' looking so close to a demon without bein' a demon. Then the only words he said to me were 'Dummerston calls,' and he just disappeared out of thin air."

Goosebumps formed up and down Flatlander's arms. Bronson took a hearty gulp of his beer, and shook his head, disturbed, at the memory. *Dummerston*. The name provided no recollection.

"What's Dummerston?"

Bronson nodded and put his smoking pipe on the table. "Aye, it's a town far down in Southern Vermont just outside of the Brattle. Close to the wall."

He recognized the name. *The Brattle.* "That's where Henry's from and he's supposedly there right now."

"Ha! Forgot about that, figurin' that the man spends more time up north then ever. I heard that some in the Brattle joke that last many of them had seen em, he was unable to grow a beard," replied Bronson with a chuckle. "But anyways, this entity's been called the Demon of Dummerston ever since. And there's been a few more sightings from what I hear; both up here in Burlington, and down in Dummerston, but nowheres else."

"The Demon of Dummerston," repeated Flatlander.

The idea of a demon was unsettling. And as he glanced at the assortment of artifacts, gemstones, weapons, and bones gracing Bronson's walls, Flatlander recognized that Bronson was literally surrounded in lore and the paranormal. The notion of there being a demon was in and of itself, farfetched; but, somehow, in this place of sorcery and magic, the idea became more conceivable by the second.

"Aye. I owe the King a favor. Ya see, he was kind of enough to pardon me of some pretty nasty things. Threw a man out the window for breakin' the colony sticks. Got ugly. Coulda spent a year in jail if it weren't fer the big man. As we got to talkin', turns out he took a real interest in my story 'bout the demon. When I asked, he told me fer a friend. I didn't push. Savin' me from jail was a good enough explanation fer me, I told em. I even offered him money for his kindness."

"He took your money?" Flatlander asked, astonished. He was having a difficult time envisioning Henry as the type who would accept a bribe or kickback.

"Nah. He wouldn't have done that, I don't think. He told me that he'd collect in a different way when the time was right," said

Bronson, as he twirled a glass of water in his hand. "I've gotta assume that this is the time."

Bronson neared closer, and spoke in a soft voice. The shadows under his eyes seemed to expand under the waning candlelight.

"We're leavin' for Dummerston on the 'morrow. Got a cot upstairs you can crash on, and if I were you, I'd find a way to bring that moose of yers in to stay too. Even a creature that size could be in trouble round these parts if it's left outside all night unattended."

Flatlander was surprised that Bronson had noticed Pete on the darkened street corner.

"You saw him?"

"A bartender sees more than you'd think."

"Wow," replied Flatlander, impressed. "And just like *that*?" he said with a snap of the fingers. "It's decided that we're going to Dummerston together? Don't you have the tavern to watch over?"

Bronson nodded. "Don't meddle with my concerns, sonny. I've got one who can work the tavern and you've no other jobs as far as I know," said Bronson. "And like I said, I owe Lord Henry. Big time. I never go back on promises."

"I suppose I have no choice," muttered Flatlander to himself, dejectedly.

Bronson gave him an encouraging smile. "I'll fix us a nice breakfast."

Bronson then began dimming and shutting off the assorted lanterns and candles scattered throughout the tavern. Before he dabbed out his last lantern with moistened fingers, a loud crash, followed by a woman's scream could be heard from down the street. Flatlander jumped, rigid and alert; yet Bronson didn't so much as flinch. Amused by Flatlander's reaction, Bronson allowed himself a smile and nodded to the unlit streets.

"Welcome to the Old North End, Flatlander. The creatures of the night flock within the shadows. Bring in the moose as soon as you can, and remember that yer safe here. No matter what you see and hear outside these walls."

While refreshing to hear such a reassurance from Bronson, Flatlander had already come to dread his sleeping arrangements, especially before a long journey to Dummerston. And that night, as he lay on his cot upstairs, nestled in an old, lamb wool blanket; eyes opened wide, Flatlander attempted sleep. Amid the near and distant crashes and screams of the night, he shifted restlessly in a constant state of trepidation. *This is my punishment for Lowell. You have received your vengeance, Henry! I never want to visit another mill again, I swear. I won't even look at another mill if given the chance.*

The wall stretched the forest floor as far as Jess could see. Consisting of large slabs of granite, schist, gneiss, basalt, and fieldstone, it rose to fifteen feet high, and nearly half again as wide. Moss covered nearly half its surface near the base, while nests, spider webs, and animal dens filled many of its nooks and crannies. Certain sections were crooked or lopsided. Yet it stood nonetheless, just as it had the past forty-five years since the last stone was laid down in Sandgate[47].

Henry and Jess had day-hiked the banks of the Connecticut River southward, past the market of the Brattle and the acropolis, while Menche fished the Pleasant Valley reservoir. They hiked and talked until they reached the base of the wall, whose side came an arm's length from the banks of the Connecticut.

"These stones at the first mile were taken from right here at the river," remarked Henry, as he rested his palm against its smooth, black stone. "The rest, mostly from our quarries in Dorset

---

[47] The last stone before the wall's completion took place in the town of Sandgate in the year 2065.

and Danby. I never took you here before, have I?" Henry asked with a pause. Her silence spoke volumes.

"I didn't think so. Do you know why this wall was built, Jess?"

Jess scoffed. "To bore daughters to death with its story."

Henry chuckled. "One would think, dear Jess. One would think. But, no. They built these walls long ago to protect us from Flatlanders. It stretches from where we now stand, up the eastern border with New Hampshire, across our southern border, and hugs the southwest to western border all the way to Addison County where Lake Champlain begins to open up. The northern border to the Quebecois as well."

"Oh, that's so interesting," mocked Jess, her tone dripping with indignation.

"You sound bored," observed the Humble King.

"No, I'd *much* rather be doing *this* than hanging out with my friends at home. Donna Jean was going to come by."

"Jess," replied Henry, as he collected his thoughts. "One of these days, maybe not today, or even tomorrow, or even the week or month from now, you're going to realize that there is more to life than just hanging out with friends. Even if it's Donna Jean. There is a history here in which you should be aware of. Sure, to you, this looks like a rickety, old wall," he said, as he peered into a crevasse, exposing an enormous spider web covered in dew, "but your way of life would be drastically different had it not been here all of your life. My life too."

Jess picked up a fallen branch, and restlessly threw it aside. "Okay dad, what do you want me to say? Whatever. It's an *amazing* wall."

"Have you studied the wall in school?" asked Henry.

"Not really. Other than the fact that it's just around. Like, nobody even talks about it."

"A shame, a real shame," mumbled Henry as he shook his head.

"Great," sighed Jess, as she rolled her eyes, "here comes another lecture."

Henry dipped a hand into the shallow current of the Connecticut. The water was frigid, instantly numbing his fingers.

"The wall stands, and yet we share the same water as the Old Country. The wall stands, and yet we breathe the same air as those in the Old Country. See, we are still connected. This wall was *put* here, Jess. Put here for a purpose. I'm not naïve enough to believe that this wall, and this wall alone, is foolproof in keeping out the undesirables, although it seems to have done an admirable job for the time being. What I *do* believe, however, is that there will come a time when we have to decide, as a people, to tear it down. I'm just not sure how I'm going to convince the people of the republic…if and when that time ever comes."

Henry looked wistfully down the southward bend of the river, scratching his head, momentarily entranced in a vision. Nearby, a group of playful squirrels rattled up the trunk of an old pine. Jess readied herself for another rude remark, but thought better of it. She had already made it abundantly clear that she didn't really care about his history lessons. *Didn't he get the message by now?* She hesitated then broke the silence more tactfully.

"Dad, I'm getting cold. Can we start heading back?"

Suddenly breaking himself from his trance, Henry smiled. "What was that? Oh, why, yes. Yes, of course, Jess. Another time, another time."

As the two resumed their trek back north, Jess noticed her father turning back on occasion, just to take one last, fleeting look at the wall, fading deep within the hardwood forest. Despite her best efforts to look completely uninterested, Jess's curiosity was piqued. The wall was devoted to keeping out flatlanders and outsiders? What could have warranted such a thing? Why hadn't she been taught any of this? The records of Vermont's history were kept mum to the young ones from the elders, monks, and teachers; yet the mere mentioning of 'flatlanders' often evoked curses from the seemingly gentlest of souls. And as her father talked passionately about the history of the Connecticut River and its importance to the republic, Jess found herself thinking of the moss-covered wall again. These thoughts lasted for the entirety of their walk back to the Pleasant Valley Reservoir.

The road to Dummerston was longer than Flatlander had anticipated, but it gave him ample time to soak in the rich mountains and countryside of Vermont. The road, which cut across much of the republic to the southeast, was nicknamed "The Rolling Road." True to its namesake, it dipped and dove, bended and swirled, hugged mountainsides and crept through valleys. It was a critically important road, connecting not only the capital of Montpelier to the heavily populated Burlington, but also served as the corridor north of Burlington, and linked all the way to the eastern fringe city of White River Junction. Lush, green vistas coupled with the crisp air of late spring; at times Flatlander could see miles beyond the rolling hills and the valley's treetops. Marveling at how pristine and remote much of the land appeared, he sighed in deep satisfaction. *Untouched. Almost as if mankind had never even set foot upon this piece of earth.*

For breakfast, Bronson had baked them pancakes doused in maple syrup, fried eggs, bacon, and served with custard. He called his creation a "breakfast of champions," and it made both men quite content before their long, arduous journey to the south. Bronson had been able to harness Pete to his covered wagon, and in addition to Bronson's tan and white draft horse, Mooney, the duo made quite the formidable, albeit comical, sight. Earlier in the trip, Mooney had been very irked by having to share his space with Pete, going so far as to even shoulder-check Pete on occasion, and nipping at the moose when he got too close. However, shortly after passing through Richmond, they strode together as a team, their gaits in near-perfect unison.

He came to find that the bartender was full of tales. He discovered that when Bronson wasn't tending to the needs of his tavern, he devoted most of his time pursuing leads regarding the paranormal. Ghosts, monsters, cryptids, wizards, and creatures of the night: the bartender had a near encyclopedic knowledge of such matters. He had witnessed for himself the Pigmen of Northfield[48], traded with Fedor the Alchemist, seen with his own eyes the figure of Vergil of the Camel's Hump, evaded an attack from one of the Glastonbury Monsters[49], and had even spent an evening in the splendor of Abenaki Island[50] under the spell of the island's chief. These were just a few of his exploits, according to the Old North End mystic, and he spoke fondly of his adventures in the republic, though he declared that there was much yet to be discovered.

Near the end of the first day of their journey, they passed through the notorious abandoned city of Barre, now a stripped-grey wasteland of dust and bedrock. Not a single tree stood for miles within Montpelier's neighbor to the south, and no longer were the sounds of birds and insects audible. What use to be the city was now a square-shaped, manmade depression bored deep into the earth three hundred meters or more. A handful of buildings, which used to comprise the old downtown, now stood vacant, as broken windows and rusted iron littered the

---

[48] A mysterious, rarely-seen creature(s) who show up periodically in the town of Northfield.

[49] A large, aggressive family of humanoids that (allegedly) reside amongst Glastonbury Mountain.

[50] An island created by the wizard, Vergil, as a gesture of goodwill to Abenaki people, the first indigenous race of people in Vermont, who were stripped of their land and rights.

ground. The travelers kept a safe distance, for Bronson deemed the abandoned city unsafe.

"To think that it's so close to Montpelier. They're like two different planets," muttered Flatlander, as he licked his parched lips. "Even the air here is dryer."

"They don't call it a desert fer nothin'," replied Bronson. "But ya can't fault Barre, Flatlander. Nobody can. After all, it was *yer* people who are ultimately responsible for this."

"*My* people? How?"

"Well," he chewed at his tongue, contemplating. "Long ago, Barre would sell its rock to the Old Country like it was candy. Not the worst of things; it made Vermont a lot of money, but it squeezed out a lot of stone, maybe too much. But then, years later, after supplyin' the wall to keep the Flatlanders out, that's what really did Barre in. Never stood a chance after that. Every stone that could be dug out was mined and sold."

They then passed a series of one story, wood-frame, horseshoe-shaped granite sheds, tucked under a man-made ridge. In the distance, several hundred small, wooden cabins and tents formed a massive cluster, though not a soul could be seen striding the dusty paths between them. The cabins of Barre might look appealing for a weary traveler searching for shelter, explained Bronson, but they were better off sleeping in the woods. The cabins were full or derelicts and undesirables; those who had flocked to the abandoned city not in search for a better life, but to evade the reach of the law.

Flatlander wondered to himself what their group would look like to an outsider: a tamed moose, a nasty-looking draft horse, a behemoth of a man, and Flatlander, with his buttoned blue shirt and khakis. He felt insignificant while in their company; a mere babe in a caravan of giants. Bronson's size was daunting. His features were dark and pronounced. And when the sunlight shone at the right angle, a hideous scar emerged that ran from his lower neck around his right ear.

An hour later, they made camp in the woods along the Rolling Road in the town of Brookfield, often passing various carriages and horse drawn flatbeds. Two carriages passed bearing the official togas of the Brattle, but most of the travelers were simple folk from the country, presumably going to either White River Junction, whose abandoned rail stations now served as the republic's preeminent honeybee farm, or Rutland, or official business in Montpelier. They even observed a carriage with two monks aboard, dressed in their customary green robes. Exchanging a friendly nod with the two older men, Bronson mentioned that they were only a stone's throw north of the monk's stronghold of Braintree, a land shrouded in mystery and fiercely protected by the brotherhood of the republic. Shortly after they set up camp, they ate then slept in a slight gully surrounded by pines.

On the second day, Per Flatlander's request, Bronson revealed his masterwork tattoo on his back, depicting a small stream, which bubbled a yellowish-green at its base. "The Ripton water," remarked Bronson without prompting. "Gives man and woman alike unspeakable vitality. I found it, Flatlander. Though between you and me- nobody must know of this."

Flatlander soon learned that the bartender's family had a long, troubled bloodline, which played a pivotal part in Bronson's upbringing. A poor, difficult student at much too young an age, he became the sad byproduct of his parent's failed marriage, combined with the undue economic hardship from his parent's measly wages. Phillip, his father, was a street cleaner and his mother, Vera, a part-time apprentice to a local hat maker. They lived in a squalid house on North Street, with the only thing separating the family from death being a small, unkempt woodstove, and large glass jar containing all of the family's earnings. Sometimes at night, Bronson would often take his favorite coin from the jar, a copper piece from the 2050's, and flip it repeatedly, calling heads or tails to important questions, begging to the gods what was to become of his own fate, and that of his family. The gods, though, according to Bronson, 'only provided him the answer he wanted half the time.'

By the age of sixteen, he left school at a young age and became self-taught; though the bulk of his interests lay in the paranormal, mysticism, and cryptids. Well versed in everything from Abenaki lore, to legends of the republic, Bronson learned mostly by listening to stories in his tavern from both the wayfaring traveler and familiar, old soul; more so, he would attest, than any book had provided him. Tending the bar earned him a living, but investigating the paranormal of the republic earned him a reputation: a reputation as a no-nonsense, well-versed hunter of the paranormal, highly respected in his field. Frequently sought out by the Monks of Middlebury, his select knowledge in such matters appealed to even the most reputable experts.

On the third day and last leg of the trip, Bronson followed the southward flow of the Connecticut River on Vermont's Southeastern border, past White River Junction, Quechee, Windsor, Ascutney, Springfield, Westminster, Bellows Falls, Putney, and even the Eastern flank of Dummerston. As they passed a thick pine forest, a bed of auburn needles at its base, Bronson pointed to the east.

"The West River lays less than an hour's travel that ways. That's where we're soon headin', though we gotta make a pit stop in the Brattle first."

Flatlander nodded, and stared cheerlessly into the clustered pines of Dummerston. An hour later, the deep woods slowly melded into farmland and meadows, which eventually gave way to the outskirts of the Brattle itself. Small, plain-looking farmhouses and cabins formed a loose perimeter around the city's downtown, as more than one villager raised their eyes in silent attention. As the group marched directly into the quaint downtown of the Brattle, Flatlander could see a large river in the distance, and several streets lined with red brick buildings grace the city proper. They passed over what Bronson referred to as the Whetstone Brook, babbling loud underneath, a rich, earthy aroma filling the vicinity. The smell of spring heavy in the air, the citizens seemed underdressed compared to their northern counterparts. Men walked solemnly down the cobblestone streets, their pants torn just below the knee. Flatlander observed many of the common men dressed in white, light, neatly arranged robes, which Bronson referred to as 'togas.' Many of the women, wary of the group of strangers, tugged their togas lower to cover more leg. Some of the citizens also wore intricate braches and leaf patterns around their heads, which Bronson clarified were laurel wreaths.

"And *that* is the acropolis," muttered Bronson, pointing to the east, as the view opened up from the wooded town.

Across from what Flatlander presumed to be the Connecticut River arose a great wooded hill. Numerous great wooden buildings, many stories tall, graced on and near its summit. He recognized the outline of one temple from a painting at Henry's house, a square pyramid-shaped building. A giant wooden aqueduct spanned its western ridge.

"It used to be Hampshire land, Flatlander. Was once called Wantastiquet Mountain. Over 1,300 feet high at the summit. The Brattle doubled its land sixty years back, took most of Chesterfield too, and it's the only land the republic's taken from the Old Country besides Valcour Island[51], fer that matter, before or since. Lots of temples up there, mostly built by the monks and the Brattle-folk. An amphitheater. Gardens. That aqueduct supplies water to the farmlands of outlyin' towns. They built three of 'em durin' the drought of the 30's and 40's. One here, one in Bennington, and one up by Jay."

As Bronson explained, the Brattle embraced the concept of the republic to such an extreme measure, that they had taken to dressing the part, much like the ancient Greeks, in the spirit of cultural revival. Their leaders were poets, scholars, philosophers, artists, and musicians. As Flatlander passed the marketplace, he saw dozen of merchants behind their merchant tables, engaging in thoughtful dialogue with their customers. Crafts, produce, fruits, and art lined the street by the scores, as the storefronts looked mostly empty and quiet. Bronson clarified that the marketplace of the Brattle was devoted to the free exchange of goods *and* ideas, large and small, as citizens debated everything from taxes, education, farm-to-table distribution, whether or not the wall was detrimental or beneficial to the republic's overall mission, and more.

"This is no common market," mused Bronson as he scanned over the merchant-philosophers; "if Middlebury is considered the gatekeepers of knowledge in the republic, then the folks of the Brattle are the traders of this knowledge. But one of these days, the Brattle may very well become the gatekeepers of the republic," considered the mystic, "considerin' it lay so close to the southern wall, so near to the Old Country. That's is to say if the Old Country ever wanted us back. Let's hope that day never comes."

---

[51] The 4th largest island in Lake Champlain outside of Plattsburgh, New York.

Bronson continued: "But the Brattle folk are a friendly folk; more in-tune than most of Vermont, but the air is different 'round here. If the arts were truly the roots of power, then the Brattle would serve second to none, as I see it," he stated with a smirk. Flatlander could see exactly what the bartender was implying. Within plain view, a dozen artists, placed at various corners of the city blocks near the marketplace, were painting on canvases. Attempting to capture the vitality of the city streets, they worked independently and in complete silence. Nearby, a large group of men dressed in odd, red suits were congregated in a park, playing various horn instruments slow-tempo. Three female belly dancers, dressed in multi-colored, jeweled dresses, writhed as they danced to the smooth instrumentals. A dramatic play was unfolding on the opposite side of the park, attracting a crowd of delighted bystanders. An actor in a long, flowing blue cape held out a glowing sphere high into the air, and recited something about "dear equilibrium." The spectators adorned various colors and styles of togas and watched in appreciation.

Mesmerized with the eclectic life of the Brattle and its people, suddenly Flatlander felt Bronson slap his arm. The group had come to a sudden stop, as Pete shifted uncomfortably in his harness. To their left stood a building painted green with orange trim called "The Riverbed Brewpub." Its namesake rattled back and forth on an old cardboard sign written in a bright, gold, chalky substance. The bar looked dark and unloved among this vibrant city street, so much so that very few people ventured near its entrance.

"We stop here, Flatlander. May not look like the finest establishment, but Eli Donlon is a stand-up man if I ever knew one. A character, true and true. Got a few questions to ask 'em."

As Bronson dismounted from the carriage and nearly took the whole thing down on its side. The few residents who had neared their wagon in subtle fashion now scattered like flies. The men playing their horns in the park went silent mid-song, and looked on with morbid curiosity. The painters, once fully engrossed in their pieces, also threw wayward glances in their direction. Even the actors struggled through their lines, as much of their attention was now devoted to the unfamiliar assemblage arriving at the Riverbed Brewpub. Flatlander harnessed Pete and Mooney to a sturdy lamppost, waved sheepishly at the onlookers, and followed Bronson awkwardly into the bar stoop.

A man of about fifty greeted the pair upon entering the Riverbend Brewpub. He was thickly built, with a full head of gray hair, and a bushy white beard. He wore a brown toga, though it hung on the man awkwardly on his broad shoulders, and over another layer of blue overalls and a white, wool shirt. His boots were, dark, rugged, and mismatched. His face was freckled and full. Bronson and the proprietor embraced as old friends.

"What brings ya here in the Brattle, Bal Ryeah? Not enough barley in the Queen City for yer fixin'?"

Bronson grunted and gave his friend a playful shove. "We've enough barley at the tavern, alone, to dump on ya 'till we bury that gods-awful face of yers," he replied, chuckling, then nodded. "Headin' to Dummerston, Eli."

"Dummerston, ay? What brings ya there, I wonder?" Eli paused, adding lively. "Never mind, I never could get much outta ya. But word on the street is yer losin' money on that ramshackle tavern of yers quicker than the flood of '99."

Eli ushered the two into the bar brusquely, his toga fluttering in the backdraft. As their host closed the door, a piece of the door's blinding clattered to the floor. Eli thought of picking it up, but quickly dismissed the notion with a wave of his hand. Bronson playfully slapped the man on the back.

"Ahh, ya never were much of a good gossip were ya, Eli? My business is like my daytime habits: no concern of yers. Plus, seems yer ain't fairin' much better."

And by the looks of it, Bronson was right. Although it was close to four o'clock, not a soul lingered at the Riverbed Brewpub. Eli moved to behind the bar, and fixed himself an afternoon cocktail. Spastically, he diced the fiddlehead and squeezed its juices into a glass full of whiskey and water. Eli then handed Bronson a bottle of Northmind Lager.

"Oh c'mon, Bronson. I've seen ya takin' a barrel of somethin' down the street, middle of the night, barely dressed, and spun as a web. Don't go actin' so pious all a sudden. Everyone knows yer business from the wall to wall[52], and I ain't no different."

Bronson took a swig of the drink, and smirked. "True as that may be, I'm a changed man, Eli."

Eli chuckled, and took a quick sip of his unique concoction. Flatlander surveyed the interior of the Riverbed Brewpub; which brimmed with an odd sense of décor. The bar was small and dimly lit, with one half devoted to the bar itself, while several eating booths, furnished with red, leather cushions, filled the other half. Odd fodder lined the walls: a large, framed painting of Eli fighting a dragon by a brook, an oversized colonies stick with a number of initials carved into its body, and a silly looking duck mask looked outwards, cross-eyed. What caught Flatlander's attention most, however, is what appeared to be a life-sized model of a pig's buttocks embedded among the wall, with the words "Punch Me!" written on a sign above it. Flatlander wandered over to the peculiar model, and noted that the solid pink wore thin at the center of its backside.

Eli's voice boomed from behind. "Ya gonna introduce me to yer daydreamin' partner here?"

Fully delighted with the pig bottom, Flatlander ignored the inquiry.

"What is this?"

"Aha, see ya found Old Sally! Quite a specimen, don't ya think? Part of the Central Scare some years back." Eli downed a

---

[52] A Vermont expression denoting great distances.

portion of his cocktail. His face soured, as he pointed squarely at the rounded model buttocks. "That pig had to weigh a good 800 pounds when it was all said and done."

Bronson sighed. "Here we go again…"

Eli shot his friend a dirty look. "Shut yer trap, Bronson. The lad asked *me* a question, not you. Believe what ya want. This pig woulda knocked even *you* senseless."

Bronson shook his head with a smirk.

Flatlander was almost at a loss for words. "Why did you do this?"

"Why? Oh, *stuff it*, ya mean?" Eli pondered the question for a moment. "Ya ever try butcherin' an 800 pound pig, son?"

Flatlander scratched his head. "I can't say that I have."

"Neither had me or my buds before Sally here," muttered Eli as he nodded toward the buttocks. "To make a long story short, between the four of us, that pig dislocated three arms, sprained an ankle, bloodied a nose, bruised a knee, and gave the four of us enough pig fer a lifetime. Don't even eat the damn stuff anymore unless I gotta! Decided to stuff the backside to make a punching bag out of ol' Sally. Can't say that I don't get a few licks in on Sally myself just about every week for good luck."

"Delightful," muttered Flatlander, as he backed slowly away from Sally's shameful memorial.

"Now, if I may be so impolite, may I ask what's the occasion? I figure it's business that brings ya down these ways. Eh, Bronson?"

Bronson laughed. "I suppose ya can say that."

Bronson turned fully around in his barstool, his boots perched high on the backrest of a chair. He folded his hands, and rested them on his lap. Flatlander stood by Bronson's side, as Eli sat at an adjacent booth, its table covered in neatly arranged menus.

"Seen the demon," muttered Bronson, hoarsely. "Some time ago."

Eli sat back in the booth for second, then looked at Bronson with renewed interest. "*The demon*? Yer kiddin'. Ya sure? Still look the same?"

Bronson nodded. "Ay, ay and ay. Goin' to make a little visit to Dummerston with this fella here, see if we can figure somethin' out."

Flatlander reached out his hand, suddenly aware that he hadn't introduced himself.

"Flatlander, nice to meet you."

"Eli Donlon." After a few seconds, the proprietor turned to Bronson, as Flatlander's name seemed to ring a bell. "Flatlander? *The* Flatlander? This the fella I heard about in the paper I take it? Causin' trouble with them wardens in Irasburg, cuttin' the head off that Fish, lord knows what else ya been doin' up here!"

Flatlander blushed. "That's me."

Luckily, Eli hadn't apparently gotten wind from their debacle in Lowell, which was chiefly of the reason he was down in Dummerston in the first place.

Eli's shock soon morphed into playful banter. "Sir Bronson Bra Ryeah! Ya got the Flatlander runnin' yer scare tactics now? Knew you were a strange bird and all, but this is gettin' weirder by the minute."

Flatlander saw an opportune time to interject. "Almost as weird as a mounting a pig's bottom and using it as a punching bag," he quipped.

Both Eli and Bronson glanced at Flatlander, surprised at the newcomer's audacity. After a few awkward seconds, the two old friends bellowed with laughter. Flatlander exhaled long and hard. *Don't press your luck.*

Eli patted Flatlander's arm. "Got me there, kid. Ya fit in here nicely, I think. But I want to hear more about this demon, bud. For the first time ever, I actually wanna hear that sorry voice of yers."

Bronson then recounted his latest demon sighting to Eli the same way he had to Flatlander, but with slightly less emphasis in certain parts. He told him that the spirit had told him to come to Dummerston. Bronson intimated to Eli that Flatlander was brought on the quest as a favor from Lord Henry, to which Eli whistled emphatically.

According to Eli, he had encountered the entity no longer than several months ago. His story had placed the demon in a doorway of a backroom, after hours. He caught it watching him with its red, glowing eyes. Upon seeing the apparition, Eli fell to the floor, breaking several empty bottles of beer in the process. But when he had looked up, the demon was gone. His description of the figure was exactly the same as Bronson's. Though he made great efforts to speak with confidence and strength as he retold his tale, Flatlander noticed Eli's hands oftentimes shook uncontrollably.

According to Eli, business had suffered tremendously after the Brattle's rumor mill went into full effect. For though the market was often a blessing in keeping its citizens engaged in important dialogue, it was also a curse when it came to spreading mere gossip. He had only told a few close friends, by his account, and hadn't expected the rumors to spread so fast. The people of the Brattle were frightened of the demon of the Riverbend: for these were a superstitious folk, more so than the farmers and lake men of the north. Although Eli's rugged nature stuck out like a sore thumb in the world of the Brattle, he had accumulated hundreds of friends who had come to appreciate his unique personality.

Yet now, that didn't seem to matter. Eli's fishing buddies rarely came by. Neither did the casual tourists from other reaches of the republic. His only patrons nowadays were a handful of regulars, and even they had become fewer in number. Worse off, Eli's business was on the verge of being shut down. He hemorrhaged money by the day. Recently, he had to fire his two trusted bar hands, for he was unable to pay them fair wages any longer. As Eli delved deeper and deeper into his story, his demeanor noticeably saddened, and on more than a few occasions, his eyes reddened. According to Eli, it hadn't been the first time he had seen the spirit. But the most recent sighting could have very well signaled the end of his business.

As Bronson and Eli neared the end of their exchange, Eli looked over to Flatlander, who had been listening patiently from his stool.

"Yer in good company, I think: despite my teasin'."

Flatlander smirked. "A friend of Henry's is a friend of mine."

Eli nodded then looked at his friend, gravely. "Before ya head off, just do me one thing: take care of yerself, Bronson. That ain't no man we're dealin' with out there in Dummerston. You should knows better n' most."

Bronson stared vacantly at the bar top. "And I'll be damned to find out."

They left soon thereafter. In one last fleeting glance of the Riverbend, Flatlander saw the figure of Eli receding back into the shadows of his bar. The city, which had moments ago been teeming with energy, had now dwindled to a fraction of the crowd. The band was nowhere to be seen, the artists were in the midst of packing up their supplies, and the group of actors now scurried across the far side of the park, dragging their costumes carelessly in tow. Up above, a bulbous, dark-gray storm front was spreading rapidly from the east, drowning out the wisps of cirrus clouds, and reflecting a yellowish tint.

As Bronson grabbed Mooney's reins, he glanced up at the sky ominously. "Dummerston calls."

Flatlander also cast a worried glance at the sky. "We're leaving tonight? Shouldn't we stay the night in the Brattle?"

"We can only see this entity durin' the night." Bronson handed Flatlander the reins to Pete. "Pony up, little man, and wear somethin' dry. It's gonna be a wet night in Dummerston and the day's growin' old."

The notion of carrying a sword for protection against an entity was silly to be sure, thought Flatlander, yet it provided him limited comfort on this cold, damp trek into the small town of Dummerston. The downpour alternated between a torrent and a light drizzle, with little to no wind. The road had become so muddied during the rain that it had become nearly unmanageable. Several times, Pete had tripped and nearly fallen over, just about taking everyone with him. His farm in Irasburg had great filtration, and he hadn't quite adapted to walking in mud effectively like his wild ancestors. Mooney, on the other hand, was built for such journeys. His hooves powered through the thick sludge with ease. Franklin had warned him of the muddy Vermont spring, as the term "mud season" became interchangeable with the much-anticipated spring. And although Dummerston lay only nine miles north of the Brattle, the unspeakable road conditions made for a laborious journey.

"Do we even know where we're going?" asked Flatlander through clenched teeth. Even Pete was tired; he could hear it in the creature's labored breath.

Bronson nodded and pointed ahead to a wooded hill. "The road leads past that crest, if my map's correct. We're lookin' fer a bridge over the West River. Can't say fer sure that we'll find what we're lookin' for, but it's the first place they seen the demon."

Flatlander nodded. He hadn't the energy to argue, and though his oversized deer hide coat, courtesy of Bronson, kept him relatively dry, the bitter air bit through him to the bone. He could see his breath beginning to steam in thick clouds, as an unexpected, gentle wind shook his fading senses awake.

Night descended upon them gradually, as the surrounding hills blocked the last vestiges of sunset. As they navigated the final leg of the journey through the Dummerston woods, the sky to the west was consumed by a burst of vermilion. The sound of the rippling West River overtook them before they reached the bridge. The bridge was unique in the fact that it was covered; and to Flatlander, it almost resembled a barn or country house, which had been stretched unnaturally above the river's surface. Even in the growing twilight, he could clearly discern the faded grey sidings of the exposed bridge, bleached from the constant elements of the West River Valley. A cold chill worked its way into his bones as he surveyed the surrounding land.

They soon found a relatively flat, well-sheltered campsite close to the riverbed, and no more than thirty meters from the bridge. As Bronson fixed them a fire with flint and knife, humming a traditional tune, Flatlander gathered wood. He helped construct a crude shelter aside a large sassafras tree. The smoke thickened quickly around the campsite, as the wayward drop of rain from the canopy would sizzle upon the fire's flames. Bronson had thought it appropriate to separate Pete and Moody to opposite sides of the camp, for they had 'walked shoulder to shoulder fer much too long.'

As the night grew dark, the fire grew in size and warmth. They fed it log after log, and yet the dampness muted the fire from reaching its true potential. The rain had seized for over an hour. He removed his shirt and jacket and placed them near the fire to dry. He shored up a fallen log and placed it next to Bronson to sit on, while the mystic cooked venison jerky with the end of a crooked branch.

"Ya may think me crazy fer sayin', but part o' me feels safer out here than in the tavern certain nights," he said before ripping the tough meat in two parts while handing Flatlander a half. Nodding in gratitude, Flatlander peered closely at the fire.

"How so?"

Bronson breathed the country air deeply. "At least out here, ya can sit back and relax. Let the air soothe ya."

"I'd prefer less rain." Flatlander took a long, savory bite from his piece of jerky. "Your friend Eli's a character."

Bronson chuckled. "That he is. More trouble than a bear on wheels[53], I tell ya'."

---

[53] An expression meaning one who presents troubling or mischievous behavior.

"How long has he had Sally at the bar?" asked Flatlander, with a chuckle.

Bronson scratched his head, contemplating. "Well, not too long after I met him, really. Don't believe every word he says though, Flatlander. The pig roughed him and the boys up some, but Eli has a way of exaggeratin' tales, spinnin' yarn, if ya catch my meanin'. The Central Scare spooked some, but that's about it."

"Do you think that he exaggerated *this* one? The story about the demon?"

Bronson paused. "Some Vermonters, not all, they like to stretch the truth, Flatlander. Just like a lot of people in the Old Country, I'd imagine. They're usually the ones who become bored in their life and need a way to spice things up. Put on a nice show fer the town drunks. But, as to yer question, the simple answer is no. I don't think Eli made up anythin' he told us at the Riverbend. I saw the same thing with my own eyes, and me and Eli haven't talked fer years."

Swallowing the remaining jerky in one big gulp, the spices and juices coated his tongue. Bronson threw several dry, large branches onto the fire that Flatlander had salvaged from a small, sheltered cave near camp. The lips of the flames shot high, almost to chest-level. He noticed that the sounds of frogs and crickets began filling the night air. And the din of the river continued, unabated. Occasionally, a mysterious splash or gurgle sounded faintly in the background.

Bronson gazed at Flatlander from above the flames. "Ya never asked me why I brought you to this bridge, did ya? I mentioned the sightin', but you didn't even care to know about it."

Flatlander sighed, taking the bartender's cue. "Why did you bring me to the bridge, Bronson?"

Bronson smirked and looked off into the distance. "The demon. The man of shadows. He's been seen in three places: the tavern, Eli's Riverbend, and this bridge right here. The young man said he tried crossin' this bridge after an evenin' with a lady, not too far from town, and left in the dead of the night to avoid her parents. He told only a few of us at the time. We vowed never to spread the rumor. He's an important man now with a great career. We didn't wanna stir the pot fer no reason. Probably the right decision, 'specially after seein' Eli's business."

Bronson continued hesitantly, looking towards the bridge in the distance. "He said, and I ain't makin' this up, Flatlander, he said that the demon came through the side of the bridge, dressed in a black robe. Glowin' eyes. Small, but fierce. Approached the young man, its robe billowin' in the river's draft. He said it moved fast and grew in size as it approached. Completely silent, it was. The young man dropped his beer, and ran as hard as he had ever run in his life. Didn't even look back till he was a full mile away, all the way back to the girl's house. He snuck in a tree house out back, and spent the night there, alone. Too afraid to wake up her parents and too afraid to revisit the bridge, his only route back home over the West River. They say he never passed through the bridge again after that."

"Was he a local?" asked Flatlander, as he leaned against the base of a tree.

Bronson sighed. "He was."

Warming his hands on the fire, the bartender looked around the campsite. Pete leaned against the trunk of a nearby tree sound asleep. Mooney looked uncomfortable, shifting around restlessly in her stationary position near the campfire. And though Flatlander tried not to show it, he was scared. While the idea of being nearby the formidable Bronson Bal Ryeah was in itself a comforting thought, the combination of being in a foreign land, the growing sounds of the night, and a gnawing sense in his gut made him dread what might come in the dead of the night.

Flatlander placed his sword beside him and sighed, weary from three days travel. "Well, thanks for the story, Bronson. It was impeccably timed. I'm looking forward to trying to sleep tonight."

Bronson chuckled to himself, and threw his cooking spear into the campfire. "I aim to please. Night, Flatlander. But if I were ya, I'd keep one eye open."

"Flatlander."

The sharp whisper awoke him without warning. A mere foot away was Bronson's face, a terrifying silhouette of bulk and hair in the confines of the moonlit shelter.

"It's here."

Flatlander jerked himself awake within the haphazard shelter of limbs and branches. It took several moments to come to his senses. He figured that he must have had shed his deer hide in the middle of the night, and used his coat as a pillow. Yet now, in the cold of the deep night, he was chilled and shaking profusely.

"What is it?"

Bronson looked off into the direction of the covered bridge and whispered. "The demon. I can sense him."

He dressed quietly in the cramped shelter, gathered his sword, which had been lying near his bedding of leaves and shaved moss, and scampered out to meet Bronson. The fire still smoldered, leaving a gentle glow on the surrounding trees and bushes. The occasional pop or crackle rang out. As Flatlander looked around, he saw both Pete and Mooney standing alert towards the rush of the West River, their snouts angled high. He walked a dozen paces to the opening of the campsite, where the ridgeline broke, as the West River and its covered bridge came fully within view. His eyes had not quite adjusted to the dark of the night, though even now, he was surprised by the still of the evening and the brightness of the moon. The heavy clouds had fully dissipated. The covered bridge, no more than fifty paces upstream, seemed to shine.

Flatlander scanned the landscape with intensity. "My eyes are bad, Bronson. Where did you see it?"

Bronson cleared his throat quietly and whispered. "Heard somethin'. Thought I may have even seen something', but the eyes aren't what they use to be neither."

Flatlander kept squinting, but still he saw nothing. No movements. No shapes. Not even an animal to provide him a momentary distraction. Bronson placed a hand on Flatlander's shoulder, and spoke in a soft voice.

"C'mon. We've gotta go check it out."

"Why? It doesn't look like there's anything there. You even said so yourself."

"Something's there, I'm tellin' ya."

"But…"

"I didn't haul all the way down here, on a four day trek to Dummerston, to wimp out at the last second, Flatlander," he interrupted, his whisper growing with agitation, "we came here to see it fer ourselves. Remember? I came here of my own free will. Coulda been tendin' the bar, makin' money, but a favor's a favor." The bartender poked his pointer finger into Flatlander's chest. "And *you* came here cuz the big man wanted ya here. We've got jobs to do. Gods willin', we don't see nothin' and head back with the news."

Compelled to argue, Flatlander had to admit that Bronson had a point. Whether or not the quest was explicitly laid out in fine detail, there was no mistaking that finding and stopping the demon had been its driving purpose. There was something about those hills that spooked him, though, and the rippling of the river seemed to dull his senses. As he peered down the river's length, he was temporarily transfixed on the moonlight shimmering off of the small rapids, like a thousand pulsating eyes.

Bronson didn't wait for an answer. "If it makes ya feel better, I'll take the front, you take the rear. And one thing ya should know 'bout demons, Flatlander- they only show themselves when they want to, or to people they think would care."

Bronson tugged Flatlander by the arm, placed a finger slowly to his lips, and gestured for him to follow. They made their way slowly through the brush of the ridge, rarely keeping their eyes off of the bridge's hollow. They let the moonlight guide them, for the fire's light merely became a faint, orange speck, fading fast in the distance. From time to time, Flatlander turned to see if anything, or anyone, was behind them, but only saw the still forest shrubs already coated in morning dew.

As they turned onto the road that passed through the covered bridge, he was taken aback how dark it was inside. Only a few openings on each side of the bridge existed, diamond-shaped, and eighteen inches across, they provided little relief from the blackness. The roar of the river seemed to amplify within the bridge itself; every splash, spatter, and groan could be heard with alarming lucidness. Bronson removed a small, patterned object from his pocket. It looked to be a gem attached to a necklace. He dangled it loosely in front of him, staring expectantly into the bridge's darkened interior.

"We know yer in there and we mean ya no harm. Just want some answers."

They were met with utter silence; even the river itself seemed to quiet down, and the night calls of the crickets receded. A cold gust of wind met them head on through the bridge, damping them slightly with what must have been the bridge's hanging droplets. The sensation on his cheek felt like spittle.

Then, as Flatlander brushed the droplets from his face, Bronson clutched his arm tight, pointing. A figure dressed in a loose, black cloak from head to toe, emerged slowly from the inside wall. It stood upright and motionless, staring straight ahead. Flatlander's heart skipped a beat, as the hair on his neck stood completely straight, as he strained his eyes even harder for details of the figure. Even Bronson seemed to shrink away, as he lowered the necklace slowly, in utter shock. Neither made a sound.

As Bronson prepared himself to speak to the demon, it looked straight at the two, its eyes shining a menacing bright red. Flatlander couldn't help himself; fear had taken its icy grip. Without so much as a word, he began running as hard as he could back to camp, horrified. Bronson called his name, but he may as well have been yelling at a disobedient dog.

He arrived to find Pete and Mooney thrashing violently in their harnesses. The moose was scraping its antlers against the trees loudly. He picked up some of the stacked kindling nearby and threw it on the fire. The flames grew by the second. Bronson came lumbering into camp shortly thereafter, his eyes wide with adrenaline, as he shot Flatlander an accusatory look.

"Flatlander, ya shouldn't have run! Ya need to stand and be brave!"

"We're better off by the fire, I think," answered Flatlander, short of breath, and floundering for excuses. "Was that the…"

"I'm tellin' ya, it was the *demon*!" said Bronson, adamantly. "And it'll be here soon."

Flatlander looked around the campsite frantically, searching for any signs of the entity. "We need to get out of here!"

In two giant steps, Bronson moved close to Flatlander and slapped him hard across the face. The sound of the hard slap resounded throughout the surrounding forest, and the side of Flatlander's face went fully numb. His panic dissolved into shock. The bartender looked through him to his very core.

"Stop. I won't have none of it. Ye hear me? Ya need to stop it and stand tall with me."

Bronson stood rigidly and puffed his chest out towards the path to the bridge, gemstone held aloft. Flatlander reluctantly obliged, as he stood by Bronson's side. Looking out in the direction of the path from which they had come, he readied his sword. He could then see a shadow coming through the brush. It didn't make a sound, gliding deftly above the forest floor. Its eyes were small, red and humanlike, and he could see, even in the relatively dim glow of the fire, that it was small in stature.

As the demon approached, Bronson held the necklace and gemstone high up in the air, and mumbled an incantation.

"Al-Katira, Al-Madid, Al-Sapher-cull."

Both Pete and Mooney bucked so violently, that Flatlander worried their tethers would snap in half. Without realizing it, he had slowly positioned himself partly behind the large mass of Bronson. Through the darkened hood, Flatlander saw a snouted, devilish scowl. The apparition appeared to have the face of a dog, though its snout was smaller, and its teeth, more human-like. Its visible skin was dark and wrinkled, and its face was covered in a matted, coarse fur. Here, in the light of the fire, he could also make out that the demon was partly translucent, as he was able to see the forest landscape straight through the being.

As the demon approached, it raised a hand, and a circle of green flames shot up and surrounded their camp. Pete and Mooney bucked even more fiercely, as the flames danced wildly near their hooves. Flatlander recoiled from the sight, panic-stricken, as he dropped his sword at his feet. Holding the gemstone high over his head, Bronson repeated his incantation.

"Al-Katira, Al-Madid, Al-Sapher-cull.

"Dummerston calls," the demon gasped.

"Curses! We're in trouble! The Dummer-stone ain't workin!" stammered Bronson, as he tucked the small gem back into his pocket. "I suppose that's what ya get when ya buy magic goods from a mountain trader!"[54]

The demon seemed to grow in stature, as the wall of green flames rose with it. The demon cackled high and loud, and tree branches above the two began snapping and flying through the air, dangerously close to their faces. Flatlander turned from the awful sight, unsure if he could stomach any more.

"Gus Boomhover," a familiar voice then boomed out from behind them, "I order you to halt at once." The demon stopped its cackling. The green flames died out in a hurry. The flying branches fell lifelessly to the forest floor. Flatlander turned, and to his amazement, saw Henry standing a mere ten yards away,

---

[54] Mountain traders sometimes had reputations for ripping people off.

atop an adjacent hill. He was dressed in a tight, undersized toga, and wore a small laurel wreath above his right ear. Although he looked somewhat comical to Flatlander, his facial expression and demeanor showed that Henry was all business. *And he couldn't have had better timing*, thought Flatlander, *whatever he had in store.*

Flatlander felt dizzy. "Lord Henry, what are you…I thought… you were in…"

"The Brattle? Yes. Yes, I was, Flatlander. But I decided to make a little side trip while Jess and Menche were sleeping. A very important side trip, you might say."

The Humble King turned to face the demon again, and neared the fire. "It all ends here. All of it. I'm tired of running away all this time. I'm not scared any more, Gus. Do you see these clothes? Take a good look at them. They're the same clothes that I wore that night, some thirty years prior. I haven't forgotten you, Gus. Your memory still lives with me."

"Who's Gus?" mumbled Flatlander.

"Hush!" whispered Bronson hoarsely to his side.

Henry stood alongside Bronson and Flatlander, an air of confidence about him.

"Take what you need then leave us. Your time beyond this world should be taken in peace. I'm sorry about what happened to you all those years ago, truly Gus. And if I could turn back the hands of time, I would. In hindsight, we were young and lived too much for every moment, every emotion, every…. relationship, and relationship lost. You were loved by all, Gus. But now," Henry struggled with the words, his lip quivered in the morning still, "now is time for you to go and rest in peace. Leave Dummerston and the Brattle. Leave Burlington. Leave the republic, and take your peace."

It was all beginning to fit together for Flatlander. *Bronson had kept Henry's identity secret this whole time. Henry was the man whom the bartender had referred to in one of his stories at the tavern.* He chided himself for not piecing together the whole mystery sooner.

The demon stood in silence for several seconds, as if considering things through. As a deathly quiet overtook the camp, Flatlander could hear the entity breathing heavily, each breath like a death rattle. It appeared to scan the campsite. Just as Flatlander breathed a sigh of relief, the demon began floating around the large campfire towards the three men. They circled around at the same pace, keeping the fire between them and the demon. Instinctively, Flatlander kicked Bronson's bag towards the demon. It floated over the bag.

Opening the half-ripped bag with little effort, it removed a bottle of Bronson's Northmind Lager, one of six bottles that he had brought down for the journey. Nodding to the three men with beer in hand, the demon then disappeared quietly into the dark of the night, back towards the direction of the covered bridge. Jaw agape; Flatlander simply couldn't believe his eyes. Bronson and Henry also exchanged equal looks of bewilderment.

Flatlander gasped in relief then turned to Henry.

"Gus..."

Henry sighed and discarded his laurel wreath into the fire. "Why don't we all sit down. I may need a helping of your jerky before I tell my tale."

The three men assembled by the fire. Relaxed and poised, Henry seemed much different from how Flatlander remembered him in Montpelier. Bronson boiled a cup of water to make a celebratory batch of dandelion and warmed more of his venison jerky at fire's edge. Henry helped himself to a strip and made sure that he had their undivided attention.

"When you're twenty two and in love, sometimes you refuse to see things outside of your periphery for what they *really* are.

I was young and in love with a girl. Her name was Kylie. And as is often the case with young love, so was another man. Gus Boomhover. He was the Brattle's toast of the town, an incredible athlete. Handsome. Great student. Great guy, really. Gus and Kylie were friends for some time before she became his love interest, and he thought it was all but destined that they should be together. But there was one slight problem." Bronson handed Flatlander and Henry steaming canteens filled with tea.

Henry took a cautious sip and shook his head. "Kylie simply didn't love Gus. She had always felt pressure from others to love him, but something inside of her told her differently. Here I was, some skinny, nerdy teenager from outside of town whose family had just moved from the West Brattle on a whim, and he was from a very established, well-liked family. His father taught at the school, his mother worked as a nurse. And Gus was a fine gentleman too. But for whatever reason, Kylie wasn't feeling the love.

"Kylie and myself began our relationship awkwardly enough. I tripped and fell directly onto her picnic while flying a kite, and smashed a basket full of blueberries all over her cloth. Knocked her bread into the dirt. Suffice to say, it was a real mess. She didn't berate me like she should have, nor did she speak an unkind word. Instead, she was just…laughing. I was smitten. We talked for a bit. We both laughed. I commented on my own shortcomings. Truth is, I saw something in her heart that day that spoke to me, and I think that she felt the same way. I asked her out shortly after helping her pick up the mess. *My mess.* After a few dates, we eventually became quite an item.

"When Gus saw that Kylie and myself were getting closer, he sank into a dark, crippling state of depression. He relinquished his captaincy on the pumpkin regatta team. He took up drinking, and hanging out with some local undesirables. Though he was barely old enough to drink, Gus became a regular at many of the establishments in the Brattle, Dummerston, and Putney alike. Kylie felt horrible, guilty for contributing to Gus's complete disintegration. As did I. We tried to reach out to him, but he was too embarrassed to discuss things with us, at least not in a rational sense. It's a complicated thing, Flatlander: love. For some, it's as elusive as a bobcat in Bennington[55]. For Gus, it was even more so."

Henry paused. "One night, Gus disappeared. At first, most of us chalked it up to a late night escapade after the bars. But when he didn't come home the next day, and the day after that, however, we were all very concerned. In fact, the whole community became very concerned. A large search party fanned out across the region scanning every road, house, and park in sight. Sadly, somebody found an empty beer of Gus's liking on that covered bridge you see down this path," said Henry, as he pointed to the covered bridge nearby, "as well as a sketch he drew of himself and Kylie scraped up in the mud. They cleaned the sketch and posted it on the inside of that bridge, and it remained there for years to come."

Flatlander threw a pair of moistened branches onto the fire, as a handful of sparks shot out.

"That's horrible. He drowned?"

Henry nodded. "Presumably, yes. Yet it was no less a presumption than the moon arising in the night sky. We were devastated, Flatlander. It took Kylie years before she was able to forgive herself completely. Some in the town even held us both accountable for Gus's deterioration. I'm sure now, as I was sure then, that it was Gus who haunted me at this same bridge over thirty years ago. Under that very moon. There are few that I've told of that night, gentlemen, and I'd like to keep it that way.

"I left the Brattle only months after the incident, as I soon began to grow distant from it. Part of it was my desire to explore the republic, but it was also in large to avoid Gus. One haunting was one too many. Kylie and I eventually married, and raised Jess

---

[55] Bobcats and lynx had a tendency to stay in the northern Kingdom and not wander further south.

together in the heart of Montpelier, living quite happily, yet the story of Gus always simmered just underneath the surface until the very end. Kylie and myself parted on amicable terms several years back, but the subject was always difficult to broach, and even harder to resolve.

"I'd heard of Eli's run-ins with the spirit, other sightings at the bridge, and eventually Bronson's encounter as well, and it left me no doubt as to who it was. He had been haunting my dreams for much too long. I hadn't ventured a foot into downtown Brattle or Dummerston since and I figured enough was enough. All this, despite the mounting criticism of the press as to why I had forsaken my hometown and built my political career in Montpelier and Burlington. I couldn't explain this all to the public. They'd think I was loony. I knew that something had to be done about the demon sooner or later, and that time was now. I decided to pack my old childhood toga and wreath with the hope that I would find him and he might recognize me."

"Well, ya came at the right time," muttered Bronson between sips of his scalding-hot tea.

"But how did you know where to find us?" asked Flatlander.

Henry raised an eyebrow. "Where else could you have been? I knew that I had previously told Bronson about the location of my sighting. I've come here the past two nights to find you. I made sure that both Menche and Jess were sound asleep, and snuck away on Bella. The funny thing is, I was worried that Jess wouldn't tire tonight, but I figured after a hour long history lesson on the Stony Mahoney's, and the wall, and the history of the temples of the Brattle, she'd be more than a little sleepy-eyed."

Henry then took a deep breath, and looked regretfully at Flatlander. "One more thing. I owe you an apology, Flatlander. Politics has a way of changing a man. Sometimes, I lose sight of that. I regret speaking to you in the manner in which I had after Lowell. I regret speaking to *all of you* that way. Jess may be void of many things in her life right now, but she wasn't void in providing sound feedback on the matter. I feel as though I'm failing you as a host, and that must change. I need to show you more of the ways of our people, more of what really matters in our culture, as Vermonters. Shortly after we reach Montpelier, and I tidy up a few things, I want to take you to a few special places. You haven't had the time to swim, to hunt, to see the stars; to truly see some of the things that make this lifestyle here in the republic worth living."

Flatlander nodded and he two shook hands. "I'm sorry too. We were out of line. It won't happen again. I've been an easy target for Shay Bromage."

Henry dismissed the notion with the wave of his hand. "Nonsense. Bromage is the only man who can make a target out of a litter of kittens[56]." After receiving a hearty laugh from Bronson and Flatlander, Henry nodded. "Apology accepted. Then all is forgiven?"

Flatlander smirked. "Without a doubt. But just to be clear- this counted as one of my quests, right?"

"Absolutely. You kicked his fancy directly at him without even knowing it! Four down and six to go," confirmed Henry. "You have also assisted the Humble King to return to his homeland, helped scourge the republic of a frightening entity, and befriended one of the most legendary figures in the entire republic. Does that count for naught?"

Flatlander nodded humorously in agreement.

"And Bronson," continued Henry. "Consider the old favor more than paid for. Your services were invaluable to this quest. And by chance, if you or Eli should encounter this demon again, let me know. I might be tempted to involve the monks of Middlebury, or perhaps even the Abenaki in such a crucial matter."

---

[56] This reference applies to an actual piece Shay wrote criticizing a litter of kittens in August of 2109.

"Many thanks, big man," praised Bronson with his hand raised to his temple. "If yer ever in the likes of the Old North End, ya know where to find me!"

Henry nodded then shrugged. "Of course. Then, if you'll excuse, I have to get back to my daughter and adopted man-child before sunrise. I didn't want to burden them with talk of demons, as you can imagine. Flatlander, I'll meet you two back in Montpelier in three to four days? We're leaving tomorrow morning shortly after sunrise."

Henry stood upright to leave, then stopped and admired the sight of the two partners sitting by the fire.

"This really is a satisfying feeling. I've missed the Brattle to no end, and to see the both of you safe, as well. What a treat."

"One last thing," said Flatlander. "I'm still trying to get my head around this. Why the beer? Why did he go for a beer?"

Henry was quiet, considering the question for a moment.

Bronson cleared his throat. "Big man, if I may be so lucky to know, what beer was the lad drinkin' the night he went missin'?"

Henry searched deep into his catalogue of memories. It seemed far from an important detail, yet much of that night was permanently etched into his mind, down to every last, minute detail. He remembered that he had seen a brown bottle, with a blue label and several stars lining on the top. Though the bottle was broken close to the neck, the brand was unmistakable.

"The only beer I've known Gus to drink."

"Northmind Lager?" asked Bronson.

Henry's eyes widened with surprise. "How did you know?"

Bronson smiled in satisfaction. "He was drinkin' the same thing at the bar. That's also been Eli's flagship brew going on thirty years strong now. I'm thinkin' he never lost a taste fer it, even in death. Probably was his last real comfort before he threw himself into the West River, his last *real* joy in life. Musta been what he was after, what he thought would provide him closure."

"Very interesting," muttered Henry.

Bronson nodded firmly. "It's time to find a new beer to tap at the tavern, and if I see anyone bringin' in Northmind, they'll be flyin' out my bar quicker than they can say my name!"

The three men howled with laughter, as a trail of thickened smoke soared high over the hills of Dummerston. The West River gushed quietly in its pre-dawn slumber. Soon after sunrise, the remaining five beers of the six-pack of Northmind Lager sat abandoned at the base of a wooded hill, left in homage of a thirsty spirit.

CHAPTER 6
The Swimming hole

FAR UP IN THE MOUNTAINS, some twenty miles northwest of Montpelier in the woods of Bolton, Flatlander thought that it felt like an entirely different season altogether. Nearing the end of May, Vermont's spring was soon coming to an end, as flowers and trees in the valleys were now in full bloom. Up here, however, was a completely different story. This was no spring, thought Flatlander. The mountains must be misinformed: not while his breath still came out as a gentle mist under the late afternoon sun.

After hiking the banks of the Winooski River for several miles, Flatlander, Henry, and Franklin briefly followed a tributary called the Joiner Brook until they came upon a swimming hole along its path. A tier of rushing water, broken up into several chains of rapids, accumulated into a large basin twenty-five feet across. Henry paused and looked at the water, a form of recognition sweeping over his face.

"Ah, just where I remembered. Welcome to the Bolton Potholes, Flatlander. Not a bad place to stop if you ask me," said Henry, as he unloaded his leather pack on a flattened boulder.

Flatlander scanned the hole. The water shone an emerald green, to which he could see straight to the bottom. Above the watering hole, a small waterfall cut through giant, angular slabs of schist, which rose to over forty feet high. Yet from their vantage point, they were no more than a few feet above the potholes' circular surface. A slight spray formed by the impact of the waterfall, sprinkling on Flatlander's face.

With flint and steel, Franklin started a small fire near the nook of a large boulder. Dried twigs and leaves from year's prior matted the ground below a slight overhang. 'A blessing,' Henry had said in delight, 'considering the amount of rain that we've seen in recent weeks.' The trio collected the kindling, and sorted it out in three separate piles: leaves, twigs and branches. Placing an aluminum teakettle on a branch of fallen spruce, the northerner completed a makeshift hanger.

As Flatlander turned to where Henry had previously stood, he discovered that the Humble King was gone. Already disrobed, and a dozen paces back, Henry was engaged in a full-fledged sprint towards the basin. Before Flatlander could voice his surprise, he was flying through the air, hollering. His howls were immediately followed by a tremendous splash, which soaked the bottom of Flatlander's pant legs. Inching back, Flatlander smiled nervously. The water felt extremely cold on his legs.

"Is it safe?" he asked, timidly.

Henry chuckled, his head bobbing on the surface of the swimming hole. "Flatlander, *please*. Our children swim here, some as young as four. Of course it's safe."

Before Flatlander could respond, a flurry of movement on his right caught his eye. Franklin's naked torso passed him like a furious ball of black hair and muscle, as he made a surprisingly athletic jump into the watering hole, flipping midair. Henry laughed, as the resulting surge from Franklin's dive sent huge amounts of spray over the rocks. Flatlander couldn't evade the scope of the splash, and within an instant, was soaked thoroughly from head to toe.

"C'mon, Flatlander. Don't be an old cow," teased Henry, as he treaded lightly amongst the waters. "It feels fine."

"Whiskers and syrup!" he cursed, as Franklin came up for a large gasp of air, the shock of the cold water stunned even that of the seasoned northerner.

Flatlander eyed the two curiously, and quickly reminded himself that this was now late May, late spring. He hated the cold. He hated the dampness of the mountains and the green color of the water. Calculatingly, he placed the tip of his finger in the water to gauge its temperature. It was downright frigid. *This is crazy*, he thought. *How are they even able to stand it?*

Henry backstroked several strides, and spit up water like a human geyser, his speech slurred by deep breaths and the intake of water.

"C'mon, Flatlander. The water'sh so clean you can shdrink it while shwim! Your body will adjush!"

"This isn't swimming weather, fellas," declared Flatlander plainly.

"That isn't for you to judge, young one," exclaimed Henry. "You're in our country now, Flatlander. You live by our rules. As the old Vermont saying goes, 'if there isn't ice on the surface, it's fair game.'"

"King Henry speaks true," confirmed Franklin, while attempting a lazy breaststroke. "C'mon, Flatlander. It feels better by the second."

Unconvinced, Flatlander shook his head. "I'm good."

Henry then paused from his swimming, and looked straight to Flatlander, whom had gathered distance from pool's edge.

"It's part of your tests, Flatlander. Consider this a rite of passage."

"Aye," agreed Franklin, "I've seen youngsters no taller than yer knee jump in with less fightin'."

Flatlander approached the swimming hole, tentatively. "I'll just put my feet in. It'll be nice to clean them up for a change after all this walking."

"Yer already soakin' wet from head to toe!" cried Franklin, incredulous at the newcomer's reluctance. "Ya can't get that much colder than ya probably already are! What's it matter?"

"Maybe some other time," replied Flatlander.

Henry conferred with Franklin for several seconds in a huddle, then faced him with a sudden stern expression, which seemed ridiculous to Flatlander, considering the context.

"Flatlander, I, Lord Henry of the Republic of Vermont, hereby order you to strip and join us in the water immediately. Failure to do so will result in your immediate expulsion from the republic."

There were no more outs, no more excuses. Flatlander marveled at the scenario: *he had just been ordered to disrobe into a swimming hole by the most powerful man in the land. Surely, it couldn't get any weirder. Could it?* Flatlander sighed long and deep, then reluctantly began taking off his clothing, one article at a time, in defeat. Franklin laughed in joy, as Henry clasped his wet hands together in celebration.

"Yes!" exclaimed the Humble King in joy.

"The boy's doin' it!" said Franklin in glee, as he bobbed up and down. "Never in my forty two years on this globe did I ever imagine I'd see a Flatlander swimmin' at the Potholes in May!"

"Yeah, yeah, yeah," grumbled Flatlander.

He noticed, through his smile, that Henry was watching him intently. Studying him, testing him, challenging his will. Flatlander realized that this moment was a lot bigger than three naked men swimming alone in the Vermont wilderness. This was an issue of trust, of acceptance, of understanding. Stepping outside of one's comfort zone, Flatlander reassured himself, *even if just for a minute*, would look good to these men.

A thought then occurred to him. Perhaps this area, or other swimming holes, no doubt, had been a fixture from their youth. The two men looked completely at ease while they swum, free spirits. Surely, even they, at one point, had confronted their very own fears and anxieties. Even they had to prove to themselves that they could summon up the courage. He soon realized that he had to walk in their boots in order to gain their respect, even if it seemed awkward, particularly for a man his age. *Whatever age that might be.* Henry and Franklin swam away, creating space in the water in anticipation of Flatlander's dive. They waited with glee.

"Don't panic when you hit the water. We'll be here for you," called Henry.

Disappearing behind a nearby shrub, Flatlander reappeared seconds later, stark naked and in full sprint. A couple of paces before launching himself, he slipped on a wet rock, taking a very ungraceful plunge into the icy water below. Howls of laughter were muted instantly his upon impact with the watering hole.

The shock of the freezing water numbed his body immediately. His eyes bugged out of their sockets as he tried to regain his senses. Despite its small surface area, the basin was deceptively deep, and yet his feet still struck the rocky bottom at an awkward angle. Air was already starting to leak rapidly out of his nose and mouth. Even while completely submerged, he could hear the muffled shouts and laughs from his two companions at the surface. His heart beat hard and fast, and it was a few seconds before he could properly regain use of his arms again to propel himself to the surface. He came up gasping and spitting. Although partially deafened by his clogged ears, and the sound of his own coughing, Flatlander could now distinctly make out the voices of his companions. He wiped away a trail of snot from under his nose, as his sinuses reeled from the sudden intake.

"And it looks like we made the boy a man yet!" exclaimed Franklin with a broad smile.

Henry laughed quietly to himself then swam across the basin gracefully. Lifting himself from the chilly waters, he reached into his knapsack, removed a cotton towel, and proceeded to dry himself off vigorously.

Flatlander felt a small measure of pride in his feat. He hoped that he had earned their approval and respect. After Franklin had exited the swimming hole, Flatlander followed suit, and used Henry's towel to dry off. Dangling Flatlander's soaked clothes on a branch above the fire's flame, Henry gestured with his free hand towards the flames.

"Spruce burns fast but true, and these logs look drier than the deserts of Barre," he said. "You'll smell like smoke for the remainder of the day, but you'll be nice and warm, and relatively insect-free."

Franklin laughed, as he wrung out the water from his thick, long hair. Henry came beside Flatlander, and handed him a steaming hot cup of brownish liquid.

"Chaga tea. Or *Inonotus obliquus, the monks often call it*[57]. 'Nectar of the white birches', others have named it from the deep wood[58]. It looks rather unsightly before it is grounded, Flatlander: like a dirty black fungus. Though its properties are widely lauded throughout the republic, and the men who drink it swear by its virtues. Here, drink."

Flatlander carefully sipped the steaming hot cup of tea, which scalded his lip when Henry tussled his damp hair.

"You did well. I know that wasn't the most pleasant of experiences, but I think that it's something that every Vermonter should go through at some point in their lives, young or old, man or woman. We'll dry up warm up by the fire, and eat well tonight."

[57] Chaga tea is wildly popular with the monks of Middlebury and Braintree.
[58] Slang for a remote forest.

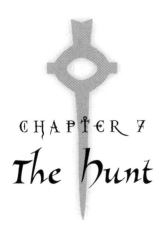

CHAPTER 7
The Hunt

"**S**UCH A PRETTY, YOUNG THING," whispered Henry softly, as he steadied an arrow at the grazing doe.

The Humble King strained in concentration. Flatlander glanced briefly at Franklin, crouched awkwardly amidst their undersized tree blind, his fingers gripped on the blind's edge, balancing his enormous weight. The wandering doe, which had been in their sights for close to five minutes, continued her grazing oblivious to the impending danger.

Then in one swift action, bowstring fully drawn, Henry released the arrow with great velocity into the animal's lower neck. The deer fled with great speed down a forest trail overgrown with bushes and weeds.

"Yes!" exclaimed Franklin, as he threw up a celebratory fist.

"Curses! Not quite the shot that I wanted. Yet, twenty plus years of pushing papers and little rust to show," bragged Henry, as he smiled broadly in Flatlander's direction. Flatlander, clearly disturbed by what he saw, gulped heavily.

Henry took notice of his new friend's reaction. "Oh, come now, Flatlander, I thought that you'd have a stronger stomach than *that*."

"Perhaps ya can pick a few berries on the way back!" laughed Franklin, as he mimicked a person picking at invisible berries. "But we wouldn't wanna accidentally prick Flatlander's finger!"

"It just seems cruel," retorted Flatlander.

"This is a cruel world in which we live in. It would be crueler if we slept hungry for another day."

Henry slung the bow on his shoulder, roughly, and helped Flatlander to his feet.

Flatlander gazed off in the distance to where the doe had run off. "Did you kill it?"

Henry looked at him with great befuddlement. "Did you see where I hit it? The arrow went straight through its neck. I'd be surprised if the creature made it a mile."

"*A mile?*" yelped Flatlander. It pained him to think of the animal running that type of distance, a bloody arrow protruding from its neck. "How would it make it that far?"

"Deer are resilient creatures," answered Henry, as he started down the rungs of the tree blind. Flatlander followed. "They need to be. Every living thing in the forest wants to eat them, including Franklin and I."

"We'll be makin' quite a few venison steaks tonight, lord!" exclaimed Franklin excitedly, as he descended the blind's ladder quite clumsily after the two.

Flatlander stood still, and looked out once more to the path where the deer had run. Branches and twigs still fluttered in the air from its hastened departure.

"I just don't get it," said Flatlander. "What makes you want to kill? You have fruits, vegetables, grain."

"You will some day know why, Flatlander," replied Henry with certainty. "This is simply the Vermont way. It's a matter of necessity. Living off the land isn't limited to gathering, farming and fishing. We use anything that we can get. Meat contains much-needed protein. Since the dawn of humanity, mankind has eaten animals. Unlike the privileged, fat people of the Old Country, we don't have unlimited resources at our disposal. We don't get to be as discretionary in our tastes. I'd like to think of us as opportunists."

Something that Henry had mentioned caught his attention. "What's this about fat people from the Old Country?"

Henry shook his head and sighed. "Your memory doesn't serve you properly, but to put it simply; it has to be pointed out to you that the people from your region enjoy the fruits of the land, without so much as getting their hands dirty. Well, to be frank, us Vermonters get our hands dirty. Always have and always will."

Henry extended his bow to Flatlander, who accepted the weapon with profound distaste.

"Flatlander, I'm requesting you take the next shot today."

He shot the Humble King a pained look. "But I've never shot a bow."

"It matters not."

"My eyesight is poor."

Henry dismissed the notion flippantly with the wave of his hand. "Excuses are the currency of the meek."

"What's that suppose to mean?"

"Exactly how it sounds." Henry gestured for Flatlander to follow him through the narrow forest trail. "Come with me. We have more game to find. Watch Franklin track this doe. He's quite good."

Franklin had already started down the path of the deer, pausing intermittently to glance for any signs of the animal on the forest floor. Flatlander took a deep breath. He felt weak. *Not my cup of tea. Not in my memory, and more so, not in my heart.* The hunters embarked downward the twisting trail of blood and broken weeds, and one hunter, in particular, with a very heavy set of legs. Blood spots and scattered footprints laid out an obvious path through weeds and brush. It wasn't until a full two miles later that they found the doe's lifeless, black-eyed carcass.

From their vantage point on the ground, the turkey loomed larger than expected. Henry had made the executive decision to start Flatlander out with 'smaller game', though the turkey appeared anything but. Henry could attest to the lack of a turkey's intelligence, elaborating: 'Flighty, yes. But intelligent, heavens no.' He then proceeded to tell a story of how he had once seen a turkey chase a warden's daughter. According to Henry, he hadn't seen a swifter death 'since the immediate aftermath of the Stony Mahoney's eighth studio album, 'Flood of the Quarry[59].'

The three hunters worked in silence, turning to a series of gestures to communicate with one another. Turkeys, as Flatlander had come to find out, were easily spooked. As he shifted his weight gingerly on the forest floor, Henry looked at him stern-faced, and immediately gave a halting gesture with his palm facing outward. After recognizing the turkey hadn't taken any notice of the three hunters crouched behind the bushes, Henry gave the thumbs up.

Flatlander drew back the bowstring. The action was tougher than it had looked. Despite the fact that he had taken a few warm up shots while Henry and Franklin gruesomely dressed down the doe, he couldn't quite find the fluid motion that he had hoped for. After trembling for several seconds, bowstring taut, Flatlander then unleashed the sharpened arrow upon his prey.

[59] A generally agreed-upon low point from the popular folk band.

The strike was devastating. Although he missed the preferred head or neck shot, the arrow struck the turkey squarely on its side. Feathers exploded from the bird's body, which sent the animal thrashing wildly to the forest floor, squawking loud and horribly.

"Excellent!" exclaimed Henry as he thumped a hand into the earth.

"He's a pro, alright!" said Franklin.

After an agonizing twenty seconds of watching the bird squirm helplessly on the ground, Flatlander was relieved to see the turkey finally succumb to its mortal wound. The forest seemed to go quiet afterwards.

"That was tough to watch," muttered Flatlander, finally, his eyes fixated on the ground. His face had paled and his stomach worked itself into a tight knot.

Henry patted him softly on the shoulder. "Be thankful. I once saw a turkey struggle for nearly five minutes from a similar shot. We forgot our knife and didn't want to approach for fear of getting cut by its talons. Turkeys can inflict more damage on a person than one would think. You suffered but little. That turkey, on the other hand…"

Henry faltered for words and shook his head.

"Thanks, that's so reassuring," remarked Flatlander.

Throwing Henry's bow to the ground, he sunk his head into the fold of his arm. *The swimming hole was one thing*, thought Flatlander. *Killing innocent animals seemed to take things to an entirely new level.*

"I'm happy to be of service," quipped Henry, as he gathered his fallen bow, and approached the fallen animal with Franklin. Reluctantly, Flatlander followed.

"Yer a natural, boy!" said Franklin as he drew the bloodied arrow from the turkey's corpse with a rough yank. "Need to take ya with me on more huntin' trips from now on! It's hard fer this large fella to hide, ya know?"

"I appreciate the offer, Franklin, but something tells me that I'll find alternatives for leisure," replied Flatlander, dryly.

"Leisure? Who said anythin' bout leisure?" asked Franklin, confused. "We're eatin' this thing, whether ya want to or not. More to go round if ya don't."

Henry shook his head in disappointment, as he approached the fallen bird. "I just hope that the meat isn't spoiled. Struggling animals don't make the best dinners. The stress taints their meat."

"Ay," replied Franklin.

"It is also worth noting, Flatlander, that it is customary in Vermont for a father to lend his venison to his daughter's suitor or else bad luck may befell them[60]," said Henry with a smile. "Rest assured, however, I have no such intentions with you. Jess is much too young."

"He speaks truth," confirmed Franklin, with a chuckle.

Henry cast a wary eye on the surrounding wood. "Let's make haste. Our venison and turkey await us, and I don't want to test the other animals' patience of the forest any longer than I have to. Many a wildcat, bear and wolf[61] lie await in this forest hungry, and they could be closer than we'd like to believe," said Henry. He turned to Flatlander, and patted him on the arm. "Take compliments whenever you can. In my day and age, they come more seldom than the Underhill sun[62]."

And before he knew it was over, Flatlander had completed his first hunt. In all truth, it had been bittersweet. Both kills of the day had disturbed him immensely. The bloody trail, the arrow piercing the cute doe's neck, the feathers, the thrashing body of the turkey; the sheer devastation of it all made Flatlander's head spin. But he tried to put the day within its proper context. *This is who they are, and this is what they do.*

"Yer kill, yer lift," said Franklin as he held the turkey out by the neck for Flatlander to grab.

As he wrestled the turkey from Franklin's grip, two things struck him: the sheer weight of the animal, and the fact that the

---

[60] This ritual was practiced mostly in the countryside of Southern and Central Vermont.

[61] Wolves migrated back eastward after the dissolution of the Old Country.

[62] A reference to a Vermont town literally sinking into the earth between two cliffs.

bird still felt warm in his hands. Holding it at an awkward angle, the turkey swung back and forth like a pendulum. He cringed each time a claw or feather brushed against him inadvertently, much to Franklin and Henry's delight.

And oddly enough, the thing that tugged on Flatlander's mind the most was something that Henry had referenced during the deer hunt; what of *the Old Country and its unlimited resources*? *What was that supposed to mean*? Flatlander thought this question over in his head, ignoring the joint laughter from his companions. *There's a lot about my homeland that I need to know.*

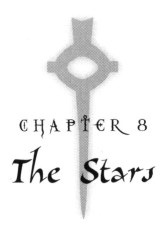

CHAPTER 8
The Stars

T WAS A CLEAR, CRISP early June night in the city of Montpelier. Clouds of fertilizer dust drifted from the countryside into the city streets, yet it was not wholly an unpleasant smell to Flatlander. Rather, he noticed, it reminded him of an aged cheese. Close to the farmlands, the city of Montpelier absorbed the dried pasture mists like a sponge. A faint, brownish haze coiled in and out of the city streets, staining the horizon. Henry assured Flatlander that the dust would settle soon after nightfall.

Invited to Henry's rooftop drink to stargaze, Flatlander felt obliged to partake. The Humble King had recently brought a bottle of red wine, fresh from the vineyards of Huntington, a fact that he couldn't stop bringing up. Drained by the endless wave of paperwork that had consumed her for weeks, Ellen also gleefully agreed to join them. As Flatlander came upon the open rooftop, he noticed Henry and Ellen sprawled out among long chairs looking up to the sky. Two lit lanterns hung from stand-alone hangers at their sides. A large telescope rested above Henry's chair, held in place by a fragile, wooden tripod. In between them sat a third empty chair, presumably for him. Three full glasses of wine lay beside each of the three chairs on small tables.

"Flatlander, the stars are bright tonight! This is a real treat!" called Henry.

"Wine and stargazing don't mix," quipped Flatlander.

"On the contrary, they seem perfectly suited to one another," retorted Henry, as he shifted the focus of his giant, white telescope, and peered intently through its lens.

"Sit down and shut up, Flatlander," said Ellen playfully.

Henry continued gazing through the giant telescope, while mindlessly plucking at a package of wild blueberries.

"It's not too often that you get such a pleasant, clear night like this. No clouds, no worries. The manure has settled. A rare occasion for the three of us to talk and relax."

Flatlander scanned the rooftop, a small stone patio, wedged between two gables. "How have I never seen or heard about this part of the house?"

Henry shrugged nonchalant. "You never asked."

Flatlander sighed, and took his seat between the two. As he sipped his wine, Flatlander rested deeply into the broken-in lawn seat. Henry smiled and a winked at him, before resuming his stargazing. As he looked up, Flatlander was amazed at the clarity of the night sky. Millions and millions of stars sparkled, as the rising moon lower on the horizon enveloped the darkened hillsides of East Montpelier.

Henry nudged the telescope in Flatlander's direction. "You want to try?"

Positioning his body below the eyepiece, he gazed through the telescope, and the sight that appeared before him left him breathless. No matter which area he focused on, the endless depth of space came into greater focus. The stars grew in color and size, pulsating dots of red and blue. Some looked as if they were moving, some like they were playing tricks with his eyes.

A minute of silence passed between the three, before Ellen took a tentative sip from her wine and cleared her throat.

"Legend has it that the stars are harder to see from much of the Old Country. Too much light pollution and smog."

Flatlander frowned, as he toggled the telescope's focus. "Your tales from the Old Country keep getting worse and worse. Who told you that that one?"

"My grand uncle, Robert," replied Ellen. "He worked as a ship hand, and had been down the old Champlain Canal[63] once or twice for business, transporting rugs. Uncle Bob was one of a handful of men from the republic who had been there and back, and among other things, told me that he had a hard time seeing any of the stars while he was down there."

"Sounds crazy to me," replied Flatlander. "Why would it be so much harder to see the stars?"

"I believe it," agreed Henry, as he shuffled slightly in his chair. "Flatlander, here in Vermont, they tell a parable called "Broke as Night" or "Broken Night." I know this may sound redundant, as your memory is short, but do you recall ever hearing that name?"

Flatlander's blank expression told Henry all that he needed to know, as the Humble King sighed.

"Well, it's an interesting tale. The gist of it is this: a successful businessman reaches the pinnacle of his career by attaining and selling resources that surround him, one by one. Trees. Rocks. Animals. Crops. Diamonds. You name it. Soon every aspect of

---

[63] A sixty-mile, narrow stretch of water that connects the southern end of Lake Champlain to the Hudson River in New York.

his life has a price tag and is summarily sold. As such, he also begins to sell qualities of himself, things that make up his being, like empathy, joy, humility, generosity. He gets *so* greedy, in fact, that he wants to harness the very stars themselves, and turn them for profit. Yet, one by one they fade behind a screen of smog from his factories, which he has now built for his business, and they are also drowned out by the lights from the large metropolis that he himself helped build. He ends up selling all of his remaining human qualities to an ancient, omnipotent being, in an attempt to regain sight of the stars, in hopes that he can harness and sell them too. But upon seeing the stars once more, they bear no impact on him in any meaningful way… for he has sold the very emotions which had him yearning for them in the first place."

Flatlander peered up at the sky. Some of the stars continued to pulsate, while some appeared to move at a snail's pace across the vast spectrum of the universe. The sensation was slightly dizzying.

Henry continued quietly. "Somewhat contrived, I know. Not to mention scientifically impossible, like many tales. But the message is strong. You see, without his humanity, the stars are just glittery dots on a pitch-black canvas. Free of reverence, free of context. Quite profound, I think. Isn't it?"

Flatlander lay in silence, as he let the moral of the story sink in, and realized the lesson spoke volumes. He had to admit, if he had observed one thing of Vermont's culture during his stay, and one thing only, it was that there was a certain value, *a certain emphasis*, on the natural world and one's humanity. How deeply the two were intertwined, and how one could easily affect the other. He thought back to Henry catching Menche trying to steal his chickens. He remembered the sheer joy of Henry and Franklin splashing around in the water hole. He even remembered Franklin bursting into joy when he, rather clumsily, removed the sword from the stump. Flatlander had begun to understand some of the roots of Vermont culture, and couldn't help but feel that these were important values to live by. Simple values, he reflected; yet vastly important, nonetheless.

Despite the oddities in this land, and the difficulties in adjusting to this new life, there had been a creeping sense of familiarity overcoming Flatlander for days. There was no rational explanation for it, he realized. His breathing had become easier. His demeanor had eased up. No more did he dread the dawn of the next day, as he had done so throughout his first few weeks in the republic. He had simply become more comfortable with the idea of staying put in the republic. He was beginning to appreciate Vermont's quirks, though the very notion terrified him.

"I'm beginning to like it here," admitted Flatlander spontaneously. Even in the dim lantern light, he could discern Henry's smile and Ellen's raised eyebrow. "And it may sound strange, but I sometimes feel like this has been my true home all along. Dummerston besides."

Ellen chuckled and turned to Flatlander, floored. "Even with all of our eccentricities, Flatlander? I don't believe it."

"I like the fact that it's weird," answered Flatlander plainly. "It's an odd land, but also a beautiful land, and easy to love. Same goes for its people."

Henry, smiling from ear to ear, nodded and voiced his agreement in a low voice. "You're beginning to see the fruits of our sacred republic, Flatlander, and why we love it so. We protect it fiercely, as a mother bear protects her cubs from a wandering stranger, though she knows not his true intentions. For her trust has been violated for thousands of years, in a cycle of torment and misfortune, and she knows not that all men bring with them ill will."

"Lord Henry, I couldn't have said it better," agreed Ellen, as she gulped a large portion of her wine and turned to Flatlander in earnest. "We're happy that you appreciate Vermont, Flatlander."

Looking through the eyepiece of Henry's telescope, Flatlander focused on one of the constellations, which he later came to find out was the Little Dipper, and imagined himself floating through the night sky, weightless and swift, rocketing through the vast emptiness of space. Whizzing past stars and nebulas, they shifted and rotated, ever so slightly, barely noticeable through his lucid, tunnel-like vision. Then a cool breeze blew through his hair, and the now-faint smell of manure met his nostrils, gently reminding him that he was, indeed, still sitting atop a roof-side patio in Montpelier, Vermont. Relishing the wine's tart aftertaste, he waited until the wind died down, and his brief, but lively dream, fully departed.

CHAPTER 9

Superpac

T HE STATEHOUSE'S HIDDEN COUNCIL CHAMBERS were a well-guarded secret to the press and public alike. Constructed beneath the statehouse itself, it was designed to be one of the most important units available to the government in the event of an emergency. The room itself was rectangular and made of heavy stone, quarried from the deepest chutes of Barre. Windowless, any occupants who wanted to see properly had to make sure to light several lanterns aligning the walls, as well as several large candles on the table.

One of the most unique and distinguishable features of the room, however, was a small brook diverted from the waters of the Winooski River, which actually ran its course through a corner of the room. The exposed surface of the brook was very narrow, no more than a dozen square feet in total. A large net rested nearby on the stone floor. According to legend, the builders of the room wanted a place where the leaders could sustain themselves for days or weeks, if need be. The brook would provide, in theory, an endless amount of freshwater and fish if and when times ever grew desperate enough. Henry sometimes remarked he hoped such a day would never come.

On this day, the 24th of June, the council convened for an emergency meeting at the prompting of Sir Trombley of Middlebury. Details concerning the nature of such a meeting were scant, but Trombley was well respected by Henry and the other lords alike for his discretion, and he trusted that his fellow lord took such matters seriously.

At one end of the table, sat the formidable Yuro, Lord of Burlington. Yuro had been minted Lord of Burlington two autumns ago. The title of Lord of the Queen City, the largest city in the republic, was among the highest honors in the republic. His long, dark curly hair flew wildly underneath a studded, jeweled crown. An elaborately decorated garb of purple, kingly robes, gold buttons, and shiny, red rubies covered the man head to toe. Pale and thin, he was noticeably shy in his demeanor. His eyebrows were thick but handsome, exaggerated within the darkened council chamber.

Yuro was the last to acknowledge Flatlander prior to the meeting; his eyes studied the stone floor more than Flatlander's face. Henry sat at the other head of the table with Ellen to his right and Flatlander directly to his left. Lord Trombley of Middlebury, Lord Andreas of White River, and Lord Sarmus of St. Albans also sat in nervous anticipation.

As pleasantries neared an end, Lord Trombley spoke. "I would like permission from the council to commence this emergency meeting. I hope that I have not inconvenienced you all too much, but we have a pressing matter to discuss."

Henry cleared his throat. "Before we begin, and with all of your blessings, of course, I would like to introduce the newest member of our emergency council, Flatlander."

Flatlander heard a couple of soft grumblings from Andreas and Sarmus, but nobody voiced an objection. Yuro gave him a courteous nod as his crown slipped precariously lopsided upon his forehead.

"Welcome, Flatlander, your reputation precedes you," said Yuro.

Although his compliment appeared genuine, Andreas and Sarmus chuckled softly in amusement. Flatlander even thought that he heard Andreas murmur something to the effect of *'it sure does'*.

Flatlander nodded. "Thanks, it's an honor."

Wish I could tell those guys how I really feel about them.

Lord Trombley placed a large stack of paper on the table. "I welcome you too, Flatlander. It's not often that we hear an outsider's perspective on matters of such concern. Your methods are...unique."

Flatlander nodded silently in gratitude.

Trombley then placed his hands on the stack of papers, and nodded. "Very well, I shall begin without further ado. There is a peril that's gripping at the heart of Burlington and surrounding communities that is reaching a pitch in recent weeks. We've known it by name for a few years now, but it's been steadily rising, in both quantity and demand, to now staggering levels. And although we have long suspected its problematic nature, I'm afraid that this intervention cannot wait any further."

Lord Sarmus fidgeted uncomfortably in his chair. "Tell us, Trombley!"

"Alright," replied Trombley. "Superpac usage in the Queen City is reaching epidemic levels."

Henry leaned forward, his familiarity with the drug well noted. "How do you know this?"

"Investigators and inside sources alike have confirmed it," said Trombley, as he thumbed through the papers like a deck of cards. "We have reason to believe that a huge supply is reaching our people daily. We need to disrupt the supply chain before superpac gets loose to the rest of Vermont if it hasn't already. There have only been a few reports of the substance found or suspected outside of Chittenden County[64], yet even those cases will grow enormously if we don't do something soon. We need to contain it and eliminate it."

"How do you eliminate an entire supply of a drug? It would take years," said Ellen. She had a look of concern to match Henry's.

"Well, that's why we're calling this meeting in the first place," replied Trombley, swiftly. "To consider our options."

"What's superpac?" asked Flatlander. He had heard the word referenced before.

Lord Andreas smiled thinly. "The new member may require some lessons beforehand if he wishes to partake in finding a solution, Lord Henry. Please allow me to field the Flatlander's question. Do you ever wish you were really, really good at something in your life, Flatlander? Wreaking havoc, besides..."

Flatlander ignored Andreas's below-the-belt comment. "Of course."

Andreas stroked his white, mink coat, whimsically. "Like what?"

"I wish that I could wield my sword better. Franklin says that I've improved, but I always feel clumsy with the thing."

"Flatlanders wieldin' swords, remind me to stay in the house at night," interrupted Sarmus. Everyone at the table, including Henry and Ellen, laughed. Flatlander frowned in disapproval.

---

[64] The county containing Burlington and surrounding towns and cities.

"Alright, alright, go easy on the lad, Sarmus," replied Andreas, as he toyed with the feather of his quail pen. "Well, just imagine yourself taking a drug that instantly made you one of the best swordsmen alive on the planet," Andreas paused then snapped his fingers, "in literally an instant."

Flatlander smiled nervously. "How would work? A drug that makes people better swordsmen?"

"No, Flatlander," replied Henry, offering graciously, "a drug that gives one certain advantages at virtually anything and everything in this world. A drug that lets one reap the victories in life without the hard work."

"I'm confused," said Flatlander, dumbfounded. The idea of a supernatural drug sounded farfetched and silly, but judging by the intense concern of the council members, it was anything but. Uncomfortable glances were exchanged from across the table. "How can that be?"

"There are some well-guarded secrets in this land," replied Ellen, as she brushed her hair back and looked to Trombley to help clarify.

Trombley, accustomed to such cues, did his best to oblige. "Unknown, yes, and rarely seen in use. The people taking this drug, Flatlander: it's like a secret society. They know that their actions essentially amount to a serious form of cheating, and they also know that Vermonters frown highly upon such a thing. It's what you would call 'taboo' in our society. The drug is often done alone, rarely in the company of others. Nor is it spoken of much, besides that of the lone transaction between dealer and buyer."

"But I don't get it," said Flatlander, "I mean, so what if I guy becomes a better swordsmen? So be it. Maybe it'll make him happy, and maybe, just maybe, he saves a few lives as a result, right? Kill a few bad guys in the process? I mean no harm, no foul."

"If only it were that easy," replied Trombley, with a small sigh. "Flatlander, you must be forgetting about human nature. While the drug could be a godsend for purely noble causes in this land, and oh, what a temptation that would be, most of what we've been told from our investigators would indicate the complete opposite. In short, people, *and even animals*, are using superpac in bad form, for selfish, unnatural and destructive reasons."

"Animals?"

Trombley paused, then flipped through the thick document on the table, stopping at a bookmarked page. "It was reported that a batch of stashed superpac in the woods was accidentally consumed by a herd of deer in Williston. Small traces of residue were found in a large paper bag. No more than an hour later, a family of black bears was found trampled to death in the woods."

Flatlander raised an eyebrow. "Your point..."

Trombley paused and swallowed. "Our investigation concluded that it was the *deer* that killed these bears."

"*What?*" Flatlander said. He was tempted to laugh, but thought better of it. "Have you also considered your investigators might be complete quacks?"

"Flatlander," said Henry with a look of admonishment.

Trombley shook his head. "The monks and wardens, alike, say the same. They found hoof marks all over the bodies. Hundreds. In fact, they were trampled so violently that they were near unrecognizable."

Flatlander shrugged. "So? Good for the deer. For just once, the cycle gets broken and the deer have their day in the sun."

The lords, clearly not amused by his assessment, shuffled in their seats. "Don't you get it, you twit?" exclaimed Lord Andreas, his eyes full of rage. "Even for a thick-headed Flatlander, you must truly have cotton for brains!"

"Lord Andreas," gasped Henry.

"Oh, c'mon. Don't 'Lord Andreas' me, King Henry! Don't you see, you fool? It changes the way things are *supposed to be*. You can't be cheating through life like it's for nothing. What good is it for the people who live their lives naturally? What of *their* morale? *Their* victories? If we tell our children that hard work will pay off for them all these years, and it doesn't, should we suggest a daily dose of superpac? Will that suffice? What good does *that* do for our future? What if the superpac runs out? How useless will they be then, this republic, full of future generations who don't know the meaning of honesty and hard work? C'mon, Flatlander. Use your brain."

"Flatlander, please excuse Lord Andreas's choice words, he has devoted much of his time to this investigation as of late, but he does have some points on the matter," interjected Trombley. He eyed the thick report. "This drug flips the very fundamental law of nature on its head, the very core of reality as we know it. Nothing will be predictable any longer. Nothing will be sacred. Any object of desire can be attained with the simple act of ingesting a baggie worth of superpac. It may not seem harmful to you right now sitting here in the protection of the statehouse, but when you see this drug in action on the streets, you and everyone else will feel cheated. Duped. And chances are, you'll only realize that you were duped in hindsight. The drug is creating a growing flood of deception throughout the county, but has peaked in and around Burlington. It's a terrible trend for a city which has such a strong sense of pride."

Though stung by Andreas's blunt words, Flatlander tried to remain focused on the issue at hand. If the reports were true, and this mysterious drug was giving unnatural advantages to its users, the possibilities were endless. Yuro, who had kept silent throughout the meeting, finally spoke, though timidly.

"We need to put an end to this."

"Very well. Then there's only one thing that must be done," declared Henry, his face strong with fervor. "We will aggressively investigate this superpac, pursue its sources, and cut them off like the poisoned tendrils they are. If a man should be a bad fisherman, then he needs to be a bad fisherman and win his victories through heartache and perseverance. If a man is a bad chef; then let him cook bad food. If a bear pursues a deer, then that deer should become the rightful meal of its pursuer! I will not have a city overrun by charlatans, liars and rogues. The war on superpac is starting now. Say 'ay' if you agree."

The six members emphatically replied "ay" in turn, the shouts echoing loudly throughout the chamber's stones walls. Flatlander stood and stretched, nodding politely as the lords filed out of the room in a single file. Afterwards, Henry approached Flatlander from the side. Ellen hesitated, looking like she wanted to mull things over with Henry, but after gauging Henry's look; she too followed the lords out in a hurry. Only Henry and Flatlander remained. The Humble King faced Flatlander directly, his look of annoyance evident for the new council member to see.

"I didn't want to embarrass you at the table by bickering, but this is a bigger problem than you think. I need you to be sharp for me on this, Flatlander. We're not just fighting a drug here; we're fighting the woes of human nature. We need to be ready in the morning for our trip to Burlington." Then, as if reminding himself, Henry said, "And one more thing- at our next meeting, please don't do so much talking. It would do you good."

It was the deepest sleep that Flatlander had received in weeks. Between the sounds of the Old North End, the haunting in Dummerston, and most recently, the sharp words from the lords at the emergency council, Flatlander was relieved to find his bed made nice and proper by Gabby. It wasn't long after his head hit the pillow that he found himself transported to another world, free of the northern wood.

He dreamt of a clear and sunny day, while sitting on a bench on a boardwalk overlooking a large body of water. Out in the distance, a jetty of stones bent to the left, cradling a calm bay of several acres in its protective barrier. Miles beyond the rock jetty, Flatlander barely discerned a thin strip of land just beyond the horizon. Though the sun stung his eyes, he felt neither pain, nor a lost sense of vision. The pungent smell of sea salt and a faint coconut scent filled his nostrils, and though the beach was empty, he could hear what sounded like groups of people laughing and playing.

To his right sat a dog. Medium sized with well-defined muscles, it sat facing outward to the sea, huddled closely to his legs. The white, spider-webbed cataracts plaguing the center of the canine's eyes were still in their infancies. The dog was shiny and black, with a brown underside on both its belly and face. Its bulging eyes and floppy ears were disproportionately large for its head, and it turned to him slowly yawning long and hard. Feeling an overwhelming sense of comfort and contentment, Flatlander lightly stroked the top of its head, and in turn, the canine leaned heavily against his legs.

This seemed to go on for some time, him and this affectionate dog, just sitting there on the bench enjoying the sea breeze. Further along the boardwalk, a curious seagull poked at a bare paper plate, a string of what looked like melted cheese plastered on its edge. Flatlander looked back to the dog at his side, which was now staring straight through him with two tremendously cute brown eyes. Something about the way the dog looked at him, something about its expression, seemed to exude human qualities, human emotions. But despite this strange observation, Flatlander felt neither threatened nor disturbed by such a sight; but instead, a deep sense of companionship and love. Only the subsequent breeze diverted the animal's attention, as it stared with Flatlander out to the ocean once more, its ears flopping lazily in the wind.

The sound of a dropped glass downstairs stirred him awake, followed by the mournful groan of Menche. Though disappointed that this pleasant dream had ended, Flatlander turned on his side, glowing at what he had just experienced. *This was more than just a dream*, he thought, *this had to be another memory. I once had a dog. Name besides, I once had a dog.*

It was barely past noon on Saturday and Church Street of Burlington was bustling. Up and down the cobblestone stretch, food vendors, buskers, and pedestrians alike walked about. It was a hot summer day with temperatures pushing into the low 90's. Many on the street wore light cloth shirts and tunics. Some were bare-chested. Lamb Gyros steamed from a nearby grill, while Franklin made the whole group wait while he purchased one. In all of the time in which Flatlander had spent in Vermont he had yet to see anything quite like it. His senses were near overwhelmed within the sounds and smells of Vermont's largest city.

The party garnered a good deal of attention from many folks on the street. Henry's presence often was met with a mixture of friendly nods and waves, yet when one factored in the dubious reputations of Flatlander, they also quickly became a beacon for negative attention. The fiasco of Lowell, compounded with Shay Bromage's damning articles, Henry noted as they walked, would take some time for the public to forget. Their priority at the moment, however, was finding superpac.

"It's a tricky thing, Flatlander. We've known of the drug's existence for a few years after initially dismissing it as heresy. Yet I don't heed the warning lightly. Say what you will about the lords of the council. They can be power-hungry, envious, and petty, except Trombley perhaps, yet they are just as concerned for our republic as I."

Flatlander shook his head. "And yet you keep them all on the emergency council?"

Henry turned and chuckled. "Is that how you see it, then? I surround myself with wasps waiting to turn on me? You underestimate me, Flatlander. For every political relationship, there is a hand waiting to be played just out of reach."

Ellen cleared her throat from Flatlander's side. "Trombley is mart and has high aspirations. He's also well connected with the Monks of Middlebury. But he knows that he can't possibly attain the highest office in Vermont. He has too little charisma, and prefers burying himself in books rather than speaking to the general public. We appease him by providing him with ample work and create enough committees to keep him occupied and involved."

"Sarmus is a loose cannon," added Henry, thoughtfully. "He's spent the past twenty years trying to redeem his reputation after being caught stealing a wagon full of maple syrup from a transfer line at the St. Albans/Georgia border. One thing that you'll learn quickly here in Vermont is that you can tease a man endlessly, pester his family, or sell him out to the press, but may Braintree save your soul if you steal another man's syrup. Sarmus found *that* out the hard way."

Flatlander narrowly avoided colliding with an elderly couple.

"Sarmus stole syrup? He always struck me as a little rough around the edges."

Henry nodded. "Made a living of it, apparently, for quite some time. And this one time, he had stolen 5000 pounds of it. He spent several years in prison and developed quite a mean streak in him. I keep Sarmus at more than an arm's length, for he'll bite off the whole thing off if given a chance."

Ellen dismissed the notion with the wave of her hand. "Lord Henry and I disagree on the matter. He's mostly bark, no bite." Ellen laughed. "As for Andreas, well, Andreas is another story."

Henry nodded. "Yes indeed. Another story entirely. But we neither have the time nor patience for such a tale."

As they walked past a relatively busy corner of town, Flatlander noticed a pair of teens taking turns dancing while a group of peers around them clapped in rhythm. A few shoppers had gathered around to watch. One of the teens performed a series of remarkable acrobatics, spinning rapidly on his head like a top, somersaulting to and fro. He finished his routine with a dramatic front flip into a full split much to the crowd's delight. His fellow dancers went wild, clapping and screeching in adoration.

All of this hadn't gone unnoticed by Franklin. The northerner shoved his way through the crowd, making his way towards the skinny, blond haired dancer wearing a brown beanie. Flatlander and company followed closely behind.

"Some fancy moves ya got there, lad," said Franklin.

The dancer, his shirt soaked in sweat, adjusted his beanie hat. "Umm, thanks, sir."

His clothes were tattered and frayed.

"I wish I had moves like that," said Franklin, as he then inched closer to the dancer. "But with a big frame like mine here, don't think I could last twenty breaths."

"I'm not sure what you mean by that..." was all the teenager could utter, as he backed away.

Franklin was too quick, however. He grabbed the teen by the collar, as the dance group and assembled crowd dispersed in a panic. With both hands, Franklin then lifted the boy a full two feet off the ground.

"Franklin, no!" said Henry. "Put him down!"

"Gimme the drugs, kid! Gimme the drugs!" said Franklin, ignoring the commands of his lord.

"Drugs?" the young teen asked in fright, as he was shook like a ragdoll. His hat fell to the ground, his hair becoming more disheveled with each shake. "Mister, I have no idea what ya mean!"

"Ya take me fer a fool then?"

Henry wrapped an arm around Franklin's arm. "Franklin, let him go! I *command* you to let him go!"

The northerner released his grip, as the frightened dancer scurried off into a crowd of shoppers on the opposite side of Church Street.

Henry's breathed heavily, as his gaze followed the frightened boy. "I've been seeing that chap dance like that for some time now. He's good. *Very* good. *Naturally* good, some might say. It's highly doubtful that he uses superpac." The Humble King paused as he shot his bodyguard a stern look. "Franklin, I beg you, we can't just go around roughing up anyone that we suspect on the street. We need to be clever about this. Subtle."

Franklin looked to the ground. "Sorry."

Henry unwrinkled his light grey robe. "It's quite alright, Franklin, although I'm sure that our little blonde dancer may have nightmares for weeks to come."

"How ya know he wasn't usin' that pac stuff, sir?" said Menche at Henry's side. "He did have some nice moves, if ya asks me."

"I guess that we'll never know for sure, and therein lies one of the toughest parts about finding superpac. We're playing a guessing game, completely at the mercy of the Gods themselves," said Henry with an audible sigh. "I think you now all see the difficulty that lays ahead in our quest."

As the party wandered around town for another hour looking for suspects, they decided to take a break and get something to eat. They had stopped several pedestrians for questioning, talked to some of the storeowners and shopkeepers about what they had seen in recent weeks, and intensely studied a group of young men loitering in front of "Maury's Meat Market." But loitering appeared to be their only crime, and nothing else. Thus far, the investigation proved fruitless.

As they sat themselves at a table outside Fatty Dumplings, a restaurant specializing in fried cuisine, Flatlander felt compelled to share his latest dream regarding his dog. He told them about the sun, and the ocean, and how his dog looked so human-like in its expression. Ellen, Franklin, and even Menche paid close attention, yet it was obvious that Henry's gaze wandered up and down the stretch of Church Street.

A juggler soon took up a nearby residence near to where they sat, setting up a low-mounted barrier of retractable fencing. He removed several pins, balls, and hoops from a large, black bag. Dressed like a jester, he wore a red and white polka dot one-piece suit. A white, heavy powder covered the juggler's face, with several odd, swirling stars and trees drawn on his cheeks and forehead. Henry, captivated by the presence of the street performer, had positioned his chair and body so that he faced the juggler with full attention.

Henry turned to Flatlander with a boyish grin. "Flatlander, this man is amazing. You have to see him."

"Have you been listening to *anything* that I've said?" cried Flatlander.

Of all his companions, Flatlander had hoped Henry would be the most helpful and encouraging.

"Yes, of course. You had a dream last night…" muttered Henry, as an unfocused gaze washed over his face.

"It was more than just a dream. It was a *memory*," countered Flatlander. "I'm sure of it."

"Dreams. Memories. It makes no difference. In the end, we're all dreams and memories to somebody," said Henry distantly.

It was no use, though Flatlander, as he sighed in frustration. Henry's attention was now purely fixated on the juggler. The man began his routine, juggling three and four pins with ease, as the crowd clapped and giggled with each successive act. He spun twice in mid-juggle with five pins, and caught them seamlessly.

"How's he do that?" exclaimed Menche, perplexed. "Some magic, I think."

Henry's eyes remain locked on the juggler. "He's good, Menche. The best in the business, without a doubt. I've seen him here before during a trip with Jess a several years ago. They call him Ertle. He performs all around the republic."

Ertle then juggled every object that he had brought, including a few nearby chairs, which he had borrowed from Fatty Dumplings. A crowd of several dozen or more residents stopped to watch. Menche got up from his seat, and stood behind Ertle's retractable fencing, completely entranced by the show. At the climax of the performance, Ertle had climbed a simple ladder in the middle of Church Street with no supports. While he stood atop, Ertle lit several of the pins on fire and began juggling them flawlessly. The audience swooned with delight and after half a minute of the impressive display, Ertle descended his ladder and took a deep bow. Flatlander's party, like the entire crowd around them, stood up to give Ertle a standing ovation. Adoring whistles and applause rung out amongst the fans. Ertle beamed with pride, and took several more deep bows in the process.

Then from the corner of the crowd, another man entered the ring where Ertle stood. He was dressed in similar garb, yet he wore blue and black stripes, and on his nose, he wore a dark yellow beak that protruded several inches. Taller and thinner than Ertle, his thin black boots were gleamed clean with polish.

Ertle, visibly upset, pointed an accusatory finger at the intruder. "Stop stealing the show, Alonso! Leave me be!"

Alonso then shot Ertle a look of pure mockery. "Afraid that I'll show you up?"

"Never," replied Ertle in sheer contempt.

"Too late for that," answered Alonso.

The crowd laughed. *How clever. A live, improvised show for the unsuspecting audience,* thought Flatlander. Alonso closed the distance between the two, and the two circled around one another like a pair of gladiators.

Alonso began picking up several of Ertle's juggled objects from the ground. In turn, Ertle grabbed the items one at a time from Alonso's clutches. This continued until Ertle's arms were near bursting full of all of the hoops, pins, and balls that he had used in his act. He wobbled slightly, and then, as elegantly as ever, Alonso removed a ball from near the bottom of the oversized pile collected in Ertle's hands, causing the entire bundle to fall dramatically to the street below. The crowd exploded with laughter.

"It's not funny!" said Ertle, prompting the crowd, especially the little children, to laugh even louder.

Menche grew red in the face from laughing so hard, and even Ellen and Franklin were beside themselves, chuckling. Flatlander smiled. When he turned to Henry, however, he was surprised to see a scowl spreading quickly across the Humble King's face, his brow furrowed in concentration. Unlike the others at the table, Henry had not so much as smirked at the act.

"Not liking what you see?" asked Flatlander.

Henry remained silent and looked on. Ellen and Franklin turned to Henry as well, and were soon startled by his stoic demeanor. Flatlander returned his attention to the show. Ertle stomped off through the crowd, vanishing into the night. Alonso resumed his act, picking up some of Ertle's rings, yet juggled them even better than Ertle: faster, more efficiently. Instead of juggling ten objects, Alonso juggled thirteen. Whereas Ertle spun twice while juggling five rings, Alonso performed cartwheels, flips, and triple-axel spins between catches. To top things off, Alonso stood on one foot atop the ladder which Ertle had left, juggled fifteen hoops, balls, and pins, on fire, while singing the alphabet. The crowd went wild as the show came to a conclusion. Alonso bowed deeply several times, threw all of the juggled objects to the ground emphatically, and mingled with some of the families after his performance. Many had watched the show with glee, as young boys and girls were chanting for more. Flatlander presumed that

Ertle would return to take a bow, but oddly, the juggler never came back. In fact, he was nowhere to be seen.

Menche hopped excitedly back to the table. "I wants to see Alonso agains, lord. The juggler that one is, I says!" he raved.

"Impossible," muttered Henry through clenched teeth.

"It was an act, my lord," replied Ellen.

Henry cast his head advisor a somber glance. "Doubtful."

"Why would you say that? It looked like they were both in on it," said Flatlander.

Henry folded his hands upon the table. "Looks can be deceiving. For starters, Ertle has not yet returned to pick up his objects. That is odd, no? It's been five minutes or more. Secondly, Ertle has been, without a doubt, the best juggler in Vermont for the past five years. Nobody even comes close. He has won that honor ten consecutive years in the making, since its very inception. This Alonso character is an aberration. Thirdly, Ertle *never, ever* works with partners. Fourth, that act seemed *too* authentic to me. I swear by all the trout in the Otter Creek that was genuine anger I saw in Ertle's eyes. I've never seen him that shaken at one of his shows."

"I don't know, it seems a little farfetched, doesn't it?" countered Flatlander.

Henry sighed, and sipped his mead. "Therein lies our challenge. We'll never know until we follow each lead down to the very end. One thing that I do know is this: Ertle would never allow anyone to show him up in public, be it real or staged."

One by one, the group began following the movements of Alonso, who was shaking hands with adults and children alike. He plucked his oversized beak from his face, and gave it to a young child who had been standing in the front row, and in turn the little, the brunette boy held it up high over his head, as if the beak were made of pure gold. The child's parents applauded Alonso's generosity, thanking him repeatedly for his random act of kindness. The party watched on in complete silence. Henry didn't miss a beat, his eyes completely fixed on the new juggling prodigy, Alonso.

"It looks like we have our first target."

Sunset had come, as its dying refractions shone from window to window of the western storefronts. Families flocked from the cobblestone streets by the order, as the citizens of the night slowly took their stead, streaming into Burlington's local eateries and pubs. The city was metamorphosing before their very eyes as families returned home, and the deviants and hedonists converged on the streets of Burlington.

Flatlander and company kept close tabs on the street performer, Alonso. After lingering near the site of his act for twenty minutes or so, Alonso stealthily made his way through some of the back streets. Flatlander and company watched from a safe distance as the juggler entered a small, light green café, Bacherman's Bistro. Franklin, Flatlander and Menche feigned interest in buying goods from a street vendor, while Henry and Ellen intently stood watch for Alonso. Franklin had eaten several chicken kabobs under this guise, and Menche had bought a candy necklace for a mere Vermont dollar, which kept the mood light, considering their humorless task. The party then spied a man leaving Bacherman's in a hurry. Dressed much differently than Alonso, his walk, size and demeanor were unmistakably that of their target. He had changed out of his jester attire into a light, blue sleeveless shirt and a pair of brown trousers. His hair was a thick orange-red, and his eyebrows were all but shaved, as thin traces of makeup were still visible on his brow.

Henry motioned for the group to follow, as Alonso dipped away from the crowd into a back alley. As they paused at the corner of a flower shop, Flatlander slowly peeked around the edge of the building into the alleyway. There was Alonso, shaking hands with a very heavyset, baldheaded man in a brownish-beige robe. The conversation seemed formal. Money appeared to be exchanged from Alonso to the unidentified associate in a not-so-subtle handshake. Flatlander twitched, on the verge of jumping into action.

"Not yet!" said Henry. "We need to be careful and deliberate. We mustn't tip everyone off all at once."

Flatlander nodded and turned back to their target. "You were right the entire time."

Henry sighed then stared scornfully at the juggler. "Though it gives me no satisfaction."

As the meeting concluded, the fat man nodded and walked off in the opposite direction of the alley disappearing into the growing shadows of dusk. Alonso clapped his hands together and smiled contently. Placing an object in his pocket, the street performer walked back towards the crowded sidewalks of downtown. Flatlander and company waited patiently around the corner of the alley for their first suspect. As Alonso turned the corner, northbound, he was completely oblivious to the group's presence. Within seconds, Henry caught up and walked in synchronization with Alonso, side by side. The group tailed closely behind.

Henry spoke to the juggler midstride. "It's been years since Ertle has been defeated, you know. Quite an impressive feat for an unknown such as yourself, emerging from complete obscurity."

Alonso peered to his side curiously, then wide-eyed, exclaimed. "Lord Henry, the Humble King! My goodness! It's quite an honor to meet you, sir!"

"I wish that I could say likewise, Alonso."

Miffed at Henry's response, the street performer raised an eyebrow. "Sir?"

Henry continued. "You see, I've been watching Ertle juggle for years now. Talented man he is, I'll give him that. I'd even take my daughter, Jess, to see the man any chance I could get. The thing is, and what a lot of people don't understand, are the subtleties behind quality juggling. It's like a dance, or a ballet: the eye-hand coordination, the timing, the memorization of movements, the endless amount of *practice* that you have to put into your craft." Henry paused. "You do put lots of *practice* into your craft, don't you?"

"Aye, sir. More than my share," said Alonso, yet his words betrayed the growing anxiousness in his voice and on his face. He looked behind him, and was quickly startled to see the company of four following him closely, completely focused on his every movement.

"Keep yer face forward, and keep walkin'," said Franklin.

"I'm a reasonable man, Alonso," continued Henry in a casual tone. "I'll try to frame this in the fairest way possible. It's come to my attention that a certain drug has reached epidemic levels in Burlington and beyond. As leader of Vermont, this has me gravely concerned."

"Really?"

Henry glanced suspiciously at the performer. "You wouldn't happen to know of such a drug, would you?"

"And what drug might this be, sir?"

"Superpac," stated Flatlander from behind.

Alonso stiffened at the mention of the word and glanced down a nearby side street. Flatlander moved to Alonso's other side and Franklin crept up to within a two feet of Alonso's back.

Alonso's voice quivered. "What do you want?"

"We only want the truth, Alonso," stated Ellen.

"I don't know what you're talking about," he said through clenched teeth.

"Folks, I think that we need to take a detour," replied Henry, casually. He and Flatlander put a friendly arm on Alonso's shoulders, as they guided the juggler down the side street. "Everyone, just smile and remain calm."

They then guided Alonso to an underground stone walkway on the side of a redstone building. There were very few people in the immediate vicinity, only a small green and yellow parrot in an outdoor cage. The air grew darker by the minute, as soon, a large, raucous group of youths passed by overhead. The five companions then surrounded Alonso at the bottom of the walkway.

"Who was that man that gave you the superpac?" asked Flatlander.

Alonso scowled. "Get out of my face."

"Wrong answer," muttered Franklin, as he violently grabbed onto the front of Alonso's shirt. Alonso squirmed frantically within Franklin's grasp, but no matter his effort, he couldn't so much as budge. The others inched in closer.

The Humble King, only inches away, glared upon Alonso. "It looks like that you're upsetting my friend, Franklin, here. He's a good man, but has a pretty bad temper too," said Henry. "The gig's up, Alonso. We've been watching you. It'll be in your best interest to start talking. Now."

The caged bird in the window above started chattering loudly. Franklin grabbed Alonso's collar, and slammed him, back first, into the wall. A second time he slammed the juggler. On Franklin's third slam, a baggy of white substance fell to the ground, unbeknownst to the group except for Menche. All of the attention was placed squarely on Alonso. Menche put his foot over the baggy in one swift motion. Dragging it underfoot, he picked up the superpac and put it in his pocket.

Alonso put up his hands in resignation. "Okay, okay. Just please, don't kill me," he stammered.

Henry motioned for Franklin to let him go, and as he was released. Alonso exhaled sharply, clutching his back in excruciating pain. Franklin aggressively searched the juggler's pockets, but found nothing.

"Dino Paraletti," Alonso murmured softly.

"Say again?" said Henry, unsure if he had heard the man correctly.

"Di-no. Par-a-let-ti," repeated Alonso, this time much louder and with much emphasis on every syllable.

"The opera singer?" asked Ellen, wild-eyed, from the side.

Alonso nodded silently, looking down to the walkway. The bird had gone silent, and so had the crowd up above. Suddenly, a door from above swung open.

"Everything okay down there? I hear voices. I'm armed with sword and not afraid to use it."

Henry hid his face in the fold of his arms, hoping that he wouldn't be detected. Flatlander stood behind Franklin's large frame. A man's head protruded from the top of the walkway. Even in the dark, he resembled a large rodent, all ears, on a small, pointed head.

"Our apologies, sir," said Ellen in the sweetest voice she could muster. "We must have gotten lost. Wasn't there a tea shop down here at one point?"

Agitated, the man muttered a curse under his breath. "Feel like I go through this once a week! At one point, yes! The place closed up seven years ago. Lodi's moved out of town to Essex."

"Oh gosh, is that right?" replied Ellen. "I'm so sorry for the disturbance. Thank you."

The rat-like man shook his head and reentered his home in a huff. The group then turned their attention back to Alonso and his crumpled form leaned against the wall in defeat.

"Dino Paraletti?" said Henry, quietly. "I hope for your sake that this is no joke. Or trust me, you will pay. It is doubtful a man of his reputation would sink to such a level."

"Who is Dino Paraletti?" wondered Flatlander. The party was too consumed with their thoughts to provide him an answer.

"Although the man in the alley *was* rather large..." reflected Henry to himself.

"Am I going to jail?" whimpered Alonso.

"Yes, my friend," replied, as he cuffed his sleeves, Henry. "We can't have you tip off our investigation. But if it's of any consolation, your stay shouldn't be long. Franklin here will escort you to the authorities. Alonso, you have helped us all immensely. You have helped Vermont immensely. For this we thank you. But I never want to hear of you challenging Ertle on my streets again. I never want to hear of you challenging anyone in the republic again." Henry paused, smiling faintly. "But for now, we have an important event to attend."

"Where are we going?" asked Flatlander.

"Oh, you didn't hear?" remarked Henry, "I'm taking you all to the Opera at the Flynn Theatre tonight. My treat." Alonso's eyes darkened, but before he could respond in kind, Franklin dragged him up the walkway, through the streets, all the way to the stockades of the North End. Henry waited until their suspect was well out of earshot.

"I've heard that Dino Paraletti's voice is pure perfection."

A thought occurred to Ellen. "But don't you find it strange we didn't find any superpac on him? I never saw him throw it away."

"Perhaps." Henry considered it for a moment. "But perhaps not. He probably ingested it all before we got to him, Ellen. That's what addicts do, you know."

Slowly, the party made their way out of the walkway. Yet as Flatlander, Henry, and Ellen began debating their next move, Menche's mind wandered with reckless abandon. He patted the full baggy in his pocket. He'd always wanted to become a superhero. He'd always wanted to be better at a lot of things, he supposed. Pondering the near-infinite possibilities, Menche scanned the scene before him, as the group walking hurriedly through the hustle and bustle of Church Street. He found that his attention kept redirecting towards Ellen. Her lean body marched gracefully in her faint yellow garments and her plush, Bristol boots. *Ellen,*

I've never told ya how much I likes ya. Menche always knew'd what your answer would be. It don't have to be like this forevers, though."

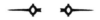

Dino Paraletti was known to have the loudest, deepest baritone of the entire republic. Known as "Dino the Dynamo," he was a featured performer in many classical performances around town, and was the subject of many rave album and performance reviews. Nearly as wide as he was tall, and keeping a long, twisted mustache, hardened by pine sap, Dino was an unmistakable presence on Burlington's music scene. Often times, his shows sold out within a matter of hours, while fans sometimes paid upwards of 300 Vermont Dollars for front row seats to a single show.

Tonight, Paraletti was part of Vermont's only opera group, "Sola," as they performed a fan favorite, "The Barber of Waterbury." Adorning a heavy fur coat and a pair of rusty scissors, Paraletti looked more the part of northerner than singing virtuoso. Flatlander watched the performance next to Henry and Ellen, captivated by the incredible vocal arrangements of Paraletti. The singer's booming falsetto echoed throughout the vast hall of the Flynn, sometimes even vibrating Flatlander's seat in the process. Franklin had returned from jailing Alonso just moments before the start of the show. During the show, Flatlander would also steal glances at Ellen, whose facial expressions fluctuated between straight-awe and, oddly, utter disappointment.

At the end of the performance, Paraletti received a standing ovation for several minutes from the audience. Several bouquets of flowers rained down upon him from the balcony, and despite several attempts at vacating the stage, the continuous roar of applause, whistles and shouts of "encore" kept Paraletti coming back for more. Flatlander and company, however, refrained from clapping.

Luckily for the party, traveling with King Henry had its perks, one of which was being allowed backstage without much hassle. They hurried from their seats out a side door and then backstage, as the lone guard nodded at Henry in acknowledgement. After Paraletti took his final bow, unbeknownst to him was the odd welcoming party awaiting him in his changing room. Paraletti barreled into the changing room in a huff.

"What's the meaning of this?" he snapped, as the singer stopped dead in his tracks.

Henry had made himself comfortable in Paraletti's chair, with Franklin and Flatlander at either side. Ellen and Menche sat at an adjacent table, helping themselves to his cheese and crackers. As Paraletti recognized Henry, his eyes grew wide and his face went red.

"*Lord Henry*? Oh, I'm sorry for my crassness. Heavens. What brings me the honor?"

"Dino Paraletti! Just the man that I wanted to see! Magnificent performance, I must say!" said Henry, as he slow-clapped, emphatically.

"Sir, thank you. It's not often that I entertain the king himself," exclaimed Paraletti in his deep, yet timid, baritone. "I'm just curious what brings you back here. I wasn't expecting you."

"Nor should you have. Dino, I've got a bit of a problem and I think that you're one of the only people who can help me. It seems we've a bit of a drug problem around this city. Something called superpac," Henry paused, and looked the singer sharply, "you wouldn't happen to have heard of this particular nuisance, would you?"

Paraletti approached a dresser in the corner of the room, and brusquely wiped the sweat from his forehead with a handkerchief. Briefly, he glanced into a broad mirror next to the dresser, while unfastening his thick coat, button by button.

"Heard of it, yes. What of it?"

Henry nodded. "That is quite an amazing voice you have."

After a few second delay, Paraletti rapidly turned to Henry. "Lord Henry, with all due respect, if you're somehow insinuating that my voice is the product of some...artificial enhancer, you not only insulting me, but my entire lifetime of work. You have no idea how hard I worked to get to where I am today."

Henry flipped through a thin catalogue, which listed the lucratively priced tickets for his performances. "Indeed. I don't know how hard you've worked. I *do*, however, recognize how desperate a person can get while on the road to success. I *do* know how a person can lose sight of their integrity," said the Humble King, as he waved the catalogue in the air, "when there's so much on the line."

Paraletti scoffed and turned a bright red. "I don't need to hear this. I'm leaving."

Henry gestured to behind the opera singer. "Now, my friend Franklin here might have a problem with that."

Franklin nodded, and blocked the doorway. Paraletti seemed to shrink in response, as he wobbled back from the door.

"I'll call my guards."

"And you certainly have the pipes to do so," quipped Henry, as he twiddled his thumbs. "But that might also be a problem. See, I gave them both vouchers for McSwanky's Pubhouse tonight. I reckon that they're far away at this point, enjoying one another's company and some fine spirits to boot."

Flatlander assumed a position next to Franklin, blocking the door, as he leaned his full weight near its handle.

"What's the meaning of this, Lord Henry?" asked Paraletti. "I demand answers!"

"As do I," countered Henry. "Give us names, Dino. I give you my word that not a soul outside of this room shall know of our little interaction. I just want to know who's supplying you."

Paraletti scoffed. "Forget it."

"That's an unfortunate response," answered Henry. He gestured with his left hand. "Franklin."

Franklin drew his axe and chopped a nearby makeup table in half, as splintered wood shot across the room. Then, with the butt of the axe head, proceeded to smash what appeared to be Paraletti's empty wine glass from a counter into a thousand little shards. Paraletti panicked and backed into a corner.

Henry smiled crookedly. "See, my friend Franklin here takes a liking to breaking things. It's a nasty habit, it really is. We've all tried to talk to him about it. Yet it does come in handy from time to time."

Paraletti cast his eyes to the ground. *The 'Humble' King,*" he said, dumbfounded. "Who would have figured these are his true colors? A pure phony. I must say: I would not have taken you for a bully."

Henry sternly pointed a finger at the singer. "You will reserve your shock of my true nature for a more suitable time, as well as for those in your company that truly care. I still wear my nickname as an honor, but this issue brings about another side of me. Unlike you, I'm obligated to protect this republic, not tear it apart at the seams. And you still risk suffering worse indignities yet than merely a broken table and wine glass."

Paraletti let out a deep sigh. "Alright. I'll tell you all I know..."

Henry smiled. "That's better."

The singer moved to a desk in the room, and opened a drawer. From there, he produced a small sheet of paper and scribbled some notes, thoughtfully. The party watched him curiously. Upon finishing, Paraletti threw the pen aside and breathed deeply. Henry picked up the note and read it aloud.

"He's everywhere and nowhere at once. Drives the heart of Church Street. Is a walking miracle if there ever was, yet can be seen as a nuisance to some. Put him in any other context, he stands out like a sore thumb."

Flatlander couldn't help himself. "Cut to the chase. What's his name?"

"I can't reveal his name," replied Paraletti.

"I'm not one for riddles," countered Flatlander.

Paraletti tensed and threw down his sweat-soaked jacket, revealing large, black suspenders. "He told me if I reveal him, then I'll be cursed. I'm sorry. I'm sorry to all of you, but it's the best that I can do."

"*Cursed*? C'mon." Flatlander approached the singer with clenched fists. "If we don't get a real answer…"

"Flatlander, *stop*," order Henry from his side. "Fine, fine. We will take you up on your clue, but understand that if your riddle turns out to be falsehood, then you shall suffer unimaginable consequences."

Paraletti nodded in defeat, and slumped into a guest chair near the far side of the room. The color had all but gone from his face, and he loosened his suspenders in silent disdain.

"Ellen, are you okay?" asked Henry to his side.

Flatlander turned suddenly to where Ellen was seated at a nearby table. Her hands covered her face. Trails of makeup streamed down between her fingers, as she wiped at one of her eyes.

"I'm fine," she replied in a muffled sob.

"Ellen?" inquired Henry further.

Swiveling the chair with her back turned towards the group, she sobbed softly to herself. Flatlander looked on in confusion. *Did he miss something?* Ellen often had the coolest head of the group, a prevailing calm in a sea of fools. Yet this was neither the time nor place to inquire, he figured.

Henry turned his attention back to Paraletti, sitting awkwardly in the corner. "I thank you, and you have my word that none shall hear of your misdeeds. Though I suggest you start practicing soon without the help of superpac. Your supplies might be soon hard to come by."

Franklin and Flatlander moved away from the door, allowing the singer to pass. Paraletti nodded reluctantly, then hurried from the room. Henry had a few quiet words with Ellen, who was still sitting in the chair, back turned. The Humble King then stood up rigidly, a determined expression on his face.

"Let's go," said Henry, as he strode past Flatlander. "We have our work cut out for us tomorrow. We'll be staying at the Hotel Burlington tonight and it's getting late."

The group marched away briskly. After briefly discussing sleeping arrangements and the next day's itinerary, Flatlander's curiosity got the best of him.

"What's wrong with Ellen?" he asked, as the group traveled down the red-carpeted entrance hall, past the oversized, brightly colored posters of the fur-covered Dino Paraletti.

Golden and red drapes hung from both sides of the hall, embroidered in golden yellow swirls. Stragglers from the performance remained cluttered near a small group of merchants selling treats and beverages.

"Ellen suffers from a broken heart," replied Henry, simply.

Flatlander met the news dumbfoundment. "*Why*? I don't understand."

Henry sighed. "In short, she has come to the painful realization that the person she has long adored was not whom they made themselves out to be. I'm sure that she will fill you in when she feels ready."

"Did she know Paraletti?"

"In a sense," replied Henry, sadly, as he glanced at the wall, where the last poster of the singer was on display. "I told her to take some time for herself tonight and have a drink at McSwanky's. Enjoy the town. We all need a break sometimes."

His assistant, though dull of mind, had heard all that he needed to hear. Menche moved close to Henry's leg.

"Excuse me, lord, but I gotsta stop I wants to take."

"But we need to get our sleep, Menche. Have you been daydreaming this whole time? We have a long day ahead of us."

Menche nodded. "I knows it. But it'd mean a lot to me, sir, if I could grabs a bite to eat at the gyro stand. Won't be more than twenty minutes, if it pleases ya."

Henry stopped and gave Menche a long, hard look, probing his assistant's face for clues of his intentions. A sheepish grin covered formed on Menche's face, as he began jingling what sounded like change in his pocket.

"Been savin' me money this week for a nice Gyro on Church Street. Seen Franklin eats ten of 'em."

Henry studied the reactions of his two other companions. Flatlander smiled, and gave Henry a wink. Franklin shrugged. With great pause, Henry then rested a hand on Menche's shoulder.

"Very well, Menche. Go have your fun. But I don't want any shenanigans from. Eat your gyro and come to the hotel immediately. Here are clear directions," he said, as he handed Menche a map of the city, "and knowing you, you'll need them. I don't want this to be a decision that I regret."

Yet before Henry could finish his sentence, Menche was a blur of motion, running through the Flynn's hallway in his signature waddle. Henry raised an eyebrow to Franklin and Flatlander, who were likewise a mirror in perplexed amusement. *The night was getting stranger by the minute*, thought Flatlander. Free on his own accord, Menche skipped merrily into the revelry of Burlington's downtown and straight into uncharted territory.

Love is a woodstove on a cold winter's day.

Paraletti's lyrics, though contrived to some, used to warm Ellen's heart to no end. The lyrics were part of the song "Woodstove" that the opera singer had performed once aboard a Lake

Champlain cruise boat, the one in which Ellen had attended with her then-love-interest, Francois Villeaux. A visiting Quebecois[65] who had been granted permission through the Northern Wall to investigate his ancestry, Francois and Ellen had hit it off shortly after a chance encounter at the Burlington Library. A week later, they took a cruise together. That night, the lyrics, along with Francois's icy gaze, stole her heart. They had spent the early part of that evening savoring the purple and pink sunset fading behind the Adirondacks. For Ellen, it was unforgettable. The lyrics, in fact, had carried such sentimental value to her that she often used them as a way to sign off on personal letterheads. The quote was also engraved on a large wooden sign that overhung her bedroom door.

Fool's lyrics, thought Ellen, bitterly, as she twirled her near-empty glass of whiskey. Her relationship with Francois had lasted only two months. *Never fall for a visiting Quebecois,* she reflected. Ellen often struggled in her fight against loneliness and seasonal depression; yet this was a burden of a different nature. During those moments backstage at the Flynn, she felt as if her entire worldview had been flipped upside-down. *Dino Paraletti. A phony?* She would have laughed at the notion had she not been so sure of it.

As the clamor began to die down at McSwanky's Pubhouse, Ellen saw that the only remaining dwellers were lonely, older men spaced several barstools apart from one another. None of them talked to one another. *Funny,* she thought, *even the men nearest to one another, those who probably share the very same values and passions in life, are so far apart. What a lonely world we live in sometimes.*

She took another sip from her glass, and used the sad sight as her cue to leave. They were getting closer to their target supplier. Ellen was thirsting to know who was supplying such an evil

---

[65] One who hails from the Quebec region of Canada to the North.

concoction. After tonight, the mission had taken a much more personal nature for her.

As she readied the coins in her pocket, a tall, dark, handsome man entered the bar. His movements were fluid, his steps confident. His five o'clock shadow, well groomed. Even in the gloom of the pub house, Ellen could discern that this was a handsome man, a well-manicured man. He wore a pair of tight, rugged green overalls, an extremely tight brown velvet tunic, and his mustache was smooth and well groomed. He also wore a look of blissful ignorance, evident by his vacant stare. *Perhaps he had been drinking?* Inadvertently, she made eye contact with the newcomer, then turned, embarrassed. It wasn't long before the man sidled on a barstool next to Ellen's.

"Hi."

"Hi," replied Ellen, nervously, as she twirled a loose strand of hair between her fingers.

"Ya like candies?" he asked.

Taken aback by the odd question, Ellen chuckled. "Are you offering me sweets? At this hour?"

"Got some in my pocket if ya wants it," said the strange man, as he patted his pocket.

"Umm, no thanks," stuttered Ellen. *Was this his attempt at a pickup line? What a creep.*

He pounded the bar in frustration with his fist then resumed conversation nonchalant.

"Ya come here often? To the pub house, I means?"

Ellen pushed her stool further away from the odd gentleman. "Not at all, really."

"Name's Trent," he said, as he stuck out his left hand. Ellen repositioned herself, awkwardly, and met his handshake.

"Ellen."

"*Ellen,*" he paused for dramatic effect. "Dat's a beautiful name."

Ellen gave the man a look of indifference. "Not really."

Trent nodded. "You're right, it isn't," he replied, without a hint of humor.

She was too tired to play these games with an obvious desperate suitor. "Look bud, I don't know who taught you how to talk to women, but you need a lot of work."

"Nobody taughts me," said Trent, pathetically, his eyes cast downward.

Ellen softened her tone. "I really have to get home. Sorry. It's not you, it's me. It's been a long day, and I really need to get to bed."

"Trent can talk to ya 'bout it if you'd like. I likes to help people. Really, I do."

"I bet that you do, Trent."

There was something about that dialect. She couldn't put her finger on it. As Ellen moved to place her coins on the bar, Trent moved in close and kissed her squarely on the lips. She swung wildly and struck him open-handed flush on the cheek. The bartender and several of the patrons looked on with morbid curiosity. Trent just stood there, stunned. Glaring hard at the man, Ellen was at a complete loss for words. But before she could admonish the awkward suitor and tell the bartender about Trent's boorish behavior, he hustled out the front door of McSwankey's awkwardly, holding his cheek like he had just had his face ripped off.

Ellen shook her head, incredulous. She felt violated, though she wasn't sure that the man had the mental capacity to truly understand his actions. Something felt off about the entire exchange, something odd. His mannerisms and speech: it was almost, oddly enough, familiar. She shrugged off the gnawing feeling with a safer, more generalized observation, particularly in light of Dino Paraletti's unmasking and now, this. *Men. They're nothing but a series of unpredictable letdowns.*

Menche was fortunate that Henry hadn't checked his room at all, because by the time he arrived home, it was close to two hours after his prearranged curfew. And the superpac took longer to wear off than he had anticipated. As an inexperienced user, it would have been impossible for Menche to know that he had taken an exceedingly large dose for the occasion. As such, he was trapped in Trent's body; imprisoned long after the superpac's intended usefulness ran dry. Before he entered the hotel, Menche uttered a curse, and spilled the remaining contents of the drug down a storm drain.

Back in his hotel bed, Menche went to bed that night feeling very ashamed of his actions. A slight welt had formed on his left cheek from where Ellen had struck him, and his sudden growth spurt had ripped and ruined his favorite brown tunic. Yet it was the mental anguish that kept him up until the wee hours of the night. Not only had he embarrassed himself thoroughly for acting as "Trent," Menche had secretly taken advantage of one of the only people who he trusted.

Where'd things go wrongs at McSwankeys? He wasn't sure. *Maybe she was too smarts than most. Maybe that's where I went bads.* The peppermint candies that he had purchased with his limited allowance were now crushed within his pockets, but Menche didn't care. *An hour's wage wasn't worth this feelin'.* His only hope was that nobody ever found out about this failed experiment.

Church Street often exuded the perfect mixture of charm and seediness. The cobblestone streets were typically clean; the street sweepers made sure of that. Many of the bars and restaurants had outdoor seating, adding to lively crowds perusing the streets for activities. Buskers played their respective instruments at half-block intervals, giving each particular area of Church Street its very own atmosphere; its very own vibe. Teenagers loitered near storefronts exchanging gossip. Merchants peddled food from various carts and stands. Families walked the strip with excitement, for no other city in the entire republic afforded its citizens with so many opportunities for fun and excitement.

From a visitor's perspective, Church Street provided a unique getaway, with a venue for just about any interest: sports, food, comedy, trivia, crafts, goods, apparel, books. Its energy only waned in the dead of the night. Yet from Flatlander and Franklin's perspectives, as temporary investigators, it proved to be a very difficult environment to pinpoint superpac's source.

Seated at a park bench in the heart of the city, Flatlander watched the crowd come and go through the famed street. To his right, Franklin glared at various strangers. They had spent the better part of the past hour in complete silence. That had been the order given directly from Henry himself, though Franklin lacked the same attention span as Flatlander. When he wasn't glaring down his imaginary foes, Franklin spent the better part of the hour sharpening his axe head with his whetstone.

Flatlander buried his face into his palms. He had felt it was important to share his most recent dreams with Henry. He had done so with the intentions that maybe Henry would have offered him words of advice or encouragement. Yet the king had looked wholly disinterested, completely consumed by the happenings of Ertle and Alonso. *Certain things could wait*, he supposed, *but for how long? Were the dreams a calling for him to take action?*

Henry would sit this phase of the operation out. 'Much too risky a proposition' to involve the king, Ellen reasoned. Likewise, both Ellen and Menche were spared from this phase as well, for neither had been of right mind in the morning, and the party decided it best they stay at the hotel.

Flatlander thought long and hard. Paraletti's words reverberated in his mind as he looked at the singer's crumpled note. *He's everywhere and nowhere at once. Drives the heart of Church Street. Is a walking miracle if there ever was, yet can be seen as a nuisance to some. Put him in any other context, he stands out like a sore thumb.* As he scanned the passing droves of people, he was aware that nearly everyone was capable of rousing his suspicions. The attractive group of blonde women standing by the corner: had they enhanced their features with superpac? The two short painters across the street, working furiously at finishing a storefront: had they been provided energy boosts from using the drug? The nearby vendor who sold crafted jewelry by the bundle: how was she able to create so much jewelry in such a short period of time? Eying her items suspiciously, Flatlander wondered.

Weren't all forms of work, all forms of action, all forms of service a way to make ends meet? Was there ever a justified form of cheating? From a moral standpoint, would the hypothetical cheating of crafting jewelry be any worse than the actions of Paraletti or Alonso, in their desperate bids for success and monetary gain? Were the byproducts borne from superpac any less valid to its purer counterparts? Could there be any possible way to harness the drug in a positive way? Flatlander's mind spun with a near endless stream of questions.

He recalled Lord Andreas's harsh words. *'Don't you get it? Even for a thickheaded Flatlander, you must truly have cotton for brains!'* He then recalled Trombley calmly stating at the meeting that *'People are using it in bad form.'* The faces of passing pedestrians seemed to morph into gruesome shapes and sizes then darken in the open sunlight. *People are using it in bad form.* Briefly, he looked upon an ocean of monsters. The sounds of the street seemed suffocating, rendered into a series of dissonant chords and atonality. *Bad form.* Flatlander swore and shook his head. He could have sworn that he was going crazy. His felt dizzy and rested his face in his hands for a moment. *Bad form.* The northerner simply sharpened his axe while humming a tune from the Barber of Waterbury, completely oblivious to the inner turmoil of Flatlander.

Then came a strange, low rhythm. A cacophony of snares, bass drums, cymbals, clarinet, and guitar filled the air. What had first sounded distant and muffled now grew in both volume and clarity. Raising his head in curiosity, Flatlander noticed that Franklin had paused his sharpening.

"What in the jeezum crow..." said Franklin.

The two men watched on, as a man in his early to mid fifties, and playing a variety instruments, appeared through a parted channel of people. He wore green corduroy overalls and a faded violet flannel. A bass drum hung tightly on his back, and an assortment of tambourines, blocks, and metal plates were held in place by metal arms. In his mouth, he blew into a polished clarinet. Strumming a worn-looking acoustic guitar with an air of authority, his eyes were completely expressionless and partially obscured by a brown fedora tipped to the side. Residents began hovering around the multi-instrumentalist in amazement.

Flatlander watched the man carefully. The advancing musician took rest upon a park bench a few storefronts down, as a can attached to a string from his waist plopped on the cobblestone road. He noticed men and women coming right up to the man, and placing coins into the large can, resting at the musician's feet. It was a familiar scene he had watched a dozen times or more with the buskers of Church Street, though with one crucial difference. As the men and women, one by one, placed a donation in the can, they also picked up small objects that were too difficult for Flatlander to ascertain. *That's odd*, thought Flatlander, as he scratched his head. The instrumentalist's rhythm and timing were perfect. *Too perfect.* Flatlander bumped Franklin with an elbow, and leaned in towards him. Something wasn't quite right.

"This might be it," he whispered.

Franklin nodded. Removing a pen, Flatlander scribbled on an old piece of tattered cardboard he had saved from a discarded box from Henry's house. He waited for the crowd to thin out, then whispered again in Franklin's ear.

"Look calm. Look happy."

"Aye."

The two slowly approached the multi-instrumentalist, who was in the midst of a smooth guitar solo. Franklin's oversized shadow engulfed the man where he stood. With a casual flick of his wrist, Flatlander threw the piece of cardboard beside the man, and nodded towards it. The man didn't so much as break rhythm, yet in an instant between chords, used an available hand to flip the cardboard right side up. Shortly after reading the note, his face soured. The note read:

Come with us.

The musician obliged without protest and they walked towards the southern end. Cradled in Franklin's arm, the can full of superpac baggies seemed insignificant; yet both understood the power of the drug in their possession. As the suspect led them down the southern end of Church Street, the multi-instrumentalist continued playing at the urging of Flatlander, so as to minimize any suspicions. But as a result of Franklin moving in too close, the multi-instrumentalist was briefly thrown off rhythm and off key. His walk became staggered; as discorded notes resounded down the hilly Main Street clear through to the Lake.

"Franklin, move away from him," he ordered through clenched teeth.

Franklin moved aside a safe distance, but it was too late. Several onlookers sensed that something was amiss. As Flatlander turned, he could see at least four men from various locations on Church Street suddenly perk up and watch the trio as they rounded the corner. Once on Main Street, Flatlander hurried his pace. Now, nearly a dozen people had congregated on the corner, their facial expressions ranging from curiosity, to surprise, to expressive rage.

"What's your name?" asked Flatlander, as he scanned the neighboring buildings and streets.

The man removed his lips from his clarinet. "A blessed dawn arrives…"

"The man asked you a question!" barked Franklin.

"Everyman," answered the musician.

His eyes were a gentle blue and youthful looking, though his nose was hideous and scarred. His face was taut, like it had been stretched back by an invisible force, and sweat began dripping down his pointed sideburns.

"It ain't a time fer jokin'!" said Franklin, as he nudged the suspect on the back.

The man staggered then regained his balance. "I said it before, and I'll say it again. Everyman."

Flatlander raised an eyebrow. "*Everyman*, is it? You're going to lead us to where you keep the stuff, and then we'll decide on what to do with you then. In the meantime, when we turn this next corner and walk a ways beyond the crowds, you're going to strip off those ridiculous instruments and start running. Run like you've never run before. You try to flee and Franklin will have your head."

"If you must," Everyman answered. "Red Rocks is where we're going and it isn't far."

"Just shut yer mouth and follow our directions," commanded Franklin.

As they turned down left on Pine Street from Main, Flatlander stole a subtle glance towards the corner of Church and Main. The group of onlookers from just two minutes ago had swollen to close to a hundred people strong, and they were just now beginning to follow their trail. In a flurry of motion, he ripped off the assortment of instruments from Everyman, as they crashed to the ground. Franklin grabbed the man by the collar and shoved him forward, also knocking his fedora to the ground.

"Run!" exclaimed Flatlander, as the three broke into a fast jog southward, down the long straightaway of Pine Street.

With sheer determination, Flatlander sprinted with all of his power. Turning intermittently, he saw the crowd losing ground. Everyman ran in complete silence, but oddly, he showed no ill effects. His gait was steady, flawless. Not even a bead of sweat dropped from his brow. The northerner's voice rattled him from this queer observation.

"We get in over our heads, kiddo?" he asked with a chuckle, as he struggled onward, his fur breeches loosening with every step.

"We'll know soon enough," panted Flatlander, who then turned to Everyman. "These are all your paying customers, I presume? All of your addicts?"

"Call it what you will," replied Everyman flatly.

"No, I'll call it as I see it," he snapped, sharply.

Minutes later, they turned a corner down a side street. The following crowd was nowhere in sight. Careening down a sloping path in the woods, the three approached a small, abandoned grey barn surrounded by barbed wire gating. An outcrop of bright-red rock soared twenty meters over the roof of the barn. The rock looked smooth, as strips of crimson and bluish-purple ran its height like veins and arteries.

Flatlander pointed to the anomaly of red rock. "Franklin, what is this?"

"Aye," replied Franklin. "Red Rocks. Just a park, nothin' more. Though a strange one at that."

Everyman picked at a lock with a key and let them through the gate, gesturing for them to follow him towards the barn.

"We'll be safe here," said Everyman.

"Why should we take the word of a pac-sniffin dog such as yerself?" asked Franklin.

Without a response, Everyman led them to the rotting doors that lay entrance to the decrepit, old barn in the center of the property. Its foundation had been chewed away by water, time, and pill bugs, which still moved about its wooden boards. The barn reeked like an old basement, as if the air inside hadn't circulated for a hundred years or more. Though it was doubtful the crowd had seen their route, a sense of urgency tugged at Flatlander sensibilities.

"You first," he commanded.

Everyman nodded and strode into the barn with Flatlander and Franklin in tow. It took several seconds before Flatlander's eyes adjusted, as the stagnated air filled his nostrils. Franklin removed his axe from his back and readied it. Inside there was a large wooden container to the side, and what appeared to be a pulley system with a revolving string of buckets slowly streaming up and down a chain through a deep, black hole. As each bucket came up and reached the pinnacle of its trajectory, it dumped a handful of a white substance into the large wooden container. The buckets were moving incredibly slow, emerging once every minute or so, and creaking every bit of the way.

Flatlander inched himself towards the hole in order to gain a peek. He could spy another bucket in the depths, but nothing else. Ten feet down, the chain disappeared into utter blackness. The creak of the pulley was loud enough to produce a short echo.

"Wow," exclaimed Flatlander, before looking at his companion, "Franklin, could you hand me a rock?"

After scanning the room for a moment, Franklin produced a rock the size of a fist from the floor and handed it to Flatlander. He lightly chucked the rock down the abyss, listening intently for a bang or a splash. Neither came. It was a half minute later that Flatlander gave up, and turned to Everyman, suspiciously.

"Where does this pit lead to? Tell us."

Ignoring the question, Everyman scooped a handful of the powder like substance from the wooden container as the drug spilled from his clutches like sand.

"Is it such a bad thing, sirs? The sugar that is..."

"The *sugar*?" asked Flatlander, dumbfounded.

"*His* sugar," corrected Everyman with a smile.

"What are you talking about?" he demanded.

Everyman pointed to the gaping hole. "His."

Flatlander stared at the hole. "Are you telling me that this is the work of the devil?"

"I ask you: is it such a bad thing? Have you not seen the fruits of the sugar? How the lovely angels open their wings at its sight? Has it not crafted man and woman in perfection, in reflection of their lord and savior?"

"We seen the fruits, and didn't like 'em," responded Franklin, as he spat into the hole. "And I got the feelin' yer lord is different than mine."

"Of course it's a bad thing. Superpac's unnatural," replied Flatlander, readily, attempting to extract more information from the multi-instrumentalist. "Your drug has people cheating, lying, stealing from the fine folks in this city living the right way. It's the principle of the matter."

Everyman sighed. "Yet do we not encounter the unnatural *every day*, in every walk of life? The brute's tears? The five-legged deer? The oversized baby? Who are we to say what's unnatural and what's not?"

Flatlander drove a fist into a nearby bucket, spilling some superpac into the black maw. "I didn't come here for a philosophy lesson, you scum, I came here to find the source of this stuff and destroy it."

"I can make you a prince," said Everyman.

"You've lost your mind," laughed Flatlander.

"A prince. Father and I can make you a prince if you let us be, and let His sugar be, as well."

Flatlander ignored the bribe, gesturing for Franklin to come close. "Do you have your flint handy, Franklin?"

"Aye," replied Franklin, as he handed him a piece of flint and a steel bar.

Everyman's eyes opened wide with sudden realization. "That's not a good idea, sirs. Father would not be happy."

Franklin turned towards Everyman, his axe ready to strike at the slightest hint of interference. Flatlander worked the flint and steel over a matted clump of hay. After a few minutes and some labored breaths, he produced a small flame. He placed the growing flame on a small batch of superpac resting on a metal trough, the amount no larger than a fingernail. In a crackling burst, a two-foot flame shot up, knocking Flatlander clean on his back.

"Goodness," muttered Flatlander, as he stood up slowly, brushing dirt and hay from his clothes. "Packs quite a punch."

"That it does," agreed Franklin with a nod.

"You mustn't!" pleaded Everyman, as he looked on, horrified.

"But we must," replied Flatlander.

He gathered a patch of hay, and lit it with his flint. He then ripped his sleeve at the elbow and used it to wrap the burning hay in a tight ball, before throwing it down into the gaping maw. Without hesitation, Flatlander and Franklin darted from the barn, leaving Everyman standing there beside the hole, his wails emanating throughout the surrounding wood. They ran the length of Pine Street, kicking up dust as they traversed through dried puddles and sunbaked mud. The crowd was nowhere to be found.

It was a full two minutes later when they heard and felt the explosion at their backs. As he turned, Flatlander watched as a multi-colored, pulsating mushroom cloud forming over the peak of the glowing Red Rocks. Large chunks of the barn and surrounding trees rained back down to the earth in smoldering chunks. Flatlander kept a wary eye on the explosion and the vapors that rose over the remaining tree line, for he feared breathing in the fumes of incinerated superpac. *Heaven only knows what would happen.*

While police and bystanders alike began making their way towards the devastation, Flatlander and Franklin strode away casually. And as the fiery inferno of Red Rocks raged at their backs, Flatlander smiled in satisfaction. *That was it. They had destroyed the source of the superpac, and oh, what an odd source it was. Who was that? A deranged superpac addict? A Satan worshipper? Ridiculous,* Flatlander chided himself. Still, he had seen what he had seen. How could he properly convey such a series of odd occurrences to Henry? Then Flatlander reminded himself that this was an odd land; unusual occurrences seemed to be the norm since his arrival. A sense of calm overtook him amid the roar of the soaring flames. Sparks shot loudly in the air like gunshots. *Five missions complete. The game is halfway over.*

Shay Bromage pounded his fist against the kitchen table. *The blasted Flatlander and his band of fools were up to no good again.* It had been a mere two months since their renowned folly in Lowell, the execution at the waterfront, and the debacle of Irasburg, and yet his trusted sources pinned Flatlander to the large superpac bust earlier in the day. Even from his home in the Old North End over a mile away, he had heard the explosion, and immediately his journalistic instincts kicked in. Shay had eyes all over the city, and for a pretty penny, and the occasional returned-favor in his revered paper, he had his fingertips on the ready for any new information. It wasn't long until a contact at the Marble Street record shop, Jeanie, had stopped only an hour later with the news, which was also confirmed by several other associates and friends.

Flatlander! In a matter of weeks, you have single-handedly destroyed my favorite aquatic childhood fancy, strained my relationship with Dawn, and now...and now...

The day before his paper went to print, Shay was always an emotional wreck. After all, he had a reputation to live up to, and no intentions of settling for less. He was Shay Bromage: proud owner, writer, reporter, and columnist for Burlington's strongest paper. Somebody had to keep the people informed, he reminded himself; well protected from the hidden agenda of outside agents. It would be important to keep his cool.

But now he was rendered completely and utterly unhinged.

Dawn had told him, minutes ago that she needed to run an errand, something about getting spices at the farmer's market. *No matter*, thought Shay, hopefully, *more peace for my writing to flourish.* Their fighting had been one of the only consistencies in recent days. The topics of their shared tension ranged from politics to finances to Shay's hygiene. The topic of Flatlander also lingered. Though rarely broached since their fight in the yard, Shay could feel the issue's presence. The way that she frowned the other day after he had made a joke regarding Flatlander's stupidity. The pitiful glance that she gave him while he listened to an old bootleg vinyl recording of Fish. Even more disturbing was the fact that Dawn had actually suggested running a glowing article of Flatlander, profiling his expanded role in Vermont politics. *Ridiculous*, thought Shay. *It would be like running a flattering article about the neighborhood skunk.*

He stormed up the stairs in a rush. *Time to get writing.* Shay had less than a day to finish the paper, as he still had twelve pages to go before meeting the quota. He needed to hurry. He stretched his back and arms in exaggerated fashion, as several large cracks and pops sounded. *When I'm a feeble, decrepit old man confined to my wheelchair, I'll send Flatlander a bill for all of my stress-related medical expenses.*

Breathing a sigh of resignation, Shay made his way to his desk and opened the top drawer. He fumbled through its cluttered contents for the secret compartment at the back of the drawer, but the object of desire was nowhere to be found. Frantically, Shay searched his pockets in a desperate bid, hoping he had not misplaced the forbidden item.

"Looking for something, dear?"

The voice cut through him like a knife.

Shay turned, alarmed. Dawn stood motionless in the doorway. Her hand was extended with a small paper baggy. Her face was the perfect mixture of disgust and ire. With a small gulp, Shay slammed the desk drawer shut and stood tall to face his wife. The gig was up.

"It's not...Dawn, I..."

She held the damning evidence up high for her husband to see. "Oh, no. You don't need to explain. I get it, Shay. As a matter of fact, this entire picture has become a good deal clearer to me now." She paused, and tried to collect herself, but failed. Trembling with rage, Dawn squinted at Shay. "You've been doing *superpac*? *Superpac*?"

"You don't know what kind of pressure I feel every hour of every day, Dawn," he stuttered. "If you walked in my shoes for just a few minutes, you would see..."

"Are you really *that* dense?" said Dawn, as she approached, "Or am *I* that dense for staying with you in the first place? I *do* walk in your shoes, Shay! I walk in your shoes every day. I'm a journalist too. Remember? But unlike you, I don't need to cheat with a drug to gain an edge on my competitors!"

"It's never too late to start," said Shay, with a twisted smirk.

Dawn was livid. "Cute, Shay. I didn't know that you were starting a comedy column this week."

"I'm sorry, Dawn."

"Is *this* your motivation for badmouthing Flatlander in your upcoming column? Is it?" Dawn held out the empty baggy with emphasis, so close to Shay's face, it nearly swiped him on the chin. "The big, mean old Flatlander busts a cheating, conniving, drug-addicted writer, and cuts off his drug supply, but ohh, let's go after *Flatlander*, and make *Flatlander* look bad. Because he's the *real* problem, right? Sounds really great, doesn't it, Shay! You can credit me for your next article!"

Shay recoiled from his wife's scorn. "You don't understand."

"You're right, Shay. I don't understand. I don't understand how I could have ever been so stupid to actually believe in you and stay with you all of these years! You're not the man that I fell in love with. You've changed. Every conversation, every article, every comment, is so angry and demeaning with you all the time. But I should have seen it coming. I really should have."

"Dawn, if you would just allow me a chance to…"

Dawn ignored his pleas. "How long has it been going on, Shay? How long have you been using? One month? Two months? Longer? Give me some idea here."

"Dawn…"

"Answer the question!"

Shay swallowed, and gazed at his meticulously shined shoes. "Over a year."

The silence was palpable. Shay tapped his fingers nervously against his frayed, leather belt. It was hard to maintain eye contact with Dawn; he had never seen her this enraged. He could tell that she wanted to cry; but she appeared too angry for tears. Without another word, Dawn threw down the empty baggy onto the ground and stormed off. Shay didn't bother following.

"Honey, where are you going?"

"To give you a taste of your own medicine," replied Dawn from the bottom of the stairwell.

Several drawers and closets opened and shut throughout the downstairs. He heard his wife stomping recklessly from the kitchen and living room in her boots. A wine bottle crashed into the sink. Bags were hastily packed. Shay followed and tried to summon up the wits to plead with her, to convince her of his sorrow, to halt her drastic actions. Before he could articulate the right words, the front door slammed with such force that it rattled Shay to the core.

Shay walked back to his office. He leaned over to pick up the empty baggy, and inspected it under the light streaming in from his office window. Small crystals were still encrusted to the bag's innards, glittering in the light. *So much. You've given me so much, and yet to lose it in a matter of seconds.* Shay thought long and hard about Dawn's parting words. '*To give you a taste of your own medicine*'. He felt rotten to the core. From the window, he then watched his wife walk briskly down the street until she was long out of view. He knew that things would never be the same again.

CHAPTER 10

The Moran Plant and The Thinker

I T WAS A WARM LATE July's day underneath a smattering of cumulus clouds on Master Yuro's estate. *Comfortable enough to take in one's own leisure*, Flatlander reckoned. From his side, Yuro yawned from his spot on a recliner, his large, jeweled, golden crown rested on a nearby display table shimmering in the sun. Though it was midsummer, Yuro's skin was a rare shade of pale, for it almost seemed to glow in the strong sunlight.

Sitting on a stone ledge, Flatlander admired the view of a vast wildflower garden, which covered a vast expanse of property. Blue, purple, yellow and white flowers were intricately planted in the design of Yuro's face, down to the very last detail. It had taken a moment for Flatlander to catch the design at first, for the grandiose and scale were incredible.

Yuro's estate was lush, his mansion half coated in a patch of English Ivy; the rest constructed of the finest red brick from Highgate. Large white pillars were erected on either side of the front door. Flatlander watched as dozens of butterflies fly gracefully over the wildflowers, fighting over the sweet nectars yielded from

Yuro's garden. And just beyond the wildflower garden, isolated patches of spruce hedges were shaped into a variety of objects: wheels, cups, hats, books, crowns, mountains, and birds. Far in the distance, Flatlander spied the outline of an angel, complete with a spruced halo and branch-like wand. The garden sculptures, while bizarre, were remarkable in their detail.

Yuro called out to his butler standing at attention near a sliding door. "Bart, will you be a good man and get Flatlander a drink? What will you have, Flatlander?"

Since tasting chaga at the swimming hole, Flatlander had craved the black fungus. "Iced chaga tea, please. Where did everyone go?"

Yuro laughed. "Where do you think? Surely, they're playing colonies as we speak."

Flatlander chuckled. His party had grown an affinity for the game, and luckily for them, Yuro's Colonies table was one of the finest in the republic.

"Thank you, Bart," said Yuro.

Bart nodded and hurried into the house. The butler wore brown work trousers and a tight, checkered purple and white tunic, the colors of Yuro's family crest. His oversized leather belt was studded with pearls, a recent holiday gift from Yuro. A man of his late fifties, the rosy-faced, flat-topped butler served his master proudly.

Yuro sighed. "You impressed a lot of people with your heroics at Red Rocks, Flatlander."

"I aim to please," responded Flatlander, his face expressionless.

"With superpac no longer plaguing our streets, this city can move forward once again. I owe you, Flatlander. If and when the time comes, just name it. I have many resources at my disposal."

Flatlander smirked. *I'm sure that you do.* Yuro was wealthy. In fact, he was one of the wealthiest men or women in the entire republic. Henry had mentioned this fact shortly before their departure for Burlington. He had amassed his wealth through a series of deals, trades and transactions that involved property, objects, and services. He won acclaim for his calculating economic maneuvers. Emerging as a leader of a political faction called the Prosperates, he had won his bid to become Lord of Burlington by a small margin against the formidable leader of the Worker's Party, Fletcher Posey. And though he attained office wdespite much scorn and resentment from his rival parties, The Worker's Party and The Contrarians, the residents also yearned greatly for new leadership after the downfall of Burlington's previous lord, Emile Babakiss.

Bart delivered an oversized chaga tea to Flatlander. It was served in a goblet with a combination of ice, flowers and plant stems spilling over the edge. Yuro caught Flatlander's curiously playing with the drink.

"Wildflowers from my garden. I've experimented with a number of them in my drinks. Marsh Marigold and Great Blue Lobelia. Mountain Mint with White Aster. Your chaga has a blend of Bergamot, lavender, and a splash of fresh lemon," he paused, and twirled his own cocktail. "I'm a bit of a dabbler."

Flatlander marveled at the strange creation. "I can see that."

Yuro sighed. "But the real reason that I had you over is to talk about a thorn in my side. I know that Henry and your party are out and about in Burlington, tending to their own affairs for the time being, but I wanted to speak with you personally first. A problem festers on the shore of the lake and I'm at a loss."

"Again? But Fish has already been killed."

Yuro chuckled. "Indeed, but unlike Lord Henry, it is not Fish that presents me with bouts of sleepless nights, Flatlander, but another issue entirely. The Moran Plant."

Flatlander delicately peeled a few of the stems and flowers from his drink, and placed them on a nearby stone ledge. Sucking his fingers to better gauge its taste, he tried to recall the unfamiliar name.

"The Moran Plant?"

Yuro nodded. "If you peer out from the eastern hills of Burlington Bay, a great challenge lies in a dilapidated building resting near to the sloped hill of Depot Street. It's called the Moran Plant and it has become quite a heated topic around town. And if you're willing to listen, I'll tell you the tale to the best of my knowledge."

Flatlander reclined against the stone ledge. "Tell me."

"Very well." Yuro breathed deep. "Well over a century ago, the Moran Plant was a coal-operated power plant. I'm not sure if you're aware of what coal is, Flatlander, but back in the older days, it was a popular energy source for the masses. A fossil fuel. Cheap, abundant, and able to burn for long periods of time, it was an ideal energy source for the Old Country. Unfortunately, it was also a very dirty substance. Flaky and black, its smoke clogged the air, produced acid rain, enough to wear down buildings and statues, and sometimes killed off all life in ponds, near and far.

"But I digress: the once elderly owner of the Moran Plant, Connie Riley, knew how to turn a profit. She did quite well when Vermont was growing, and desperately seeking energy sources. Riley would import the coal from various parts of the United States to meet Vermont's energy demands, but that was back before the fall of the Old Country."

Yuro meticulously removed a piece of stem from between his teeth. "Some in the community didn't take too kindly to Connie's profits, nor the dirty energy that she produced en masse. Truth be told, with the emergence of alternative energy markets, combined with a shifting policy of wanting to decrease Vermont's dependency on imported energy, the supporters of the Moran Plant became few and far between. Connie herself may have fared better had she not been such a thorny woman. She had quite a reputation around town as being rough around the edges, hard to work with.

"But, no matter. The Moran Plant was her baby, and she, its rightful master. She loved that plant, more than her family, friends, and quite possibly, life itself. She'd reportedly skipped her daughter's birthday for late night sweeps at the plant. One story goes that while her son placed second in the lumberjack championship, Old Connie was single-handedly cleaning out one of the Moran's furnaces. Then, nearly four scores ago, her dream came crashing to an end.

"Connie was willed out of the Moran Plant, plain and simple. The records indicate that it was closed due to a string of safety violations, but anyone who knew Connie knew her to be a stickler for cleanliness. Something just doesn't add up, Flatlander. If you dig a little deeper into the records, and read over her police interview transcripts before she died, which I have, you walk away with the distinct impression that this was, indeed, a setup. Sabotage, if you will.

"The violations were clear as day. A train-car of coal spilled over to the side of the tracks with no reasonable explanation, and very little follow-up in the investigation. A series of coal spills in the factory itself. Large fissures rapidly appeared on many of the pipes. A small fire broke out on the ground floor. And what did all of these incidents have in common? They all took place under the supervision of one of her subordinates, Eugene Hecht, a key partner in constructing the Winooski hydroelectric dam just to the north, no more than six years later. See the connection?"

Flatlander raised an eyebrow. "Hecht orchestrated its demise."

Yuro nodded. "I believe so. But here's when things get interesting. The Moran Plant shut down, Connie's license was revoked, and she was never to be seen or heard from again. Just as mysterious as her disappearance, so too was the upstanding form of a new statue in the field by the front of the building. 'The Thinker', they called it, and it still stands to this day. Shaped in the form of a man sitting on a stone, his chin resting atop a closed fist, he seems to be lost in thought. It's made of the strongest Vermont Marble and stands over twenty feet tall from its base. More stupefying is the fact that nobody knows how it got there, who brought it or constructed it, or why it's there in the first place. Nobody has staked its claim. One day, it was just…there."

Flatlander chuckled. "Hmm. It just appeared?"

"So they say."

"So what's the problem?"

"Since the very day that it shut down over one hundred years ago, there has been debate on what to do with the building. My fellow Prosperates tell me that they want to turn it into a high-end restaurant, with its very own self-sustaining greenhouse, a garden-to-table operation. The Contrarians, or "people's party," as they refer to themselves, in their incomprehensible rambling, are screaming bloody murder to make it a public park, free of businesses, like another one of their non-profitable hangouts, without ever once listening to others' ideas. And most outrageous of all, the Worker's Party is actually proposing that we just turn the whole thing into a giant ice-climbing wall. An ice-climbing wall!" he marveled, dumbfounded at the thought. "Have you ever heard of such folly, Flatlander? I've been in my lordship for less than two years, and have heard more insane ideas than I could have dreamt in a lifetime."

Flatlander chuckled. "Nobody's moved into the Moran this whole time?"

Yuro took a deep breath. "This is where the tale gets even stranger, Flatlander. People have tried. But what has frequently occurred, according to local legend, is that the Thinker turns its back on the Moran, and therefore, renders the project cursed and doomed to failure. Businesses that moved in lost income rapidly. Fires started out of the blue. Rampant acts of vandalism took place. People vanished. People became very ill. Something's happened every time a new business started in the Moran without fail. Therefore, it's widely accepted that the spirit of Connie Riley curses the old factory out of spite, and the Thinker plays a critical role in protecting her beloved structure. For every time that the Thinker has turned its back, a project is cursed and a life is altered."

"Why doesn't somebody just knock the freaking thing down?" wondered Flatlander. "You have enough manpower."

Yuro looked out towards the expanse of yard, scowling. "Alas, that had also has been tried, and it resulted in tragedy. The one man who tried bringing down the statue with nothing more than an oversized sledgehammer was instantly struck dead by a bolt of lightning. He was found face down in the morning rain, a sizeable burn mark entrenched on his shirt, and his melted boots scattered a dozen yards away. Since then, others have had second thoughts."

"You've got to be kidding me."

Yuro sighed. "I wish that I was, Flatlander. Truly. I wish that I was."

"Every time I've visited the waterfront, it's packed with people. I can't believe that building is abandoned. Seems like such a wasted business opportunity."

"You're telling me." Yuro nodded, sadly. "Now the political parties bicker near every day over the building, from the meetings at city hall to the statehouse of Montpelier to the foreground of the building itself. Nobody can decide on what to do with it, and few seem brave enough to even present an ideal solution that's beneficial for all parties. The fear of change lies deep in the collective psyche of the populace. As such, Flatlander, the growing dilemma has had worrisome implications."

Flatlander sat up and shot Yuro a hopeful look. "But *you* have the authority, don't you? Why don't you just take a vote and give the command?"

"Technically, yes, I have the power," replied Yuro, in earnest. But he then returned to Flatlander a sickly look. "But I have learned in my two years as Lord of Burlington that navigating these political waters can be very murky territory indeed. People always wants your 100% commitment on every issue, and if you don't fully appease them, then you suddenly become their target. Also, I'm wary of contributing a failed idea, only to have the blasted Thinker turn on me and run me to ruins. I have worked hard for my assets, Flatlander. I don't intend on losing them." Yuro paused and admired his stretch of property. "And on this particular matter, I have been pounced on like a swarm of turkey vultures by my opponents. So this is exactly the type of scrum I would like to avoid."

Flatlander tossed aside the remaining contents of his chaga into a nearby cluster of ivy. "So you want to send *me* in to do clean up this mess." It wasn't a question.

Yuro smiled faintly. "It *is* what you do best, is it not?"

Flatlander brushed his hair back, mulling over the lord's request. "So what do I do?"

"Simply find a solution, Flatlander. There is no hidden agenda, I promise you. I recall Lord Henry saying it best when he introduced you to this republic 'we need another set of eyes, an outsider's vision.' You have proven yourself a worthy protector of the republic. Well, as it stands: Burlington needs you at this hour. I need you. It was barely a fortnight ago when I heard rumors that the political factions meant to do battle soon, all stemming from this Moran Plant debate. While these rumors often spread irresponsibly from the dregs of the Old North End, I take such matters very seriously. I don't want any bloodshed in this city, and I will do everything in my power to prevent that from happening."

Flatlander sighed. He realized the opportunity to capitalize on making the Moran Plant his sixth quest. Henry's relationship with Yuro was an important allegiance to maintain, one that he didn't want to compromise.

"Okay. Okay, I'll do it. Just promise me one thing…"
"Of course."

Flatlander picked out another bit of stem from between his teeth. "Go lighter on the stems from now on."

After a lazy day of sipping wildflower drinks, Flatlander retired to his chambers on the third floor of Yuro's sprawling mansion. From his bedroom window, he saw the lawn stretch out as far as the eye could see, until the spruce sculptures and gardens dimmed into the faded, auburn sunset.

Upon taking his rest, he became immersed in yet another dream. Again, he rushed headfirst down the familiar river. Its rapids were treacherous, and the rocks pained his hands and legs upon each braced impact. Pain soon became numbness, however, and his body adjusted. It felt sort of like a game, he realized, as he propelled himself from rock to rock like an amphibian. He was in more control of his movements this time around; he had more wits about him. As he rushed past a steep bank, Flatlander saw a lone baby sprawled out on a rock. In its hands, it shook a blue and red rattle with playful-looking flowers on its handle. *I know that rattle.* He wanted to call to the infant I to see if the baby would respond. *Where were this child's parents? Who would leave a baby so close to a river like that? What was happening?*

He then spied another child, a little boy on the same bank, no older than two years of age, chasing a monarch butterfly with a net. The boy giggled uncontrollably, and despite the cold water and devastating current, he almost found himself laughing along with him. It was there, plain to see: pure, unadulterated joy. *I know this scene. I've seen it before. I've lived it.* Flatlander tried in vain to swim to river's edge to get a closer view. He made little progress despite his efforts. The river was going to bring him wherever it liked, at whatever pace it liked, and there wasn't a single thing that he could do about it.

Up ahead, he saw a bend in the river, as it rushed between two imposing cliff sides. A large, loose tree limb had wedged itself between two rocks that lay before him, creating a shallow bridge for Flatlander to grab a hold of. At the last second, he grasped the limb: his cold, wrinkled fingers searching desperately for any type of grip. But the last fleeting vision that he had before being rushed away by the current was of the boy waving at Flatlander, smiling, the words haunting him far beyond his waking.

"I love you, Daddy!"

Somewhere high on the Green Mountains, a series of wolves' howls echoed among the valleys. A nasty wind whipped back Shay Bromage's hair, as he struggled to tether his mule, Harrison, to a nearby spruce. Peering back at the steep ridge from which he had traversed, Shay wondered if he had come the right way. He wasn't so sure. As he caressed Harrison's head, he scanned the imposing wall of stone ahead of him. This high up in the Mountains, the weather was simply unpredictable.

Intent on traveling to Camel's Hump under the cover of darkness, Shay had foolishly forgotten just how rugged this terrain was. Harrison had lost his footing on several occasions, and even he, an experienced hiker by his own right, experienced some difficulty negotiating the land in the dark with nothing more to guide him than a worn out mule and an old, secondhand lantern. Shay placed his hand against a cold stone as he held the lantern aloft. He knew these stones intimately, even in the dead of the night. He could have sworn…

From the corner of his eye, Shay noticed a faint orange glow dancing on a boulder. Rarely did people venture this far in the Green Mountains, especially at night. Just down its eastward flank, the journalist could make out the border of a cave entrance.

Bingo. Another howl ripped through the mountainside, disrupting Shay's train of thought. Harrison jerked anxiously, as the mule pummeled the spruce with a leg kick.

"Harrison, good boy, stay. You'll be safe up here, I promise. The wolves love to call to one another, but rarely do they venture up this high," he said with a pause, as he stole one last glance of the light emanating from the cave. "I have business to tend."

Wolves. Not one of the more welcome additions to the republic since the great fall, thought Shay, *but perhaps that subject can be a future article of mine?* He walked cautiously up and around the slight bend in the trail, leading directly to the entrance of the cave. *If I have a future.* Smoke billowed through several small holes high above his head, and he watched it dance along the steep stones above before disappear into the clear night sky.

Collecting his breath, he took a few gentle steps into the cave, mindful that his presence wasn't wholly expected. Along the sides of the room, oversized, ancient books filled several bookshelves. Jars of liquids, in all colors and consistencies, rested on a carved stone table, which appeared to be made from a natural stone formation of the cave itself. A few liquids bubbled; others emitted colored smoked; and others, yet, blinked as if powered by an electrical current. Much of the walls were lined with fur. As Shay brushed his hand against its coarse surface, he recalled his revulsion during his first visit here when he discovered that these were all, in fact, deer hides. *Dozens and dozens of deer hides.* The cave reeked of smoke and oil, but was oddly mixed with the faint, delicious, scent of cooked Venison. And there, sitting with his back to Shay, close to the fire, sat the wizard with whom he had come to see.

"Mr. Bromage," came the booming voice from behind the chair. The wizard didn't so much as flinch or move a muscle. "How kind of you to pay me a visit at this hour."

"My apologies, Vergil. You are an otherwise difficult man to get a hold of," replied Shay, as he sat in an empty, stone carved chair to Vergil's right.

Vergil glanced over the journalist with mild interest. The wizard wore a thick, dark green robe, with white and golden symbols adorning it. Individual stars, constellations, and animals marked various points on his robe, and his hood was lined with rabbit pelt. He was an imposing figure, at close to seven feet tall and wiry thin. He was completely bald, with several pronounced scars running the length of his scalp. His wrinkled face looked almost non-human. He cradled his favorite staff, a gorgeous creation of both marble and walnut; its head molded into the face of a deer, next to that of an eagle. His olive eyes bore a tremendous depth, and his brow protruded greatly, as if buckling under the tremendous weight of his brain.

"I hope that the wolves didn't sour your mood, Mr. Bromage. The neighborhood just quite isn't the same with them around. Wouldn't you agree?"

"Harrison and myself would prefer not to linger long."

Vergil turned to the journalist with a sinister smile. "Sometimes I think that mule has more sense than you. I really do."

Vergil stoked the fire with his staff, as the sparks glanced wildly in all directions. The fireplace, tucked ever so slightly below the floor, was comprised of quartz and greyish-green chlorite schist. Vergil kicked some loose kindling back into the gut of the fire, placed his staff beside his chair, and turned to Shay.

"Mr. Bromage, what can I help you with? I wasn't expecting you."

"It's Flatlander."

"And what seems to be the problem with Flatlander'?"

Shay thought for a few seconds. "Well, it's not quite as simple to kick him around any more. He's actually beginning to become quite popular and has even made himself quite the fan club, including, I regret to say…my wife."

"Carol?"

Shay winced. "Dawn."

Vergil nodded. "Oh yes, of course."

Shay watched the fire grow in volume, as he leaned in closer to seize the heat. "I hate him. I hate this Flatlander."

The wizard looked upon the reporter with concern. "Tell me, Mr. Bromage, what has upset you so dearly?"

Shay became flustered. He didn't even know where to begin. "Well, for starters, he has killed Fish, the only singer whose voice could make the gods themselves cry upon the lake. This world shall never know another quite the same."

Vergil scoffed. "I see that you have not lost your touch for hyperbole, Mr. Bromage. But it must be said. Fish was a greedy, aquatic abomination, so enraptured by its own selfish needs, it would have sooner been a bloating bag of puss on the shore than a facilitator of good in this world. I gave him his powers, if you recall. And he squandered his potential like the tick that is the Old Country[66]."

Irritated by Vergil's curt assessment, Shay continued nonetheless. "He has also turned my own wife against me."

"But surely not from your own devices?" asked Vergil.

Shay knew that he couldn't divulge the full truth. Nobody had known he had been consuming large amounts of superpac all of these years, not even Vergil. He wanted to keep it that way. Dawn's thinly veiled threat disturbed him. She had been so vindictive in recent weeks, it seemed; anything was possible. *How could I word this lie as delicately as possible?*

"Through the work of black magic, most likely." he stated.

"The Flatlander knows magic? Nonsense," spat Vergil.

Extending his hand to the fire, the wizard made a fist. The fire rapidly turned a bright blue, and before Shay's eyes, he could see an overhead view of Harrison resting on the ground outside,

---

[66] Vergil has often compared the Old Country to a parasitic tick.

his energy all but drained. The hazy, blue figure of his mule let out a long yawn then glanced around the tree nervously. Vergil's released his grip. The fire became sweltering hot, and within a second, resumed its original form and color.

"There are very few in this world whom possess the skill and wisdom to work magic, Mr. Bromage. Keep that in mind when speaking of such matters."

Shay nodded and cleared his throat. "My apologies, Vergil. I suppose what I'm trying to say is I'm not sure I want to keep playing this game. I'm not sure I want to continue trashing the Flatlander needlessly. My family and career are at stake. Please understand."

The wizard looked sternly upon Shay, his dark, black eyes glaring fiercely. "But you have signed a pact, Shay, if you recall."

Vergil pointed to a framed piece of paper resting on an adjacent mantle, its glass frame reflecting the light of the fire. Shay glanced at the document in a pained, almost fearful, expression. He hated to be reminded of this artifact, this object of scorn. *Quite possibly the biggest mistake of my life, though in light of recent events, perhaps that was debatable...*

"Yes. Yes, I know, Vergil. I ask this of you in good faith."

Vergil grimaced. "*In good faith*, he says," mumbled Vergil to himself. "Ha. You don't mean to tell me that you're reneging on our deal? We both know the terms, do we not?"

He isn't going to compromise. Shay was sure of it. If only he could travel back in time ten years prior, to the time in which he had written extensively about Vergil in an article, he would. He would have never had written the piece at all if he had known the implications. Shay had just found the subject of Vergil so invigorating, that he just couldn't help it. It called to him, spoke to him. Young and full of energy, Shay was in the throes of embarking on an exciting, new career. The concept of Vergil was deeply ingrained in the folklore of Vermont, and yet the mysterious figure had only been sighted a handful of times. The townsfolk who had reportedly seen him were labeled as loons, and the mystery of Camel's Hump's wizard and First Vermonter, lived on.

The title of Shay's piece "Vergil Uncovered," had been a hit, and served as one of the premier articles to help launch his newly minted Shay Chronicles. The piece had convinced an otherwise indifferent part of the population that Vergil, was, in fact, real. People's curiosities were piqued, and a renewed interest in finding the wizard was stoked by a cocky, young journalist. The story was a hit with the people of Vermont, all but with one exception: Vergil himself.

The Wizard of the Camel's Hump didn't take well to this newfound attention, and through the works of his magic, had found out a deep, dark little secret about Shay that he had used as leverage ever since. Shay still keenly remembered the day when Vergil had found him, amid a solitary hike in Bristol, whereby forcing the young reporter into an ominous pact, a pact eventually used to demean and push away the outsider simply known as Flatlander.

If I could just go back in time…

"No, I have not forgotten," answered Shay, defeated.

"Good," replied Vergil, as he twiddled at a few loose strands of his beard. "Because it would be absolutely terrible if I had to remind you of the consequences. Wouldn't it?"

Shay frowned and got up to leave. He hadn't received the answer to which he had hoped, and it would be a long, grueling descent down Camel's Hump in the dead of the night. He wasn't even entirely sure that he'd see Dawn upon his arrival home. *Perhaps she had decided enough was enough, and moved out*, thought Shay, despondent. Sick to his stomach, he contemplated her whereabouts. But just as Shay readied to depart Vergil's cave, he turned to ask Vergil one last, burning question.

"Why do you make me do it?"

Vergil frowned. "Do *what*, Mr. Bromage?"

Shay threw his hands in the air. "The articles, Vergil. The anti-Flatlander pieces."

Vergil took a deep breath and, out of habit, spun his staff in a circle. "Every day, the sun duly rises and falls among this beautiful carpet of greenery, laid out among the mountains and valleys of my domain. Every day, I have sworn a primordial allegiance of sorts to the forces which have kept me company through moments of unbearable monotony and, conversely, of the utmost ecstasy. You simply don't understand, Mr. Bromage. You don't understand that Vermont is under attack from an enemy that comes and goes under the guise of a well-to-please Flatlander. *That* is why I fight. *That* is why I continue to carry on as such. And *that* is why I *insist* on you continuing this journalistic deed. For the overall good of the republic, for the land in which we all consider home." Vergil paused momentarily, then took a jab at Shay, referencing the journalist's ill-conceived article concerning the wizard, "And if you can, keep *that* quote out of the paper too."

Shay then parted ways, defeated. Harrison perked up when he saw his master, and rubbed his head against Shay's chest for warmth and some much-needed affection. The wind was now stiffer than he had remembered. Kissing Harrison's head gently, Shay proceeded to untether the mule from its harness. They then gently descended the slopes of Camel's Hump side-by-side, Shay's lantern dimming under the milky moonlight.

Shay stroked the back of his mule's neck. "Harrison, sometimes I feel like you're the only creature who understands me. Now, come. Let's leave this godsforsaken place."

Dawn adjusted the settings of the typewriter, her makeup smeared from streams of tears. Ruffled tissues littered her office desk, and the smell of steaming tea hung in the air. For the past two nights, she had taken up residence in her cozy office at the Burlington Daily. Needing time away from the man that she *thought* she knew, the man she *thought* she loved, Dawn would have never predicted this dilemma. Shay now reeked of treachery and greed, and she wasn't sure if she could even face him for the time being. *Superpac. He'd been on Superpac the whole time, and I hadn't even the common sense to see it.* Dawn wept aloud, while she began formulating titles for her newest piece, before crossing them out.

~~Prominent Local Journalist Uncovered~~
~~Shay Bromage: A Superpac User Amongst the Elite~~
~~Cheat: The Rise and Fall of Shay Bromage~~

With each proposed title, a bit of Dawn's heart ached. It was too much weight to bear. Should she leave Shay? *Could* she leave Shay? If so, where would she go? The questions stung hard, for she hadn't the answers. A thought then occurred to Dawn: her article must state that there is a conflict of interest based on her relationship with the subject at hand. She typed frantically at the bottom of the page.

Editor's Note: Dawn Bromage is the wife of Shay Bromage.

There, noted Dawn with pride: considerate *and* transparent. Pausing, she glanced at a sketch that she kept above her desk, something that Shay had drawn. It depicted the two of them embracing outside of a corn maze in Danville, dwarfed by the corn stalks in the background. Dawn smiled at the memory. She recalled that she had been so distraught that day; the two had gotten so utterly lost. At that point in her life, the feeling of helplessness had felt alien to Dawn. In almost every facet of her life at that point in time, Dawn had excelled in, whether editing, gardening, and cooking.

On the other hand, Shay had kept his sense of humor during their ordeal in Danville, Dawn reflected with a smirk. He joked that if they never found the proper exit, he would be content with the love of his life, and an endless ocean of corn on the cob to feast on. Dawn chuckled; contrived, yet quirky. *That was Shay in a nutshell.*

The event seemed insignificant at the time, barely noticed, in fact. Yet the adventure in the corn maze bespoke to the qualities of the man to which Dawn had fallen rapidly for: handsome, intelligent, and fiery. Shay had a way of massaging her insecurities, of helping her see the truth behind some of life's complications and its endless maze of delusion. Hubris aside, even Dawn would admit, Shay was a prodigal talent, a true champion of ideals, a man who, unflinchingly, brought out the best and worst in the people around him.

But now, his legacy, and more importantly, their marriage, all seemed to come crashing down in a web of lies and deceit. The piece of paper rested stiffly between the typewriter's table and platen. Wiping a tear from the corner of her eye, she groaned. Dawn thought long and hard about what she was about to do to the man she loved. *I'll destroy him. I'll destroy everything that he's ever worked for. I'm angry with him, furious, really. But I'm not a bad person. I can't. I just can't.* In one swift motion, Dawn reeled the paper out from the typewriter's clasp and crumpled it up. With a cry, she threw it into a nearby trash.

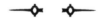

My kids. Those were my kids! Flatlander woke, his sheets dampened by sweat. The dream of his children by the river shook him to the core. *'Daddy,' he said. Was that my boy?* He needed to share his dream with Henry. And this time, Flatlander told himself, he wasn't going to be brushed aside so easily. There was too much at stake: his past, his future, his happiness, the question as to whether or not he should reside in Vermont, or travel back solo to the Old Country. He had done so much for his new friends in Vermont, he reasoned; there needed to be some measure of reciprocity.

He hurried down the large, spiral staircase. He had a hunch as to where his friends may be lingering: down in Yuro's basement at the colonies table. Henry and Ellen had grown a fierce rivalry in the game during their brief stay at Yuro's. Though the competition was highly amusing at times, the craze seemed to be getting out of hand. They had had rushed from the superpac collection event, and literally ran to the table to get in a game before dinner the night prior.

Yuro's mansion was vast and abundant in rare antiques, custom paintings, and handcrafted furniture. The main entrance and living room were large enough to fit over 100 people comfortably, as painted vaulted ceilings rose to a height of over twenty-five feet. Ornamental blue and purple carpets, Yuro's family colors lined the floors from wall to wall. A large, intricate painting depicting his family tree dominated one wall of the living room, weaving family murals within the branches of a strong looking maple. Every family member along the family tree shared a resemblance to that of Yuro, though his or her facial hairs and hairstyles differed wildly. At the center base of the maple was Yuro himself, the one distinction being the jeweled crown that sat atop his head. Flatlander chuckled as he passed the odd painting.

He passed the door that led, according to Yuro, to an older, abandoned part of the mansion, though it remained locked to its guests. Above the door, the word "Forbidden" was marked on the wall in thick, black lettering. Earlier, when Ellen had inquired about this part of the house during their brief tour, Yuro had intimated that the section was going through renovations, and quickly changed subjects. Flatlander and Henry had exchanged a look. And though Flatlander found this to be peculiar, he learned that it was proper guest etiquette in Vermont to respect one's host and obey the house rules. Therefore, they disregarded the mysterious door for the time being.

Sure enough, he soon found Henry and Ellen deep into a game of colonies. Lord Henry twirled his elm branch gracefully between his fingers as he scanned his remaining balls on the table. Yuro's marble table was much fancier than the one that he had seen at Bronson's, polished cherry wood so clean that it glowed among the torch-lit haze. On its side, large "Y's" were inscribed on the wooden frame in purple lettering.

They hadn't notice Flatlander standing in the doorway; for their attention was completely transfixed on the game at hand. Ellen stood across from Henry, awaiting his shot. Mumbling softly to himself, Henry aimed his elm stick and shot at the rainbow colored stone ball into the far corner of the table. The ball traveled gracefully across the polished marble, and hit the colored target with a gentle click, sending it deftly into the nearby corner hole. Ellen slammed the butt of her elm branch into the ground with a look of pure agony on her face.

"Yes!" shouted Henry in celebration.

"You know, for politicians, you seem to spend a lot of time playing around," said Flatlander.

The two turned towards the doorway, startled.

Henry saluted him and ushered him in. "Flatlander! You've found us!"

"Forget what you just saw," grumbled Ellen, as she shook her head, and shot the table one last admonishing look. "Henry must have the luck of the gods on his side tonight!"

Flatlander made his way into the room, inspecting the colonies table apathetically.

"Is it as addictive as they say? Bronson told me about the colonies junkies at the tavern."

Henry swung his arm around for Flatlander to take in the full view of the basement room. All of the king's clothes were strewn sloppily on the floor, while used cups and dishes lined the bookshelves and countertop. The only natural light that penetrated the basement was through two narrow windows on adjacent sides, the rest by large torches.

"Use your breathtaking power of observation, Flatlander. What do you think?" he laughed. "Truth is, I must receive one of these for Montpelier before our trip home. Perhaps Jess would agree to have it in her room."

"I'd caution against that," remarked Ellen, as she placed her elm branch roughly onto a golden wall rack. "Sounds like an unmitigated disaster in the making."

"You always manage ways to ruin my dreams, Ellen, even in the throes of victory. Thank you," replied Henry with a sigh.

Flatlander noticed the rest of the party curiously absent. "Where are Franklin and Menche?"

Henry shook his head. "Up to no good, I presume. Those two have been acting like little children as of late, even more so than usual."

Flatlander nodded and sat at the seat of a nearby table. "I need to talk to you both about something that I dreamt last night."

Henry cocked an eyebrow. "Is everything okay?"

"I think so," replied Flatlander.

He then proceeded to retell his dreams to Henry and Ellen. He told them about the fishing dock and the dog. He told them about the reoccurring river, and the game of propelling himself off of the rocks. Most of all, he told them how he saw two separate children on the banks of the river, which stirred something instinctual in him. Something profound. Ellen sat stoically as he spoke, and Henry became choked up as Flatlander talked about the children that he saw, in all their vivid detail: the rattle, the butterfly net, the shouting of 'Daddy.'

When Flatlander finally finished, Henry took a deep breath.

"Flatlander, I must say, whereas once I thought these dreams of yours to be a lingering effect from some type of head trauma, it's becoming more and more apparent that these are fragments of your memories trying to get back to you."

"So, you think that those were my children?" asked Flatlander, tentatively.

The idea that he might have two children, whose whereabouts and livelihoods were unknown, left him feeling unsettled and terrified.

Henry loosened his sleeve, which had been tightly wound at the elbow. "I can't say for sure, but I would venture to guess. Your brain is trying to tell you something."

"Your mind: it could be choosing the memories that you've held most esteemed," said Ellen.

Flatlander nodded and drew in a sharp breath. "I need to find out."

A great pause ensued, as Henry placed a reassuring hand on Flatlander's shoulder. "In time. In time. And if and when the time comes, and you should be beckoned back to your home, regardless of whether you accomplish your quests or not, I'll shall do everything in my power to assist you. You have proven your hardiness and value. It's the least that I can do. You have my word."

"Mine too," added Ellen.

Flatlander was slightly caught off guard by their kindness, for he had only accomplished half of his assigned missions. *I could leave tomorrow if I wanted.* He found himself giving the idea of returning home some serious and thought. He wondered what his children's names were. He wondered about where he lived, worked, and presumably, if he had a significant other. He wondered about his hobbies and interests. Though it was extremely frustrating to grasp at straws like this, he was alternatingly grateful for those small, but wonderful, glimpses into his past.

"Thanks."

Henry nodded and moved back to his seat across from Flatlander. "You're very welcome. Tomorrow, however, we shall see the Thinker with our own eyes, and your quest will continue unabated." Flatlander frowned. Perhaps he couldn't leave tomorrow. *Yuro told Henry as well?*

"Yuro told you about the quest?"

"Of course," smiled Henry, thinly. "While you were asleep. He wouldn't be so foolish as to keep his king in the dark, don't you think? After all, I choose your quests."

Flatlander remained silent.

"And while we're on the topic of families," continued Henry, unabated, "I've been meaning to tell you more about Jess the other day."

The colonies table lay bare, as the three friends sat there, exchanging stories of their lives and loved ones. Henry spoke of Jess and his ex wife. He spoke of childhood dreams and old jobs, long before he became elected and dubbed the Humble King. Also, for the first time since he had been in Vermont, Flatlander saw Ellen in all of her humanity for the first time. She spoke of her distant mother to the south and her troubles finding true love. She spoke of the Montpelier wind and how it seemed to call to her at times. She spoke of the future and how she planned to one day win a lordship in the republic. She spoke elegantly and honestly, free from her shield of infallibility. It was a rare and pleasant experience for Flatlander. Yet unbeknownst to the group, just outside the confines of Yuro's basement, a dangerous shadow trailed their two friends on the periphery of the mansion.

"Quiet, Franklin! Ya wanna get us *caughts*?" chided Menche from behind the lumbering brute.

Letting their curiosities get the best of them, the two had entered the forbidden door to the darkened half of Yuro's mansion. Menche had picked the lock with little more than a thin copper wire that he had found in a drawer in Yuro's kitchen. Out negotiating deals for the Moran Plant at Burlington's City Hall, Yuro and his butler, Bart, had left the house close to thirty minutes ago. The rest of the company, consumed with colonies, hardly stirred from Yuro's basement. This left Franklin and Menche ample time to do some exploration.

As the door slowly creaked open, Menche peered nervously through a darkened hallway. Streams of light shone out from a few bedroom doorways further down, as clouds of dust circulated from a ceiling-borne draft. The air was stale. To Franklin, it reeked of a mixture of mothballs and pine tar. The hallway was in a state of utter disrepair, several floor planks had buckled and the white ceiling was caked a thin layer of mold and rippling spider webs. Much of the walls were so badly peeled that scales of paint lay piled on the floor below.

"I fancy it hasn't seen a mop fer some time, huh?" chuckled Franklin, softly, as he wiped a small spider web clean from a wall.

Menche giggled. "Or a broom."

Franklin lit a small lantern, which he had found near his bedside at Yuro's. The two ventured carefully down the hallway, side-by-side, peering into each abandoned bedroom as they passed. While the conditions of both rooms were in a similar state of dilapidation, the beds were, oddly, still neatly made, the beds, dressers, and desks in their familiar positions. Thick tangles of dust-covered spider web filled each missing floorboard, wall panel and ceiling pane. Despite this, moths and black flies buzzed about.

As they passed the third room on the right, they noticed an object sitting on a bed. A porcelain doll, dressed in red satin with blond hair, leaned awkwardly against a pillow. Its large beady eyes seemed to be trained solely on Franklin. Franklin recoiled from the ghastly sight.

"Whiskers and syrup…" he muttered under his breath. "I hate dolls."

"Whose doll, I wonders?" asked Menche.

"I don't like this place," declared Franklin, as he shoved his little friend back into the hallway. "Seen enough."

"Not gettin' an argument outta me!" replied Menche in agreement.

As the two turned back down from where they had came from, a loud clattering sounded from the far side of the hallway. It sounded to Menche like a horse stomping on the floor. He was the first to catch the sight, yet it appeared a shadow from the distance. Grotesquely large, the shadow moved with extremely agility for its size. Every couple seconds, long arms or appendages slapped the walls of the hallway violently, each louder than the last. It grunted and roared madly, as the creature began moving towards them in a hurry.

Menche emitted a high-pitched squeak, as the two explorers sprinted down the hallway in sheer terror, and back through the forbidden door. Upon exiting, Franklin slammed the door shut and gestured madly for Menche to refasten its lock. Once completed, the two walked quickly, out of breath, to the empty deck outside the kitchen. It was half a minute or more before either one spoke.

"What was it, ya thinks?" asked Menche through heavy breaths. His skin was a ghostly white and his hands shook uncontrollably.

"Don't know. Don't *wanna* know," stammered Franklin, as he took a moment to collect his wits.

"Ya think, ya think it was one of dem, dem monsters from Northfield?"

"T'was no pigman," dismissed Franklin. "They'd never come this far north."

"Then whats could it been?"

Franklin eyes then went wide. "Ya see the way that doll looked at me? Ya saw it, didn't ya?"

"I thinks I'm gonna be sick," muttered Menche, as he dry heaved.

The two spent almost a full five minutes collecting their breath, attempting to process what they had just seen; or what they *thought* they had seen. Then both noticed suddenly that Bart the Butler was giving them a curious look from a window inside the kitchen. Franklin did his best to compose himself, hoping that the butler hadn't caught wind to their misadventure. Waving to Bart in feigned delight, Franklin wondered why he had arrived home so soon from shopping. Shooting the northerner a suspicious look, the butler then disappeared back into the kitchen.

Franklin exhaled sharply. "Menche, ya can never mention this to the lads. This stays between us. Promise."

Menche wheezed between gasps. "Promise."

Franklin nodded: "Good."

But all was *not* good. It was rare form for Franklin of Walden to become so spooked. *Should I tell Henry? No*, decided Franklin, *ain't worth the trouble*. Whatever lurked in the darkness of Yuro's mansion was sinister, pure and simple, and something told him that they hadn't seen the last of it.

The Thinker sat on its stone pedestal amid a clearing next to the Moran Plant. Portraying a naked man lost in thought, the statue's chin rested plaintively on a closed fist. His body was muscled and defined, his privates well guarded by an outstretched thigh. The statue was made of pure bronze, yet had been covered by traces of blue-green lichen over time, and parts had even rusted brown by the incessant lake squalls.

As Flatlander circled the Moran Plant with Yuro and Henry, he was taken aback by the condition of the building. Its windows were all gone or partially smashed, as a large flight of pigeons fluttered to and from the upper reaches of the factory's lofts. Depressed and lifeless, the Moran's red brick was darkened by years of coal production, and afterwards, sheer neglect. Its shape was unique, observed Flatlander, like a group of three boxes cluttered together in a disproportionate staircase, with the tallest column or "stair" soaring to nearly ninety or more feet in the air.

"A bit of an eyesore, I know," muttered Yuro, as he kicked a piece of grime loose from the Moran's outer wall. "I have a hard time explaining it to those traveling from other regions of the republic. 'Is it a prison?' they ask. 'A mental institute from the Old Country?' The troubling thing this, I am sometimes at a loss for words. It's a simply dreadful sight."

Cautiously, the three neared the statue of the Thinker. Flatlander noticed Yuro's walk stiffening. Gazing at its multi-colored surface, Flatlander took a deep breath, reminding himself of the tales told by Yuro. And while he doubted some of the tales' authenticity, Flatlander wasn't about to test his luck against this mysterious power. The Thinker was larger than he had previously thought: it simply soared over the three men. Yuro had trouble even looking directly at the statue's face.

"You say that it once struck-down a man dead?" asked Henry. "How can that be?"

Yuro nodded. "Yes, though there's no definitive proof according to the skeptics."

"No need," replied Henry, swiftly, as he glanced warily at the Thinker's face, deep in the throes of contemplation. "We don't intend on making the same mistake. Luckily, we have some time to come up with a plan."

Yuro shuffled nervously. "Yes, umm, about that. Hmm. That, umm, may or may not be true any longer."

Henry turned to Yuro. "What do you mean?"

Yuro blushed. "I suppose that it's time to come clean. You see, yesterday while you were all lounging at the house playing colonies, I was summoned to an emergency council regarding the future of the Moran Plant. Well, it doesn't look good. Somehow, word got out that Flatlander and yourself have your eyes set on the building." Yuro looked sheepishly at the ground, then swished his tongue in his mouth, looking for the right words to use. "Let's just say that the warring groups in this city are mobilizing. In fact, it may even be unsafe for us to be here at this very hour."

"And you're telling us this *now*?" asked Henry, as he approached Yuro, scanning the surrounding hills with a wary eye. "Master Yuro, I took you as being smarter than that!"

Yuro shrunk away. "Many apologies, Lord Henry. I take full responsibility and deserve your criticism. The emergency council tried to vote on a temporary resolution, yet the attempt was futile. It ended with a shouting match and an all-out declaration of war between the Contrarians, Prosperates and Worker's Party."

"*And*?" asked Flatlander, his curiosity piqued.

Yuro swallowed and closed his eyes, bracing himself for the incoming verbal onslaught. "And there is much trouble to come to this field by tomorrow at noon. The groups are intending to meet here to do…" he paused before swallowing, "battle."

Henry was flabbergasted. "*Battle*? How can this be? *Over a building*? Master Yuro."

Yuro pointed at the Moran Plant. "Lord Henry, you must take three things into account. First off, this has been a contentious issue here for over a century. To dismiss its historical implications is to dismiss common sense entirely. Secondly, there is a lot more going on here than a dispute over a building. This is a power grab. These three groups, including my own Prosperates, hate one another, and will do everything in their power to destroy the other two. They squabble over every issue imaginable, from who receives city money, to taxes, to what color they should paint road signs. Third, it's, never mind."

Henry grew impatient. "Master Yuro?"

"It's Flatlander," Yuro admitted shamefully. He turned to Flatlander with sorrow. "Many apologies, brave one. While you have built up many supporters, particularly since your courageous victory against Superpac, there are still many who don't trust you, or what they perceive as your 'agenda'. Furthermore, some have seen that you mostly bring a wake of destruction upon any task you are given. They smell your scent, so to speak, and they are panicking. There are still many who want to help decide the Moran's fate without the help of an outsider, let alone a *Flatlander*. They've invested years of energy and emotion into their ideas, and they aren't about to go down without a fight, in the most literal sense."

Flatlander was tempted to tell Yuro off, but thought better of it. Taking his frustration out on the Yuro would amount to nothing. It was the common people of Burlington, not the lord, who perceived Flatlander as the threat.

"So what do we do now?" demanded Henry, as he paced back and forth near the base of the Thinker. "We haven't the manpower to help you defeat two or three separate militias on such short notice. It would take days for me to mobilize the republic's volunteer army."

"Nor would I expect you to," replied Yuro with a pained expression. His crown nearly tipped over, but he saved it instinctively. "All that I ask is that you help me try to maintain peace. It's all we can hope for. If we let this fray get out of control, it could end up throwing the entire city into complete disarray. And that, my friend, could spell trouble for even the likes of you." The lord glanced up to the hilly Depot Street, towards to foot of Burlington's downtown. "Vermont's largest city could break out into an all out war, Lord Henry."

Henry placed a hand on Flatlander's shoulder. "We need to leave here at once. This place isn't safe," then turned to Yuro, "Master Yuro, we thank you for your time and will meet you back at your house by dinner. I must have a private word with my advisor."

"I'm sorry, Lord Henry."

"Save the pleasantries until we get this matter resolved," replied Henry brusquely. "For now, we need a plan."

As the two walked away, Flatlander soon came to find out that Henry needed to remove himself from the conversation before he exploded on Yuro, and said some terribly regrettable things. He also came to find out, via Henry's tirade, about some of the intricacies behind Burlington's political scene, including Yuro's perceived weakness in power. The city was on the verge of erupting, as Henry likened the evolving situation to the recently found abyss of superpac, ready to ignite with the slightest spark.

Flatlander turned back towards the Thinker, and saw Yuro standing in the distance watching them leave. His purple, kingly robe fluttered like aired laundry on a clothesline. The statue glowed an unnatural aquamarine in the afternoon haze. Behind the Moran Plant and beyond, the lake stirred greatly under stiff winds and a semi-obscured sun. The Adirondacks were the clearest he had ever seen them. It was a quite a pretty sight, but Flatlander had neither the wits nor the time to appreciate it. There was much to mull over.

The next day was gray and still. They met shortly after dawn at the front of the Moran Plant. Flatlander, Henry, and Yuro had convened at the site early to try to come up with plans to prevent an all-out battle. Franklin, Ellen, and Menche arrived soon thereafter. Yuro had suggested that perhaps they should cordon off the property with ropes, but doubtless, argued Henry, a mere barrier wouldn't stop the men from doing battle. Henry proposed to use non-violent means, like covering the fields in fish guts collected from the fishing vessels at port. Yet fishing in the Queen City had been slow that morning, and it proved to be an insurmountable task after they had seen the scant morning's catch. Flatlander suggested that they create a diversion to buy them more time to plan, but what kind of diversion; he hadn't the slightest clue. All morning, the group debated on what to do, but as time dwindled, they had come up with nothing.

At 11:32 AM, the Prosperates, Yuro's own member party, came marching to the Moran's lawn, one hundred men and women strong. They were dressed in their party's colors: purple, blue and gold. A fickle-faced minstrel, wrapped tightly in a purple and violet trench coat, sang an ominous tune, as he led the group closer to the building of contention. They looked determined, yet their attire seemed to be more suitable for a tea party, not the theatre of war. Their garments were soft and silky, like Yuro's. In addition, Flatlander saw that many of the Prosperates wore an excessive amount of jewelry, limiting their freedom of motion. Behind their forlorn minstrel, a redheaded woman in her late fifties wielded a torch in one hand and a cross in the other.

She halted the party with a raised hand and addressed the embattled lord. "Master Yuro. Such a pleasant surprise, though it would be better to see you fighting by our side rather than spectating."

"Hester, stop this madness at once!" demanded Yuro.

Hester bristled at the suggestion. "I *am* stopping this madness, though, dear Yuro. I'm stopping this *hundred years* of madness, for once and for all. For every day that the Moran lays empty, a Prosperate sheds an unseen tear."

The Prosperates cheered at her words. Hester was a soft-faced woman, slightly portly, and she had a pair of round, beautiful blue eyes, which now glowed in the late morning gloom. Unlike the majority of her party, which traveled in purple and gold, she wore a bright blue robe, a tan, silk dress, and her hair was braided in the shape of a halo. Hester was second in the chain of command of the Yuro's Prosperates and had been at a sharp disagreement with Yuro in his handling of the Moran Plant. She pleaded desperately for the high-end self-sustaining restaurant at meetings, citing the need of such a business by the waterfront. In spite of Yuro's disagreement, she had rallied enough support within the party to make a last-ditch stand. It was a damning statement of Yuro's slipping clout, and the dispute now completely fractured the once-strong party. Yuro, most of all, was both shaken and ill with grief when he discovered her plans for battle while at the emergency council meeting.

"Hester, I've trusted you like family. The Moran will see no victor today, only bloodshed. One cannot barge into a room with blind rage and expect positive results. Please, I beg you. Let's talk this through."

Hester glanced back at the formidable party gathered at her back, then back to Yuro. "My apologies, Master Yuro. You have been a worthy mentor, but the time for talking is over. The time for battle has begun."

Yuro shrank back into the shadows of the Moran Plant, a defeated shell of himself. Recognizing many in Hester's party, he tried, futilely, to convince them to turn back around. Not a single member obeyed. Then, looking to Henry with a blank expression, he threw down his lucky rabbit's foot to the ground.

"Much blood will be spilt here today," he spat.

Flatlander and Henry traded an ominous glance, as Franklin scanned the hills of Depot Street for more signs of trouble.

Sure enough, more trouble came. At 11:48 AM, the Worker's Party began flooding the Moran's lawn. Though not quite as large a group as the Prosperates, they were a burly, fearsome bunch.

These were the farmers, loggers and builders of Burlington. Most bore weapons of blunt force, and even a few wardens appeared amongst their ranks carrying rifles. Nearly all wore menacing scowls; looks that revealed a deep-simmering hatred for the Prosperates and their agenda. Some wore brown and beige furs, while others, the camouflage that had been associated with the hunters of the north. Unlike the Prosperates, not a single woman was seen in the crowd, nor a single bare face, as their beards ranged in length from half a foot to waist-length. The Worker's Party was fiercely proud to be Vermont-born and saw the Moran Plant issue as being the last straw in destroying the image of their republic. They also carried with them an immense distrust of Flatlanders. Anticipating this deep prejudice, Flatlander came wearing a deer coat on this hot, summer day, courtesy of Yuro, in anticipation of the Worker's Party. *Though it probably wouldn't do much good*, he had been warned.

Their leader, Fletcher Posey, the imposing farmer and former political rival of Yuro's, stood at the lead, a scythe coated with mud firmly gripped in his hand. Posey's beard was long and trimmed into a near-rectangular shape. His brown overalls were tattered and stretched. He wore a torn, faded brown fur coat, no doubt the ill effects of being bleached by the constant sun at his back, a badge of pride amongst republic farmers. Occasionally, Posey was advised to replace his coat by his family and peers alike, though he would have none of it. He perceived his jacket as he perceived the republic as a whole: keeping Vermont entrenched in its more traditional roots was critically important. For in his view, the second republic, in its splendor of infancy, was built on the backs of those whom dwelt and labored the farms, logged the land, fished its lakes, and oversaw construction of the wall and aqueducts.

Posey motioned for his men to stay at bay, as he continued onward to the shadows of the Moran towards Flatlander and party. He sneered as he neared Yuro and Henry.

"If it ain't our darlin' the Humble King and Yuro decidin' to play leader for a change. What a treat."

Yuro ignored the ribbing. "Your ice wall is nothing but mere fantasy, Posey."

Posey flushed with rage. "We need out boys to grow up strong, skilled and brave. An ice climbin' wall will toughen their hands, toughen their skin! If they ain't climbin' ice, they might end up on the streets doin' superpac!"

Yuro sighed. "Superpac is no longer a threat. Besides, we can make ice-climbing walls in other places. The Moran is much too important."

"I ain't stupid. Ya been listenin' to that damned Flatlander too much. I'm sure he'll turn the whole blasted thing into his own apartment, rent-free with the Lord Henry's approval," countered Posey, as he glanced towards Henry. The Humble King held his tongue.

"We would do no such thing, Posey. The mere thought is preposterous," replied Yuro, assuredly. "We must reconvene and work hard to achieve a solution to this insanity."

Posey grunted. "And what would ye know of hard work, Master Yuro? Ye can probably count on one hand the days in which you have truly toiled, truly worked till yer barrow-back't like the lot of us!"

Henry flushed red with anger. "How dare you speak to your leaders in this fashion! Have you no shame? The Flatlander has nothing to do with your petty squabbling. And ice wall or not, that is no excuse for a precursor to war!"

"Don't speak to me of *shame*, Lord Henry," countered Posey. "The only pool of shame rests behind yer backs, ten stories tall." Fletcher Posey glanced up the full height of the Moran, and then circled back around to face his men. "When the day is through, our boys will be climbin' their ice walls 'till their hands go numb."

The Worker's Party cheered and grunted in approval.

"Then you have sealed your fate, and those of your men," declared Henry.

Posey whipped his scythe around in the air, much to the delight of his small army of men, who continued to cheer on their fearless leader with sheer abandon. Many of the Prosperates looked on nervously, as Hester began conferring with a priest, deep in prayer.

At 12:05 PM, and in a sudden rush, the horde of Contrarians came sprinting into the fray from the hills of Depot Street. They wore no single uniform, nor carried one uniform weapon. They brought plungers and branches, daggers and clubs, stones and brass knuckles, spears and sharpened steel bars. They came in droves over the hill, shouting and screaming. They streamed onto the Moran's lawn, as the two other armies inched slowly backwards to make room for the unruly group. Despite their fierce appearance, their proclaimed leader was a feeble old man named Wilson Willard. Carried on a portable throne, Willard wore his fur coat inside out. It was a custom that many of the Contrarians adhered to, as the party was known to persistently defy most logical conventions, as well as anything perceived to be conformist.

"This could get very ugly very fast," mumbled Yuro.

The Contrarians rushed closer to the field of battle, and soon gathered en masse between the competing factions. Willard could not speak, but delegated members of his party by merely gesturing and pointing in various directions.

"Do something," urged Ellen desperately to Yuro. The three armies yelled and sneered at one another, daring the other to make the first move.

Henry turned to Yuro, and spoke sternly. "If you refuse to speak to them, then I will."

Yuro nodded, reluctantly. Soon he emerged from the shadow of the Moran, and blew into an oversized bullhorn, which he had brought for the occasion. The sound echoed from the hills of Depot Street out into the lake. After another half minute of clamoring, the armies settled down and watched the Lord of Burlington standing afoot the Moran.

Yuro cleared his throat. "Friends. Burlingtonians. Vermonters. Prosperates. Worker's Party. Contrarians. Hear me. For once in my life, I am fearful for our future." He paused, before pointing at the gathered masses. "Look at us! This is sheer madness. Long after the last bit of blood from today's battle is washed from these grasses, the Moran will still yet stand, and nobody here will be claimed the victor for their troubles. Long after the children of this town have lost a father or mother in battle, the Thinker will still occupy his pedestal and tempt the fate of others. Long after our political structure has devolved into a state of disarray, the waves of Lake Champlain will still beat true to the same shore, the same wind will come shooting from the west, the same starlight will come flooding from the heavens, and still, the same Thinker sits in his same state of timeless reflection."

In response, the various groups shouted unintelligible, horrible things at Yuro and company. The shouting escalated, as several stones and farming objects were thrown within mere feet of the group. Franklin wielded his axe in loops, ready to knock away any objects that sailed too close for comfort. Flatlander unsheathed his sword.

Yuro tried to plead with the crowd again. "Please. I stand here with Lord Henry himself, leader of our great and free republic. If only he could have some words with you, then perhaps you could give into reason."

From deep among the Worker's Party, a spear was launched in the direction of the Contrarians, striking a man flush on the thigh. His scream was ungodly awful, the mere pitch sending chills up Flatlander's spine. It took only seconds before the Contrarians responded, and charged the other two groups in a frenzied craze.

The mud on the field was awful, shot up in spurts by the furious storm of boots. Ellen removed her dagger at the ready. Seconds later the groups clashed, Yuro gave his companions a look of pure dread.

"My friends, I apologize. The city is lost and there is nothing that we can do to stop it."

The ensuing battle raged on with great savagery under the watchful eye of the Thinker. The yells, screams and moans rang out among the field of battle. An occasional gunshot sounded off presumably from the wardens, prompting a series of shouts, and the intensified clattering of arms. All-out chaos reigned supreme. There was very little organization from all the opposing factions, and it showed within their scattered ranks.

The field soon stunk of sweat and blood. Though many of the troops engaged in battle made efforts to avoid Yuro and company, the Contrarians and Worker's Party weren't shy about sending a "stray" arrow or spear in their general direction. With Henry's prompting, Flatlander took cover with Henry, Ellen and Menche behind a large piece of scrap metal leaned up against the Moran's outer wall. They could still view the battle from rusted-out openings in the metal frame. Franklin dragged Yuro away from the action, and took cover behind the Moran Plant per Henry's orders. The northerner guarded Yuro fiercely.

Then, just as the battle hit a fever pitch in its intensity, Flatlander noticed a peculiar thing. An errant arrow smashed through a window overhead, shattering it. From the corner of his eye, he caught a strange movement in the statue. Its head looked straight ahead; though its original positioning had the statue facing downward. He then watched as the statue's fist slowly unclenched itself. Flatlander shook his head, unsure if he was imagining things. *It couldn't be.* Yet, there it was, plain to see. Nobody else in the vicinity seemed to take notice. The turbulence of battle festered all around the base of the Thinker. Flatlander began searching for explanations. *It must have been knocked into hard by a soldier or horse.*

While Flatlander was still trying to digest what had occurred, a nearby brick on the Moran chipped off from the wall from a wayward bullet. Flatlander then focused intently on the Thinker, and sure enough, it moved again, placing both hands at its sides.

It's coming alive. Then a realization began dawning on him, providing a glimmer of hope in their grave situation.

"Lord Henry, the horn! Please! Hand it to me!" pleaded Flatlander, as he pointed to Yuro's dropped horn, lying near to the entranceway of the Moran near Henry.

Henry shook his head emphatically. "Flatlander! Do you want to get us killed? What antics do you have planned?"

Flatlander reached out his hand for assistance. "No, you don't understand. I think that I figured it out. Please, Lord Henry. It could be the answer!" said Flatlander over the roar of the battle. Henry grimaced, and quickly retrieved the horn, before diving back under the shelter, unharmed.

"You're not calling attention to us, are you?"

"Stay here," replied Flatlander to the group.

Flatlander then emerged from behind the piece of scrap metal, blaring the bullhorn in one hand, holding his sword in the other. The clanging of metal on metal began to subside. The yells and screams faded to a near mute. The plopping of boot steps, deeply entrenched in the mud, came slowly to a halt. Flatlander kept blaring the horn. He sounded it until he was sure he had everyone's full attention. The militias slowly hobbled together, staggering into rank and file. The Contrarians, Worker's Party, and Prosperates looked upon Flatlander expectantly. Dozens of wounded on the field of battle continued groaning in pain, filling the void of near-silence.

"What are you *doing*?" gasped Henry from behind the scrap metal.

"Watch."

Flatlander took a deep breath. "If I could only have such a moment of your time. I want you all to see something. Watch me, then watch the statue."

The crowd slowly obliged and watched him intently. Some were already startled after recognizing the changed posture of the Thinker. Flatlander took several steps away from the Moran, picked up a fist-sized stone, and threw it hard at a near half-cracked window. The window shattered dramatically, as the men and women exchanged curious looks with one another. Then, as if on cue, the Thinker splayed his legs out from his cross-legged position, and lifted its head ever so slightly. On its face, a smile formed among its thin, corroded lips. The assembled factions wooed in amazement at the sight. Yells of confusion and panic filled the air. Posey, convinced that Flatlander was behind some sort of trickery, grumbled about the use of black magic.

Just to prove the point further, Flatlander dropped the bullhorn, charged the plant, and struck his sword against a loose piece of wood obtruding from a post. Though it was a clumsy strike, it hit with enough force to sheer it off clean. Seconds later, the Thinker slowly stood from his sitting position, and straightened. The statue was clearly beaming with delight, his hands clasped together in a hopeful repose. Murmurs, coupled with a few scattered shouts, resounded from within the crowd of men and women.

Flatlander picked up the bullhorn again. "Don't you people get it? This is it. This is what the Thinker wants. He wants the Moran Plant gone. He wants it eliminated. There's no other way. He can't speak but he's telling us something right now. If you'd all just stop and listen."

"And what does a *Flatlander* know about listenin'?" countered Posey from the crowd, his face bloodied and crazed.

"More than you think. I plead with you all. Let's bring it down!" said Flatlander into the bullhorn valiantly.

A large bulk of the crowd had ignored Posey's indignation and approached the structure ready to inflict damage. Some came aggressively, while others neared the Moran cautiously, baffled over what they had just witnessed. Flatlander peered behind the sheet of metal at his friends.

"You guys better get out from under there! Fast!"

They moved a few dozen paces from the building and watched the flurry of arrows, sword glances, and gunshots obliterate windows, doors, and brickwork. Spurring them on was the Thinker himself, a smile slowly crawling on his once-expressionless face. It began raising its hands in celebration. Flatlander motioned for the party to hurry from the crowd, as they soon watched the scene unfold from atop Depot Street.

A group of Contrarians doused the plant in a clear liquid and then ran away in excited yelps. Seconds later, a dozen flaming arrows embedded in the roof and foot of the building, and within a minute, the Moran Plant ignited under a mountain of flame and smoke. Residual coal dust in the building gave the smoke a thick black, acrid quality. The battling had now come to a complete stop, as nearly every assembled fighter stopped what they were doing, and looked upon the famed structure in astonishment. An unsuspecting tranquility seemed to come over the battlefield.

The Thinker began glowing a bright blue, cutting through the grey of the wet, cloudy afternoon like a knife. The crowd alternated between the Moran Plant, aflame before their very eyes, and the Thinker, whose color had now grown a radiant, shimmering turquoise. The statue then began radiating so much light and energy, that many in the warring crowds were wary of it exploding, and ran for cover, far from the Moran's bloodied grounds.

Then in one brilliant flash of light, the Thinker transformed itself into three separate beams of blue energy, and then shot out to the heavens at breakneck speed. The explosion sent out a shockwave of energy to the waterfront below, sending people hurtling for cover. The boom was so loud, in fact, the rumble echoed loudly off of the Adirondacks to the west a second later, and continued to thunder on the lake's surface long after the thinker was gone. All that remained were the skeletal, burning innards of the Moran Plant, fully engulfed in an inferno. Periodically, came with it a crashing of metal, a slight explosion, or falling brick, barely discernable over its roaring flames. Small groups of wounded and weary scattered in all different directions. Several Prosperates and Contrarians passed by Flatlander and company with small, acknowledging nods.

A calm then fell over the land. Flatlander looked to Henry and Yuro, who were watching the blaze intently. Franklin, Menche, and Ellen stood idly by the side of Depot Street. Flatlander briefly caught Ellen admiring him, but upon locking eyes, she quickly turned away in embarrassment. He then lost himself in the falling embers of the Moran's Plant, as burning sections of scaffolding fell to the concrete floor, each emitting a loud bang. The eyesore that was the Moran, another relic from the Old Country, continued to wither away; the very ashes of its predecessors spread freely among the winds of the Champlain Valley.

CHAPTER 11
The Obelisk of Highgate

"LET'S EAT," SAID LORD HENRY as he lifted his spoon. Never were two words more comforting to Flatlander during those late morning hours, for his pangs of hunger had become near unbearable. Henry and he had recently arrived at Sweet Tooth Sweeney's, a restaurant specializing in high-end deserts and pastries. In front of him lay two gold-coated pastries doused in a truffle oil and caramel and smeared in a generous portion of maple syrup. Situated on Bank Street in Burlington, Sweet Tooth Sweeney's was a popular destination for many. A small outdoor patio enclosed with ivy-covered gates graced the front of the restaurant, which fit several tables snugly. Housed in a giant, hut-looking structure made of various stones; it was originally erected during the republic-wide drought of the 30's and 40's. Used as a shelter for unfortunate local farmers, many who had lost their crops at the peak of the dry years, the building had now transformed, quite ironically, into a center for decadence.

It was mid August in downtown Burlington. A month had gone by since the destruction of the Thinker. Henry had thought it pertinent to give Flatlander a much-needed break. During Flatlander's time off, he had spent the better part of late July and early August swimming, reading up on the republic's history, taking Pete for strolls, and exploring the forest trails in the foothills that surrounded Montpelier. Yet as summer winded down, Henry warned that another mission was soon lurking on the horizon.

"I'd like to personally congratulate you on your success thus far, Flatlander," said Henry, his voice garbled from simultaneously consuming a glazed, raspberry pastry. "Six of your assigned ten quests are now complete with only four more to go. I hope you should know that I'm considering making this a full-time job for you in the future."

"I'd be expensive, Lord Henry. My services are in high demand," quipped Flatlander.

Henry nodded. "Yes, of course. You'd be showered in gifts from the various regions of our republic," replied Henry, playfully, "flowers from the miller, gems from Yuro, and a three gun salute from the wardens."

The friends shared a laugh. The Humble King paused momentarily while he ate and looked at Flatlander curiously, as if he noticed something unusual. Out of instinct, Flatlander wiped his mouth with his napkin, expecting to find fudge smeared about his lips or frosting on his cheeks.

"Have you been growing out your facial hair?"

Flatlander rubbed his cheeks and felt a rather thick layer of stubble greet his fingertips. The truth was that it hadn't been a conscious decision.

"I hadn't realized how long it had gotten."

Slowly, a smile began to form across Henry's face. "Well, by the Gods themselves! If it isn't the makings of a beard, then my name isn't King Henry!"

"I don't know about that," mumbled Flatlander, slightly embarrassed. "I just haven't the time to shave…"

"Yes, I can see that! You're beginning to look more like a Vermonter by the day! Wait until Franklin sees this! Oh,

Flatlander, this is so exciting!" exclaimed Henry, as he clasped his hands together in delight.

"You don't have to..." began Flatlander.

But as he watched the pure joy in Henry's face, he held his tongue firmly in place. *Let him be happy.* A joyful Henry was much more tolerable than a stern Henry.

As the excitement wore off, they began discussing the political fall-out from the Battle at the Moran Plant, and how Yuro had tightened his grip of power in Burlington after the others had looked foolish in their plans. Henry spoke of Jess and her slow transition to normalcy, and how she had begun caring for Pete. He also spoke of Flatlander's future in the republic and how he wanted to keep him around longer than his allotted ten quests. Intentionally ambiguous on the matter, Flatlander still needed time to arrive at a decision. Near the end of their meal, Henry received a bill from a waitress and held it up for Flatlander to see.

"By chance, does your memory recall how to tip properly, Flatlander?"

"It has something to do with giving money, right?"

Henry nodded and removed a wad of cash from his pocket. "Correct. It's customary to leave 15% gratuity of your total bill at a minimum. 20% is standard. Tipping 25% or more is very generous, but seldom done; spare only by the wealthiest clientele." Henry glanced at the bill again. "Our bill comes out to roughly forty-eight dollars, so I will leave a tip of ten dollars. Pretty standard, I'd say."

Flatlander sensed there was something that Henry was not telling him.

"I appreciate the math lesson, but I don't see why..."

"See here," said Henry as he nodded at the table of patrons seated to their left. "I want you to observe this exchange."

Two couples occupied the table of interest; dressed in brightly colored pastel coats, and adorning tightly laced pants. The men wore quilted aviator hats, and the women wore their hair down, long and silky smooth. As Flatlander focused his attention on the group, it had become quite evident that they spoke a different language. The tongue sounded more romantic than English, more rushed in its pronunciation with a heavier nasal twang.

"Who are they?"

"Shh. Listen."

As the waitress came by to give the table their final bill, he heard the men and women confer with one another in confusion. She then took a noticeabley deep breath and went back inside. Seconds later, the very same waitress peered out of the window at the patrons, casting them a doubtful glance. The group continued their confused conversation, placed a wad of money on the tabletop, rose awkwardly, then left. Waiting until the couples were out of sight, she rushed outside to the recently occupied table. Upon counting the wad of money, the waitress let out a heavy sigh of frustration. In jerked motions, she then cleaned off their table, slid the thin wad of money into her apron pocket, and walked back towards the inside of Sweet Tooth Sweeney's.

"What was *that* all about?" inquired Flatlander.

Lord Henry's contemptuous gaze followed the recently departed party.

"Those people hail from a region even north of Vermont, beyond the wall, in the northern reaches of Lake Champlain. The region is named Quebec, formerly a territory of Canada until they too seceded. They are called the Quebecois. They come mostly by boat through the Northern Gate, or on foot through a small entrance in Highgate. Many of them live in Montreal, the great city of the North. The Quebecois are a very mysterious kind. Few here understand their culture and inner-workings. Fewer so, in fact, understand their tipping habits. That waitress, most likely, didn't receive the appropriate tip from the service that she just provided them."

"But how do you know that? Is this common?"

"Yes." Henry sighed. "More common than any of us would like. It could be a slight; an affront, a damning statement of what they perceive as inferior service and food, or the unmistakable gesture of indifference. Perhaps it's a sign of a possible gloomy Quebecois economy? All of this is merely speculative and conjecture. The possibilities are endless. If Lord Andreas and a handful of other senators get their way, however, there would have been a ban against the Quebecois traveling here until the case is resolved. This would be a terrible mistake, in my estimation. Montreal is said to be massive, though they care little for war. Through the Montreal Compromise[67], we are fortunate enough to enjoy a peaceful relationship with them, including a trade agreement that keeps our maple syrup markets separate. But this trend is becoming an unfortunate pattern. Some here, like that waitress, can't afford such a loss of their income."

"Is it really that big of a deal?" asked Flatlander. He thought back to the waitress's reaction. "How much did she lose? Ten or twenty dollars, at most?"

Henry nodded. "She may have only lost ten dollars, but those ten dollars could have paid for her next meal, her next date, a pound of her favorite tea, her boot polish expenses for the coming winter or more. Multiply that ten dollars by the thousands every day throughout the entire year, and it adds up to quite a hefty sum, Flatlander. In the past five years, in Burlington alone, losses from Quebecois tipping habits are estimated to be close to six million dollars."

Flatlander whistled. "Well now that you put it that way..."

"Which is why it's important that we get to the bottom of this. This may require guidance from our greatest minds in Middlebury. Certain rumors point to a mysterious object in the woods of Highgate, on the same road that once leads to the Great

---

[67] An economic and peace agreement in 2036 between Vermont and Quebec.

City of the North. I need to speak with Lord Trombley on the matter."

Flatlander's attention drifted to the waitress inside of the restaurant, her face now buried in her hands. As she glanced up, he could see her eyes were red and puffy. Tears streamed down the side of her blushed cheeks. A female colleague came by, draped her arm around the young woman and hurried her away from the watchful eyes of the restaurant's remaining patrons. Neither Henry nor Flatlander missed the sad sight.

"I'm in," added Flatlander, with a renewed sense of purpose.

"I knew that I could count on you."

"Only a fool shall suffer alone," whispered Shay, vacantly, as he peered into the fire.

The words had been those of Walt Newsome, Burlington's legendary journalist: reporter, philanthropist, philosopher, and model for Shay Bromage during his early years in the profession. Newsome was considered the godfather of journalism in the city of Burlington. Prior to his arrival, the news consisted of a condensed report of criminal activity, business deals, and upcoming events. There was no mention of myths. No mention of lore. No mention of the thousands of untold, unseen stories that unfold before the population on a daily routine. To his credit, Shay noted wryly, Newsome achieved his success with only hard work and intelligence, not with the use of superpac. Shay shook his head in shame.

The air felt thick and oppressive, the summer heat was barely reduced by nightfall. Shay stoked the small fire pit in his backyard with a crooked tree branch. As the flames brightened, Harrison body emerged from the dark into better detail; its eyes shone a bright red. The mule glanced at its master in curiosity.

"Pay me no heed, Harrison," muttered Shay flatly, as he pointlessly continued rearranging the enflamed logs. "Shouldn't be too hard. Plenty of people are doing it as of late."

He dinged one of the logs roughly with the branch, causing sparks to shoot out.

Only a fool shall suffer alone.

He rubbed at his face in marked frustration, thinking long and hard about the direction of his life. Since discovering his secret addiction to superpac, and according to mutual friends, Dawn had been temporarily living in her office. Vergil had shown him no mercy relating to their pact of smearing Flatlander. And meanwhile, Flatlander, once the scourge of the republic, had made positive news once again for his role in eliminating the Moran Plant and the Thinker. *And this, shortly after destroying the supply of Superpac.* Shay sighed in discontent. *The fool was now hailed as a hero. A hero!*

Inside, a blank sheet of paper lay upright, inserted through his typewriter's spool. The future article in wait: his condemnation pertaining to Flatlander's handling of the Moran Plant. Yet Shay had already made up his mind on the matter. He wasn't writing it. Vergil would be furious, of course. The repercussions would be swift and fierce.

The Shay Chronicles had been one of the last things on Shay's mind, yet his newspaper was one of the few aspects in his life that he could still exert some control over, something that he could still love unconditionally. *Well, that…and Harrison, I suppose.* He smiled at the sight of his mule; now sound asleep against a fallen tree. Shay sighed long and deep.

Only a fool shall suffer alone.

Three days later, Vergil's pact with Shay Bromage came to a screeching halt. The wizard, discouraged to see Shay's newest edition of the Chronicles void of any anti-Flatlander sentiment, felt it necessary to teach the reporter a much-needed lesson. Not all magic had to be of grand nature, mused Vergil, for much of his craftiness lied in his ability to perform trickery, or manipulation. In fact, he considered it a form of guidance: showing people the right things at the right times; objects or ideas they otherwise would have been blinded from. It was amazing to watch how a simple guidance could lead to chain reaction of epic proportions; something Vergil took a perverse pleasure in. In the case of Shay Bromage, specifically, it required Vergil getting the attention of Dawn's newsroom assistant, Maya Mornier, who was working the night shift at the Burlington Daily.

"Look into the garbage," came a whisper at Maya's back.

Maya froze from her crouched position above the stack of articles for the next day's paper. Turning rapidly, she expected to see one of her colleagues. But the office was empty. No colleague, deliveryman, nor late night tipster appeared in sight. Then, on the adjacent side of the room, the garbage pale next to Dawn's desk began to glow an unnatural green.

Maya swallowed, as a chill ran up her spine. Was she seeing things? She had always suspected the Burlington Daily's headquarters of being haunted. It had been one of the main reasons why she often refused to work in the building late at night. Yet never had Maya seen or heard anything that would reinforce those beliefs. She considered running, but instead made her way towards the glowing whicker garbage container.

As she peered inside, a crumpled paper began to also glow green at the top of a clump of scrapped, ruffled papers. Maya recoiled from the sight. Was this a sign or the work of black magic? Or was she the target of some sort of prank? The crumpled paper ceased to glow. Summoning up the courage, she leaned over, picked up the crumpled paper, and brought it to her desk lamp. And it wasn't long before Maya figured out who had written the piece and why. Soon thereafter, Maya found herself in the largest moral dilemma of her short career. Reading what she presumed to be Dawn's disposed article concerning her husband, Shay, Maya thought at first that the article was a joke. *Dawn and Shay certainly shared a dark humor between them*, she thought, *perhaps this was just an extension of that?* But the language, the crossed out titles, the tear smudge on the paper's edge; each clue told her an entirely different story. *Shay Bromage. A superpac user. It made perfect sense, in hindsight.*

Yet for all of the goodwill that she felt towards Dawn, her mind strayed to a memory in which Shay had visited the paper two, maybe three years ago. There he was, arriving at Dawn's office on lunch break, decked out in his ridiculous flannel jacket and slick, blonde ponytail. He had picked up an article that Maya had recently written about a successful flower shop downtown. After reading the article in a most condescending tone, Shay then remarked out loud that 'this Maya Mornier had no idea how to write' and even went so far as to suggest firing Maya on the spot.

However, neither Shay nor Dawn knew that Maya had been listening from the adjacent bathroom, ear cupped to the wall. Afterwards, neither Dawn nor Maya spoke of it, but it troubled the younger newsroom assistant to this day. Maya subconsciously clenched her fists. Shay had bruised her professional confidence that day more than anyone she had ever known.

Alas, a wicked smile slowly spread across Maya's face. She studied the piece of paper between her fingers. Maya could just explain to Dawn tomorrow that she had found the paper, and assumed it to be part of this week's edition. After all, Maya was in charge of the layout, the last worker in the small assembly line of editors before the paper went to print. The matter was then decided.

Sorry, Dawn, some things just have to be…

For the first time in days, Shay left his house with an extra hop to his step. He wasn't quite sure why he was in such a good mood, really. Perhaps it was the emotional numbness that he had come to embrace. It could have also been a defense mechanism, a forced blindness to whatever repercussions were surely to come. Perhaps he was turning over a new leaf, free of drugs, negativity, or pacts with devilish wizards? Regardless, Shay Bromage was bound to seize the day; free of concern or inhibitions.

The walk had been peaceful enough, yet soon it became apparent that something just wasn't quite right. As he passed several neighborhood friends, they looked at him crookedly, refusing to return his greetings. From a nearby porch, the Petersons, an older couple he had become friendly with, swayed back and forth on their dual rocking chairs, staring bullets through him. *Odd*, thought Shay. *I don't recall any previous qualms with the Petersons.* And while he exchanged a few pleasantries with the passing milkman and town priest, Shay couldn't shake a gnawing feeling in the back of his mind. Could the elderly couple have been quarreling prior to Shay's passing?

He felt his jacket and readjusted his spectacles to make sure that his appearance wasn't the source of such disapproving stares. Nothing. His ponytail was meticulously flattened and fastened tight with his copper hair clip. His jacket was firmly pressed to perfection; his spectacles perched at an odd angle, giving Shay his trademark whimsical, sophisticated edge. Still, the premonition lingered.

By the time Shay arrived at the Burlington farmer's market, it was quite evident that something was amiss, *something major.* He had walked this same route dozens of times, maybe even a hundred times or more. And yet this time it felt like his first. The marketplace still buzzed with the same life and excitement to which Shay had grown to love, and yet something still felt different. As he passed various townsfolk, his mere presence seemed to suck the very life from every conversation, as they would stop mid-sentence and glare directly into his eyes.

It couldn't be. If this is what I fear it to be...

Shay approached a merchant named Stan, who specialized in crafting small, wooden carvings of Vermont gods and lore. The carvings sat on display at the front of his counter, each no larger than a child's hand. Gone was his familiar smile, once a routine fixture.

Shay nodded to his merchant-friend. "Stan. Good day to you, sir. I hope that you've been having the most pleasant of mornings."

"And to you too, sir," replied Stan, hesitantly, averting Shay's gaze. His tone lacked any and all form of dignity or respect. Shay cringed inwardly. *What was going on?*

Shay scratched his head. "Umm. Is everything okay, Stan?"

"Sure. Why ya ask?" asked Stan as he shuffled some of his carvings around the table in a rearranged pattern. Shay recognized it immediately as a hollow gesture suggesting that he was preoccupied.

Shay lifted a finger. "It's just that...never mind."

He left Stan without saying goodbye. It was as he passed an empty table, he spied the cover of the "Burlington Daily." His heart skipped a beat as he read the title, not believing what he was seeing. Shay Bromage: Superpac Addict. Never had four words stung so much. He felt naked, exposed. *How could this be? Dawn! How could you?* In a meaningless and desperate bid to dispose of the article, Shay rolled up the paper and threw it to the ground.

"Hey, I was readin' dat!" said a portly, toothless woman in a light yellow robe from nearby.

"Then you need better taste in reading material, my dear," Shay barked back.

A massive panic attack overtook him. He couldn't believe it. He could not believe that Dawn would actually follow through with her act of revenge.

The woman snorted. "Hey! Yer dat pac-sniffin bastard *himself*, aint cha? Yer a disgrace to this city, I say. I, fer one, never liked yer writin' anyways."

Yet Shay barely heard the woman's hoarse voice. His mind was much too occupied. Heart racing, he wanted to get away and fast. Making his way through the maze of the people and stands at the farmer's market, he stopped at the steps of city hall. Trying to catch his breath while simultaneously trying to prevent himself from vomiting, he doubled over and dry heaved. *She's done it. She's ruined me. Dawn's ruined me.* Tears welled up in his eyes. *No. I've ruined me.*

Karma had come full circle, Shay supposed. *All empires, no matter how powerful and mighty, must eventually come crumbling down. I'm no different, in a sense. Maybe it's not over? I can always write a long, heartfelt apology. The Vermont people are an understanding lot, despite the lack of credit I give to them. Flatlander's come almost full circle as proof! I can rectify this situation somehow, some way.*

And it was at that moment, in which Shay noticed what was to be, without a doubt, the most painful image he had ever laid eyes upon. Hung high from the rafters of city hall was a massive forty by twenty foot sign with Shay's face and namesake, with big, bold lettering next to it. It read:

Shay it ain't so! Breaking news! Shay Bromage is a Flatlander. Born in New Jersey. Moved to Vermont while in grade school. See pamphlets below and copies of Burlington Daily for more details.

"Oh, no. Gods, no! No, no, no, no, no..." stammered Shay as he stumbled backwards from the sight, before falling clumsily on his backside.

But the journalist barely felt the impact at all. He had gone completely numb. The banner was larger than life, spanning half the width of city hall. His complexion went as pale as cotton, his mouth as dry as the Barre wind. *Vergil. This was the work of Vergil, no doubt,* thought the broken Shay Bromage, as he lay motionless on the stoops of city hall. A pact broken and a secret disclosed, and the only person in the whole republic who knew of Shay's early past. *Dark forces were indeed at work from the wizard of the Camel's Hump,* thought Shay. *I'm ruined. My life is ruined.*

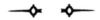

The Champlain Road to Middlebury revealed to Flatlander the gorgeous terrain of Addison County in its summer splendor. Large swaths of fertile farmland hugged Lake Champlain for much of the first leg of the trip, amid the daunting peaks of the Adirondacks from across shore. The aroma of fresh manure for late summer crops blew steadily with every gust of wind, which Flatlander had oddly grown a certain likeness to. He didn't find the smell overpowering any longer. It reminded him of why he loved the purity of the Vermont countryside. The land seemed old, the farmhouses unchanged.

Shortly after they entered the town of Ferrisburgh, the road began taking the party further inland. Taking a bathroom break, Jess disappeared behind a group of hedges on the left side of the road. Flatlander scanned their surroundings. On either side rested two dairy farms with dozens of Holsteins in pasture. They feasted peacefully on the lush valley grass, as their tails wagged lazily in the breeze. Across the lake, a ways out, the outline of a large, white ferry churned through the water with serene grace. Its black and red hull dwarfed many of the other boats near to it.

"Ah, you've noticed the Ticonderoga," remarked Henry from Flatlander's side. "Quite a beauty. The last of the paddle-wheel passenger steamers, they use to call them. It hauled cargo, passengers, soldiers, and even fronted as a casino for a short period of time. Years afterwards, the Ticonderoga had become a museum among the artifacts of Shelburne. Not long after the great fall, however, Vermonters decided to put her back into the lake. Just around the Shelburne Doctrine. Nothing had ever replaced the Ticonderoga's beauty while it was decommissioned and nobody has since." Henry paused and took a moment to admire the ship. "Even the greatest of critics had a hard time justifying she stay in the fields of Shelburne. What good is such a boat, Flatlander, if it spends its time solely on dry land?"

Flatlander squinted hard at the famed vessel. "It certainly doesn't look like she's in much of a hurry."

Henry chuckled, as he too shielded his eyes from the lake's glare. "If the roles were reversed, would *you* be in such a hurry, Flatlander? She has the best seat in the house. The mountains on either side, beauteous farmland in raw abundance, fellow boats as companions. The Ticonderoga has quite the life."

From down the road, they heard Jess shout out. Both Flatlander and Henry rushed to the sound of her voice, weapons drawn. Franklin, Ellen and Menche followed closely behind. *Bandits were rare here*, Henry had told him, *but not entirely out of the question*. Soon, they saw Jess crouching over a section of dirt road where the dirt had eroded away. In its stead, a hard, cracked black surface emerged from the earth.

"Dad, what *is* this?" asked Jess, as she poked at the black rock.

"How does she not know about this?" asked Ellen to the Humble King, dumbfounded.

Menche whistled. "The Old Road, I thinks, them teachers use to say. Not seen it in some time."

Henry smiled nervously as he inspected the black surface. "That's asphalt, Jess."

"Asphalt?" asked Jess, as she peered at the alien material. "What's asphalt?"

"It was what the roads use to be made out of, back in the days of the Old Country. Have they not taught you such things in school, young lady? This should be common knowledge at your age." Henry chuckled lightly, and raised an eyebrow. "Perhaps you were too busy tending to Fish?"

Jess squinted hard at her father. "Actually, *dad*," replied Jess, "they never said anything about *this*."

Henry smiled thinly. "Well, consider this a crash course then, my dear. It troubles me that you have yet to learn this in school. I may need to have a word with your professors when we get back as it pertains to their curriculum."

"A lot of history gets overlooked in the republic. It's not her fault for not knowing," said Ellen, as she patted Jess's back. "Spend a day with me and I'll teach you all you need to know."

"Are they all like this?" asked Flatlander, as he kicked away more dirt, exposing more brittle asphalt. "The roads, I mean. Why don't you still use asphalt in the republic? It's a lot smoother than what you've got now."

Henry nodded. "Fair questions, Flatlander. For starters, roads require a good deal of maintenance, and it isn't long before they begin to crack, erode, and disappear. Factor in Vermont's terrible winters and our messy mud season, and the roads revert to their natural states rather quickly. And yes, many of the roads are like this underneath the layers of dirt. As to why we don't use the asphalt, *that* is a more complicated issue entirely."

Henry chuckled and nodded painfully. "For some, it reminds them too much of our plight with Flatlanders and the Old Country, a painful collection of memories if there ever was. Also, keep in mind since we mostly use horse and oxen for transport, their hooves weren't meant for long travels over such hard, flat terrain. It wears down their shoes or hooves. Either way, six or seven years after the creation of the republic, we figured that we'd be better off without them. Many roads were uprooted during the purge[68]. Many of the others have completely disintegrated. Does that answer suffice?"

Henry's question was met with silence. Jess used her fingers to sift through the small traces of dirt atop the black asphalt roadway.

"You could have told me," she muttered in a small voice.

"Since when have you cared about what I've ever had to say," retorted Henry, rolling his eyes.

Jess's face pinched in anger. "Dad, quit acting like a jerk."

"I wanted to teach you, but you just kept, kept..."

"I kept *what*, dad?"

"Fish this, Fish that."

"Hey, hey, hey" interrupted Ellen, as she stood between the two. "You two are family. There's no reason for either of you to be this upset with one another. Consider it done and move on. We need to get to Middlebury before nightfall. Consider this a learning experience. For you both."

"Yes, consider it done and move on," repeated Henry, vacantly, as he looked upon the road, avoiding his daughter's glare.

As the group readied to move on, he deftly neared the patch of road where the asphalt had been unveiled. Kicking up some of the surrounding dirt on top of the protruding roadway, Henry frowned. The Humble King's thoughts then carried him back to the imposing wall near the Brattle with Jess by his side, gazing up at its moss-covered head. *It's not her fault; there is much for her to learn*, he thought. *Too Much.*

"Middlebury: Town of the Silver Tower."

---

[68] During the first several years of the republic's existence, many artifacts from the Old Country were systematically destroyed.

The name had all but been decided amongst the senate two decades prior, but subsequently died upon the monks' objections. *Too ostentatious*, they had decried, for the sacred land of their people needn't a valuable element attached to their namesake. And despite the impressive tower, which dominated over their stronghold, the monks lived but a humble life.

The monks of Middlebury were a mysterious, yet vital, component to Vermont. Long considered the guardians of knowledge of both old and new, they served as the needed conduit between Vermont, its history, and its role to the rest of the world and universe. Each devoted a lifetime of work and research to the longevity of the republic. Though the more senior ranks took root in an area named Braintree, which lay fifty miles due east through the Green Mountain Forest, Middlebury was considered home to the majority of their sect.

The silver tower soared high and mighty at the heart of town, thirty stories tall, complete with a main spiral tower and several large turrets near the top. The Otter Creek rushed through the heart of downtown, culminating into the eighteen-foot Middlebury Falls. Aged buildings of Middlebury's old campus, now serving as its giant monastery, were covered in thick layers of English Ivy and moss. Monks often walked in pairs, or groups of three, with hands clasped behind their backs (as was customary). They dressed in their green lamb wool robes, with the hoods of Braintree draped completely over their heads (as was also customary). What wasn't customary, however, on this particular day was the procession of folks following Lord Henry, the Humble King, across Otter Creek. Lord Trombley met the six travelers near the foot of a small bridge near Middlebury Falls.

"Greetings, Lord Henry. It is a great honor to host you and your party."

Trombley's glasses shone in the afternoon glare. He was without his traditional golden robe, reserved for his dealings in

Montpelier, and he too wore a green robe with adjoining hood. For it was considered sacrilege, by monks and outsiders alike, to step on holy ground without wearing the proper attire of the monks. And Trombley was popular amongst the monks. Though he lacked the experience in the brotherhood, his lifetime pursuit of knowledge and his devotion to protecting the republic remained firmly aligned with their cause.

Henry waved as they neared. "Greetings, Lord Trombley. The journey was spectacular, as usual."

Lord Trombley bowed. "You're too kind, Lord Henry. Though I must agree that few places rival the pastures of Addison County in raw beauty. I trust that you and your company are tired?" asked Trombley, as he scanned the group. "Flatlander. Ellen. Franklin. Jess. Menche. Good to see you all. Welcome to Middlebury. Home to the monkhood and friends of Braintree."

"What's the Braintree?" whispered Menche. "Don't like the sounds of it."

"Shh. We've discussed this before, Menche," chided Henry, and then, as he cleared his voice. "We thank you for your hospitality, Lord Trombley. There are some important matters to discuss."

"Yes, of course, Lord Henry. I must request, however," replied Trombley, as he tugged at his robe, "that your party wears our traditional garb when entering our sacred land. There are extra pairs hanging in the shed behind me. Franklin, it shall please you that we have robes large enough to accommodate even the likes of you."

"What's that s'pose to mean, Trombley?" asked Franklin in jest, as he patted his full belly.

Trombley smiled crookedly. "Nothing more and nothing less. Please, everyone, follow me."

The Lord of Middlebury then led them to a small shack with numerous robes hanging from a series of crudely constructed, wooden coat hangers. Flatlander felt awkward putting on the robe, for it was so long in the back that it trailed behind him two feet.

Franklin fought clumsily with the robe, losing his balance on several occasions, while nearly taking out Jess in the process. Yet after only a few moments of struggle and confusion, the group soon departed for the library.

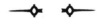

Judging by the queer looks that the group received from the assortment of monks gathered at the library, visiting strangers were seldom. Small trees and bamboo sprung up in the walking lanes by the bookshelves, and English ivy decorated much of the walls, shelves, and lantern stands. The air was fresh and earthy, as drops of transpiration lopped off much of the ivy. To the group's right, a lone monk watered a perennial with a wooden, grail-like pitcher. Several large oaks spread the roof and floor with their massive boughs, and were intersected by beams of stripped pine.

"Could use a bit of trimmin' if ya ask me," whispered Franklin in Flatlander's ear.

"Tell me about it," agreed Flatlander.

Henry caught wind of their conversation. "I would keep that sentiment to yourself, gentlemen. The monks hold nature in the highest esteem, owing much of their origins to the miracle at Braintree. Take heed. It is said that even the plants have ears where the monks dwell."

Flatlander bristled at the thought. "You mean to tell me that the plants can…"

Henry cut him off with a warning stare. "I think that it's wise to err on the side of caution."

As the group ventured forth throughout the vast library, Trombley gestured at the vast expanse of volumes. "Most of the books you see here were written by the monks themselves. Every year, a monk is commissioned a certain aspect of Vermont to research, and every year they produce a book that encompasses the collective research of their subjects. Failing to do so would jeopardize their chances of making the highest rank of the priesthood. Here in Middlebury, they serve as the channel, so to speak, of Braintree and beyond. The books in which we *allow* are then released to the public."

Flatlander resumed their pace in silence: this, despite his growing number of questions. *Why were certain books or subjects disallowed? Why hadn't the monks ventured outside of Vermont? Or did they keep such missions secret?* Trombley took them to a spacious corner of the library, and motioned for the group to sit at a long, antique table. Into its edges were carved several engravings depicting mining tools. Several books were stacked in the center, and a large candle burned high in the air, despite the late afternoon sun, which blazed through the array of windows.

"My apologies. The older books can get badly damaged from the sun."

Jess shifted from side to side. "Dad, can I look around for some books?"

Henry cocked an eyebrow in surprise, and peered over to Trombley, who was re-adjusting the window blinds to a slightly darker, more ambient, atmosphere.

"That is a question better reserved for our friend, Lord Trombley."

Trombley turned his head, while pulling on a twisted cord. "What was that, you say? Oh yes, of course, little misses. How could I refuse the daughter of our noble king?" asked Trombley with a lighthearted smile. "But please be gentle, Jess. Many of these books are very rare. In fact, some are the only remaining copies in existence. Many haven't been copied for public use yet."

"I will!" replied Jess shrilly, as she sprinted carelessly off to the other side of the library.

Henry blushed. "This is a strange sight, Lord Trombley. She usually doesn't like books."

"Well, this is a good thing. Is it not?" replied Trombley, dismissing Henry with the wave of a hand, "We were all young once, if you recall. Let her explore. This is an exciting place for a newcomer." He paused. "Though I have to assume that you have came here for more than just mere sight-seeing, Lord Henry?" he asked, cocking his eyeglasses, as he made his way to the head of the table.

Flatlander smiled. He was beginning to like Trombley. Sure, many labeled him as smug or intellectual to a fault, but the Lord of Middlebury had a great sense of humor, and stood by his principles.

"Indeed. A problem grows in Burlington proper, quite an underestimated dilemma."

Trombley cocked an eyebrow. "Which is…"

Henry adjusted his belt. "It is a problem that you're well aware of, Lord Trombley. It was discussed several months ago at the emergency council when we convened over the winter."

Trombley hesitated. "The fiasco at the chili festival? I assure you that Inepticus was dealt with properly after his antics. No man should be capable of consuming that much spice in one sitting without dying."

"No, not that." Henry shook his head at the unfortunate reference. "We've come to discuss the tipping issue regarding the Quebecois."

Lord Trombley's brows furrowed with deep concern. "Getting that bad, is it?" Henry and Flatlander exchanged a pitiful look. Trombley observed their quiet exchange and smirked. "I take that as a yes."

Flatlander winced. "I saw it all. They just got up and left, the whole group of Quebecois. The poor waitress just stood there, crying."

"It ain't the proper Vermont thing to do," added Franklin.

"It's troubling, to say the least," confirmed Henry. "Yet I figure now that we have the help of Flatlander, we can try to tackle this problem head-on."

Trombley nodded. "Hmm. Well I can personally attest to the difficulties that this issue presents. During our emergency council meeting on the subject, Lord Henry, we estimated that city employees have lost a small fortune in lost tips. But I agree that the hardest thing to stomach is the *human toll* that this issue has wreaked on our bartenders, waitresses, and other fine people in the service industry. Yet," the lord paused, as he looked distantly at a nearby section of book shelves, "I wonder if there's more here than meets the eye."

Henry leaned forward. "How so?"

Trombley left the table without another word, and walked down a nearby book aisle with his dignified gait. The group watched him closely, as the Lord of Middlebury delicately removed a massive, grey book from the shelf and carried it over, placing it upon the table excruciatingly slow. He blew on the book's edge, stirring up a cloud of dust.

"It baffles me why I haven't referred to this text earlier. 'Vermont and the Quebecois,' written by a deceased monk, Arthur Crowning. Perhaps I downplayed the significance of the problem? My schedule maybe didn't allow for it. Regardless, it matters little," stated Trombley. He began turning the darkened, oversized pages. "It's apparent that there is a language barrier of the strongest sort at work here. We cannot understand them and they cannot understand us. From this perspective, we'd have similar luck communicating with seagulls."

"Yet the Quebecois don't tip, as is customary in our republic..." started Henry.

"Customs are just that, Lord Henry. They are particular to a specific region. One cannot assume that just because it's custom here in the republic, that it should be a custom in Quebec and the Great City of the North," interrupted Trombley. He pointed to an open page from the book, and pointed at a passage. "Which brings us to this extensive history of the Quebecois and our border region of Highgate. Here, on page 114, this book speaks of an obelisk in the woods, which acts as a translating stone for Vermonters and Quebecois. There is a section that addresses rumors behind the problem. Let me read it aloud:

'For years, it has been well documented that there exists a large communication gap between Vermonters and the Quebecois, and troubling those whom seek discourse where discourse is void. They need not know of the supposed Obelisk of Highgate. The unfounded rumors, which have spread throughout much of the Northern Chittenden and Franklin County, tell of such an obelisk. The same folks who spread this comical rumor also stand by their story of seeing a large and terrible masked guard in the supposed area. They often cite this fellow as standing ten feet tall, discrediting any and all attempts at being taken seriously. Still, a small, informal search party was assembled to canvas the Highgate woods, and as of today, no trace of evidence, such as the obelisk, or its guard, could be found. The rumor should most likely be chalked up to folks whom seek asylum in the realm of fantasy and magic, rather than the insufferable boredom suffered at the hands of reality.'

As Trombley finished reading the passage, he scanned the faces of his guests. Henry couldn't hold back his disappointment, as he rubbed at his forehead. Ellen kicked back her chair and pressed back her hair.

"Then this whole trip was for folly," reflected Henry, as he scanned the ancient book and re-read the passage.

"And to think with all of the paperwork that I have waiting for me in Montpelier, and we just wasted an entire day for *this*," muttered Ellen.

Trombley held out his hand. "No, no. Please. You both misunderstand."

"Misunderstand *what*?" demanded Ellen.

"You need to read between Crowning's lines. There are a few things that you must be made aware of on the matter. For starters, the witnesses to this obelisk and guard were far from crazy. They were surveyors and former soldiers working for a wealthy landowner. These workers witnessed these sightings by Proper Pond, and tell us much in their accounts. They describe the appearance of the obelisk in the finest of detail, to that of the guard, whom they describe as standing ten feet or more, and as broad as a horse is wide. They describe him to the very armor that he wore, to a giant, carved bear mask, and the weapons in which he wielded, namely a whip and a mace.

"Second, Crowning was found to be partly affiliated with the Quebecois, and there is the lingering question of whether or not he received compensation for his book's stance on the matter from the Quebecois. It may not be as farfetched as you believe. It was rumored that Crowning's mother was, in fact, a Quebecois.

"Third, if you re-read this passage, and others relating to the topic, Crowning's passion for discrediting these rumors almost takes on a comical tone. He's so incredibly dismissive of the notion, so flippant; it almost makes one curious if he is hiding something. This is the same man whom had no trouble mocking the concepts of magic and fantasy in *this* passage, and yet, in *other* works, he has no reluctance in believing and writing extensively of the Pigmen of Northfield or Champ the Lake Monster. There *is* magic in this republic. Even you, Flatlander, in your short time, can attest to that. Something doesn't add up.

"Fourth, there is a lot of money at stake here. Millions of dollars, in fact. Is it truly outside the realm of possibility that someone, or some group, would want to keep this obelisk a secret?"

The group sat in stunned silence. Ellen shook her head, incredulously. "How do you know all of this?"

"Miss Ellen, the truth is, I don't know," replied Trombley, as he reached for the book from Henry's clutches, "yet you mustn't forget that I spend countless hours in this library, pouring over countless documents, seeing as to what research best helps our republic. Though the monks do thorough jobs researching these matters, it is partly my job to analyze their writings, to make certain connections. I've always been intrigued by this issue. Though I must admit it's been some time since I've revisited it."

Henry looked at the group. "Then we must go to Highgate to see this obelisk for ourselves."

Trombley adjusted his spectacles. "Lord Henry, a word of advice: do not advertise your trip to the north. This should be a stealth mission. There may be certain forces that may not wish you well on this venture. Do it for the waitress and her tears. Do it for the strength of the republic. Do it for Burlington's lost revenue. And if for nothing else, do it for unbound curiosity. If you find it, all must know. While you search, however, *nobody* must know."

Henry sat up from his seat. "I always know that I can trust you and your people, Lord Trombley. Please keep this between us, my friend. I will send a unit to Highgate to verify these tales. But we must be on our way. Nightfall is coming, and Jess has many chores to do around the house."

As if on cue, Jess hurried back to the group with an unsettled look on her face. Her face had gone considerably paler, as a thin ray of light came searing through the blinds.

"*Jess*? What's wrong? Are you okay?" asked Henry as he scanned his daughter's face.

Jess turned quickly, averting her face. "I'm fine, dad. Can we go?"

Henry looked at his companions in utter confusion, then back to his flustered daughter. "Umm, yes. We were just on our way." He bowed to the Lord of Middlebury slightly. "Lord Trombley, I thank you again. You will hear back from us soon."

Trombley waved to his guests. "I would hope so, Lord Henry and guests. Thank you for gracing us with a rare visit."

Henry and company prepared to leave. But as Trombley scanned over the opening page of Crowning's book, a horrid illustration caught his attention. The Red Guardian. Wielding a tremendous mace and a long, leather whip and cloaked in heavy armor, the enormous bear-masked knight looked ready to hack an approaching man to death. The victim cowered low in the foreground, his arm splayed, futilely, as a protective barrier. In the background, smeared in mud and strewn leafs, stood the obelisk at shoulder-height, partially obscured by the guardian's massive frame.

Trombley cleared his throat loudly. "One more thing."

The party paused and turned.

"I've read more about this supposed guardian, and if the rumors mentioned in this book are indeed true, then this being, this warrior guarding the obelisk is a killer. He is ruthless. I advise you to take extreme caution. It's stated earlier that even the Abenaki now avoid the area as if it's cursed."

While her father and company had deliberated with Lord Trombley, Jess had ventured off to a section of the library devoted purely to Lake Champlain, and specifically, to the legend of Fish. She spied the subject name on the wall shortly after they had first entered the main lobby. Salvaged driftwood, advertised to be from the lake, served as shelving units. A painted three-inch model of fish in mid-song sat atop the bookshelf. Jess stared at it, a well of emotions building up inside of her. Then, reluctantly, she hid the object from sight behind a rather thick, marble book stop.

It was the most extensive collection covering the topic of Fish Jess had ever seen. They ranged from various biographies; to the cultural impact the creature had on Vermont, to criticisms of its music. To Jess, however, one book stood out from the others. "The Complete Authority on the Legend of Fish," by John Waters, was an immense, illustrated, comprehensive collection of history and memories related to the Champlain legend.

Jess flipped through the book in amazement, savoring every rare illustration, snippet of history, and story from various eyewitness accounts. A chapter entitled, "The Cult," was solely devoted to the legion of cult members whom followed the legendary lake creature. As Jess perused the chapter, an illustration caught her eye. Surrounding Fish in the shallow waters were its cult-like members, kneeling in worship at their deity. Their faces were muddied and crazed. Their eyes looked upon it as if for the first time. The symbol of Fish was imprinted on all their foreheads. *Was this how I use to look? Is this how the world perceived us? Perceived me?* Jess repelled the disturbing thought, and continued thumbing through the book, searching for any interesting tidbits regarding her once-esteemed passion. Chapter Fourteen, titled "Influences of Fish," caught her fancy.

"Though it's hard to pinpoint exactly which artists were direct musical influences early in Fish's life, a dozen reputable music critics cite "The Stony Mahoney's" as being one of Fish's primary inspirations. Verified eyewitness accounts confirm The Stony Mahoney's once played at a Waterfront Festival while Fish was still developing its own sound. A noted change in Fish's style was observed after that performance. Shortly thereafter, several songs were added to Fish's catalogue, most of which have a near identical melody to the Stony Mahoney song, "Siren of the Lake." Though impossible to confirm, due to Fish's inability to communicate, extensive research on this matter has been completed by several Monks of Middlebury, and confirmed with near certitude."

Jess couldn't believe what she was reading. *It couldn't be true. The Stony Mahoney's? Dad's band? No chance! Two of the band members played rocks for instruments*! Yet, the writing was there plain to see. The Monks of Middlebury had even sealed the back cover of the book with their signature stamp, a vine of ivy coiled around a staff[69], validating its authenticity. Jess shut the book in dismay, and hurriedly joined the rest of the group, as she tried in vain to digest the impossible.

After Flatlander and company had returned from Middlebury, it was decided that due to the dangers of Highgate, the party should go their separate ways. Jess was to tend to her studies. Menche was to pick a round of fresh vegetables from the various gardens on the property. Ellen was to assist with paperwork from the legislation. In the meantime, King Henry continued to lead talks with Yuro and the three main political factions on what to do next with the empty Moran Plant property. And it was in this pretext that Flatlander, Franklin and Pete left for the northern reaches of Highgate.

Shortly after they returned to Montpelier, Flatlander wanted to make greater efforts to *look* the part of a Vermonter. He had taken to one of Henry's thin, sleeveless leather tunics, specially made for the warm, summer months. It fit him nicely; its leather hide providing the necessary protection and flexibility he found lacking in other coats. Two tufts of fur protruded from each of the jackets' shoulders, a signal of higher rank in many parts of Vermont's outlying communities. His facial hair growth had now become a short and trim beard, and though patchy, it suited him well. Flatlander's newfound beard hadn't helped keep him cool from the summer heat, however, and he often found himself itching it incessantly as they neared Highgate. And though he may

---

[69] A stamp from the monks required 90% agreement from the order or higher.

have looked the part, Flatlander couldn't help but feel vulnerable with such a small party this far in the northern borderlands of the republic.

This knight guarding the obelisk is a killer. He is ruthless. I advise you to use extreme caution. Trombley's words echoed in his head as he peered deep into a surrounding mist. Flatlander tried to ready himself for his potential meeting with the guard and the obelisk. As he peered onto the uncoiled parchment, the map now confirmed that they were close, three miles to be exact.

He had sharpened his sword upon returning from Middlebury. Under the tutelage of Franklin, he had used a whetstone, metal file and oil to his instrument. Around his neck, he wore a necklace assembled with Henry's medallion. Before he left Henry's home, he had elicited whistles from the Humble King and Franklin alike.

"A Vermonter, through and through," Henry had marveled.

The passed the Winooski Bridge and through the domed city of Winooski and the famous Winooski Circle, which by nature, was packed of slow moving bodies and carriages. Each exit of the circle pointed traffic in different directions. In the middle of this circle lay a vacant grass park. The most famous branch of the Winooski River passed underneath the bridge, as a series of rapids and waterfalls rushed past old mill buildings, their foundations now resembling old castle-like ruins. Flatlander marveled at the size and scale of the clear dome. It soared a few hundred feet or more above the red brick buildings that made up downtown.

They then took the Highgate Passage. Soon after passing through neighboring Colchester, a dense fog had rolled in during the morning of their departure, blanketing the surrounding landscape. The visibility of the road had diminished to a dozen yards or less, and though the two companions agreed that such conditions were favorable to the covert nature of their quest, it gave them great unease.

They passed the occasional farmhouse on the northern road, though much of the adjacent properties were all but obscured by the thick fog, which seemed impervious to an easterly breeze. The humidity was oppressive. The subsequent heat, maddening. Franklin remarked that such a fog was rare during the summer months; but Flatlander paid the observation little heed. Intent on finding this obelisk, and wrapping up his seventh quest, he was trapped in his own mind. After passing through Colchester, they encountered townsfolk during their passage through the towns of Milton, Georgia, St. Albans, and Swanton. None dealt the strangers welcoming looks. All looked forlorn. Finally, they reached the border town of Highgate.

"What's crawled up his fanny?" asked Franklin after passing a particularly bare-chested, menacing-looking farmer. Between swooping cuts of his scythe against cornstalks, he gave the two a dirty look. His stringy, curled black hair was drenched with sweat, and grime and manure stained much of his torso.

Flatlander smiled and patted Pete's hindquarters. "Perhaps the sight of two unsightly men and a large moose creeping near his crops."

Franklin spit on the ground. "I say to hell with 'em."

After a several second pause, Flatlander looked back at the farmer, now at their backs. "They're pretty far from the action up here. They could probably care less about Quebecois and tipping."

Franklin nodded reluctantly then gazed upon Flatlander and his black tunic. "Ya know somethin', Flatlander? Ya look different, somehow. Never thought I'd be sayin' this, but ya kinda look like a Vermonter now. Not sure if ya should be honored or scared."

Flatlander chuckled. "Me neither."

Franklin scanned the surrounding farmlands and woods, as he downed a gulp of water from his horse-skin canteen.

"Never seen this land aside from winter. One of the coldest, windiest nights of my life was spent huntin' up here in Highgate."

"Is that right?" asked Flatlander, as he pinched the fabric under his armpits, attempting to air out his sweat-stained shirt. "I have no concept of what cold is on a day like today."

Franklin grunted. "Oh, you'll find out. I promise you that. A Vermont winter will remind you real quick of what cold is. Real quick. A land of extremes, I'm tellin' ya. And no lesser than in the dreaded Highgate."

Flatlander stopped dead in his tracks. A feeling gnawed at him since their departure from Montpelier: a kind of nervousness that he had felt from Franklin and others regarding the town of Highgate. In the back of his mind, he had hoped for a larger contingent of men, though he understood the risks of compromising their position. Still, the question lingered in his mind.

"What kind of danger are we in?"

Franklin paused, but resumed walking. Unhappy at being ignored, Flatlander followed his friend.

"Franklin, talk to me."

The northerner looked ahead. The pastures ended abruptly in a maze of forest. The sun lay completely obscured though the heat grew in intensity. A small flock of birds carried across the roadway into the dense thicket of wood, as their chirping faded into nothingness.

"The kingdom, nor Highgate, is a place for the meek."

Flatlander scanned the adjacent forest.

Franklin grunted, and seemed to consider the question thoughtfully. "It's but a subtle land with a awful feel, if I may say so. Keep yer sword handy and yer wits about ya. Danger may be close."

The two companions then ventured forth into the woods of Highgate, becoming fully enveloped into its fog. The volume of bugs began to intensify, as swarms of gnats, blackflies and mosquitos ate away any exposed flesh of both Franklin and Flatlander. Flatlander swatted several mosquitos that had bitten him simultaneously on the neck, as he withdrew a bloodied palm. The black flies were relentless, biting at every opportunity they had. The pain was unbearable. On a few occasions, Flatlander had been reduced to a series of cries and groans as he slapped at himself blindly.

Then, as Flatlander readied to hack away at a particularly thick cluster of vines obstructing their path, Franklin caught his arm with alarming speed. He shook his head furiously, and the message from the northerner was abundantly clear: *they were getting too close for that.*

They proceeded to peel each bush and vine back, stealthily, and though arduous, they maintained their tortoise-like pace for over an hour. Neither wanted to attract an ambush from whatever might be lurking in the mist. Referring to the map, Flatlander estimated their current distance from the northern road and eyed his compass.

"We're close," he whispered.

"Think I'd rather be freezin' near to death than getting' eatin' alive by the mosquitos of the Missisquoi," whispered Franklin with bugged out eyes, as he pulled away a drape of Bittersweet vine.

"Agreed," replied Flatlander in a hushed voice. "This is awful."

The two proceeded through the growth with soft steps as they gently brushed by each bit of foliage a quietly as they could muster. Flatlander counted a dozen tree stumps carved thoroughly by beavers. At intervals, the ground soon became covered in a few inches of black water, back to muddied, to dry land, and back again. This pattern continued for twenty minutes or more of their trek. A small woodchuck, which had been standing on their course, scattered away in a hurry through the undergrowth, as Franklin and Flatlander went on high alert. Breathing a sigh of relief, the two plodded onward. According to the map, they were nearly at the marked location.

Several dozen more paces and without warning, the fog dissipated, and they came upon a small clearing in the bramble. A field no larger than fifty yards in diameter appeared before them, as tufts of swamp grass scattered around a floor of thick mud and fallen branches. In the center of the field, amid a slight depression, a black, four-sided obelisk arose to sixteen feet in height.

Wide-eyed, Flatlander drew in his breath. "Trombley was right."

Franklin's jaw dropped. "Well I'll be...", he then traded a sharp glance to his partner. "Quick, get out the tracin' paper. I'll stand cover."

Flatlander rummaged through his satchel, and grabbed several sheets of coiled tracing paper and a charcoal block. The northerner peered around the clearing, waiting for any signs of their foe. Racing to the obelisk with Franklin close at his back, Flatlander wasted no time. On each of the obelisk's four sides, the text of four distinct languages marked its surface. One side was clearly written in plain English, and the others in unrecognizable languages. Flatlander had neither the mindset nor the time to closely inspect the words. Frantically, he began rubbing the charcoal with spastic swipes.

Franklin then grabbed his shoulder, and pointed in the distance.

"Look! He's here!"

From across the clearing, a tall, dark figure emerged amid a tangled mixture of vines. Standing half again as tall as Franklin and dressed in a scarlet and black tunic, he carried a large mace in one hand and a whip in the other. His face was obscured by pale, wooden mask, which was shaped into the shortened snout of a bear. His eyes were all but hidden under an oversized visor. Rope was tied around the knight's elbows and knees, tightened so much that his muscles were taut, and his veins exposed freely among his arms. Flatlander paused from his rubbing of the obelisk. The guardian of Highgate had arrived.

From underneath the mask came a low, menacing voice. "Who goes there?"

Franklin twirled his axe through his crooked fingers. "Our business ain't none of yers, big man. Be off, and consider yerself lucky."

The massive knight approached, his footsteps thudding against the soft earth.

"But you see, my business *is* yours. And I take major offense to your tone, Northerner."

Franklin whispered in Flatlander's ear. "Keep up yer tracin', boy. Leave this lad to me."

"But Franklin…"

Franklin pointed at the paper and coal. "No buts. What's more important is you bringin' back them scrolls."

"Franklin, this is crazy."

Franklin shook off Flatlander's concern. "My mind's been made. Quick, or you'll be usin' yer own blood fer the tracin'!"

After a brief hesitation, Flatlander resumed his tracing of the obelisk with the scrolls of wax paper. His palms became greasy with sweat, making the task that much more difficult. Franklin cleared his voice then spoke loudly in the direction of the guardian.

"See, we like it here if it's nothin' to ya. Great view. Great company. Lovely day here in the bog, if I says so."

The guardian raised his mace and whip for combat. "Suit yourself."

Franklin removed his axe from his back holster. "Bring 'er here."

The guardian leapt forward with surprising speed, his steel-toed boots throwing up small clumps of mud from the moistened sod. In one fell swoop, he snapped his whip from mid air, nearly catching Franklin's chin in the process. Franklin charged the guardian, axe held high, and rained several tough, well placed blows onto the guardian's armor. On his final hit, he smashed off the giant's metal shoulder guard, sending it soaring into the surrounding bog. The guardian leapt backwards and cracked his whip into Franklin's right cheek. The northerner looked momentarily stunned, and brushed off a fresh gleam of blood from the side of his chin.

"Franklin!" called Flatlander from the base of the obelisk. "It isn't worth it. Please, I'm begging you. Let's leave. Now!"

"Keep scribblin' I says!"

Flatlander obliged, his eyes frantically shifting from the obelisk to the two titans before him battling to the death. In just under a minute, he had traced two of the obelisk's sides. The guardian, now acutely aware of Flatlander's progress, began taking several strides towards him. With the crack of his whip, he struck the edge of the obelisk, nearly taking the worn charcoal block from Flatlander's hand. Flatlander jumped instinctively, using the body of the obelisk as a shield. Tripping over an exposed root, Flatlander fell squarely on his side. Wielding his mace to strike a devastating blow upon the fallen Flatlander, the guardian coiled his weapon with all of his might, ready to smite his opponent.

But in an instant Franklin tackled the guardian, blindsiding him, using all of his weight to bring the giant to the ground. They fell in a tumbling heap. Franklin tried to use the butt end of his axe to his opponent's helmet, but his was caught in the giant's steel-like grip, as the guardian threw him effortlessly into a pile of branches and twigs. Franklin burst from the pile rapidly, bits of leaves scattered amongst his hair and beard. He charged the guardian once more with a ferocious burst of speed, but before he could make contact with his axe, the giant connected his mace into the side of Franklin, hurtling him through a nearby patch of shrubbery. The guardian, without missing a step, then followed Franklin through the brush.

Flatlander finished his tracing of the third face of the obelisk, just in time to see Franklin stumble through the underbrush. The guardian towered over his friend, drool smeared down the length of his mask. Writhing on the ground in pain, Franklin struggled to find his fallen axe. The guardian held up his mace for a final blow.

At that moment, Flatlander could think of nothing else than protecting his friend at all costs, and in a split second, threw his sword at the guardian with all of the strength he could muster. It rotated twice in the air, then pierced the guardian straight through the side of his head. The giant fell with a sickening thud, as his mace plopped into a shallow pool of murk at his side. His body convulsed violently. But after several seconds, it was all over. Their foe lay still among the marshes of Highgate.

Flatlander rushed to his friend's side. Spiting up a large glob of blood, Franklin squirmed slowly on the ground. Flatlander tried to sit him up straight, but the northerner grimaced in severe pain and fell back to the swampy earth. Inspecting the side of Franklin's coat, he saw the source of Franklin's pain. The mace had been wielded with tremendous force, breaking ribs, ripping skin, and potentially puncturing Franklin's lungs. A terrible purple-blue bruise formed the length of the northerner's side.

"Water," muttered Franklin.

Flatlander unlatched his canteen and poured a desperate helping of water in and around his friend's mouth.

"Gave me a good smack, he did," gasped Franklin.

"We need to get you help," replied Flatlander, as he too took a swig of water, then nervously screwed back the lid of the canteen. "We need to get back to Burlington fast."

Franklin placed his hand on his side to comfort his wound. "Ya saved my life."

Flatlander shook his head. "We're not out of the woods yet."

Franklin smiled and spat out a mouthful of blood. "I owe ya one, kid." Franklin chuckled, then immediately regretted the action, as he winced in pain. "Did ya finish the tracin'?"

Flatlander lied. "I did."

In fact, just three of the four sides had been successfully traced, but Flatlander knew better than to tell Franklin. He couldn't sit by idly and finish the job in good conscience while his friend lay dying, potentially bleeding to death internally. Knowing Franklin, the northerner would be adamant that Flatlander finish the tracing and stay true to the quest's objectives. The sheer amount of Franklin's blood spattered on the ground, however, was reason enough for Flatlander to abandon the task. *Another day, perhaps.*

But not today. Flatlander collected the charcoal and trio of coiled up wax papers and stuffed them into his satchel.

"Then get me outta this forsaken mud hole, bud," muttered Franklin. "The Gods of Highgate wished upon me hell. And they've succeeded.[70]"

Flatlander reached underneath Franklin's armpits, and dragged the northerner's massive frame along the bog in frantic spurts. The task took hours and was beyond painstaking. In some of the thicker sections of brush, he requested Franklin use his own feet to hop clumps of branches and weeds. In the final leg of the trip, Flatlander was unsure if he could drag the brute under his own power. Yet drag and support him he did, until they met up with the Pete again close to the roadway.

Once on the Northern Road, Franklin remained unusually quiet, which made Flatlander nervous. It was unlike the gregarious bodyguard and right-hand man. Dressing his friend's wound with a temporary bandage of cloth and tissue, Flatlander then situated him atop the back of Pete. The guardian of Highgate lay dead at their backs, yet it was all the death that Flatlander could stomach for the day. Panic-stricken and dry-mouthed, he rushed southbound to Burlington, hoping that Franklin had enough fight in him to weather the pain and live another day.

"Ten minutes, Gentleman," the nurse told the onlookers, her voice void of any emotion.

Henry and Flatlander gathered at the foot of Franklin's bed, looking down at their compatriot with marked concern. Bags of fluids hung at his side. A nasty laceration looped around the side of his face from the lash of the guardian's whip. His broken arm

---

[70] In later years, Franklin would confess that this line was designed to be his final, dramatic line before death.

lay wrapped in a hard cast, and a ventilator helped him breathe through his battered lungs.

Franklin stayed in a secretive unit among the hospital's ward, the nature of his quest and injuries staying highly confidential. On his official medical paperwork, Franklin was admitted due to a 'horseback accident'. As such, Flatlander was noticeably scant on such details when recounting the ordeal to doctors and nurses.

"It wasn't supposed to be like this," stated Flatlander, devastated.

Seeing the strongman from Walden bedridden was a tough thing to see, yet he couldn't take his eyes off him. Franklin was covered with bloodied bandages. Though his beard was properly cleansed of dried blood, small bits still stuck to the inside of his nostrils.

Henry tapped the bed frame. "He just needs rest, friend. Franklin is a tough fellow, the toughest I've come across in my lifetime."

"He is," replied Flatlander plainly. "And he saved my life."

"I understand your pain. He's been a good friend of mine for ten years and counting." Henry drew in a sharp breath. "If it's any consolation whatsoever, Flatlander, your scrolls have proven invaluable. Trombley and his monks have already cracked the code of the obelisk, and translated the languages. The key translation was simple," he paused, "there *was* no translation."

"*What*?" Flatlander blinked back his surprise, and took the news like a punch to the gullet.

Henry continued. "There was no translation for 'tip.' Nothing. A blank space lay in its stead. Amazing, isn't it?"

"So Franklin's life now hangs in balance because of a term lost in translation? A mix-up?"

Henry shook his head. "Not lost, Flatlander- never there to *begin with*. And take solace, all is not in vain. Trombley's men were able to reconstruct enough of the language to translate the concept of tipping into the Quebecois' tongue. Their culture simply lacked the equivalent definition. In their homeland, the tip is built into the total of the bill. The Quebecois felt just as embarrassed as we did. No matter, though. Let bygones be bygones," said Henry, as he turned to Flatlander. "You've done the city well again, Flatlander. Franklin told us, prior to losing consciousness, that the Guardian was sure to kill him had it not been for your intervention. Your deed was heroic." He paused. "And in case you've lost count, there goes seven of your ten quests. Three more and you will become a Vermonter both in name and virtue. Or, sadly, leave us."

"That's swell," replied Flatlander, curtly. Then his voice grew an edge. "I'm glad that things worked out with the translations and all, but right now I'm just thinking about my friend."

"Your bond has become strong," observed Henry, with tempered satisfaction. "I understand, Flatlander and I apologize. I didn't mean to be insensitive to your plight. If you would only allow me one word of advice: get some rest. You must be exhausted from the day's events."

"I'll sleep when I'm ready."

Henry nodded in acceptance of the situation. "Very well. I shall see you in the morning. I have no doubts that he will stir when the time is right. Good night, Flatlander. May the night bring you comfort."

As Henry departed the hospital ward, Flatlander listened to the assortment of nurses and doctors bidding goodbye to their esteemed king. A chilled draft briefly sent goose bumps up Flatlander's arms. The fluids continued draining to and from Franklin's arms in spurts, as the gentle sound of his breathing filled the room. Perhaps it was from sheer exhaustion or the way Franklin looked; so peaceful on his pure white quilts, but Flatlander soon became overcome with drowsiness. His pained body ended its stubborn battle against sleep. He took his rest upon the wooden chair beside his fallen friend, as the sounds of murmurs ebbed away.

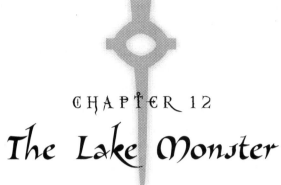

CHAPTER 12
The Lake Monster

TWO MORNINGS AFTER THEIR ILL-FATED quest to Highgate, Yuro called Henry and company to assembly. To the relief of all, Franklin was beginning to show signs of life, yet the doctors advised for him to stay an additional week for observation. And despite his semi-delirious, drug-induced protests, they didn't budge. Flatlander had spent the past two days in Burlington with Franklin while Henry and Yuro oversaw the negotiations of the Moran Plant. According to the two, the leading proposal was to incorporate all of the different factions desires for the property, which included the ice climbing wall, free park, and high-end restaurant. While the idea was met with less overall opposition, the proposal was turning out to be a logistical nightmare. Yuro had rolled his eyes on a number of occasions at Henry during the talks, but if it meant eventual peace between the political factions, he would have to uphold the ridiculous proposal.

Yuro greeted Henry, Ellen, Flatlander and Menche at the door of his sprawling home. "Welcome, King Henry. Ladies and gentlemen! We have much to discuss," he declared grandly, as he beckoned the party inside. He raised an eyebrow. "I see Franklin is missing?"

Flatlander cleared his throat to answer, but Henry spoke up before he could provide an explanation. "Indeed. He is feeling ill at this time, Lord Yuro."

Yuro frowned. "I'm sorry to hear. I've taken a great liking to that lug. Give him my regards, will you? I must confess, Lord Henry, my mood has brightened considerably since I learned of the solution of the Quebecois tipping problem. I suppose it was right there before our very eyes. Who would have thought the answer was so simple, yet so elusive?"

Ellen replied, whimsically. "Sometimes many of us overthink such trivial matters, Lord Yuro."

Yuro nodded. "Indeed, Lady Ellen. Indeed. Well, nice work. Please, take a seat."

They arrived in Yuro's meeting room. A golden lance was framed on one wall, and on the other, a purple and green tapestry hand-woven by the merchants of the Brattle, and hung on metal spirals. Helpings of olive bread and Tarrenteise cheese were spread generously on a long, rectangular table made of ebony, a butter knife resting between saucers. An overhead map of Yuro's hometown, Cornwall[71], was glued to the ceiling. The lord's trademark mixed drinks lined the middle of the table in a spectrum, sequenced according to their color. Bart stood proudly in the corner of the dining room, admiring his work.

"Fine preparation, Master Yuro," declared Henry.

Yuro nodded at the exquisite presentation. "Bart and myself would spare nothing less to please the Humble King."

"I'm curious, have any of you received the news regarding Shay Bromage?" asked Yuro.

"What of him?" asked Henry.

Yuro nodded, smugly. "A few days ago, there was a report that he is a Flatlander from New Jersey. And a superpac user too."

"Preposterous," replied Henry.

---

[71] A town bordering southwest portion of Middlebury.

"*What*? Shay Bromage is a *what*?" Ellen stammered.

Yuro shrugged. "I've no idea. It was only in the papers."

Flatlander couldn't believe what he had just heard. "Shay Bromage is a flatlander like me? Do you have the paper here?"

"I don't."

Then why had the journalist been so biased against him? It didn't make any sense. Flatlander thought briefly that he should be celebrating the news of his number one detractor being brought down to his level, but instead, felt rather sad. *What could have prompted Bromage to take such a stand against me?*

Yuro held a wine glass aloft. "Well, regardless, thanks for making it. Please, let's dine. Forget that I even brought it up."

The group dined for a few minutes in relative silence, still shell-shocked from the news of Shay Bromage. Then Yuro then whispered something into Bart's ear, and the servant left promptly. Shortly after taking a sip of a greenish-yellow fluid, Yuro spoke.

"Though I'm delighted by the progress of the Moran talks and the discovery of the Obelisk of Highgate, I've always been taught that complacency often leads to disaster. I think that you recently said something to the same effect at the statehouse. Did you not, Lord Henry?"

Henry perked up. "I did."

"As I thought," said Yuro, with a pause. "And while I thought of your words, and the fact that Flatlander has been striking it hot as of late, a thought then occurred to me. For there is something that I have set my sights on for quite some time."

"Surely not another garden patterned to your face, Master Yuro?" asked Henry with a smile.

"Very funny, my lord." He laughed faintly. "But, no. I want to find the Lake Monster, Champ. He might have something that I want."

Ellen chuckled, mockingly. "Lord Yuro, for generations, thousands have tried, and not a single one has produced a shred of credible evidence that the lake monster exists."

"Perhaps they just weren't looking in the right places," replied Yuro, defiantly. "Many efforts to find him have been thwarted by the pretense of disbelief. Other turned out to be hoaxes, peddled by swindlers and attention-seeking miscreants. Experts on such matters are unusually rare and unusually honest. Yet, alas, as it pertains to the lake monster, I think that I have found that expert."

"Born on a fool's whim," dismissed Ellen, as she scribbled a note in her journal. "The legend of the lake monster is as old as the Abenaki themselves. Yet even *they* cannot muster proof to this day of its existence. Vermonters have accepted this to be legend, and legend *only*, Lord Yuro. Nothing can change that."

Yuro cocked an eyebrow. "Hadn't you and others also not felt the same towards the Guardian of Highgate? And yet your beliefs proved untrue from what I've heard."

Henry's jaw dropped. "How did you know?"

"Worry not, King Henry," said Yuro, as he spread a generous portion of butter on his bread. "Your secret is safe with me. I only hope that Franklin recovers from his wounds. One forgets that I have many eyes and ears in this land."

Ellen bristled. "The guardian was another matter entirely. The lake is open for all to see. Hundreds, if not, thousand of eyes train its surface every waking second. The lack of reported sightings speaks volumes. You're chasing a literal phantom."

"But I disagree, Lady Ellen. Recently, my agents have gathered intelligence that suggests, that, for all intents and purposes, Champ is real and carries an object of immense value for the city of Burlington."

"What quack suggested *that*?" demanded Ellen, cockeyed.

"Ellen!" admonished Henry.

"It doesn't matter." Yuro ignored her tone of indignation. "What matters more is that I'm inviting you all to take part in this special quest. I have an important contact on Grand Isle who may yield the answer to this riddle. Retrieve the special key from the lake monster, and you will be rewarded, financially, beyond your wildest dreams. The real folly, at least to *me*, would be if you refused."

Henry mulled it over. "While your quest sounds intriguing, I must side with Ellen here, Master Yuro. The legend of the lake monster is likely a concoction from certain deranged individuals, or a series of optical illusions. It is wishful thinking to assume a plesiosaur, some prehistoric beast, roams the waters of Lake Champlain. Besides, I have left my daughter unattended for much too long to take part in such an endeavor. Montpelier beckons for better or worse."

Yuro nodded. "I understand, Lord Henry. You have spent a great deal of time in Burlington as of late. It's a long time to be away from home. But surely your cohorts would consider such a quest?"

"Tell us more about this key," said Flatlander.

Yuro pursed his lips. "Hmm. That, I cannot tell. Not yet. Though I trust each of you, my opponents have many spies throughout this city," replied Yuro, and then he gazed around the room wild-eyed. "I feel as though sometimes the walls themselves have ears."

Flatlander was surprised to hear Yuro speak with such paranoia. *Who could he be referring to?* He then thought back to the battle at the Moran, and just how divided much of the city of Burlington was. The opposing parties were at his throat. His own party begrudged him. Flatlander also remembered Henry's description of Yuro's weakening grasp, and his inability to bring unity to the Queen City. It was no wonder he felt under siege from within. Ellen leaned forward, resting her elbows on the table.

"Don't take this personally, Master Yuro, but it sounds like you want us to go on a wild goose chase. I can think of better uses of our time."

Yuro nodded ever so slightly, an exaggerated frown spread on his mouth. For a moment, Flatlander thought Yuro looked like a defeated child. After resuming his meal and drink for several seconds, he then paused and cleared his throat.

"Did I mention that there is likely millions of dollars at stake?"

Henry inadvertently dropped his fork, as it clanged loud against the side of his plate. Menche looked at his company excitedly. Flatlander wiped off the remnants of his mint-julep drink, which had accidentally spilt down the sides of his whiskered chin.

"Millions..." whispered Flatlander in wonder.

"*Seventeen* million to be exact," replied Yuro emphatically.

Henry looked to both Flatlander and Ellen with a calculating glance, and placed his napkin gently on the table.

"Lord Yuro, if I may have a moment with my party alone."

"Of course," replied Yuro, with a crooked smile.

Seventeen million dollars richer sounded a lot better than seventeen million dollars poorer, thought Flatlander, *even if finding Champ was nothing more than a giant stab in the dark.* Yuro left them alone to debate. It wasn't long until they reached an agreement. Minutes later, Yuro knocked softly on the room door and reentered.

"Master Yuro," stated Henry, cautiously, his eyes fixated on Yuro's jeweled crown, "we will take you up on your offer."

Henry assembled a team to help find the famed Lake Monster of Flatlander, Ellen and Menche. Franklin needed more rest to mend his wounds, and Henry, more time to spend with his daughter. This was to be Flatlander's eighth assigned quest, Henry noted with a measure of awe, and the end of his journey was drawing near.

According to Yuro, they were to meet with a man named Ramsey Devereux on Grand Isle, whose expertise of the lake was renown. Ramsey was also rumored to have information on the Lake Monster's whereabouts. He was to be found at a restaurant named the "Catch and Eat" at Keeler Bay, on the eastern shore of Grand Isle. According to Yuro, Ramsey was a jack-of-all-trades: merchant, fisherman, and charter boat captain. He owned and operated several boats from his own personal dock near the restaurant. He was highly selective in whom he engaged in business with, and was esteemed and respected by his peers and customers alike.

The party was to travel before dusk; apparently Ramsey was usually found at the establishment during the early hours, for his days lake-bound were usually busy. *The Vermont Islands were like another country unto themselves*, stated Henry during their planning. *The people can be thorny. Island life had ways of changing a person, and yet, there were few greater beauties in our republic than the fabled islands of Lake Champlain.*

Flatlander, Ellen, and Menche readied horse and carriage and departed for Grand Isle two hours before sunrise. An offshoot from the northern road, the way to the islands wasn't terribly complicated to navigate. Yet the further they ventured west, the more darkened the road became, until they were completely engulfed in utter blackness. Yuro and Henry had warned of the occasional bandits along this particular stretch of roadway, yet luckily they encountered no such persons.

They reached the causeway at sunrise. A small, thin, slightly elevated stretch of roadway; the causeway was a path that connected the islands to mainland Vermont. As they ventured across, it provided the group a spectacular panoramic view of the lake. A stiff, steady wind blew in their faces. The Adirondacks to the west of the lake were as clear and large as ever, and even the Green Mountains to the east were, for Flatlander's first time, visible in one continuous north-to-south profile. Silence consumed them, as the group basked in the cherry red reflections that the rising sun spilt on the lake, a welcomed sight after a dark and chilly night on the road. The lake shimmered like an endless, dancing sea of fire, as these flames morphed slowly from red to orange to yellow.

And for the first time, Flatlander truly came to realize the sheer scale of Lake Champlain. For it was neither the drinkable grail nor the cute basin for the western mountains which he had perceived while shore bound. Now, with the waters of the lake surrounding him and the mainland at his back, Champlain's true size and grandeur left him awestruck. And Grand Isle loomed closer and closer, as they had soon entered the realm of the lake folk.

The Catch and Eat lay only two miles up the island roadway in a town called South Hero on Keeler Bay. A small peninsula protruded from near the middle of its southern shore. A relatively small stretch of water separated South Hero from Milton of mainland Vermont, so the waters were often calm and pleasant, an ideal docking location for fishermen and merchant boats.

Housed in a white, rectangular building, the Catch and Eat caught Flatlander's eye right away. In front of the complex, a man-sized wooden statue of a lamprey, a parasitic eel-shaped creature with a toothed, funnel-like mouth, was erected. Pierced into the lamprey's body was a spear. A long, wooden dock led to the entrance of the Catch and Eat, which floated on the surface of the lake. Built upon large columns of basswood and white pine, and stabilized with a series of water-filled sacs and buoys lying just below the lake's surface, the Catch and Eat was incredibly stable. A dozen or more boats were docked nearby- skiffs, rowboats, sailboats, one houseboat, and a medium-sized freighter.

The party arranged for their carriage to be looked over in the establishments' nearby barn, horses included (a fee donated by

Yuro himself). Ellen ensured they tie their carriage down firmly, and take any and all belongings of any value, for the "safety of possessions wasn't guaranteed by the establishment," as was posted in bold print in multiple locations. They then ventured into the restaurant.

Once inside, in Flatlander's brief assessment, the Catch and Eat Restaurant was named quite literally, as it was the most unique of eateries. Inside, an assortment of fishermen, freight men, and travelers were seated at tables on the outer rim of a large sixty by sixty foot pool. The pool, an exposed surface of the lake, undulated in the still of the hall. The room was without roof, and it would have been darkened at this time of day despite the sunrise, had it not been for the multitude of lanterns and circular scuttles outlining its walls.

Several patrons actively fished in small pairs and trios, sharing stories and laughs with one another, as they searched for an early breakfast. Some wore the blue of the lake men, others, a mixture of flannel and wool, and still others, the traditional light tunic of the republic. A woman, presumably a worker for the eatery, sprinkled what appeared to be flaky fish food on the surface near a pair of fishermen. One of the fishermen, an old fellow with a long mustache and snug, yellow-checkered flannel, groaned while she spread the food, complaining that he'd prefer to 'catch his meal the old fashioned way, hook and worm,' prompting the worker to halt her baiting. Several other fishermen grunted and nodded their approval.

Flatlander turned to his companions. "Let's find Ramsey."

Ellen whispered in his ear. "Be mindful of your tact, Flatlander. The island folk are a salty lot."

He nodded and made his way to the counter, feeling the stares from every patron in plain sight. The woman working the counter looked old and haggard, her face the likely unfortunate byproduct of years of winter squalls and lake effect. She wore her hair short and pinned up in a bob, and afforded neither a smile nor welcoming greeting for the party. Flatlander had done his best to begin looking the part of a Vermonter. His beard growth had thickened considerably, and his fur coat resembled that of many of the residents. Still, it didn't take much for most of the patrons to see through this façade. His hands were still soft, his gait, rushed, his eyes; frantic, and most importantly, his footwear; flat.

"Shipwrecked I takes it," quipped the woman, evoking laughter from several nearby fisherman.

Flatlander nodded and smiled, then tried his best attempt at Vermont dialect. "Map told us Grand Isle's a stone's throw from the Moran."

This prompted more laughter from the fishermen, as the worker placed her elbow on the counter, and peered at the new patron curiously.

"I take it yer lost, hun?"

"Depends on who ya ask," replied Flatlander, in his best imitation of a Vermont accent.

"I take that as a yes," countered the gritty woman. "Ya came in here as wild-eyed as a puppy."

Ellen thought fast. "No more lost than Ol' Stannard would be at a talkin' contest."

Most within earshot were familiar with the reference to the notoriously inarticulate Stannard of Milton, earning Ellen and company some smiles and a few laughs from the men seated around the bar.

"Ha! Ya got me there, lady," the woman at the counter said with a cackle.

She crouched low and retrieved a trio of fishing rods, and spread them on the counter before the party.

"That'll be twenty for the three of ya, hun. Remember, no fishin' in another man or woman's space, or I can't protect ya. I'll leave that fer yer own troubles. *You* catch it, *we* cook it, and *you* eat it. But don't be expectin' gourmet if ya catch one of them dumpy things. We do what we can."

"Of course," agreed Flatlander, as he grabbed the three rods, and placed a twenty-dollar bill on the counter. "Thank you, mam."

"And one more thing, honey," continued the lady, crossly, "don't make yerself the center of attention 'round here. These folks come here to relax, not to listen to you city folk jerkin' them fish around like ya had the lake monster itself on the other end. Any troubles and yer outta here. Do I make myself clear?"

"Crystal clear, mam," replied Ellen. "Thanks for your hospitality."

The company grabbed their rods and made their way to an empty bench, situated close to the side of the open lake water. The clerk had given them a small metal can of worms, which was taped snug to Flatlander's rod.

"Now what?" asked Flatlander.

"We sit and we listen and we wait," replied Ellen matter-of-factly.

"Can't waits to get me some fishies," remarked Menche with a broad smile on his face.

Flatlander studied the clusters of fishermen gathered at pool's edge. Some were lost in thought. Others were likely enraptured in their own tales of the lake, which they'd likely been sitting on for too long, joked Ellen. He heard some express frustration at their lack of success in the day's catch. Flatlander sighed. They didn't know whom to look for, or even what this stranger Ramsey looked like. He resisted the notion of asking around. Then, after a few minutes of clumsily attaching their tackle to their lines, they heard a voice across the pool call out.

"To hell with ya, Ramsey. Why dontcha bring some of that luck this way?"

Ellen's gaze focused on a man on the opposite side of the pond and to the right, whom was in the process of reeling up a foot long fish as it thrashed wildly from the end of his line. He was a black skinned fellow, dressed in navy blue overalls and a grey woolen sweater. His head was bald and he wore the look handsomely. High cheekbones and crisp eyebrows betrayed his experience on the lake. He wore a wide grin, as he cut the fish loose from his line, and placed it in a small wooden bucket to his side.

"Need to get fattened up before old man winter shows his terrible face, Haren," replied Ramsey to his heckler. "A fine day's dining for a fine morning."

"Yer too much, Ramsey. Hope ya choke on the chum," replied the tall, lanky man in a heavy bleached blue cloak and brown trousers.

Ramsey gave the fellow an exaggerated bow. "Same to you, good sir. Same to you."

Flatlander nodded at Ellen.

They watched carefully as Ramsey soon left his bench, and conferred with one of the cooks standing ready by the kitchen door before handing him his fish. He then proceeded to the end of the bar, waiting for his catch from the kitchen while enjoying a moment to read an old copy of the Shay Chronicles. As he read with concentration, Ramsey would raise an occasional eyebrow or grunt with suppressed laughter.

Though the island folk were a fair distance from the hustle and bustle of Burlington, rumors spread with the traveling men and women of the lake, as many were grossly familiar with current news and politics. According to Ellen, there were few in the republic, besides elected officials and spies, whom had more up-to-date information on the happenings of Vermont's political scene. Reading and speaking of such things greatly passed the time during lake travel, and oftentimes, the shipmen disseminated the news even before the papers. Ramsey, however, was an exception. To observe him reading in his off time was rare. He spent such a vast amount of time lake-bound, that he was often a month or more behind on gossip.

Ellen figured this would be the best time to talk to the man, if any, as she prodded Flatlander with her elbow. They waited a few minutes then ventured towards Ramsey, fishing rods and all.

Ellen passed the lake captain a friendly smile. "Any news worthwhile?"

Ramsey flipped a page, but refused to meet her eyes. "It's a month's old, but I like reading up on events that slip under my nose. Sailor's gossip leaves a lot of holes to be filled, my lady. I'm reading about the Battle of the Moran Plant. I heard that explosion from four miles away. I would have loved to see that circus."

Ellen exchanged a mischievous smile with Flatlander. "Me too."

"Says here that the Flatlander fellow prompted each of the three militias to destroy the building outright. Bold move, I must say."

"*Reckless* might be the operative word," replied Ellen, as she glanced again to Flatlander, who had, at this point, buried his head firmly into his hands.

"You won't get an argument from me," declared Ramsey with a grin, as he kept reading. "It was once rumored that Posey ate a man for arguing with him. A mean man if there ever was. This Flatlander was lucky he didn't die on the spot. I thought that the story of the Thinker exploding was pure fake, exaggerated by the lake men. Incredible. It's a wonder how Shay Bromage ignored such insatiable fodder."

Ellen smiled. "You didn't hear?"

Ramsey perked up. "I'm behind."

Ellen took painstaking pleasure in revealing the news. "It was discovered that he too is a Flatlander and superpac user. Outed on the steps of city hall," she raised an eyebrow. "I'm surprised that the story never reached the likes of you."

The boat captain received the news of Shay with a look of utter confusion. "These are strange times that we live in, strange times," mumbled Ramsey, wide-eyed, as he concentrated on finishing the article.

Ellen grinned. She decided the time was right. "Unless my ears deceive me, I presume that you are the infamous Ramsey Devereux, boating extraordinaire of the islands."

Slowly, Ramsey dropped the paper and looked squarely upon Ellen. "That's the first time I've heard of such a full, esteemed title, my lady, but I'll accept it, begrudgingly." Ramsey extended his hand and they shook. "Captain Ramsey."

"Nora," replied Ellen without missing a beat. She nodded towards Flatlander and Menche, seated to her right. "These are my companions, Fiddle and Crip."

Ramsey nodded at Flatlander and Menche.

Ellen looked over her shoulder to ensure nobody was listening. "I wish to buy your service to assist us with a task. It's of a highly sensitive nature, so I cannot speak freely of it at the moment."

"I don't take secret offers," replied Ramsey flatly, as he resumed his morning reading. "My apologies, but it's general policy."

"Perhaps we can change your mind?"

"Miss Ellen, I have a fishing party to ferry on my merchant boat, the *Shelburne Sky*, whom I gave my word to last week. They pay generously. I cannot fall back on my word, you know. It would be bad for business."

"How much are they paying you?" asked Ellen.

Ramsey rolled his eyes back, thinking back to the agreed-upon amount. "Five hundred proper for the day."

"Double it," replied Ellen.

Ramsey shook his head. "Miss Ellen…"

"Triple it."

Ramsey was adamant. "A man of the lake is not easily swayed by money."

"Tenfold," declared Ellen. "We will pay you tenfold."

Ramsey bit his lip and collected his wits. He paused to look at the activity in the kitchen before muttering to Ellen in a low voice.

"Seldom am I offered five thousand dollars for a day's work, yet seldom do I agree to such arrangements without knowing the nature of such an excursion."

"It'll be two days work. Three days maximum. Nothing more," said Flatlander.

Ramsey smirked, his dimples running the full length of his cheeks. A small, thin-faced man came out of the kitchen with Ramsey's catch cooked as a filet, steaming hot, and served in a basket with paper lining the bottom. Flakes of red pepper and herbs coated the fish, and a container with melted butter was tucked in the basket's corner. Menche licked his lips. Ramsey readied his silverware and napkin with anticipation, his eyes growing large as he scanned his breakfast with pure delight.

He fastened a bib around his neck. "And if I refuse?"

"Then we'll resume our fishing and be off on our merry way," answered Ellen.

Ramsey studied the group cautiously, and spoke low and with certainty. "I expect to be paid in cash. I'll meet you out by pier eight in fifteen minutes. A man of the lake needs to savor his breakfast every chance he gets. He never knows when the next meal will come. I hope that you've all got your lake legs ready. Now, if you'll excuse me, I'd like to eat alone."

Ellen nodded then gestured for Flatlander and Menche to follow. The party left Ramsey without protest, returned their rods, and walked outside. The woman at the counter mumbled something to the effect of city folk lacking the necessary patience. The wooden beams bordering the entrance to each dock was labeled with a number, and it wasn't long before they reached pier eight. When they reached the proper slip and its vessel, however, Flatlander was unsure if they had found the right ship- or if it was a ship at all.

"This isn't a boat. It's a floating house."

Ellen's assessment was curt, yet accurate, thought Flatlander. For the vessel that lay in wait at slip eight defied most logical conventions of what constituted a boat. Above the traditional-looking hull, the bulk of its body was shaped eerily similar to that of a log cabin, constructed of mature cedar logs and coated in a dark finish. It reached almost thirty feet long, consisting of a small felted deck at the stern, a cockpit near the bow, a very small bathroom and kitchen near the cockpit, a small cabin, and a larger common area complete with a woodstove and chimney. The boat's mast, though awkward and out of place, soared high over its deck. A beige canvas sail wrapped around an adjoining beam. On the side of the hull, "The Bethel" was scribed in faded, block white paint.

"It's a houseboat," remarked Menche with glee; but his companions paid him no heed.

Ellen inspected the side of the bow, which was covered in Zebra Mussels. "I'm not sure if it can make it a stone's throw without sinking."

"This *is* slip eight," replied Flatlander, with a sigh. "Maybe Ramsey confused the number."

"If this is the boat we're taking, then we may as well swim," replied Ellen.

"Oh, *stop* it," Flatlander said with a laugh, as he peeked into the common area. "Ramsey strikes me as a man of his word. And I kind of like this boat. It has character."

Ellen raised an eyebrow. "You actually *like* this thing?"

"It's a houseboat," corrected Menche once more.

Then a familiar voice chimed up from behind. "I never confuse my slip number, dry walkers. And your small friend is right, indeed. It is a houseboat."

"Told ya," said Menche, triumphantly.

Ellen turned away and blushed in embarrassment. They hadn't noticed Ramsey coming. The captain looked upon his vessel with his chest puffed out.

"She's a beauty, isn't she?"

"Hardly," replied Ellen.

Ramsey patted The Bethel's side. "Aesthetics aside, The Bethel has guts. It's been through some of the toughest weather this side of the Green Mountains. It laughs in the face of the winter squalls."

"And as a result, how many times have you had to retrieve it from the bottom of the lake?" countered Ellen, as she twiddled with one of the boat's rusted cleats.

Ramsey's lip twitched. "My apologies if it isn't the Ticonderoga, Lady Ellen. My funds are somewhat limited, though I see that yours are not. Which brings me to my next question," said Ramsey as he eyed the three companions suspiciously. "Who pays five thousand Vermont dollars for a two day charter? Before we board, I'd like to know who you are. I'm not one for secrets."

Ellen cocked an eyebrow. "That's not what we've heard."

Ramsey opened his mouth to argue again, but the insinuation soon sunk in, unmistakable. He had harbored only one true secret, one profound secret; one to which he had sworn to a friend. Ramsey moved in close to Ellen, his face contorting with anger and confusion.

"*Who are you?*"

Ellen sighed. "Well, I suppose the game is up. Ellen Parthen, King Henry's head advisor. This is Flatlander, a new friend of the king. And this little man here is Menche, our assistant. We've come to find Champ the Lake Monster, by direct order from King Henry and Yuro, and we hear that you're the man for the job."

Ramsey eyed Flatlander as one would an unwanted houseguest. "A Flatlander? Wait a second, are you the same guy…"

"From the article? Yes," replied Flatlander, as his face reddened. "But I can assure you, Captain Ramsey, Shay Bromage has had it out for me since day one."

Ramsey shook his head in disbelief. "Oh, this is just great. Now I'm chartering Flatlanders around the lake to find the lake monster! Better yet, a Flatlander, a gnome and a paper pusher from Montpelier, all whom bear no connection to the lake or the plight for the people who roam its surface. The folks at the Catch and Eat will love this one. It's a story for the ages."

Now it was Ellen's turn to be outraged. "Enough of the snide talk, Ramsey. We promised you five thousand. Make jokes of it all you want, but there must be *something* you're not telling us."

"And if I choose not to?"

Ellen hesitated. "If not, then I suppose we'll have to leave and report to King Henry. I'll make sure to mention that a really rude, unpleasant shipman rejected our bid. He may not take the news well. Him and Lord Yuro were both counting on us tremendously."

Ramsey scanned the piers to make sure nobody else was near. The winds died down, and Ramsey saw that they were alone in conversation. His eyes grew intense.

"Pray, I ask, why would you want to track down Champ?"

Flatlander interjected. "He might carry a treasure."

"A treasure! A treasure, the flatlander says! Ha! But the lake monster *itself* is a treasure," retorted Ramsey. "Do you mean him harm? Because if you do, then, mercy unto your souls, I will resort to unspeakable acts against you."

"Of course not," interrupted Ellen. "He carries the key to the city, the key sought after by Lord Yuro."

The revelation bore little recognition for Ramsey, his face pure blank. "*What key?*"

"The key to the city," replied Ellen. "Vast amounts of money may be at stake. It could be a very expensive mistake if we don't pursue this lead, Captain Ramsey."

"How expensive?" asked Ramsey, with a smirk, which seemed to test the strangers: *try me.*

Ellen inhaled. "Seventeen million dollars."

A southern gale moved in, as Ramsey's eyes grew large. "Seventeen...*million*? This is madness. Seventeen million dollars is enough to buy every lake man for a month," marveled the captain.

"Indeed," agreed Ellen.

"Well, I suppose that I can come clean to you, though it burdens me to say," replied Ramsey with a sigh. "I have seen Champ, yes. But only three times total."

"I find that hard to believe," replied Ellen.

"Believe what you will. It's as true as a lakeman's appetite," Ramsey replied before hesitating. "What if we don't find him? Nothing is guaranteed."

"Then we move on," replied Flatlander.

"And what would my cut be if we do find him?"

"We can talk about that later."

"We can talk about that *now*," retorted Ramsey.

Caught off guard by the question, Flatlander hadn't devoted sufficient enough time thinking about compensation, nor had Henry or Yuro given him or Ellen a figure. He recognized that much was at stake, however, and trusted his instincts as best she could.

"One million."

He noticed a brief but intense glare from Ellen.

Ramsey whistled, resting his back against the hull of the Bethel. "*One million dollars,*" repeated Ramsey distantly. "Why do I get the sense that this is too good to be true? I appreciate your tenacity, Flatlander, though I cannot make any promises to your party. Yet, if you're true to your word, then this is truly an offer I cannot refuse." He paused then stood up rigidly. "However, you must promise me three things."

"Name them," stated Ellen through clenched teeth.

"First off, no harm shall be done to Champ. He's dwelt in these waters long before you and I," he said as he glared hard at Flatlander, "or before this train wreck named Flatlander wreaked havoc upon our land. I won't have any of it. Got me?"

"Yes," replied Ellen without hesitation. Flatlander blushed in embarrassment and turned away from the conversation before he let his mouth get the better of him.

Ramsey held out a second finger. "Second, this shall remain *our* secret and *our* secret only. If any soul gets wind of this, we may have much trouble on our hands. I have no idea how Yuro dug up this information, but it's the type of knowledge that can get a man killed, and I have no desire to end my life prematurely, nor take another's. I want you blindfolded three hours before we even reach the location. This is to protect me, you, and most importantly, Champ itself. Understood?"

"Just between us," agreed Flatlander.

"And last," said Ramsey, as he removed his extended fingers and gazed upon the three strangers fiercely, "I'm the captain of the Bethel. I call the shots. I can tell that you've got mouths on you," said Ramsey as he sized up Ellen and Flatlander, "but if I feel like, *at any moment*, you're trying to run my ship, we'll be turning tail back to shore faster than a horse-on-a-river."

"Not a problem," replied Ellen.

"Then we've got a deal, Ms. Ellen. We'll depart in ten minutes sharp. Don't be late. And Flatlander," said Ramsey, "If you do anything stupid that risks the integrity of this boat, I'll have your head on a platter. No shenanigans like up in Irasburg or Lowell. I may be a bit behind on gossip, but I'm no fool."

Ramsey took off his shirt and threw it on the deck of the Bethel. From a side compartment, he removed a harpoon and and slung it around his back. In rapid successions of motions, the captain removed several large fish from a metal storage container onboard, and placed them in a large gunnysack. Flatlander watched as the captain made his way down the pier towards the Catch and Eat with a quiet confidence.

"I need to go relieve myself," Ramsey called out in mid-stride. "We'll depart in ten minutes."

Ellen looked upon Flatlander with pity and smiled gently. "You hear that Flatlander?" she joked. "No shenanigans."

"No foolin," agreed Menche. "Captain scares me."

"I consider myself lucky that he didn't kill me on the spot," joked Flatlander.

"Don't celebrate too much. We haven't departed yet," replied Ellen.

Flatlander watched as Ramsey disappeared into the Catch and Eat. *Seven quests deep. Seven good stately deeds done.* And yet, he knew better than to believe that the rest of Vermont was excited with his rise to fame. Though denied of some measure of dignity by Ramsey, he also felt a certain level of relief at the upcoming quest. Flatlander had felt a fondness of the lake since he had first laid eyes upon it. Lake Champlain fascinated him, drew him in and called to him. He knew, deep down, through some

inexplicable intuition, that his time in Vermont would be incomplete if he didn't get to see the lake as the lakemen saw it. Hopefully, he reasoned, they would find the mythical lake monster, and his head wouldn't end up on a platter. Flatlander observed the position of the sun in the sky through a thin strip of clouds, and subconsciously began scraping zebra mussels from the Bethel's bow with his moccasin.

Two things became quite evident soon after the Bethel's departure. First, Ramsey wasn't quite the hardheaded tyrant that he had made himself out to be. Second, he took quite a liking to tobacco. Though his commands were direct, Ramsey exuded a high level of patience in helping Flatlander man the jib and halyard, while Ellen handily controlled the spinnaker. Even Menche, who managed to tangle himself in an assortment of ropes, drew more laughs than scowls from the captain, whom had taken a fondness of Henry's assistant. In short, he enjoyed being a leader of his vessel and took great pride in his knowledge of how to run it properly.

Ramsey was also inseparable from his pipe, which was often filled to the brim with fresh tobacco from the fields of Charlotte[72]. A light blue pouch rested at the captain's console near the steering wheel at all times except bed. The windows of the Bethel were kept open to vent the vessel properly of Ramsey's smoke, though the steering room was thick with its scent. The three passengers didn't like it, but they endured the smoke dutifully, having but no choice in the matter.

Since leaving the islands behind in their wake, the sun had rose spectacularly in a hard red blaze, setting the tone for what was to become a magnificent day on the lake. The voyage had been full of excitement; operating a houseboat, particularly one as unique and difficult to maneuver as the Bethel was challenging work, and required a steep learning curve. Flatlander made efforts to pause at opportune moments and absorb the beauty of the Champlain Valley. The Adirondacks to the west were imposing, and he could get a better sense of their scale from his vantage point. He wondered what lay beyond...

The Bethel anchored outside of Burlington for lunch, near the famous Dunder Rock[73]. Flatlander and company then watched

---

[72] A town just south of Shelburne.

[73] A small rock island close to Red Rocks that is revered by the Abenaki people.

as dozens of freighters and cargo ships came and went, as close to a hundred shipyard workers frantically unloaded and stacked cargo with machine-like efficiency. He was amazed at the amount of activity on the shore, the sheer depth and complexity of the operation was startling from their new perspective.

"Impressive, isn't it?" asked Ramsey, as he noticed Flatlander's admiring gaze. "Meat. Smoke. Produce. Syrup. Hops. Hay. There's barely a product in this republic that slips by the wayside that isn't hauled in or out of those crates by the creeps."

"*Creeps*?" asked Flatlander.

Ramsey chuckled. "Ah. Ship-talk for the port workers. Good men, they are. Unfortunate nickname. Derived from the mistakes made by a 17-year-old boy a long time ago. But yes, they perform their job well." Ramsey then pointed to the shores. "But you'll see more than that, for only a handful of the creeps have been beyond the wall of the lake, Flatlander. It's not common, nor encouraged by the republic or sailors alike, but some venture out through the gate in the Northern Wall of the Lake[74]. It's just wider than a common road, a natural risk during high seas. Quite a few men, *good* men, have met their demise attempting to pierce the narrows, as its called, only to find their hulls shattered upon the gate itself, and their corpses sunk like stones to the depths of Champlain. Their bones later wash up on some poor fellow's shore."

Ramsey paused. "So, on that note, who's hungry?"

He chuckled sinisterly and retrieved a small cardboard box, which he had purchased from a friend at the Catch and Eat. Four cooked, blackened walleyes stewed in their own juices. Ramsey had been reluctant to fish during their excursion, for though it was his preferred method of dining while lake bound, he had

---

[74] The northern wall immersed in the lake is considered by some to be a greater engineering feat than the wall itself. Quebec assisted Vermont in its construction.

committed most of his time overseeing his new crew. There was much for them to learn in the early goings.

As Ramsey pointed out various locations of the lake, each with their conjoining story, Flatlander realized how much he was enjoying his time exploring Lake Champlain. Sailing had been a blast- and in partial jest, he questioned to himself if this could be a future career for him. His thoughts shifted with the millions of ripples and waves scattered across the black expanse of lake water. A school of fish surfaced briefly near the Bethel, as thousands of bubbles soon took their stead. A seagull call stirred him from the lake's hypnosis. There was something so grandiose about the lake life, something so solitary. As if the sights and sounds of the lake were meant for him and him only.

When the day's work was complete, and the Lake Champlain sunset filled the heavens with layers of purple and orange, the Bethel anchored near the outskirts of Shelburne Bay. Atop a table of knotted driftwood, Ramsey placed a salvaged bottle of red wine from the vineyards of Shelburne. Twenty years prior, he told the crew, it had the unfortunate distinction of being sunk to the bottom of the lake during a particularly nasty storm. The cargo ship, "Thatcher," had been en route to its destination in St. Albans, full of select wines and cheeses. Despite the sentiments of his crew to abandon the route on that particular day due to impending weather, Captain Hungerford defied them and followed through with his plans to travel to St. Albans Bay. It was the spelling of their demise. A violent, fast moving tempest from the west caught them in the middle of the lake. A particularly nasty gale capsized The Thatcher, and only three of the ten-person crew, minus Hungerford, survived the ordeal. The bottle of wine was one of Thatcher's last relics, which Ramsey had attained through bartering in the markets of Waitsfield.

Prior to uncorking the bottle, he made sure to honor those whom had fallen on that doomed excursion. Lighting a small, orange candle, Ramsey mumbled a lake man's prayer in homage, 'to those who explore and not sit idly.' Cooked lake trout and walleye were stacked four inches high on an oversized plate, as the aroma of basil and spices filled the small space of the cabin. Earlier, Ramsey had caught the dinner with a bit of help from Menche, whom did the honor of whacking their wriggling bodies before clipping the hooks from their gaping mouths.

"So, why *'The Bethel'*?" asked Ellen through a mouthful of crisped walleye. "I presume that you've been?"

A beautiful, quaint town in Central Vermont along the Rolling Road, Bethel was located snug between the rural towns of Royalton, Rochester, Stockbridge, and Randolph. Its charming town center, complete with a splendid white church and an old, antiquated series of storefronts. From the high vantage point of the Rolling Road, the view of Bethel was often a nice reprieve for travelers shortly after venturing through the gravel-strewn, skeletal remains of Barre.

Ramsey nodded. "I have, good lady. And just so you know; I name all of my vessels after places that have some meaning in my life. I spent many a year in Bethel working as a farmhand for a sugaring operation near Brink Hill. I was poor and indentured to the owner of a maple farm, a doctor, who I loved yet loathed. He had saved my father's life. You see, one day my dad had thought that he had a bad case of the "craps," as he so eloquently called it then. As it turned out, his appendix had been burst for hours. Doctor Yohan performed emergency surgery, a procedure that my family couldn't afford. Rather than risk running afoul of the law by not paying him, I promised this man two years of my service tending to his farm and maples to pay off the debt.

"He had a log cabin at the back of his property, close to where he had built the sugar shack. It was this one-room cabin: with nothing but a woodstove, chimney, and bed. Sugaring was tedious work, but I came to love it all the same. I'd wake up to the smell of boiled sap every morning, and let me assure you, there are far worse odors to awake to."

"I take it that was your inspiration for the boat design?" asked Flatlander.

"Yes," replied Ramsey with a laugh, "but when I designed and built the Bethel, I became the laughingstock of every lake faring man and woman from the islands to the shores of Crown Point. Yet twenty years, six vessels and several thousand clients later, some have been whistling a different tune in regards of my repute."

"You're a trailblazer," said Flatlander.

"*Madman* is more like it. The houseboat was not designed for elegance, that much is sure," replied Ramsey. "But I appreciate your kindness. We'll make a sailor out of you yet, Flatlander."

After they ate, Ramsey excused himself to take a nap in the captain's room, while Menche followed suit on a small cot in his quarters, leaving Ellen and Flatlander to enjoy the soothing sunset to the west. It splashed above the Adirondacks in a fiery spectrum, shimmering off the surface. The scores of boats, which had previously dotted the lake's surface, were now gone spare a few remaining schooners and ferries in the distance. With bellies fully engorged, Ellen and Flatlander sat back upon two cushions upon a bench.

"I worry about Franklin," said Flatlander with a sigh. "I hope that he's okay."

"He's the toughest man I know. He should be fine."

"I hope," replied Flatlander under his breath.

Indeed, he hoped Ellen was right. Something felt off to Flatlander about the whole notion: while they were able to enjoy Lake Champlain, his friend lay bed-ridden in a hospital ward.

"Ramsey's quite the character," remarked Ellen, attempting to change subjects. She scanned Flatlander's face for any sign of humor.

"My head is still attached; so I've got no complaints," replied Flatlander.

Ellen sighed. "I don't know how you do it. In all of my years, I've never seen anything like it."

Flatlander looked at Ellen defensively. "Do *what*?"

Ellen chuckled. "Whatever you've been doing since you arrived here," replied Ellen as she looked upon Flatlander, amused. "You know, when you came to Montpelier with your silly shoes and that baby face of yours, I kind of hated you. Honestly, I really did."

"*Hated* me?"

"Yes."

"Hmm. Change comes to the best of us, I guess."

Ellen nodded. "I guess you're not as bad as I thought."

Nearly a minute passed as the two lost themselves in the deepening colors of the sunset. A group of seagulls hovered nearby, clattering amongst themselves, as they eyed down a surfacing school of fish. Flatlander and Ellen watched quietly as they circled in figure eights, then dove down individually for their meals. The Bethel, meanwhile, rocked sharply from the wake of a distant freighter.

Ellen shuffled slightly. "Do you still dream of home?"

"Bits and pieces come to me from time to time," answered Flatlander, plainly. "But I'm convinced that there are pieces I'll never get back."

"Lost in time and space I suppose," muttered Ellen. "I'd be curious to see the Old Country some day."

"Same, and it might not be long until I'm back home." Flatlander paused then turned to Ellen. "You know something? I'm noticing you never really talk about yourself."

Ellen stiffened at the direction of the conversation.

"It makes no difference," she replied flatly.

"Oh, *c'mon*," replied Flatlander with a chuckle. "Up until now, my life has been like an open book to you guys. I've told you my dreams and memories. Half of the republic thinks that I'm the village idiot thanks to the fine reporting of Shay Bromage and the good folks of the senate. You're telling me that you can't even so much as tell me *something*, *anything*, really, about yourself?"

"Well, what do you want to know?" asked Ellen, as she shifted restlessly in her seat.

Flatlander thought for a moment. "Where are you from?"

"From a small town called Bridgewater- it's in the south."

"What kind of things do you like?"

"Flatlander, I hardly think this is important…"

"*Please*, I barely know you," interrupted Flatlander.

Wearing the blue of the lake men looked odd on her, he had to admit. The heavy, navy blue, buttoned wool shirt was large for her frame. Still, Flatlander thought, she looked cute in the awkward garments.

Ellen sighed. "Fine. I like Vermont lore. I like watching opera at the Flynn. Use to, really, before our run in with Dino Paraletti. And it's kind of embarrassing to admit this, don't laugh, but I enjoy watching birds during my free time. I enjoy reading. I like working for the republic, as frustrating as it can be, even if it sometimes drives me to the brink of insanity."

Flatlander chuckled. "Does it ever get to be too much though, you know, with the paperwork and stupid politics and games?"

"It certainly has its frustrations," admitted Ellen, carefully. "But I guess that just comes with the territory like any job."

"I suppose," replied Flatlander nonchalant, wondering how he could phrase the next question without drawing Ellen's ire.

He wasn't sure of his feelings for Ellen, or her feelings towards him, but he figured if there was a perfect time to find out, now would be it. Adjusting his chair back slightly, he glanced in her direction, biting his lip.

"I've noticed you looking at me in a certain way."

Ellen straightened up in her chair, horrified. "How so?"

Flatlander swallowed. *Uh oh. This could go poorly.*

"I noticed it after the Thinker burst into the air. I noticed it during our trip up to the islands. I've noticed a few other times as well."

Shuffling in her seat, Ellen gazed starboard near the foot of the mountains. "I never took you as the type for such an ego. I've simply grown a lot of respect for you, Flatlander. That's all."

Flatlander raised an eyebrow. "Is that all?"

"Take the compliment while you can still get it," answered Ellen brusquely.

"Is that all, though?" asked Flatlander again, as his eyes searched desperately for any sign in Ellen's face suggesting what he wanted to hear. He waited several seconds.

Ellen averted her eyes. "Yes," she replied with a raised voice.

"I didn't mean to…"

"Stop," urged Ellen loudly, as she then sat back and sighed.

Taking the hint, Flatlander also sat back in his seat, leaned back, and stayed silent for some time. The gulls began cawing loudly then collectively traveled northward searching for better yields. Their calls soon faded into the soothing ripples and waves splashed against the hull of the Bethel. The sunset had proceeded into the more advanced stages of lazy indigo and gray, as the sun was nearly fully enveloped behind the Adirondacks. It was apparent that Ellen was uncomfortable with the conversation, but it seemed too late to change subjects.

"I'm enjoying the moment. Just leave it at that," said Ellen finally.

Flatlander sighed. "Okay."

Then, without warning, Ellen grabbed Flatlander by his shirt collar, and kissed him passionately in a warm embrace. Initially taken off guard, he then gradually reciprocated. He lifted her bangs back to see her closed eyes. Ellen's body relaxed under the warmth of his arms, like a weight had been lifted from her shoulders. Despite several moments of pauses and awkward smiles, the kissing continued longer than either had anticipated.

Nearby, Menche awoke shortly before sunset, well rested after a tiring day on the boat, and a full meal to boot. The day had left him exhausted. His muscles tensed with every dip and bob of the waves. He needed to develop his lake legs, as Captain Ramsey had so aptly framed it. Menche made his way to the door of the porch to check in on his friends. Instantly, he caught sight of Flatlander and Ellen on the deck, kissing. He rushed back into the cabin, plopped into his bead, and pretended that he was fast asleep. Meanwhile, he listened to the sounds from the deck with a mixture of jealousy and curiosity. The sun then sank away from sight and left the Bethel to the night.

A sage lavender-scented candle sat aflame on a desk near the bedside flickering faintly through each of Shay's labored breaths. The shadows of his bureau and grandfather clock loomed large on the opposite wall. The sound of a passing horse-drawn buggy filled the room, as Shay pulled his oversized bed covers closer to his chest. He tried in vain to ignore the coldness now left at his bedside in Dawn's absence.

Emptiness. That's all Shay felt; all he knew. His bed lay empty. His house lay empty. Worst of all, his heart lay empty, abandoned of all hope after the revelations of him being a superpac user *and* Flatlander. Shay laughed tragically, as his unmasking plagued his every thought. A superpac user *and* a Flatlander. *Either one of those revelations would have been enough to ruin a career,* thought Shay, *but two? It's simply career homicide.* Admittedly, the scenario would have provided him a snicker had Shay been writing about somebody else, some other subject, some other poor sap. Yet it was *he* who was the subject of this cruel joke. *He* who had to bear this new burden for years to come. *He* who had to deal with whatever consequences there were to follow. *There isn't a hole big enough to hide in,* thought Shay, miserably.

Vergil had retaliated with vengeance. It shouldn't have come as a shock, really. The wizard was as ruthless as he was powerful; not the type of man whose ire you'd wish to seek. To plot revenge against such a foe was folly. He knew of Vergil's power almost to a fault. *For Fish's sake[75], he had written extensively about the man,* thought Shay, *which was the main reason he had gotten caught in this predicament in the first place.*

The truth was: Shay was indeed a Flatlander who had migrated from a part of the old country named "New Jersey" when he was just a boy. His memories from that distant land and time were vague, at best, but real. Very real. His family, which consisted of himself, his parents, and his sister, Natalie, had secretly moved to Vermont while he was still in grade school. They had snuck in through a gap in the wall near the town of Pownal. He was too young to understand what exactly they were fleeing from, only that they were seeking a new and better life in the north. When they migrated to Vermont, they exchanged their currency for Vermont dollars through a woman whom the family had befriended during their travels, Gina Allen. The residents of Pownal had thought them to be relatives of Gina's from the north. Gina tutored his family in Vermont's language, history and culture. She even let them stay with her through the spring months. Eventually, when she was comfortable with their collective transformation, bought them a one-way ride to Burlington on a public carriage.

Adjusting to their new lives was hard. His family claimed to folks in Burlington to be from the town of Pownal, for they could recall certain places, shops and landmarks with ease. Hoping that

---

[75] An expression used more frequently by Shay after Fish's demise.

each time they spoke their lies, that nobody from that town, or with contacts from Pownal, would call them out, or attempt to corroborate their differing stories with other residents. Luckily, the town of Pownal was small enough at approximately 4,000 people to nearly swallow their secret whole. *Nearly.*

His parents had left back for the land of New Jersey ten years later, unable to adjust to the harsh Vermont winters and the vast cultural divide. At that point, Shay and his sister were attending the university, paying their way through school by serving as delivery workers for the Burlington Daily. Natalie eventually left for the artistic collective of the Brattle, exploring the industry of glassblowing. And to this day, he had limited contact with his sister, which had now dwindled to an annual excursion. On more than one occasion, this excursion coincided with a tasty story down south. On one such occasion, Shay had interviewed the past acquaintances of Lord Henry and brought up embarrassing tales, ranging from an incident involving a dirty diaper to the Lord's less-than-inspiring grade school transcript. *Surely, Natalie didn't mind that I killed two birds with one stone.*

Bringing up another's dirt for no other reason than to belittle them was a specialty of Shay's since his early days in journalism. *No more*, the reporter cursed. *No more.* Shay wondered how Vergil could have discovered such a private thing. But he reminded himself that little, if anything, escaped the timeless gaze of the wizard.

If only he could, Shay would grab a firm hold of the grandfather clock at the opposite side of his room and slap the hands of time back to happier, more joyous time. He remembered swinging with Dawn in the kitchen on her birthday: a sloppy imitation of ballroom dancing. He remembered the smile on her face, as she kissed him with chunks of cake still smeared on her lips. Her kisses made him happy, like nothing else mattered in the world at that moment. But that all seemed so distant now.

He had tanked. Bottomed-out. The proverbial rug had been pulled out from below. His world had changed drastically in the blink of an eye, evidenced by earlier in the day, when Shay had spent a great deal of time repairing damage done to his house by vandals. They painted "Flatlander, go home!" on his front door. And for good measure, these same delinquents had thrown a stone through his window while he tended to his garden. By the time he reached his porch, it was too late. The perpetrators were gone. In the aftermath, it had taken him the better part of two hours finding a matching coat of red paint in town and finding a handyman to fix the window.

But the real damage was to his psyche. Shay no longer felt comfortable in his own home or his own skin. He knew in the deepest of both heart and soul he needed to repent and fast. He needed to turn over a new leaf. Shay wondered earlier in the day how such revelations would affect his newspaper's sales, but soon realized that was an absurd thought. There were much bigger matters at hand.

There was no obvious fix, yet three things remained certain: he had to make amends with Dawn. He had to make amends with Flatlander. And despite the recent spate of vandalism to his house, perhaps partly *because* of the recent spate of vandalism to his house, he needed to make amends with the people of Vermont, specifically, his fans. His community.

Walt Newsome had said it best in the twilight of his career, as his body of work largely went unheralded. *Just because a bridge is burnt doesn't mean that it can't be rebuilt.* So simple and Vermont-like, thought Shay, yet so brilliant, logical, and applicable at the moment. He hoped, for the very life of him that he could mend the broken pieces of his life together into some semblance of happiness again. *Things will then be different, I promise.*

Franklin drifted in and out of consciousness in his small hospital room, his mind ambling through memories old and new. He watched himself grasping the medallion in his hands, shielding it from the eyes of the Miller. He watched his hair being soaked. He re-lived the memory of barreling down the mountain road of Lowell at breakneck speed in the dead of the night, narrowly missing en embankment. The conjured images soon opened up a Pandora's box of memories, releasing the floodgates to his time spent in the north. To the nurses and doctors who came by his bedside to check up on the brute, there was no indication that Franklin was now transported to another era, in another part of the republic. The same hustle and bustle filled the ward's hallways. Nor did his sedentary, peaceful pose on the plain, white hospital bed give away the nature of his remembrance.

Yet in his dreams he was now traveling on foot through knee-deep snow in the far reaches of Lowell. The memory came to him in greater focus, like a felled tree in mid-fall. The easterly winds carried with it the brutal cold of the White Mountains[76] to the east, and yet Franklin of Walden paid it no heed. Fine winter powder glittered on his beard from the unfiltered moonlight, and his footsteps carried an unusual grace in the fallen snow for a man his size. There had to be a good twenty inches of fine powder that blanketed the ground, fresh from an afternoon storm. Even in the limited glow of the moonlight, the sprawling countryside of Lowell was visible for a half mile just east of a cluster of barreling clouds.

His axe head was made of the finest, heaviest steel, forged from an acquaintance in Maidstone Village and assembled with an ash-wood handle. Markus was the man's name, and his home doubled as a forge. Markus had been highly recommended by Franklin's friends from both near and far, from the Kame Terraces of Caledonia to the paper mills of Hyde Park. Franklin grinned, as he gripped its handle tight.

---

[76] A large mountain range in New Hampshire.

With weapon drawn, he began smashing any obstructions into sheer oblivion: trees, shrubs, even an awkwardly shaped woodpile, which lay coated by a thick layer of powder. He destroyed these things less out of aggression and more so from self-disgust. Nearby, a brown, wooden sign, made of a cutout cross section from a tree, with "Richard Brantley" inscribed on its surface. Posted at eye level, the sign marked what appeared to be a long driveway. He swung his axe upon the sign with such force that several wooden shards spurted into the dark. Unconcerned of his loud arrival; Franklin knew it would be near impossible to hear anything with the squalls screaming through the valley as they were. A great, dark mass of clouds retreated to the west. The white birch forest pitched and bent in unnatural directions, as blasts of air shot out from wood's edge sporadically. For a moment, it all looked so pretty, until he remembered his purpose for being there in the first place.

"Brantley would make a nice ornament on my wall, wouldn't you say? My wife always complains about my sense of décor."

These were some of the last words spoken to Franklin by his superior, Sir Peter Breen, High Lord of Caledonia, before his departure to commit the unspeakable: assassinating a fellow high lord of the North. Franklin's reputation for being a hard-nose preceded him; his exploits in bar fights, barehanded hunting expeditions, and his law enforcement became the stuff of legend. Local rumors told of a time that Franklin knocked out three drunken men in a fit of rage and when they had finally come to their senses, the trio found themselves hanging upside down, tied from the bar ceiling.

And for the past several years, Franklin had acted as bodyguard and servant for Breen, one of the most powerful men on the farther reaches of the Northeast Kingdom. Breen had found himself in several trading disputes with Richard Brantley of Lowell, and his dislike of the man grew after finding out that it was he, according to various rumors, who had plotted to overtake

Caledonia in a power grab. The tipping point came to a head when a party of Brantley's men roughed up Breen's nephew at a local watering hole. Breen soon promised that for every bruise his nephew suffered at the hands of Brantley's thugs, a limb was to be lost as a returned favor. After a thorough inspection, it appeared as if the nephew suffered five substantial bruises, which presented Franklin a slight mathematical quandary in the event he found one party liable. Luckily, for Brantley, Breen never followed through with his threat.

Franklin traversed through a deep snowdrift towards Brantley's house. He had disliked the proposition from the start. The likes of Breen and Brantley were nearly indistinguishable in his eyes. *Both squabblin', pampered high rollers,* he thought; the few accustomed to a life of luxury in the far reaches of the kingdom. Thus far, for all of Franklin's toils and grunt work, the fifteen by twelve foot shack on Breen's property was all that he could show for it. He often confided to his closest family and friends that he bore no love for his boss.

Still, Franklin had been promised an extra year's pay and twelve acres near Breen's Caledonian estate per completion for the terrible deed. He had even toured the prospective property a day prior to his journey to Lowell and fell in love with the sheer ruggedness of the land. Several large pines dominated the center of the property, reminding him of his freewheeling childhood, playing in the evergreens of Walden. Throwing pinecones at his sisters, rubbing the sap from his hands, and oddly enough, enjoying the sensation of its glue-like quality. Most of all, he remembered laying on his back among those thin, yet surprisingly comfortable sheets of pine needles; and how the smell of pine and tree sap would soothe his nerves, and how close the squirrels came to his fingers without a care in the world. Truly, he loved those pines. They represented to him something intimate, something endless. Yet his current task was a thankless task. There was no glory in killing a man in cold blood. Though tough and ruthless, Franklin was far from a cold-blooded killer.

The howling winds slowed to a soft breeze, and a deep silence took its stead. The black clouds rolling to the east soon faded in the distance, and the great light of the moon drenched the Lowell landscape in all of its grandeur. Meadows, woods, and hills lay as far as the eye could see. The occasional squall whipped up from the distance in the open farmland below. Franklin shook his head from the sight. The view was great, yet not on such a night as this. The Northerner continued his haunting passage through the white birch forest, albeit, in a more subtle manner. He would soon be too close to Brantley's home to test fate. The head sign of Richard Brantley lay half-buried and scattered amongst the fresh drifts. The mist of Franklin's breath could be seen easily discerned in the evening moonlight.

He drew in a breath before the doorway of Brantley's house, mentally preparing himself for the inevitable bloodshed. The bleached cedar boards creaked sharply under Franklin's weight then died off rapidly into the thick snowfall of the night. Franklin grimaced, leaning snug against the porch wall, listening for any hints of life inside. A loud thump sounded to his right caused Franklin to jump and instinctively draw his axe. Quickly, he realized that it was nothing more than a thick clump of snow falling from the roof. Breathing a quick sigh of relief, Franklin readied his instrument of death.

Heaving his axe with tremendous force, Franklin struck the door hard, splitting it directly down the middle. One of its large wooden panels exploded back into the house, as the door's hinges bent awkwardly. After three more devastating strikes, the door lay completely smashed upon the entryway, as snowflakes gathered on the inside floor. He saw the main hall illuminated by three large oil lamps, which sat on a long, wooden mantle. Franklin expected a flurry of confused shouts from Brantley, followed by footsteps and more shouts.

Yet he heard nothing of the sort. It was completely silent.

The interior of the house was bleak. There was little furniture to be seen, aside from two old rocking chairs and cube-like stone table. No paintings hung on the walls. A musty, stale smell with a faint hint of garlic hung in the air. Several deer racks looked out to him from a high wall in the living room, their expressions blank and lifeless. To his left, Franklin observed a wide staircase, its bannister worn and smooth. *Second door to the left. Second door to the left. Breen had better be right!* Franklin raced up the stairs as his heavy footsteps resounded throughout the hall. He found the door. Lowering his shoulder, he plowed through with all of his might, falling to the floor face first.

Frantically, Franklin picked himself up, only to find ten burly guards surrounding him, weapons drawn. The withered, diminutive Brantley stood at its periphery. All pointed sharpened blades directly at Franklin's head, all except Brantley, who seemed to be reveling in the moment. A wicked smile spread on the High Lord's face.

How could the bastard have known? Cautiously, Franklin dropped his axe to the floor. He knew these men to be fierce, loyal and unforgiving. The largest of the men, the notorious Oludor[77], dwarfed Franklin by a foot, his horned helmet barely fitting inside the bedroom. Franklin knew he was strong enough to hold his own in a fight on pure adrenaline alone, but a dozen northerners? Even Franklin recognized he didn't stand a chance. Brantley took a step closer to the humbled would-be assassin.

"Franklin of Walden, we've been expecting you."

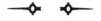

---

[77] Richard Brantley's right-hand man.

Franklin spent the next few weeks in a makeshift prison housed in an abandoned shack on his property. Subsisting on a simple diet of carrot, root and stew slow-boiled in a oversized, granite ware pot by Brantley's guards, the northerner yearned for a brighter days. Subjected to regular beatings at the hands of Brantley's guards, he often wondered if he was to spend his dying days at the hands of the High Lord's men. The shack was kept partially warm by a cast-iron wood stove in the corner; yet it was barely enough heat to keep Franklin alive through the harsh winter chill. He shook violently during both day and night. The guards knew this, and manipulated the amount of heat as if it were a torturing device, depriving the prisoner of his primal need. It appeared that they had had some practice with such cruelty. Franklin quickly came to loathe the guards, as he did the woodstove.

There were several occasions, while bound in shackles, that Franklin felt the life drain from him. Several times he saw himself lying on the smooth, flattened pine needles of his childhood memories. He saw in the distance sight the cabin of Breen's promise no more than several stone throws away. But now the cabin of his dreams looked empty and plain; a bounty not worth its plight. *What a cruel joke*, thought Franklin. *Been so foolish. Bargin' into a northern lord's home in the middle of the night like that, expectin' nothin' but the best of things.* He had a feeling that there was much more to the story than met the eye. *There's nothin' natural 'bout a dozen men waitin' in a bedroom that hour of the night.* Franklin smelt a rat, and a rather large one at that.

A gash had opened wide on Franklin's forehead. The big fella with the horned helmet had hit him harder than he'd ever been hit in his life. 'Oludor' they had called the man. Franklin had heard tales of the man even before his migration from Walden. He had even developed a sense of competition of sorts through their respective legacies, though the two had never met. Until now. A mean, redheaded enforcer, his name evoked the strongest of fears throughout the Northeast Kingdom and beyond. Oludor wore his long red beard in a double braid, studded with rubies and garnets. He wielded a maul of such size and power that it would take two average-sized men to lift it properly. Oludor of Lowell, or "Brantley's Red Fury," as some in Walden had previously referred to the giant, was a man not to be reckoned with.

It was near the end of the third week that Franklin received a special group of visitors. To the northerner's shock, Peter Breen walked in with Richard Brantley. Accompanying him were an ugly stranger in a wool cloak with long, matted hair, and a third man, with a large nose and flattened forehead, whose presence appeared to be of a more sophisticated nature. The man's gait was proper, the air about him, dignified. He looked squeamish when he viewed Franklin's bruised and battered torso.

Brantley gestured to Peter Breen. "Lord Breen, here is your pet. Good timing. I was tempted to feed him to the wolves more than once."

Breen looked like he had put on some weight since Franklin had last seen him. The High Lord's long locks of grayish-brown hair fell clumsily to his shoulders. The lines below his eyes had grown considerably darker. His cheeks looked rosy from the cold. Breen looked on disapprovingly as Brantley produced a paper, then came so close to Franklin that their noses nearly touched. His warm, moist breath, which reeked of tooth decay, actually provided relative comfort for Franklin, who was intermittently losing the feeling in both his ears and nose.

"You've gotten yourself into some major trouble here, boy," Brantley muttered.

Franklin winced in pain. "Just followin' orders."

"I told you no such thing," snapped Breen, from Brantley's side. "I told you to deliver a message to Brantley, pure and simple- a message of truce."

Franklin trembled with pure rage, straining his chains and shackles to the very limits, as every muscle fiber in his body tensed. The chains pulled and rattled but would not give out.

"Still as stubborn as an ox too, I see," remarked Breen, with a dismissive wave.

"Runs like one too," mocked Brantley, recalling the northerner stumbling gracelessly into his bedroom after plowing through the bedroom door.

"Yer lucky ya have yer gang here," snarled Franklin, as he glanced at the towering Oludor, waiting patiently outside of the shack.

"And your lucky I haven't had you gutted like a fish for your crime," retorted Brantley. "Never before has there been such a brazen attempt on a High Lord life, at least as far back as I can remember."

"He looks like hell," said the unknown third party.

His elegant speech, neatly trimmed pants, and Cerpelli boots suggested he came from the more cultured cities of Burlington, Montpelier or the Brattle. His stubble was thick but short, and his nose, though abnormally large, wore his face well. He wore a black fur coat with a grey wool undershirt.

"Keep talkin' like that, city boy," spat Franklin into the direction of the stranger. "And you'll look the same."

Breen wound up his arm to strike Franklin in the face, but the stranger grabbed his arm before the blow could land.

"No. Let him be."

Breen glared hard at Franklin. "You just insulted the newly elected King of Vermont, Lord Henry Cyrus of the Brattle. Amazing. Your insolence knows no bounds."

Franklin sized up King Henry. "The Kingdom don't care fer lords of the republic."

"Please, call me Henry," replied the stranger in an oddly pleasant tone. "And I bear no ill will."

Breen neared Franklin, close enough that Franklin observed several boils on his neck in fine detail. Averting Breen's gaze, he squirmed more, as the chains began to rub his wrists raw.

"He's a wily one all right. Hit this one with the full force of a battering ram, and you'll have yourself a broken ram through and through." Breen turned slowly from the prisoner, and took a few steps aside. "You'll be happy to know, Franklin, that I have arranged a deal in order to spare your life. King Henry, in his quest to find a hardy right-hand man, has offered to purchase your services. I was tempted to sell you to my friend here, Ernest the Miller, for a hefty exchange, for he has made some enemies during his time in Lowell: miners, naturalists, minstrel neighbors, and such.

"But, ultimately, I've decided to sell you to King Henry for a large fee, despite the fact that we operate close to a near autonomous level here in the north, outside of the kingdom's jurisdiction. A northern lord can never afford to be too…thrifty."

"And I have approved of such a transaction," added Breen, smugly.

Ernest the Miller cleared his throat from the back of the room.
"Hear me now: if things go astray,
The Lowell Mills is where you stay."

"And I, friend, welcome you with open arms," exclaimed Henry, with an ever-so-slight bow, as the two warlords chuckled.

Franklin eyed the northern lords. "Ya set me up, ya no-good, filthy, scummy liars! *Why*??"

"Are you *that* dense, Franklin? Never mind, don't answer that question." Brantley replied, as he shook his head. "Because neither of us felt safe with such a reckless, dangerous man so close to our homes and loved ones. Neither of us wanted a man of your repute within a dozen leagues of our towns. So, here it is. From henceforth, you are not to take step foot ever again into the land of the north. You are now an outcast of this land, Franklin. Understood?"

He had finally had his admission from Breen and Brantley. He had been perceived as a threat; too dangerous to keep close by. Yet there must have been some soft spot in one of their hearts, some little speck of loyalty, thought Franklin. Otherwise, they would have had him killed right there on the floor of Brantley's bedroom.

Franklin twitched. "Where's my axe?"

Brantley replied. "Nowhere close by. We have given King Henry the key to unshackle you, but not until we are safe in our house, under the careful watch by two-dozen of our fiercest guards. Enter at your own peril. But please, consider this before such a course of actions: we have spared your life in graciousness."

Breen smiled thinly. "This is all for your own good, Franklin of Walden. Understand that this could have been much worse. You have served me well, and for that I truly thank you."

Franklin spit on the ground in front of Breen's shoe. Holding up his head, defiantly, a frozen shoot of snot clotted Franklin's nostrils, rendering his breathing to a pathetic rasp.

"I'm sorry that the feelings aren't mutual," concluded Breen. Brantley skirted close behind like a stumbling fool. "Farewell, friend. I hope that we never cross paths again."

The lords and the miller left the shack at a brisk pace followed by Oludor. For a half minute, Henry waited for the men to enter Brantley's home before unlocking Franklin's shackles one by one. The brute of Walden collapsed to the ground in a heap. King Henry struggled greatly in trying to get Franklin to his feet. Draping a blanket around the northerner, Henry rushed him to the dying embers of the wood stove. There, Franklin held his hands so close to the fire that he was nearly touching them. He could have sworn that he smelt his own burning flesh. Slowly but surely, feeling returned to his frostbitten fingers.

"Ya should have just left me to die," muttered Franklin.

"Nonsense. A dog deserves a better death," said Henry, as he scanned the brute's deteriorated form. "Let's get out of here."

Franklin followed Henry, draped in a blanket in a slow and awkward pace. His muscles and joints numbed from the cold, made stiff by their stationary positions. They had walked about halfway down the driveway when Henry spoke.

"They set you up, Franklin. Both you and I know that now. Furthermore, I overheard them talking of it in the next room as I relieved myself in the bathroom. They were in on it together from the start. Breen gained a swath of land and a fat purse, and Brantley, one less mortal enemy."

Franklin clenched his fists tightly, and turned towards the house, wanting nothing more than to run back and kill them all. *Burn it to the ground.* His murderous facial expression must have been plain for the king to see.

"Easy, there," Henry placed a reassuring hand on Franklin's shoulder. "You are outnumbered, outmatched, and with all due respect, look like you've been run over by a herd of moose. Your days in the north are behind you, Franklin of Walden. I'm sorry that they have ended so bitterly. Yet if it's any consolation to you whatsoever, you will now serve me, the king of all Vermont's lands, in the heart of our beautiful capital city, Montpelier."

"I wanna tear 'em to shreds," replied Franklin through clenched teeth.

Henry glanced at Brantley's house and nodded. "And I can't fault you for that. There is no worse taste to bear than that of treachery." Henry turned to him: "But Franklin, my friend: take solace. You have your sanity, what's left of your health; and most importantly, your life. You will start anew. I promise."

The King walked through the snow-laden fields of Lowell with his newly minted yet badly bruised right-hand man. Seething with rage throughout most of the trip to Montpelier in Henry's carriage, Franklin was in little mood to talk despite the King's best efforts. During the ride home, he asked Franklin about his family and his hobbies. He even talked to Franklin about his own love for Vermont and his daughter, Jess. And after some time, Franklin began to open up. He recounted his upbringing in Walden. He recalled his adventures with his sisters, whether climbing trees or floating down small icebergs in the Morril Brook. The memories conjured up smiles and laughs alike from both men. And soon, without realizing it, talking to the king made him feel better.

It wasn't until they were riding through the village of Morristown, about twenty miles into the ride, that Franklin began to really appreciate the man. *He saved me from dyin'. Me. He's a king, and he's speakin' to me of all people, and best off, he's speakin' to me like a friend. Askin' me about me life. He's either the best conman in the republic or the most humble king I've ever heard.* And it was with these sentiments in which Franklin changed his future forecast, and the nickname of Henry was born. *May not seem noble in his looks, but's noble in his deeds.* And from that day on, Franklin made a vow to himself to avoid the Northern Kingdom at all costs. He would now serve proudly and unconditionally under Henry of the Brattle.

A horn sounded off through the evening gloom, echoing faintly through the Champlain Valley corridor. According to Ramsey, this signaled the late-night arrival of cargo from the islands. Off the eastern shore, bulb-like smoke drifts floated lazily above the assorted tanneries, smokehouses, and factories at the foot of Burlington Bay. The lake had become still; its onyx surface oscillated fluidly. The moon was full and unusually bright, illuminating bits and pieces of the rippling water in a milky, white film.

It was Flatlander's second night on the lake. True to his word, Ramsey had required his crew of greenhorns to fasten their blindfolds a full three hours before arrival to his secret location. It turned out to be a much more tedious experience than Flatlander had anticipated. Initially, they passed the time in utter darkness by telling stories and jokes. As the evening wore on, however, so too did their energy for conversation. The leisurely lopping of mini waves on the Bethel's hull was the only constant.

Flatlander wasn't sure of what to make of the previous night. Kissing Ellen had felt so good, but now he felt strange about the whole affair. She was his associate, his colleague, and besides that, Henry's counsel. He was unsure how Henry would receive such information if he ever got wind of it. In addition, Menche's behavior had become very peculiar; he often lumbered around the houseboat sad and expressionless. His actions, from spitting out line for anchor to cleaning up deck with broom in hand, seemed sullen and labored. It was unbefitting of his quirky companion. Flatlander thought that perhaps he had developed an acute sense of lake sickness.

Ramsey's voice shattered Flatlander's thoughts. "Blind's up, greenhorns."

They removed their blindfolds, revealing a location a mere fifty yards from shore. They found themselves on a remote section of the lake with no discernable cities or towns nearby. The shore was comprised of black, dense hardwoods. The muted hush of waves kissed a rocky strand, spilling against the smooth stones, gurgling faintly as they receded.

"That is one experience that I wish to never live through again," muttered Ellen, as she hastily tossed it carelessly to the deck.

Ramsey laughed, and patted his tobacco pipe loose over the deck of the Bethel. "Many apologies, Lady Ellen, but a rule's a rule."

"Moon hurts me eyes," remarked Menche, as he shielded his vision.

"So this is it?" asked Flatlander. He scanned the surrounding section of the lake.

"This is it," replied Ramsey simply, as he hurled a huge anchor overboard.

Flatlander attempted to catch any sign of a structure to give away their location, but to no avail. Ramsey had been thorough in preventing such things to be known. Shortly after the crew donned the blindfolds, he had sailed the Bethel in several concentric circles, all but eliminating any and all sense of direction. Luckily, he had not bothered so much as catch a peak, for Ramsey held a watchful eye over the group for the duration of the voyage.

"Hold on just a moment," stated Ramsey, as he disappeared within the cabin of the Bethel.

When he reemerged, he carried with him a polished, wooden box. Placing the box at the foot of the deck, Ramsey gently unlatched its metal buckles. Inside, lying on a neatly folded pile of cloth, lay a corroded bronze horn. Roughly the length of Flatlander's forearm, the horn consisted of a simple grip, and a uniquely shaped funnel, its lip peeled upward like a blooming flower. Ramsey crouched over the instrument, caressing its funnel.

"An older fellow traveling to Milton was short of cash and used it as payment. My general policy that I only deal in money, but my thinking is that a man who walks away from an offer empty-handed is a foolish man indeed. I hadn't used it for some years, had no idea of its purpose, and had even given thought to selling it on several occasions when I found it too unsightly or useless. From a lake man's perspective, it doesn't take much collecting to clutter a boat."

He then removed the horn from its case and held it in his hands for the crew to inspect. "Three years back, I got stuck in the mud near this exact location during a fishing trip. It had been a dry year, and I had greatly underestimated the water's depth. It was also late at night and the chances of anyone finding me, on mere sight alone, were slim to none. I thought, on a whim, it was wise to try this horn. It was more to humor me than anything, to be honest."

Ramsey blew hard into its mouthpiece, his face straining against the pale moonlight. Though low and earthy, the sound emitted from the horn had a fine, melodious quality. Flatlander thought it sounded like a cow, but more phonically pleasant.

Ramsey continued his tale after the noise faded into the night. "I watched and waited. I swore at my own stupidity. I laughed at the fact that I had used the thing in the first place. Then something incredible happened."

"It followed the horn's sound," said Ellen.

Ramsey smirked. "It was a sight that I'll never forget; a sight that challenged my very notions of what was real. I thought it to be flotsam at first. But it then came up beside my boat, the *Allison Cleary*, and greeted me. Its head stuck several feet out of the water then it was gone. It happened so fast, but I swear to you by all the gravel in Barre, it happened."

"What did it look like?" asked Flatlander.

"One of dem plesiosaurs? Dem long necks, like snakes? Read all 'em books," said Menche, looking for a shred of affirmation.

Ramsey nodded. "It looked like a long-necked serpent with a large body. But it wasn't as big as some of the legends say: he was roughly the size of large deer. Its skin was black by the looks of it. Its eyes were dark slits. First, the beast looked at me curiously. And just before it splashed its head back down underneath the water, it gave me a distrustful glance. I swear to you. Its face had a very human-like expression."

"Did you tell anyone? Sounds like the sort of thing one would have a tough time keeping to him or herself," said Flatlander.

"I told one person and one person only," Ramsey replied. "Whose name is not worth mentioning. But yes, I told him and he nearly laughed to death at the time. But apparently he didn't seem to find it *that* funny. For he must have been the one to eventually share this information with Lord Yuro or one or more of Yuro's dozen spies."

"Money can buy you all sorts of things," stated Ellen, as she patted the hull of the Bethel.

Ramsey nodded in acknowledgement and looked out into the night. "But in the end, happiness is the truest measure of wealth. Is it not, Lady Ellen? I've primarily come across two types of people who work the lake- the bitter and the glad. The former are affected by every issue that can go astray, and my, how things can go astray when you take a land-born animal and put him or her on a lake-faring vessel. The latter, however, ride into the lake squalls with excitement. They see life's imperfections as hidden opportunities for adventure and knowledge. And a deeper knowledge than that of any Brattle merchant-philosopher tries to bark at you. The knowledge of the soul."

Ellen glanced upon the boat captain with appreciation. "Wise words for a man of the lake."

"The water of which solely bears the recognition," replied Ramsey.

Ellen looked out towards the main body of the lake, and proceeded to make her way to the Bethel's edge. Removing a large pouch from her pocket, she proceeded to sprinkle a powdered yellowish-white substance onto the lake's surface.

"What are you *doing*? What is that?" demanded Ramsey in a harsh whisper. "If you mean any harm to Champ…"

"Relax, Captain Ramsey," replied Ellen, softly, as she emptied the last the pouch's contents overboard. "It bears repeating: I mean the lake monster no harm."

Ramsey clenched his fists. "Then what have you got there?"

"Grounded Buttonbush," said Ellen, as she placed the empty pouch back into her pocket, and faced the group. "While preparing for this trip, I spent a night researching any and all eyewitness accounts of the lake monster despite my doubts. Few offered true glimpses of the monster, only accounts of its shape and size from a distance. All, of course, except for a small passage that the Monks of Middlebury uncovered from an ancient Abenaki text named 'Tatoskok,' a pseudonym for The Lake Monster."

"Heard that name before," replied Ramsey, curiously, in a small voice. "From the Abenaki themselves, I think."

"I'm sure that you have, Captain Ramsey," said Ellen, hastily. "One doesn't share the passion for such an animal for so many years without stumbling upon its more ancient surname."

"What's with the Buttonbush, though?" asked Ramsey, as he pointed to Ellen's pocket. Clearly agitated, Ramsey set the horn onto his lap and stared at Ellen, perplexed. "If that *is* poison, I swear by the northern gate, I'll see to it that you pay."

"The Lake Monster will be fine, Ramsey. This is only meant to aid our efforts."

Ramsey nodded reluctantly. He then blew into the horn several more times at ten-second intervals, with virtually the same clarity, pitch and volume each and every time. Though the inlet in which they had anchored swallowed the sound whole, the echoes of the horn proceeded to barrel across a large swath of lake facing outwards toward the main body of water. The group waited, listened and watched, as their eyes had now adjusted fully to the moonlight. Every wave, every ripple, every breath, carried with it a calmness, though Flatlander found his nerves to be on edge. The sitting and waiting felt impossibly long.

Then, from the portside a disturbance on the surface of the water caught the group's attention. By the time they rushed up close to face the water, however, whatever had created the sound was gone. All that remained was a fresh set of ripples spreading rapidly outward. Ellen cursed under her breath. Ramsey held on to the metal railing tightly in his grip, his knuckles whitening under the strain. Seconds later, a separate splash sounded from starboard, and there in plain view, raising its elongated neck and reptilian head, was the lake monster. The crew stared at the creature in awe as they froze into position. Moonlight coated its features.

The lake monster's sleek, black body shimmered just above the surface. Rising from the water, the beast's neck reached the height of a grown man. Its small, reptilian head scanned the passengers on the boat, as its neck moved in large, swooping motions from side to side. Though difficult to gauge in the dark, the lake beast's torso was seven feet at most, though its head was small enough to fit in a breadbox. A fishy, mossy aroma filled the air.

"Whoa there, Champ. Easy, boy," muttered Ramsey quietly.

"Champ," marveled Menche like a little child, as his boots clambered giddily on the deck. "Da Lake Monster, I says! Lord Henry won't believes it!"

"It can't be," said Flatlander, as he backed up slowly from the creature, grabbing a rail for support.

"Oh, it *can* be. It's just as I told you, is it not?" asked Ramsey in a whisper. He turned to Ellen slowly. "Whatever you have planned you better do it soon, because this isn't going to last long."

Ellen didn't so much as twitch, her attention squarely focused on the mystical beast.

"Lady Ellen," Ramsey barked a reminder through a heavy breath. "You need to act fast."

Snapping to attention, Ellen addressed her captain. "What's done is done."

Ramsey blinked. "*My Lady*?"

The creature sank back below the surface like a fallen stone, as the boat rocked gently in its wake. Ellen closed her eyes in deep concentration and breathed deeply. Ramsey grabbed a hold of Ellen's shoulder and nudged her.

"Lady Ellen, you may have missed your chance. It's doubtful he'll resurface."

In silence, she focused on the spot from which Champ had sunk below.

"Lady Ellen," continued Ramsey. "I'm not coming back out again. Once is enough, no? I'm sorry. You paid handsomely, of course. But a deal is a deal. The creature has a mind of its own and I don't want be calling it out here every day like some common dog. I've already got one of those waiting at home for me. Speaking of which, I can't…"

Without warning, the lake monster emerged from the water with a burst of speed, splashing the Bethel's crewmembers in the process. Its neck moved backwards at an awkward angle and then curved into a c-shape, as if intending to strike the Bethel with its head. The crew shifted to the other side in a hurry, as Menche scurried behind the body of an oversized anchor for cover. Yet Ellen stood firmly in place.

"Ellen!" said Flatlander. "Are you crazy? Move!"

"Lady Ellen!" barked Ramsey, "as the captain of this vessel, I command you to move this instant! Remember: it's a wild beast!"

The Lake Monster's neck lunged forward, but halfway through its motion, the creature coughed violently, shooting projectile mucus from its mouth. Ellen bore the full brunt, as it slimed her face and shirt. A small, metal object clanged against the deck several times before coming to a halt at Ellen's feet. The lake monster then dipped below the lake's surface with an emphatic plop. Flatlander and Menche hurried to Ellen's side to check on her health, as Ramsey kept a safe distance.

Ellen turned and picked up the metal object from the deck, and displayed it for the crew to see. It was a key that was roughly the length of a pinky finger, and corroded into a sickening brown. The throating and bit of which had now misshapen over time. A thin cover of algae suited the key's stem.

"To answer your question: yes, this is the key to the city sought by Yuro," said Ellen excitedly, as she turned the key over in her palms under the moonlight. Ramsey lit a lantern near the steering wheel, and brought it close to get a better look. "A pretty little thing, isn't it? Ramsey, you're a rich man now."

Ramsey poked at the key, unsure of its authenticity. The recent series of events had unfolded in such rapid succession, that Ramsey found himself in a state of utter disbelief.

"This is Yuro's key?"

"Not Yuro's," corrected Ellen, and then added. "The republic's."

"How did you know?" stammered Flatlander. "How did you know to get the key?"

"The Abenaki know the beast better than most," replied Ellen. "It took some digging in Burlington's City Hall, but I found an excerpt from a book about the history of the Abenaki and the Lake Monster, in which the author suggests that the lake monster is allergic to Buttonbush, vegetation which is more of a common occurrence upriver. I figured it was worth a shot. I harvested and ground some up before we left for the islands and dried it by open flame."

"You were counting on an *allergy*?" marveled Flatlander. "What was your backup plan? Shooting the monster between the eye?"

"I'll admit, it was all on a whim," replied Ellen slowly, as she gave him a wink, "Plus, I was just enjoying this trip on its own merit. This," she said as she wriggled the key in her fingers, "is a giant added bonus."

"Amazing," said Ramsey, as he gently took the key from Ellen and placed it against the lantern's glass, as the glossy digestive fluids smeared his palm. "Though it may be the last time I'll see Champ. He'll never trust the horn again."

"Drawing assumptions is the lazy man's strategy," replied Ellen, as she inspected her phlegm-soaked shirt curiously, picking at globs, and flicking them to the Bethel's deck, "but we have what could amount to the most prized possession of Burlington, and a memory of the lake monster which few could attest. That's more than enough for me. Now if somebody could fetch me a towel and clean set of clothes from my room, then my night will be truly complete."

"A sight to behold, despite its unsightliness," remarked Yuro, as he inspected the key between his fingers. "I owe all of you a good deal of gratitude. I promise that you will be well compensated for your troubles."

They had arrived at Yuro's house bearing the key, which Ellen had hid the key in her sock during their journey back to Burlington. Though robbery was a rare occurrence among the northern highway, it did happen on occasion. They couldn't take any chances.

Ellen bowed. "Our pleasure, Lord Yuro. I hope that we haven't disappointed."

"Far from it," replied Yuro, as he shook his head. "Far, far from it. Your research pertaining to Buttonbush was genius. I'll have to give Lord Henry high marks for choosing such a wise advisor, Lady Ellen."

Ellen blushed, mentally congratulating herself. Henry, according to Yuro, had been visiting Franklin in the hospital ward and tending to various functions in town. Flatlander wished that the king had been present, but was happy to hear that Henry was keeping his wounded friend company.

"I'm honored," replied Ellen.

Yuro dropped his key on a pink handkerchief, walked to a nearby window and closed the blinds, dimming the inner office to a comfortable, orange glow.

"I'm curious, though. Tell me more about the beast. What did it look like?"

Ellen hesitated. "The lake monster is as true as the lake from which it hails. It's sleek, black, eight feet at most, besides the neck, which is another six to seven feet. Like a plesiosaur."

"Indeed?" Yuro took a moment to consider, trying to form a picture in his mind. "So Ramsey proved to be useful after all?"

"Yes, he was," replied Flatlander. The mentioning of Ramsey reminded him of their promise to the salty lake boat captain. "And while we're on the subject: he expects to be compensated for his role, Master Yuro. He was quite insistent on that matter."

"Dare I ask how much?"

Flatlander grimaced, expecting the worst of reactions. "One million."

Yuro whistled, but retained his calm. "I will have his money personally delivered to him by chariot by the end of the week to ensure he receives what is owed. However, his fee will depend on whether or not this is truly the key. There is much yet to be known."

"But we saw the lake monster itself cough it out," pointed out Flatlander.

"Proving little at this point, I'm afraid," interrupted Yuro. "We'll know by tomorrow when we test out this rusted, little trinket out on the vaults."

Flatlander opened his mouth to argue, but received a swift jab to the side from Ellen. She spoke courteously.

"We thank you, Master Yuro. Could we assist you in your venture to the vaults?"

Yuro smiled. "Of course, Lady Ellen. It's the least I can do for bringing me such a wonderful gift."

Before resigning to bed, Yuro placed the key into a wooden box atop his fireplace mantle ten feet high. To ensure its safety overnight, he had meticulously guided it with a pair of five foot, metal fireplace tongs. He waited until his guests had all long gone to bed, when the only sounds in the night were the peepers and crickets in his vast backyard. Yuro even refused to delegate Bart to hide his newfound treasure. The fewer people who knew about it, the less Yuro had to worry. He trusted Bart unconditionally, but this was much too valuable an object to be careless about. *I mustn't worry so much*, Yuro chided himself, for tonight was the only night that he intended keeping the key on his property, before transferring it into a more secure location. Yet, not even an hour later, as Master Yuro lay sound asleep, a shadowy, dark figure moved through the mansion with a dreadful purpose.

"Gracious, no! It can't be! Impossible!" came the scream from downstairs, as shrill as it was loud. Throwing off his blanket off in a huff, Flatlander rushed from his bedroom to the top of the grand staircase. Rubbing his eyes, he saw Yuro standing on the bottom floor, near the fireplace. In his hands, the Lord of Burlington cradled a fallen wooden box. His face was pale and distraught.

"Master Yuro?" inquired Flatlander, as he scratched his head.

Yuro shot him a pained look, and threw the box on the ground, as it clanged against the side of the fireplace, empty.

"It's gone!"

"What's gone?" asked Flatlander, although he had already guessed the answer.

"The bloody key! It's gone. Oh gracious. Oh gracious. *Oh gracious*," muttered Yuro, as he paced frantically around his living room, desperately searching under couches, tables, and bureaus.

Flatlander's heart skipped a beat. The thought of someone taking it right under his or her noses was highly disturbing. He wondered, darkly, whether it could have been somebody they knew, somebody on the inside. The servant? Yet there was Bart, assisting fervently, scanning the floor for any possible crevasse where the key might have been lost.

"Where did you leave it, Master Yuro?"

"In that cursed box, you blundering buffoon!"

"Master Yuro!" Flatlander replied in astonishment, taken aback by the indignation.

Yuro took a deep breath. "My apologies. But this isn't the time for pleasantries."

Ellen's bedroom door opened from across the top of the stairway. She looked tired but alert, as a look of concern spread across her face.

"What is going on with all of the commotion, you two?"

"Well, it's curious to see you all made up so early," remarked Yuro, suspiciously, glancing at her white satin gown. "I trust you slept well."

Ellen glared at the lord. "What's the meaning of *that* tone, Master Yuro?"

Yuro pointed her an accusatory finger. "Be true with me, that's all I ask. Have you taken it?"

"Taken *what*?"

"The key! Have you taken the key?" replied Yuro in agony. He brushed aside some ashes in the fireplace with a small, wooden broom.

"Oh no…" Ellen muttered as she hurried down the stairs, Flatlander in tow. "You can't be serious."

"Do you have any idea what kind of trouble we're in?" muttered Yuro, as he then swept the innards of the fireplace, scattering ash and bits of burnt log amongst his hardwood floor.

At that moment, Menche arrived from one of the downstairs guestroom, yawning, arms stretched high above his head.

"What a night's sleeps, I says. Slept them lake legs away, I thinks."

"Be quiet, Menche," said Ellen. "The key is gone."

"Gone?" gulped Menche.

"Menche, listen," stated Flatlander gently, "have you seen or heard anything around here that may have been suspicious last night? Anything?"

"Nothin' I seens. Nope," answered Menche. "Besides Champ."

"Think hard," urged Flatlander.

Menche's eyes rolled into the back of his head. "Well, now I comes to think it, there was this one time…"

Menche caught himself before he divulged more, but it was too late. He blushed slightly and looked at the ground sheepishly.

Flatlander peered hard at his friend. "Go on. There was this one time that *what*?"

Menche shuffled his feet. "We didn't means nothin' by it. Me and Franklin wents lookin' in the old part of da house."

"Menche!" said Flatlander, as his face reddened.

"You *what*?!" shrieked Yuro, whom had overheard Menche's admission from deep inside the living room. In a flash, he hurdled a couch aggressively, closing the distance between him and the little man in the blink of an eye. "But I told you that that part of the house was strictly forbidden!"

"Master Yuro, please," urged Ellen, as she extended a protective arm in front of Menche. "He doesn't know any better. Go on. Tell us everything."

Menche continued. "Well, we's went in there, but we's got scared. Was only in for a minute, tops. Saw a doll and ran. May have seen somethin' else too. It was big and ran in dem shadows, I swears it. Ran till we couldn't no more. Was Franklin's idea, it was."

"Why didn't you tell us before? Why did you keep this secret from us?" asked Flatlander.

The trio had formed a perimeter around the shamed form of Menche, who seemed to shrink by the second. Henry's assistant whimpered softly into his hands.

Yuro's face went deathly pale as he backed away. "Oh, gracious. It can't be true. Tell me that it can't be true."

Ellen raised an eyebrow. "Master Yuro, is there something that you're not telling us?"

Yuro turned to the group, as Bart strained to lift the nearby couch to inspect underneath, dropping the furniture with a resounding thud. Facing his guests, Yuro wiped the sweat from his brow and pointed to the empty box alongside the fireplace.

"First, I need your words that none of you touched that wooden box."

Flatlander gave Yuro a clueless shrug, and both Ellen and Menche shook their heads adamantly.

Yuro sighed. "Friends, we are in big trouble. We must summon Lord Henry at once. For I can think of no other culprit than that of Emile Babakiss."

Ellen's face lit up in recognition. "*Emile Babakiss?* Impossible. There hasn't been a trace of the man for years."

Yuro looked down at the floor with a measure of disgust. "Lady Ellen, I regret to inform you that isn't the case. Emile Babakiss, or what form now takes his name, has been dwelling in the abandoned part of this home since shortly after his disappearance. We had an agreement years ago that he could stay here if he didn't bother me, or I, him. He has most likely taken the key to the vaults, for it was *him* who stocked the vaults in the first place. I foolishly overlooked the possibility that this could happen."

The collective anger, which up until this point had been pointed squarely on Menche, had now shifted to Yuro. Flatlander and Ellen looked sharply upon the lord.

"Who's this Emile Babakiss?" asked Flatlander.

Ellen fumbled for the words. "Lord Yuro, why?"

Yuro held up his hand defensively. "Now's not the time, Lady Ellen." Quickly," he urged frantically, removing a sharpened dagger from a nearby desk, "we haven't much time."

Henry had been enjoying his time back in Montpelier. Though he missed the company of his party, he truly cherished the time he got to spend with Jess. She had excelled at her studies at the high school. He had been receiving rave reviews from professors and administrators alike.

Henry noticed the change in his daughter. No longer was she an empty shell devoting herself solely to Fish. Without even having to prompt her, the posters and rebellious clothing had been scrapped for more sophisticated memorabilia, including portraits of the republic's wall, a mural of the popular play "Equilibrium," and a branch of hope purchased from the Monks of Middlebury. A comprehensive encyclopedia about Fish was generously lent to her by the Monks of Middlebury, and now lay open on the floor beside her bed. Jess had even joined the chess team at school, which did

Henry very proud, for the Humble King was once considered a
novice player in his own right. He looked forward to sharing the
beautiful game with his daughter, and hoped secretly that her
skills hadn't yet surpassed his own.

Jess had also begun spending time with new peers- good
influences, by Henry's judgment. Her new friends Sarah, Morgan,
and Casey were all respectful, pleasant teens. Long gone were her
days of ignoring her responsibilities to see Fish with less desirable
peers, like Donna Jean.

The day before his company was to return from their quest on
the lake, and after a long and grueling cabinet session deliberating
on new windmill construction, Henry left the statehouse weary
in both body and mind. He had also made the trek to Burlington
twice since Flatlander's departure to check on Franklin, whom
had stabilized, yet still remained in the ICU. It seemed that he had
barely a moment to himself.

After checking on his compost tumbler sweltering in the sun of
his backyard, Henry entered his home through a side door seldom
used. It was late afternoon, and he moved through the house
quietly, so as not to wake Jess from her occasional after-school nap.

From upstairs, Henry heard a faint yet familiar tune, one
of his favorites from his youth. "The Swells of Irene" by the
Stony Mahoney's reverberated through the house. The melody
immediately transported him to his days working on a sugaring
farm in Putney, where the owner played the vinyl record "River
Hymns" by the Stony Mahoney's like clockwork. Paulson was
the man's name, recalled Henry whimsically, and his affinity for
the album was extreme. In fact, Henry had listened to it so often
during those early spring days that he could fingerpick each guitar
solo perfectly in the air, hitting every imaginary note dead-on.

But who was playing it now and why?

Henry ventured up the stairs quietly. In the hallway, he could
see that Jess's door was slightly ajar. As he peeked in, he saw his

daughter shuffling through his many Stony Mahoney albums one by one, while periodically looking into her book about Fish. *It cannot be. A dream come true.* For fear of getting caught and spoiling the moment, Henry quickly slipped away from sight, leaving the door ajar.

Smiling wide, Henry skipped merrily to his office, ecstatic, whistling along softly to the tune of "The Swells of Irene." He wanted to shout, to celebrate, and bask in the moment. He thought better of it, however. *Let it be.* For fear of overwhelming his daughter, he decided to keep his discovery a secret. Yet it was a defining moment in his perception of Jess and their relationship. For now, at least, they had one thing in common: good taste in music. Henry continued humming the tune in his head for the entirety of the day and much of the night as well.

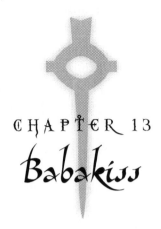

CHAPTER 13
Babakiss

MILE BABAKISS WAS ONCE CONSIDERED a man of esteemed title and reputation. Having built his political platform as being a warrior for the poor and needy, his campaign had taken on a multitude of promises, ranging from affordable housing, to a cleaner living environment for Burlington's residents, to implementing higher taxes for social programs. Though considered a champion for the poor, many of the wealthier residents and socialites of the Queen City viewed Emile as a dangerous idealist: the type of man who could potentially stomp their beloved city into financial ruin. For even generosity had its limits, they reasoned, and Babakiss toed perilously close over such a line.

The son of a struggling fisherman and midwife, Babakiss found out at an early age the importance of money. On numerous occasions, the family had run short of food and savings, forcing Emile and his father to fish the Winooski River for sheer survival. And an unsuccessful day fishing meant a hungry, sleepless night for the family of three, a destitute all too familiar for the Babakiss clan.

They lived in an abandoned tin shanty along the banks of the Winooski, deep between the farmlands of the Intervale and

Winooski, tucked back into the adjacent wood. Its walls consisted of rusted, aluminum outer sheets, which had been defaced years ago by vandals with paint. And yet this small shanty is what Emile Babakiss and family called home, and they made do with what they had. For his father, ever the optimist; saw their plight as a necessary evil for attaining future wealth. Sometimes, when the fishing became futile on the Onion River, his father would look up to the sky and decry praise and gratitude among the gods of the wood despite his hardships.

Emile excelled in his studies, and due to the plight of his youth, entered the public sector to ensure that others didn't have to experience the same level of poverty from his youth. This came to a head, when encouraged by his friends and family, Emile decided to run for Lord of Burlington for the Contrarian Party. The city had been struggling for years, and Emile rapidly and systematically secured the votes of the needy. Winning a close election against his opponent, Burt Bright, Emile became an instant political sensation, and a true leader of the people was born.

The citizens respected Emile Babakiss for his remarkable "rags to riches" story, from the elite of Burlington's hill section to the hardened folks of the Old North End. He kept a painting of the shanty from his upbringing on the wall of his office, despite the fact that it had long since been torn down by city officials. On the inscription of the frame, the quote "remember your roots," was engraved on a copper plate; a quote which paid homage to Amos the Monk's famous speech at Middlebury, and more importantly, Emile's tormented past and relentless fight for the needy.

And just like so many men who have come and gone from the political limelight throughout the republic, Emile Babakiss's downfall involved the element of money. Controlling countless millions came with it special responsibilities and pressures. Managing the taxes of Burlington's citizens was considered an honorable task, an important bridge of trust between the government and its people.

But Emile Babakiss never embraced this duty wholeheartedly, and slowly, the insidious hands of political corruption exploited this fact. This corruption personified was named Jon Park, Emile's special counsel. Park had been clever enough through the years to craft an inspiring portrait of himself to the community. He headed a charitable organization called "Logs for Love" which supplied firewood to the needy. He provided money and political influence in the statehouse on behalf of a group he co-founded called the "Sad Hunters," a group of despondent men who had been banned from hunting for various reasons (neglected wives, indiscriminate hunting practices, accidentally shooting other hunters, etc.), and had formed a support group. He also attended church on a regular basis and donated such generous sums over the years, that the monks of Middlebury had constructed an honorary plaque to Park on the walls of the entryway.

All of this was an act.

Park was also perceived in town as a formidable investor. Few knew how he came to attain his wealth. Some thought that he was the product of old Shelburne money. Others thought him a benefactor from a series of successful investments. Yet his bloodlines were virtually unknown. He spent his money freely, often buying the sharpest blade, the warmest coat, and the finest boots. His investment history, at least that on public record, was minimal at best. Despite this, Park suffered no hesitation in flaunting his supposed knowledge of investing to even the flimsiest of friends.

All of this, too, was an act.

Beneath Park's choirboy exterior dwelt a man tainted by the foul, insatiable appetite for money. His name had surfaced in political circles regarding his ties to Lord Andreas's syrup smuggling operation, though he was never implicated in the courts. Without definitive proof of Park's connections to Andreas, Emile refused to act. Complacent in demanding Park's ouster from his circle, if Emile had dug just a little bit deeper, the truth would have eventually surfaced. Sadly for Emile Babakiss, his inaction turned out to spell his own undoing.

One day a bill was left on Emile's desk. The bill was nondescript, no different from the thousands of others that had run their course through his office for some two years. Millions of dollars were often shifted on a daily basis, yet Emile Babakiss barely batted an eye, for this was routine.

Yet unbeknownst to Emile, approximately fifty-three signatures prior, he had signed his name, unknowingly, as the president of a fake company named "Green Skies," a supposed non-profit specializing in herbal research. Thirty-nine signatures prior, he had given the green light to allocate 17 million dollars of funding to this fraudulent creation. And sadly, the final bill that he signed was to assume personal liability for the company in the event should it collapse. And collapse it did: in a fraudulent flooding accident staged in a storage unit of City Hall. This calculated mode of deception was orchestrated by none other than Park himself, who had been keenly observing Babakiss's disinterest in his growing pile of paperwork.

The stage had been set.

Babakiss had been living a life of luxury in the meantime, able to afford the best food and entertainment one could buy in all of Vermont. His mansion soon began filling with rare and valuable artifacts. He justified his expensive appetite to his modest upbringing, as if it were a calling card to spend the republic's money freely. His frivolous spending irked many in his own Contrarian Party, for this self-indulgence clashed with the party's ideals. Opposing parties called him a hypocrite.

He did all of this because Park had assured him that this Green Skies was raking in the profits, and was convinced that he was merely spending his share. But the majority of the money, with the conniving Park at the helm of the operation, was brought to the abandoned vaults underneath the city, and mostly in small increments so as to not attract attention. With walls three feet thick and made of solid steel, his fortune was more than well protected. The only known key belonged to that of Emile, which he hung from his wall merely as an ornament, completely oblivious to its use outside of some symbolic value. Time would reveal that Emile Babakiss had been spending the city's tax money instead of what he presumed to be his profits. The repercussions proved to be brutal.

Emile found out the truth while in session at a budget meeting, as he noticed large expenditures of the city's coffers next to the line of Green Skies. At first, the budgetary committee attributed the unsavory numbers to faulty accounting. Then, after a short investigation, two days at most, they realized that Green Skies was a smokescreen, an imaginary company with a vanished paper trail. The budget committee added up the total monetary loss, dug up the signed paperwork, followed the long paper trail as far as they could, and realized that they had been scammed- to the tune of seventeen million dollars.

Emile was livid with Park. He denied his involvement in the clandestine operation, citing that he thought his share of the profits were of a different nature, from private earnings and that he, himself, had been duped, a mere victim of naivety. Yet even for Emile's staunchest defenders and Contrarians alike, the lord became increasingly more difficult to defend, as they too cried for his ouster. A hypocrite of the worst kind, they reasoned, a man who built his entire legacy as protector of the poor, all while harboring a disingenuous agenda. Emile Babakiss wore a large bulls eye on his back and he panicked.

Before the debtors and authorities came to repossess the key to the city to unearth the vaults, Emile set off among the lake with little more than a canoe, and threw the key into the depths of Lake Champlain. Years later, rumors emerged that Champ himself had swallowed the key whole. Others insisted that the key was fed to Champ by Vergil himself as a means of punishing all of Burlington for Emile's misdeed. The most commonly accepted tale, however, was that the key was destroyed or hidden beyond the wall.

Park emerged from the scandal unscathed. In fact, the counsel had made a tidy profit from his deception. A year later, Park had run unsuccessfully for Lord of Burlington. In his platform, he had taken a strong stance against political corruption as a response to Emile's handlings. The irony of his campaign was unsettling even for Park, whom often marveled during his moments alone how could he have pulled off such a diabolical plan.

But Emile's actions hadn't gone unnoticed; in fact, they attracted the attention of Vermont's mightiest. Vergil of the Camel's Hump saw the harm that this treachery had done the community, *his* community, and the republic, at large. And the wizard remained firm in his near-infinite quest of protecting Vermont's interests. The night that Emile returned from his venture on the lake, undetected, Vergil cursed Emile while he slept, rendering his body into that a deformed monster: part horse, part squid, part ape. The next morning, his cabinet, appalled by discovering Emile's creature-like appearance, fled his mansion in droves; leaving what little office possessions they had behind. Politicians, journalists, and concerned citizens alike assumed that Emile had fled the Queen City in the night, never to return again. Shay Bromage wrote a satirical obituary. Few believed eyewitness accounts from his former staffers.

In the years since, Park disappeared from the ready eye of the public, enjoying the fruits of his plot amongst the hillside mansions of Burlington. Meanwhile, Emile dwelt in his abandoned quarters alone, cursed as an abomination. He feasted upon the smattering of rodents, cats, bats, small dogs, and insects that had invaded his once beautiful home. Yuro, the next elected lord, moved into the house, but only under the condition that the haunted section be cordoned off and sealed with Emile inside. Despite the occasional sound from the decrepit part of the mansion, the presence of Babakiss was a mere afterthought as the scandal drifted into past history. From what Yuro had read concerning Emile Babakiss, it left him pitying the former lord, and praying a similar fate would not bestow him, Contrarian or Prosperate.

Never would Emile forgive Vergil for his curse, nor would he forgive the actions of his once trusted partner, Park. He gave every waking thought to opening the city vaults, and how he would exact revenge on those whom had hurt him so dearly. Never would he have expected the very key delivered to his home, years later, by Yuro and some strangers. Emile Babakiss would make the most of the opportunity.

Jon Park emerged from the steamy innards of his bathroom wearing his favorite red velvet robe, fresh from a morning shower. His greying beard was neatly trimmed and fashioned with a generous helping of berry-infused conditioner created by Fedor the Alchemist. Park was tan and well toned from the abundant amount of jogging he had done amongst his affluent hill section of Burlington. Despite his impressive health, Park's hair had receded vastly in the past several years, exposing a swath of blemishes and freckles along his bare scalp.

He fumbled around his room in the gloom of the dawn, darkened more so by an impending rainstorm from the west. Glancing briefly outside his bedroom window at the massive rain clouds, Park estimated he had twenty, maybe thirty minutes maximum, before rainfall. He had not always been a morning person, and though most folks would assume retirees should take more liberties in taking their sleep, Park had found quite the opposite since he stopped working. Sleeping difficulties had become the norm. He knew the reason; *at least he thought he knew.* Yet he would not speak of it freely.

He contemplated what kind of shirt he should wear for the day: his navy blue t-shirt, woven from the fine silkworms of Morrisville, or a light, brown vest comprised of fisher cat pelts. He reminded himself that it was much too warm to be playing with fur, like some of his odd compatriots, and opted to wear silk instead. As he opened his sock drawer, Park poured over which pair he should wear as well. He needed his socks to breathe well, in case it rained, he concluded, as he grabbed at a lighter pair. *Retirement can be such a hassle,* lamented Park in earnest, as he departed for the kitchen.

But upon entering the kitchen, he noticed something was not quite right. The cup of tea which he had left steeping while he showered was now spilt and shattered on the floor, leaving a pool of black liquid at its center. *Odd,* he thought. His wife, Mindy, had gone to stay with her sister's in Shelburne for the week to help care for her ill mother. *Tea cups don't just spill over on their own accord,* thought Park. *Perhaps she had forgotten something at home and had come to retrieve it?*

"Mindy? You home? What happened in here?" called Park into the living room adjacent to the kitchen.

He heard what he thought was a footstep by the front door and froze. Could someone be playing a trick on him? *Perhaps his daughter, Julie? Doubtful,* thought Park. It was enough of a chore waking her up in time for her morning classes at Hilltop University. *Had she been out gallivanting all night, only to sneak in during the wee morning hours?* Making his way to the doorway of the living room, Park lit a candle on a nearby bureau.

"Julie? Is that you?" he asked in an empty voice.

No response came. Suddenly, a shuffle of movement came from the pantry near the bottom of the spiral staircase. A gurgled breath came from the small, darkened hallway that lay afoot. Park soon came to the terrifying realization that this couldn't have been a family member. They weren't the type for pranks, and surely Julie would have burst out laughing at this point. There was someone, or something in the house. Startled, he grabbed a large steak knife near the door to the kitchen, and moved cautiously to the hallway to inspect the mysterious noise.

"Who's there? I demand to know. This is private property," he said into the darkness as he glanced from side to side. "I have a knife."

Breathing hard, and shaking terribly, he came to the pantry door at the end of the hallway, and opened it slowly. There he saw the usual non-perishables: pickled peppers and fiddleheads, cans of Barney's mushroom soup, and several packages of maple infused crackers from a small farm in Bakersfield. In the corner, a hidden package of dried apple straight from the Mills of Lowell remained unopened. Park breathed a sigh of relief. *Mindy must never know of those.*

In mid thought, Park was blindsided by a hideous, black form. He was hit with such force, that his knife flew from his grasp and imbedded in the opposite wall. Park's muffled screams, obstructed by a fur-covered tentacle, soon went silent. Dragged by the monstrosity outside of his house and into the woods of his backyard, the former advisor soon passed out from sheer shock. Seconds later, all that remained of Jon Park's presence was his knife, planted firmly in the wall, and his spilt tea, which had now collected into beads upon the cold floor.

Former leader of the republic, Lana Bremille, had constructed the vaults over seventy years prior. Located below a two story red brick building on 200 Church Street, its original purpose was to store any and all of the remaining artifacts of the Old Country, from traffic signs, to auto manuals, to electronics, to handbags. Anything that hadn't already been destroyed by the republic-wide purge[78] was brought to the vaults in troves. The building itself was partially obscured by some strategically placed hedges, but if one wished to snoop carefully in the back, they would find a long stairwell leading to a heavy, iron door. The door was virtually impenetrable; therefore no guards were needed to watch its premises.

Six years after the vaults had been accumulating artifacts from the Old Country, near the end of Bremille's tenure, all of the contents had been mysteriously burned. Crews spent the better part of the month clearing the fabled vaults of ash, warped metal and plastic. The cause of the blaze was a mystery. Some pointed towards the strong and protective reach of the monks; others blamed rivaling political factions, while some even implicated Bremille herself. Regardless, most in the republic cared little for the fire's implications aside from a handful of scholars who wanted to keep the items for future research. For the general populace cared little for flatlanders and their painful technologies.

And the vaults long sat vacant until shortly after the election of Emile Babakiss. During Babakiss's tenure and disappearance, Park had the vault rented out in secret. The fortune, most of which he had siphoned illegally in Emile's name, had rested and grown in the vaults for years. Park had also rented them out to powerful crime families for a monthly fee, so that the authorities couldn't trace their fortunes. From time to time, Park visited the vast treasure and took what he pleased, unconcerned about potentially squandering his fortune. He reckoned that it would take several hundred years before he made any *real* dent.

---

[78] During the first ten years of Vermont's second republic, many traces of the Old Country were systematically destroyed.

Flatlander and company arrived at the building, frantic and short of breath. They followed Yuro's lead, whose movements appeared both confident and strong. Descending the long stairwell behind the brick building at 200 Church Street, they neared the massive iron doors of the vaults. Flatlander noticed them slightly ajar.

Yuro glanced at the doors. "A curious sight."

"He beat us here," stated Flatlander.

"But why would Emile leave them open?" Yuro wondered aloud, as he tried to peak in through the dark, narrow opening.

"It might be a trap," said Ellen.

Yuro took a reflexive step backwards.

Menche whimpered. "Don't thinks I like this. May be goin' back home."

"Oh, no you don't," Ellen chided Henry's assistant. "You and Franklin really screwed up this time. You're coming with us."

Menche shuffled uncomfortably. "Hmm. If it pleases ya."

"Keep your guard up," said Yuro, as he removed a small dagger from his cloak. "Emile Babakiss is both unpredictable and angry. Gone is the man he once resembled. Stay on your toes."

Flatlander readied his blade in a quick draw, his every nerve on high alert. Removing a hunting knife from her waistband, Ellen swished its blade against a loose piece of ivy against the wall, severing it completely. Menche cowered behind the others. In unison, the four companions exerted all of their strength to push open one of the doors, as its massive hinges groaned deafeningly under their collective strain.

A dark, narrow passage appeared several yards ahead in a crude, dirt entryway. To Flatlander's surprise, the ground of the entry was comprised entirely of packed dirt, and several holes of various sizes, presumably animal burrows, bore deep into the earth. Old, chipped concrete walls rose a dozen feet to both side, and sizeable green, bacterial stains smeared downward on the walls like excess paint. It smelt vaguely like a brook during a heavy rainfall, *like back in Dummerston*, reflected Flatlander. Only then the aroma was somewhat refreshing among the open air, yet in the confined hollow of the vaults it stagnated and smelled of moistened rot.

"Follow my lead," commanded Flatlander.

The others did as they were told and fell into order, making their way cautiously down the narrow path.

"Dark," said Menche from behind Ellen's leg.

"And mighty noisy too," retorted Ellen in a harsh whisper. "Pipe down or you'll get us all killed."

"Flatlander, Ellen, I meant to tell you both about him," said Yuro, as positioned himself at the rear of the pack, and looked back intermittently to ensure there was no ambush from behind. "I meant to tell you all, in fact. I really did. It's just that I...I... *pitied* the creature. I assumed that he was sealed in that house like a tomb. It had been months since I saw any signs of him. I swear to you."

"Master Yuro, though I appreciate the apology, now is not the time for rationalization," replied Ellen. "Watch our backs, please."

Yuro looked briefly at the ground. "As you wish, Lady Ellen."

The path then opened up to a vast room, which stretched back as far as the eye could see. Flatlander didn't think it was conceivable that a room so large could exist under such a small structure. The room, all of these decades after the fire, still smelt faintly of ash and soot. It would have been pitch black, except for a row of large torches outlining the perimeter of the vaults, fluttering wildly, while shadows danced amongst its outer walls. Scattered on the floor, without any rhyme or reason, were opened boxes of jewels, garnets, and gems, most with their contents spilt partially, while others appeared full to the brim. Coins and precious stones littered the ground like gravel, amid large clumps of Vermont dollars, bunched together with string. The torchlight would sometimes catch a reflecting jewel or coin, like eyes in the night.

On the far side of the room, Flatlander observed an unrecognizable thin, balding man in a blue shirt locked in a tremendously large steel cage.

"Oh, thank goodness! Please, help me!" he said aloud as he rattled the bars of his enclosure.

Yuro squinted. "By the heavens, if it isn't Jon Park."

Following Yuro's lead, Ellen peered through the darkness towards the caged man. "How can you tell, Master Yuro?"

"That voice is unmistakable," replied Yuro. He cupped his hands. "Park! Is that you? In the name of Vergil himself, what is going on here?"

The man appeared distant, his voice even more so. "Master Yuro...I....it's just....I'm so happy you're here," replied Park awkwardly, as he halted his frantic rattling of the cage's bars. "I was brought here against my will."

"Well that much is obvious, friend. Is it whom I suspect?" asked Yuro. His question was met with an unsettling silence.

Ellen shifted restlessly. "Master Yuro, please. This isn't the time for shouting matches. Let's go see. Be careful. He can be lurking anywhere. Be on the lookout."

Flatlander ripped one of the many torches from the wall, and held it at arm's length. Slowly, the party ventured across the cavernous vault, over half opened chests, over precious stones every color of the rainbow, over Vermont dollars scrunched or wilted amid the cave-like humidity, over solid silver and gold blocks stacked like a season's firewood. Flatlander was at a loss for words, for the amount of treasure in the vaults was simply shocking. Every now and then, a small rodent would dart from a pile of valuables then disappear back into the shadows.

"The legends were true," remarked Yuro softly, in awe.

Flatlander tried his best to estimate the value of what he saw, but soon came to the conclusion that such efforts were useless. *Seventeen million was likely a low estimate.*

"He's coming!" yelled Park, who now stood a mere dozen paces from the group.

From the near side of the room, Flatlander heard the rapid stomping of hooves against the ground coming nearer, as coins rang loudly and echoed in the vault's vast chambers. Flatlander swung the torch in the direction of the sound, but the light couldn't reach far enough to see what lay ahead. He held his sword high, waiting for the monster to pounce at any second.

"The gig is up, Emile," said Ellen into the darkness. "We know it's you. We can end this game right now and all will be forgiven. The Humble King would understand."

"Lady Ellen speaks true," confirmed Yuro, as he frantically eyed the darkness, searching for any sign of movement. "Release Park and return the key. No harm shall be done to you."

"Grahhh," came a high-pitched squeal. It came from just beyond the reach of the torchlight.

"S-s-same things we's heard back at d-d-da house," stuttered Menche from behind Yuro's leg.

Flatlander tightened his double grip on his sword. "Show yourself, Emile, you fiend!"

In slow, horrible movements, the aberration better known as Emile Babakiss willfully stepped into the light. It was an awful sight to behold. Close to seven feet tall, the creature had two sets of arms, and two sets of furry, brown tentacles. Though it looked to have humanoid facial features, its skin was scaly, grey, and coarse-looking; like that of an elephant, yet shaped like an ape. Instead of feet, the creature stood on worn down hooves. Its legs were powerful, shaped like a horse's. The most gruesome feature of Babakiss, however, and the one that would still haunt Flatlander's nightmares for years to come beyond their venture into the vaults, was a large appendage that Babakiss carried on its back. As the creature turned briefly to check on Park, Flatlander observed the politician's former body and face were attached to the creature's spine like an unwanted tumor. Emile's former face, now positioned slightly above the creature's shoulder blades, still wore a look of horror. The rest of his body looked like a large sac of puss; the contours of its shape and size rendered into a horrid state of indistinctiveness.

To Flatlander, the sight was nauseating. He recalled seeing a replica of this creature at Bronson's Tavern, but no replica could do sheer justice to the hideousness that stood before him. *To think, just for a second, that this creature was living right under our noses while at Yuro's.*

"Stop!" commanded Flatlander. Surprisingly, the creature obliged, settling on its rear quarters. "My name is Flatlander. We come in the name of Lord Henry and the Second Republic. You have taken a special key from us to which has been entrusted to Master Yuro. We order you to give it back. We also order you to release this prisoner as a gesture of goodwill."

"Grahhh!" the creature called in response.

Flatlander flinched at the gruesome response, but remained steadfast in his demands. "If not, you will leave us no choice than to settle this matter by force."

"Urrrghhhh," the creature gurgled, as it then leapt for Flatlander.

He tried to connect with his sword, but the creature was too quick and strong. He missed wildly. It bowled him over with the force of a bull, instantly knocking the wind out of him as he hit the ground hard. Dropping his sword and torch, Flatlander lay on the ground squirming in pain. Babakiss then whipped Yuro with a lashing tentacle, sending the Lord of Burlington hurtling backwards a dozen feet. Yuro's hard fall sent him colliding with Menche, who also flailed to the ground. Menche scurried under a sizeable collection of silver coins to hide. Upon seeing the sheer power of the beast, Ellen turned to run, but another lashing tentacle tripped her up, and she crashed shoulder-first into the side of an open chest full of garnets.

"Ellen!" said Flatlander, as he struggled to regain his footing. He noticed that Babakiss had grasped onto the fallen torch with one of his tentacles, and waved it in the air furiously, attempting to set Ellen aflame. Rapidly crawling away from the beast, Ellen's movements were greatly impeded by the sea of jumbled treasure. While the monster's focus had shifted entirely to Ellen, Flatlander snuck up from behind the beast and swung his blade down with a fierce stroke, severing one of Babakiss's tentacles and causing him to drop the torch.

"Maaahh!" Babakiss cried in agony, as blood spurted from the wound like a faucet.

In one quick motion, it turned its body like a slingshot, as a tentacle slammed Flatlander directly in the face, catapulting him into a fractured wooden barrel. His sword clanked amongst a pile of jeweled crowns.

Dizzy, Flatlander felt his face as blood began dripping freely from his nostrils. He also felt a sharp pain in his palm. Looking down, he noticed a three-inch splinter protruding from the tendon between his middle and index fingers. Grimacing, he pulled the splinter out, just as Babakiss rained down another blow upon the small of his back. Flatlander went sprawling again, rolling several times over a darkened mass of booty. His face began going numb. Blinking stars and streaks obscured his vision. The beast's massive shadow, magnified by the light of the fallen torch, grew over Flatlander's near-motionless body. Its smell was repulsive, like a slab of rotting flesh.

"Stop, Emile!" he heard Yuro shout from the darkness.

"Mrrrrggg!" the creature called.

A large green emerald came sailing out from the black of the vault from Yuro's direction and struck Babakiss squarely on the back of his skull. Momentarily stunned, the creature grunted in pain and crouched to tend to its head wound.

Flatlander willed himself to a sitting position and scanned his surroundings carefully for the fallen blade. He saw it resting behind the hooves of Babakiss, gleaming faintly in the pale torchlight. He also made out the figure of the crownless Yuro, his dangling black curls disheveled. The Lord of Burlington huddled next to the fallen form of Ellen. He sliced his dagger through the air spastically. Ellen held her hunting knife ready beside her waist, ready to launch an attack of her own.

The creature turned to Yuro and Ellen, and began marching towards his victims in a horse like amble. Hissing and gurgling as it moved, Babakiss spit large globs of blood from the side of its deformed mouth, as mucus bubbled at its lips.

Yuro squeezed the handle of his dagger tightly. "Lady Ellen, I wish the Gods themselves had made me bigger and stronger to protect us."

Ellen shot Yuro a stern look. "I appreciate the sentiment, Master Yuro, but spare me the chivalrous banter."

Yuro looked at Ellen in earnest. "You never mince words, do you?"

"No."

Babakiss moved closer, its slimy appendages nearly within reach of Ellen's arm. Yet even in the gloom of the vaults, Flatlander began to see strange movement near the foot of the beast. He caught a brief glimpse of Menche sneaking underfoot, his potbelly form perfectly visible in a silhouette. Menche collected the sword and threw it to Flatlander clumsily, and immediately absorbed a crushing blow to his chest from the creature's remaining tentacle.

"Menche!" exclaimed Flatlander, as he quickly picked up his fallen sword.

Flatlander's fear quickly metamorphosed to sheer rage, as his three friends lay wounded. Twirling his sword through the air with a renewed grace and energy, Flatlander ignored the throbbing pain in his head and his wounded hand. Babakiss hesitated to strike Flatlander, wary of his blade's might. Unexpectedly, it then sprinted towards the cage of Jon Park in a full gallop, its hooved strides clamoring through the sea of treasure.

"He's going for Park!" screamed Ellen.

"Emile! This has gone way too far! Your wits have abandoned you!" screeched Yuro.

Jon Park had been helplessly watching the scrum from his cage, but as the monster stormed ever closer, he retreated hysterically from the prison bars. Without thought and relying on pure instinct, Flatlander swung his blade back behind his shoulder, and heaved it with all of his might towards the sprinting creature, just as he had done in Highgate. The sword missed Babakiss entirely, though, soaring right by its head. Instead, it struck a leg to a large metal shelf, stacked with countless pots full to the brim of copper pennies: one of the last remaining stashes of Old Country currency currently in existence. Within an instant, the entire shelf collapsed sideways onto the beast, crushing it with a sickening crunch.

Flatlander rushed to the scene, ready to finish the job and slay the beast where it lay. His adrenaline now surged through his body. Walking upon his fallen enemy, Flatlander gazed upon its deformed shape, now partly hidden by pots of spilled pennies. Cradled in Babakiss's limp hands was a coiled scroll. Flatlander kicked at his downed enemy, awaiting a response, as Yuro and Ellen took up his flank with caution. Blood from Babakiss's severed arm drenched the pennies a liquid crimson, and the creature emitted an even more repulsive odor, like putrid gas.

Up close, he could see in fine detail the tumorous sac resembling Emile's body, which had now ruptured and deflated like a bad case of bursitis. Foamy white ooze poured from a series of lacerations from his collision. Its face resembled a near ape-like creature with grey, coarse skin. Its horse-like legs lay twisted and motionless. A single tentacle lay stretched at its side, hair protruded from the top, while the bottom was covered in suction cups. One bulbous tumor jutted several inches out the left side of the creature's forehead, while a second tumor, nearly as large, protruded from its right jaw.

Soon, Flatlander's anger quickly morphed into pity, as the body of the creature afoot looked as tortured in death has it had in life. An anatomical monstrosity, thought Flatlander: part horse, part squid, part ape, part man, a strange, repulsive combination not only unfit for the light of day, but even the dim vaults of the Queen City.

Jon Park clapped his hands together and sang praise. "Incredible shot!"

"You did it, Flatlander!" panted Yuro, as he hurried to Flatlander's side, with Ellen trailing closely behind. "A fine marksman indeed!"

"Are you alright?" inquired Ellen, as she scanned Flatlander's wounds.

"I'm fine," answered Flatlander with a sigh, as he inspected his injured hand. "I'm cut, but fine. You okay?"

Ellen grimaced and rubbed her shoulder. "I'm tougher than I look for a paper pusher."

Flatlander turned to the Yuro, whom he had grown a new appreciation of. It was evident that Yuro was out of his element in the heat of battle, yet he had not fled nor froze, as Flatlander had originally feared.

Ellen glanced at the limping lord. "Master Yuro?"

Yuro brushed dust and grime from his purple robe, as he wiped clean his dagger with a handy kerchief.

"It could have been worse, Lady Ellen. A few bruises here and there, nothing more."

"Menche?" called Flatlander.

The little man limped his way near the beast's skull, gaping in awe of its extreme deformities.

"Ugly beast is deads. Gots me good there, must say."

Then Flatlander did something unexpected, something that he hadn't planned. Taking a knee near the head of his broken opponent, Flatlander bowed against the hilt of his sword.

Muttering quietly above the battered corpse of his opponent, he then turned to his party.

"We must give Emile a proper burial."

Ellen was almost at a loss for words. "But why?"

"Because it's proper," answered Flatlander.

"That can be arranged, I suppose," replied Yuro.

"I found it!" announced Ellen, as she held aloft the sought-after key to the vaults. An opened rosewood box lay at her feet.

Yuro rushed towards Ellen's find. She handed him his object of affection.

"Oh, thank heavens. Goodness gracious, thank you, Lady Ellen! You shall not elude me again!"

He kissed the key and swiftly tucked it into his back pocket.

"Oh, thank the heavens you came!" said Jon Park from between the bars of his cage. His clothes were tattered and covered in his own perspiration. "I've no idea how you found me, but there are no limits as to what I owe you all."

"I *am* curious as to why you're here?" asked Yuro, suspiciously, as he approached the caged prisoner. "What would Emile want with you?"

"I haven't the slightest clue," replied Park quickly, who then hesitated, and raised an eyebrow. "Wait. You mean to tell me that this creature, this beast, was Emile Babakiss? *The* Emile Babakiss?"

"I'm surprised you didn't recognize him," said Ellen, as she moved a torch towards the grotesque, emptied face of Emile attached to the creature's back. "You were his lead advisor, after all."

Park looked upon the monster's back, at the mutated shell of Emile's face, then quickly averted his eyes, gagging in disgust.

"So it is, I'm afraid," said Park as he pointed at the beast, "but that appendage is *not* Emile, not the man that I knew. And it's as dark as the nightlife of Barre down here. And while I'd love to talk with you more on the matter, I would request you first free me from this hellish cage."

"No need," replied Flatlander.

He was holding the fallen uncoiled scroll in his hands, found near the corpse of the deceased monster. He motioned for the group to come near, and read the print with the assistance of Ellen's torch. It was an old letter. Flatlander read it aloud emphatically.

"My friend,

A parting word- nothing but Green Skies until the day we die. You were right. There isn't a paper in this world that the man wouldn't sign. The storm will pass by if you allow it.

Stay well, my friend and be alert. Will see you in greener pastures. –JP"

"The whispers were true," declared Yuro, aghast. "Emile was cheated from his seat. Stabbed by the very hand in which he fed…"

"Lies! I did no such thing," replied Park vehemently. He peered suspiciously between the bars of his cage. "What are you reading? Where did you get that information?"

"I found it here on the floor," replied Flatlander as he handed the letter to Ellen.

"It's clearly fabricated!" replied Park. "Anyone could have written it. I was nothing but a humble servant to Emile from day one! I was more than just his advisor. I was his confidante, his manager, his accountant, his friend, his, his…"

"His worst enemy," interrupted Ellen, as she recoiled the letter and tucked it underneath her arm. "It was because of your treachery that this man lost it all: his wealth, his family, his estate, his title, even his own body for pity's sake. And while Vergil cursed this man into an abomination, you lived a life of luxury. From one advisor to another: you have cast a foul stench on this profession."

Park blinked rapidly. "Lady Ellen, you must believe me."

Ellen approached the prisoner. "Jon Park, you must pay for your sins. As these men my witness, this letter will be used as evidence against you when your case is heard."

Flatlander glanced at the document snugged beneath Ellen's elbow. "And you know this to be true, Ellen? Why would this letter be here on Emile's possession?"

"Emile must have brought it here for us to see," stated Ellen. "It might also explain why the door to the vaults was left open."

Yuro rubbed his bruised elbow. "But then it must be inquired, Lady Ellen, why would he try to kill us if he wanted word of Park's deeds to get out?"

Ellen gazed at the form of the fallen creature. "A valid question, and yet one which I do not know. Perhaps Emile was scared. Perhaps he had a difficult time trying to communicate this to us. Perhaps he was torn between outing Park and killing him altogether. He might have known that there was a chance his fate was sealed with death, so he decided to bring this document to ensure justice to Park. Don't forget, the Emile that we once knew and loved was all but gone, a host to some parasitic monster; we can only guess at its true motives."

"That *thing* kidnapped me from my home!" cried out Park, while pointing to the corpse of Babakiss. "And now I stand here only to have my name dragged shamefully through the mud, while you take pity on that horrid freak."

"Your name was dirtied years ago," replied Yuro.

"Though, in hindsight, it was just the tip of the iceberg," agreed Ellen.

Park crossed his arms defiantly. "Then I look forward to awaiting my day in court. My lawyers will have a field day."

Flatlander then approached Park's cage and gave a menacing look to Emile's former advisor.

"And I'll do everything in my power to make sure that you spend a long, long time in jail for what you've done to this man."

Park glanced at Flatlander dismissively. "And who is this strange one who speaks to me as if a commoner, with flattened shoe and swollen tongue?"

Flatlander paused. "Flatlander. My name is Flatlander. And you will know my name and remember my name for years to come. Bye, Jon. It's been lovely speaking with you."

On cue, the group turned slowly and began to leave.

"Come back, you bastards! Come back! You're fools! All fools!"

Park shouted and banged at his cage furiously. His rage echoed throughout the great treasure room. With every step, Flatlander felt a dreaded sickness, for the treasure took on a whole new meaning to him. This was blood money, a trove of betrayal. Yet Flatlander was comforted by the fact that a form of justice had taken place, even as Babakiss's hideous corpse lay still at their backs. Yuro paused and stole one last glance of the fabled vaults.

"I'd never thought I'd say this in my lifetime, Flatlander, but I have seen way too much treasure for one day."

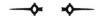

Park was promptly arrested. Emile Babakiss's corpse was given a proper burial, complete with a ceremony among the meadows of the Intervale, the land of his upbringing. It was well attended, for as the mountain of evidence implicating Park for his wrongdoings began to grow, so with it came new empathy in the populace for Emile's plight. After the jury found him guilty of embezzlement, fraud by deception, and investor fraud, Park was sentenced to fifteen years in prison. He was also expected, per conditions of his sentence, to visit the gravesite of Emile Babakiss once a year (supervised) and apologize to his headstone.

The vaults were scraped clean by the authorities, with the fortune amounting to the tune of 40 million Vermont Dollars, far surpassing initial city estimates of 17 million. This included other criminal fortunes and Park's other investments/hoardings. Lord Henry used the valuables found in the vaults to refill the city coffers, and as a result, morale around Burlington skyrocketed. Residents of the Queen City were subsidized by this fund in their taxes and energy needs, and though Yuro and others called for restraint in spending too rapidly, these new found assets gave reason for many in the area to celebrate.

Yuro hired a local company of lumberjacks whom specialized in demolitions, aptly named "Axes of Destruction," to eradicate the older section of his mansion where Emile had dwelt. He donated the resulting scrap wood and stone to be erected for Emile's memorial in the Intervale, a mighty tomb amongst the Winooski River. *It was as if a burden itself was lifted from the house*, Yuro had remarked shortly thereafter.

Henry had partially reconnected with Jess, though he never spoke of witnessing her listening to the Stony Mahoneys. Devoted to her studies, Jess continued to be more respectful to her father and others. She asked questions about his life and the republic. She tended to her chores, particularly caring for Pete. Even the barn, which Henry had often left cluttered and neglected, had been cleaned and transformed by Jess, without even so much as a prompt from her father. Henry was pleasantly surprised by her newfound maturity, and felt, for the first time in years, that he had his daughter back.

Franklin's condition had stabilized, but he was kept at the hospital an extra few days for observation. In the immediate aftermath of Babakiss's death, Flatlander tried to visit his friend, yet the northerner often remained in a deep sleep. Flatlander chose not to awaken him.

Captain Ramsey was rewarded his one million dollars by Yuro, which was delivered to him as promised. While aboard the Bethel, fresh from a routine fishing run, a carrier came by chariot, burlap sack in hand. To the dismay of his fellow fishermen, Ramsey broke down and cried in sheer joy as he peered into the sack of money. He dismissed his company before they were to find out the nature of this gift; and more importantly, *why* he had received it in the first place.

Flatlander's popularity was now at an all-time high. A dramatic shift in the public's perception had been occurring. Shay Bromage had taken a month off from putting out his paper to 'confront his personal struggles.' Meanwhile, Dawn had been writing glowing articles of Flatlander's accomplishments, and even for those whom despised the man's native roots, even *they* were impressed and grateful for the retrieval of such a large chunk of their hard earned tax money from the secret vaults.

And with Henry officially accepting the slaying of Babakiss as Flatlander's ninth completed quest, all that remained on his horizon was his tenth, and final, mission. He only hoped that his string of luck would continue. He also hoped that his convictions would grow stronger, one-way or another, for the time when he would have to decide on his future. Becoming a citizen of the republic gave him another option to mull over, an option that, if he chose to accept his future role, could pave the way for a happy and prosperous life among his newfound friends. And though he could tell Ellen made concentrated efforts avoiding him, part of him was convinced that theirs was a chapter far from over. And it was only two weeks later that his final quest came calling, beckoning him to the statehouse of Montpelier, along with every other lord, lady and noble in the republic.

CHAPTER 14

Inepticus and the Fiskle Cliff

"And it was with great merriment in which the people of Underhill reveled: a celebration of the ages. Equilibrium rested mercifully within the hands of the chosen one. The cliffs ceased to grow impossible heights, and the town itself again was no longer fully engulfed within the realm of shadow. The great spire fell to nothing more than a column of dust amid the unveiled landscape. How great was that day. How joyous was that day. How well deserved for Underhill. For another night would come and bring with it, finally, this time: the gentle, intoxicating glow of the sun."

- an excerpt from the play "Equilibrium," by Penelope Witt. 2108.

THE LORDS AND MASTERS FROM the various regions of the republic poured slowly into the assembly hall of the statehouse like a colony of ants. Those who hailed from the far south and east looked haggard, for their journeys had taken as long as three days time. An armada of carriages and horses collected on the grounds, as workers frantically tethered their vehicles among the long rows of iron bars. A crisp air blew through the streets of Montpelier, as vendors, salesmen and women, merchant-philosophers and mountain traders swooped in to meet the rush of lords to take advantage of their business, peddling everything from food, to drink, to jewelry and trinkets. A large murder of crows cawed from a giant elm, and had gathered into such a large display, that they had rendered the tree into a fluttering, blackened mass.

A visual sometimes says a thousand words, and nowhere could this be any truer than by looking at the vacant desk in the statehouse where normally sat the Lord of Underhill, Brookes Desmairis. On the surface of his desk lay a treasured branch from Braintree, which served as a traditional symbolic gesture of hope among Vermonters. His plight, and the plight of his people, after all, was the very reason the lords of the republic had convened.

Flatlander arrived in the company of Lord Henry, and was greeted with considerably more respect than that of his first visit to the statehouse. Applause rang out from all directions, as shrill whistles resounded from the balcony. As he passed through the corridor of desks leading to the center of the chamber, lords and masters even mustered the courtesy to shake his hand and thank him for his services, while a scattered few still watched his every move with heavy scrutiny.

As all of the men took their seats at eleven sharp, Greg Ulger slammed his gavel with authority onto the warped surface of his desk.

"Lords, Ladies, Masters: the meeting is now in session. I welcome you all. Ahmed Haque, the Duke of Stowe, will provide us with opening statements."

The floor went eerily silent, as Haque limped haggardly to the center of the floor. Gray-haired and in his mid fifties, Haque was coated with the greyish-brown fur of the coyote. His hair was collected in a Dutch braid reaching below his shoulders. His pronounced chin all but covered and shaped properly in a triangular goatee. He spoke from a prepared statement, which shook mightily within his hands.

"Greetings. It is with great delight that I see so many familiar faces here in the gem of our beautiful capital. Sometimes I forget how large our republic is, at least to me," he said, as he glanced in wonder around the room, stopping and smiling at a few recognizable compatriots. "There are some faces here which I haven't seen for over a year or longer. And I couldn't be prouder to call you all my brethren and sisters as we head into another splendid autumn. But this season is also different, for it is also with great sadness that we have come together here today. For the man whose town I share a mountain with, Lord Desmairis, much like the townspeople from which he speaks for, has fallen peril to the bleak tidings from Underhill. Still."

Haque nodded towards Desmairis's empty desk, then continued: "But I look to his unoccupied desk, and upon the branch of Braintree, and I have hope. Brookes is a strong man. It bears mentioning that on a certain occasion, I once witnessed him removing a fallen tree from the roadway with ease- the same trunk, mind you, which later required three men to load it properly onto their carriage bed. As I know, only his heart matches his strength, as Brookes has been, consistently, one of the most generous and giving members of the senate."

He continued, forlorn, as he suppressed a muffled sob. "But now, even a man with such considerable strength needs the collective aide of his republic. Brookes and his town need our help, and they need it *soon*. Time is running short. Many of us know at least one resident of Underhill; and their fate is one that I would not wish upon my worst enemy.

"Underhill has fallen quite literally almost completely into shadow. You all know of that, but perhaps are unaware of how awful it has truly become. Nobody can pinpoint the exact cause; rumors vary from an imminent earthquake, to a geologic anomaly, to, and believe me that I hesitate to even entertain the gibberish, an ancient curse. For 'why' exactly, we cannot be sure. What we *do* know is that the ground outside of Underhill has inexplicably arisen into harrowing cliffs; a body of earth joins Mansfield as an extension of the mountain. The new part of Mansfield we can see from many, many miles away. You all know them as the 'Fiskle Cliffs.' And while this formation did not occur overnight, the cliffs have grown nearly double in the past year alone.

"In the center of town, a giant, black spire has grown. Atop this spire lays a sphere of uttermost importance, for there are some whom claim that retrieving this sphere, this 'equilibrium' will undo these terrible changes. People have tried climbing the spire, but it's much too steep, smooth, and high above the ground, making any and all attempts futile. Four have perished in their heroic attempts. Their plaques remain showcased in Stowe's city hall."

Haque paused, and collected his breath. "You may be asking yourself why such desperation? Why must this deserve our attention now? The answer is simple: the land has become cursed and winter is afoot. Crops are long past dead, and what land is left lies mostly fallow. Most trees have fallen and died; their supply of firewood is dwindling rapidly. Water sources have been cut off; spare the squalid runoff from the cliffs or a touch of rainfall from which to soak their thirsts. The Browns River and all its tributaries, as well as the underground aquifers, have altered their course with this sudden upheaval of rock. Daytime in Underhill consists of a three-hour window of gloom. We can only imagine the pain that our brethren from Underhill are enduring, and I'm sure that Brookes and his people are fighting, and fighting well, but by the day, it looks more and more like a fight that they cannot win.

"For months now, myself, and the good people of Stowe and the neighboring communities of Jericho, Cambride, Westford, Essex, and Bolton, have tried valiantly to assist. We have dropped food and water for the people by rope and by parachute, notes of goodwill, books, clothes, but even these items in gross abundance cannot prepare the town for the deathly grip of Vermont's winter, which will soon rear its ugly head, soon visible on the horizon on our frosted peaks. And even Stowe, despite its prodigal wealth, has its limits. We have offered its residents to be saved by rope, one by one, but most will not leave the land for which they love. But now, Underhill has fallen so far into shadow that the town has all but vanished into this newfound abyss. This leaves us with one of the greatest challenges that our republic has faced.

"So, we appeal to you, the fine leaders of Vermont, to assist our friends during this time of need. We come as their voice, their hope, their potential saviors. As homes and businesses fall further into the earth, drowned out by both distance and shadow. Thank you."

Haque gathered his statement, and limped from the podium, which Flatlander could now see was the result of a foot injury, wrapped thick in bandages. The statehouse erupted with applause, which carried on for a full minute and a half, until Ulger once again pounded his gavel.

"First words from our Humble King, Lord Henry of the Brattle. Then the floor is open for debate."

Henry swiveled in his throne from the podium to the lords before him. "Very dire words, indeed, for our brethren in need. Thank you, Lord Haque. You have done you and your republic proud by serving your neighbors. Your words and actions speak highly of your character."

Henry paused. "While we've all known of the plight from Underhill, it's become more and more apparent that something must be done, and soon." He pointed to the Lord of Underhill's vacant desk. "I look upon that single branch from where our friend, Brookes Desmairis, regularly sits, and I feel a mixture of emotions. I miss his laugh. His whistle. I even miss, and I never thought I'd say this, but I even miss that gods-awful weasel of his that simply won't stop climbing all over him. Where did he even get such a creature, I wonder?"

The lords and masters laughed heartily.

Henry's smile slowly morphed into a look of concern. "But in earnest, our window is closing. This all began five years ago. Since then, the play 'Equilibrium' has been written and performed a hundred times, its actors and actresses have received countless accolades, a mural of the town has been painted on the side of the Center of Echoes, and yet, truly, what has been done for the residents of Underhill? And I ask you, who besides the gracious Lord Haque and Underhill's handful of neighbors have made a real effort to help those whom need us most? I admit that I am just as guilty as you all. But today is the day that we change that. Today is the day in which we all pledge to save Underhill." Henry pointed up and across the room at the painting of the woman in white kneeling before Mount Mansfield. "And something tells me that we knew this day would be coming all along."

Ulger glanced at Henry to see if the Humble King had finished his words. Henry nodded a silent acknowledgement. The majority of lords still gazed upwards at the large mural. Ulger pounded his gavel.

"The floor is open for debate."

Lord Riegelman of Addison stood up rigidly. "Jeezum, King Henry, what *could* we do? They refuse to be rescued by rope! Lord Haque said so himself. Addison can supply them with enough supplies to last a week at most, but little else."

The familiar grunt of Lord Sarmus of St. Albans followed. "Eh, a little cliff never hurt nobody. And plus, cursed ground is cursed ground; the land don't just rise and fall like that. It ain't natural. If they don't wanna leave, let 'em stay. It'll be their own damned fault!"

"The Monks of Middlebury have focused much attention on this subject," stated Lord Trombley of Middlebury. A thick open book lay on his desk. "And the consensus among the few who I've spoken to confirmed that this could very well be a curse from an ancient civilization. They attribute this abnormality to the powers of a mountain god, a subterranean spirit. Even my sources in Braintree cannot recall a similar geologic phenomenon on our planet. They say that only by returning this stone to its proper place in the mountain can we undo the devastating effects left by the Fiskle Cliff. This is odd and troubling to many of you, I know; for many of you work under the presumption that there is a rational explanation for everything. I, for one, differ. We seem to be dealing with an ancient form of magic here."

Riegelman shook his head. "Trombley, curse or no curse, the residents of Underhill are sealing their own fate. What are we going to do? We can't move mountains."

"Are you so sure?" answered Trombley, mysteriously.

"Trombley, you have gone mad!" barked Riegelman. "One cannot move mountains from the very ground, no matter how much time you spend camping in the monk's library!"

Chuckles echoed throughout the floor. Lord Trombley sat in deep concentration, and then flipped through a dense notebook at his desk.

"But what of *Underhill*?" pleaded Henry, in an attempt to redirect the conversation. "Are you all telling me that you're all okay with a fellow town of this republic permanently sinking into the earth? What if this was *your* town? One of *your* brothers or sisters? *Your* fathers or mothers? What *then*? Lord Haque delivered a fine speech, a fine speech indeed; yet it is up to us to cultivate ideas to save our befallen brethren."

His white fur coat standing out like a dandelion's blow ball, the lord of the White River Junction, Lord Andreas, cleared his throat.

"There is word of a messenger's son in Stowe who is practiced in the art of flying."

"And who would this be?" asked Henry.

"Danario, Stowe's most famed messenger, has a son," stammered Andreas, as he placed a thoughtful finger on his chin. "Though I fear I have forgotten his name…"

"*Inepticus?*" interjected Lord Haque. The name spewed from his mouth like a foul taste. "The messenger's son? Surely, this cannot be your recommendation, Lord Andreas. This must be some sort of joke."

Henry's face soured considerably. "I know that name."

"Yes! Inepticus is *indeed* the name," replied Andreas with a nod.

Henry leaned forward in curiosity. "While I'd love to sit here and discuss bloodlines of Stowe, I'm curious where you are leading us, Sir Andreas."

Riegelman was visibly outraged. "*Inepticus?* I have heard this name before, as have we all. Is this the same man whom was hospitalized at last year's chili contest for consuming too many peppers? The same man whom ran over several cows with his horse and carriage, all because he was chasing a dog? The same man who began a forest fire while trying to fully oil-fry a frozen turkey? I have seen this name countless times come up in the papers, Andreas, and it is usually for his renown misdeeds and blunders."

"I know too of Inepticus," stated Trombley, as he stared in confusion at Andreas.

Henry sighed long and deep. "I *too* have heard of this man. Why conjure his name, Lord Andreas? This is a serious matter we're discussing, not potential fodder for a Shay Bromage column."

"Hear me out," replied Andreas, defensively, amid a wave of laughter. "I'm merely suggesting an option to my colleagues, just as I was asked moments ago by yourself and Lord Haque. Underhill is surrounded by these cliffs, nearly swallowed. Is it not? Though this spire is presumably lower in elevation than the supposed Fiskle Cliffs that surround it. Correct? Would it then be wholly unreasonable to suggest somebody fly from the edge of these cliffs, grab this 'equilibrium', and return it to its proper place?"

"Man cannot fly," answered Trombley flatly. "It's a biological impossibility."

"Your keen powers of observation and foundational knowledge of the sciences astound me, Lord Trombley," replied Andreas, to the crowd's continued delight, as he turned to the Lord from Middlebury with an evil smirk. "The monks have taught you well."

Haque interrupted before Trombley could respond. "Inepticus has been troubled since he was a lad. His father, however, is a standup fellow. He has two brothers and a sister who are wonderful community members. Inepticus has always been cursed, though, like the shores of York[79]. He has tried to follow his father's path, but has not been equal among his steps."

"Though he is studied in the art of flying, is he not?" retorted Andreas.

"If you consider gliding down a steep hill 'flight', then I suppose so," replied Haque, his voice laden with sadness. "However, I wouldn't trust Inepticus with shining my pair of Cerpellis."

The crowd both gasped and chuckled at the form of showmanship from the usually dignified and reserved Haque. Riegelman looked pitifully upon Lord Andreas.

"Is this the best you can come up with, Lord Andreas? Is it? The flying turkey, the living gaffe; better known as Inepticus, charged with saving an entire town?"

---

[79] A reference to the abandoned warehouses in Plattsburgh, NY, across the lake from Burlington, that are rumored to be haunted.

"Do *you* have any better ideas? I suppose not, as usual. You haven't had a single one since your appointment to the senate. The Critic of Addison[80] strikes again," mocked Andreas with hostility.

"I beg your pardon…"

The crowd of lords chuckled, as the statehouse resembled more and more a circus. Riegelman blushed and shook with anger. Andreas turned back to the crowd of assembled lords and winked with self-satisfaction.

"Gentlemen! Enough!" shouted Henry. "Order!"

Ulger slammed the gavel to resume order. Silence returned, at which point Andreas took a deep breath while looking directly at Lord Henry.

"Lord Henry, what about your friend, Flatlander?"

"What *of* Flatlander?" asked Henry, his eyes squinting at the mere mention of his valued associate.

Flatlander straightened from his view in the front row. Though he expected his final quest on the near horizon, he didn't know it would be this soon or under such dangerous pretense. He was also surprised to be recommended by an actual sitting member of the senate, let alone the likes of Andreas. Mere weeks ago, he would have thought that quite implausible.

Lord Andreas straightened. "Oh please, his track record has been simply stellar, Lord Henry. You have even said so himself. He has freed Pete, slayed Fish and Babakiss, eliminated Superpac from our streets, defeated the curse of the Moran, delivered goods from the Miller, retrieved Burlington's key from the vaults. Heaven knows what else! Is there nothing this man cannot achieve? Maybe you were all correct in bemoaning me foolish for suggesting Inepticus's name…he is but a thick-headed twit."

Henry's tone dripped with suspicion. "Since when did *you* become such an ardent supporter of my associate, Andreas? It was

---

[80] A disparaging nickname of Riegelman coined by Shay Bromage

merely a season ago in which you cursed Flatlander's name among every member who sits before you this day."

Andreas smiled thinly. "Call it a change of heart, Lord Henry. Don't we all sometimes have a change of heart? But let me ask my fellow Vermonters. How does the senate feel about the idea of Flatlander tackling the darkness of Underhill rather than Inepticus?"

A thunderous applause rang out from virtually every lord and master in the senate. A standing ovation ensued, as some looked to where he was seated near to Henry. Flatlander's heart pounded, and though he was flattered by the recognition, a part of him was troubled by Andreas's tone. The Lord of White River's support felt insincere, sneaky, like there was an obvious agenda. Henry wasn't easily fooled.

Lord Henry motioned for Ulger to sound the gavel. When the whistling and applause died down, Henry spoke.

"Though I'm delighted in the senate's newfound appreciation of Flatlander, I utterly disagree. Flatlander's extremely valuable to me and to the republic as a whole. It would unwise of me to send him on such a dangerous mission."

Riegelman threw his hands in the air. "But what of Underhill? What of our brethren? A few thousand men and women lay stranded at the foot of Mansfield. Are we to do *nothing*?"

"He is a servant to the republic, Lord Henry. Not for your personal use like some household pet," argued Andreas.

Henry trembled with anger. The lord from White River was now cornering him. He couldn't contain himself.

"Gentlemen, Flatlander has been nothing but a selfless agent of the republic. You owe him more than your gratitude. As for him being a "household pet," watch your tongue, Andreas. He is no more a pet than the snake of White River, whose intentions remain hidden, unseen in the tall grass."

Lord Andreas grew red in the face and clenched his fists in tight balls, but Lord Haque beat him to a reply.

"Gentlemen! Now, now. It still begs the question, Lord Henry, what to do about Brookes and Underhill? Though I'm disappointed to hear that Flatlander is unavailable for this cause, we must respect Henry's wish as leader of this republic. Yet for an urgent matter such as this, I appeal to you to provide as much help as you can. I urge you to look upon the branch where Lord Desmairis once sat, and look inside yourself, Lord Henry. For the gem of Eastern Chittenden will be no more if we indulge in simple complacency."

Henry and the senate gazed upon Brookes Desmairis's desk in unison with a silent, dreaded pity. Several of the lords chattered quietly amongst themselves, as Andreas still stared at the Humble King with utter scorn.

"Very well," answered Henry after a lengthy pause. "I will do my best to appease you and the republic, Lord Haque. In three days time, I will commission Inepticus, at Lord Andreas's original recommendation, to charge the rescue of Underhill. I will also deploy Flatlander, two selected monks, his father, Danario, and myself to assist Inepticus in his frightful journey. I offer no promises to those seeking them, yet Lord Haque speaks true. Something must be done. I will hope, as we all must, that this is the day that Inepticus has lived for. I now order this session adjourned."

Ulger's gavel signaled a vociferous uproar from the various lords and masters, many of which had relatives or friends in Underhill. The decision in appointing Inepticus to such an important matter had caused a major stir. Few, if any, lords believed in such a cursed man for such a sacred quest. His name had slowly become a punch line to many over the years. Trusting such a man was insanity, they argued out loud to one another. Yet there were no easy answers for Lord Henry. He swiftly exited the angry, confused senate hall, himself, angry and confused. Underhill was sinking further into shadow, reflected Henry, and so would his political career if his handling of the matter should prove weak.

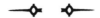

Flatlander left the statehouse immediately following Henry's departure while the lords of the republic squabbled amongst themselves in disbelief. Acting on a hunch, he walked briskly to Henry's home only a block away. Opening the door to Henry's office, he found the space engulfed in darkness. Henry's chair swiveled slightly towards the far wall, his frame silhouetted fine against the pale light emitted through an office window. Jasmine incense burnt at the front of his desk, as grey strings of smoke worked their way through the room like a meandering serpent. A nervous tapping of Henry's foot rattled a pen and several coins on his desk.

"What would you have done?" came the Humble King's defeated voice from behind the tall chair.

Dumbfounded, Flatlander brushed back his hair. He faced a dilemma. Truly, there appeared to be a divide amongst the king and himself. But how could he bring it up? Clearing his throat, Flatlander took a tentative step into Henry's office.

"Actually, this is one of the rare times in which I agree with the senate, Lord Henry. Inepticus doesn't seem like a good choice."

"So you're siding with them, I presume?"

"Since I've lived here, all I've heard about are Inepticus's screw-ups."

"Sounds familiar, doesn't it, Flatlander? It wasn't too long ago that you were in a very similar boat." Henry chuckled, mockingly. "Then, please, enlighten me. What would the *godly* Flatlander have to say about such a matter?"

Flatlander blinked in surprise. "Is that a hint of *jealousy* that I hear in your voice, Lord Henry? My number one concern is that we might be sending this young man to his death!"

Henry turned rapidly in his chair to face Flatlander. His face was flush.

"Never speak to me in that tone again, Flatlander. My patience wears thin. You have no idea, do you? A leader makes decisions that eat away at his very soul, his very essence, and this occasion is no exception." He looked upon Flatlander crookedly. "And pray, what do *you* think should happen with this Fiskle Cliff?"

"My apologies, Lord Henry. I didn't mean to offend," replied Flatlander, as he leaned against the wall, arms crossed. He took a moment to collect himself. "All I know is that there's one last quest for me to complete. I've been living in the republic for months and it's all now coming to a head. And you've even said yourself. I have no home. I have little possessions. No family to care for. I have no 'horse in this race.' So tell me why *I'm* not the one leading this quest?"

Henry shook his head. "Times have changed, Flatlander. You have proven much too valuable."

Flatlander shook his head in disagreement. "But I have completed nine of ten quests for you thus far. Haven't I earned the right to make this my final one?"

Henry cracked a knuckle nervously. "Andreas is up to no good. It was his intention all along to corner me into appointing you."

"This has nothing to do with Andreas," countered Flatlander. "This is something that I want to do for the republic."

Henry sighed. "But you *will* help. All that you need to do is merely assist Inepticus and you will be done. You will have completed your tenth and final quest, and most importantly, you will live to see another day. For Inepticus's sake, I cannot be so sure."

"And yet you knowingly send him to his doom?" retorted Flatlander, in disbelief.

He had always taken Lord Henry as a leader of great moral convictions, a man of sterling reputation. Though now, Henry's appointment of Inepticus to the Fiskle Cliffs made Flatlander question those beliefs in earnest.

"Flatlander, see here," replied Lord Henry tersely, as he rose from his seat. Pulling open the shades of his office, the light revealed dark bags below his eyes. He trembled as he spoke. "As leader of the Second Republic of Vermont, I need to make balanced decisions. Decisions which to live by, and eventually, to die by. I cannot risk losing you, and though I'm deeply concerned over the wellbeing of Inepticus, he *has* prepared his entire life for this moment, as he is one of few in this land who has studied flight. His failures in other facets of life shouldn't predetermine his worth in others. He sees this as a great honor, and he *should*. For, potentially, in his act of heroics, Inepticus will be fighting for the republic as a whole, and striving for something that he hasn't garnered much in his life: respect. There isn't a monetary value to be placed on such a thing, nor can deductive reasoning quantify such a thing in simple terms of logic. Men and women rise and fall to meet expectations, and you must entrust them entirely; whether by sheer madness or reason." Henry paused, gathering his wits, and looked to Flatlander solemnly. "Do you trust me, Flatlander?"

Flatlander turned and opened the office door to leave. Lord Henry repeated his inquiry with desperation.

"I asked you a question. Do you *trust* me, Flatlander?"

Pausing at Henry's office door, Flatlander toyed with the brass knob, and reflected for a moment, while carefully choosing his parting words.

"Yes, Lord Henry, and I will support you unequivocally in your decisions, including this one. But I hope, for your sake, and the sake of the republic, that this does not come back to haunt you."

And before Henry could reply, Flatlander left Henry alone in the smoke-filled office. Flatlander's mind scattered in a thousand places. Sweat beaded across his brow. The Fiskle Cliff had already dealt the first blow, Flatlander decided, and they had not yet even reached its overhang.

Inepticus was the youngest of four. The son of a local messenger, Danario, and his wife, Cynthia, of Stowe, he was born into a wealthy and respectable family. For Danario Talcott was Stowe's premier messenger, delivering important documents and goods to its various residents day and night. Though he charged a handsome fee, Danario was inventive and hardworking in his methods of transportation, and the people of Stowe had few other options among this rugged, mountainous land. For heavier fare, the messenger sometimes traveled with his blond mare, Bitsy, whom pulled a customized carriage. To reach more desolate locations high up on the mountains or through washed out roads, Danario would outfit his personal yak, Smudge, to carry him up cliff sides and treacherous mountain paths. For tasks that relied purely on speed and little else, the family had raised and trained a carrier pigeon, Celia, for the lighter fare. Though Inepticus sometimes abused the privilege of using Celia for such mundane tasks like calling out sick from school.

It was demanding work and rarely did Danario take a day off. Relentless and thoughtful, the people of Stowe relied heavily on the man and developed a glowing respect for the messenger. And it was in this light that Inepticus viewed his father growing up. Danario put a lot of pride into his work, and he was able to make a fairly lucrative career of it. Still, with three sons and a daughter reaching their teenage years, Danario was more than ready to hand his business to his children in due time.

The last day he had taken off was when he had to rescue Inepticus from a nearby drinking well. That day he would never forget. Lowering a rope for Inepticus to tie around his chest, greasing the well's sides with a container of pig lard, pulling the boy up with the help of Bitsy. He recalled for every five feet of progress, Inepticus would fall another four feet, thereby making the task incredibly long and taxing. In fact, the endeavor had taken the better part of two hours, he remembered, and the rope burns on his hands had lasted for a week, stinging sharply with even the slightest of pressure. Afterwards, Danario had chastised the boy. Inepticus, desperate to explain himself, had told his father that he was merely trying to fetch water for the family dinner. Yet the family had just recently replenished their water supply the day prior. This caused Danario to be very suspicious.

Inepticus had two older brothers, Robert and Garret, and an older sister, Enchantment. Robert was the oldest of the four, and his academic prowess became the stuff of local legend. As an eighth grader in school, he had resolved the school's electricity shortage after a severe storm by designing and constructing a biomass generator. It burned the fallen trees and branches from the heavy winds, and converted the heat into electricity, keeping the school open while surrounding schools remained closed. And though many of his fellow peers were sore at him for this accomplishment, the deed had earned him the recognition and admiration alike from parents and staff. Since then, Robert was close to graduating high school and matriculating to Burlington's Hilltop University to pursue a degree in Engineering. He also offered his father aid by helping to manage the office's future finances.

Garret, one year Robert's junior, was the tough brute of the bunch. A standout athlete in both mountain ball (Stowe's premier sport) and the lumber games, Garret was blessed with the unexpected gift of strength. Though fairly short at five foot six, he made up for it in his tenacity and brawn. He competed against men twice his age in the lumber games, and often left his competition in awe after his jaw-dropping performances. Once he had axed down a seventy foot black tupelo, a tree known for its hard, heavy wood, in a matter of one minute; a task no man or woman had ever accomplished in the history of Stowe. Inepticus often relied on Robert as a source for wisdom and on Garret's brute strength if he needed protection from a bully at school. Because of Garret's talents, there was never a shortage of firewood stacked at the Talcott household. Four separate piles out back stood close to fifteen feet tall. Garret offered Danario his future services for clearing mountain roads, or creating new ones for delivery purposes.

Enchantment, the gem of their parent's eyes, was regarded as the most beautiful girl in Stowe. Having won ten consecutive beauty pageants by the age of sixteen; the trophies and medals lined a ledge in her bedroom from wall to wall. She had the largest, bluest eyes of any child Stowe had ever seen, and some in town even swore they could even see the color in her eye in the dead of night. Cynthia had made it one of her missions in life to see her Enchantment act lady-like and proper, and it filled her heart with joy to see her daughter flourish in the role of Stowe's princess. But good looks weren't the only qualities that benefitted Danario's daughter, for Enchantment also went out of her way to help out the few needy in her community. She often looked after her father's valuable animals, and promised Danario that she intended caring for them in the future.

Inepticus, however, was an entirely different story. Danario struggled to find duties in which his youngest son could excel. Sometimes, he had Inepticus hand-deliver messages to a few of the nearest homes out of fear that the boy would get lost with more distant destinations. True to his fears, the boy still became lost. He even tried giving Inepticus maps. Still, the boy would get lost. Twice he had to use his carrier pigeon, Celia, to find the boy amid the endless wood of Stowe.

Cynthia attempted to train Inepticus as her assistant chef for family meals, but Inepticus often botched measurements, gave himself pepper burns on undesirable bodily parts, and burnt crucial ingredients. After one particular kitchen fire, Garret had thrown the smoldering pot off of their home's balcony into the snow some fifty feet below. After replacing her hand-woven window curtains and the family's favorite cooking pot, Cynthia figured that the kitchen was simply no place for Inepticus.

Yet Danario would not give up on his son. Committed to the idea of supporting the wayward Inepticus, he convinced his three children to give their sibling a hand in finding his way. For every week his children would allow Inepticus to assist them in their duties, they would earn small piece of ownership in Danario's business. He thought that it would be a nice incentive for them to overtake the family practice, while simultaneously allowing Inepticus the much-needed support that he required in his day-to-day existence.

Though reluctant, one day Garret brought Inepticus along to chop and stack firewood. He was doing fine, according to Garret, until Inepticus lost the axe head as he swung back for a strike. It had flown over the side of the embankment into their vast back yard, smack right into a fresh snowdrift several feet deep. It had been Garret's favorite and sharpest axe head of his collection, for he had thought that his weaker brother would benefit from using such a quality instrument. The axe head was eventually found, but not until several months later, when the last of Stowe's snow had melted into the earth, and its days of use during the winter months had passed. Suffice to say, Inepticus did not cut any more wood with Garret from that point forward.

Robert thought that Inepticus might find strength in books, like himself. He brought his brother down to the basement and lent Inepticus a book to read, "Thetford Manor," by Malcolm Lourdes; the story of a struggling farmer that Robert thought would appeal to the foolhardy boy. To Robert, Inepticus appeared to be reading quite diligently, yet he was surprisingly mum when

Robert asked him comprehension questions about the details of the text. At first, Robert chalked it up to his brother being several years his junior and unpracticed in his reading and articulation. Upon further inspection, however, and after several days of this same routine, Robert soon discovered that Inepticus had been secretly staring, quite oddly, at pictures of birds smuggled within the pages of his novel. Robert was so angry that he demanded from Inepticus the book in which he had lent him, vowing never to help him again.

Even Enchantment tried her hand at helping her brother despite Garret and Robert's warnings. Every Sunday afternoon, Enchantment had brought Inepticus to the Stowe General Store, where she had spent much of her time collecting and packaging non-perishable goods for the poor. Though Stowe was a rather wealthy town, there were some less fortunate souls living in the lower reaches, whose income washing dishes at the high-end restaurants or working at one of the larger farming operations was meager at best. Not all in the mountain towns, Enchantment told Inepticus, were people privileged enough for a panoramic view of the valley[81].

And it wasn't until the third week that Enchantment noticed something amiss. That day, as she went to check upon the progress of Inepticus, she noticed him missing from his duty of readying cardboard boxes for canned food. Noticing a trail of emptied meat cans, Enchantment followed it until it brought her to the back yard of the Stowe General Store. And there, by the large metal dumpster, stood Inepticus petting two large Siberian Huskies. Three empty cans of cod lay nearby.

The truth hadn't been hard at all to get out of Inepticus. He had simply 'fed the animals out of pity.' 'They looked so hungry,' he had said. But while Inepticus had done this deed with noble

---

[81] It was commonly accepted that in many republic towns, the higher in elevation one is, the higher in socioeconomic class.

intentions, Enchantment reminded him that two families were likely affected by his mistake, forcing them to look elsewhere for food. To make matters worse, the two Siberian huskies at the heart of the matter were actually owned by the neighbor of the general store. Both were actually very well taken care of and content, according to Gage Myers, the general store's owner and manager. This only darkened his sister's mood; for Enchantment had felt no greater fury in her life.

Years later, as all of his siblings grew old and moved elsewhere in the republic working successful jobs, Inepticus stayed at home with his parents to help them with the family business. Danario was bitter at the situation, though he would never admit it in the presence of Inepticus. *At least the boy was loyal*, Danario tried to remind himself. *Thick as an ox, sure, but loyal.* The others were waiting out the days in which Danario would pass them the reigns of the business, though they cared not for its current state of affairs. In the meantime, the aging messenger of Stowe struggled to find Inepticus duties that the boy wouldn't botch, but just as always, they were all met with varying degrees of failure.

It was during this prolonged predicament that Danario would sometimes sob in his sleep. And it was on one such night that Inepticus heard his father's cries, despite his mother's attempts to comfort her husband with the gentle strumming of a harp. Inepticus, stubborn but not dumb, knew the reason for his father's agony. He realized that something inside of him needed to change. Yet, as Inepticus juggled his mother's plump, fresh tomatoes over the family's sheepskin rug, he just couldn't figure out exactly what those changes would look like.

It was only weeks later that Inepticus became enamored with the idea of flight. It happened as he went for a breath of fresh air one morning on his family's deck. He noticed a voracious hawk swooping in and around the Stowe valley. He watched the bird of prey from the deck of his house, which overlooked a large, steep decline. In large, gliding loops, the hawk chased several smaller, black birds, interspersed with several rapid charges. Occasionally, the hawk would call out "Kee-eeee-arrrrr." The resounding echo that rang across the valley would make Inepticus's heart skip a beat and his face teem with excitement. It was as if the boy was deeply immersed in a dream, one in which he had no intentions of waking from. He imagined himself flying with the bird, seeing the same views and vistas, the same winter landscape stretching out for miles and miles, blanketing the Vermont countryside. Every night in his dream, he'd fly over that same hillside chasing the same flock of birds. Yet despite his borderline obsession, he felt no closer to flying. Doubt oftentimes transmuted into despair.

One morning, Inepticus decided to tell his father of his new found plan. He found him in his office rifling through some business papers. A dozen boxes or more of various sizes lay stacked at the side of his desk.

"Father, one day I want to invent something that will allow me to fly."

Danario shot his son a queer look. "Can't you see that I'm busy?" His father slammed an envelope into a box. "Besides, Inepticus, how could you possibly achieve flight? You haven't even mastered how to read properly or how to chop wood like Garret. You cannot even be considerate, like your sister, for heaven's sake! Temper thy dreams before they become your undoing!"

Inepticus continued, unabated. "It came to me while in a dream, father. I was flying with the hawk that circles our valley for prey. Their calls are all I look forward to each day."

His father gazed out his office window at one of his carriages knee-deep in snow. A slight frost misted some of the windowpanes as the rising sun shined bright on the new layer of snowfall.

"Well then, that is very strange and a troubling indicator of your grasp of reality. Hark, Inepticus. While it pains me to dash thy dreams upon a floor of doubt, you need to set your sights on those goals less ambitious, less lofty. Like my carriage- it may need shoveling out."

Inepticus eyes grew large. "But to fly…"

"But to fly *would* be a dream come true!" interrupted Danario, as he stood from his task of organizing orders for the day. Gripping the handle of his glass mug, Danario downed the remaining contents of his chilled water. "But Inepticus: consider this just a moment. Do you think that you're the first to dream of such a thing? Heavens, no! For years, it has been a goal of dreamers and thinkers alike. Man was made to walk the ground, though, not wander the sky amongst the birds and bats and insects. It would take a miracle for such a thing to occur! For a fish could not breathe our air just because he *wanted* to."

Inepticus knew his father to be wrong, as tales from Burlington told precisely of such a miracle.

"But that's not true! There *is* a fish that breathes our very…"

Danario shook his head vigorously. "Enough, Inepticus! Such foolish talk is better reserved for the nursery school at the base of Mansfield! I will hear no more of this as long as the Little River flows through the veins of Waterbury."

Inepticus paused. "And what then? When the river stops flowing?"

Danario looked at his child incredulously. "You must be kidding, child. The Little River will never stop flowing, Inepticus! That's the point. Gracious, you are even too dense for idioms!" He paused. "And grab that shovel and get working!"

Inepticus left in a huff, directly past the shovel leaning crookedly against the wall. The talk with his father did little to quell his dream of flying. It gave him a purpose, *a drive*. For the first time in his life, Inepticus felt the actual need, the actual desire, to work for something bigger in life. For once, despite his father's resounding cynicism, Inepticus readied himself for the day in which his dream could come true. Then, and *only* then, would life be kinder. His resolve, rooted within the context of his father's stinging judgment, grew with each passing day; for Inepticus then decided he would craft his very own wings.

Despite Danario's growing trepidation with his son's new passion, he reluctantly decided to help him design and build his very own pair of wings. He considered it a way to appease the boy as well as wake him up to reality. If Inepticus were to *see* the actual folly in his fantasies, to actually *feel* it there in front of him, perhaps he would then reconsider his desire to fly. They worked together in Danario's personal woodshop in the basement hours after a hearty dinner of beef and carrot stew.

"How many times have I told you, Inepticus! You must use heavier materials!" scolded Danario, as he inspected his son's wings. "If you want to actually be successful, which I *still* think is madness, mind you, then these light wings will snap in the wind like a twig."

"Speak for yourself father, for I have had a vision, a dream, of seeing myself flying high above the clouds."

Danario capped a bottle of glue with a free hand. "In your dreams, I'm sure that you have attained quite a few accomplishments, but in the real world, Inepticus, *the real world*, you have faltered. As such, your wings are nothing more than a jumble of broken tree branches with a sloppy glue job. And as such, your attempt at flight is a misguided, ill-conceived foray into a world we cannot possibly enter, for it defies physics."

Inepticus grabbed his wings from his father's clutch. Inspecting the tight leather material binding the skeleton of the wings, he saw he had stretched it as thin as possible. Taut as his father's wagon cover, its surface sparkled by a waxy sheen.

"Then how would *you* construct your wings, dear father?" asked Inepticus, with an edge to his voice.

"I'll tell you how, son. I would construct wings in my dreams, and in my dreams *only*. Man was not made to travel through air. Trust me, Inepticus. In my thirty years as a messenger, there's plenty that I've seen and learned, and I can at least attest to *that* much."

"Then I look forward to the day to which I prove you wrong," replied Inepticus, as he thumbed a splotch of excess glue from the wing's edge.

"And I will not hold my breath for you for such an occasion, Inepticus, for I would surely suffocate in due time," replied Danario, as he stormed from the workshop, grabbing his trusty wrench in the process.

Inepticus sat alone on a stool, overlooking his pair of wings resting on the desk. Just minutes ago, they had looked so promising, so fitting, his future as expansive as the very skies themselves. His mind had expelled all doubts; cast them out like the Flatlanders of old. After just a short while in the presence of his cynical father, however, the motley set of wings now reminded him of all of his limitations, all his weaknesses. The glue lay smeared on a wing's underside. A supporting branch was placed at an awkward angle on its frame. Some of the sloppier connectors of his wings had become more apparent, and with a keener eye, he sought to make the necessary adjustments.

Thumbing through his sketches of the local hawk of which he drew on a regular basis, Inepticus smiled with hope. Though far from the most accurate, nor the most artistically inclined of sketches, they still pervaded his every thought and action. *I will fly.* And with a drawn-out yawn, Inepticus readied himself for sleep in his stationary, land-dwelling bed. *I will fly.*

On a frigid day in February, several weeks after the spirited debate in their family workshop, Danario sent Inepticus on a relatively short excursion down the mountain to deliver a letter to a the Pomfrets, a neighborhood family. Though the home of Wilson and Amelia Pomfret lay only half a mile down road, the only way to reach it was through a rather winding stretch of road that looped to the west. As Danario processed a new, large batch of items to deliver in the coming days, Inepticus snuck out of the back door with both the letter, and, unbeknownst to his father, his pair of wings, which he had recently modified for such an occasion.

The boy ran down the country road at a steady clip, for if Danario caught wind, he would surely be upset. The wings were never to leave their respective hangers in the basement, per Danario's order. There had even been a sign posted on the wall saying as much. *Father must not find out*, thought Inepticus, as he ran frantically, his wings catching the occasional gust, and throwing him off balance on several occasions. The snow on the roads had been well removed by the horse-drawn plows. Yet in the adjacent woods, nearly three feet of snow had accumulated in recent weeks. Once out of sight of his house, Inepticus slowed his pace; worried that such reckless form might potentially destroy his fragile creation.

He neared a sharp bend in the road and looked down fifty yards or so to where the Pomfret's home lay at the bottom of a steep embankment. *The short cut of short cuts.* Deep snowdrifts surrounded the mustard yellow home. Two narrow, shoveled paths led from their driveway around the house. A small wooden shed stood half buried in among the drifts, seldom used. The Pomfrets were elderly folk, some of the oldest in all of Stowe.

Inepticus walked to the edge of the embankment, turning in both directions to make sure that nobody was watching. Nothing stirred from either direction. Inspecting the wings closely, he made sure that every joint, every piece of metal, every screw and nut, every slither of wood, was in working order and unblemished.

He then thought of the hawk he had keenly observed; how it must have briefly felt as a chick, the moment before the mother forced it from its nest with little to no warning. How scared it must have been. *At least I'm afforded the luxury of preparation*, he thought. Fastening his wings to his specialized suit with a series of buttons, ties and buckles, he prepared swiftly for his endeavor. He flapped the wings slowly to make sure the movements felt right, and sure enough, they did. The stretched leather, covered with glued feathers, captured the wind's every movement.

Taking a deep breath, Inepticus peered over the edge of the embankment and closed his eyes. He pictured himself as a hawk, circling the Pomfret's house in wide, lazy arches, and coming to a perfectly timed and graceful halt perched atop their mailbox, quiet as an owl. Taking a few sharp breaths, which misted in the frozen air, Inepticus looked straight ahead to the coated white pine forest canopy, then leapt fluidly from the bend in the road.

Immediately, his heart nearly leapt into his mouth, for his wings had yet to find the proper air channel. He dropped like a stone. Adjusting his body in a more elongated form, Inepticus straightened, and hoped for the best. Luckily, his wings then found life moments before his landing, and the boy glided with newfound direction, gliding over the mounds of drift. Sailing past the mailbox headfirst, he came to a screeching halt as he made impact in one of the deeper outlying snowdrifts surrounding the Pomfret's house. After several seconds of collecting his senses, Inepticus lifted his head through the surface of the drift, and spat out a mixture of snow and blood. He had cut his gum, but it could have been worse, much worse.

As the gravity of his accomplishment began to sink in, Inepticus hooted with glee, pumping his fist cheerfully in the air. Despite the fact that his wings had broken apart on impact, the fact remained that he had flown. Even if just for a few short seconds, at best, Inepticus had actually flown and directed himself towards an intended target. It was a triumph for the ages for the seventeen year old.

"I did it!" said Inepticus at the top of his lungs as he shook off his broken set of wings, arms extending towards the sky. "*By the Gods*! I did it!"

From the front of the house came a gentle, gravelly voice.

"*Inepticus*? Is that you?"

Standing on the front porch was Mrs. Pomfret, dressed in pink pants and brown dyed wool jacket. Her oversized bonnet nearly covered her eyes, as she adjusted it slightly with her cut-off gloves. Inepticus, wrapped up in the excitement of the moment, had momentarily forgotten why he had been sent to the Pomfret's in the first place.

"Mrs. Pomfret," began Inepticus in his most polite tone, as he attempted to collect himself. "A rare pleasure to see you on this fine day."

"And to you too, Inepticus," replied Mrs. Pomfret curiously. She eyed his bloody mouth, the broken tangle of material on the ground and the gaping hole in the nearby snowdrift. "My goodness, dear. Are you okay? What on earth happened?"

Inepticus stood proud. "Think nothing of it, dear Mrs. Pomfret. The herald of Stowe is friends to all; and is neither stymied by mountain nor injury." He removed the letter from his pocket, and handed it over proudly. "I present to you a letter from your daughter, Bonnie."

Mrs. Pomfret placed a hand on her hips. "I can see that, Inepticus, and am delighted. But I worry what your father would think. And what is that contraption on my lawn? Why is your mouth bleeding? What have you to say?"

Inepticus turned to his wreckage of his wings then back to Mrs. Pomfret. "I say that it is a beautiful day to deliver mail on such a fine morning, and there is no neighbor whom I would rather serve than you, Mrs. Pomfret."

"Your father teaches you well," replied Mrs. Pomfret with an appreciative chuckle. "I'll let you butter me up good for the time being, young one. But you really should see a doctor when you can. Farewell, Inepticus."

"And to you, my dearest of neighbors," said Inepticus, as he took an exaggerated bow before departing.

"Such a curious, young thing," mumbled Mrs. Pomfret under her breath as she entered her house, mail in hand.

From the small, octagon-shaped pattern of miniature windows on the front door, Mrs. Pomfret watched as Inepticus gathered his broken contraption and carry the objects awkwardly on his back, making his way up the drive to the mountain roadway. The object began looking semi familiar from certain angles. *Are those...wings? Can't be*, decided Mrs. Pomfret. *Must be the eyes going from old age. Yet, Danario's son is surely one of a kind*, she thought, whimsically. *Yes, one of a kind.*

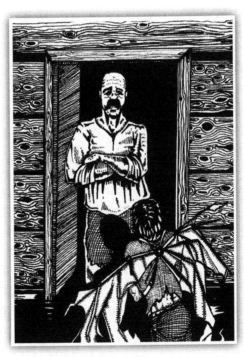

As he approached his house, Inepticus's rush of unbridled joy swiftly morphed into fear when he saw the look of Danario awaiting his arrival, arms crossed, at the foot of the stoop. He momentarily considered throwing his broken wings aside, but it was much too late. It would be a futile gesture, for his father had seen plenty. Propped up against the wall of the house, Danario's eyes squinted hard at the boy.

"How was your trip to the Pomfret's, Inepticus?" asked Danario, the cadence of his voice suggesting an exaggerated naiveté.

"It was fine. Thank you, father," replied Inepticus, as he swallowed a drop of blood from his wounded gum.

"I see that you have brought your wings, surely just to show the Pomfret's your fine work, I presume."

It wasn't a question.

Inepticus decided to engage in his father's game of wits. "Yes, father. They have showered me with praise, and have given me hope where you have given me nothing but despair."

As Inepticus neared his father, he paused. Danario peered closely at the broken wings attached to his son's back.

"Doth mine eyes deceive me? Your wings! Heavens, Inepticus, you must have taken quite a rough fall walking on the roadway. The horse's plows surely must have missed a few spots if thy eyes prove true. Is this not so?"

Inepticus nodded. "Aye, father. The main roadways were treacherous, yet I was able to muster through, despite layers and layers of ice. My wings, on the other hand, weren't so lucky."

Danario nodded. "Still, you have made excellent time. No man or woman, at least that I can recall of in my age, has made that route so fast. One second, I was sorting through mailing addresses as you left the house, and next I know, Inepticus, I see you returning, the letter fully delivered, and you, in fine spirits."

Inepticus blushed at what he perceived as an enormous compliment. "I take my errands seriously, father. My speed is that of a sparrow downwind and my..."

"Do you think me a fool, Inepticus?" interrupted Danario in full outrage as he approached his son. Inepticus threw the cluttered pile of wings on the snowy ground and recoiled from his furious father.

"A fool? Nay, father. Nay."

Danario pointed to the road. "I know that the horse plows have done the roadways fine, for I myself traveled on them this morning while you were asleep in bed like a babe! I also know that it is not humanly possible to make the trip to the Pomfret's and back again in the time that you made it today. I know this mountain as well as the earth itself, from every nook, every corner to cliff face, just as I know the dishonesty in your face and in your words! Tell me truly: you must still possess the letter to which I entrusted you to deliver. Do you not?"

Inepticus could not hide the truth any longer, and beamed, despite himself. "Nay, father, for I elected to *fly* to my destination despite your attempts to stifle me. I flew from the hill overlooking the Pomfret's and landed successfully near their house. You'll be pleased to know that the letter is safe with Mrs. Pomfret."

Danario eyes lit up. "*Pleased*! You thinks me *pleased*? You have knowingly defied me, Inepticus! You know, just as well as I that you were *not* to attempt flying under any circumstance while you share the same roof with your mother and I. You *know* that, son. And speaking of which, how will *she* handle this bit of troubling news?"

Inepticus swallowed. "But I have flown, father. I have been one with the heavens. A pity, you cannot even congratulate your own son on such an incredible feat. I traveled the route faster than any man or woman in history, you have even said so yourself. Did you not? How else can you explain my expediency?"

"Flight, you say," spat Danario, disgusted at the very suggestion of the word. "That was a *controlled fall*, Inepticus! It bears little resemblance to our modern understanding of what it means to fly! To truly fly!"

"And yet I am in one piece," countered his son.

"And what of your wings, Inepticus?" interrupted Danario, as he pointed at Inepticus's ripped, tattered wings, now rendered to a loose collection of sticks and materials. "Take notice, I beg you! What of *them*? I have seen less damaged goods after a pony-run down the goat's trail at nightfall."

Inepticus smiled briefly at Danario's reference. For it transported him back to the times of his early memories of his father and the stories he would come home with regarding the harrowing paths he had taken to deliver goods. In his father's more daring youth, the goat trail was reserved only for wild goats. But, Danario of Stowe, in a desperate bid to deliver a lover a bouquet of roses, garnered Stowe's respect for his heroics and timeliness for using the trail with his mare. Stories such as this fueled his legacy as master herald. Inepticus cherished the memory, but it unsettled him. Was his dad any less reckless than he?

"The landing was harder than I had expected, father," admitted Inepticus, quite reluctantly.

"Of course!" replied Danario, wide-eyed. "That has been the common sentiment from all of the fools who have ever attempted the endeavor of flying. The art of landing becomes a mere afterthought, buried foolishly amongst the excitement of flight."

"But, I flew…" replied Inepticus stubbornly, his voice lacking the same certainty from just moments ago.

"Right. You *flew*," replied Danario, mockingly, as he buried his face deep within his palms, deep in troubled thought. Danario then looked upon Inepticus. He had worked himself into a sweat despite the cold. "No sooner will you or anyone know the true nature of flying until they revive the bodies of the machines of flight from the Old Country. And we both know that my workshop is not up for such a task, Inepticus." Danario's gaze had wandered up to the sky, but soon again fell upon his son with scorn. "Yet perhaps you will fly one day, son. For I may kick you straight in the backside with such force, the impact and your subsequent upheaval may temporarily defy the very laws of gravity. Though, for now, I demand you go to your room and write a letter of apology to the Pomfret's for your dangerous, reckless, and above all, stupid method of transportation. And I want you to *walk* it to them in the morning! If I see those wings within an arm's reach of your person, you will be grounded for a year!"

"A whole year?" Inepticus cried. "But father…"

"Yes, Inepticus! Grounded both on earth and in sin. I will speak to you no further tonight; for I need a moment to collect my wits."

Danario then stomped crossly into the house, slamming the door behind him. Inepticus stood motionless in the bone-chilling air. His wings were a sad sight indeed. They now sat disassembled, a pile of scrap resting at his feet. He felt ill with rage and sorrow, the words of his father hurt and swirled in his head, warming his cheeks with discontent. *A controlled fall? How could that be? It was more than that, it had to be!* He was adamant that he had, indeed, flown. *I will build another set of wings. I don't care what father has to say. They will be better, I'm sure of it, and then I will show him,* thought Inepticus. *One day, I will show him.*

Underhill had long been considered a charming town. Twenty miles east of Burlington, it dwelt under the shadow of Vermont's most colossal mountain, Mt. Mansfield. If Addison County were considered Burlington's gem to the south, and the Vermont Islands, Burlington's gem to the northwest, then Underhill was surely considered the gem to the east. Besides its impressive height, Mansfield was unique from other mountains in the republic. For when viewed from the east or west, the mountain's profile resembled that of a human face, complete with nose, chin, lip, and brow.

The western section of Mansfield fell under the jurisdiction of Underhill, the eastern part, Stowe. It was several years ago that Underhill began experiencing a very unusual change. According to various forms of lore, a very powerful stone was unearthed from a hidden mine on the mountain. And according to this same lore, the man who found this stone was a miner looking for garnet deposits deep in the abandoned mines of the mountain. Ervin Fiskle was his name.

Fiskle, 44, was the youngest of four deceased brothers and a sister, Paige. He lived as a recluse in the woods of Underhill. For even when the days grew bitterly cold and the nights, impossibly long, Fiskle rarely sought out the company of his fellow man and woman. The few townsfolk whom had encountered Fiskle described him as being somewhat quiet and well spoken for a man of the far wood. He frequently explored the mountain on his lonesome, having discovered several small unofficial, non-commissioned mines amid its base and vast wood. He thought that they were most likely the work of treasure hunters and prospectors from older generations.

On October 20th, 2105, the day in which he supposedly discovered the fabled stone, later dubbed "Equilibrium," witnesses described a flash and thunder echo across much of northern Vermont. A prolonged series of tremors shook much of the republic, where eyewitness accounts varied from small objects falling from shelves in Milton, to men being thrown like ragdolls in nearby Stowe. Regardless, the majority of residents in Northern and Central Vermont would recall where they were and what they were doing on that fateful day. Fiskle himself, wary of the blue glow from within the mountain seam, felt this thunder from deep within the mountain, and thought, with each subsequent tremor, that he was that much closer to death.

It was a gorgeous rock, equilibrium: half its body was a sky blue, and the other half an earthen brown, with a band of white separating the two. Perfectly spherical in shape and barely larger than the size of a closed fist, the stone glowed unnaturally. He carried it from its place of origin among the mountain's seam, wrapped it in a small gunnysack, and departed for his cabin.

It's said that the night of his discovery, as he attempted sleep, Fiskle was visited by a spirit, and told to bring the stone where he had found it. This visitor took the form of a scarecrow, and demanded that the stone be returned by the next sunset, or else he and Underhill would reap disastrous consequences. He assumed this to be a device of his own madness. Undeterred, Fiskle kept the stone well hidden under his bed, ignoring the spirit's pleas.

Within days, the folks of Underhill and the surrounding communities began to notice a strange occurrence. The land moaned and buckled. The air rumbled for hours on end. The mountains themselves grew on both sides, creating a circle of incredibly high cliff ridges. Most light could not penetrate the deep shadows enveloping the town. This all happened over the course of two weeks, as residents from neighboring Stowe, Jericho, Westford and other communities watched much of Underhill disappear from sight. Fiskle, horrified of the wrath that he had unleashed, told only his sister, Paige, of this stone, which was later named Equilibrium by the monks after they researched its origins. His sister, ever the voice of reason, advised her brother to give up the possession immediately. Still, Fiskle refused to part with his stone, lamenting that it was some sort of treasure meant for him to find and him only.

Undoubtedly, his inexplicable love for the stone spelled his certain doom. It is said that one day soon thereafter, as he admired it, even in the near utter darkness of Underhill, the ground underneath him uplifted suddenly and violently skyward. Fiskle found himself being propelled upwards at an alarming rate. He then saw, with utter alarm, that he sat atop a spire no wider than two arm spans. When he came to his senses, he estimated himself to be at least several hundred feet off the ground or more. It was difficult to tell. With no way of getting down, or anyone from Underhill immediately aware of his plight, Fiskle slowly withered away atop the cold, black spire. He died in a matter of five days from exposure and hypothermia. Afterwards, it was said that for an entire hour, every bird in Underhill converged upon the spire to feast upon Fiskle's corpse, bones and all. A thousand birds and bugs filled the sky above the spire, adding a dark, ominous tone to an already dread-filled town. Yet, the stone remain untouched and unmoved. And it was there that the legend of the Fiskle Cliff was born.

The day prior to Inepticus's impending leap from the Fiskle Cliff, both father and son occupied the home's basement carefully planning out the cursed son's attempt at flight. A rocking chair still stirred from where Danario had just sat, as the father paced the room nervously, stewing in troubled thought. A pair of snipped pigtails sat unceremoniously at the base of an adjacent sink; Inepticus's meager attempt at enhancing his aerodynamics

"Take my wings," ordered Danario from the depths of his workshop, as he emerged from the darkened room adjacent to the main workshop with an unfamiliar pair of platinum wings draped over his shoulder. They looked sleek and powerful, though heavier than his very own.

"*Your* wings? *You* have made wings? But what of *mine*?" replied Inepticus in surprise, as he pointed to his own wings lying before him on the work table. "Father, I have labored greatly in building these wings for many a fortnight. I have studied the hawks during hunts. I have scavenged wood and materials for years, perfectly suitable for the construction of flight. You know this, father, for you have seen me toil. Have you not?"

His father rubbed his eyes. "Inepticus, it pains me to say this, it really does. But as your father, I feel but no choice. I promised myself that the next time you attempted flight; I'd rather have you use my wings than your blunder-ridden rubbish. At first, I thought it very foolish, for a busy man such as myself has better things to tend than to build a pair of wings for his dimwitted son, incapable of flight. But as flawed as you may be, I still love and care for you, Inepticus, for you are my son. So I beg you to use my wings. I'm more skilled and experienced in crafting, just as I am more skilled in understanding unique methods of delivery."

"But what of *mine*, father?" pleaded Inepticus, desperately.

He looked upon his wings wistfully. He had even inscribed his name on the wooden frame that very morning. In fact, the carving knife still rested nearby on a workbench.

"I will keep them safe and cared for, and you can still be proud of them, son. Until the day I see you fly in my wings, you shall not use your own, spare the foolish hill jump if it so pleases."

Inepticus glared hard at his father's platinum and silver wings. Its wax paper surface seemed too thick, and his use of wood heavy was in sheer contrast to Inepticus's design.

"Father, I've waited all of my life for a day like this. My wings are all that I have trust in, all that I have to show for…"

"Foolish boy," interrupted Danario. "We're talking of life and death. The Fiskle Cliff is no mere hill jump to the Pomfret's. It drops two thousand feet or more into a darkened abyss. You must navigate towards the top of the black spire, which is no more than a dozen feet wide, and clutch with you this sphere, this equilibrium, in a split second. And then, in order to safely navigate your way down, Inepticus, you must find the proper wind currents to propel you to cliff's edge or land safely on the sunken land of Underhill and pray for rescue. The Gods must be heavily in your favor on such a task. Though I can attest, wholeheartedly, they have not been so kind to you thus far."

"But father…"

"I can change my mind at a moment's notice," chided Danario with the wag of his finger. "Consider it a privilege then, Inepticus, that I am even allowing this insanity to go on in the first place. Lord Henry, bless his heart, is entrusting you with this sacred undertaking, and though I think it a sham, a travesty of logic, I will support my son *and* the republic. I will therefore cheer you on as a feller of trees cheers on his fallen bounty."

Inepticus missed the barb, nodding reluctantly. "Then I will do my best to serve you and our beloved republic, father. Though I'm wary of these new, mysterious wings, which you have bestowed upon me at a moment's notice, I will oblige. I will travel with you, Henry and Flatlander at the week's end to tackle this Fiskle Cliff, and then you will see that I am not a worm of a son. Then maybe you'll see, father."

Danario promptly scooped up Inepticus's wings, and placed them back onto a pair of hangers embedded in the wall. Inepticus gave them one final, mournful look, as a father would impart on his wayward son, now squandered of his glorious potential.

Danario sighed. "One can only hope, Inepticus. One can only hope."

The party left shortly after the break of dawn and ascended Mansfield's massive face, mere specks on its barren tracts of land. The caravan of hikers included Flatlander, Henry, Inepticus, Danario, and two high monks: a young man from Middlebury named Zachus, and the other, an older fellow from Braintree, Helphon. Supplies were carried en masse with two of Danario's trusty mules; manpower and knapsacks were used to haul the rest. Zachus brought a single lamb guided by leash, which was to be sacrificed in homage to the gods of the mountain, a rare yet important gesture derived from the traditions of Braintree.

Zachus had dirty blonde hair, and sparkling blue eyes, and at 28, was young for the monkhood of Middlebury. He had risen quickly through the ranks of his brethren. Respected for his thorough research on the rivers of Vermont, Zachus was sometimes dubbed the 'River Monk.' Seen as a visionary by his peers, Zachus's ideas ranged from hydroelectricity, to proposed canals, to improvements on the aqueducts, to controlled flooding to fertilizing farmland. He was chosen to assist in overcoming the Fiskle Cliff for his young legs and strong mind, both kind assets on such a quest. Short and nimble, his beard patchy and weak, and a green robe sagged loose on his body.

Helphon, all of sixty years of age and counting, had grown up most of his life in Underhill before joining the brotherhood in Braintree, and two of his siblings and their respective families lay currently lost in shadow. As such, he was knowledgeable in the layout of Stowe, Underhill, and Cambridge, for they had all been called home at various times. Helphon was chosen for knowledge of Mansfield, including that of the prevailing winds, which circulated around its summit day and night. Though old and wrinkled, Helphon was quite strong for his age. His beard, which reached down to his bellybutton, had grown a distinguished charm, of which he had cultivated for twenty years.

Flatlander's main task was to carry sufficient kindling for the sacrificial fire. For there was little time to spare when the group summited, much less find suitable firewood in the wet, cold alpines of the highest reaches of the mountain. It sounded simple enough when Henry had revealed his role. Yet the oversized bundle of firewood smacking on Flatlander's lower back reminded him, with each passing step that it was more of an undertaking than he had assumed.

There was ungodly tension in the wind. Flatlander felt it with every leap and bound past boulders and narrow, mountain streams. The march felt more like a funeral procession, thought Flatlander, as he studied Zachus and Helphon walking solemnly, side by side, gliding up the slopes smoothly as if ghosts.

Inepticus struck him as strange: his bowl cut bobbed with each stride, and his tattered magenta tunic and sandals were ill suited for the near-freezing temperatures of Mansfield. The young man held, with great discomfort, the wings in which he bore up the steep mountain trails. The boy's talk and demeanor suggested that he was in his teens, yet Flatlander was surprised to find out that Inepticus was twenty-five. Disturbingly thin, thought Flatlander, Ineprticus's pointy, bare elbows reminded him of a body part that he'd more likely see on a bird. *Hopefully that will help him today*, he thought optimistically. He likened his company to a boy amongst men.

The winds then became heavy, as a cold front pushed through the northern reaches of the republic towards Montreal, the Great City of the North. Yet despite the less than favorable conditions, Danario and Inepticus held steadfast that today would be their day of judgment. Lord Henry, ever the source of stories and good-humored ribbings had fallen deathly quiet during their hike. No matter the efforts he made to appear relaxed and confident, Henry's eyes betrayed troubled thoughts.

When they finally summited, after a grueling four-hour affair, the group set up camp and started a fire amongst a cluttering of stones arranged in a semi-circle. Zachus blessed the fire with a branch from Braintree, the sacred wood, which when fully engulfed, burned an eerie green. Helphon removed the sheep from plain sight, only to return with its lifeless remains, limp and dangling over his shoulder. He proceeded to skin the animal and fillet it with knife and hook. Water was boiled from the mule-carried bucket, filled from a mountain stream, and boiled with the fungal tea of the Chaga. The lamb was skewered, glazed with the finest honey of Middlebury, and cooked for all. Inepticus took little for himself, for in his mind, every ounce gained counted against his favor. While the others ate, the boy viewed the vast depths of the cliffs in dismay.

When all had finished their lamb and Chaga, Zachus and Helphon recited incantations to the group, the dialogue alternating oddly between Zachus's melodic voice and Helphon's raspy speech, as follows:

Helphon: May the wind sail smooth and your wings hold true.
Zachus: The republic as one. All hopes on you.
Helphon: Inepticus, of Stowe, while all Underhill's in woe.
Zachus: These blessings we bring from tower and tree:
Helphon and Zachus: Go!

The group then cheered the hero Inepticus, and accompanied him to the edge of the Fiskle Cliff. Upon arriving at the precipice, Danario inspected the craftsmanship of his wings and looked his son straight in the eye.

"If you should fall, Inepticus, fall like the leaf and not the stone."

"I shall make you proud," replied Inepticus in a choked voice.

"Shall that be as such, Inepticus? One can only hope," replied Danario, as he patted his son on the shoulder. "May the northerly winds carry you safely home, son."

Flatlander gazed upon the darkened spire, emerging from the abyss like a twisted needle. Its surface gleamed smooth, though several cruel twists and knots interrupted the otherwise uniform shaft. Father and son embraced amongst their onlookers, all shook hands in good luck, and then Danario took a tentative step back. Creeping close to the edge of the precipice, Inepticus froze in place like a statue, looking out into the abyss where Underhill lay.

Its depth looked impossibly vast, as Flatlander could barely make out the outlines of several buildings and structures along the cliff's base, catching a small angle of the sun's rays. Using his light sandals, specially crafted and donated by the merchants of The Brattle, Inepticus gently brushed a patch of gravel over the cliff's edge, testing for a firm foothold. His platinum coated wings reflected the closest cumulus clouds and blue skies into a series of grey refractions. He sucked his finger, and pointed to the heavens, testing for the prevailing wind. Pointing north, Inepticus exchanged a nod of approval from Helphon, whom himself was testing the winds by dangling a loose string from a steady, wooden spool.

"Say a prayer for the man, Flatlander, for if nothing else, his courage is unrivaled," muttered Henry.

Flatlander gazed upon the poised messenger's son, who was now spreading a delayed adhesive created by Fedor the Alchemist to his hand in order to tether the spire's stone effectively upon contact. Flatlander thought of a prayer, but his mind drew a blank. Rather, he generated an image in his mind of Inetpicus's flight being a success, as he stood triumphantly among the free citizens of Underhill, equilibrium firmly within his clutches.

They waited and they watched, and for some time all that passed was the faint howling of the wind. Then, in a sudden rush of movement, Inepticus spread his wings wide like a startled heron, and leapt. He dropped fast, as if thrown downward by an invisible force prompting gasps from Henry and Danario, and a startled silence from the rest. About three hundred feet down, Inepticus was then pushed from the cliff's sheer walls, and aimed his torso directly for the top of the black spire. Flatlander was surprised to see how fast the boy traveled, for in no time, he looked little more than a hawk hunting the plush valleys for game.

Lord Henry spoke Flatlander's mind. "Goodness. Man has achieved flight. He moves like the birds."

"He has mastered the winds thus far, like Wuchowsen[82]," observed Helphon.

"I cannot believe the speed," muttered Flatlander, astonished. Even in the distance, Inepticus spanned the abyss incredibly fast, his wings barely beating.

Danario remained silent, lips pursed, as he settled a cautious eye on his son's soaring form, his platinum wings sparkling in the distance. Inepticus was locked into his target and gaining on it with tremendous velocity.

But the group's excitement quickly turned to horror, as Inepticus was blown hard upwards by a stray tailwind, knocking him far off course, as he grossly overshot the dreaded spire. By the time Inepticus recovered, he was hurtling perilously close to the opposite cliff wall, turning just in time to avoid a large outcropping.

"No, Inepticus!" yelled out Danario, instinctively.

Inepticus regained his control, yet it was clear that scraping the top of the spire was no longer a possibility, for he now flew a hundred feet or more below its zenith. Unless saved by miracle, Inepticus had missed his opportunity. He circled around the abyss in a wide, controlled arc. Zachus's held the binoculars with trembling hands, as he observed a troubling sight directly in Inepticus's flight path: a flock of geese in a V formation.

"Turn, Inepticus!" commanded Zachus from across the gorge. "Turn, for pity's sake!"

Yet Inepticus couldn't hear a thing save the autumn wind roaring past his ears at a near-deafening pitch. He struck a goose on the edge of the formation blindly with his right wing, killing the bird instantly upon impact, but also ripping his wing thoroughly. He twisted and turned out of control, plummeting

[82] The god of wind in Abenaki lore.

violently towards the floor of the abyss like a fallen rag. The group of onlookers cursed in sheer terror, as Flatlander averted his eyes from the tragic scene. Danario recoiled from cliff's edge, and fell to his knees in despair, physically sickened by the sight of his failed son.

"Curse Fiskle, every bit of 'em," muttered Bailey Payne, looking well past her forty-two years of age, as Underhill's bitter lookout positioned herself uncomfortably in a braided hammock.

Her eyes sunk deep; her face was pale and lifeless. The observer's cheekbones jutted out beneath her eyes like the stones of the Browns River, the once-strong tributary that use to grace this now-forsaken land.

Bailey watched the brim of the cliffs from atop a hill in the backyard of her home, as she had done every day from noon until dinner. It was her assigned duty. She often watched for any signs of Lord Haque's people, who would protrude a large group of branches from cliff's edge, like darkened lettering amongst the skylight of the valley. Each shape communicated to the people of Underhill a different supply they were furnishing. A sphere meant more food, a cube represented drinking water, a wooden-cross signified medical supplies, and a star shape meant that oil and firewood were on their way. Shortly after, heavy crates outfitted with silk parachutes, compliments of Stowe, or other neighbors, fell gracefully from the sky in troves. And Bailey's job, appointed to her by Lord Desmairis, was to alert the townsfolk and bark out one of the four symbols attached the branch, while simultaneously ringing a large bronze bell.

In recent months, the branches had appeared less and less, and far fewer crates had fallen from the skies. As a result, Underhill's supplies had dwindled rapidly. Bailey's hopes dimmed, and she'd often find herself prone to excessive sleep as a means to forget her plight.

Light did weird things in Underhill, reflected Bailey, as she gazed to the edge of the darkened cliffs. The way it shifted on the cliff walls and focused in certain areas in focused beams. Traces of light still found its way into town, but it often resembled the gloom of twilight. Her eyes had adjusted to this fate, as had all of Underhill's residents.

Nearby, Bailey's four daughters played in the yard under the gentle glow of several candle-lit lanterns, firmly encased in thick glass to prevent a fire in this now-arid land. The rivers had dried up or had been directed elsewhere by the sudden uplift of land: the Browns River, Cranes Brook, Mill Brook, and Stephenson Brook had all but vanished, their river beds now comprised of nothing more than a brittle, dry clay and smoothed stones. Her daughters, though malnourished and scared, still found time to pass the days and enjoy themselves as best they could. Bailey smiled at the sight.

As she considered her plans for preparing their meager supplies for dinner, a peculiar sight appeared overhead from the cliff's highest reaches. An extremely large bird darted from the edge of the cliffs towards the black spire at the center of town. Bailey peered at the animal intently through her binoculars, toggling its lens for better focus. Its movements looked unnatural and clumsy. She toggled the lens further. Then, for a split second, Bailey caught a glimpse of what was clearly a human outline.

"A man!" she barked loudly to anyone within earshot. "A man takes flight for the stone! People, look! One has come to our rescue!"

As groups of neighbors collected at her side, Bailey followed the flying man's movements closely, as he arced around the spire in a huge, sweeping circle. Her daughters stopped their playtime in the yard, and ran to their mother's side with hopeful grins. But then something went wrong. *Terribly wrong.* On the man's next come around, he collided with a formation of geese, tearing a hole in one of his wings. He began tumbling towards the bottom of Underhill like a shot duck. Bailey gasped; her binoculars now felt too heavy to bear. The observer halted her watch and rung the bell repeatedly.

"Oh, curses! He has fallen! A flying man has fallen from the sky, a half mile due west of the spire!"

They stood there under the shade of scraggly ash tree, all in memory of Inepticus. His burial plot was modest in both size and appearance, wedged between two large, cubed, granite mausoleums. Two dozen people came to Stowe to pay their homage, despite the fact that many of them felt obliged, for they had other important duties to attend: birthday parties, weekly gossip at the markets, the lumberjack games. The list was truly endless. Still, those gathered on that fine, autumn day came so for Inepticus's sake and the sake of his family.

From a behind a row of tombstones came forth a monk, Father Clive Orton; dressed in the customary garb of the monks; the green robe and hood of Braintree. A neck chain constructed of beads and slate from the Connecticut River hung from his neck, the same rock used for the construction of the wall in his hometown, the southeastern border town of Guilford. In his youth, Father Orton had helped construct parts of the wall like many other young men as a means to earn extra money. He was a man of medium build; his hair was a greyish brown and well kept. His beard was trim and even, as streaks of grey ran their course across his chin like spider webs. Orton's strangest feature, though, were his eyes. They shone a bright green.

Flatlander sat apart from Inepticus's family, though he was close enough to be within earshot of their conversations. Some spoke of looking forward to attending the lumberjack festival after the funeral. Others, he overheard, were rattling off the names of the gravestones which they had passed on their way. The visitors recited many old, yet familiar names, which had been cemented into Stowe's unique history. Few spoke of the passing of Inepticus.

And yet, there was the young man's name engraved sloppily onto a slab of sandstone, carved into the shape of his favorite bird, the hawk. Underneath it read: *Here lies Inepticus: You Almost Made it.* Flatlander thought of the epitaph as odd. He regretted deeply the fact that they had never retrieved the young man's body, which was now certainly rendered unrecognizable at the foot of the Fiskle Cliff. Rather, a model wooden hawk occupied Inepticus's coffin in his stead.

Father Orton cleared his throat. "Welcome all and thank you for making it. I stand before you today, humbled to speak, and grateful to pay tribute to one of the Gods' loving children. Blessed are those whom dignify the deceased, such as you, with whom in this woeful time of mourning and distress, hold one another tight in the loving memory of Inepticus. I welcome you in light, in love, and in blessings. Good tidings to all."

Father Orton paused then his face pinched tight with emotion. "Oh Inepticus! As your lifeless corpse fluttered through the sky like a maple seedling, twisting, turning, spinning and wheeling, like a spoiled bird of death, as you still lay writhing, imbedded awkwardly in a crag amongst the mountain, as a detached goose beak still likely remained, punctured within your wing, crushed by impact with the wall, ravaged by carrion, your body became nothing more than a churned, dismembered slither of bacon crashing to the canyon floor...think not of the gruesome details of his death, but more so, the loving spirit of this young man."

Flatlander exchanged a curious look with Lord Henry.

Orton continued: "Inepticus, you were a loving son and brother. For when your brother, Robert, asked for some help once moving into his new bedroom upstairs, you were unremitting in your efforts to assist."

Enchantment cleared her throat. "Actually, that was Garret."

"But *surely*, Inepticus must have promised to lend a helping hand?" inquired Father Orton.

"No," replied his family in unison.

Orton sighed. "Yet he *would* have. Would he not?"

"That's certainly debatable," spoke Danario. "His excuse was that he needed to do homework, yet not a book was to be found in his room that night; only sketches of birds. That was all."

Father Orton quickly tried to change direction of the eulogy. "Nevertheless, Inepticus died a hero. Soaring amongst the heavens in which he dreamt of traversing as a boy, capable of a profound innocence, yet also a fierce determination when faced with incredible odds. Oh, sweet Inepticus! Raise your tattered wings once again, yet this time, they will be held aloft on the Gods' shoulders: for They, and only They, can bear this blessed weight. All burdens. All sorrow. All joy and love. For only They will show you the light in the darkest of the night."

"Inepticus had bad vision," interjected Robert. "Lights oftentimes confused him."

Father Orton ignored the interruption. "Then let Them take your confused, wandering soul, and take you to a steady path to the lands beyond this physical realm..."

"Inepticus wasn't good with paths, never stayed on them. Always got lost," mumbled Garret, to nobody in particular. The family unanimously voiced their agreement.

Father Orton was lost for patience. "Stop it! All of you! This is a funeral and you are Inepticus's family! Have you no mercy?" said Father Orton. The crowd of mourners shrugged with indifference.

Father Orton collected himself, shook his head, and continued: "Fine. So be it. Inepticus. Son of Danario. Brother of Enchantment, Garret, and Robert. The dreamer of Stowe. Hawk of the valley. May your soul soar to new heights among the heavens. May the wind, from here on out always be at your back, and the prize clear within sight. For you are Inepticus, and your wings will never be forgotten. Equilibrium may yet remain aloft on its impossible perch, but alas, your death was not in vain."

The family got up and began to leave before Father Orton had even finished his last sentence. Flatlander watched the Inepticus's parents and siblings in disgust. *Inepticus had died a hero.* It was plain to see. To what fault had Inepticus lived his life, so that his death was mere routine to his family, their emotions buried just like their fallen brethren? He could not leave the cemetery like this; there was something that needed to be said to them before parting.

He caught up with Danario near the shade of a large cubic tombstone. "Mister Danario, you have my condolences. I can't imagine your pain."

The older gentlemen turned around, and eyed Flatlander courteously. "Many thanks, Flatlander. And I appreciate you assisting us on Mansfield. It's with heavy heart that I lay my son to rest."

"And yet I can plainly see that this was no hero's burial," said Flatlander, as he briefly glanced back at the fresh, yet now-abandoned burial site. "Not a single member of his family spoke kindly on his behalf."

"The boy had been cautioned of flying for years, Flatlander, an absurd fantasy for a sedentary soul. It was a fool's whim from the start."

Flatlander turned a beet red. "Your son died a hero, sir, trying to save Underhill, trying to assist the republic, trying to make his family proud for once in his life."

Danario smirked. "Powerful words coming from a man who knows little to nothing of our land and of our ways. You met him but once yet you speak of him as if he were a brother."

Flatlander held his tongue, fuming. Danario turned to join his three living children, who were now readying their father's small armada of delivery horses, mail baskets still in tow. *How could a family be so cruel to its very own? So emotionless? So vapid? They hadn't even made the time or effort to disband their horses from their mail carrying gear.*

"I wonder, do you still carry your son's wings, Mister Danario?" asked Flatlander.

Danario turned from his task of readying his carriage. His three children looked on in amusement. "I suppose. And what would you want with those hideous things?"

"I would like to purchase them from you." Flatlander looked at the master herald with a look of determination.

"Why in the world would you want…" began Danario, until full realization had dawned. "No…you don't mean to…please tell me that it is not what I suspect…"

Flatlander confirmed Danario's suspicions. "Did your son not study the laws of aviation half of his natural life?"

The stockier of the two sons, Garret, called out from inside the carriage. "Don't be a fool, Flatlander."

Danario nodded and pointed in the general direction of Mount Mansfield. "Did you not see my son's gruesome death upon the Fiskle Cliff, Flatlander? You were right there with me. Were you not? Simply watching birds fly did not magically make Inepticus a bird, and you watching Inepticus, even less so."

"Maybe so, but rumor has it that *you* had constructed those wings for Inepticus. The ones in which he had used for *his* task. Is that true?"

Danario's glared hard at Flatlander and his nostrils flared. Slamming a stack of filled envelopes into the carriage, he drew close to Flatlander.

"I miss your meaning."

"I mean to use his wings to tackle the Fiskle Cliff," answered Flatlander. "My only request is this: if I should succeed, you must return to this grave on the following morn, and beg for forgiveness from your son for your callousness, and place his own wings upon his own grave."

"And if you don't make it?" countered Danario.

"Then it will all be for nothing."

"I don't believe what I'm hearing," he heard Robert marvel from the backseat of the carriage.

Danario scoffed. "Then I shall meet you here on the day of this supposed flight in the same fashion as my befallen son. For if *my* wings steered a man wrong, I can only imagine my son's in midflight. I caution you to think on the matter before you go, Flatlander. Though you upset me, no more blood needs to be shed for the lost memory of Underhill."

Flatlander listened to Danario's plea, and for a heartbeat, surely felt, as Inepticus must have during past conversations with his father. His father looked tired. Large, purplish bags lined his eyes, as his tunic rippled gently in the breeze.

"When can I get the wings?"

"I'm a delivery man by title, so there are plenty of means. I will have his wings to you by sunrise tomorrow. But I pray, Flatlander," said Danario, as he collected himself. "I pray that you think clearly and reconsider such a bold move."

Flatlander nodded, yet remained steadfast. "I want the wings by sunrise tomorrow."

He then left Danario and his family, and joined Lord Henry, whom was waiting patiently by his mare, Bella, chewing on a straw of hay. Flatlander stormed by the Humble King in a huff. Figuring that something in the conversation had gone astray, Henry followed closely behind. Flatlander mounted his horse and gripped the reins tight. And though Lord Henry cast several curious questions pertaining to his conversation with Danario, Flatlander kept mum on the details until they reached the border of Montpelier. It was then that Lord Henry's subsequent yell of surprise could be felt more than heard.

The hospital bed was empty where Franklin had once rested, its white satin sheets neatly made, and a white pillow rested unkempt by its headboard. The get-well gifts, which had once been assembled atop a small wooden desk nearby, were now gone. In their stead, an immaculately presented fruit bowl shone in the morning sun. Flatlander paused at the doorway, feeling a sense of dread, as an unfamiliar, heavyset nurse strolled in from an adjacent bathroom.

"He's gone, dear," the nurse said.

Flatlander stammered. "But..."

"No, no, no," the nurse interrupted quickly. "I mean he's been released. Went back home to Montpelier. Just yesterday, Mr. Flatlander."

Flatlander sighed in relief. "Oh, thank goodness."

"Quite a feisty one he is," remarked the nurse with a smirk. "Nearly tore through here when we gave him the clearance to leave."

"Sounds like the Franklin I know," quipped Flatlander, as he wiped a bead of sweat from his brow. "Thank you."

As Flatlander turned to leave, the nurse's voice called out. "Oh, and uh, Mr. Flatlander?"

Flatlander turned. "Yes?"

"I think it's real special what you've done so far for the republic, I really do," said the nurse with a smile, "even if some people don't like you."

"Thanks," he replied as he blushed slightly, "that means a lot."

The nurse hesitated. "Franklin told me about you and the Fiskle Cliff. Please, be careful. I'd hate to see you end up here like your friend or worse."

Feeling a momentary sense of irritation, Flatlander thought better of it and remained quiet. Though he disliked the idea that Franklin and the nurse were talking so candidly about his eventual fate, he supposed they had legitimate concerns. Franklin had been most likely informed by an outside party, most likely Henry. And it didn't sound like the northerner was pleased at the quest's prospects, just as any true friend would.

Flatlander nodded. "My gratitude for the concerns and for looking after my friend, Nurse, um."

"Nora."

"Nora."

Flatlander left the hospital joyful despite himself. His friend was healthy again. Arriving back in Montpelier in the late afternoon, Lord Henry updated Flatlander on a few small matters concerning Franklin, the senate, and a recently signed apology letter from Shay Bromage, expressing his regrets from publishing several previous articles regarding Flatlander. When Flatlander inquired of Franklin's whereabouts, Henry told him that he was out back, near the tree trunk in which Flatlander had once pulled his sword the stump.

As Flatlander made his way towards the woods in the backyard, he could hear repeated thunderous impacts every five to ten seconds. Vaguely, he made out the figure of Franklin, moving about in the forest like a wild bear. In his hands, he wielded his heavy, wooden axe as if it were a light stick. He had been striking at trees, practicing his battle skills. As Franklin heard Flatlander approach, he took a brief reprieve from his vicious onslaught.

"If it ain't the man himself!" said Franklin with a broad smile.

"Franklin!" exclaimed Flatlander, as the two briefly embraced.

"Heard about yer dealins' wit the lake monster and Babakiss. Proud of ya, kid."

"Honorable exploits, I suppose," joked Flatlander.

Franklin smirked. "Ya haven't lost it, have ya? Almost to where ya wanna be. Ten's the blink of an eye away."

Flatlander scanned his friend for any remaining injuries. A tender scar, dealt from where the guardian had struck him, still lined the brute's cheek and chin.

"How are you feeling?"

"Better than a bride on the superpac," stated Franklin, as he swung his axe hard into the bark of a nearby pine. "Thanks fer askin'."

"You sure it's wise what you're doing? I mean, you just left the hospital two days ago."

"You betcha it is," interrupted Franklin, through heavy breaths. "Need to get the blood flowin' through the veins again. Ain't no better way than swingin' the ol' friend here."

Flatlander nodded and smiled. It would be a losing battle, he recognized, trying to convince Franklin to rest. It wasn't in the man's nature. The evidence was right there in the various stumps and trees in the immediate area, utterly butchered, as divots sunk deep in their trunks, and splintered wood protruded from their wounds like sharpened teeth. Bark littered the forest floor, now reduced to yard scrap.

Franklin took several more strikes then threw his axe on the ground emphatically. "Hearin' yer taking the plunge? The Fiskle Cliff, I mean."

Flatlander regarded the subject guardedly. Franklin's face revealed little emotion, and he probed the northerner's face for any hint of emotion.

"You could say that."

Franklin shook his head. "Not a thing to be takin' lightly, if ya don't mind me sayin' so. Can't say I approve."

Flatlander looked at the ground. "So I hear."

"How'd ya hear *that*?" Franklin asked to his friend, dumbfounded.

Flatlander smirked. "I was told."

Franklin grunted. "Musta been that Nora, quite a mouth on that one."

"But she's sweet and took good care of you," said Flatlander, as he rubbed at his temple. "Franklin, it's something that I've gotta do. I'm not expecting you to understand."

Franklin glared at his friend. "Why?"

"Because I've felt drawn to this quest from the beginning, more so than any other. And if I don't do this, Franklin, I don't think that anyone will. Underhill needs our help or they'll fall deeper into shadow."

Franklin smacked Flatlander hard on the shoulders. "Won't be the only thing fallin' into shadow. C'mon Flatlander. Yer too smart fer this. Ya been here too short. Hate to admit this, fella, but the gang here's become quite fond of ya. Would be a shame if ya were to go out like that. Smashed on the rocks and all."

"Thanks for the visual," joked Flatlander.

"It ain't just a visual, ya fool," replied Franklin with a scowl. "It's yer reality if ya don't turn yer back while ya still can."

"What about *you*, Franklin?" Flatlander rebuked. "You say that I'm the crazy one, but you're usually the first to rush headfirst into danger any chance you get. *You* know that and *I* know that."

Franklin dismissed the notion with a wave of his hand. "There's a difference between bein' brave and bein' stupid, Flatlander. Chargin' into battle and jumpin' off cliffs ain't the same. What yer doin' is as stupid as a frog with sideburns."

"You're not going to change my mind," declared Flatlander. "Thank you. But a promise is a promise. I leave in two days."

"Well, then, remember this," called out Franklin, clearly winded, as he sat on a well-carved tree stump. "Even 'em hardest warriors know fear, Flatlander. They know when the tides of battle change, ya know. When to fight and when to flee. When to die and when to live. I never told ya this, but I'm an outcast of the Northern Kingdom, run amuck on a botched assassination attempt n' Lowell. Throwin' down my axe in Lowell all those years ago was one of the hardest things I done, but I'm alive now because of it. And no matter of what ya think since, I ain't plannin' on dyin' any time soon."

"Inepticus tried it too."

"Inepticus is also a dead man," barked Franklin.

Flatlander held the northerner's gaze. "I know that. I just left his funeral, Franklin."

Franklin sighed. "Which says as much fer yer wits…"

"Look. You've been a good friend. One day, I hope you understand," said Flatlander, as he patted his friend gently on the shoulder.

It took every last bit of effort not to cry, as he turned and walked away. Flatlander left his tired friend sitting on the stump, winded from both a spirited exercise and his heartfelt discussion. A lump caught in Flatlander's throat. His heart was heavy and his head was spinning. Franklin's dire warning was a cause for concern, thought Flatlander. Even Lord Henry had given him more than enough outs to avoid this quest, reflected Flatlander; perhaps it was not too late?

Dawn shuffled through the pages of her husband's first publication in over a month, holding onto his every written word as if it were his first. She had picked up a copy of the Shay Chronicles from a local grocery shop. Her heart skipped a beat as she gazed upon the cover; a picture of a single brown and tan striped feather surrounded by white, the republic's accepted symbol for offering apology. Simple, thought Dawn, yet brilliant. *Shay hadn't lost his poetic edge.*

Shay was a blowhard, sure, but he was a damn good reporter and she knew it. Dawn had casually noted to her colleagues earlier in the day that she missed her husband's column almost as much as the man himself. And though she said this with good humor in her voice, those close to Dawn knew this to be a façade. The split pained her deeply. She hoped, for his own sake, that his addiction to superpac was just a phase, nothing more. The man had more talent than he knew what to do with. She missed Shay. Life simply just wasn't the same without the love of her life present.

The apology in Shay's publication read as follows:

> "Dear loved ones, resentful ones, bitter ones, and those indifferent- I write these words with tears in my eyes, an odd first for a man who has written over 20,000 pages of newspapers in his career, traveled 20,000 miles, interviewed over 3,000 men and women, and who has the calloused fingers and beaten mule to prove it."

Dawn bumped accidentally into a man walking his dog, and mumbled an apology, all the while intent on continuing her husband's column.

> "I have sinned. I have sinned worse than anyone I know. In fact, if my powers equaled that of the great Vergil himself, I would rid myself of temptation, for that's where my folly belied all these years. But temptation, as we have come to know throughout the history of humankind, has yielded tremendous power in the lives of quite ordinary people. In truth, my problems began well before my addiction to the awful drug known as superpac. They began with my unrealistic pursuit of perfection, and my suppressing of certain elements of my past, which have now resurfaced with terrible implications."

At the entrance to her office building, Dawn fumbled for her office keys tucked deep in her pocket with one hand, while simultaneously reading the apology in the other. She dropped the keys into a small puddle, cursing under her breath, and continued reading on with renewed focus.

> "The truth is, I am a Flatlander. I am a former superpac addict. I am a flawed perfectionist. I am the biggest hypocrite and fraud to walk the lands of Vermont, and to which no editor can help smooth out in a series of revisions. I am all these things, and worse. I'm a bad husband to my loving wife, Dawn. I am a bad boss. An intellectual of the worst kind, for I put my need to sound clever above the civil duties of my humanity. I have been all of these things and worse, and as such, I have lost much. Now, I can only beg for your forgiveness."

Tears began to well up in Dawn's eyes, despite her best intentions of keeping her composure. She couldn't believe what she was reading. Never before in her life had she perceived her husband as being so vulnerable, so rattled, so humbled; yet, so honest. Dawn unlocked the front door of her office building and continued up the main stairwell, the newspaper rattling in her trembling hands.

"Never again will I take so much for granted. Never again will I belittle the very people who make this republic and its people so very special. Never again will I use Superpac to further my career. Never again. Never again will I belittle my wife. Never again will I curse the Flatlander's name for the sake of sheer hypocrisy if nothing else. Never again will I stir the ancient forces of this republic that I work so very hard to protect. Never again.

I, Shay Bromage, apologize for all of the pain that I have inflicted. I stand humbled and ask for your forgiveness.

With deepest regrets.
Yours Truly
Shay Bromage

The tears now came freely now, slipping down Dawn's cheeks as she stumbled into her office, her head cupped tightly in her palms. Dawn dropped the newspaper to the floor, sobbing heavily. They were tears of pain and joy, mixed with a touch of anxiety over what the future would bring to her and Shay. She found herself yearning for the man, for she knew the apology to be sincere.

"I presume you're caught up on the news?" came a familiar voice from within the hallway of her offices.

Dawn quickly glanced up into the face of her husband, who was smirking heavily, wearing his custom plaid jacket. He looked clean-shaven and well rested, his glasses polished to perfection, refracting the faint office light. He held a small bouquet of roses, tied together with yellow twine. His ponytail looked sleek and well kept. Dawn brushed away a falling tear from her cheek and stood there silently, unable to formulate the words.

"Shay, I..."

"Turns out I'm not so perfect, after all, love," said Shay with a wink and a smile, before his face grew flat with sincerity. "I'm so sorry for all that I've done to you, Dawn. Will you have me back?"

"I miss you," was all Dawn could muster, before she approached her disgraced husband in a hurried jog. The two embraced for a long, long time in the confines of the *Burlington Daily*. Very little was spoken, and with Shay's public apology lay splayed out on the office floor, no more needed to be said.

The summit must be yours to face alone. Henry's words reverberated in Flatlander's head as he gazed upon Mount Mansfield from its base. He pleaded for Henry or another to accompany him to Vermont's tallest peak, but to no avail. The Humble King had been adamant that Flatlander follow in what was long considered a rite of passage by many in the republic. Boys and girls, alike, stated Henry, took this same hike to the summit alone upon reaching the age of fifteen.

As Flatlander gazed upon the mountain ridge, it dawned upon him how large Mansfield's summit was. Unlike the majority the summits that he had seen thus far in Vermont, Mansfield was different. There was no towering peak. No point. No apex or pinnacle. Rather, the top of Mansfield was stretched and somewhat flattened on top, as if hammered, mercilessly, by the very gods themselves.

The leaves were bathed in various shades of red, yellow, and orange. Salmon red, apricot, and carrot colored canopies stretched for miles amid the cloudless autumn sky. A young, blonde-haired couple descended from a nearby trail, holding hands and laughing, as the sunlight reflected from their hiking branches. They nodded politely at Flatlander and then disappeared over a hillside trail to his left. The air seemed still. He knew at that moment what he must do, yet felt like an ant at the foot of this great beast. Flatlander took a swig of water from his hollowed gourd, which served as a makeshift canteen.

Although it took a half hour for his body to acclimate to the strenuous nature of the hike, the early leg was quite pleasant for Flatlander; the alluring fall colors evoked a natural serenity of which he had yet experienced. Leaves covering the ground near the base of Mansfield created a colorful carpet that was soft on the senses. A sign marking the beginning of the sunset trail stood to the right with a faded map behind a dirty glass panel. He felt reassured seeing markers along the way. This was big land for such a small republic; and he, a pebble amongst its quarry.

The trail took him through a winding passage of trees and boulders, footbridges and potholes, muddied ground and streams. Every so often, Flatlander was presented with a clear view of the land below him from his respective height, and marveled during each and every juncture. He noted with a small measure of pride that he had only lost his footing once, while hopping from one large lump of bedrock to another.

The flora gradually changed during the course of his hike, from full colorful foliage, to the hardwoods thinning in leaves, to large pines and spruces, and finally, to the miniature spruces of the alpines. Most of these spruces couldn't have been much greater than six to ten feet. The ground transitioned from being laden with knotted roots to sheer rock. Lichen-covered stone became more prevalent at the higher altitudes. The air was soon cleaner and the wind stronger. Gusts came from all directions, yet it was not as fierce as Flatlander had initially feared. Instead, it cooled his sweat-covered brow, and filled his lungs to a capacity to which he had never felt before. His legs felt numb and heavy, yet with each passing wind, and glimpse to the reddish orange potpourri of country landscape and farmland below, he began feeling reinvigorated.

On a few occasions, he was fooled into believing that he was one corner away from the summit, only to find another short and narrow path along the mountain ridge. When he finally finished the last leg of the trail, and mounted the top of Mansfield, Flatlander marveled at the view in which he beheld. He could see for miles and miles in a sweeping panoramic, the landscape melding seamlessly in the afternoon light like a masterpiece painting. The air had never felt fresher, his senses never more alive. It was intoxicating, and as Flatlander regained his composure, he tried to decipher his surroundings. Intermittently referring to a map which he had brought, Flatlander could see clearly parts of Lake Champlain and the Champlain Valley and the Adirondacks to the west, Stowe and the White Mountains beyond the wall in New Hampshire, far to the east, Smuggler's Notch and the vast forest of the north, and Camel's Hump and other assorted peaks to the south.

Directly west, a single blackened spire soared in the air between a series of cliffs. Standing a mile away, it reached nearly halfway up the mountain's height, yet couldn't have been more than ten to fifteen feet in diameter, maximum. On all sides of the spire, it appeared a great section of earth had been uplifted. The geologic feature looked deformed and unnatural, resembling more of a plateau, or mesa. In the middle, a narrow ravine cut through the plateau like a cleft before opening up into the wider area of Underhill.

The distances were vast, the mere proportions of the land, seemingly immeasurable. Flatlander contemplated his fate, knowing full well that he soon would be gliding over this beautiful land. Taking out his compass, he moistened a finger on his tongue, and held it out against the winds. Glancing down at his compass, it pointed the origin of wind trajectory to the northwest. After taking long, gulping swigs from his canteen, he removed a pen and paper from his satchel, and scribbled a question in which he intended to ask his family: *"Did we ever hike? Have I ever been to the top of a mountain? Or have you? If not, it's incredible. You should try it. Know that I love you and miss you; even as my memory still betrays me."* He folded the note neatly, placing it firmly in his pocket.

He hoped dearly that the wings of Inepticus would hold up, not just against the rough tail winds of the northwest or the unpredictable drafts from every direction imaginable, but against the very forces of common sense and logic. Flatlander carried much more on his back than that of he or Inepticus's legacy. He carried with him that of Underhill, a town in dire need of a savior. He carried with him the sense of purpose. And high above the burnt sienna canopy, on Vermont's highest peak, with an awful distance between him and the ground below, he carried with him the knowledge that he could very well be nearing the end of his life.

The next day, Henry accompanied Flatlander back up the trails of Mount Mansfield with no fanfare. Despite his fondness of both monks, Helphon and Zachus, Flatlander had convinced Henry to keep this task secret from the senate. His legs were still quite sore from his hike the day before. He experienced difficulty in negotiating the difficult terrain in his moccasins, though his foot pains were mere afterthought. The impending leap from the Fiskle Cliff was now all that consumed his mind.

When he had told Ellen and Menche of his plans, Ellen had called him "thickheaded," while Menche openly wept. "The most foolish thing she's heard in years," was how Ellen best summed up the plan. And though she spoke through the rolling of her eyes and sharpness of her words, Flatlander also sensed she spoke in pain. And though she departed under the pretense that she should get work done in her office, Flatlander didn't hear but a single drawer open, or a sheet of paper turn, the signature sounds of Ellen's busywork.

Earlier that day, Danario had arrived in Montpelier with his wings. They were neatly folded in a long, leather bag. The Messenger of Stowe trusted no other for such a critical task, and true to his word, hand-delivered them on horseback to Lord Henry's home at the break of dawn. Flatlander rushed out the door to greet Danario, but found himself speechless. The messenger just stared off vacantly, shrouded in a silence that spoke volumes. Danario then heaved the wings onto the roadway as if they were cursed, before speeding off.

Oddly, he felt for the man, he really did. Despite his callousness, Danario had still lost a son, and whether he admit it in one year or one hundred years, Inepticus's death would inevitably take a toll upon his stubborn father.

During the hike, Henry talked in circles about a number of subjects: growing up in the Brattle, Jess's transformation, his feelings about the wall and outsiders, Franklin's well-being, and in light of their scaling of Mansfield, Flatlander's need of quality boots. He spoke of his parents and their affinity for the outdoors, and the political career of Emile Babakiss, and of the Monks of Middlebury and some of their groundbreaking research.

He spoke of rivers in which he had paddled, and mountains in which he had traversed. He spoke of his love of pumpkins, and his plans to increase trade with the Quebecois. He spoke fondly, philosophically, of his nickname 'Humble King'. He spoke long but true. He spoke of anything and everything not related to the Fiskle Cliff. In short, he tried to ease Flatlander's worries. For he had previously tried to talk Flatlander from taking this insane plunge but to no avail. His presence alone rested on the contingency that he was not to speak of the deed with Flatlander for the duration of the ascent.

Henry must have realized after some time that he must have been stammering. As they came to a rest, he paused and leaned his back against a sloping stone, laughing nervously.

"My apologies. I've been babbling, haven't I?"

Flatlander took a long swig from his canteen, and spat a glob of phlegm over a nearby boulder.

"No more than usual."

Henry smiled. "On second thought, perhaps you *should* go jump off of a cliff, as far as I'm concerned."

"Gladly," replied Flatlander with a grin.

They laughed and continued their hike in near-silence. As they reached the summit, a black circle in the bedrock marked where Helphon and Zachus had built their fire, as charred wood still lay scattered about, pushed in all directions by the unrelenting wind. The familiar patches of light-green lichen covered much of the summit stone. Small white and yellow flowers filled some of the crags between the large stones, and Flatlander was again struck by the purity of the air. They walked slowly to the precipice of the cliff, very near to where Inepticus had previously leapt.

Henry gazed to the blackened abyss, forlorn. "You *don't* have to do this."

Flatlander looked down to the shadows of Underhill, before painfully averting his eyes. He handed Henry a note.

"Please give this to my family if they're ever found. And tell them, although my memories are spotty at best, I'm sure of this much how much I loved them. Tell them if they should think of me, think of me kindly."

"I will, Flatlander," replied Henry.

Lord Henry then removed a large, silver coin from his pocket, and without warning, flipped it into the abyss below.

Flatlander glanced down, as the coin vanished quickly into darkness. "What was that?"

Henry sighed. "They may do the same in the Old Country, as far as I know, but in Vermont, we sometimes throw a coin into a pond or well for good luck. I received that coin as a token of appreciation from Lord Haque several years ago during a visit to Underhill. It was just before the formation of the Fiskle Cliff. A half dollar from the Old Country, one of the only remaining in the republic. The Monks have their own superstitions. You have yours. Please let me hang on to mine."

Flatlander nodded and they began assembling Inepticus's wings to his back. They felt lighter than they had during his hike, yet their open spans amongst the heavy summit winds threw Flatlander fully off keel. Lord Henry helped fasten the wing's straps to Flatlander's arms and legs, ensuring that each buckle was firmly in place. Even amid the stiff gales of the summit, Henry's breathed heavy, nervous for his friend.

With the wings properly attached, and the sun rising high beyond the peaks, Henry faced Flatlander.

"You've become a good friend and a trusted aide, and though I disagree with this decision wholeheartedly, I trust and respect your judgment. Be brave and may the winds blow you safely home, Flatlander. Your family will receive this note in the event you fall. You have my word."

The two embraced, mindful of Inepticus's wings fluttering dangerously close. Then Lord Henry took several steps back, as Flatlander began inching towards the cliff's edge. For the first time, he could make out the faint outlines of several structures that appeared to be homes along the eastern edge of Underhill. The black spire emerged from the shadows of the town as if it were floating on air, for its base lay unseen in the dark below. The depth was hard to fathom, and Flatlander felt momentarily overcome with dizziness and nausea, and had it not been for the summit's fresh air, he thought, he surely would have vomited. He then spread the same adhesive to his hands, courtesy of the monks.

Taking a deep breath, Flatlander reflected on his life in Vermont, and all of the good things. He remembered the exhilaration of sprinting off with Pete the Moose during their escape from Irasburg. He recalled the beauty of Lake Champlain, and how nice it was to soak up its glimmering beauty among the shadows of the Adirondacks. He recalled the unique people that he had met, the monsters he had fought, the land that he had traversed, from the foothills of the Brattle to the pastures of Addison County. He reflected on the sonic explosion of the Thinker, and the surrounding militias scattering like frightened flies. He thought of Ellen, Franklin, and Menche, from their frightful night in Lowell to the romantic time he had spent with Ellen aboard the Bethel. Flatlander reflected on these things, and for the first time, realized that he had started his own collection of memories, carved out his own path, among the seemingly endless wood of Vermont.

And it was then that Flatlander leapt from the edge of the Fiskle Cliff.

"See anythin' yets?" asked Menche, behind an alpine shrub.

Ellen adjusted her binoculars from her perch on the exposed bedrock. "They're just talking." She watched as Flatlander and Henry conversed at cliff's edge. She then saw Henry throw a small, shiny object into the abyss below. "Wait, Henry just threw something over the cliff."

"What's it be?" asked Menche, as he shuffled to get a clearer view.

"I don't know- *hush*," muttered Ellen, as she watched the both of them proceed to fasten the wings to Flatlander's torso. "I can't believe that he's going through with this, and with Inepticus's wings, nonetheless…"

Ellen knew that she should be tending to matters crucial to the republic, as she had been left in charge of administrative duties with Henry's absence. She also knew that Henry and Flatlander wanted to keep this a private matter. The likelihood of Flatlander crashing to his death was great, but Ellen wanted to be there, in any event. Unable to understand the degree of personal sacrifice, Ellen had long assumed Flatlander's interest in the quest was merely a bluff, a gesture to appease the lords of the senate. Yet as she watched Flatlander at cliff's edge and Lord Henry by his side, Ellen knew her assumptions to be wrong. *If only he knew how I felt about him…*

Lord Henry and Flatlander embraced, and in the pit of her stomach, Ellen was finally convinced that this was no bluff.

"Please, don't do this, Flatlander. Please. It's not worth your blood," cried Ellen to herself, as Menche scurried from the bush to her side. "*Please.*"

"It's too lates fer that, Ms. Ellen. Too lates," whispered Menche, as he squinted out across the opposite side of the cliffs.

Flatlander then dove headfirst into the depths of Underhill. Ellen sat up suddenly, in hysterics, the binoculars nearly falling from her grasp.

"Oh my God, Menche. He jumped! Flatlander jumped!"

"Dat's a big bird, mama," came the high-pitched squeal of Bailey Payne's daughter, Risa, as she pointed upwards from the uncomfortable hole of her stationary tire swing. Bailey had been momentarily distracted from her watch by the barking of her cocker spaniel, Cloey, but hurriedly peered through her binoculars to catch a sight. A quick adjustment to the binocular's focus told her all that she needed to know. Another winged man had taken flight towards the top of the black spire.

Bailey cursed under her breath. *When would they learn?* "Oh, for goodness sake. Not again. Goodness, not again! Risa, you get in the house right this instant, darlin'. No need to be out here."

"But mama," argued Risa, as she pointed to the open slither of sky. "I wanna see the bird."

"Risa Janet Payne, you get your butt in that house now or I'm sellin' that swing for kindlin'! I'm in no mood for arguin'," said Bailey impatiently; the binoculars glued to her eye sockets.

She didn't wait for her daughter's response before she began reciting a prayer that a local monk had once taught her early on in Underhill's plight.

"And though we fall into shadow, may the prevailing winds prevail, though the sun grows dimmer by the day, the spirit of Underhill sails. And though we fall into shadow, may the prevailing winds prevail, though the sun grows dimmer by the day, the spirit of Underhill sails. And though we fall into shadow…."

During the first few seconds of free fall, Flatlander's heart stopped completely, his blood froze, and his face went numb. It was an explosion of the senses inherent with the violence of the fall. The world suddenly became a spinning torrent of rock, wind, and tortured thoughts. Convinced that he had indeed leapt to his death, it was only then that Flatlander had recognized the recklessness of his decision. The roar of the wind was deafening, drowning out all other distractions. His wings rattled with the growing velocity. The physics of his descent tested any and all of Flatlander's preconceived notions of flight, and yet despite this, Inepticus's wings held true.

He was flying! Shifting his body to a lateral position, Flatlander was able to balance himself and control his direction more efficiently. The spire of Underhill grew in both size and detail as he approached its flattened head, impaled into the earth like a corroded nail. It amazed Flatlander how small a movement could impact his trajectory: a slight shrug of his left shoulder threw him off course substantially. A mere twitch in his feet rotated his form vertically. He learned quickly to calm his body, and he traveled as a glider would at a slight gradient. Before long, the dastardly sight of the black spire grew immensely within plain view.

Coming upon the top of the spire faster than he would have liked, Flatlander saw equilibrium for the first time, true to form- a small sphere, the lower half, a glowing light blue, and the upper half an earthen brown. The top of the spire looked impossibly small in comparison to the grandeur of Mansfield and the cliffs. Equilibrium, alight with phosphorescent blue, sat in the middle of the spire's flattened crown. Flatlander then began to panic, for his flight path seemed to be undershooting equilibrium. He focused solely on the stone, and held out a sticky palm to tether his target, while his other arm instinctively braced for a potential impact with the spire.

Flatlander held his breath, when just then he saw, much to his horror, that he was headed directly for the top of the spire's upper walls. Too late to try to change course, Flatlander felt the hand of death coming from the pit of his stomach. Too late to turn, Flatlander was consumed with dread, until one of the finest miracles ever to occur in the republic took place.

From below, a single gust propelled him upward, and he proceeded to skim over the surface of the spire like a hawk on open water. In a single, downward thrust, Flatlander extended his right arm, palm open and facing forward, towards the glow of equilibrium. The stone smacked violently against his hand, and he winced, for the pain was immense. He looked down.

Equilibrium now stuck to his palm like an oversized fruit, and the changed weight distribution hooked his trajectory too far right. Equilibrium, the very stone in which the republic had so strongly sought, was now acting, quite literally, as a death-anchor.

Continuing to hook around the spire's shaft, Flatlander contemplated ditching the stone to regain his balance. But it was too late. The special adhesive, made in secret by the monks of Middlebury, was meant to dry hard and the stone held firmly in his palm. And as he continued to arc around the spire in a dangerous fall, Flatlander knew that death was upon him once again, as his world grew darker by the second.

Then, an even greater miracle occurred. A strong current of warm air rose from the depths of Underhill, and Flatlander found himself completely at its mercy, like a fluttering moth. It warmed up his chilled bones. It spun him and pushed him. It lifted him and turned him. It filled his wings with new life, and Flatlander, with renewed hope. There wasn't enough time to contemplate its source, Flatlander merely wanted to land safely, and he hoped that the source of warm air would continue elevating him above the walls of the Fiskle Cliff and onto solid ground. The air pushed him hard and unevenly, hurtling him upwards relentlessly, as if the breath of the earth itself was exhaled upon him. The frames of his wings strained under the relentless pressure.

Soon, Flatlander tilted his body so he could ride the wind current, and he made his way to the edge of the cliff. From his peripheral vision, he saw the movement of people along cliff's edge running towards his destination. With one last great heave, Flatlander swooped upward, then came crashing down several feet short of the Fiskle's edge. The warm air current suddenly died out. He collided then fell forward upon a small rock perch protruding just a foot or so from the sheer cliff wall. His right wing snapped and crunched under his weight, its frame now painfully dug into his back. He turned rapidly, clinging to the smallest of finger holds: a natural indentation in the cliff. Flatlander held on with all of his strength, while his other hand clutched equilibrium firmly in place. Over one thousand feet separated him from the canyon floor below.

"Help!" he called.

His fingers strained to keep him from falling, but Flatlander knew that he couldn't hold on much longer. One miracle was enough a blessing, but now with his mangled wings, it would surely be a sheer fall all the way to the cursed town of Underhill. Just as his last bit of strength left his fingertips, a short leather belt fell down beside him. Flatlander looked up at the panic-stricken faces of Menche and Ellen.

Flatlander couldn't believe his eyes. "Menche? Ellen?"

"Flatlander! Grab ons, sir!" said Menche, as Ellen moved swiftly into position behind, and held firmly onto Menche's legs.

Flatlander grabbed onto the belt. He now dangled precariously over the cliff wall, as both feet searched frantically for a foothold. Using equilibrium as a climbing device, Flatlander wedged it between a pair of narrow fissures.

"You didn't think through how'd you get back up, did you?" came Ellen's voice.

Flatlander grunted, his every muscle taut and near collapse. "Not the time for smug observations."

"Didn't know ya weighs so much, sir," muttered Menche.

"Shut up and get me up this thing, Menche!"

Suddenly, Lord Henry's face also appeared, sweaty and red-cheeked. Without a word, he grabbed onto Menche's left shoulder, as Ellen grabbed Menche's right arm, and together, they pulled Flatlander with all of their collective might until the four collapsed backwards onto firm land. The four lay on the ground, panting so heavily they were unable to catch a breath.

Lord Henry crawled his way to Flatlander lying on his side then gushed with unbridled joy.

"Ha! You damned fool! I don't believe it! A miracle! You flew, Flatlander! Even when the wind failed, you flew! I felt the warm air myself! It was warm, was it not? I've never seen anything like it before in my life! A miracle, I say. Ha! A miracle!"

"Yers a hero, sir! Flew like them birds," exulted Menche, as he jumped up and down with joy.

"Amazing, Flatlander," agreed Ellen, as she knelt over his crumpled form and gave him a hug. "The biggest bird I've seen in flight yet."

Flatlander rolled to his other side, wincing in pain. His fingers were raw. His nose was bloodied from the impact with the cliff and his muscles, sore to the touch. Inepticus's wings draped broken from his shoulders, as he displayed equilibrium for Henry to see. Lord Henry gazed upon the exotic stone, caressing it softly with his index finger. His eyes grew large, for he had never expected the stone to shine like the tales had told; its blue half glowed as if fueled from within.

"So this is the stone," he coughed, rubbing equilibrium like a crystal ball, "the stone in which fables have been born and plays been made. Who would think that something so beautiful could unleash such destruction on our people?" Henry caught himself from fawning, and laid a comforting hand on Flatlander's shoulder. "Are you okay, Flatlander?

Flatlander grimaced in pain, then sat up. "Ugh."

"A miracle from Underhill," muttered Ellen. "Like I've said before, Flatlander, there is much in this land that is unknown."

Henry nodded, and detached Inepticus's shattered wings from Flatlander's back.

"As true as Inepticus's fine gift, a marvel of engineering. I suspect quite a few people will be eating crow for years to come. I can see the headline now: 'Flatlander Takes Flight Over the Fiskle Cliffs With Wings Made From Republic's Village Idiot.' Danario and Shay Bromage's heads will undoubtedly explode."

Ellen chuckled. "Bromage and the senate will deny they ever doubted Flatlander in the first place."

"Politicians have short memories when it's convenient for them," quipped Henry with a wink. "But the important things are that Flatlander is alive and we have equilibrium in our possession. Come, let's share with the republic this fine news."

"Please get this thing off my hand," pleaded Flatlander, as he shifted his fingers uncomfortably against the body of the stone.

"Yes, of course. My apologies," said Henry, as he poured his remaining water from his canteen onto Flatlander's hand. The adhesive moistened enough for Ellen to pull it, roughly, from his palm. She offered Flatlander the brown, non-sticky half of the stone.

"Your trophy, your lift," confirmed Henry with a familiar smile.

Flatlander reached out a hand and accepted equilibrium. Its colors resembled a miniature globe, half blue, half a rocky brown. The milky white adhesive smeared upon the blue half like a broken web, with two of Flatlander's fingermarks still easily apparent. From close up, Flatlander could see the extreme complexities of the stone. Its texture was smooth, yet the shades and patterns of blue and brown varied greatly, with pearly quartz-like beads imbedded within.

Ellen glanced at the stone. "We must bring it to Trombley and the monks and decide what to do with it, and don't forget, Underhill still needs us. The legends say that it must be returned to its site of its discovery or nothing will change. Nothing at all."

"Indeed. Underhill still needs us," agreed Henry, as he looked out into the darkened town. "And, sadly, the corpse of Inepticus still lies rotting away among the valley of shadow. We'll bring the stone to the senate to see what they think. But, in earnest, I'm tempted to bypass the statehouse and find the source of this stone myself. Decisions in the senate tend to get, umm, bogged down. Yet I'm already in the proverbial doghouse, am I not?"

"You are," confirmed Ellen plainly.

"Then let us descend and get Flatlander help. Then we may reach a decision," replied Henry.

The party left Mansfield's summit with their prize in hand, and more importantly, their hero, Flatlander, alive.

They marched down the trails of Mansfield in single file, cautiously maneuvering between sunken boulders, mountain streams, and collections of spruce trees tangled at the roots. The lichen-covered landscape gently gave back way to the mist-soaked stones of Mansfield's wooded crest. Flatlander kept equilibrium close to his body, shielding it from that of suspecting eyes, though they hadn't passed a traveler or mountain trader yet. Though Flatlander's body ached, he couldn't shake the feeling of pride that he had acquired since plucking equilibrium from its perch atop the black spire. He had completed his tenth and final quest, and in spite of the looming decision he faced in whether to stay or leave Vermont, he took certain solace in what certainly had to have been his greatest accomplishment. And though it nearly cost him his life, Flatlander had little regret.

Their hike was excruciating and descending Mansfield's trails actually meant sometimes hiking higher in elevation to find an alternative way down to bypass the Fiskle Cliffs. Every mile traveled took its toll upon their weary bodies. Each subsequent closer view of the surrounding landscape was greeted with muted celebration; a sign they were nearing home.

The group deliberated on what to do with equilibrium during their descent: should they find the mine that Fiskle found it in and return it? Keep it in a museum? Seek out the wisdom of the monks? Seek out the Abenaki? Seek out Vergil? What of Underhill? Why hadn't the predicted change occurred? Though it was agreed that they needed to bring the prize to the senate, they also wanted to do what was best for Underhill and the stone itself. Even Lord Henry had to admit that both of those goals could prove to be mutually exclusive.

From the front of the pack, Henry paused suddenly and looked to the earth below. Several seconds later, Flatlander felt a thundering rumble from deep below the ground. His teeth chattered uncontrollably, as the mountain quaked from within. Dead branches fell. Menche's face paled to a deathly white.

"Off the mountain! Now!" order Henry to the group, as he hurried to a fast jog.

A wagon-sized boulder shook from its foundation, rolling two-dozen feet from where they had just traversed.

"Me shoelaces untied, lord!" yelped Menche from the back, as he stumbled from rock to rock awkwardly. Ellen and Flatlander followed behind, scrambling for their lives.

"Let's go, Menche! The mountain's coming down, you fool!" called Flatlander at his back. He knew that he was too tired and hurt, and the terrain too difficult to carry his friend.

"An earthquake in Vermont?" asked Ellen. "What's happening, Lord Henry?"

"I don't think that it's an earthquake," replied Henry in a huff, as he skipped over a fallen branch.

Flatlander lost his balance while trying to climb down a steep embankment, as equilibrium came loose from his grip. Bouncing off several rocks, it finally came to rest in a shallow gully. Flatlander rushed to retrieve it, but right before his eyes, the stone was engulfed by the earth, as the gully transformed to a similar viscosity of quicksand. In mere seconds, it was gone.

"No!" exclaimed Flatlander, in dismay. "I dropped the stone!"

"What? Flatlander, of all the things we could not risk losing..." said Henry, as he turned from his frantic pace, and looked to Flatlander in shock. "Where is it?"

"The ground swallowed it up whole."

Henry eyes bugged from his head. "You're trying to tell me the ground swallowed it up? That should go over well with the senate. 'Sorry that we couldn't produce Equilibrium for you. The ground swallowed it whole'!"

"The ground doesn't just swallow things, Flatlander. It has to be around here. Look harder," stated Ellen in agreement, as she began scanning the ground for the lost stone.

"I sees it happen too," said Menche, as he took to Flatlander's side. "He ain't lyin'."

Before Henry could answer, the four looked out to a clearing overlooking the formation of the Fiskle Cliff, and it became quite evident what had been causing such a stir. The giant spire wobbled unsteadily from the depths of Underhill, as a series of horns and bell chimes bellowed from the valley below. The cliffs rumbled from their base, throwing up giant clouds of grey and brown dust, as entire slabs of the cliff walls, some the size of the statehouse, fell lifelessly into blackness. The spire severed from the bottom of its stem, like an invisible sword had hacked it clean. In slow motion, it came down as a whole, and as it impacted Underhill below, an enormous cloud of dust and rock burst from the ground up. The impact from the fallen spire rattled Flatlander to the core, and the group jumped behind a nearby hill to seek shelter from the spreading dust, whose shockwave now spread through the valley below like a stubborn ripple.

The extraordinarily loud rumbling and shaking continued on for a full minute, as Flatlander could only hope that the ground underneath held steady. When the earth stopped groaning, and all that remained were slight reverberations sounding out beyond the extended countryside, the group ventured from their shelter and looked out into the valley. Flatlander's jaw dropped. The Fiskle Cliff was nowhere to be seen. The Town of Underhill had fully emerged, as a large ray of sunshine broke through the heavens and cast over the dusted and dreary-looking homes and shops. Men and women, mere dots from Flatlander's vantage point, spilled out from their dwellings and into the valley below, congregating en masse, as shouts and horns clamored in the distance.

The dried riverbeds in the valley below slowly filled again with water from the shifting highlands, and the afternoon sun shone strongly through a dusty haze above Underhill. It was only a matter of time before the residents of the neighboring towns of Stowe, Westford, Cambridge, Jericho, and Essex and beyond saw with their own eyes the miracle that stood before them. And word would spread fast around the republic, reasoned Flatlander, because the Fiskle Cliff formation and Mansfield's immense profile could be seen from as far as forty miles or more from certain reaches. Undoubtedly, much of Vermont had bore witness to this dramatic geological event.

Lord Henry laughed. "This cannot be real. It's as if I'm watching the play Equilibrium itself. I cannot believe what I'm seeing."

"Underhill's back!" said Ellen in celebration. "Underhill has returned! Flatlander, you've done it!"

Tears welled up in Flatlander's eyes, as he watched the quaint town of Underhill come back to life.

"It's a beautiful town," said Flatlander. "More beautiful that I had expected."

"That it is," agreed Henry, as he looked upon Flatlander proudly. "And they have *you* to thank."

Ellen hugged Flatlander out of sheer joy, as Menche did likewise against his leg. Lord Henry kept his distance, but his look of joy and adoration said all that needed to be said. He wept tears of joy for the resurrection of Underhill. He wept openly for how much this would mean to his republic. He wept for Inepticus's memory. Most importantly, he wept for the selflessness and courage displayed by his friend and associate, Flatlander, who had sacrificed his life for a town of people he had never even met. Looking out beyond the mountain, Henry wiped away a track of his tears.

"Come. Let's go greet Desmairis and our newfound friends."

It took an hour for the dust to fully settle onto the town of Underhill, and even with this new layer of dirt and debris, the people rejoiced in sheer ecstasy. The spire, which had loomed ominously for five years, now lay broken and scattered among the hilly, sun-soaked countryside. Children played on its fallen form like a giant, felled tree. Word spread fast amongst the republic. The people and animals of the adjacent towns and cities were drawn to Underhill in droves; as it were an obligatory pilgrimage. They came in admiration of their hardened neighbors, they came in morbid curiosity, but mostly, they came to share in the collective joy of the newly freed peoples of the republic.

Reunions of all sizes sprouted up amongst the country roads of Underhill. Brothers embraced Brothers. Mothers embraced their sons and daughters. Grandparents danced the streets like children, while grandchildren recounted stories with skill and wisdom that betrayed their age. Children laughed and sang songs of joy and hope, taught to them mostly by the monks. Musicians came with instruments in tow. Clothes, food, and medical supplies arrived in caravans from Chittenden, Addison, Washington, Lamoille and Franklin counties, small but kind gestures from the regional lords and business leaders whom saw to the people's wellbeing. The finest craft brews and wines were delivered by the barrel and hand-poured among its citizens. Schools and businesses from surrounding communities were closed for the remainder of the day, and the next day too.

Families sat near the banks of the Browns River in wonder, admiring the waters for the first time in years, grateful for its deep, healthy currents. Bailey Payne, binoculars still dangling from the small of her neck, waded into the river's shallows followed by her children, as they skipped and splashed one another in glee.

The Fiskle Cliff had been engulfed wholly by Mt. Mansfield and the surrounding woods, and the only trace of its existence was a wide circle of shredded trees and exposed earth, which had become disfigured in the wake of its violent collapse. Brookes Desmairis was found, pale and malnourished, as were most of the residents of Underhill, but only a dozen of the three thousand residents had perished during their five dark years afoot the Fiskle Cliff, a strong testament to the hardiness and determination of Underhill. When Brookes Desmairis stood upon a nearby hill to greet the assemblage of Vermonters pouring into his town, a friend who was nearby to the beloved lord heard him utter:

"The sun has never felt so good; and friendship with the republic, no better appreciated.[83]"

But perhaps the biggest surprise of all in the reemergence of Underhill was the discovery of Inepticus, who, despite popular belief, hadn't become a worm-ridden corpse after the terrible fall

---

[83] A quote that would later be written above the door of Underhill's Town Hall.

from the cliff. He was alive and well, save a fractured arm. His fall had been partially broken by a giant pile of leaves, which had been blown into the depths from the surrounding forests and collected into a giant pile by the townspeople by means of preventing an accidental fire. A dozen yards to either side of the pile, and Inepticus would have surely perished upon impact. When a farmer named Earl Reed found Inepticus later on that day, he was delirious from his fall, mistakenly believing that he had actually grabbed equilibrium and dropped it mid-flight. Several farmers searched their properties fruitlessly for hours for the stone, but the found nothing.

When word of Inepticus's survival reached the ears of his father, Danario, he made sure to cancel his planned tag sale of Inepticus's belongings, and rushed to meet his wounded son in Underhill, who at this point was celebrating in the fine company of Flatlander, Henry, Ellen, and Menche at Reed's home. The townsfolk pointed Danario in the direction of his son, and he hurriedly made his way around small, close-knit circles of family and friends laughing and hollering. He saw the group assembled through the windowpane of an old, grey farmhouse. Henry the Humble King stood at Inepticus's bedside, as did a small, gnomish man in overalls and a blonde, well-dressed woman in white sat by an opposing wall. On the other side of the bed, his back facing towards Danario, a man sat nearest Inepticus. Even from the back of his head, Danario was able to determine this man to be that of Flatlander. In his hands, Danario saw him holding a battered pair of wings. The waxy sheen and tightly bound leather told him what he had already suspected: that these were, in fact, Inepticus's wings, presented to him by Flatlander.

Danario then concluded, in complete shock and bewilderment, that his son's wings had proven successful. It was in that moment, when Danario viewed his bed-ridden son laughing and beaming simultaneously, that he felt something for Inepticus, which he had never felt ever before; an insurmountable pride. *So it stands that I may be the fool, after all. Perhaps the boy could fly all along.* Reluctantly, Danario walked briskly into the home to welcome back his son from death before this alien feeling departed.

Meanwhile, a helix-shaped wizard's staff lay unattended at the base of Underhill, wedged between root and stone, adorning the wood-sculpted head of the Abenaki wind eagle, Wuchowsen. Beside it, laid Vergil, peacefully, in a deep slumber. He slept near a cave in Mansfield's base, a shadow within the once shadowed land, far removed from human senses. And shortly before that first true sunlight dawned upon the town of Underhill, and before the first townsfolk stirred from their celebrations aplenty, Vergil would be gone, departing through the route of the mountains.[84]

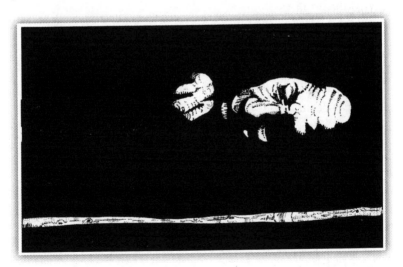

---

[84] A generalized term for the thousands of mountain trails in Vermont.

CHAPTER 15

A Vermonter he Is

THE CITY HALL OF BURLINGTON played host to Flatlander for his ceremony of citizenship. Master Yuro made sure to treat his friend to a fine and well-attended celebration. The guests of honor were treated by the Horns of the Brattle, Lord Henry's second favorite, more accessible hometown ensemble. Delectable cheeses, wines, beers, and pastries were brought from the finest merchants in Chittenden County, and spread out before the guests on tables covered in red satin sheets. The familiar faces of certain lords stood out to Flatlander: Andreas, Riegelman, Haque, Stannard, Hamish, Sarmus, Trombley, Ann Weston, and Brookes Desmairis all made appearances. Several monks also attended, including Orton, Zachus and Helphon, their faces all but hidden by their hooded cloaks, as they sat behind Lord Trombley, quiet, but content. Franklin, Ellen, and Menche had front row seats. After the visiting nobles had finished their plates and downed their wine, the last trumpet played for the full-bellied guests, and they were directed to their seats in the assembly hall. The atmosphere was jovial and informal.

Shay Bromage quietly took notes from a dimly lit section of the back of the room, barely visible. His station consisted of his old beat up typewriter and side paneling for privacy. It was a needed humble return from his long hiatus. Shay felt each of the nobles' crooked, satisfied smiles as they passed his desk to find their seats. They stewed in his recent scandal, perceiving it as instant karma from his history of hit-pieces. But Shay accepted the smug looks as a small price to pay for his sins.

Lord Henry adorned his golden silk fleece, a recent gift from Master Yuro for Lord Henry's recent assistance in matters big and small. Nothing in the laws indicated this a crime, reasoned Henry to Ellen. He had also groomed his lengthy stubble with a brush and buck knife for the occasion. In front of Henry's throne, Flatlander sat towards the crowd in an oversized chair. He fidgeted nervously, awaiting Henry's formal introduction. Lord Henry had bestowed upon him one of his black bear jackets and leather gloves. Flatlander's beard was full now, a drastic departure from his first visit before Lowell. His sword rested against his chair. His metamorphosis into a Vermonter was nearly complete.

Henry rose from his throne and joined Flatlander's side.

"Thank you, friends, colleagues, nobles. I'm grateful for you attending this special event. As I'm sure that you don't mind spending some quality time outside of the *excitement* of the statehouse."

Those in attendance laughed.

"Today, I present what is, without a doubt, the most significant citizenship ceremony in all of my life, and likely, the most significant ceremony in the history of the republic."

He then turned his attention to his friend. "Flatlander, when you first came to us, you were but a babe, your hands as soft as an infant's bottom. Your facial hair was as thin as a November frosting. You'd wilt up like the common hydrangea at the smallest chill in the air. But my, how you've grown. Now, as I look at you, I see the face of a fellow Vermonter. With your scraggily beard and sword. Even your speech now resembles that of a Vermonter more than even some who are native-born. In short, you've changed before our very eyes."

Henry paused, and grinned ever so slightly. "Most don't know this, but Flatlander and myself have gotten naked together."

Howls of surprised laughter rang out among the audience. Even Shay Bromage laughed, as he struggled to take notes. Flatlander blushed a deep red.

"Yes, it's true. Now, I know what you're thinking: what were the elected leader of Vermont and Flatlander doing naked together? I can assure you that it's not what you think. Flatlander proved his mettle by jumping into the near-freezing Bolton Potholes this past spring, and from that point forward, ceased being simply a Flatlander from the Old Country, and slowly began his transformation into a man *of* the republic, *for* the republic."

The audience applauded lightly. Henry paused, cherishing the spirited memory of the potholes. "You see, Flatlander had never been short on intelligence or wit, yet he lacked a fundamental trait that's found in abundance within even the simplest of Vermonters. The sense of freedom. Freedom as an individual, freedom as a citizen of this republic, and freedom through space, land, and mind, which pervade our everyday life. Vermont is more than just a place. It's a state of being. Some in the Old Country surely saw us as little more than oddballs, radicals, or "fringe folk." Nonsense. Why does the Old Country value freedom so little? Since when did those in the Old Country lose their way? I would rather be labeled a fringe-dwelling fool, than subject my beloved republic to the oppressive nature running afoul in the Old Country."

The crowd applauded ferociously, while a few lords in attendance sprung to their feet briefly in adoration for Henry's words. Lord Trombley smiled broadly.

Henry continued: "You must understand, Flatlander, that Vermonters rarely complain about the cold, nor do they dwell on the length of the winter. We don't need other hands to feed them, nor do we expect to be waited on like pups, waiting in turn for each succulent nipple from their overwhelmed mother.

"We do not wallow in their own problems, instead we wallow in their solutions. We do not abuse or speak unkindly of nature, for it's nature and nature only in which we give our thanks to the Gods. Even the harshest of Vermont winters can yield benefits: from an early harvest, to the merchants who thrive selling winter goods, to the way the country landscape looks so pretty and regal among the barren trees and farmlands.

"We do not seek out material goods for the sole reason to seek out material goods, for the material that we often seek cannot be bought, sold or traded under the guise of economic thirst. We take what we need in such a way as to not harm mother earth. Vermont is mostly excluded from a culture of excess. A Vermonter should bear no judgment onto others for their physical appearance, nor do they expect to be judged by others in kind. A Vermonter needs not be reminded of their size, as a republic, for we hold our small size proudly in our hearts and in our minds.

"A Vermonter is of the loving, caring, kind. But do not mistake that kindness for weakness, friend, for behind the simple mask of every Vermonter lies a fierce energy of independence, which influences nearly every facet of our lives in common brotherhood. Tease the bear and you will feel its claws.

"A Vermonter is generous, and when our neighbor's sugar maples leak slowly, we give to our neighbors what we can, much like a good neighbor should. A Vermonter is smart, and though this notion may be occasionally challenged due to the simplicity of some of our dialects, even the seemingly simplest Vermonter can be chockfull of wisdom if you listen to him or her properly. A Vermonter grows his or her own food, kills his or her own meat, and often builds his or her own home. And when there is an exception, that exception is made with the thought that it is better for the republic as a whole than for them as individuals."

A tremendous applause ensued, as even the likes of Sarmus and Andreas beamed with pride.

"Flatlander, you came into this land removed from your memories, from your past, from the mother from which you were born, and from the culture from which you grew. You came to us a blank slate, an empty canvas. However, as I see the folks in front of me from near and far, and the strength behind your eyes, I can see that you will leave this room a tried-and-true Vermonter.

"You have released our symbolic animal, Pete the Moose, from impending doom. You have killed with mercy the anomaly known as Fish and released an entire generation of lost cultists to their relieved families. You have delivered special goods from the Mills of Lowell, creating an important economic bridge between eastern and western Vermont. You have eradicated the local supply of superpac, which wrought havoc on the good people of this republic. You have eradicated the Thinker, and allowed for the redevelopment of the Moran. Some might not know this, but you have vanquished the Guardian of Highgate, and discovered ancient translations to solve our Quebecois tipping crisis. You have helped return countless stolen money and valuables to the fine people of Burlington, and now, singlehandedly, you have saved the poor citizens of Underhill from the sinking basin of the Fiskle Cliff."

Henry paused and let the audience cheer wildly. A streamer flew down from the upper reaches of the balcony. Brookes Desmairis clapped the loudest of the audience. His eyes became bloodshot red.

"You have swum with us. Hunted with us. Watched the stars above with us." Henry paused. "And now, it is past time that you *become* one of us, in both title and in claims. It's said by some that it takes one hundred years of lineage before one can be considered a true Vermonter. Well, I say- nonsense! For adhering to this outdated notion would require us to overlook a gem amongst our midst."

From the recesses of the assembly room, Shay Bromage nodded his head approvingly.

"Flatlander, please stand up," said Henry in a loud, booming voice.

Flatlander obliged, smiling nervously, as the Humble King circled slowly about.

"It's also with great honor that I announce you one of my official advisors. You join a wonderful group whom I consider friends and colleagues of the utmost professional integrity. I will leave your title up to you. You have earned it, just as you have earned my respect and the respect of many others throughout this fine republic.

"I ask you to take this oath," continued Henry, as he recited the lines from memory. "I, Flatlander of the Old Country..."

Flatlander repeated: "I, Flatlander of the Old Country..."

"Solemnly swear..."

"Solemnly swear..."

"To be strong when others grow weak..."

"To be strong when others grow weak..."

"And wise when others lose wit..."

"And wise when others lose wit..."

"To be kind when others grow sour..."

"To be kind when others grow sour..."

"And to be true when others grow false."

"And to be true when others grow false."

"Forever and more."

"Forever and more."

"For a Vermonter you shall be."

"For a Vermonter...I shall be."

Lord Henry paused emphatically. "So, to you, I bear this honor, Flatlander: you are an official brother and a citizen of the Republic of Vermont, for now and for all eternity! May your travels take you near and far across this magical land, which you can now call home, and may the republic serve you in the same fashion for which you have served the republic."

Lord Henry embraced Flatlander, and shortly thereafter, handed him a contract for his new appointed position as Henry's official advisor. He looked at the contract with a wide smile, then bowed deeply for those gathered in attendance. The statehouse erupted into a raucous of applause and cheers, and it wasn't until a full three minutes later that it began to subside.

As the applause began to fade, Henry took Flatlander aside by the arm and led him to the side of the stage where none could see.

"Flatlander, may I have a private word with you?"

"Of course, Lord Henry," replied Flatlander as he followed him beyond the reaches of the stage's curtain.

He placed his sword against the wall, and stood proudly in his new black bear jacket.

"Now you look like a man I would not want to cross," stated Henry, half-jokingly.

"Thank you," replied Flatlander with a smile.

Henry nodded proudly. "Flatlander, I never told you about when I was first elected, did I?"

"I don't think so. Ellen once mentioned that you won quite handily."

"Yes. But there was a much larger, more important battle, that I had to win outside of election numbers," said Henry. "One of the first things I did *after* winning: can you guess what it was?"

Flatlander raised an eyebrow. "You celebrated with a vacation?"

"Hardly."

"A local tavern?"

Henry smirked. "Spirits were consumed the first night, surely, but only in moderation."

"You exacted vengeance on your opponents?" joked Flatlander.

Henry chuckled. "No, Flatlander. Quite the opposite, actually. The first thing I did was I went to the home of my cousin, Beatrice, who lived in the meadows of East Burke, and proceeded to help her de-clutter her barn, a task in which I had avoided for several years. I worked for twelve hours straight. The next day, I visited my father's grave and apologized for not spending enough time with him. Two days later, I cooked a meal for the homeless of the Brattle, for I had previously introduced anti-loitering legislation three years prior, which had jeopardized their dignity. And two days after *that*, I sang amongst a local choir which I had badmouthed as a teenager."

Flatlander shuffled uncomfortably. "Why are you telling me all this?"

"Are you not seeing a pattern? Are you not seeing a common thread?"

Flatlander shook his head, confused.

"This wasn't just merely some publicity stunt, Flatlander," continued Henry with a deep sigh. "That all came *before* the election. These actions, on the other hand, were completely genuine. These tasks were a way for me to move beyond the shadows of my past. And though many more remained, like Gus Boomhover, at least I did my best to right those whom I had wronged."

Flatlander nodded, courteously. "That was noble of you."

"*Noble*? No. It was *necessary* of me, Flatlander," corrected Henry. "As it is *necessary* of *you*." Henry rolled up the sleeves of his golden fleece, and unbuttoned his collar. "After my election, I visited the Chamber of Echoes in disguise, and called out into the well for advice. In return, a voice called back *'make amends, young one.'* There's no rational explanation for those words, or who said them to this day, but I saw to it fittingly. In retrospect, I'm now counseling *you* to follow that very model, and amend for your mistakes. Right those of which you have wronged. You have my permission to use a small cut from our discovery in the vaults. Put it to good use."

Flatlander considered the request with unease. His heart still pounded furiously from the incredible reception he had received at the ceremony just moments ago. Yet this was an unexpected turn. Had he not accomplished enough? Had he not earned some breathing room? Still, although he resented this additional request and its present timing, he also knew Henry to be right. Despite the republic's paradigm shift in appreciating his deeds, there were still surely some who resented him, even the *idea* of him. He thought of the men and women from his various quests that would still harbor ill will.

"Right those of which I've wronged?" mumbled Flatlander under his breath. "But I'm not running for office…"

"Yet you're now a public figure in good standing with me." Henry nodded solemnly. "You will not regret it. Showing the prowess of body and mind is easy. The prowess of heart, however, is truly the most important. Respect is not won; it's earned. Begin to make amends with those you may have wronged, Flatlander. Begin to make amends and you will see the fruits of your labor. You will also earn a loyalty that remains intact throughout even the strongest of winter melts. I have worn the label of Humble King proudly, despite the enormous paradox that it represents."

Flatlander nodded. It was understood. Though he accepted the challenge reluctantly, he knew that there were plenty in the republic who he could apologize to. He knew that there were enemies he'd be better off making friends with.

Flatlander smiled. "Consider it done."

Shortly after his talk with Flatlander, Ellen requested a moment of Lord Henry's time while he schmoozed with the various Vermont lords and ladies in attendance. Henry obliged, and followed Ellen into one of city hall's meeting rooms. When Ellen was sure they weren't being followed, she turned to Henry tentatively.

"It's time that he meets the other."

"I'm not sure what you…"

"The other Flatlander," interrupted Ellen. "We've held on too long."

"Ellen," replied Henry, dumbfounded, "the man's hardly had a moment to soak in his victory. For pity's sake, and here you are bringing up that he meet the other one. Frankly, I'm in disbelief. I thought better of you."

Ellen glared at her boss. "Spare me his pity, Lord Henry. For it was pity, and pity alone, which influenced you to bring Flatlander to our home in the first place."

Slightly ashamed for her harsh words, Ellen walked away briskly and pretended to examine a large mural on the wall of the Brattle's acropolis. She felt Henry contemplating, searching for the proper words. Ellen could almost guess his facial reaction.

Softly, the Humble King inquired in earnest. "Ellen, what has gotten into you?"

"Nothing. It's only fair."

Henry approached his advisor. "Ellen, you know me as many things- a nagger, a talker, a country boy at heart, a dreamer, but I can wager you not think of me a fool. Tell me what troubles you."

"I'm fine," replied Ellen emphatically, as she turned back to Henry, her face flushed.

Her hand trembled as she straightened her bangs. In the distance, the faint sounds of lords laughing permeated through the walls.

"You care for him," declared Henry. It wasn't a question.

Ellen chuckled. "If you mean I *respect* him. Then, yes. I do, Lord Henry. I respect the man. He's come and done much for our republic, for our cause."

"No, Ellen," replied Henry as he looked deep into her eyes. "You *really* care for him."

Ellen averted her eyes. "Lord Henry."

"Look, don't think that I haven't noticed you two sharing looks. I don't know what kind of funny business occurred during your excursion on the lake, but with the way Menche talked after your return, there was more magic at work going on in that houseboat than the sighting of Champ."

Ellen flushed a bright red. "Nothing happened."

"I think of it nice, Ellen. I really do. You and Flatlander," said Henry, as he smiled and shook his head. "I never would have thought, not in a million years, that you two would be compatible. Yet I suppose love knows no bounds."

Ellen's lip twitched, as long seconds passed. "Will you arrange for the meeting or not?"

"My only question is this: *Why*? Why the urgency? Has Flatlander done something to hurt you? Has he already endured his first struggles with a Vermont-born woman, and you, your first with a man from the Old Country?"

Ellen replied with nothing more than a heavy stare.

"I think I see it now, I really do" remarked Henry in amusement. "You feel for him, and yet you push him away. You care for him but cannot accept him for what he is or who he is. You thirst for him, and yet you fear what the republic would think of such a relationship. Ellen, if this is your way, your *strategy* of pushing the man away, then I take pity on you. Flatlander has made his mark in more ways than one, and is at the least deserving of your respect. And though it is not my business, nor my decision to make, he is also deserving of more. I'll say this much: whether he stays or he goes, Ellen, you will still be in the same place as before. Alone, and no closer to what it is that you seek."

"Will you arrange for the meeting or not?" asked Ellen, teary-eyed.

Henry watched her closely. Ellen's chest heaved in tormented spurts. Henry nodded reluctantly.

"As you wish, Lady Ellen."

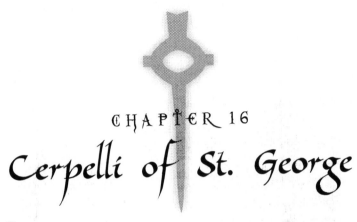

CHAPTER 16
Cerpelli of St. George

THE FOLLOWING MORNING, LORD HENRY confided to Flatlander that there was one more gift that they had forgotten to impart to him. According to Henry, it was 'a gift that no true Vermonter should go without'. So after a night at Yuro's, they set out shortly after the crack of dawn by horseback to the nearby village of St. George, due south of Burlington and east of Shelburne. During their venture, they discussed potential towns that Flatlander could move to, including the pastures of Addison, Burlington, and the shores of Colchester. Lord Henry pressed him diligently to stay on as his advisor. And though Flatlander thought it premature, they also discussed preparations for the long Vermont winter: how to cut and store firewood, insulate a home better, and store food if need be. It was as if in Henry's mind a decision had already been made concerning Flatlander's fate: he was to stay. Yet Flatlander hadn't the heart to tell Henry that his decision was still very much up in the air.

On a small road off the main drag, shortly after entering St. George, laid a cordwood home[85] constructed amongst a hillside. Aside from a few decorations, it seemed to blend in with the

---

[85] A building method utilizing debarked tree and mortar that was popularized after the dissolution of the Old Country.

rocks seamlessly, as if the home were almost an extension of the hill itself. The road was vacant, save one small, plain blue home directly across the street. A small row of hedges lined a walkway to his door, as a clutter of fallen leaves marked their base. A giant statue of a boot made of bronze dominated a small stone patio, with tied laces spread a girth as wide as Flatlander's arm. Tall grass and weeds partly obscured the property from the roadway, as a pair of ravens feasted on the swarm of insects that hovered over the meadow like a halo. A gentle smoke rose from its chimney top, as the putrid aroma of decaying flesh made Flatlander's stomach turn. He took a moment to collect his breath.

"At ease, Flatlander. Do not let your nose deceive you. Cerpelli's work is unparalleled."

"I think that I'm going to be sick," said Flatlander, as he swallowed hard.

"No matter, you'll honor him as you honor me, for he is a living legend amongst the republic."

"What is this place?"

Henry gazed off at the sight of the stone hut, ignoring Flatlander's inquiry. "You'd pass right by and think nothing of it if you didn't know what treasure it harbored inside," muttered Henry in mild admiration. "In fact, many do as such. Flatlander, you're about to meet a special man to me. I consider him as I would my own father."

Before the duo made their way to the front door, it swung open wildly.

"Master Henry! Such a pleasant sight to brighten my day, I should say," stammered an old, bearded man behind a pair of thick, foggy, scratched up goggles.

The old man wiped the smudge from his lenses, and shook Henry's hand firmly. He wore a dirty rag on his shoulders, which was covered in black and brown grime. Sweat had formed at his forehead and dribbled down his cheeks, wetting his beard and shortened grey hair. He wore a light, black sleeveless shirt and navy blue pants as thin as silk. His arms were covered in soot and dirt. And he was genuinely delighted to see Henry by the look of it.

"And to you as well, dear friend," replied Henry as he shook the man's hand and gave him a strong embrace. They separated, as Henry gestured to Flatlander. "And this is my new friend and advisor, Flatlander."

"Word reaches these parts fast," replied the man with a grin, as he shook Flatlander's hand. "Your reputation precedes you, Flatlander. Jonathan Cerpelli. Pleased to meet you."

Flatlander grinned. "The pleasure is all mine."

Cerpelli then looked to Flatlander's footwear and sighed gravely. "Amazing, I say. A pair of moccasins? Brown and flat-soled- they neither provide much in the ways of support or traction, Flatlander. Yet to many who dwell in the Old Country, where comfort is a key virtue, the shoe could be worn without shame. Whether in the privacy of their home, or out in the public eye, these moccasins were constructed by those whom call the Old Country home, with little to no regard for the rugged terrain of the north." Cerpelli crouched to get a better look at Flatlander's footwear, and caressed the surface with this thumb. "These shoes haven't been made privy to the prolonged winters of Vermont, which make men and women harder, weathered, rugged, and in turn, prone to appreciate the more primal needs in life; fire, food and drink. These shoes have never trekked down a mountainside at the break of dawn with the sub-zero wind howling, and the brittle snow squeaking underfoot, with the sun observed from the distant horizon providing no more comfort than that of a dying lantern."

Flatlander shot a look of bewilderment with Henry.

"Cerpelli speaks wisely of such things when he makes first assessments," observed Henry in appreciation, as he cocked an eyebrow at the now-bashful Flatlander and his worn-down moccasins, Cerpelli's source of scorn. He shared a timeless smile with his host. "Old friend, I trust that you've prepared for our visit?"

"Indeed, I have. Come in and have a seat, gentlemen," mumbled Cerpelli as he stood and brought the men into his home.

The walls were lined with short pieces of debarked trees, and between certain areas, colored glass bottles were embedded within holes in the wall. The light from these bottles covered the room in various soft tones of yellow, red and blue. Once they passed the antechamber, the home opened up into a larger, circular room. At the top of the ceiling, the roof opened into a two by two foot hole.

Almost immediately, Flatlander found the source of the rancid stink. High above the open flame of a subdued fire, the hide of a bear spread taut on a series of poles in the floor. Nearby, a wooden bucket containing its blood, flesh and organs sat alone. The heat and smoke did a sufficient job at keeping the flies at bay, though a number of strays hovered near the bucket.

Flatlander recoiled at the sight.

"I'm a boot maker, Flatlander. Worry not," said Cerpelli.

Flatlander pointed at the bear hide. "Then what is the...why do you have a..."

"A bear hide? It makes for fine leather when processed correctly. I take what I can get. Drying its hide out before I treat the leather with crushed Hemlock," replied Cerpelli calmly. "Just got a new batch, fresh from the bark mill of Lowell. The barkers have strewn too much from the Hemlock in this area. Now I get it shipped from the Northeast Kingdom. The small Hemlock farm I care for is only in its juvenile cycle, not mature enough yet for use. Never thought I'd see the day where I'd be buying from halfway across the republic, but oh well, here we are."

"Yes, here we are," repeated Henry with a wink to Flatlander. "This man, my friend, is the greatest boot maker in all of the republic," declared Henry with absolute certainty. "Though those of lesser taste, I regret to say, claim Vacca of the Brattle[86] his superior."

"Bastard," said Cerpelli under his breath, as he spread open a velvet curtain for better ventilation. With it came a heavenly breeze.

"Bastard," echoed Henry.

"Makes pure rubbish, plain and simple," continued Cerpelli, like he'd devoted extensive thought to the subject. "To claim Vacca my superior is folly. His leather is made from cats, or so I hear. Five cats to a boot.[87] The man has no shame."

"Five cats, at least," agreed Henry.

"But, as you can see," stated Henry, as he took a seat on a metal chair, and placed one of his right boot up on a leg rest, displaying its craftsmanship, its plush, brown leather shone in the light of the fire, "this man is a true artist, Flatlander. He made these boots for me twenty nine years ago."

Flatlander turned, inspecting Henry's boots. Aside from a few small blemishes and scratches, the footwear was in remarkably fine condition.

"Thirty two," corrected Cerpelli with a proud nod.

"I stand corrected," admitted Henry sheepishly. "Thirty two. I forget sometimes that he has a near perfect memory, a trait quite uncommon for one his age. But note the subtlety of the design, right here with the Hemlock leaf. Note the sheen of the leather. These boots are thirty-two years old, Flatlander. Thirty-two! A pair of Cerpellis age like a fine wine. Polish them twice a year, and it's like they never age at all."

"The bone oil works wonders," remarked Cerpelli, admiring the same pair of boots which he had crafted for Henry three decades ago. Flatlander nodded in agreement.

---

[86] Vacca is a competing, popular boot-maker whose products are particularly popular in southern Vermont.

[87] This was an unsubstantiated rumor spread reportedly by Cerpelli's friends and family.

"Excuse me for one second," said Cerpelli, as he removed a pair of brown boots from a nearby shelf. The old man pulled over a nearby stool, and sat near his customers, putting browned boots on an aged, stone display table. "The laces originate from the horses of Dover; specially bred for the strength of their hair. They can hold upwards of a ton if need be. The leather is calf-hide, specially treated in my trademark Hemlock tannin. Leather soles, patched with lynx fur at the seams. Thick rubber soles. I've polished them till they sparkle with a combination of mink oil and cow bone."

"They're amazing," replied Flatlander, impressed.

The leather was surprisingly moist to the touch, and as Flatlander removed a probing finger from its surface, he had expected there to be trace of brownish liquid lining his nails. Yet his fingertip came up dry.

"They're yours," stated Henry plainly, admiring Flatlander's attentiveness.

"But how much are they?" asked Flatlander quietly.

"On me," replied Henry. "Think nothing of it. Consider it a gift or a necessity as you deem fit. And during the cold winters in the Green Mountains, consider it both."

Flatlander tried on one of the custom-made boots on his right foot, delicately tying the laces through its chain of steel loops. The boot felt bulkier than his accustomed moccasins.

"They feel heavy."

"As expected," answered Cerpelli, with a slight chuckle. "The one Flatlander whom I fitted years ago said as much. In time, they'll feel like an extension of your body. Have patience."

"You fitted another?" asked Flatlander in surprise.

"I must have misspoke," replied Cerpelli, curtly, as he glanced cautiously at Henry. "Though I see customers from near and far, rarely do I share gossip unwarranted. Except as it pertains to Vacca."

"It's often a code of sorts among boot makers to refrain from such talk. They think that it brings bad luck upon them and their craft," offered Henry, diplomatically.

"I see," nodded Flatlander. "Sorry I asked."

Wiggling his toes around, Flatlander tried to flex the boot's sole, but it gave very little flexibility at the base. Still, he imagined himself back again in the mud of Lowell, Dummerston, and Highgate, or the rough rocky terrain of Bolton and the Fiskle Cliffs. *How much agony this footwear would have saved him during those times!* They had bestowed upon him an honor that transcended any monetary compensation or title.

"Lord Henry, Mr. Cerpelli, I cannot thank you both enough."

"It's the least that I can do," replied Henry, as he removed a wad of money from his pocket. "A man without proper boots in the republic is like a bird without wings, incapable of true ventures. This way, you can see more places, travel at a higher level of comfort. And must I remind you, they will fare you well as the coming winter descends upon us."

"Just don't buy that Vacca rubbish," reiterated Cerpelli, as he dutifully accepted payment from Henry.

An hour later, and after learning the intricacies between Cerpellis and Vaccas, Henry and Flatlander left with straws protruding between their clenched teeth, bellies half full of porter, and Flatlander's first pair of Vermont-made boots. In some ways, it was an even greater honor than his citizenship ceremony.

CHAPTER 17
Carloscious

TWO DAYS AFTER RECEIVING HIS boots from Cerpelli, Flatlander and Henry rode to the nearby town of Colchester on Pete the Moose and Bella. He had been told to bring three days' supplies, for according to Henry, they were going camping on the shores of Malletts Bay. Though he wondered, upon leaving, why Ellen had looked so forlorn while completing her paperwork.

They came upon an area called Niquette, a tract of wooded land that hugged the northern shore of Malletts Bay, which connected to Lake Champlain at its western inlet. The homes were well spread as they reached the border of Niquette. The mist, which filled amongst the trees, tingled Flatlander's skin in a fine spray. Henry halted his mare, Bella, and turned abruptly to Flatlander.

"I have a confession to make. What if I told you that I had no intentions of us going camping?

"Whoa, Pete," said Flatlander, as he tugged on Pete's reins, coming to a stop mere yards ahead. "Come again?"

Henry sighed. "What if I told you that I had no intentions of camping in Colchester tonight?"

"What are you talking about?"

"Relax." laughed Henry, as he dismounted Bella. "We've come here for another reason entirely, but fear not. It's still a monumental occasion, I'd say."

Flatlander had actually gotten his hopes up for a few days of camping, and this time they were far removed from the haunted lands of Dummerston. To be on the water, to be in the peaceful town of Colchester, to be done with his quests: every indication was that this experience would undoubtedly be more enjoyable. But if Henry had tricked him, he thought, the Humble King better have good reason.

"What's going on?" asked Flatlander, as he too dismounted, clumsily, from the towering back of Pete. "You mean to tell me that I've been carrying all of this gear for nothing? Can you please then explain to me why we're here?"

Henry's mouth opened, but he hesitated and instead tethered Bella to a nearby set of wooden ground posts.

"Please follow me, Flatlander."

Following Henry's lead, the two marched down an old country road, at the end of which was a yellow house with black trim and a large black solar panel on its roof. The lawn was littered with mechanical waste, trinkets, gadgets, and partially chopped wood. Several bird feeders hung from a small elm tree, which bent awkwardly midway up its trunk. In the feeders, colorful white, pink and blue candies were intermingled with seed. A couple of fat squirrels lingered nearby, eying Flatlander and Henry warily before scurrying away through the underbrush. Several carved stone statues depicting birds in various motions stood in the lawn, each roughly a meter high.

"What a mess," exclaimed Flatlander, bluntly, as he scanned the property. "Have the owners passed on?"

Ignoring the question, Henry crossed his arms, lost in thought. "When I was a child, probably around the age of five, there was a wolf pup found in the woods not too far outside of the Brattle. It was without mother and food, and the fine people who worked at the animal shelter cared for it as if it were one of their own, like kin. Such a cute thing, it really was. When I read about it in the paper, I couldn't help but visit. The wolf had led a happy enough life; but there were those that worried, rightfully so, both at the shelter and elsewhere, that he had not been properly socialized with his own species. That he had not, according to the shelter folk, lived truly as a wolf should live. They worried that this would complicate any efforts to reacclimatize him to his natural habitat. And truth be told, they were probably right."

"Where are we going?" asked Flatlander, stopping in his tracks, a mere dozen paces from the small, yellow home.

Henry turned to his companion and sighed. "It's time you met one of your own. I want you to meet the other Flatlander."

Flatlander paled, his eyes opening wide with surprise. "The other Flatlander? So, this is the one that Ellen brought up all of those months ago? The one in which you never told me about, even when I asked? You could have warned me. Better yet, you could have been honest about this from the get-go."

"My apologies," replied Lord Henry, coolly, as he gazed at the door of the little, yellow house. "But I needed to ensure your compliance in the matter. I couldn't risk you getting cold feet, like at the Potholes, so to speak, before we had even departed for Colchester. It may seem trivial to you. But, I assure you- it's not. I ask you to study this man before you finalize your decision to stay or go. And then sleep on those thoughts. It's only proper."

As the wind picked up, a set of wind chimes hanging from the limb of a mature spruce rang pleasantly. A spattering of birdseed, left piled on the lawn, flew away in wisps. Flatlander stroked his beard.

"What's his name?"

"You'll find out shortly. But worry not, though some dislike his ways, I find him to be quite a pleasant man in his own right. I think that you'll like him too."

Flatlander sighed, as he too eyed down the yellow home.

"Flatlander, please, just spend one night with this man and his wife, and then come back to us in Burlington with your final decision. I ask this of you as a friend."

"And what if I refuse?" he asked.

"Then you will face a long walk home," replied Henry with a smile and a wink. He patted Flatlander on the back. "In all earnest; I ask you to do me this one last favor."

Flatlander sighed. "Fine."

"And that's all that I ask," said Henry with his own sigh of relief, "well then, shall we meet our hosts? They're expecting us."

A sign hung near the front door with "How ya doin?" inscribed in large, bold print, and a picture of frowning anthropomorphic duck looking outward with its hands placed on its hips with a rather unpleasant predisposition. A doormat lay at the home's stoop, and in large, block silver lettering, stated "It ain't the Ritz Carlton, guy." Flatlander raised a curious eyebrow, as Henry knocked on the front door and awaited a response. From inside, they heard a pan drop to the floor, shuffling down a staircase, and a tense exchange of words in unfamiliar, harsh accents.

"Dee, da guests have arrived! C'mon, sweethawt! This place looks like a pig-sty," came a hoarse, breathless voice in a rushed crescendo.

"Quit yellin' at me, ya bald-headed freak!" a woman's voice responded, clearly agitated. "If you weren't playin' with ya stupid gadgets all day, you coulda been helpin' me pick up this whole time."

"Da gadgets pay da bills, sweetheart," replied the male voice. "Da gadgets pay da bills."

"It ain't only da gadgets dat pay da bills…" she mumbled back.

Flatlander looked at Henry curiously, who proceeded to knock on the door again, while grinning mischievously at Flatlander. The Humble King took pleasure in stoking whatever fire had been simmering behind those closed doors, thought Flatlander. The hosts were clearly in no state to be rushed.

"Alright, alright. Didn't realize we was hostin' the prince of Vermont, here. Hold ya horses," stammered the male voice.

"That's no way to talk to our guests," snapped the female voice. "Have some mannas, fer cryin' out loud!"

"Great. Now everyone's a critic! I can't win. I just can't," replied the man.

The door finally swung open. In the open doorway stood a portly man, who at only several inches taller than Menche, came up just above Flatlander's belly. He was almost completely bald, except for a thin curtain of straight, brown hair on the sides and back of his head. A thick mustache obscured parts of his upper lip. He wore a red robe, which draped down to his sides like a blanket, and though he wore it loose, his belly formed a sizeable lump at his midsection. Around his neck, he wore a chain of gold amid a swath of chest hair, and dangling from the bottom of this chain hung a small, framed picture of an elderly woman. There was a juvenile quality to the man, though thick, black hair grew in abundance from nearly every inch of exposed skin.

Beside him stood a rather tall woman with dark, curly hair. She wore a cream-colored dress with black stripes running her form horizontally. The woman smiled vainly, and twirled her hair nervously between her fingers. In her mouth, she appeared to be chewing a piece of gum.

The man held out his arms in welcome. "Lawd Henry! Good to see ya 'round deez pawts! If it wasn't fa da papers, woulda thought you'd croaked yea's ago!"

"Master Carloscious," replied Henry, as he bowed in greeting. "A king has many duties, as I'm sure you're well aware of."

"Yeah, yeah. Well ya neva lost dat sense of huma, did ya?" replied the man with a crooked smile, as he shook Henry's hand heartily.

"Depends on who you ask," retorted Henry with a wink.

The small man pointed to Henry and looked humorously to the woman. "Get a load of dis guy, Dee."

The accent sounded harsh to Flatlander; a grating dialect, which bore no semblance to the common dialects of the republic: whether the roughshod New England accent of the common people, the nasal twang of the Quebecois, nor the more smooth, pleasant tongue of the aristocracy. This was something entirely different.

Carloscious smiled at Flatlander and extended a small, hairy hand. "You must be Flatlanda," remarked the host with a smile. "Welcome to my abode. I'm Carloscious, and dis is my ol' ball and chain, Dee."

"Oh, shut up Cawloscious. Hi, Flatlanda," greeted Dee in a high, squeaky voice, her smile bordering on flirtatiousness. "We've heard lots about yous."

"Nice to meet you both," replied Flatlander as he shook the couple's hands.

"Been readin' about you through that Bromage guy in da paper," said Carloscious, then he grabbed Flatlander's arm and spoke to him closely, "but just between us, don't listen to dat knucklehead. Not sure if ya heard, but news came out dat he's a Flatlanda too. And one of dem pac-sniffas to boot! How bout that? A flatlanda! Just like us! A regula wolf in sheep's clothin' da guy is, if ya know what I mean."

Flatlander and Henry exchanged a humored glance, as the latter's eyes widened. "So we've heard, Master Carloscious."

Carloscious looked sternly at Henry. "And what about dis stuff I'm hearin' bout hikin' up Colchesta taxes? I'm already payin' an arm and a leg!"

"Taxes are out of my control," replied Henry, in earnest. "And no, I haven't heard about that yet."

"You been livin' unda a cave dis past year or *what*?" replied Carloscious, incredulously. "You tellin' me that the mighty king, lord of all da republic, neva heard about dis? Not even a peep?"

"No, Carloscious," answered Henry, as he crossed his arms.

"You getting' all dis, Dee? It happened right unda this man's big ol' nose."

"Cawloscious, where's ya mannas? Leave da poor man alone," said Dee, as she rolled her eyes. "He's ya king, ya know."

Carloscious shook his head in disbelief. "I mean, I just figyad a guy like dis, ya know, wit all dem books and people and things, I figyad they'd know dis kinda stuff."

"Enough already," scolded Henry, whose patience had worn thin. "Shall we move on to more important matters?"

Shaking his head, Carloscious whistled, then nodded reluctantly. "I guess so, ya honorable Lord Henry."

Through clenched teeth, Henry began. "Very well. You know that I've brought Flatlander to come spend the night with you. As you may have read in the papers, no doubt from Shay Bromage himself, Flatlander and myself have been quite busy as of late. I arranged this meeting because I thought that it would be wise for him to see how well you've," Henry paused, "adjusted to the ways of Vermont, Carloscious. To act as somewhat of a spiritual guide for Flatlander. May we come in?"

"You bet, come in, guys. Come in," motioned Carloscious as he gestured for the pair to come into their home.

Two navy blue suede couches rested against the walls of the living room. Upon a small, black table, rested a collection of unique seashells underneath a glass display. Small stone sculptures, no larger than the size of a hand, of animals and people stood on various mantles and shelves. A large mural of Carloscious and Dee hung over a small fireplace, which had now been polished clean. Carloscious's face looked fatter and a bit more distorted in the mural, and as a result, Flatlander felt himself on the verge of laughter. Carloscious picked up on Flatlander's wandering eye.

"Oh, dat? The guy didn't like flatlandas, I'm tellin' ya! I'm not *that* fat!"

"So, how *has* your adjustment been?" asked Henry, his pained expression clear for all to see, as he sat on one of the couches. "Indulge us."

"It's a piece of cake, Flatlanda." The small man dismissed the notion with the wave of his hand. "Twenty five yeas, and I ain't got a complaint in da world," remarked Carloscious, who then hesitated. "And even if I did, who'd wanna listen?"

"Nobody," Henry and Dee replied in unison.

Carloscious chuckled. "Ugh, foget about it. He doesn't wanna hear it. Don't blame da guy, really, Flatlanda." Backing up, he sat on the adjacent couch. "All da man does is hear da loons yack it up at da statehouse. Nothin' I'd wanna get into. No thanks. Not fa dis guy."

Clearing his throat, Henry looked at his host expectedly. "Please, tell Flatlander about yourself Master Carloscious."

Carloscious sighed. "From Brooklyn, New Yawk City. Bensonhurst, near dis little deli called "Sal's". Best balboa sandwiches in da five boroughs right there. Met da love of my life right here, Dee. Introduce yaself to da boy, Dee."

"I already did, ya bozo," replied Dee.

Carloscious recoiled slightly. "Okay, okay. Give a guy a break. Anyways, as I was sayin', I worked a bunch of em jobs, but neva really liked none of 'em. Always liked makin' tings and workin' wit my hands, ya know? Went from stackin' boxes in a factory to makin' a move nort wit Dee here. Truth is, Flatlanda, I neva even planned on comin' hee. I kid you not. I was lookin' for somethin' to do at Lake George. Took a wrong turn, climbed a wall cuz I thought it was just a roadblock, and found my way through da republic, and da rest is history. But, hey, where are my mannas? Flatlanda, tell me a bit about yaself. Sorry if I'm yappin'. Been a while since we had company 'round here. Where ya from? New Yawk? Connecticut? Joisy[88]? Mass[89]?"

Overwhelmed by the outrageous pace of the conversation and near-unintelligible speech, Flatlander did his best to keep up.

"I don't know. I lost my memory before I came here."

"Lost ya memory?" replied Carloscious, his speech slightly impeded by his bushy mustache. "Dat's terrible. Terrible stuff, really. Ya rememba nothin'? Like, nothin' nothin'?"

"I've dreamt of an endless lake."

"Da ocean. You saw da ocean, I bet."

"I had a dog with me."

"Ah, dat's cute," remarked Carloscious with a smirk. "I use to have one of dem."

Flatlander collected himself, breathing heavily, as he recalled one of his more painful memories. "I also saw what I thought were my kids. I think. I saw them both by a river. One called me 'daddy'..."

"Aw, ya poor thing," interjected Dee in a nasal tone and puckered lips, her eyes looking to Flatlander like a lost puppy dog. She turned to Carloscious with a pronounced frown. "He had kids, Cawloscious."

Carloscious nodded grimly. "I know. It's a sad ting, Dee. A sad ting."

"I remember in one, I was fishing and being grabbed from behind..."

"Whoa, guy," quipped Carloscious. "What kinda fishin' were you into?"

"It was just a dream. I was just a child," replied Flatlander defensively.

---

[88] Carloscious's term for the state of New Jersey.

[89] Carloscious's term for the state of Massachussets.

Henry glared hard at Carloscious. "Let the man speak and stop interrupting, Master Carloscious."

Flatlander continued: "I just want to see my family, to make sure that they're okay. I need to know that they're okay. And sometimes, when I'm tempted to stick around here for a bit, I need to remind myself of that as much as possible. Who knows what I've missed in their lives? They could be struggling. I wouldn't even have had the slightest clue."

"It sounds like a tricky ting, Flatlanda," replied Carloscious. "Whateva I can do to help, lemme know."

"I feel for ya, honey. Hang in there, will ya?" comforted Dee.

Flatlander nodded. "Thank you."

In an instant, and despite Flatlander's sad story, Carloscious sprung up like a cannonball.

"Before ya go, I wanna show ya one mo' ting, Henry. Check dis out, around back of da house."

Carloscious led the group to his backyard, which was no bigger than a quarter acre, bordered by a short stonewall with various carvings of scripts and characters embossed in its side. Rusted contraptions, from small frames to towering poles, lay scattered in the yard. The wall was covered in ivy, moss, and metallic waste. A series of small stone statues were lined neatly in a row adjacent to the garage. Several stone cutting devices lay at the foot of the statues, as scrapings of grey rock dust layered on the grass below. The statues looked stylistically familiar to Flatlander.

Flatlander pointed at the figures. "Where have I seen these before?"

"There's some little hole-in-the-wall in the Burlington's Old North End. Ya wouldn't of heard of it, Flatlanda…"

The memory came to Flatlander suddenly. "Bronson's Tavern?"

He looked upon Flatlander, shocked. "How'd ya know?"

"I stumbled upon it."

Carloscious nodded and gazed at his handiwork. "See, I'm an odd duck. A little masonry hee, a little dare. I sell my sculptchas; I build gadgets and devices for the schmucks up in Colchesta and Essex. Some work, some don't. I kinda keep to myself. Don't have much in the ways of neighbas, but I guess that's the way Lord Henry wants it. Can't argue wit da big boss. Ain't dat right?" Carloscious exchanged a playful glance at the Humble King.

"It's for your own benefit," replied Henry. "The people of Colchester would have a field day watching you make a mockery of Vermont life."

"Oh, so now da truth comes out, huh?" replied Carloscious, as he entered the small woodshed on the side of his property.

A rusted-out shell of an old battered vehicle sat lifelessly under the shade of a black poplar tree. On the front of the vehicle, a large blade resembling an oversized axe head, gleamed in the sun. Despite the dilapidated appearance of the contraption, the interior had actually been well maintained: the red leather upholstery and dashboard looked faded, but properly cared for and polished. Beside the vehicle, wood was stacked in an unusual formation, as if it were on the verge of tipping over entirely at any given moment. After careful examination, Flatlander observed that the reason for this was because the smaller logs were stacked at the bottom of the pile, while the larger logs rested at the top. Carloscious then emerged from the shed with a large plastic container, and poured a noxious smelling liquid into a small hole at the vehicle's side.

Henry watched the spectacle unfold, biting his lip in embarrassment, as he tried to interpret what they were witnessing.

"In case it's escaped your attention to this point, Carloscious has had a difficult time assimilating to our ways," whispered Henry, out of earshot from the eccentric inventor.

Flatlander smirked, following his host's every move.

"But he's been here for 25 years," whispered Flatlander back, as Carloscious finished pouring the remaining contents of liquid into the engine. "You'd think he'd get the picture by now."

Henry nodded. "Now you partly see my reluctance in letting you stay in Vermont in the first place, Flatlander. Do you not?"

"I suppose so," agreed Flatlander with a laugh. "What a peculiar man."

"A regular gem," marveled Henry. "Carloscious sometimes gets his hands on gasoline. How? From his illegal trading and smuggling, no doubt. I sometimes wonder whether or not he will burn down his house accidentally."

Carloscious sat at the driver's seat of the vehicle, and after a series of groans and mechanical whistles, started its ancient engine. After letting it purr for a moment, he revved the engine by stepping on the gas several times, as the remnants of stagnated fuel burned up into thick, grey clouds of smoke. Flatlander and Henry waved the smoke away furiously, coughing loudly.

Carloscious spoke loudly coarsely over the thunderous noise, his voice barely discernable. "Ya see, Flatlanda, I get deez awful blistas on my hands from splittin' wood. Did it twice when I first moved here. Since then, no tanks. Save da axe work for da axe men, if you catch what I'm sayin'. I figured since my biz is makin' stuff easier for folks for luxury livin', which between us, is hard wit deez loons in Vermont, I even decided to make splittin' wood easier. Watch dis."

The vehicle lurched forward towards a log resting against a metal plate a dozen yards away, its sawed end facing Carloscious and his creation. Stepping rather firmly on the gas pedal, the vehicle emitted a cacophony of pops, whistles, and hums. All the while, Henry grimaced at the preposterous sight, intermittently exchanging humorous glances with Flatlander.

In a rather slow, anti-climactic impact, the axe blade struck the log weakly, causing nothing more than a shallow dent. Upon seeing the log still intact, Carloscious cursed under his breath. Embarrassed, he backed up the vehicle, and struck the log again, and again, and again. Twelve times total, Carloscious backed the vehicle and accelerated into the log, until finally, on the twelfth attempt, the log split in half, awkwardly.

"It's painful to watch," muttered Henry, as he shook his head in dismay.

Flatlander nodded in agreement.

"Badda bing, Badda bang, badda boom," said Carloscious as he clapped his hands together, beaming with pride. "And I neva even had to break a sweat!"

"And on that note," declared Lord Henry, as he pulled up his trousers. "I believe it is time for me to go. Enjoy your night, Flatlander. Master Carloscious is a generous host and a wealth of information regarding the Old Country. Utilize him. I'll see you in the morning."

"See you in the morning, Lord Henry," replied Flatlander, glumly.

"Bye Henry," said Dee with a pleasant smile.

"Bye Dee."

"Take it easy, Henry," said Carloscious, as he waved Lord Henry goodbye. "Me and dis guy got lots to talk about."

Henry nodded. "I'm sure that you do, Master Carloscious. I thank you for your hospitality. I'll see you both in the morning."

He watched Henry take off with Bella, camp gear still draped behind his saddle. Henry soaked in one final, humorous look at the two Flatlanders standing side by side before disappearing into the mist of Colchester. Pete remained roadside. The mare's thunderous stride was still heard for half a minute before Flatlander and Carloscious were thrown into an incredibly long, awkward silence.

"Is dat Pete da Moose, da one I been hearin' about?" asked Carloscious.

"That's him," confirmed Flatlander.

"Oh, Flatlanda, you and me are gonna be pals, mawk my words," declared Carloscious, as he brushed the oil and rust from his hands with an old washrag. "Wish we had a tousand nights wit all da stuff I gots to tell ya."

Flatlander nodded solemnly. "I bet you do."

There was no turning back or running away. He would have to remain in Niquette Bay and get well acquainted with this most unusual man and his wife. *So this is 'the other one' whom his party had initially referred to.* Yet despite his concerns, which were many, Flatlander met his task with newfound curiosity. Because he *did* have a lot of questions, questions to which he hoped he could get a lot of answers to.

The day was young, and the better part of it consisted of Carloscious telling his entire life story. A former laborer living in Brooklyn, his true love had always been masonry, stone cutting, and devising wild inventions to ease many of life's woes. During his tale, Carloscious proudly displayed his meatball catapult to Flatlander, and successfully launched a premade meatball into a simmering pot of tomato sauce, much to Dee's consternation.

He had traveled to Vermont accidentally, according to Carloscious, for the land he had originally sought out was nearby Lake George, New York. He knew little of the Republic of Vermont, for the folks of the Old Country rarely mentioned it. That was another thing, mentioned Carloscious, nobody from the Old Country referred to themselves as "Flatlanders." It was a term unique only to Vermont and various other remote parts of the Old Country. Carloscious and Dee mistakenly took a daytrip to the border region near Poultney, Vermont. A narrow breach in the wall existed along that border at the time, likely the work of faulty construction or the trail of an illegal trading operation. Regardless, Carloscious was looking for adventure near the Ticonderoga border, and had unknowingly wandered into the sovereign republic of Vermont.

Then the story got more interesting. He and Dee had ventured into a nearby bar. Carloscious mocked the locals and partook in a game of cards, owed money to a gambler after a night of drinking, stole a horse to escape (though he had never rode before in his life), and ended up on the receiving end of a bad beating by the locals. As a result, he faced at a yearlong sentence in nearby Castleton Prison.

His lawyer sent out a call to the statehouse, asking for any lords or assistant lords to grant his client leniency. His case was so unique, argued the attorney, for Flatlanders rarely visited the republic. Lord Henry, Lord Maroney of Montpelier's assistant at the time, soon took up the cause and convinced his superior to pardon Carloscious. No other lord would take the risk. Lord Maroney did so, but only under the condition that Carloscious relocate elsewhere in the republic and do his best to assimilate to the ways of Vermont. Maroney and Henry both thought of this man as an experiment. And though likely to fail, Henry considered it an important experiment nonetheless.

At the time, Henry would never have believed that Carloscious would last a year among the water-folk of Mallets Bay. Lord Maroney has passed away several years prior. Yet twenty-five years later, the Humble King stood corrected, and was often reminded by Ellen of Carloscious' shockingly long residency. Since that time, Carloscious had, somewhat surprisingly, fallen in love with the land with which he accidentally stumbled upon- through bruises, incarceration isolation, and extreme prejudice. Sadly, there were few in the republic that the outsider could call friends. He often traveled incognito while venturing into town, disguised with a fallen hood and fake beard. Luckily, he rarely went out, for most of his work was done from home. He was contracted to cut statues for businesses, politicians, and private homes. Granite, marble and other fine stones were delivered to his home monthly by clients near and far, then left by the roadside in the morning for the carriages to pick up.

Dee had experienced a bit more luck in making friends in the neighborhood, two of which accepted her unconditionally despite their cultural differences. She worked as a beautician, which was important, because she was able to apply her knowledge from her experience in the Old Country. The women of Colchester came to her often in secret, for they were justifiably reluctant in divulging to the husbands that they were having a flatlander give them makeovers. Dee didn't mind, however, and embraced this role wholeheartedly. It both kept her from public scrutiny, while earning a side income to boot. He was unsure of what to make of the man. Carloscious had virtually no filter for his thoughts, but he was kind-hearted and amusing to no end. Throughout much of the conversation, he thought to himself whether he had, previous to his amnesia, talked and acted like this odd man before him. The notion was met with intrigue.

One of the more enlightening topics of conversation related to Carloscious's desire for products that reminded him of home. He purchased these forbidden products, most of which were deemed illegal during the republic's "Purge" in the 30's and early 40's. He got them mostly in the mists of the Lamoille River Valley by the Milton/Colchester border; one of the only trafficking sites of Old Country goods away from the wall and mountain trails. In the early mornings of autumn and spring, Carloscious would venture to this region, and purchase smuggled goods in a group that fluctuated between five to eight men and women. Most were native Vermonters whom paid handsomely for outside goods, and the two travelers whom sold the goods were more than happy to unload their contraband to the grateful customers. This man and woman were of mysterious origin, and based on their threatening looks and weaponry, their customers took great heed not to question them about such matters.

Carloscious purchased everything from the cheaper syrup from the Quebecois, hot sauce from the south, clothes from New York, seafood from Maine, and cheaper bread and tobacco from Massachusetts. He bought coffee from a smuggler who made the New York run, but at seventy dollars a pound, Carloscious was only able to splurge on his missing love several times a year. He also sometimes indulged and purchased nuts, including almonds and pistachios from the west, and citrus from the south, for the climate of Vermont was ill suited for such crops. Occasionally, these traders would bring trinkets; toys and gadgets from afar, from wristbands to watches to books, and the small congregation of buyers would bid aggressively for the desired objects. As Carloscious told it, the dabbling in illegal trading and buying wasn't so much attributed to him disliking Vermont products, as much as enjoying the variety and waxing nostalgic.

If a product was brought in from a bordering state, like New York or Massachusetts, or New Hampshire, Carloscious claimed, it was labeled a "first line good" and priced somewhat reasonably. Second line goods came from the further reaches of the Old Country or the neighboring countries of Canada and Mexico. Third line goods, the most expensive sort, like coffee or chocolate, originated from regions well outside of the Old Country, and these were often extremely rare to come by, and harder to afford.

And though trading and purchasing smuggled goods was extremely risky by nature due to its potential legal repercussions, there were some great benefits. He often received gossip from travelers from the Old Country. Those who were familiar with Carloscious's home city of Brooklyn, and favorite places from around the state, like Niagara Falls. The folks from New Hampshire, which bordered Vermont's eastern flank, had seceded from the Old Country a decade after Vermont, but unlike that of their walled-in counterpart, had suffered a tougher transition in becoming a sovereign state. Maine, just north of New Hampshire, still harbored elements of the Old Country, despite its sovereignty, and dominated the fishing industry along the Atlantic Ocean. Massachusetts, due south of Vermont and New Hampshire, strong-armed New Hampshire into relinquishing territory along their common border and

regions bordering the Atlantic, for their heavier population meant heavier supply. True to Henry's word, Carloscious turned out to be an encyclopedia of information regarding Vermont's outlying states and other matters, and Flatlander began studying his words more carefully.

"Dee, could you pass dem meatballs, hun," asked Carloscious from the head of the table, as he grounded cracked pepper onto his spaghetti from an oversized, red shaker. "Don't mind me, Flatlanda. Sometimes I gotta spice dis stuff up real nice. Dee likes her sauce bland."

Dee gave her husband a crooked look, as she stood behind her chair. "Maybe I just won't cook fa ya no mo, ya ungrateful mutt."

Carloscious gestured to his wife. "See? No respect, Flatlanda. It's the story of my life."

Flatlander chuckled, helping himself to generous portions of the spaghetti and meatballs. The tart tomato sauce mixed perfectly with the garlic and herb meatballs. Relishing this unique plate, it was almost like Flatlander was rediscovering a familiar taste.

"I gotta give you credit where credit's due, kid. You've been dynamite hee in da republic, simply dynamite," Carloscious marveled through a mouthful of dinner. "Ain't dat right, Dee?"

"We've been rootin' for ya," agreed Dee, as she took a seat beside her shorter husband, with her neatly arranged meal. "Cawloscious is a big fan of yaws."

"Thank you," replied Flatlander, as he wiped traces of spaghetti sauce from the corner of his lips. "It's been a long ride."

"I hee ya, kid. Look, if dere's anythin' dat Dee and I can do, you just ask. You gots family here, I hope you know dat."

"Many thanks," replied Flatlander, as he took a swig from a cup of maple infused soda, "but why stay here so long if you feel like a misfit? Couldn't you be sculpting and enjoying the goods from the Old Country in the *actual* Old Country?"

Carloscious dropped his fork, and nodded solemnly. "I hear ya, sounds like a bad choice, huh? But let me tell ya a couple things, Flatlanda. First off, dis whole Old Country business is in shambles. Da whole ting sounds like it's goin' down da toilet. Not da type a place I'd like to be enjoyin' my time, if ya catch what I'm sayin'. Secondly, where else can I get da tings I love and still enjoy da outdaws? The idea of nature down in da Old Country is a square pawk half da size a' dis room. Can't have dat, Flatlanda. Just can't have dat. It ain't nature, I tell ya that much."

"But what about your family? Friends? Loved ones? Don't you miss them?"

He considered his own tormented thoughts.

Carloscious downed a sizeable meatball and belched, as Dee smacked him playfully on the head with the back of her palm. "Ouch. Look, one ting I came to realize is dat you gotta look out fa one thing in dis world: yaself. Or in my case, just me and Dee. Don't get me wrong, Flatlanda, there's plenty a' people I cared fa down there, but in da end, their version of a good life just ain't da same as mine. What's that sayin' again, Dee? Dat Frost guy said somethin' once about some trail…"

"C'mon, hun, you should know dis," Dee said, as she shook her head is disbelief, and then jogged his memory as best she could. "Ya took da road less traveled by, Cawloscious, and dat's made all da difference[90]."

"Yeah, *dat's* da one," confirmed Carloscious, as Dee smirked proudly. "Point is, ya not missin' much down there, Flatlanda. A lotta pain and a lotta drama."

Flatlander wasn't willing to give up so easy; his own dilemma consumed and clouded his feelings. "But the boys in my dream,

---

[90] A reference to Robert Frost's "The Road Less Taken."

they were *my* boys. I'm sure of it. I can't let my kids grow up without a dad, or my wife all alone to raise them."

Carloscious shrugged and cut his remaining meatball into smaller pieces. "They may know, Flatlanda. The powa of da soul is stronga than ya think. Do whatcha gotta do, but if I were you, I'd have trouble leavin' behind a good ting like what ya got here in Vermont. Ya been makin' a strong name fa yaself. It may be a crazy republic, you betcha, but it's a good home, regawdless."

"I'll think about it," Flatlander mumbled, as he twiddled with a forkful of spaghetti.

"Mull it ova," replied Carloscious. "But just rememba what dat Frost guy said. Choose ya own path, he said. Don't worry about nobody else. In da end, it's *you* dat matters most."

The conversation continued for some time under a similar pretext, and eventually shifted to lighter topics, such as the men and women of Colchester, telling the difference between real and fake maple syrup, and the layout of Malletts Bay, which Flatlander came to find out, served as the ideal setting for canoeing. He attempted to bring his dish to the sink, but Carloscious and Dee were on top of it immediately, clearing and cleaning the kitchen like a well-trained duo. Afterwards, Dee excused herself from their guest's company to work on some of her clothing designs for her side business. Carloscious waited until she had gone upstairs, before turning to Flatlander with a wink.

"Flatlanda, I wanna show ya somethin'. Not sure if dis'll change ya mind or not, but it might be an eye opena."

He then led his guest to the doorway of the basement from across the kitchen and turned on several lanterns running the length of a short, wooden stairwell. He shuffled excitedly down its steps, making sure he beat Flatlander well before he reached the bottom. As he followed closely behind, Flatlander then stood in awe, as a hundred or more carved sculptures rested against the grey rock walls of a large cellar, resting on a simple, dirt floor.

Carloscious lit more lanterns outfitted in various locations among the walls and hung from the ceiling, focusing the details of each and every statue within sight.

There were white marble sculptures. Dark granite sculptures. Basalt and serpentine sculptures. There were ghastly sculptures, monstrous sculptures, and animal sculptures. The sculptures varied in size from the size of a small dog, to the size of a full sized man. Flatlander approached the detailed waist-high sculpture of a black bear with its paws over its eyes, as if trying, in vain, to hide. The details on the bear were exquisite, down to every pattern of fur, to its sharpened claws and teeth. Flatlander was dumbfounded, speechless. Perhaps there was more to this man than met the eye; Carloscious's talent was profound. Carloscious began placing a number of dusty chisels into an opened black and red toolbox, as they clanged loudly at its bottom.

"Here it is, Flatlanda. Dis is mostly where I keep my work, ya know? For dose darka ones, I need to do 'em outside to see betta. Whaddya think?"

Flatlander brushed back his hair in disbelief. "It's amazing. How do you carve in such detail?"

"Much appreciated, Flatlanda. Learned it a ways back in da Old Country when I was a mason. Neva thought I coulda made a livin' off it, though. I guess ya just neva know, huh?"

Flatlander peered hard at another statue that piqued his interest; depicting two ducks arm wrestling. He shot his new friend a curious look.

"So what? I gotta ting wit ducks," stated Carloscious plainly.

"I noticed," replied Flatlander, lightly. "You are quite incredible, little one."

Carloscious sighed. "Hey, not fa nuthin', but can ya stop talkin' like dat?"

Flatlander was confused, but couldn't take his eye off of Carloscious's creations. "Talking like *what*?"

"Talkin' down like one of dem prissy royal-types. Ya jus sounded exactly like Henry. Love da man, but hate da way he talks."

"It's not like I try."

Carloscious gestured frantically with his hands, as he relived their previous conversation.

"Yeah, yeah, yeah- ya memory's gone- ya copy dem othas without even thinkin' of it. I get it. I just don't like it."

"Umm, sorry," mumbled Flatlander awkwardly as he began scanning each and every sculpture with an intense interest.

One sculpture depicted the tower of Middlebury and the giant tree of Braintree standing side to side, connected by a short footbridge, with the heading "The Bridge of Knowledge." To its right, was a sculpture of a hand, with the crumbling form of Vermont's shape inside, and crumb-shaped rocks dotting down the side of its palms. The next sculpture was a scale size model of Fish, his head arched to the sky in song.

"Oh, I betcha like dat one, huh? Heard all about dat Fish ting. Bravo, Flatlanda. Bravo. Interestin' story, but I neva liked his stinkin' music anyways." Carloscious paused. "I get da rock sent from Procta and Danby, where I got my guys. I get buyas from all ova da republic. Tavens. Baws. Gawdens. Dey love 'em even down in da Brattle, 'specially them artsy ones. Middlebury. Burlington. Montpelier. You name it, kid. In a good week, I'm pulling five figures, easily."

"I don't doubt it at all. You're a talent," marveled Flatlander.

"Thanks, guy," replied Carloscious as sidled his guest. "But da real reason I brought ya down here is over there in da corna. You gotta see *dis*."

Carloscious led him to the far left corner of the basement, halting in front of one of his creations. Flatlander stopped dead in his tracks, as his head tingled oddly from the sight. In front of him rested a marble statue of a man standing nearly five feet tall. The shape of Vermont provided the statue's base. He held a sword with both hands, which divided his visible torso in two halves. One half was dressed in a button down shirt; the other was dressed in a sleeveless tunic with a fur collar. On its plaque, it said "Unity."

"How 'bout dat?" asked Carloscious excitedly, seeking his guest's approval.

Flatlander quickly scanned it over. "Again, it's wonderful Master Carloscious."

Carloscious shook his head and pointed to the statue's temple. "Yeah, but look at da face, Flatlanda. Look closely at da face."

Flatlander obliged, squinting closely at the statue's face. And it didn't take long for him to recognize what was painfully obvious: that the sculpture had *his* face. Flatlander's shook his head in utter confusion.

Carloscious studied Flatlander's reaction. "See? See da resemblance?"

"You sculpted *me*?"

"I wanted to make a statement 'bout da inna conflict between Vermont and da Old Country, ya know? Somethin' I been goin' through a lot, ya know?"

"Strange. But you hadn't even met me yet," noted Flatlander. "How did you know what I looked like? I suppose Shay Bromage could have described me well enough in his articles."

"See, dat's da thing, Flatlanda," replied Carloscious in a near whisper. "I made dat piece a year befoe ya even came to da republic."

Goosebumps formed along Flatlander's arms. A sudden silence enveloped the basement; except Carloscious's raspy, shallow breathing. Flatlander moved close to the face of the near-identical statue, until his nose almost met his stone counterpart's. He felt the shape of its jawline, and traced his fingers over the eye socket, nose, and lips. Seconds later, he felt his very own. It was as if his exact form had been frozen in time and cast in rock, and his wide-eyed wonder slowly morphed into something more akin to discomfort. *How could this be?*

"How did you make this?" inquired Flatlander, a hint of suspicion laden in his voice. "Tell me, Master Carloscious."

Carloscious shrugged nonchalant. "It came to me in a dream, Flatlanda. Would ya believe it?"

"You're telling me that this image was conjured to you in a dream..." mumbled Flatlander, distantly, as he admired the craftsmanship of his model's unlaced Cerpelli boots. "I wonder what this means?"

"I think ya already know, kid. I really do," replied Carloscious, as he patted Flatlander's shoulder from behind. "I think ya already know."

After Carloscious and Dee took to sleep, Flatlander went to look upon himself in the mirror near the living room sofa. His beard had grown to over an inch long with patches of white and blonde streaking along his lower cheeks. A small mark was left near his nose from his collision with the Fiskle Cliff. Dark bags under his eyes spoke a simple truth: his time in Vermont thus far had taken its toll, both spiritually and physically.

He hadn't really had time to relish in the completion of his tasks, and oddly enough, the completion of his tasks brought him little closure to his plight, for the same questions remained. Should he remain in Vermont? Who had he been in his previous life? And perhaps more importantly, who had he *become*? Were all Flatlanders as complicated and odd as Carloscious? Flatlander wrote these questions and more in his notepad.

Flatlander had grown fond of the fellow, but it was easy to see why the Vermonters kept him at arm's length. They were mostly a quiet people. Carloscious was loud. They were self-sufficient.

Carloscious went out of his ways creating shortcuts in his life. Most importantly, it seemed that Vermonters had grown up with the sense that Flatlanders were not to be trusted under any circumstances, and despite Carloscious's valuable skill set, it was, unfortunately, only the negatives in which many saw in him.

Had Carloscious foreseen the future through one of his sculptures? Was it a prophecy? The idea that he was to be a savior was a flattering but unlikely outcome, thought Flatlander. He thought of Carloscious's statue wearing an identical pair of Cerpellis. If there was anything that this land had taught him, any *one* thing, it was that superstition often paralleled reality closer than one would ever believe. He had encountered ghosts, cursed mutations, statues with unforeseen powers, mountains emerge and sink back into the earth like giant blocks of the Gods, lake monsters, forest guardians, and substances of unimaginable power, and yet, oddly enough, the past that he yearned so desperately for was the biggest mystery of them all.

CHAPTER 18

Amends

"IT AIN'T ROCKET SCIENCE, BOYS. Keep them sights calibrated," said Hal Gaudette, as he squinted hard at the paper targets fifty yards ahead.

The shooting range in the warden's headquarters of Warren portrayed mature bucks in various poses of obliviousness. The targets were posted on wooden stakes. Most were laced completely with bullet holes.

Hal continued: "I don't know about you boys, but I ain't goin' home this winter with one measly six pointer for the fam. If the fam can't count on the us for good venison stock, then they can't count on us for nothin'."

One of the key roles for the wardens in recent years involved traveling to towns around Vermont with surplus of deer, then aggressively hunting them down. In some unfortunate towns, deer became severe pests for gardeners, carriage drivers, and children (for fear of getting Lyme disease from the deer tick). The wardens were one of the few groups to carry firearms in the republic, as they were extremely hard to come by since the fall of the Old Country. The only gun manufacturer in the republic, based in the far reaches of Newport, was both limited in quantity and incredibly expensive in what they could offer. And while the majority of hunters collectively stewed in the difficulties of hunting with mostly bow and arrow, Hal and his friends had little trouble amassing the season's bounty.

The wardens' latest order was to travel to Pittsford soon, due north of Rutland, to curb a hike among the deer population. As part of their bonus on such excursions, the wardens charged a 30% commission to any and all deer shot; which meant a good hunting season brought ungodly amounts of venison to their homes. In essence, it bode well to have a prosperous hunt before the long Vermont winter reared its ugly head.

"Looks like a bunch of pea-shooters out there, the lot of ya! Couldn't hit the broad side of a barn if ya tried!" stammered Hal, assessing his wardens' accuracy.

Several splintered trees on the periphery of the shooting range served as a prime testament.

Weekes turned from his gun with a scowl. "Ya know it'd help if ya stopped barkin' for just one sec, Hal."

"Somebody's gotta," replied Hal matter-of-factly. "Excuse me if somebody's a bit too sensitive for a little honesty!"

"Why don't ya just shut up, grab yer gun and get shootin' with the rest of yer minions," piped in Dougie, as he licked off a shot, which landed squarely on his intended target's head.

He spit a wad of chew on the ground, and reloaded his gun aggressively.

"Yep," agreed Jimmy.

Hal sighed, and grabbed his shotgun in frustration. "Time to show you folks a thing or two 'bout shootin'. Watch papa bear closely, little cubs."

As he approached a vacant shooting lane next to Weekes, a voice shouted over the gunshots.

"Hey boys, you might wanna come over here and check this out," called Sam, who was squatted over a large wooden crate, his eyes wide with excitement. Its doors were sprung open. Nearby, a crowbar lay on a small pile of dried oak leaves. The ten wardens slowly got up from their positions, locked their firearms, and placed the smoking barrels under the cool shade of a tool shed's awning.

"This better be damned good, Sam," grumbled Hal under his breath.

He hated when target time was interrupted for any reason. This was their time to shoot, and in the thirty minutes they had spent on the range, it was abundantly clear to Hal that the wardens needed their practice. He neared the men, who were now crowded around the crate, laughing and smiling. Peering inside, Hal's breath caught in his throat. Removing his aviator sunglasses, Hal tucked them into his vest pocket, reexamining the contents of the crates. Inside lay a dozen hunting rifles stacked and in mint condition. Each rifle was complete with a scope, a polished cherry wood handle, and a polished, black barrel.

"Son of a..." remarked Hal in exasperation. "What have we got here?"

Weekes turned to Sam, who was wearing a mirrored image of confusion. "Who sent 'em?"

"Don't know," replied Sam, with a grin, as he toyed with one of the rifles. "But we've got our names on 'em too!"

Sure enough, Hal turned over each of the rifles in the crate, revealing each of the dozen or so warden's names on the side of the barrels. The engravings were written in gold cursive lettering.

"Think I got a good idea who sent 'em," remarked Weekes to the others, as he cradled one of the rifles in his hand, turning the bottom of the handle to his friends.

On the sole of the handle was the engraved depiction of a man on the back of a moose, riding hard, one hand gripping the moose's neck tuft and the other was raised in the air, signaling victory. Below the picture, it stated: Be Free.

"Tell ya what, boys, I'm startin' to like this son-of-a-bitch more and more," stated Hal with a laugh. "I'll be thankin' the lord each passin' day that we didn't shoot that boy up in Irasburg when we had the chance."

"I'm with ya," concurred Jimmy, as he tipped his cap in appreciation.

There was no mistaking it, thought Hal. It was a gift from the man once named Ripley, but actually named Flatlander. One by the one, the wardens inspected the engravings on their customized rifles until they were all hooting with laughter. Hal took one long, deep, satisfying breath, and smiled broadly at the blue-lit sky. This would be a well-fed winter indeed.

Flatlander sat cross-legged on a park bench near the waterfront admiring his work. In the morning rays of light, the rich blues of the mural shone bright, as pedestrians stopped to admire the piece with quiet gasps of delight. Lord Henry and Yuro had commissioned the new addition to Frederico's Tea Shop by the Waterfront three nights prior, with permission from Frederico himself. Flatlander had started shortly after nightfall and worked until the wee hours of the morning. He was equipped with three lanterns, ten buckets of paint, paintbrushes, and an iconic image of Fish from which to model his piece, taken from Jess's massive collection.

After completing his project, he sat and waited at a distance. Word must have gotten around fast. Within an hour, groups of former cultists, the once-ominous mark of the fish swiped clean from their foreheads, congregated en masse at the foot of the mural. Flatlander estimated a hundred of them, then quickly lost count, as former cultists and casual admirers alike poured from every direction. Several from the group embraced among the image of their former deity; others gently smoothed over the mural with their hands, as if they could touch, hear, and smell the presence of Fish.

Per request, the former members of the Stony Mahoney's set up instruments mere yards from the group of onlookers, and began playing one of Fish's classic songs, titled "Tempest" by the cultists. The band members strummed their guitars and struck their stones and barrels with heightened fury, as the crowd delighted and reveled in the aquatic-themed melody. Sal Solomon breezed through his soloing, just as he had done thirty years prior. In the distance, he saw the form of Shay Bromage peeling through the crowd on his clunky-looking mule on his way to the mural and Stony Mahoneys. A broad smile filled the journalist's face.

Flatlander made his way quietly past crowds of young folks, yet not a single person noticed the man who was responsible for the creation. He knew that he shouldn't linger long. When the inspecting eye of a female cultist finally caught sight of Flatlander's signature at the bottom of the mural, he was far from sight. He had seen what he had come for. After all, there were more deeds to be done; more amends to make.

The miller cursed under his breath, fumbling in his pocket for a loose collection of bolts. As he steadied himself atop a wobbly, wooden stool, a loud groan came from behind the gears of the windmill blade. He had labored heavily all day trying to fix the parts of his successful new mill, which specialized in grinding tea leafs. Massive shipments of Mint and Chamomile had been shipped in from nearby Eden and Craftsbury to be processed. Yet the wear and tear was corroding several joints and bolts of the machinery, bringing production to a halt and holding up a large order in the process.

It had been tough work readying the mills for the Vermont winter after a busy fall season. Shortly after the miller's run-in with Flatlander, his luck had been mixed. With the publicity from

Shay Bromage's article, word had spread near and far of the miller's goods, attracting more business. But, sadly, it had also exposed the miller's vulnerabilities, in both his relationship with Sonia and a potential hostile republic ransacking his products. Though business was great, much of his clientele was new, which brought with it an entirely new set of demands, personalities, and pickup schedules. The miller simply couldn't afford to have his mill non-operational. Not at a busy time such as this. And while a deliveryman from Chittenden County whistled impatiently in the driveway amongst his empty carriages, the miller reddened with frustration.

"Of all the trials that plague my mills,
The tea blade strikes a nerve to kill."

"Three hours," called the deliveryman.

"In three hours *what*?!" asked Sonia from Ernest's side, frantically, as she toyed with an oversized wrench, working to loosen the mill's withered bolts.

The man sighed. "That was my planned departure time, lady! Three hours ago. I'd be better off having the statehouse pass legislature!"

The miller shot the deliveryman a deathly stare then glanced at Sonia.

"Please tell that man to quiet down,
My patience thins. Please, not a sound."

"It'll just be a little while longer," replied Sonia to the deliverer, politely, ignoring her husband's request.

The deliveryman slammed a rolled newspaper against his carriage in disgust.

"Ernest, we need to hurry. There's two thousand dollars riding on this order."

While the miller worked furiously trying to realign the gears of the tea grinder, a stranger in a green hooded cloak approached the deliveryman standing in wait. At first sight, the deliveryman looked apprehensive, nervous. An exchange was made between the two. The deliveryman then smiled broadly, as he stuffed a large wad of cash into his trousers. Without so much as a word, he took off down the Lowell ridge with his light horse and empty carriage.

"Wait!" called Sonia to his fleeing carriage. "Please! Let us reward you for your wait! We have the goods! It will only be a moment longer!"

But the man was well gone. The miller threw down a wrench in frustration, as it clanged loudly against a metal bar near a set of rotors. Their attention was soon drawn to this hooded figure, standing alone in their circular driveway.

"Can we help you?" called Sonia to the mysterious figure. The miller sighed and stood beside his wife, greeting the mysterious guest with a curious look. Sonia worked an oil stain from her wrists.

"You just cost us a day's work, blockhead," she said.

"Your fee has been paid," a male voice responded. The hooded figure remained still.

Sonia squinted at the man suspiciously. "Come again?"

"Follow me," replied the stranger.

He turned to the right and made his way into the mix of mills that dotted the miller's yard. He proceeded to a corner of the property, which they seldom ventured to, spare for the collection of sifters and screens that they used for some of their juicing. The miller grabbed his hunting bow, which was perched on a shed wall, and followed the strange man with caution. Sonia tentatively followed suit.

"Who are you?" called Sonia to the man's back.

Still, the man refused to answer. His gait remained the same: calm and deliberate. The miller remained quiet. As they made their way to the southwest corner of the property, Sonia's heart skipped a beat. To the left of the hooded stranger stood a countless number of wooden crates. To his left, a newly erected miniature windmill, constructed with serpentine and wood, standing nearly ten feet tall from top to bottom.

"How did you...what...I don't..." stammered Sonia.

The stranger lowered his hood, revealing that of a bearded, smiling Flatlander.

"You'd be surprised how little one can hear from the outside while working in the mills, especially at night."

The miller tensed with a quiet rage, clenching his fists with such force that his knuckles lost all color. The memory of Flatlander and his company's deeds seared deep. Sonia, however, placed a calming hand on her husband's shoulder.

Flatlander took a knee. "Sir. I owe you a big apology. I took your hospitality for granted, and your kindness for weakness. Never again. I have learned much. I cannot change the past, but I *can* do my best to make amends. I'm sorry. I truly am."

The miller hesitated, then breathed a sigh of relief and gazed upon the presents, the appreciation slowly forming on his face. Sonia simultaneously wiped away a tear from the corner of her eye.

Flatlander continued. "Your delivery has been compensated two-fold. This is a financial gesture of goodwill from Lord Henry and the republic after our profits from the vaults. Also: the goods in which you were so kind to donate to the republic are now returned to you," stated Flatlander, gesturing at the stacks of wooden crates. Franklin and Menche emerged from behind the crates and joined together at his side. "We constructed a mill right under your very noses built from the stone and trees of Lowell itself. All this, as a token of our appreciation of your services, to make amends for our mistakes."

"We's feels bad," agreed Menche, as he pulled up his falling overalls.

"Milady. Sir," nodded Franklin to both the miller and Sonia, as he took a deep bow. "Many apologies fer me actions. I hope there's no hard feelins."

"I don't know what to say," replied Sonia, as she choked back tears.

"But that's not all," replied Flatlander, as he motioned for them to follow him again.

He then led the group to behind the nearby shed from which his partners had emerged. At their feet lay a thirty by thirty foot circular pond. A pile of dirt, shoulder high, lay beyond their property in the woods. Two wheelbarrows rested bottoms up against the surrounding fence, their wheels muddy and deflated. On the far shore, a pair of large swans plucked at several strands of duckweed underneath its surface. Several decorative rocks lined the banks of the pond, and a wooden park bench rested easy among the shade of a several nearby yellow birches.

Flatlander motioned to the new pond. "The three of us men dug the earth for three nights straight. On the third night, a blessing from nature filled this pond with rainwater. Let this be known, Lady Sonia: a piece of Ryegate follows you still."

Sonia stood speechless. The miller removed his work gloves and tossed them to the ground, stunned. He gazed upon the water with utter delight, as his eyes grew watery. Looking at his wife, the miller felt every bit as happy. For her joy meant his very own.

Sonia embraced Flatlander, as she sobbed softly in his arms. "How can we ever thank you?"

Flatlander returned her embrace and spoke softly, his head resting upon her shoulder.

"By continuing your important service, Lady Sonia. Rarely a day goes by that I don't regret my actions on that night. But we hope for a better friendship as days of future pass, and the hum of Lowell's wind blades fill the night air like music."

Sonia then strongly embraced both Franklin and Menche each, showering the group with cries of praise and gratitude. The two blushed in turn, as she also blessed them each with a wet kiss. Despite this, the miller flashed his toothless grin.

"Whatever grudge for me to bear,
Has vanished like the morning air,
The gift of which you've brought is grand,
Amended now, like waves to sand."

Luckily for the party, they later made off unexpectedly with several crates of processed chamomile and mint. More importantly, there was one less enemy of Flatlander's in the republic. Somewhere, from the recesses of the ridge, Flatlander could have sworn that he heard the minstrel, Benegas, strumming away a joyous tune.

Leyton Myregard threw fistful after fistful of birdseed around his lawn in rapid succession until his palms were stained a brownish-yellow and his arms became heavy. His movements were guided by sheer memory, though graceless and hobbled. The cardinals and blue jays loved the sunflower. The sparrows and juncos feasted mostly on the millet and cracked corn. That big, foul-looking woodpecker, which Leyton had named "Bug" (for his odd, buggy eyes), loved his safflower seed. They all wanted. They all needed. And Leyton provided the best he could for them, broken-ass and all. It would be another six months until a doctor in Burlington could remove the remaining bullet from his backside. Six months of labored movement and constant pain. Six months of toil. Leyton cherished the thought of being healthy again, though he was no fan of knife and needle.

It was a bright and sunny autumn day in Irasburg after two days rain. The scent of the rain-soaked leaves enveloped the surrounding farmland. Earthworms surfaced in abundance. Most of the leaves had begun to turn a brownish red or bright yellow. This time of the year brought the old farmer back to happier days. He recalled a time when he fetched buckets of apples from his orchard in the back of the property with Pete in tow. The moose feasted on the occasional apple that would periodically spill from Leyton's brimming bucket.

He missed Pete. He really did. Things just weren't the same around the farm. Bits and pieces of the animal's old presence remained. Pete's favorite chew toy, a discarded metal rake, had not been moved from its resting spot against the feeding trough. The same breakage in tree bark, caused by Pete rubbing his antlers, remained on a number of old elms on the property. On one occasion, Leyton even recognized his hoof print in some old, dried mud under the protective awning of his tool shed.

Around breakfast time, Leyton would also often instinctively move toward the windows while cooking eggs and sausage, expecting his furry friend to be greeting him with its tongue out. But, no more: his pasture now never looked so empty. He had since covered the window with a dark, heavy blind. Leyton had never felt so alone, and there wasn't a bird in the world that could fill the void left by Pete. *Not even Bug*, he was sure of that much. Just as the old farmer was about to fix himself a bowl of mushroom soup, a voice called at his back.

"Leyton!"

Turning from his front stoop, Leyton observed a man walking in the distance, side by side with a small, awkward animal, roughly the size of a medium-built dog. Seventy years had done a number on his sight, for he failed to make out any details of the two unannounced guests. Realization soon dawned upon Leyton, however, as the man with the familiar gait came within view from a dozen paces away. *If it isn't the ol' bastard, Flatlander.* Beside him was a leashed baby moose. Flatlander looked different, more Vermonter, Leyton thought. He wore a thick, dark brownish black, neatly trimmed beard, and a light beige catamount coat vest. On his back, he wore a sheathed sword, and he walked with a quiet confidence.

"Flatlander? That you?" asked Leyton, as he removed his hat and placed it at his side. "What brings ya up 'round these parts?"

Flatlander smiled. "Figured I'd pay you a visit here with my friend here."

Leyton cocked an eye at the moose. "And who's this? Pete get shrunked or somethin'?"

"Just a friend," replied Flatlander with a laugh.

Leyton smirked despite himself. "Hope ya don't bring the same trouble as last time."

Flatlander shook Leyton's hand. "Can't make any promises, Leyton."

"Nope. I won't stand fer that. How's Pete?"

Flatlander nodded. "He's doing great. He's living with Lord Henry and is cared for properly by Henry's daughter. I would have brought him, but Pete needed rest. Next time. I promise."

"Ya don't ride him, do ya?"

"Sometimes," replied Flatlander, as he subconsciously rubbed the small of his back.

Leyton whistled softly. "Wouldn't have thought so, I must say."

"Henry wants you to visit some time. He tells me that he's sent you several letters."

"Right. Those." Leyton grunted. "Once the backside feels better. Can't do much of nothin' round here nowadays, let alone march halfway 'cross the damned republic fer a visit."

Flatlander nodded in understanding. "I was so happy to hear that you made it through the ordeal. We were worried. I heard the shots."

He thought back to the day when they had rescued the moose, the farm falling rapidly at the wayside from atop Pete. He had thought Leyton and Menche were dead men. The memory gave Flatlander a slight chill.

"Ya did yer job, boy. I made it, but took a bullet in the hindquarters," said Leyton, wincing, as he rubbed his bottom.

Flatlander recalled a passage from the subsequent article after the Irasburg affair. "At the time, Shay Bromage wrote that you'd make a full recovery within the week."

Leyton's face went bright red, as he shook, incensed. "To hell with that! Tell ol' Shay Bromage to come up here, shoot 'em in the ass, and then tell him he'd be fine in a week! I'm old enough to be that boy's grandfather, and now they've gotta pull a bullet from my bum like seed from a pumpkin! It ain't right. Not a walk in the park for an ol' timer like me! You tell Bromage *that*!"

"If I see him," answered Flatlander with a grin.

Leyton inhaled deeply, and hesitated. "Ya look different," he remarked, as he examined Flatlander's new beard.

"I hope that's a good thing," quipped Flatlander, as he stroked his facial hair.

"As good as yer gonna get comin' from my mouth, that's fer sure."

Flatlander laughed. *The old man had not lost his ways.*

"I'm flattered."

"And what's yer friend's name here?" asked Leyton, as he gazed curiously upon the baby moose.

"Suzie."

It dawdled about playfully yet clumsily. Leyton observed that it was having trouble balancing.

"A baby moose takes a while to grow into them legs. Poor thing. Pete was the same way."

Flatlander steadied the moose in his arms and patted the crown of its head. The animal began suckling Flatlander's fingers like a nip, to the amusement of Leyton.

"They found her wandering in the forests of Fletcher. A friend of Lord Henry's wished her a good home, and I thought of a great place for her. Right here in Irasburg." Flatlander then glanced at the old farmer expectantly. "Right here with you."

"*Me*?" chirped Leyton, as he adjusted his sun hat properly. "Wait. Now, hold on here. I ain't ready to be takin' care of no damned moose again. Things eat more than a badger in a garbage pit. 'Specially them young ones."

"Leyton, I didn't know who else to turn to," pleaded Flatlander, as he patted his small companion on the snout. "She's less than a few months old. If you don't take her, they may have to put her down. There are no other people in the republic who know more about caring for moose than you."

"Then that's the price she gotta pay," remarked Leyton, as he crossed his arms, defiantly. "I ain't havin' none of that! Last thing I needs around here is another round of them wardens knockin' on my door!"

"But just look at her," begged Flatlander, desperately, as he directed Leyton's attention to Suzie.

The baby moose looked aloof, frolicking awkwardly among a cluster of dampened leaves, as it kicked at them playfully.

"Please, Leyton."

"I just don't know."

"*Please.*"

Leyton eyeballed the creature, just as he use to survey potential quarry sites. "Well, I s'pose I do get bit lonely up here on the farm from time to time," he conceded.

Flatlander kept pressing, sensing momentum. "She's really well mannered."

"And I still gots some of them toys from Pete, I s'pose."

"Then I think it's a no brainer if you ask me," declared Flatlander, as he crossed his arms in anticipation.

After a moment of consideration, Leyton sighed then slapped his knee. "Ahh, to heck with it," he laughed. "Bring the little feller, here."

Smiling wide, Flatlander walked the animal to Leyton, as the elderly farmer crouched above the nervous animal. He itched her behind the ear.

"How ya doin', sweet thing?" Suzie initially hesitated accepting Leyton's pets, but in seconds, cozied up to her new owner. After a minute of petting, she sat beside the old man's leg.

"She likes you."

Leyton shot Flatlander an evil grin. "Just don't tell those damned wardens about this one."

"You have my word," chuckled Flatlander. "Plus, I think that I may be in better favor with them from here on out."

Gauging the time by the sun's position, a skill recently taught to him by Henry, Flatlander grimaced. The sun hovered a palm width from the forest canopy, signaling roughly four o'clock, a wise time to depart for Henry's.

"Well, Leyton, I'm a long ways from Montpelier, and the day isn't getting any younger. It's been nice catching up with you again, and thank you for agreeing to care for Suzie. You're always more than welcome in the capital. I hope you know that."

Leyton nodded. "You got it. And same goes fer ya. Well, come by any time with Pete, or say hi to the little one here whenever you can. I've gotta admit, boy, yer gettin' this whole Vermonter thing down better than I thought ya would."

"There are some things that I'll never get, but thanks," replied Flatlander as the two shook hands. "And one last thing, Henry told me that any and all medical expenses you endured and have yet to endure will be compensated for."

Leyton's weathered face softened. "Hmm. Much appreciated. Give Henry my blessins, and good tidins to you both."

"I will. Bye, Leyton."

He then strode off back onto the main Irasburg drag, alone. Begrudgingly, Leyton had to admit. He admired the man. Hell, he took his best friend away and left him with a bullet in his bum, but if there was a single person whom Leyton admired from the cities beyond Irasburg, Flatlander fit that bill. He watched him go, silently wondering if he would ever see the fellow again. At the very least, Leyton considered as he gazed at the baby moose, times at the farm would be more exciting with his new companion to watch over.

"C'mon Suzie, let me fix ya a real meal," Leyton said to his new friend, as he led her to Pete's previously occupied enclosure. "Them city dwellers wouldn't know moose snack from deer bait if it fell on their heads."

"Dad, I'm home!" called Jess, as she entered through the front door of her home.

After throwing her green and yellow book bag carelessly to the floor, she ran up the stairs to her room with a burst of energy. 11th grade had gotten off to a fantastic start. She enjoyed the majority of her peers and teachers, yet it was her developed passion for reading which had made her mind flourish in ways she would have never thought possible. The history behind the lake and the wall piqued Jess's curiosity, and she had borrowed a great number of books from a local bookshop owned and operated by former Monks of Middlebury.

Almost every day since the school year began, Jess made a habit of reading as much as she could about the republic: its history, legends, towns, and people. She ate up the information, every part of it. Her initial research into Fish's life and musical influences provided a necessary bridge to other worthy topics.

Currently, Jess was enamored with a book called "The Brattle: A Land of Poets and Painters." She enjoyed reading about her father's hometown, and the colorful personalities, merchant-philosophers and artists who led the community. When Jess opened her bedroom door, however, something felt odd. Several items were misplaced. While she was hardly the compulsive type with her possessions, Jess had also the keen ability, much like her father, of sensing change. Several shirts were moved from the floor. Her dresser had shifted from the wall slightly. Her closet door had been opened. Jess brooded, feeling somewhat violated, especially after she and her father had formed a healthier father/daughter relationship.

"Dad!" she called out. "Have you been in my room?"

Nobody answered. She assumed that he was tending to business at the statehouse. *He's not that stupid*, she reminded herself. *Dad wouldn't make it so obvious.*

Peering around the corner of her closet door, Jess looked on the floor. There, sitting on near a stack of books, surrounded by her various sets of trousers and sweaters was a fishbowl. Inside the bowl, a beautiful white-specked goldfish swam in circles around an underwater castle partly coated in algae. Nearby, a glass canister full of flaky, multi-colored fish food rested near a wooden footrest.

Attached was a note that read:

Jess,

In life and in death, it's important to note that memories never die, and ideas stay true. He may not sing like the other, but he'll stay by your side, even during the long winter months. Your father is very proud of you. Keep up the good work.

yours truly,

Flatlander

Jess hugged the note, collapsed in her bed, and stared at the ceiling, smiling. Her fondness of the man named Flatlander was now complete.

Everyman reveled in the glory of his afternoon nap from his ten by ten foot prison cell. In this reoccurring daydream, he pretended that he was back in the company of his father, in his old work shack, tending to the production of the magic sugar. He cherished this lasting impression to no end, rarely taking notice upon the cell's cobwebbed ceiling of gneiss rock, though it dominated his overhead view.

His bedding consisted of a light cloth wrapped over a shallow mattress of hay; and as such, comfort had become a relative term. He was provided only a flute for his own pleasure, which now sat unkempt on the dirt floor. Allotted two hour-long time slots, he only played his songs at noon and after dinner. The guards and fellow prisoners, alike, often regarded his music half mockingly, while others genuinely enjoyed it. An amateur painting of Red Rocks hung on a wall next to his bed, a gesture of goodwill from a former client. A small mildew-covered sink protruded from the corner wall, reinforced with steel supports. Nearby, an uncomfortable, metallic toilet with a broken lid and loose handle rose just inches from the ground.

He had barely survived the blast that erupted below red rocks, but sadly, was apprehended days later by the authorities. Charged with distributing narcotics and conspiracy, Everyman awaited his day on trial, knowing that he could face a potential sentence of thirty years in prison. The hours had felt like days and the days like weeks, here in the close confines of his stone prison cell. He also missed his instruments almost as much as he had missed the sugar itself. *If only father could help…*

"Prisoner 119! Got a visitor!" called Officer Kasia, the portly, brunette prison guard from between the bars of his cell.

A visitor? Everyman sat up straight and leaned against the wall. Kasia's face was expressionless; a norm he had grown accustomed to. Beside her stood the man whom Everyman recognized as Flatlander. He looked older now; his brownish black beard, beige fur vest, and newly minted Cerpelli boots suggested a higher stature within the republic.

"May I come in?" requested Flatlander.

"A strange visitor comes at a strange time," observed Everyman.

"You got five minutes," declared Officer Kasia, as she unlocked his cell, and slid his door open with practiced strength. Flatlander stepped into the cell, and nodded to Kasia, who then proceeded to shut the door behind him with the same declarative force. She left before another word was uttered.

Everyman eyed the Flatlander suspiciously. "You come unarmed and without escorts. Why?"

"Oh, come on," replied Flatlander with a grin, as he cracked his knuckles. "You wouldn't hurt me, would you?"

Everyman's pale, gaunt face tightened suspiciously. "What do you want?"

"I've come for advice." Flatlander gazed around the tiny cell.

Everyman chuckled. "Strikes me as ill-advised to seek the advice of a prisoner, much less the one *you* helped apprehend in the first place…"

Flatlander crossed his arms. "You want to talk or not?"

"Very well."

Flatlander swallowed. "Everyman," he said before hesitating, "that name still sounds strange to my ears. I've been granted permission by Lord Henry to extend to you a pardon for your crimes."

Everyman's eyes went wide with hope. "A *what?* A *pardon?*"

Flatlander continued: "Yes, but with it comes the stipulation that you must answer some of my questions and be truthful. And know, for whatever it's worth, that I was the one who helped convince Henry and the other lords of this idea in the first place. Let me assure you, it wasn't easy; and you will also have to complete a number of hours serving our community upon your release. But you could have paid worse for what you did."

"Blessings to you, strange one! I cannot properly express how grateful I am for your mercy," replied Everyman with his head bowed, sniffling through tears of joy.

"Don't thank me yet. You've caused a lot of pain in the republic," stated Flatlander plainly, as he took a seat on the cold floor next to Everyman's bed.

Everyman wiped at a tear. "Of which I feel terribly about, Flatlander. I thought, for the life of me, that I was doing people a favor."

"How?" countered Flatlander, "you sold the people poison, something that slowly ruined their best qualities. They became obsessed with winning. They forgot who they were, what they were. They're now lost in this world thanks to you."

Everyman rested his head in his palms, and spoke through stuttered sobs. "I'm truly sorry, Flatlander. It was never meant to be."

He waited for Everyman's sniffling to subside. "Look, I have three questions for you before I leave and make the pardon official. Are you ready to answer them?"

"I am," replied Everyman, between labored breaths.

"Very well," said Flatlander as he positioned himself cross-legged on the floor. "What is it that all people seek?"

Everyman smiled faintly, his voice suddenly becoming quite clear. "The baker sweats, the farmer toils, the boat captain shifts restlessly among the brimming lake; all yearn for a certain succession in life. Some may not even know what that particular succession looks like, let alone when it may come, but they yearn, nonetheless. For yearning is the nature of humankind, from the first time our ancestors decided to put spark to wood, or seed to soil, or wheel to ground. We all seek a place among the heavens, and yet we also strive to bring the very heavens to the earth itself."

Flatlander nodded approvingly.

Everyman tucked a knee into his chest. "And what else would you like to know?"

Flatlander considered. "What's the worth of dreams and memories?"

"Is this the second of your questions?"

Flatlander nodded silently.

"The worth of dreams is heavy, however, the worth of memories," replied Everyman with a pause, as he scratched his chin, "is however much you want to assign them."

Flatlander hesitated, before turning his head from side to side to check to see if other prisoners or guards were within earshot. He then spoke in a near whisper.

"What do you see in *my* future?"

Everyman shook his head. "I'm no fortune teller, Flatlander."

"Please, answer the question."

"But..." pleaded Everyman, as he shifted uncomfortably on his bed.

"Your pardon," reminded Flatlander, "remember your pardon."

"Ah, very well." Everyman looked Flatlander up and down, swallowing in every detail of the man, from head to toe. "My father use to tell me that leading the blind is simply the easiest task in the world, for you only need to appeal to whatever it is that they fancy. I can sit here and tell you that your fortune is strong, Flatlander. I can also tell you that it's bleak. In whatever answer I give, and however much you'd like to believe me, you may live out your dying days advancing some sort of self full-filling prophecy. There is no such thing as fate, though; fate is what you make of it. But what do I know?" Everyman looked at the prison wall closest to his bed. "I'm merely a prisoner. When I taste the fine fruits of freedom once again, and play my instruments with a newfound sense of appreciation, and smell the fresh air coming from the lake, perhaps then I will be able to answer that question with more thought, more insight. Until then, I resign to you the logic of a cynical, imprisoned musician, sickened by the sight of these stone walls."

Officer Kasia suddenly appeared at the cell door, twiddling a hefty set of keys in her hands impatiently. Flatlander nodded his head solemnly in greeting.

"Very well," he replied, "Thank you. Your pardon will be made official by sunset."

"Many thanks, Flatlander. Father will be most pleased," replied Everyman in glee, as he clapped his hands together loud. "Bless you, bless you!"

Flatlander grimaced at the troubling reference. "Yes, give him my regards. And don't make me regret my kindness."

"Good man, you have my word," answered Everyman ominously, his eyes piercing Flatlander whole. Then Flatlander left the cell.

Everyman retrieved his clarinet from under his bed, and began playing it softly, despite the fact that it wasn't his allotted time for song. The notes came out naturally, almost as if he lacked all control, as if an unseen force was at work, guiding his dexterous fingers along its shaft. He played on instinct. He played from collective memory. He played as a reflex to the wonderful news brought by Flatlander. And two hours later, prisoner 119 was still playing; much to the annoyance of his neighboring inmates by the time the prison guards came bearing his official pardon.

Bridport. Shoreham. Benson. Fair Haven. Poultney. Lord Henry's finger traced the length of the wall along the span of

Vermont's southwestern border. West Pawlet. Rupert. Arlington. Shaftsbury. Dorset. Manchester. Glossy bumps, smooth as marbles, represented the edge of the Taconic Mountains. Bennington. Pownal. Stamford. Whitingham. Halifax. The topography smoothed out, then protruded once again, as the Green Mountains grew from the southern border like a spine. He proceeded to trace the exaggerated outline of the wall, as it hugged the republic's southern border with Massachusetts.

Henry had come to Bennington to mull over an issue of utmost importance: the future of the wall. He had brought one of the three known sophisticated dioramas of the republic with him, which unfolded from its hefty case-like shell into a three by two foot spread. It came complete with marked cities and the wall. Two appointed bodyguards, Bolger and Suzuki, adorning heavy armor, hovered over Henry like twin statues. Ellen thought it prudent for the king to travel with armed protection in the absence of Franklin and Flatlander, to which he accepted, begrudgingly.

Henry reflected deeply. The erection of the wall had been a massive public works project, spearheaded by an ideologue and noted politician, Christie Renault. Renault, the elected lord of Williston, advocated fiercely to close the Republic's borders in 2031, shortly after the fall of the Old Country. Flatlanders, and the land from which they hailed had done much damage to the republic, she had argued, and the only reasonable defense was closing Vermont's borders to this proven dangerous population. Ideas for completing this task ranged from a singular giant moat, to barbed fencing, to booby traps. In the end, they agreed upon constructing a wall built of stone, ranging from five to twelve meters in height.

The stone used in the wall ranged from the marble in Danby, to nearby Dorset, Rutland, to a vast amount of granite and marble in Barre, to near anything hard and abundant in dozens of cities and towns around the republic. Barre, already one of the central hubs for Vermont's mining industry for close to 200 years, was literally picked dry to the bone; its quarries emptied a half-mile down or more. All that remained to this day were expansive depressions filled with dust and gravel, rendering the city to a hopeless, grey badlands; an unnatural desert. It had been plundered for thirty years to supply the stone for the wall; and some estimated it would take a hundred years, minimum, for the land to fully recover. It often saddened Henry to know that while his home city of Montpelier thrived, its twin city, Barre, had made the sacrifice to keep the republic intact and its borders sealed. This was another complicating factor in Henry's decision to tear the wall down. The people of Barre would eat him alive if he allowed for such a thing, he thought. *And who could blame them, really?*

Helping with the construction the wall had been a good way for needy families to earn a quick buck during the 2nd republic's period of infancy: whether it was seasonal, supplemental, or full-time. And ironically, the majority of the funding which supported the wall's early construction had been generated from maple syrup sales to the outlying cities in New York, Massachusetts and New Hampshire. After the wall's completion, these syrup trades came to a stoppage, for they had served their only purpose.

Of course, the wall was not without its breaches. The northern gate in Lake Champlain, though perilous, was a direct pathway to the lands of Canada and Montreal, the Great City of the North. The west to northwest shore of Lake Champlain was wall-free, for the lake in these regions was vast, and New York's shore bound communities had become nothing more than ghost towns-particularly that of Plattsburgh, the haunted buildings of which even the hardiest of Vermonters avoided. And although the wall protected the eastern border, it also relied on the swift currents of the Connecticut River to shield them from any potential attack from New Hampshire. Though dozens of small breaches had come and gone throughout the years, primarily in the southwest and southeast, republic officials did their best to patch them up after their annual inspections were complete.

The construction of the wall was also not without its controversies. Twenty-one farmers from various regions in the republic had refused to sell their properties to allow for its construction through the power of eminent domain. The republic was faced with a dilemma. Freedom-loving Vermont was now stripping men and women of their same, inalienable right to land. The farmers had complained about a host of issues- groundwater disruption, crop disruption, allowing strangers and large pieces of equipment on their once-private land. One farmer even complained about the wall potentially blocking out the sun for an extensive berry patch. Yet all of this was eventually sacrificed for the overall good of the land, and the republic compensated these men handsomely.

The concept of the wall troubled Henry, but it was all he had known since he was a child. The wall was supposed to make things simple and tidy for future generations of Vermonters. It was suppose to maintain a sense of sanctity and protection in Vermonters from the evils of the world. It was suppose to strengthen their cultural roots. Yet, Henry often questioned how long these qualities would last. He was fortunate enough to grow up close to the southeastern wall, for the towns of Guilford and Vernon were all that separated the Brattle from this marvel of republic engineering. On more than three-dozen occasions he had visited the wall, and on nearly each and every visit, Henry had contemplated the same things. *Why? Why go through such extreme efforts? How does this wall of stone benefit the republic? Why hide among the shadows of the outside world, always in motion? Why are we afraid? Why have we forsaken outsiders for so long? Why?*

Henry stepped away from the diorama of Vermont, and viewed the model as a whole. The shape of Vermont had always captivated Henry. Some said that it looked like a misshapen pistol, a relic from the Old Country, pointing southward. Some thought of it as the western half of an ancient-looking arch. Once a boy from school had told him that it looked like a drawing of a door in which the right half had been chewed away. And just for that single moment in time, Henry had thought the boy was right.

The consequences would be rapid and dire if he, indeed, decided to bring the wall down. The emergent variable, however, one that had flipped all of Henry's preconceived notions, was simple- the arrival and unpredictable success of Flatlander. Here was a man, a stranger, an unknown, one not to be trusted, according to predated logic and history, who then performed more good deeds for the republic than anyone that came before him. *What if there were handfuls of Flatlanders of similar constitution, similar moral fabric and wit? One hundred? One thousand? More?* The political risk of allowing more to come was high, to be sure; yet the upside could be unfathomable.

Furthermore, Henry was troubled by Jess's lack of knowledge regarding the republic's history. The wall did a sufficient job in protecting Vermont's citizens from the anguished cries of the Old Country, yet the monks of Middlebury and Braintree, and the republic's elders, had formed an even greater barrier, a wall that hid important information from Vermont's youth. *They had always called it a shield*, reflected Henry, but he sometimes likened such a policy to a blindfold. *One serves to protect, the other serves to hamper.* Henry understood the reasons, yet experienced conflicting emotions on the subject. *Why should any information be censored? When are we becoming like the tyrants of old, the very ones from which we so willingly seceded? To learn history, in theory, is to learn from past mistakes: how could this learning occur if past mistakes were now as hidden as deep as the roots of Braintree themselves?* Henry mulled these questions and others, as he studied every perforated bump and curve along his model wall.

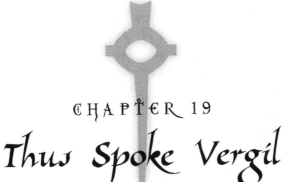

CHAPTER 19
Thus Spoke Vergil

THE NEXT MORNING, SHORTLY AFTER Henry retrieved Flatlander from Carloscious's home, he asked the Humble King if he could take a personal detour in Burlington to see the Intervale. It was an unseasonably warm October day, the type of day that he wanted to take full advantage of before winter came. Eager to explore the vast tract of land, including the burial site of Emile Babakiss, Flatlander pleaded his case. Henry agreed to this arrangement, citing a desire to visit with the workers at the nearby Biomass Plant.

The Intervale Center of Burlington was bordered to the north by the domed city of Winooski and Colchester. Providing many residents with the opportunity to use its community farmland, it had long been a staple in the Burlington area. As long as its various farmers committed a minimum number of hours per year volunteering, they were all permitted to grow and harvest their own vegetables within their very own plot. By doing so, not only did the Intervale propagate a farming culture close to the more urban-like environment of the republic; it also allowed access to the benefits that came with local farming: saving money that would otherwise be spent shopping at the farmer's market and teaching the populace a powerful model for sustainability.

As Flatlander walked a wooded trail, snug between the Winooski River and a large field packed with beds of squash and corn, he had to marvel at the concept. It was brilliant: a community of farmers who paid a small fee for their lot, who subsidized their living by growing their own food. He considered trying it out the following spring if he chose to stay in Vermont. *If he chose to.* The four words sounded strange in his head. After all, he still had a choice: a choice, which by all measures, seemed near to impossible to make.

Nearby, smoke billowed from the tower of the McNeil plant, Vermont's largest energy source. Old, rusted rail cars full of wood chips were pulled by horse and oxen on the city's old rail line to the power plant. Once there, the chips were burned to generate electricity, fueling Burlington and its surrounding hamlets. The dome covering the city of Winooski arced out above the tree line from the east, gleaming bright in the sunshine.

As the trail ended, Flatlander observed a pond covered in lilies under the shade of a drooping willow tree. Here in the blazing afternoon sun, the pungent aroma of the stagnant pond water filled the air, as dragonflies, mosquitos and gnats swarmed every which way. Nearby a decrepit red barn sat alone near a rustic, abandoned grain silo. A bench was placed at the foot of the pond. Weary from his afternoon walk, Flatlander decided to take a breather and sit.

"Flatlander," a deep, booming voice called.

Startled, he turned rapidly to face an unexpected visitor. Reflexively, he grasped for the hilt of his sheathed sword. A wizard stood in plain view. He was impressively tall, over seven feet by Flatlander's estimation. The wizard ducked below the bottom of the willow's branches and approached the bench. The dark green robe he wore was so long, that the tail end draped nearly two feet behind him like a quilt. His robe had various symbols gracing its surface, embroidered neatly on his silken robe- a half moon, a mountain, and various trees and animals. The others resembled odd-looking objects and stones. His face was pockmarked and wrinkled, as old as time, yet his features remained handsome and distinguished. The wizard's baldhead was comprised entirely of pronounced wrinkles, and he carried with him a staff bearing the head of an eagle gripped in his right palm. His eyes contained an endless depth, reminding him of the starry sky from atop Henry's roof. His hands were massive. He wore thick, fur-covered boots, worked a greyish-white from wear and tear. The wizard looked to Flatlander with a quaint smile.

"Many apologies. I do that often with my guests, whether I intend to or not. Please, relax yourself. I'd like to talk."

Flatlander tentatively took a couple steps back. "Who are you?"

The wizard ignored the question. "You perform your tasks well, Flatlander," he replied in a deep baritone.

"How do you know my name?"

"Oh, come on now. Between the Shay Bromage's glowing articles and your propensity for creating a scene, you are a modern-day celebrity here in Burlington. Are you not?"

Flatlander considered this. The man had a point.

"I'm dreaming."

The wizard chuckled deeply. "Come now, a dream would never give you an answer to such a foolish question. I will be whatever you wish me to be. But for the record, I've only shown myself a few dozen times to the common folk in my lifetime. An uncommon occurrence when you factor in that I'm well over a billion years old. May I have a seat, Flatlander?"

"Umm, I guess," replied a stunned Flatlander.

The wizard sat on the bench, which he had recently vacated. He already had a troubling suspicion as to who this was, as he slowly recalled the assortment of tales from Ellen, Henry, and others.

The wizard relaxed and made himself comfortable. "I'm being rude, I know. Startling you, inviting myself to your private bench, no introductions made. My name is Vergil. You may or may not have heard of me."

He extended one of his oversized hands. The motion spurned several frogs to jump from the sun-covered banks of the pond back into the murky water; as ripples faded into the pond's onyx surface.

"I've heard of you," replied Flatlander, as he reluctantly took Vergil's hand in his own. "You sound like a man who I wish to avoid."

Vergil toyed with the top of his eagle-headed staff. "And yet it appears that many of my *good* deeds go largely unnoticed."

Flatlander eyed Vergil, worried. "I've been warned about you."

"So we're off to a good start," said Vergil, as he shimmied his backside on the bench and stretched out his arms and legs. Several joints popped and cracked loudly in the process. "Mm, goodness, that's better. Thank you. A fellow at my age appreciates a few moments off of his feet. Thank you for sharing this bench. Sometimes I think that these younger generations are hopeless until I meet a fine, young gentleman such as yourself. Please, come sit near me."

Reluctantly, Flatlander sat down next to Vergil. *If he had intended to do harm to me, he would have done so already*, thought Flatlander. Still, to finally meet the man who had purposefully inflicted so much pain on others made him extremely nervous.

"You're not going to turn me into some creature like the others. Are you?"

Vergil roared with laughter. "You certainly live up to your billing, Flatlander. You really do. Able to provide an ample laugh when I need it most!" chuckled Vergil. "No, no, no. Of course not. Perhaps in my more bitter days. But I've tried to view you in a more fair light as of late. You seem like a reasonable man. Are you not?"

"Unless you know something that I don't," retorted Flatlander, as he looked to the ground.

Vergil clasped his hands together. "Good, because I consider myself a reasonable man too. So let's talk as reasonable men do."

Vergil gazed at the pond and its inhabitants, his facial expressions fluctuating between amusement and intellectual curiosity.

"You know, Flatlander, I've always maintained a certain fascination with ponds. Admired them for what they are. This one, in particular, there is something so serene and nostalgic about this particular pond. Wouldn't you agree?"

His senses unhinged, he paid the sentiment little heed. "I don't know."

"You *don't know*?" scoffed Vergil, taken aback my Flatlander's flippant tone. "I suppose that you're new here, and young, undeveloped in both mind and spirit, lacking the intangible skills needed in appreciating the abundant beauty in life, and in nature. I pity you to some degree. I really do."

Flatlander rolled his eyes and motioned to stand up. "If you're going to keep going on like this, I can leave right now."

"Oh, *stop* it, Flatlander," said Vergil, as he blocked Flatlander's meager attempt of escape with an outstretched arm. "I mean you no harm. When *you* get to be my age, perhaps you can be afforded a level of crassness that comes inherent with age." Vergil leaned backward on the bench, and scanned the surrounding area. "But, this pond. I want to talk to you more about this pond."

Flatlander scoffed. "Don't you have more important matters to tend to?"

"Perhaps, but I think *this* matter will do for now," replied Vergil evenly. "In this pond, by my last count, there are three turtles, twenty frogs and tadpoles, twenty five goldfish, and a family of ducks that call it home before, during, and after the deep winter freeze. Countless other smaller animals and insects dwell here as well. What people fail to realize, or understand, for that matter, is that the fight for survival is just intense here in this measly pond than any other part of this world. In fact, what lingers underneath this pond's surface is truly remarkable," remarked Vergil whimsically. He turned to Flatlander abruptly. "Let me show you."

Detaching the eagles head from his staff, Vergil replaced it with an object carved into the shape of a large human eye, yet where its pupil was supposed to be, was imbedded the fancy of a green emerald. He pointed the staff at the pond, his eyes wincing with effort. To Flatlander's dismay, the world around them darkened, drowning out all other colors, shapes, and reflections. The barn, seconds ago, no more than forty yards to their left, had disappeared into an utter blackness. The road in the distance also vanished abruptly. The willow tree collapsed to the ground into an indistinctive brown heap then blackened, its branches falling silently like braids. The pond lit up from top to bottom, as every organism glowed a greenish hue. As if being lifted by an unseen force, the pond hung suspended in mid-air, just above eye level, as its exterior shape rippled gently in the blackened void. Then it magnified to nearly three times its original size: so much so, that even the water beetles were now as long as Flatlander's index finger.

Flatlander turned, in utter alarm, and looked back between Vergil and the lifted pond, unsure what was happening.

"Stop this! What are you doing?"

"I'm sure that you have many questions, but for now, I just want you to listen," replied Vergil, smoothly. "This pond has been here for three thousand years. A mere speck in the fabric of time: though quite old, by your standards. For three thousand years, this pond has survived through droughts, floods, farm waste, industry, vagrants, polluters, property disputes- you name it. And yet, despite its longevity, despite its resilience to the trials endured at the hands of both nature and man, a battle for its very survival is being waged right now under the serene façade of its surface. Flatlander, I want you to relax, let your mind and eyes adjust, watch the pond closely, and tell me what you see."

Flatlander swallowed. He watched as a tadpole frantically chased the larvae of an unidentifiable insect, as their bioluminescence lefts traces of green in their paths. The larvae tried to reach the surface of the pond, but the tadpole was too fast, engulfing the creature in one fell swoop, as the suspended surface suffered a slight ripple of jade. Several other tadpoles raced towards the scene of the disturbance, eating what scant traces of the larvae remained.

"I just saw some tadpole eating a bug. The poor thing almost made it out," replied Flatlander, frantically, as he pointed at the trails of bioluminescence. In awe of Vergil's powerful magic, he shook his head in wonder.

Vergil chuckled. "It's amazing, isn't it? So much of life's wonders dwell just underneath its surface. And just as in all aspects of nature, both that tadpole and dragonfly larvae are acting out their necessary roles in this world. It's almost like a dance, you see, like the whole thing is orchestrated."

Flatlander shook his head. "I just don't understand how you can do this?"

"Again, now is not the time, nor the place for such an explanation. My powers are reserved for me, and me only, and that's all that you need to know. But I want to show you something else," said Vergil, as he pointed his staff at the various pond creatures. "You see those turtles on the far side? Their ancestors migrated from the Winooski River some 1,000 years ago. Those few goldfish, brought here by a farmer several decades ago to "lively" things up. Even a parasite was brought here on the feathers of a traveling duck, yet it was soon eaten by the variety of larvae in a matter of months.

"Those stringy plants you see growing on the bottom, and reaching for the top like vines is called Water Milfoil in the common tongue, an invasive species, same with that bunch of purple loosestrife near the shore, which was originally brought here for its beauty. Both came from lands far beyond our republic. Both kill the native species here. They serve little purpose as a food for the other organisms, fight for needed sunlight, and underneath the surface of the mud, and wage an attack against the native species' roots in harvesting water and nutrients among the soil. The appreciation for the species' aesthetics was short-lived, as we can now see their devastating long-term effects on our environment. That small shrimp-like pest whizzing around aimlessly, that is the spiny water flea, brought to this republic just over 100 years prior. You see: the only original residents of this pond are those several rocks at the pond's floor. Soon, this pond will be either dead or entirely alien when compared to its original composition.

"This pond: though its heavenly mirror reflects the sky so purely in near infinite resilience, I take, in kind, exception to some poetic oversimplification; for the greater reflection, with greater meaning, looks from within. What good is a pond to those whom behold its majesty, in which all creatures have now become rendered unrecognizable? Is it no different from the faces of a family, whose alien features stir no memory, no thought, nor common bond? I ask you this; at what point does the familiar become unfamiliar, and at what point does the sky, in its earth-old age and wisdom, shriek at this shifting compatibility?"

A group of rocks, no larger than Flatlander's hands, seemed to glow an eerie red, as hundred of green microorganisms fluttered around their forms.

"Why are you telling me all this?" asked Flatlander, confused.

Vergil glanced at Flatlander. The wizard's eyes probe through his soul.

"Why do you stay here, Flatlander?"

"Because I have nowhere else to go," he replied, as he stared vacantly into the depths of the suspended pond. "What would you do if you were in my place? Wander off without any idea where to go? Without even some of the simplest understandings of who you are? I'd be a fool. At least I have friends here."

Vergil raised an eyebrow. "Do you have memories of your home?"

"Sometimes," admitted Flatlander reluctantly. "But they come and go in pieces. Sometimes they come to me in dreams. Sometimes they come to me when I lose myself in the moment."

Vergil probed Flatlander's vacant gaze. "And what do they tell you?"

Flatlander thought back at some of his memories. "That I had a job. A family. Children. A dog. They've told me that I use to live by the water. They've shown me a river. They've shown me things that make me cry when I wake up." Flatlander paused. "Why?"

Vergil sighed long and deep. "Well, it sounds like your memories serve you true. I ask because I wonder what's keeping you here, if, in fact, these memories of your previous life still exist?"

Flatlander considered the question for a moment, unsure if he should reveal his innermost thoughts and feelings with the powerful wizard.

"I'm scared to find out. As crazy as it sounds, I'm growing fond of this place. I don't know what to find, or what to expect, when I leave. Maybe the dreams are just that entirely."

"But maybe they're not?" retorted Vergil with a wink.

"You don't want me here," declared Flatlander with certainty after a pause in conversation.

Vergil smiled wryly. "It would be dishonest of me to argue that fully, Flatlander. I actually *like* you. I really do. But much like a young man would grow comfortable with unsightly hairs growing from unsightly places. And it's been long and difficult to even reach that conclusion. Your exploits in this land have become the thing of legend, in spite of the fact that you bore a series of difficult tasks with little to no preparation. You have succeeded, unflinchingly. This has been a very successful but very trying time for you, I would imagine."

"You could say that."

The larvae and bugs continued their ballet for survival, carving through the floating pond like shooting stars.

"Flatlander, I've been watching you shortly after you arrived in my land. Watching you from a safe distance."

"*What?*"

Vergil observed Flatlander's discomfort and smiled thinly. "I was drawn to you by morbid curiosity, I suppose. It isn't often that Flatlanders venture into our land. Years ago, as I watched the wall being erected by the commoners, I often wondered whether its construction was in our best interest or not. Early on, I thought that it was an incredible waste of resources and energy, but my powers are reserved for protecting this land and its people. I'm no politician. Who was I to argue? I despised the happenings from the outside world which had pervaded my land, so I wouldn't impede their efforts."

Silently, Flatlander studied Vergil's wrinkles, still visible amid the bioluminescent glow emanating from the pond.

The wizard twirled his staff playfully from hand to hand. "My fate has become fully intertwined with this land, you see, and sealed with every successive sunset from my abode, high in the Green Mountains."

Eyebrows furrowed, Flatlander scratched his beard. "I thought that immortality was impossible. Unless I believe the tale about the Ripton Water."

Vergil sighed, and adjusted his pointed hat, which had sunk down the back of his head. "My trust in confiding such things has soured since my unexpected appearance in a Shay Bromage article."

Flatlander smiled at the reference. *Shay Bromage*. Despite the fact that part of him enjoyed reveling in the journalist's recent struggles, he also felt for the man. After all, Shay was one of the few who could relate to Flatlander's feelings of alienation and prejudice. Whether the journalist liked it or not, he *was* a Flatlander.

Vergil continued. "My point is *this*, Flatlander, and why I sought you out- we like ponds, such as this one, because they bring us back to our self-contained communities, our primordial roots, our mark of all that is familiar and comfortable in this world. A pond rarely grows, it just *is*. Different animals come and go, and yet a pond in its true and pure form will filter out the undesirable entities at their own pace, and in their own manner. A pond in untrue, impure form, a pond that is run rampant with outside invaders, cannot sustain itself. Some call them invasive species. I call them undesirables.

"Well, Vermont has been *my* pond my whole life, Flatlander. With each and every newcomer to this republic, comes with them an added layer of complexities and problems. History has not been kind to us from these forces. Those from the surrounding states once claimed this land as their own. Elitists came. Rowdy revelers came. Those from afar came with little to nothing, rarely ever bothering to learn or appreciate the culture of this land. People who came for trinkets, People came for sport, people who came for a cute 'get away', people who came, who still come, in fact, to fleece our waitresses and servers, people who came for maple syrup. They were unwanted, yet still, they came.

"Nuclear plants were built. Mines were mined. Pipelines erected. Lumber harvested. Mountains carved up for sport. Lakes polluted. The honeybee was nearly eliminated. Outsiders were siphoning even our quality beer from the folks of Waterbury and Greensboro. Though much of the land remained untouched,

Vermont is such a small area in comparison to the Old Country, so much so that a hurried plundering caused near-irreparable damage to our land. It was like the very sap of Vermont was being extracted, yet we were excluded from tasting the proverbial sweet contents come spring."

Vergil paused to catch his breath. Clearly the subject weighed on him, as his hands trembled slightly. He had so many questions for Vergil. *What was nuclear energy? What pipeline? What happened to the honeybees?* Yet, he now only thought of one burning question, the one that truly mattered.

"But you still just want me out? Don't you? To you, I'm just one of them."

Vergil smiled, as he rested his staff against the side of the bench, as a stray fish illuminated in green passed closely by.

"Flatlander, like you, an alien in a land unknown, I learn to pity those so like my own. Though it would be tempting, I will not force you to leave. You performed your quests well, much to the Humble King's approval," he answered. "I will not violate your agreement with Lord Henry, especially since you did so much good for our republic. I truly cannot ignore that. You have also earned much support from the republic itself, it seems. It is not *you* whom worries me, nor even the Flatlanders who have come before you, like that bald short fellow in Colchester." Vergil paused before continuing with heavy heart: "it's what will follow if you choose to remain. No, rather I am just…urging…you to explore your past, your roots. See your children with your own eyes. Kiss your lover with your own lips. Breathe the ocean air with your own nose, in your own house, with your own dog. Taste these things, and live these things, and be finally free of your chains, which if not cast away, will impede your every movement in life. Be free of your troubles, Flatlander. Go. Leave Vermont and be happy."

Flatlander sighed. "And if these memories deceive me? What then? I'm not sure what I'd do. Where I'd go."

He thought of the prospect of returning home, as a water beetle then whizzed mere feet from his face. Oddly, he tried to picture himself back at the beach from his dreams, his sword, boots and beard grossly out of place.

Vergil nodded. "Memories serve a number of purposes, but rarely, if ever, do they intend to deceive. *Misperceive,* perhaps. But I will offer you my guidance that it is wisest to find out these things firsthand. Go home to the Old Country and then make your decision, back to where you're loved and wanted. Then you'll make a better, more informed choice."

"You're saying that I'm not loved and wanted here?"

Vergil shook his head slowly. "I don't doubt that you are on some level; yet even the wisest lack the type of foresight that comes inherited with a billion years. Allowing you to stay would open up the floodgates for others, revisiting a regrettable time in our past, one in which I would rather not re-live. Also, these dreams of your family will remain but that- mere dreams. And while your children grow old, and wonder where their father is, you'll be nowhere to be found. As your wife awakes alone in her bed every day, she'll wonder what her life could have been. While you try to adjust to your new life here, the weight of the guilt will become unbearable to the breaking point. You may have won a long and arduous series of battles to earn your status as a Vermonter, Flatlander, but the true start to your life here has just begun. You have been here less than six months, a blink in the hands of time. Go back while you still can."

Vergil made reasonable points, sorted with half reasonable logic, but the underlying message still felt offensive and detached in his mind.

"But I literally *just* became a Vermont citizen."

Vergil ignored Flatlander's frustrations, as he picked up his staff, and stood.

"I've said all that needs to be said on the subject. It's all in your hands at this point, young man. We'll meet again, I'm sure of it. It's been a rare pleasure meeting you, Flatlander. Think wisely of my words."

And it was in that agitated state of mind that Vergil left Flatlander on the bench by the pond. He walked back into the surrounding darkness, fully enveloped, until he disappeared out of sight. Slowly, the pond settled back into its natural crater. The animals reverted back to their more natural colors. The sunlight began to wash over Flatlander as if a curtain was lifted. The red barn emerged in the distance, and the willow tree's branches lifted like a yellowish-green veil. The oppressive heat and sun returned in full force.

"But I literally *just* became a Vermont citizen," repeated Flatlander, dejectedly.

Wizard or not, even Vergil lacks the authority, or moral high ground, to cast me away. Yet, much of what Vergil had said made sense. He had family, he was sure of it. He was still loathed by many in the republic, he was also sure of *that*. And nothing would be worth more than knowing his family was okay. And yet, what *was* truly keeping him from pursuing that knowledge? What, in fact, had prevented him from abandoning his new life in the republic and making for his homeland outside the wall? He couldn't say. Yes, he was scared. Scared of what answers lay ahead, scared of what kind of role he would play in another, alien world. Instead of retracing his own past, he felt as if those memories belonged to somebody else: from a different time, and a different place, and made from an entirely different fabric. Though some memories felt intimate, others lacked familiarity. It was like he was back with Bronson on his trek to Dummerston, watching that tragic rendition of "Equilibrium" in the shaded park of the Brattle, but this particular act was no act at all, it was his very own, very real, life.

CHAPTER 20
Skipping Stones

FLATLANDER SEARCHED THOROUGHLY FOR HENRY in his Montpelier home, to the barn where Pete had been grazing, to the neatly organized office in the upstairs with a half finished garden salad sitting unattended at his desk, to the gazebo in which Henry occasionally used to review paperwork. Nowhere was the Humble King to be found. Flatlander had even briefly contemplated finding Jess at school in order to track down her father but decided it might be rash. Gabby, who had been busy sorting through the basement's cluttering, heard Flatlander's calls and revealed Henry's whereabouts. According to her, he was to be found near the Sunny Brook, a mile or so west, upriver the Winooski. Flatlander promptly set off to find him.

From a distance, Flatlander saw the figure of a man striding the banks of the Winooski, scanning the ground diligently, his pants legs rolled up above his knees. It was Henry, dressed in a casual brown leather tunic and beige trousers. Nearby, a black fur coat rested on a large set of stones near a park bench. The wind was still. The river, swollen from a day's rain, was moving swiftly, but appeared smooth on the surface. As Henry crouched low to the ground, he turned a few rocks over in his hands, picked up a thin, flat piece of slate, and skipped it across the river's surface with might. The stone traveled thirty yards, skipping near ten times in the process, and came to sudden halt as it collided with protruding tree root near the opposite bank. With his keen senses, Henry soon detected Flatlander's presence. He turned, the look of mild surprise covered Henry's face.

"Flatlander! Pleasant treat to see you here."

"You were quite the challenge to find," Flatlander remarked plainly, as he moved in closer to the king.

"Ah, yes, my apologies. I sometimes forget that I'm always needed. Never should I have time alone to myself."

Flatlander stopped abruptly in his tracks. "Should I leave?"

"Of course not," said Henry. "Come and talk."

The riverbank was lined with stones of all sorts, colors and sizes. The rain in the preceding days had saturated the Winooski, forcing the river to overflow its banks, leaving the ground coated with a layer of muck and silt. With every stone Henry picked up, he washed each in the leftover pools of water collected between stone and earth, remnants of the recent floodwaters.

Henry cocked an eyebrow. "Have you ever tried skipping stones before, Flatlander?"

"Not that I can remember," replied Flatlander, as he shook his head.

"Well, it's quite enjoyable. See here," said Henry as he palmed a smooth, white rounded stone with a flattened bottom, no larger than the size of a doorknob. Twirling it gently between his hands, Henry gauged the weight and shape carefully. "You choose a stone that is preferably flat and thin, but not so thin or light that it changes position midflight. Like this one. It's not perfect, but it will suffice. Then you cock back your arm, lower your center of gravity, and release perpendicular to the water and release. Like this."

Henry then hurled the stone with great velocity, his face grimacing in concentration, as it skipped the river's surface several times before dropping through the waters with an emphatic plunk.

"Try it," requested Henry, as he handed Flatlander a smooth, algae-covered stone, as water dripped down his palms. "This should work."

Flatlander reluctantly grabbed the stone, and brushed a clump of cold slime from its bottom. Attempting the same form as Henry, he threw the stone at a peculiar angle. With a sudden splash, his rock had made a sudden halt.

Henry smiled faintly. "You know that they actually hold a competition for skipping stones in the republic? Ellen has been organizing the affair every year. Quite a silly event if you ask me, but to each their own, I suppose."

"I wasn't aware," admitted Flatlander, as he twisted another stone in his hands and threw it with all of his might. This time, it skipped three times atop the swollen river.

Henry nodded, impressed. "Not bad, Flatlander! Yes, it's just one of the many quirks in our fine republic," he paused. "It would be sad if you missed it."

Flatlander sighed long and deep. "That's why I came to see you. There are things that I need to find out. I'm reconsidering my decision to stay. I'm actually, um, thinking of leaving."

Henry paused from his search for another stone, and looked upon his friend. He bit his lip, frustrated, searching for the right words to impart upon his advisor. Yet words temporarily failed him. A passing carriage in the distance powered through a muddy section of the road, throwing off gravel as it passed. Henry waited for the carriage to pass.

"Undoubtedly," nodded Henry. "But I beg for you to reconsider. Perhaps we can find another solution. Truth be told, there's been a lot on my mind, Flatlander. Lots of changes on the horizon, you see; which goes against the norm around these parts. I'm finding it all quite difficult to digest."

"Change can be a good thing," remarked Flatlander, optimistically.

Henry sighed. "Yes, it can. If nothing else, your presence here has taught me that much. Yet in my old age, I prefer it to come in more manageable spurts, not in the incredible deluge we have experienced as of late." Henry nodded upriver. "You know, it was a mere mile or so from this very spot that we first met," observed Henry, as he searched the riverbanks for another suitable skipping stone. "Barely two seasons prior. And in that amount of time, you've gone on to accomplish things that most men wouldn't have dreamt possible. It's made me reconsider a number of things."

"How so?"

"I cannot say. Not yet, at least. But you must tell me, all things considered, if your decision is final. I cannot emphasize to you enough how much I'd like you to stay. You would share the role of Lead Advisor with Ellen."

Flatlander faced his friend, his eyes heavy with regret. "Lord Henry, you've been a good friend. This is a beautiful land. I hadn't realized its true beauty until I summited Mansfield, and when I did, it was like a painting. The land, I mean. The woods are endless. Lake Champlain is magical. This whole place, in fact, is like something out of a dream." Flatlander paused. An oversized branch floated gracefully by, and assortment of sparrows perched among its branches. "But my memory's coming back one day at a time, and I feel that my life beyond the wall is calling. My wife and kids need me. I *need* to go. I *need* to know what's out there, what I left behind. Besides, it's not like I never intend on returning."

"Yet I doubt you *would*," said Henry, as he threw an undesirable rock against the riverbank with a loud clatter. "Be honest. The land beyond the wall rarely returns what it takes. It's been well documented by the monks and others."

"I have to go back," stated Flatlander, adamantly.

"But there's so much for you here," pleaded Henry in exasperation. "You'd have a home, a job by my side, your very own land and title, the respect of the people. Not to mention a potential girlfriend," added Henry with a wink.

Flatlander blushed.

Henry continued: "Oh, come now. Ellen has grown quite fond of you, I can tell. Your past is what you left behind in the Flatlands. Here, Flatlander, here, you have a future."

Flatlander hesitated. "Lord Henry, it's a decision that's troubled me for months. But it's a decision that I've got to live with."

"Very well. Just know that the door will always be open, should you reconsider," replied Henry with a sigh of resignation. "That's right. The door will always be open."

Flatlander turned and left Henry alone with his thoughts. He heard no more skipping stones upon the river, for there were no more desirable stones for the Humble King to skip.

Shortly after his lively plea with Flatlander, Henry summoned the services of Shay Bromage. Seeking a form of compensation from Shay, he hoped that the journalist would pledge his services as a repayment to Flatlander for his derogatory articles. The embattled journalist seemed surprisingly more-than-willing to oblige. The request was simple: to draft an invitation, and make copies for a great number of folks throughout the republic bearing these words:

Friends,

You are cordially invited by Lord Henry of the Brattle to personally see off our friend, Flatlander, who has decided to leave us for his home amongst the Old Country. I invite you to bid farewell to this special man, who has crossed countless paths in the republic, and completed countless noble deeds.

If you wish to attend, please meet at: Battery Park. Saturday, October 25th. Noon.

Sincerely,
Your Humble King,
Lord Henry Cyrus of the Brattle

After copies were produced at Shay's printing press, Henry was to send his fastest messengers to deliver his letters across the expanse of the republic, from the acropolis of the Brattle, to the tower of Middlebury, to the far reaches of Lowell and Irasburg. He took inventory of all the men and women Flatlander had come across during his adventures. He even requested the assistance of Danario, master herald of Stowe, who had lost face in the wake of the Fiskle Cliff crisis, and was more than willing to assist in part to repair *his* sullied reputation. In seven days time, Henry hoped that many would show up, for notice was short, and the odds of Flatlander staying, growing smaller.

CHAPTER 21
Battery Park

STORM CLOUDS LOOMED HIGH ABOVE the Adirondacks all morning, threatening at any given moment to unleash a torrential downpour onto neighboring Burlington. But the storm never came. Instead, the clouds streamlined south to north in a greyish-white channel, while the queen city, mere miles away, enjoyed a breezy, sunny day. There was an eerie quality to it all, thought Flatlander, and for a second, he wondered what conditions must be like atop the mountains.

The storm building to the west brought with it a fresh autumn chill, delighting the porters and longshoremen, who gained a measure of satisfaction knowing they'd get the cool weather without the utterly terrible lake conditions. Small whitecaps, they could live with.

Battery Park lay further down in elevation than downtown Burlington and played host to a variety of characters in the city: poets, wandering teens, vagrants, working men and women on lunch break, city officials, arborists, politicians, and more. Two elderly men occupied a table with a chessboard near a small amphitheater as they aggressively debated an allegedly illegal move. A solar panel powered a set of speakers in the lofts of the amphitheater, which intermittently emitted hawk screeches. With each screech, the pigeons and seagulls scattered in all directions. Flatlander admired the sights and sounds in humbled reflection, for these could be his last.

So, this was goodbye, thought Flatlander. *How odd.* From start to finish, it had been a strange and incredible journey. Vermont certainly had its quirks, but Flatlander could no longer deny to himself or others that he would miss it.

Still, he needed to know about his family. What had they endured at the hands of the Old Country? He also desired to understand what kind of person he used to be; what kind of things he use to like. The dreams and flashbacks had provided momentary glimpses of his old life, yet they did little to reveal his life as a whole. He wanted to get a better idea of whom he was, and once he had done that, he believed that he could make better-informed decision concerning his future.

Yuro had been generous enough to lend Flatlander one of his own horses, Putter, and a spare wagon for his quest back home. Henry had stocked him with several weeks of supplies. Canned meat, fruit, water, knives, flint and steel, iodine tablets, clothes, an extra bow and arrow. The Humble King did his best of balancing Flatlander's needs with Putter's carrying strength. Though Pete the Moose was offered, Flatlander refused such a generous gift, for he reasoned that Vermont's symbolic animal should stay put in Vermont. For the first time, though, the finality of his decision hit him upon seeing his stocked wagon and readied horse parked along the outskirts of Battery Park. *This was really happening.*

Flatlander passed the amphitheater and approached a trail next to a short stonewall overlooking a drop off before the grandeur of Lake Champlain. It was then that he saw Henry, dressed in the same black fur coat as when they first met. Sitting on a bench, the Humble King gazed out towards the storm skirting along the Adirondacks. His hands were folded neatly between his legs, and he seemed to be lost in thought.

"Lord Henry."

Henry turned and nodded. "Flatlander."

"Quite a view," said Flatlander, as he peered down towards the steep shore.

A wall of stones curled out a ways into the lake, creating a breakwater. The waves chopped against this breakwater in chaotic spurts, spitting up globs of foam. A group of dockworkers, not far from the chamber of echoes, stacked lumber into a small cargo ship. The main body of the lake looked darker than Flatlander had ever seen it during broad daylight, and it simmered in the wind like churning, black ink.

Henry nodded. "The lake is testy today. I both pity and envy the shipmen."

Flatlander sat next to his friend, watching the lake quietly. "I guess this is the end."

"Yes, Flatlander. I suppose so," replied Henry, distraught. "Tell me, did you enjoy your time in Vermont?"

Flatlander laughed, whimsically. "I did. I'm just trying to imagine how the Old Country will compare. No more singing fish or beer-craved demons."

Henry chuckled and crossed his arms in recollection. "Have hope though, Flatlander. Life is a puzzle where the pieces shift before your eyes. The Old Country may have some magic yet; you just have to know where to look. You know where to find us. Don't hesitate to ask. You'll always have a place here."

"Much appreciated," replied Flatlander, as he shook hands with his friend and boss. "You're a good man, Henry. It's been an honor. I promise to make it back when I can. Thanks for all that you've done for me. Words can't express how much you've all meant to me. And I'm passing through Montpelier to give Franklin, Menche, and Ellen my goodbyes. I'll miss you and this place dearly."

Flatlander shook Henry's hand solemnly, and embraced the Humble King. Over Henry's shoulder, he then glanced at the lake, wistfully. The waves were small but choppy; and a pair of small, brown fishing boats paddled out towards the lake from the shores of the waterfront. He imagined himself back on the deck of The Bethel clumsily working the jib, while Ramsey barked out orders from his smoke-filled cabin. His smile quickly morphed into a profound sense of sadness and guilt, as he was soon to say goodbye to the land that he had now come to love. Flatlander suddenly averted his gaze from the lake and looked to his feet. *This is torture. But I have to leave.* Without another word, Flatlander turned to leave the Republic of Vermont in his wake.

"But just one more thing, Flatlander," called Henry to his back. "I've invited some guests to come see you off."

From behind the other side of the amphitheater, came a large group of people, all of them instantly recognizable. Franklin. Ellen. Menche. The Miller and Sonia. Hal Gaudette and the wardens. Jess. Lord Trombley. Helphon and Zachus. Inepticus. Flatlander's head spun and his heart raced. Lord Haque. Captain Ramsey. Shay Bromage and Cheryl. Bronson. Flatlander watched in awe as more people streamed out from behind the amphitheater. Master Yuro. Bart. Everyman. Ertle the juggler, and even Alonso.

A pair trumpets blew from opposite sides of the park, while a massive crowd began approaching from all directions. Flatlander was startled at the size of the group, and he turned to Henry, alarmed.

"Who are all of these people?"

Henry methodically scanned the approaching congregation. "The once-faceless that you have assisted during your quests. To your left come the former cultists of Fish. To your right, the waiters and waitresses of Burlington. Straight ahead are the former addicts of superpac. Beyond them, I assume some grateful Burlington taxpayers. And beyond them, even, though you can barely see from your standpoint, a large group of Underhill's residents free from the shadow of the Fiskle Cliff. Thanks to you."

Flatlander and Henry waited until the group formed a large circle around the pair. The crowd was enormous, two thousand strong by Flatlander's estimation. They came chanting Flatlander's name, most with broad smiles. They came to within a few yards of Flatlander and Henry, clapping, brimming with appreciation for the miracle-maker. Blushing a deep red, Flatlander was unable to fully process what was now unfolding before him. Within minutes, Battery Park was packed with adoring fans, all who had come to say goodbye to their beloved folk hero.

Henry stood and motioned to the crowd with a raised hand. The men, women and children obliged, as soon it was only whispers and lake wind only that was audible.

"We're pleading for you to stay," said Lord Henry in a loud voice, to the satisfied nods and grunts of approval from the crowd. "I have had a home built for you in Montpelier. I also have created a permanent seat for you on my council. An office awaits you in my home. What more is there to say, friend? Your future lies here in Vermont."

Flatlander scanned the crowd, searching for some level of understanding. "But my family…"

Henry nodded. "I knew that had to be addressed. I failed to mention that the search for your kin is in good hands. Right now, as we stand here, our dear friends, Carloscious and Dee, have departed for the Old Country in search for your family. They left this morning at my bidding." The crowd roared with applause.

Flatlander grimaced. "But why on earth did you…"

"Find such an enthusiastic volunteer?" interrupted Henry, with a wry grin. "Let's just say that Master Carloscious owes me some big favors, and I wasn't hesitant to ask."

Flatlander swallowed. "That's not what I meant."

The Humble King continued, unflinchingly. "I've also decided that perhaps there are many like you beyond the wall of Vermont, and so, it is with great honor, that I announce, for the first time to the public, my decision to restore the old roads in and out of the republic through the wall itself. Vermont will once again allow for outsiders to come and go at will. We will once again, though with great caution, share this world with the Old Country!"

The crowd reacted with a mixture of surprise, horror, and muted dissatisfaction. Lord Henry looked around at those whom had gathered closely.

"It was a decision that gave me much trepidation; yet it is for the overall good of Vermont and its people. We've come a long way since the Shelburne Doctrine. I will present this to the statehouse on Monday with the hopes that they agree." Then Henry turned back to Flatlander standing to his side, hoping that his brief aside hadn't ruined the moment. "But I digress. Some here have something they want to say to you, Flatlander."

Shay Bromage stepped forward from the crowd, as murmurs grew through the massive gathering. Wearing a thick blue flannel jacket, puffed out by several layers underneath, the journalist gave Flatlander and Henry a jittery look. He adjusted his glasses and looked upon Flatlander face to face and cleared his throat.

"Flatlander, I've been meaning to tell you in person. I'm sorry. I was wrong about you from the start. In my ill-fated quest to protect Vermont's ideals at any and all costs, I sacrificed my integrity. It has been my privilege, correction: *my honor*, to follow your story. You have done the republic well, and because of that, I promise to be a more, um, objective reporter from here on out. I never thought I'd say this, and entertainment value aside, from one Flatlander to another, I plead for you to stay."

The crowd hooted and hollered.

Menche then emerged in an awkward shuffle. "Flatlander, sir, ain't no good at talkins, as ya probably knows. Only means to tell ya that ol' Menche is as fond of ya as I is pumpkin carvin' on a fall day. I begs ya to think of stayin, if it pleases ya."

Near to Menche, Franklin then plunged his axe into the earth, and knelt before Flatlander. "The north taught me to be tough, but none have I seen tougher than the likes of ya, Flatlander. Still think yer crazy fer jumpin' off that damned cliff, but ya got balls, kid. Ya saved me life in Highgate, and the least I could do is ask ya is to reconsider yer decision, like the rest. What'd ya say?"

Ellen then stepped forward, and brushed a dangling bang back against a stiff wind. The crowd quieted to a hush. A pained expression painted Ellen's face, her tough exterior melted away completely.

"I've been so wrong about you from the start, Flatlander. When we first met on the outskirts of Montpelier, it was me who told Lord Henry to ward you away. Even afterwards, I argued Henry's decision, as if your mere presence was a plague. It's hard for me to say this, but it was also *me* who urged Henry to arrange your meeting with Carloscious prematurely as a means to dissuade you from staying."

Ellen choked back tears. "But it's *I* who am the saddest to see you go. The truth is, I fell for you long before our excursion on the lake. I fell for you this whole time, and at first, without even knowing it. I haven't realized how much I've stood to lose until now, when your departure is here and staring at me in the face. Please, don't leave. You mean too much to the republic. You mean too much to *me*."

Ellen ran into his arms and kissed him passionately, much to the crowd's delight. Lord Henry nodded in approval, and even Menche clapped his hands together in celebration. When they finally disengaged, Flatlander gazed upon Ellen's tear-stained face. He then looked out back towards the lake, as whitecaps shifted in wild disorder. The sun shone through a heavy patch of darkened cumulus clouds, casting several beams of light on the rough waters below.

Flatlander wiped a tear from his eye. He took in the size and intensity of the waiting crowd. The seconds felt like a lifetime, as the gathered crowd greatly anticipated his reaction in near silence. In defeat, Flatlander kicked at the dirt with the toe of his new Cerpellis.

"Well, I've heard that Vermont winters are pretty tough."

The crowd exploded in shouts of joy and laughter. Ellen, Franklin and Menche hugged Flatlander in unadulterated joy. Whistles and horns echoed from across Battery Park. The wardens separated themselves off to more remote location of the park, and shot their new rifles in the air. The crowd paused in momentary confusion, yet upon seeing the smiling faces of the wardens, resumed their celebration. Children rushed off to the park's playground with their peers. Many in assemblage congratulated and thanked Flatlander individually, and then walked to the wall of Battery Park to admire the ferocity of the lake. Finally, the republic had formally accepted an outsider as one of their very own.

And in the distance, perched high in a tree, Vergil, the great wizard of the republic, Vermont's first citizen, looked upon the event with muted contentment. The distinct feeling of acceptance of Flatlander washed over the wizard like a pair of boots, which had finally broken in after two seasons. He wanted nothing more than to see those of the republic happy, and as he gazed over the crowd from the tree limb, the sentiment was undeniable. Seldom had Vergil seen such a happier sight, and he bathed in the people's happiness like a bee in nectar, recalling that for once in his near-infinite life, a man, an outsider, traversed into Vermont's borders with unforeseen incredible results. Though somewhat horrified at the prospect of opening the wall, Vergil felt once again, that it was outside of his control.

In the newspapers, Shay Bromage would recount the persuasion of Flatlander with glee, free from his promised journalistic constraints of objectivity; yet this time in a positive regard. And so began Shay's slow ascent back into the public's grace, once again embracing and nurturing the court of public opinion, which had now fallen heavily in Flatlander's favor.

Just weeks later, Lord Henry won approval for his idea of allowing multiple passages in the wall, despite strong resistance, especially from the Monks of Middlebury. A dozen road-sized holes were bored by hand into Vermont's wall over the course of a month, allowing for outsiders to pass through without harassment, disparagement, or prejudice. The groundbreaking event was met with mixed reception, as many in the republic were still highly resentful of outsiders. Flatlander's resounding success, however, had given enough residents second thoughts as it pertained to the matter of the wall. Still, regardless of where one stood on the issue, people near the open roadways watched the entrances, regularly, with guarded thoughts.

Flatlander had come to find the republic his home, a place where he could set his roots and start life anew. He waited excitedly for the return of Carloscious, for he longed to hear what his peculiar friend would reveal to him about his past, his life, and, in particular, that of his family. And days later, while Franklin painstakingly taught him the proper technique in how to split wood amid the fallen leaves of late autumn, Flatlander paused, and thought kindly of his future, as he had his past, for the coming of winter would bring with it a sense of closure.

To be continued…